THE HOLLAND FAMILY SAGA

PART NINE

COLLISION COURSE

All material copy-written and filed on site at The Library of Congress.

ISBN 978-0-09892445-7-2

ACKNOWLEDGEMENTS

I first want to thank God for giving me life, and helping me to discover a talent I never even knew I possessed. Writing this saga is nothing more than a pure joy and I so hope that I did write by you all once again as I look forward to writing more of this story so long as there is interest. Thank you, for allowing me to entertain you all.

With so many names to mention, I will say that those who've ever had a conversation with me are most appreciated. The inboxes and the questions and the admiration of the body of work makes it all worth while. Thank yous go out to Kimberly Sanders, Gina Lucas, Lizzy Linh King, Marina Chestnut, Rosalyn and Rosalind (the Rozz sisters) Pat Rice, Ruby Price, Hadiyah, Kristen, Felisha, Vanessa Speaks, Kosha, Daniella, Spencer, Sandy and Saima across the pond, Jacqui, Vanessa Nickelson, Nickee Mitchell-Joyner, Wanda McIntyre, way too many to name, but believe me, I thank you all for giving me a chance. To all the book clubs? Thank you, thank you, thank you for accepting me, holding discussions and giving me interviews. I don't always chat much, but it's only because I tend to focus on the task at hand the closer the date nears to publishing. Again, thank you all, and Happy Reading.

Clever Black

CHAPTER ONE

OLD TRADITION

December 24, 2008

Seventy-five year-old Doss 'DeeDee' Dawkins Senior had just emerged from behind a set of wooden double doors that led from the medium-sized kitchen of The Cicero Hot Dog Deli, formerly East Side Bar and Grill. It was a quarter to six in the morning on the bitterly cold and snowy Christmas Eve of 2008, two days after Mendoza Cernigliaro had been killed by a federal agent.

The bureau had kept Mendoza's death concealed the night of, but an unnamed source had leaked information to the Chicago Tribune, and a preliminary autopsy report and crime scene photo had been hand delivered to DeeDee over to his condo on Lake Shore Drive a couple of hours earlier. DeeDee read the report while dressing in the early morning hour. While going about his morning routine, he made a phone call and alerted a man close to him and Mendoza, a man by the name of Natalia Cannapolis Senior, who was the unnamed source.

"We gotta get things in order for the friends' arrivals later this morning. I'm headed to the deli once I dress," Natalia Cannapolis Senior told DeeDee as he rose from his bed.

Natalia Senior was a retired seventy-nine-year-old Cicero cop and made man. His family ran another crew inside of Twenty-Third Street Mafia. They were the family's disposal crew on top of being a valuable source of information. A lot of hits Twenty-Third had executed were committed on the streets. Many of the victims were killed in public, but those who'd pulled off the public hits left little to nothing behind by-way-of evidence. The ability to execute a homicide and leave no evidence behind was a main factor in this highly-proficient criminal organization's longevity.

Sometimes, however, a job would require the complete destruction of the intended victim. During those times, the Cannapolis Family was the crew Twenty-Third turned to in order to destroy a human body completely. The two families were close, but in respect only, as the Cannapolis Family attended no parties or celebrations. It wasn't out of disrespect or anything on the part of Cannapolis Family, to the contrary, it was the fact that they operated as legitimate businessmen before the eyes of other businessmen and politicians in the states of Illinois and Indiana. The Cannapolis Family had a lot of pull. Their affiliation with Twenty-Third Street Mafia spans back over thirty years.

"I picked a paper up on my way out of the lobby of my condo. You saw the headline in the Tribune?" DeeDee asked as he placed a coffee pot onto the grill's stove and turned the fire up high.

"Mendoza Cernigliaro, Infamous Mobster, Killed." Natalia Senior remarked as he stood beside DeeDee, repeatedly dipping a tea bag into a separate pot of boiling pot of water. "What a front-page story."

"I read the autopsy report before I called you," DeeDee stated as he looked around for a coffee mug.

"Mugs are over there," Natalia Senior guided as he nudged his portly chin towards the middle sink situated behind the bar counter. "I was surprised when you told me about Mendoza being sick and all. It's funny how, how he and Zell suffered from the same condition," the 5'8", one hundred and ninety-five pound Italian with a neatly-trimmed grey mustache and short grey hair remarked matter-of-factly.

"Pancreatic cancer," DeeDee said as he walked over to the sink and rinsed out a mug. "Both were facing death in a short period of time and handled a crisis in ways unexpected."

"When Zell agreed to make Mendoza boss and allow him to sell drugs it cost my son his life." Natalia Senior replied as he poured himself a cup of tea.

"And Mendoza's actions cost him his," DeeDee countered as he poured up a coffee for himself. "If only he would've let us know what the reasons were we probably, we probably could've done something different, Natalia."

"I was the guy who gave Mendoza the information on Chloe Sexton. He said not to say a word to no one. I never thought he would do something like that, otherwise, I would've stopped him myself."

DeeDee had always wondered what it was exactly that was motivating Mendoza to go after Chloe Sexton in such a callous manner. Now he knew: his friend was dying of pancreatic cancer. Mendoza's illness was only part of the story for DeeDee. Besides the autopsy report he'd obtained from the Medical Examiner earlier that morning, the Chicago Tribune article he'd read had chronicled the fact that Mendoza Cernigliaro had been shot dead by a federal agent while in the process of killing Chloe Sexton, who was going to testify before a grand jury against him for two murders she knew he'd committed.

The news article had given DeeDee some valuable information. Mendoza had never mentioned the feds being involved to neither he, Francine nor Naomi, but because of the article, he was now made aware. The last witness in two possible murder indictments, one from two years ago back in 2006 against Finland Xavier, and the other having taken place nearly forty years ago in 1969 in Lester Sexton, had been killed. The only person left to be questioned was Naomi, and DeeDee knew she wasn't going to talk.

With those facts aside, DeeDee knew his daughter-in-law would possibly get questioned by the feds, the one group of people who the family had always stirred clear of given their illegitimate ventures. Those thoughts and more ran though his mind as he opened a double door steel refrigerator beneath the counter and grabbed a roll of sausage and a container holding a dozen eggs. He and Natalia Senior had prepared breakfast and had eaten and where placing the upturned chairs inside The Cicero Hot Dog Deli onto the floor forty minutes later.

"I thought someone would've at least stuck their head in on their way to work. It's twenty minutes to seven already. Neighborhood's still and quiet," DeeDee remarked as he and Natalia Senior set about pulling sheets off of the tables.

"You're right about that," Natalia Senior agreed through the silence as he and DeeDee threw the sheets into a bin inside the deli's linen closet. "Times have changed, man, I tell ya'. These youngsters on the streets today don't respect no one and nothing. I mean, all the old timers, they've, they've all passed away for the most part and it's all but a handful of us left. I've been around and so have you. It's an entirely new generation of gangsters out there that care less—but don't worry, il mio amico, the ones from back in the day will show. They're up in age now so it takes a while for 'em to get going," he laughed as he shut the linen closet's doors.

"I'm an early riser myself. Been that way ever since I moved in with my daughter-in-law on the ranch after my son was killed," DeeDee said as he returned to his cup of coffee.

Natalia Senior nodded in agreement. "Our sons was in different crews inside Twenty Third but there was never any animosity. It was tension, because both crews understood the hell out of this business. But Natalia Junior should've taken my advice and stayed out of that deal with Zell and Mendoza. That's not how we operate. My son's decision pit me against my own family, the same as Mendoza was pitted against Junior. What is with the Italian juniors in this outfit? Doss Junior was a stand-up guy. So much so he was made boss of the family."

"Yeah, but he took it over at such a violent time, Natalia," DeeDee contemplated out loud as he walked over to the large, dark-brown tinted front window of the deli where a small wooden table and two tall bar stools were situated. He took a seat and began placing chess pieces into their proper position atop a Chicago Bears-themed chess board.

"See, that goes back to what we was talking about with these youngsters, DeeDee," Natalia Senior remarked as he walked behind the counter and reheated his pot of tea. "I meant to tell you the time you arrived, but we got off into other things," he added. "I got some information that may be of even more value to you than that just that Medical Examiner's report and what was leaked to the press."

"I'm all ears," DeeDee said casually as he eyed Natalia Senior with a slick grin.

"You calling me out, DeeDee?" Natalia Senior questioned the moment he turned around with his fresh cup of tea and eyed his friend sitting at the chess table.

"One of the things I know about this newly-renovated establishment is that whoever sits here at this table is awaiting an opponent," DeeDee remarked as he eyed the chess board.

"Yeah, ya', ya' calling me out," Natalia Senior stated through light laughter as he walked over and unlocked the deli's front door, his wide body wobbling over the wooden floors. "It's nearing seven so I know the family will be in soon. Now," he said as he approached the table and climbed up into a chair, almost like that of a child given his short stature and wide frame. "Bahdoon LuQman is being moved sometime after Christmas. This agent, though," he said as he moved a few pieces around on the board. "The lead agent that was working the case against Mendoza? Not only was he the one who killed Mendoza, but he's also the agent behind having Bahdoon shipped over to Stateville Prison. The Somali told the agent what he knew about the Desiree Abbadando hit over in Denver and a missing woman named Kathryn Perez down in Saint Louis."

"Do we know the agent's name?" DeeDee asked.

"That I couldn't find out. Couldn't get his name at all. Don't know who his superior is either because none was listed in the report I got. I'll see what I can pull up, but it doesn't look too promising."

DeeDee and Natalia Senior was just about to start their game of chess when the door to the hot dog deli opened. Natalia

Senior looked up from the game board and saw a voluptuous tan-skinned woman with cropped black hair and full lips. She was dressed in a dark-brown cashmere trench coat and black knee-length boots. "Hello, DeeDee," the woman said humbly as she stood with her fingers intertwined.

DeeDee turned and smiled at the image that stood before him. "It's nice to see you, Sharona," he delightfully remarked. "How'd you know I'd be here at this hour?"

Forty year-old Sharona Benson held up a copy of the Chicago Tribune. "I went to your condo. When you weren't there I figured I would find you here. This place has undergone quiet a transformation. And it still holds onto some of its old tradition," she complimented as she looked around the renovated building.

The pool tables that once sat in the floor's center and all the booths lining the wall had been removed to create more space for more tables and chairs in the room's center. Sharona noticed that one booth in particular remained, however—Zell's old booth, which sat at the far left corner in the back of the deli. Another entrance was near Zell's booth now. There was never a door there Sharona could remember. She remembered East Side Bar and Grill being a dimly-lit place where some of the most dangerous men and women in Chicago's underworld hung out and conducted business. As of the present, however, the place was brighter and more family-oriented.

"Who would've ever thought this gangster's domain would've been transformed into a hot dog deli." Sharona stated as she looked the establishment over with appreciation.

"And a damn good hot dog deli it is," Natalia Senior stated proudly.

"I believe you, Mister Cannapolis. I'm going to have to try this place out one day."

"And it'll be on the house when you does come through, young lady. Come on over, Sharona. Let me fix you a hot cup of coffee." Natalia Senior invited as he swung his stubby legs around and eased down from the bar stool.

DeeDee hadn't seen Sharona Benson since the summer of 2001, when she'd abruptly left him without saying goodbye, nor offering a reason as to why. He'd always had his suspicions as to why Sharona had left him, but he was never able to confirm it as he was never afforded the opportunity. Through his disappointment, he eyed Sharona with appreciation. She was even more beautiful than the last day he'd seen her as she walked over to him while staring directly into his eyes with a concerned look.

When Sharona neared, DeeDee stood up from his bar stool and opened his arms slightly. His ex-lover stepped into him and hugged him tightly, holding onto him for several lingering seconds.

"Are you okay?" Sharona asked as she leaned back and held onto the sleeves of DeeDee's silk suit jacket.

DeeDee looked into Sharona's dark-brown eyes and swallowed a lump in his throat. "I have the task of going down there and identify my friend's body ahead of me. Don't know if I can handle it."

"You want me to go with?" Sharona asked sincerely as she tilted her head and looked up at DeeDee with caring eyes.

"Would you?"

"I wouldn't mind, DeeDee." Sharona paused and looked to the floor. "I have to be honest," she then confessed. "For a while I've been searching for you. I have something very important to tell you, baby."

The door to the deli opened at that moment and a lone, muscular male figure dressed in a black wool trench coat and black fedora entered holding onto a black briefcase. "Granddad," the man called out as he pushed the door shut with the base of his leather shoe while eyeing the slender black man and the woman standing before him. "Who are you guys? Where's my granddad? Grandad?" the young Italian called out as he set his briefcase down and moved his hand towards his trench coat.

Natalia Senior walked from behind the bar counter and said,

"Natalia, it's okay, son. It's DeeDee and an old acquaintance of his by the name of Sharona. Sharona? This is my grandson, Natalia the third."

"Nice to meet you, ma'am," Natalia III stated as he removed his hands from his trench coat and shook Sharona's hand. "I didn't recognize you, Mister DeeDee," he added. "I come here and the place is all quiet with only two people inside. I was expecting a large turnout. Word travels through this neighborhood. Mendoza was a respected man."

"Hard to tell. I was just telling DeeDee how you youngsters don't respect the ones that came before you all," Natalia Senior remarked as he handed Sharona a hot cup of coffee.

"Not all of us, granddad. I told my crew and my guys will show sometime today. They're on their way back from discussing the new arrangement with that guy RJ down in Naptown. You was right." Natalia III responded as he pat his grandfather's chest with the back of his hand.

"I told you he was going to check out. He's connected to the Weinberger family. They're an organized group of Germans and blacks over in Cincinnati." Natalia Senior said as the group began walking over to the bar counter.

"I was the last man in Cicero to ever talk to Mendoza, Mister DeeDee," Natalia III said as he pointed to the booth at the back of the bar.

"Is that so?" DeeDee inquired as Sharona took a seat just a ways down to let the men talk while she waited on DeeDee.

"That's the truth. We kinda didn't hit it off right, you know? I mean, I was only watching the joint. Mendoza wanted this special-made hot dog and wanted to sit in Zell's booth by his self and eat it while listening to Frank Sinatra over and over and over and over again," Natalia III complained as he rolled a finger beside his ear.

DeeDee and Natalia Senior laughed lowly over Natalia III's subtle rant. "It drove me crazy, let me tell ya'," Natalia III noted. He then dropped his smile and rubbed his chiseled, neatly-trimmed black beard in deep thought. "Mendoza also told me that I make enough money to get myself killed. Said it was a business. And in business? No matter the business, when there's money to be gained from that business? Tomorrow isn't promised."

"Sounds like something Mendoza would say," DeeDee nodded as he reflected on the statement.

"He also told me I wouldn't last five minutes on the streets." Natalia III quickly followed.

"That was Mendoza alright," DeeDee chuckled as he beckoned Sharona while chuckling with Natalia Senior.

Natalia III stepped closer to DeeDee and looked him in the eyes. "Mendoza was wrong about that, il mio amico," he stated in an adamant tone. "I took it as an insult because it's obvious the guy didn't know me all-too-well and what it is that I do exactly now that I'm all grown up. My grandfather was right about one thing—times have changed. Not many guys would've taken what Mendoza said. And had it been anybody else? I would've killed the guy. But it was out of respect for who he was that I put pride aside and sat and had a drink with the last Don of Cicero—nothing more. His business wasn't my business."

Twenty-six year-old Natalia III once ran with Junior Cernigliaro. The two of them oversaw security for the cocaine shipments Doss Dawkins was having shipped in from Seattle, Washington. Natalia III knew nothing of Junior's plan to stage a coup. When Doss was killed, word on the streets soon spread that Junior was involved. Natalia III swore to his father and grandfather that he had nothing to do with setting Doss up to get killed.

Natalia Senior, on the other hand, had known of the hit against Doss, but he'd disapproved. Going against his disapproval, Natalia Senior's own son, Natalia Junior, sided with Junior Cernigliaro. Their plan was to use Q-Man and Toodie Perez to kill Doss Dawkins. From there, they were going to kill Mendoza and DeeDee and split the cities of Saint Louis and Chicago and set up their own cocaine operation.

Natalia III was made aware of the treachery by his

grandfather and was forced to make the hardest decision of his life: that of killing his own father, or holding to true to La Cosa Nostra. In his eyes, Doss Dawkins was Boss of the family, and with him out of the picture, and with Junior Cernigliaro disposed of, he knew the next in line to run the organization was Doss Dawkins' son, Dawk Holland, someone he knew in name only back in 2006. Respecting the order of things within the organization, Natalia III sided with the Holland family. He'd killed his own father on behalf of the family and had solidified his position as their top Italian connect.

Natalia III had met Dawk for the first time last month down in Saint Genevieve, Missouri. The two had discussed rackets and Dawk informed him that the family had something in the works coming on in a few months and he would contact him then. Not one to wait, Natalia III started his own cocaine operation, only Natalia III didn't pay for the product he sold. He robbed other dealers in and around Chicago and sold the bricks out of state. He was, by all means, a dangerous man involved in deadly business. As of now, Natalia III answered to no one but himself; he called the shots on the streets of Cicero. And this is the reason he'd told DeeDee how disrespected he felt when he'd conversed with Mendoza.

DeeDee eyed Natalia with a stern stare. He knew of him having killed his own father on behalf of the family and gave him a measure of respect because of that fact. "I appreciate your honesty, son," he spoke sternly. "But, I don't think Mendoza would've cared one way or the other."

"I did, though, Mister DeeDee," Natalia remarked truthfully. "Just to let you know? I still adhere to the order of things. Tell Dawk don't forget about me and my guys up here in Chicago."

"We have no rackets as of now in this city, but we have something in the works." DeeDee told Natalia III as he headed for the door while holding Sharona's hand. "Someone from the family will notify you when the time is right."

"Good. One more thing," Natalia III said as DeeDee turned back around to face him. "That hot dog meal Mendoza wanted was a special one that he wanted to share with everybody. The Cernigliaro is what he wanted it to be called. It's an Italian sausage dog with au gratin, a large order of fries and Pepsi with a full bottle of scotch and a Duke of Devon Macanudo Cigar imported from the Dominican Republic. I have a Expedition full of rolled sausages and fresh baked buns. I even stopped and got some boxes of cigars last night on the way home. I did all those things only to find no one's here outside of us. The fuck is wrong with people? Don't they have any respect?"

"You were preparing to fix my friend's last meal?" DeeDee asked surprised. "I never knew that story."

"Mendoza told me two nights ago that I would have a story to tell," Natalia III confessed. "And it's one I'll tell to everyone who sits in his booth for the first time. I'm gonna create a new menu with his meal on it, fix the booth up and place today's newspaper in there and charge two hundred bucks for The Cernigliaro like he requested."

Just then, the door to the deli was pushed open once more and an octogenarian Italian couple entered the building. "Where's Francine?" an old woman's high-pitched voice called out in the lobby. "Francine? Is Francine all right?"

"Where the hell is everybody? Did they not read the paper this morning?" the woman's husband, a man named Scoffield Cannapolis, asked in a snippy voice.

"They'll be around, Scoffield!" Natalia Senior snapped in a steadfast voice from across the room. "You and my sister-in-law come on in here!"

DeeDee eased past Sharona and greeted the portly Scoffield and his slender grey-haired wife. "You and your family are amongst the first to show, Scoffield. Thanks for coming," he remarked.

"What the hell is wrong with people? Do they not know what a legend had been lost?" Scoffield complained as he removed his wife's coat.

Eighty-four year-old Scoffield 'The Butcher' Cannapolis owned a steel shredding plant over in Gary, Indiana and another plant down in Sainte Genevieve, Missouri. He was the man who'd made Lester Sexton and Finland Xavier disappear by running their corpses through his car crusher over in Gary, Indiana. His last job was the disposal of Toodie Perez the previous month—a job in which Natalia III had overseen down in Sainte Genevieve, Missouri where he'd met Dawk Holland briefly.

The Cannapolis Family had destroyed dozens of human bodies. Scoffield had retired, but the family's disposal business remained intact, having been passed down to Natalia III, a twenty-six year-old Italian who by all outward appearances was a man who simply ran a hot dog deli.

"You know, it's still early," Natalia III reasoned upon seeing the arrival of his family. "Tell ya' what? I'll go get the sausages out the jeep, granddad will fire up the grill and we'll—"

"I hate to be rude, gentlemen, but I have business." DeeDee interjected. The long-time mafia affiliate really wanted to get the ordeal of having to identify Mendoza's body over with so he could notify the rest of the family in Oklahoma. He was also wondering what it was that Sharona had to tell him that was so important.

"Business hell!" Scoffield protested. "Mendoza's on ice, but I could hear him right now saying, saying, 'What the hell is the rush? I ain't going no damn where'."

DeeDee chuckled as he stood beside Sharona. He pulled out four one hundred dollar bills and said, "Let me be the first to honor my friend by paying for you and your wife's hot dog dinner, Scoffield. I have business."

"What is this hot dog dinner and menu you speak of, DeeDee?" Scoffield asked.

Natalia III stepped forth at that moment and, for a second time, he proudly told the conversation he'd held with Mendoza concerning his last request to his great uncle.

"The Cernigliaro," Scoffield smiled after hearing the story. "I would've guessed a T-bone steak knowing the guy, but I'll try it—bring the scotch first!" he quipped as he and his wife headed for the booth where Mendoza Cernigliaro last sat.

"DeeDee, let us know Francine's plans for Mendoza. And your money is no good here, il mio amico! Just take care of our friend!"

DeeDee and Sharona left the hot dog deli and stepped into the blowing, cold wind and were greeted by a quartet of Italian women in their seventies. The women often hung out inside of East Side Bar. Two of them had three sons for a couple of members of Twenty-Third Street Mafia, and their grandchildren now worked for Natalia III. Although waning in its power, there was still an Italian connect up in Cicero that could be a valuable asset to the Holland family if handled correctly.

The four women standing before DeeDee had been around for as long as time itself. They were basically considered whores in their younger years. DeeDee had been intimate with a couple of the women back in the late sixties and seventies, but he would never mistreat them or even view them as such. Those were the younger, wilder years, when everybody that hung out inside East Side Bar felt invincible. Decades later, they all were in the final stages of their lives and were no longer the same people.

"Is Francine inside, DeeDee?" one of the women asked in a concerned manner as the group walked up to the deli's entrance.

"No," DeeDee answered. "Thank you all for coming. The Cannapolis family is inside. They have something special going on this morning—a small farewell, but I'm going to talk to Francine before making any major plans."

"You mean she doesn't' know yet?" the woman asked disheartened as she tightened her headscarf under the falling snow. "Give her my condolences and tell her she's in our prayers will ya', DeeDee?"

"I will. You ladies go on inside where it's warm," DeeDee remarked as he placed his cream-colored velvet fedora onto his head and held the door open for the women. Once the females entered the deli, he guided Sharona to the black stretched Cadillac limousine that was idling out in front of The Cicero

Hot Dog Deli.

Once inside the ride, DeeDee raised the partition and looked over to Sharona in silence as the driver pulled away from the curb. She coughed nervously as she patted her chest while DeeDee remained silent, his eyes being shadowed by the fedora that was pulled down onto his head while he stared at his ex-lover as The Jacksons' song *Good Times* began to play over the radio.

"Will you stop gawking at me like that? Please?" Sharona pleaded respectfully over the melodic song's intro.

"It's been nearly a decade since I've last seen you, Sharona. You left me high and dry. I appreciate you coming down today, and I thank for taking this ride with me because it'll make it that much easier for me to deal with—but you owe me an explanation as to why you left me, woman."

"What do you tell your family about us splitting up?" Sharona asked as she leaned forward and removed her cashmere coat.

"I never give a reason. I just say you left me in my old age whenever the moment warrants discussion." DeeDee answered.

"You know that was not the reason why I ended our relationship, Doss," Sharona stated tenderly as she placed a hand on DeeDee's silk-clad knee.

"Hell, I know that wasn't the case," DeeDee chuckled confidently as he looked out his passenger window. "I'm as hard as the day is long."

"I can't argue with that," Sharona admitted as she briefly reflected on DeeDee's strong, everlasting lovemaking skills. The hours they'd spent together in bed could never be forgotten. The many trips to Maine, Vegas and the Virgin Islands were all times she would forever cherish. "I've started my own advertising agency, Doss," she told DeeDee, breaking the brief moment of silence. "It's called Benson and Company. I produce high-budgeted commercials for major corporations from Kellogg to Kraft Foods. I own a mansion in Rockland and a condo on the upper east side of Manhattan where my production company is located."

"I always knew you would go far in your career, Sharona. I'm happy you're doing okay in life." DeeDee smiled as the limousine cruised down the avenue under the falling snow.

"And I'm glad to know you're alive and well, Doss. You say you tell your family I left you in your old age, but why do you really think I left?"

"You found another lover closer to your age so you could start a family," DeeDee stated bluntly as he looked out the window and ran his hand underneath his chin.

"There was never another lover, Doss," Sharona admitted through a truthful stare.

"Then why? Why did you leave me, Sharona?" DeeDee asked as he looked over to Sharona.

"I didn't want our child growing up in the life, Doss." Sharona admitted nervously as she bit her bottom lip and eyed DeeDee, awaiting his reaction.

"Our child?" DeeDee asked as he sat upright. "What child?" he asked in wonderment.

"When I walked out of your life in July of two thousand one?" Sharona asked rhetorically as she leaned back into the leather seat and crossed her legs. "When I ended all contact with you I was two months pregnant. You had this, this thing you were involved in with some Asians is all I ever knew. You were going back and forth to all these different cities and all. It got real busy for the both of us, you know? We grew apart and I became afraid."

"You had no need to fear me, Sharona. I would've never hurt you."

"You hurting me wasn't the fear I had. I feared what other people would do to me and your son to get back at you, Doss. He was only a few months old when Lucky was killed. I wanted to come to the funeral and introduce you to your child, but I was too ashamed to show my face in Cicero because I'd abandoned you and thought you would never forgive me."

"You should've come, Sharona. We could've made things right."

"You left me vulnerable, DeeDee," Sharona remarked as her eyes welled. "As smart a man as you were and are still, you left me vulnerable here in Chicago. I went to bed petrified nights you were gone. I didn't want to raise my son under those conditions."

"That was something we could've worked out, Sharona. To just up and leave?"

"I realized that some time ago, DeeDee. It wasn't that big of a deal," Sharona smiled. "And I mean that in a good way. I see now I had nothing to fear. I ask your apology."

"Neither one of us owe an apology. You did what you felt was best. So, I have a son. How old is he and what's his name?" DeeDee asked.

"He's seven. His name is Doss Dawkins the third. I knew Doss was a junior, so I carried on with the tradition. I left him home with his nanny because I wasn't sure how you would react. Still aren't sure. I'm missing my song, honey. Turn it up a little, please?"

"You sure it's mine?" DeeDee asked as he adjusted the volume.

Sharona looked DeeDee in the eyes. "That is a question to be expected," she acknowledged. "DeeDee, I'm not here to ask you for one single penny. Our son is very well taken care of. I just know what a family man you are and I'm willing to put everything on the table to allow you to make your own decision as to whether or not you want to be a part of your son's life because the door is open, baby. It's open."

"Does he look old?" DeeDee inquired as he leaned back and stared over at Sharona with raised eyebrows.

"What?" Sharona laughed in a bedazzled manner as she reached out and tapped DeeDee's shoulder softly. "What made you ask that question, Doss?"

"I had to have been sixty-six or sixty-seven when you conceived, somewhere around that age. I mean, the boy might have old genes, a wrinkle forehead or a receding hairline."

"You have great skin and a head full of hair, Doss. You look years younger," Sharona complimented. "Our son is a typical boy that reminds me of his father in so many ways. He's intelligent, fearless, low key, and he's a handsome fella."

DeeDee entered a deep thought. Losing Doss was a heartbreaking experience for him. He knew he could lose Dawk each time his grandson left the ranch. Dawk had been a part of the family business for over eight years now, however; it was a life that he was bred to live and the consequences were understood.

Walee was a young player just getting his feet wet on the streets. He dealt with many females and was making money. DeeDee knew both of his grandsons were either directly or indirectly affiliated with was now deemed 'the life' and it worried him. Learning he had a young son, however, offered him a new day. He now had another chance to raise a son, and this time, he wouldn't teach him the business, he would coax him into something legitimate or at the very least place him on the right path the remaining years he had left on Earth at age seventy-five.

"He's a handsome fella?" DeeDee smiled, relinquishing his thoughts.

"Sure is." Sharona replied as she smiled back over to DeeDee.

"Well, I'm gone have to see for myself and make sure."

"You don't believe me?" Sharona asked.

"I do. But let's be real about it."

"Okay," Sharona replied as she chuckled, already deciphering DeeDee's apprehension. "Go on and say what's on your mind concerning your son, DeeDee."

"I just don't want him to look old, Sharona. Because, woman? You was loving on an old ass man." DeeDee laughed.

Sharona let go of a hearty laugh as she planted her head in DeeDee's chest. The two of them laughed together over their age differences and reminisced on the stares they'd often received whenever they were out together.

"Remember the waitress who was taking our order at that seafood restaurant inside that bed and breakfast in Bangor, Maine?" Sharona asked through laughter.

"That woman?" DeeDee scoffed as he shook his legs rapidly. "She touched a nerve when she said—"

"And your daughter is having?" DeeDee and Sharona quoted the words in unison before laughing aloud as they touched foreheads.

"You set her ass straight, Sharona!" DeeDee laughed.

"Umm, hmm. Asked her what the hell I look like getting romantic with my daddy. She knew couples went there, her behind was tryna be funny!" Sharona stated in mocked disgust as she laughed along with DeeDee. "She brought that south side out of me—just a small bit, though," she said as she pinched two fingers together. *The good times, baby...I think about it..."* she then sung aloud as she bowed her head and snapped her fingers to The Jacksons' song titled *Good Times.* "Yes, lord," she smiled through closed eyes.

"We had some wonderful times, Sharona," DeeDee said cheerfully as he tapped his foot to the music. "I dealt with a lot of women that were only after my money. It wasn't like that with you. I was your man. You took care of me, but not as a senior citizen, you was doing it for your man."

"I loved you, DeeDee. Was *in love* with you," Sharona professed as she suddenly leaned in and kissed her former lover.

DeeDee, although caught off guard, responded. He kissed Sharona deeply as he cupped her chin. Those old feelings had immediately returned for both former lovers. They held onto one another while breathing heavily as their tongues interacted. Sharona reached down and caressed DeeDee's dick through his slacks, but he pulled away and leaned back in the leather seat at that moment. "Her name is Irene," he admitted.

"So there's someone in your life," Sharona coughed as she

pulled her dress down. "I'm sorry. I should've asked first. How rude of me."

"No apology needed," DeeDee assured. "It's been secret for a while. I just don't feel right doing this. Not now. Not over the circumstances."

"I understand. And again, I'm sorry for not being more considerate." Sharona replied as she reached for her purse and snapped it open. "I'm happy you have someone. Do you love her?" she asked while grabbing a mirror and small tube of lip gloss.

"Love might be a tad too strong word to use at this moment," DeeDee admitted, "but I can say I care deeply. What about you?"

Sharona shook her head to say no after she'd applied a fresh coating of gloss to her full, sexy lips. "I haven't the time. And any man coming behind you has their work cut out. All I meet is pretenders, DeeDee. No contenders."

The limousine had pulled up to the Cook County Medical Examiner's office at that moment. "Well, this is it," DeeDee said as he thumbed his fingers anxiously.

"It'll be okay, Doss. I'll be with you," Sharona said as she sprayed her wrists with expensive perfume and dabbed her earlobes. "And, just to let you know? I respect your love life. I'm not a baby momma drama queen. The last thing I want to do is cause contention between you and the lady you adore because you and I both know we always did it with class. The offer? As far as you being a part of your son's life? It still stands. You're welcome to introduce him to your family if that is what you want. There're many doctors in town willing to give you both a blood test to end all doubt."

"Sharona I don't need a—"

"I want you to, DeeDee," Sharona interjected as she placed her coat back onto her body. "That'll do away with any suspicion in your family. I know he's yours, but to just pop up with a seven year-old child claiming to be your son would raise suspicion and motive. Am I right in my assumptions?"

"My family is a welcoming family. But you have a point. We do this the right way to erase all doubt. But not my doubt, only that of my family, because I believe you, baby." DeeDee ended as he opened the door, climbed out and helped Sharona from the car.

****

The long grey hall located in the basement of the Medical Examiner's office seemed like a lonely gateway to hell to DeeDee as he and Sharona walked side by side, approaching a set of grey aluminum double doors at the end of the hall. The nearer he grew to the doors, the more somber DeeDee grew. His eyes watered as he reflected on the fifty-plus years he'd known Mendoza.

The man had been an ally for justice on the streets if DeeDee had to tell it. He'd served up retribution on behalf of his murdered wife in the late fifties. He was a loyal friend willing to die in honor when the coup against Zell Verniche` backfired in the mid-nineties, and was a savior two times over to the Holland family when he'd given up his own grandson after Junior Cernigliaro had staged a hostile takeover. The ultimate, was Mendoza sacrificing his own life by going after a witness rather than go before a grand jury and testify against the family. The depth of gratitude DeeDee felt towards Mendoza Cernigliaro was a debt he felt could never be repaid.

When DeeDee reached the double doors he placed his hands on the aluminum, yet unable to push as he knew he would be ushering in a new era. His oldest three grandchildren and their cousin from Arizona and his crew would now lead the next phase of the family business. He wondered how they would fare, and even more so, would they survive the bloodshed that was sure to come in the very near future given the family's plan.

Brushing business aside, DeeDee grabbed Sharona's hand tightly and pushed the door open. The lone, paunchy Caucasian coroner in his mid-sixties recognized him right away. He stepped back from the body he was autopsying, removed his latex gloves and sanitized his hands in a sink beside the metal table. "I was wondering when someone would show," he said reverentially as he extended his hand out while walking towards DeeDee.

"Someone's here now," DeeDee spoke lowly as he eyed a corpse lying on one of the metal slabs, that of a black male who'd obviously suffered gunshot wounds given the darkened holes in his side, stomach and chest. The male's head was torn off halfway, only his nose and lips recognizable as the top portion of his skull was a mangled mess. "I hope my friend fared better in his condition," he said to the Medical Examiner.

"Ohh, he looks as if he's asleep, DeeDee," the man said as he waved his hands in the air. "I did what I could to sew up the damage to his body, but his face was untouched. He'll have an open casket if that is what Francine wants."

"Let me see my friend," DeeDee requested through a calm whisper.

"Got 'em over here," the Medical Examiner remarked as he walked over to a wall of freezer doors and pulled one open that was at waist level.

DeeDee kissed Sharona's temple before he walked over to the metal slab where his friend lay. On first glance, it appeared as if Mendoza was asleep indeed, but something was off about his appearance as he lay in death before DeeDee's eyes.

The Medical Examiner, sensing DeeDee's perplexities, stepped up and said, "His hair was dyed black when he arrived. I rinsed it out and brought it back to its white color as best I could. I also powdered his face with talcum and touched up his lips with a little blush because they'd darkened a bit."

"He looks like a vampire, man. Dracula." DeeDee complained. "Do away with the powder and blush."

"I'll see to it before my shift ends today. It's a mortician's job anyway."

After signing to have Mendoza's remains turned over to a funeral home back in Cicero, DeeDee and Sharona left the Medical Examiner's office. While approaching the limousine, the two were greeted by several reporters who'd been staking out the area and were bombarded with a slew of questions.

"Mister Dawkins, who is the purported witness Mendoza Cernigliaro killed and what was her connection to Twenty-Third Street Mafia?" "What kind of repercussions will Mendoza Cernigliaro's death have on the Chicago underworld?" "Were you involved in Chloe Sexton's death?" "Are you the next in line to succeed Mendoza Cernigliaro?"

DeeDee uttered not a word as he trotted down the stairs, tugging Sharona with him where the two climbed inside of the waiting limousine and left the area.

"Well, are you next in line?" Sharona asked as she looked back at the reporters snapping pictures of the limousine.

"No," DeeDee answered.

"Good. I suspect you'll be here in town through Christmas making the arrangements for Mendoza's funeral. If you want? I'll take you to your son."

"I would like that. He's seven, right?"

"Yes."

"Let's go shopping."

"Shopping? For what?" Sharona asked curiously.

"Toys. I wanna see my boy and bring him some Christmas gifts. I want my first time meeting him to be memorable."

"Really?" Sharona asked as her eyes lit up. "You haven't even seen your son and you're willing to do all of this on a moment's notice?"

"You've never been a woman to deceive me, Sharona. I don't think you would play that kind of a game," DeeDee let it be known. His eyes then caught sight of the folder he'd obtained from Natalia Senior. "How could I let *this* slip my mind!" he quipped.

"Is everything okay?" Sharona asked anxiously.

"I have to make an important phone call before we do anything, Sharona. Driver? Take me over to my condo on Lake Shore Drive," DeeDee ended as the limousine left the area.

CHAPTER TWO

HOLLAND HOLIDAYS

"...My niggaz would do anything for me...jealous niggaz in the 'hood that'll look at me funny...'cause a nigga lookin' good and he hittin' your honey...see we still up in tha' hood and I'm gettin' mo money..."

Eighteen-year-old Walee Dawkins lay sprawled out on his back atop a plush king-sized bed inside the Skirvin Hilton Hotel, just north of downtown Oklahoma City in an area known as Deep Deuce. The left foot of a naked twenty-four-year-old Jordan Whispers lay upon his chest as she slept at the opposite end of the king-sized bed on her back. The breasts of twenty-one year-old Anquette Sears was pressed to the right side of his face as Tre` Songs' remix to the rapper Game's song titled *Dreams* played over the speakers inside his suite.

Tre` Songz was ripping the lyrics as Walee stirred from his slumber amid a tangled mass of naked flesh. He pushed Jordan's manicured foot off his chest and looked around groggily, having to recall exactly where he lay as the night before had been one of the wildest nights he'd ever experienced in his young life. It had taken the eighteen-year-old playboy a while to get Jordan and Anquette together in the same room for the simple fact that they despised one another. Jordan felt Anquette, the cashier Walee had met at a Chic Fila inside Quail Mall back in 2006, was threatening to take her position as Walee's number one.

Jordan had been involved with the family since early 2002. She, Dawk and her friend Oneika Brackens had a three-way love affair going until Dawk got serious with Oneika. Jordan and Walee got tight after he'd paid her a hundred dollars to break his virginity when he was only fourteen years old. She'd basically been teaching him the art of seduction from the first day the two had sex and had been his loyal ally for the last four years or so.

Jordan's resolve did nothing to prevent the rising of jealousy's ugly head whenever she felt that her position beside Walee was being threatened, however; and as of date, Anquette Sears, the 5', brown-skinned, short curly-haired, dark-eyed twenty-one year-old was her latest threat.

Walee and Jordan made quick eye contact as they lay toe-to-toe in the bed. She plopped her foot back onto Walee's chest and laughed through sleepy eyes. "Morning, daddy," she cooed sweetly as she wiggled her toes.

"The fuck all we done last night?" Walee asked as he jumped off the bed and turned the music down and trotted over to the cameras and turned the power off. "I hope I ain't eat no fuckin' pussy!"

Anquette stirred awake at that moment and looked around as she removed hair from her face and stared at Jordan. "Oh no," she sighed as she fell back into the feather pillows. "Tell me this didn't happen."

"The things you let me do to you," Jordan spoke through a sly smile as she shook her from side-to-side.

All three participants in the previous night's ménage a trois eyed one another in the nude as they either replayed, or tried to remember what all had gone down. Three loud stems and uncountable bottles of champagne clouded memories, but the two cameras at the foot of the bed on either side facing the mattress held the evidence.

Walee was preparing to check the video when a knock on the door interrupted. "Yo, fam?" eighteen year-old Kahlil Jamison yelled aloud as he knocked on the door repeatedly.

Walee wrapped a towel around his waist and went and cracked the door to the suite where he saw a fully dressed Kahlil standing out in the hall.

"Who set up the cameras, dog?" Walee asked.

"You don't remember? You had me set things up for a eight hour strip. Let me see what the fuck happened in here!" Kahlil laughed as he made his way inside the suite to check the cameras.

Seventeen year-olds Spoonie and Tyke came running into the room at that moment. "What y'all been doing?" Tyke asked aloud. "Oooh!" she exclaimed upon noticing a naked Jordan and Anquette splayed out on the bed. "Walee got like the best Christmas gift ever for a man!"

"Yooo," Walee sang as he ushered his youngest sisters out the room. "Kahlil? Take care my sisters, fam."

"Gotcha, big dog," Kahlil responded as he walked out the room while smirking over at Jordan and Anquette. "Thought y'all didn't like each other," he declared as he strode past the bed.

"We don't!" Jordan and Anquette snapped in unison as they stared one another down.

"K-Dog." Kahlil turned around and Walee stepped closer.

"What up, fam?"

"I was fucked up last night," Walee whispered. "We all was fucked up, except for Spoonie and Tyke as far as I could remember. What you and my sisters did last night, dog?"

"We made a video too, dude." Kahlil smiled as he clicked his fists together.

Walee didn't crack a smile as he stared at Kahlil. Last thing he remembered was Spoonie and Tyke wrestling with his best friend in the living room as he, Jordan and Anquette headed for the bedroom.

"Spoonie and Tyke? Kahlil? You serious, fam?" Walee asked under his breath.

"Nahh, dog. But I'm showing you something—every film the company you plan on starting make don't have to be X-rated, ya' feel?" Kahlil asked rhetorically as he walked out into the open area of the suite.

"I gotcha. You talkin' like maybe doing a movie or something. That'll be tight. So what y'all did after me and those two come in here?"

"Spoonie and Tyke was drinkin' Gatorade all night. They ain't touch no liquor or did no drugs for sure 'cause I wasn't gone let 'em. Not that they would. Wasn't nothing like that. Come check this out."

Walee went and slid on a pair of silk pajama shorts and a silk t-shirt and walked into the living room. Tyke ran over and clicked on the plasma TV mounted on the suite's living room wall upon his arrival. "Watch this Walee," she said happily as an image of her, Spoonie and Kahlil singing James Brown's song titled *Santa Clause Go Straight to the Ghetto* began playing on the television. It was a quirky video that had Walee's youngest sisters and his best friend singing while passing around wrapped gifts for members of the family.

Walee bowed his head and laughed as he walked over and dapped Kahlil. "That's cool, dog. Thanks for looking after my babies."

"You was tore down last night, fam. But you know I always got you." Kahlil remarked as he rubbed his chin over the music and happy video playing on the wall.

Walee looked back down the hall and saw Jordan's head poking out from the room. She was beckoning him with her left hand with a smile on her face while shaking her head in disbelief. "Y'all come see this shit, man," she laughed.

Walee and Kahlil walked back into his suite and closed the door. The two walked over to the cameras Kahlil had set up the night before and eyed the footage that was running. What came across the screen was nothing short of decadence at its finest. Jordan and Anquette went at it hard. Walee could barely get in between the two, but when he did, he handled his business by taking turns on both females as they rested on their knees while tongue kissing one another. In one scene, Walee was driving into Anquette from behind as Jordan, on Walee's orders, lay up under their junction. When Walee spurted off into Anquette, Jordan's head shot forth and she sucked his juices from her crevice. She flicked her tongue into the camera before swallowing the load she'd sucked from Anquette and then took Walee's come-drenched, pussy-coated dick into her mouth.

Walee, Kahlil, Jordan and Anquette all looked way from the camera. "Damn," they all remarked as they walked off shaking their heads in disbelief.

"Y'all three can when an award in Vegas for the best money shot," Kahlil stated. "Nasty mutherfuckas," he then chided.

"We gone have to go there one day for real, y'all," Walee said seriously as he checked the time on his father's $30,000 Rolex watch. "We got a couple of hours before I head back home so let's get ready to move," he stated in a nonchalant manner as headed for the shower.

A quick stop over to a McDonald's shortly after they'd checked out of the hotel found Walee and his sisters, along with Jordan and Anquette headed east across town to the same subdivision where Bay's condominium lay. Walee pulled up in front of a condo identical to Bay's that sat on the corner of the subdivision near its gated entrance. He parked his Dodge Charger in front of the one story tan-bricked condo that sat up on a hill. "What y'all think, fam?" he asked.

"Think about what?" Jordan asked from the backseat as she looked at the condo, then back over to Walee. "This ain't Bay house."

"I know," Walee replied as he went into his pocket and came up with two sets of keys. "This our place, ya' dig?" he asked rhetorically as he handed a key to Jordan and Anquette.

The look on Jordan's and Anquette's face was one of surprise and disbelief. Anquette had never been in this upscale neighborhood dominated by high-end one story brick condominiums with manicured lawns. It was a long ways from her stomping grounds back over to Lantana Apartments on Oklahoma City's northeast side where she resided.

"This the next level," Walee said seriously as he eyed his crew. "We doing good on the DVDs we putting out and I'm thinking about going legit with it, understand? Get the necessary licensing so we can put these movies out on the market. Let's check it out," he ended as he climbed from behind the wheel of his customized burnt orange Dodge Charger sitting on 26" black steel rims.

Kahlil, Spoonie and Tyke had known of the condo Walee had purchased for over a week. Together, the three of them had furnished the apartment in order to have it laid out for Jordan and Anquette. The three of them, along with Walee, stood on the sidewalk and watched happily as the two females ran up to the home like joyful toddlers and jostled before the door, trying to be the first one to place their key into the key hole. Anquette relented and Jordan unlocked the door and pushed it open. The two ran into the condo side by side and sniffed the new interior, which was reminiscent of fresh-baked vanilla cookies and new leather.

Just like Bay's condo, Walee's pad was laced out with wooden floors, top-of-the-line appliances, with flat screen TVs and king-sized beds in each of the three bedrooms. Jordan and Anquette were shouting with joy as they ran from room to room. Their gratefulness was appreciated, but Walee had to state the terms. He called his women into the living room where everybody took a seat on the white leather c-sectional. "I know how y'all two get down," he began as he eyed Jordan and Anquette. "What I'm putting down today? I'm lettin' y'all know how serious I am about this business. In order for it to work, I can't have none of that jealousy shit going on, ya' feel me?"

"Walee," Jordan spoke up. "After last night it—"

"I'm not done talkin'," Walee spoke calmly, cutting Jordan off.

Jordan pursed her lips shut and leaned back into the sofa and eyed Walee. Anquette, at that moment, had tried to pull rank. "She need to learn how ta' keep her fuckin' mouth—"

"Closed the fuck up like your ass need to learn how to do,"

Walee snapped as he stood up from the couch and placed his hands inside of his grey suede pants and stared down at both women.

Anquette rubbed her eyebrows and leaned back into the sofa. "I'm, my bad," she humbly surrendered.

"I'm not gone have no petty shit going on between y'all two. After last night? Because we all saw it, after last night I figured y'all two would get on the same page. You wanna stay on the team you gone have to play your position. If ya' wondering? Y'all get the privileges and accommodations that come with being here," Walee said as both hands pointed down towards the wooden floor beneath his $1400 dollar Edward Green black suede boots. "But that privilege comes with a price tag."

"What's that?" Anquette asked as she stared up at Walee.

"Jordan already know, but you gotta learn, Anquette. If we gone get major money off this sex venture we gone need more recruits. I'm talking about a solid team of women willing to get down on camera for a one-time fee. They sign a fifteen hundred dollar contract for one sixty minute film and we keep all the proceeds. Each of y'all get fifteen percent off the gross every quarter."

"I know some chicks willing to get down," Anquette stated. "Lantana full of dimes that'll fuck on camera if only to pay the rent."

Walee looked over to Jordan, who was sitting with her legs crossed picking at her nails. She sensed Walee's eyes on her and looked up. "What?" she sighed. "You already know how I do, Walee. I done brought this one in, so I get fifteen percent off top if ever that video go public, already."

Anquette cut her eyes at Jordan. "If I do this, that video from last night stays our secret. I'll recruit, but I'm not willing to put myself out on front street like that. I have to see how this money go first."

"What? You don't want your friends to see you gettin' dick juice sucked out your pussy by another woman? Hell, you winnin', bitch." Jordan sassed as she shook her head and crossed legs.

Anquette eyed Jordan with a scowl before she fanned her off.

Walee looked over to Kahlil at that moment and both young men chuckled. "We all had blood tests run," Walee said, getting back to business. "Whoever get inside this circle gone have to be willing to do the same thing before we even begin shooting. Line 'em up, and I'm gone handle the business side of things so we can start filming next month some time. I'm on my way up the road. You ladies make yourselves at home," he stated as he nodded towards Kahlil and turned towards the door.

"Oh," Walee remembered as he stepped back into the living room. "The fridge stocked out with food. And I know the tree set up and all and it look like no gifts under there, but check the main suite, I left something on the pillows for the both of y'all," he ended before turning back towards the door once more.

Jordan and Anquette sat on the sofa for a couple of minutes after Walee's departure. Both were trying to hold onto their nonchalant attitudes, but they were burning to uncover what Walee had left on the bed inside his suite. When Jordan eased up from the couch, Anquette followed. Jordan started trotting out of the living room and Anquette picked up the pace. When Jordan felt Anquette trying to trot past her, she made a mad dash towards the bedroom.

Two envelopes came into view when Jordan ran into the room. She picked up one of the envelopes, but when she saw Anquette's name, she threw it back down onto the mattress and picked up the second envelope, one that'd better had her name on it. A smile came across her face when she her name and she pried the envelope open.

Both females had received $1500 dollars cash to do as they please. Jordan had had better with Walee, but she knew where he was going with it and understood what he was trying to put down. He was treating them both as equals. And for Jordan, that set right with her. The twenty-four year-old slender, blue-eyed brunette sighed as she looked over to Anquette, who was panting and fanning herself with the envelope as she sat atop the mattress.

"This, this is awesome!" Anquette stated giddily.

"Act like you been here before," Jordan scoffed as she walked out the bedroom.

"You might as well get used to me being here!" Anquette shot back as she fell back on the mattress and kicked her legs in the air happily.

Jordan walked back to the room and stood in the threshold. "I don't have to get used to shit! Your ass just here! All the fuck you is is just here! Here to make money so live up to that shit!"

"Don't worry 'bout me," Anquette laughed. "Close the door on your way out!"

Jordan had thought about walking back into the room and slugging Anquette. She hated her being around because it took some of the adoration Walee laid on her away from herself. Jordan was loyal by nature, though, and rather than get into an altercation which may lead to her strangling Anquette to death on Christmas Eve inside a condo her man, benefactor, or whatever he was, she let it rest. She had been conflicted for some time over her feelings towards Walee ever since she'd fallen in love with him over a year earlier, she opted to digress and head for the kitchen to search out a meal she could prepare while leaving Anquette to fend for herself inside the condo the two of them now shared.

****

Walee could only wonder how Jordan and Anquette would get along as he pulled up to Ponderosa an hour and a half later. "Why you didn't go around back?" Spoonie asked she and Tyke climbed from the backseat.

"They had a few extra cars around back with Ben 'nem being in town," Walee answered as he trotted up the stairs.

"Oh, okay. We ain't get nothing from McDonald's. I hope momma or Katrina have something cooked already that we can eat because I'm hungry." Tyke remarked.

Walee didn't respond as he rang the doorbell.

"Why you ain't use the key, man?" Spoonie snapped as she warded off the cold air by tightening her hooded leather jacket and stomping her boot-clad feet.

Before Walee could answer, Francine opened the door. "Well, well, well," the seventy-five year-old vivacious woman stated through a smile. She stepped aside and hugged each of the kids as they entered the home. "The only people aren't here on the ranch now is your grandfather and Mendoza. Bena and Tiva aren't home either, but they're here in town."

"You heard from my grandpa?" Walee asked as he locked the doors.

"He called this morning and said his flight was delayed. I hope everything is all right. Welcome home kids and Merry Christmas!" Francine said as she followed the kids through the home.

Francine was dressed up in a green pant suit with a white elf hat and white boots and had a glass of wine in her hand. All throughout day she'd been welcoming family and friends into Ponderosa. She hadn't heard from Mendoza in two days. He'd gone to Chicago with DeeDee to visit his doctor was what she'd been telling everyone. Francine knew her husband was ill, but Mendoza would not let her travel with him to Chicago. His actions had aroused suspicions within the woman—enough suspicion for her to request the truth. The day Mendoza left was the day Francine Cernigliaro had learned that she was never going to see her husband again.

…*"Mendoza, are you coming back?" Francine remembered asking her husband as he combed his hair in a mirror inside their bedroom on the second floor of Ponderosa three days earlier.*

"I want you to, I want you to be sure and make sure that Malaysia and Malara spend part of the summers at the ranch up in Montana," was Mendoza's answer as he set his comb down. The man whistled, seemingly in a joyful mood as he sat

on the wooden bench at the end of the bed and picked up one his black gator shoes and a polish rag. "I brought those two some bloodhounds for Christmas also. They're over to Mary's place," he said as he began to rub his shoe to a bright shine. "Make sure the twins get those dogs. Take the dogs to Montana when you all go too. They're good for the land. Everybody's welcome to visit."

Francine smiled and walked over to Mendoza and sat beside him on the bench. "Mendoza?" she asked as she looked him in the eyes. "Why won't you answer my question?"

"What do you want me to say, Francine? That this is it? That I'm not coming back?"

"If it is don't say it, Mendoza. Don't say it to me."

"Why ask me if you don't wanna know? I'm just beginning to go through, to go through everything and explain what's going on and what I want done once I leave the ranch tomorrow."

"Remember the night you went and saw Zell when he found out that you were going to kill him?" Francine asked lovingly as she placed her hands on Mendoza's arms.

"I do," Mendoza said tenderly as he stopped polishing his shoe and looked over towards his wife. "I told you that I might not be coming back that night. I told you that I may have to kill DeeDee."

"That was the most terrifying night of my life, Mendoza," Francine admitted. "If what you're going to Chicago to do is anything like that night with Zell? I don't wanna know about that. I want to remember nothing but the good times. I want it to end on a happy note."

And it did. Francine got to fix breakfast for Mendoza the morning of his and DeeDee's flight the following afternoon. The two were up early that day with their great grandchildren. Mendoza had fixed blueberry pancakes for Malaysia and Malara and they'd helped him, although making a huge mess inside the kitchen. That was the happiest Francine had seen Mendoza in a long time. He'd also made certain to say goodbye to everyone on the ranch and shared a laugh or two with them before he and DeeDee was driven to the airport by Mary and Irene.

Mendoza and Francine talked about the good things that had transpired over the fifty-six years that they'd been married the whole ride. When they reached the airport, Francine climbed from the car. After so many stories, she was wrought with laughter outside of the main entrance. And the last moments with her husband would be unforgettable for her given what he did next.

Through laughter, Mendoza grabbed hold of Francine and kissed her on the lips, leaning her over gently with an arm under her waist and his other hand clutching hers tightly, the two's wedding bands clinging against one another. Mendoza's kiss grew more intense as he pulled Francine upright. "God knows I love you, Francine Cernigliaro," he said as he stared her in the eyes.

"I'll forever love you, Mendoza Cernigliaro," Francine replied as her eyes watered. She hugged her husband once more, kissed both his cheeks and then his lips before straightening his hat and returning to the vehicle, smiling through her tears, yet all-the-while knowing she'd just kissed her husband for a final time.

"Where everybody?" Tyke called out from the coat closet, shaking Francine from her thoughts.

"All around," Francine answered softly. "Come on now, make yourselves at home."

Francine returned to the kitchen where she and Henrietta were baking pies as Walee and company walked through the home searching out other members of the family.

"I'm guessing it's not Mendoza," Henrietta smiled as she dented the edges on a homemade pie crust.

"I told you he's not going to show, Henrietta." Francine remarked dolefully as she grabbed an apron and tied it around her midsection. "I hope the family takes the news okay," she sighed.

"Don't think like that, Francine," Henrietta countered. "I

don't believe a word of what you're saying about your husband being…being…"

"What? Dead?" Francine blurted out. "This is my way of dealing with it, Henrietta. I've spent the last two days crying in my bed at night and I refuse to let what I know to be true about my husband bring everybody down. It's my burden to bear. One I willfully accept on behalf of the family."

"What if you're wrong? What if he shows?" Henrietta asked in a near whisper.

"Then I'll be dressed for the occasion," Francine stated proudly as she stepped back and showed off her outfit. "Enough of that kind of talk. Let's finish baking these pies for dessert," she ended.

****

"This one here for you, Samantha," Kimi said as she handed her cousin a small box. She and Koko were sitting on a love seat inside the main living room on the first floor of Ponderosa handing out early gifts to some of the family.

"And…this one's yours, Martha." Koko followed as she handed Martha a box smaller than the one Samantha had received. "They had some nice jewelry on Grand Cayman Island. We hope y'all like the pieces," she added as she grabbed another small bag. "How many accounts are going to be attached to that account we set up, momma?" she then asked.

"One for now, which is the company we're starting next month." Naomi said as she walked along the large fireplace's marble mantle while hanging more stocking stuffers.

Twenty year-olds Kimi and Koko knew from their trip down to the Cayman Islands they were going to be laundering money again. Having been trained by their mother for well over five years, the two were mathemical geniuses and financial magicians. They were able to calculate large sums of numbers in their head within seconds and new federal tax laws and codes inside out. Naomi's middle daughters watched every dollar going in and going out on a monthly basis right alongside their mother. Seventy-six million dollars was what they were responsible for; and as the cocaine profits rolled in, the numbers would only increase they both knew.

"What about that deal with Tropicana, momma?" Kimi followed.

"You ladies have your presentations drawn up?" Naomi asked she hung the last stocking.

"Yeah," Kimi and Koko answered in unison.

"Very good. Leave them on my desk tonight and I'll look them over in the morning," Naomi replied as she smoothened out her tight-fitting red, silk dress.

Fifty-three year-old Naomi Holland-Dawkins, the family's Head Honcho, was in the opening stages of executing a major power move after learning some things down in the Cayman Islands. The meeting with Rafael Gacha had gone well. But on the flight back to Cayman Island, she, Dawk, Ben, Phillip Tran and Grover Kobayashi had discussed the agreed upon price. Nineteen thousand was high for a kilogram. The family was paying what some were paying on American soil without the risks involved.

The advantage the Holland family held over other dealers, however, was the Levamisole formula Gacha had showed them. Using the formula, the Levamisole would allow the family to place a full cut on one kilogram and turn it into two while maintaining its potency. The family was paying nineteen thousand per kilogram, and stood to make thirty-seven thousand in profit selling wholesale. It was the family's biggest score ever. Nine hundred and ten pounds of cocaine. Sixteen million dollars after all liabilities. Good numbers for a legitimate corporation like the one Naomi was starting the following month—but the company was also big enough to hide proftits coming in from a drug organization moving nearly a half ton of cocaine every month.

Naomi had Rafael under the impression that she was going to continue doing business with his people inside of Tropicana Produce throughout the duration of the run they were going to make—but she actually had people of her own inside of

Tropicana. And if she played her cards right with the produce company, she would be able to move on to her plans for Rafael Gacha—that of subversion. In order to get close and dethrone Rafael, however, Naomi knew she needed her own land and a small army south of the border—and it all started with her and her middle daughters' meeting with Tropicana the Monday following New Year's.

"We been had our proposals ready, momma," Kimi said as she removed crepe paper from a small gift bag, shaking Naomi from her thoughts.

"I'll check it over and make any necessary adjustments," Naomi replied, getting back in focus. "Martha? Make sure those background checks on the drivers are what they are. Double check them before opening day at the warehouse next month. We're going to have to rely on a couple of those drivers to make it up to Oklahoma City from Laredo without any hang ups."

"Gotcha, sis. Everything's a go on that bonded warehouse at the border crossing, by the way." Martha replied as she placed a pair of diamond studs into her ear. "These karats are nice, Kimi and Koko," she added. "You should've seen the gifts on the island we went to, though. Five thousand dollar gift cards, expensive watches, diamond rings and whatnot."

"We had a Christmas like that a few times. And we having one like that this year," Koko stated. "Remember that year momma got daddy that thirty-thousand dollar Rolex, Kimi?" she then asked.

"Yeah," Kimi replied as she picked up a gift for Twiggy and set it aside. "Walee wearing daddy watch now," she added as she reached back down into the bag.

"When was that?" Samantha asked as she unwrapped her gift.

"In ninety-three. Me and Kimi were five then." Koko answered as she opened up a gift, that of an oyster pearl necklace for Henrietta valued at $1,100 dollars. "You think Henrietta will like this, Samantha?"

Samantha leaned over and eyed the oyster pearls. "'Yiska would love to see me in these'." Samantha chuckled. "That's what Henrietta gone say when she see those pearls. She's gonna love those."

"What you was doing on Christmas Day of ninety-three, Samantha?" Kimi chimed in.

"Christmas of ninety-three I was lying in my bed staring at a picture of my mother, father, aunt and brother," Samantha spoke casually. "I wanted this model of this air craft carrier. This big air craft carrier I saw inside this hobby shop in this little strip mall not too far from my elementary school. I wasn't expecting Manhattan to get it and he didn't."

"What he got you?" Martha asked.

"Nothing. He cussed me out and told me to stay in my room and don't come out," Samantha said as she shook her head. "He had some woman in there. The two of them started fighting after they got drunk and the police had to come to the house. That night altered my life."

"How, Samantha?" Kimi asked.

"Had I known better, I would've run straight up to that police officer standing in the living room and ask him to take me. I would've told everything. But I got scared because I thought the police, like the teachers in the school at the time, wasn't going to believe me. I thought if I told the police and they still left me there, Manhattan would've killed me. My whole life and everybody I knew in Vegas lives would've been different if I'd done that and the police had taken me or not."

"Then you wouldn't have met us!" Spoonie quipped as she ran into the living room with her arms wide, headed directly for Samantha with Tyke following close behind.

Samantha hugged her nieces as she relinquished her thoughts. The family had only been together for a little over three months and there were still plenty of stories to be told. During those times, those holding the conversations would often compare their lives based on the month of a certain year or a specific date and relate to one another what they were doing around that time. What was turning into a downhearted story had been lifted upon Spoonie and Tyke's arrival inside of the living room, however; the twins moved down and hugged Martha, Kimi, Koko and their mother as the conversation turned upbeat once more.

"I know Kimi and Koko attend Oklahoma University. What university are you guys attending again Spoonie and Tyke? And what are you two going to study?" Samantha asked as she tried on the tennis bracelet given to her by Kimi and Koko.

"We're attending the Center for Veterinary Health Sciences at Oklahoma State University." Spoonie stated excitedly.

"And we're studying to become Veterinary Pathologists." Tyke followed.

"What does a Veterinary Pathologist do?" Samantha asked as she spread out her arm and looked at the $2,000 dollar bracelet. "This here a bad piece of jewelry, sisters. Thank you," she told Kimi and Koko as she winked back at them.

"A Veterinary Pathologist treats, diagnoses, and prevents disease in animals," Spoonie answered. "Me and Tyke would like to open our own clinic to care for wounded animals and get a veterinarian research lab up and running on the ranch to find cures for the diseases many of the animals carry. Not our animals, but, you know, the ones in the wild."

"I wish we could make all the animals people eat sterile. That way they won't produce any offspring for people to eat." Tyke chimed in.

"You do that they won't have any animals left in the world for people to eat, Tyke." Kimi chuckled.

"We know that!" Tyke answered sarcastically as she placed her hands on her hips and stared Kimi up and down. "So that just means that me and Spoonie will have to put up with you animal killers the whole time we're here on this planet."

"Y'all gone get to fly around the world and do research?" Samantha chimed in.

"Maybe," Tyke speculated. "For say if we learned about a plant somewhere in the world that has therapeutic remedies or something."

"She just wanna be y'all pilot!" Kimi laughed. "Y'all be in good hands, though, because my cousin know what she doing up there. Don't forget our bet, Samantha," she added.

"We gone see tonight," Samantha assured.

"Becoming animal scientists has been a lifelong dream of my youngest," Naomi spoke proudly as she walked over to the fireplace mantle and grabbed two stockings. "And to make things easier on my babies, their younger brother brought the two of them a Christmas gift."

Spoonie and Tyke walked over to their mother, grabbed the stockings and opened them. Both twins were expecting a pair of earrings or a ring, which had been the normal stocking stuffers for the past few years. They were surprised, however, to see that each of their stockings contained a single bottle of orange scented air freshener.

"What are we gonna do with this, momma? Why Walee bought us this?" Tyke asked puzzled.

"It's to keep the inside of y'all new car smelling good," Walee said through a sly smile as he stepped into the immaculate marble-floored living room and came from behind his back with a set of car keys.

Spoonie and Tyke placed their hands on their hips and said simultaneously, "That's why you parked out front!"

"I wanted to surprise y'all," Walee said as he walked over to Spoonie and Tyke and hugged their necks.

"And you did!" Spoonie smiled lovingly as she and Tyke hugged their brother and thanked him.

Spoonie and Tyke remembered when Kimi and Koko had gotten their Maserati after announcing that they were going to the University of Oklahoma back in July of 2006. The twins were fourteen back then, and Kimi and Koko were the same age as they were now—seventeen—and just like Spoonie and Tyke, they were on their way to college.

The thought of following in Kimi and Koko's footsteps

made Spoonie and Tyke proud. Their only wish was that their father could be around to see them do the same thing their older sisters were doing. They just had to tell him the good news.

Walee was with Spoonie Tyke on that hot summer day back in August of 2008 and he'd heard the conversation...

..."*Walee do good on the grill, daddy,*" *Spoonie smiled through her tears as she knelt beside her twin staring at her father's grave. "We always talk about the day we found out about Mister Spots," she laughed as she placed white tulips atop her father's grave. "We was able to save a stinky beast, too. His name is Moses. And he has his own theme song!"*

"*Get down Moses!*" *Spoonie and Tyke sang in unison as they looked into one another's eyes and laughed aloud.*

Tyke leaned into Spoonie soon after. Her merriment slowly turned into a smile, and then a solemn stare of sorrow. "Daddy," she spoke respectfully as she wiped away tears, "me and, me and Spoonie chose Oklahoma State. We want to become Veterinarian Pathologists when we get older."

"*She wanted to tell you that and then ask you for a car, daddy.*" *Spoonie chimed in as she pointed towards Tyke.*

"*Shima, you can't ask like that! Daddy, she—*"

"*I'm telling the truth, daddy!*" *Spoonie interjected. "She scared to ask you, but I'm not."*

"*Okay, okay! God, Spoonie!*" *Tyke sulked as she raised her hands in defeat. "It was going to be for Christmas, though, daddy. Our birthday is on the twenty-ninth of December so an early Christmas gift would be perfect!"*

"*But we won't be mad if you don't say yes, daddy,*" *Spoonie chimed in.*

"*Yeah. We'll just go and ask momma,*" *Tyke followed as she and her twin laughed and playfully tapped one another's arms.*

Spoonie then pressed her head to the side of her twin's head and the two grew quiet once more as they stared at their father's grave. They'd just created how they believed the conversation would'd gone with their father if he were still alive.

"What you think daddy answer would've been, Spoonie?" Tyke asked lowly.

"We sixteen now and have our learner's permit. I think he would've gotten us one," Spoonie answered softly as she reached up and rubbed the tears forming in her eyes. "I just wish he was here so we could ask. Just to ask," she blurted out heartbrokenly as she leaned forward. "We miss you, daddy!" she cried.

Tyke grew flustered. She was going back and forth, rubbing Spoonie's back, wiping the tears from her eyes and staring back at her father's grave. "Daddy, we not mad at you!" she cried. "We just want you to be here that's all! You should be here and not, not here!" the shattered sixteen year-old screamed aloud as she extended her arms out towards her father's grave. "We love you, daddy," she ended as she grabbed hold of Spoonie and cried with her twin at the foot of their father's grave.

Walee was leaning up against a tree listening to his sisters talk to their father as his eyes filled with tears of sorrow, pity and anger. This was something his father's death had brought about for the family: the depravation of joy towards his offspring. His father was missing out on so much having been killed and times like these were hard to wacth.

Kimi and Koko got to enjoy the full experience of selecting a college and the rewards that went along with the event. For Spoonie and Tyke, however, their telling their father what college they'd chosen to attend had to be shared with him at his gravesite atop Ne`Ne's Hill, and there would be no event to follow it seemed.

Spoonie and Tyke's plight pained Walee's heart. And knowing his father the way he did, he knew Doss would've gotten his youngest, his most innocent pride and joys a car for Christmas.

Walee saw to it that Spoonie and Tyke received their driver's licenses a couple of months later. The next move was for him to *determine what kind of a car he would purchase for his youngest sisters on behalf of his father, although his reasons for doing so, which was to do what Doss was now unable to do, would remain his secret and his secret alone...*

"Y'all seen that fresh whip out back? Who that for?" Kahlil asked as he walked into the living room, shaking Walee from his thoughts.

"You already knew what was going on," Tyke laughed as she and Spoonie walked over and hugged Kahlil.

"Y'all still don't know what kind it is, though," Kahlil remarked. "What's up, family?" he then spoke to the women inside the living room.

Everybody spoke to Kahlil as he made his way around the room hugging each female. When he made his way over to Koko, there was an awkward pause. The two had seen one another countless times since the hit he'd placed on Chablis and they'd even talked about the matter a time or two. Theirs was often an uncomfortable encounter, however; Koko had a sense of gratitude, while Kahlil only sought to make sure that she was okay. The two were secretly hoping that it was nothing more to the rapport, but neither wanted to discuss the matter for fear of hurting one another's feelings. Cordiality was now their relationship after all that had gone down.

"You doing all right, Koko?" Kahlil asked caringly as he hugged her and rubbed her back softly.

Koko couldn't deny the protectiveness Kahlil offered, but she was so hoping he didn't like her, not in an intimate way as she was too complicated a female for a young man she viewed as being that of a younger brother. Kahlil was on the same level as Walee in her eyes. And just like her younger brother, he had plenty sexual attraction and potential, just not with her. She would never shun the brother she never had, though; and would only continue to treat him as such.

"I got you a gift, Kahlil," Koko stated as she reached down and came up with a large box.

"This yours, Walee," Kimi quickly followed as she came up

with a small box of her own. "It's a pinky diamond ring, Playboy," she let it be known while smiling.

Kahlil, meanwhile, had just pulled the top off his box. "Ohh snap!" he exclaimed as he removed an autographed San Francisco 49ers football helmet belonging to Hall of Fame cornerback Ronnie Lott. The great ones in sports was who Kahlil emulated. Ronnie Lott was known as one of the hardest hitting cornerbacks to ever grace a football field. Kahlil's style was similar according to early scout reports.

"Ya' man Kirk Herbstreit on ESPN say you remind him of that man right there so I thought you'd like that," Koko said as she wobbled her head while smiling proudly, knowing she'd delivered.

"This here one of the best gifts ever, Koko," Kahlil replied as he leaned down and pecked Koko on the cheek.

"Ewww!" Koko chided playfully.

"Let's go see our car!" Spoonie cut in as she and Tyke sauntered out of the living room, not really concerned if the family was following them or not as they just had to see what was out back.

"This is our first car, Shima!" Tyke whispered happily as the two strode by Francine and Henrietta.

"I know." Spoonie agreed as she covered her lower face. "We get to live on campus, play softball and we have our own car. It's gone be so much fun, Sinopa!"

"What kind of car do you think it is?" Tyke asked as she and Spoonie approached the French doors.

"I don't know."

"Y'all gone see what it is or not?" Kimi asked aloud from across the way as she and the rest of the family that was in the living room entered the kitchen. "And here!" she added as she tossed the car keys to Spoonie.

Spoonie and Tyke pulled the center French doors open and were hit with a thing of beauty. A black, two door Infiniti G37 sports coup with tinted windows and chrome wheels was sitting out behind the home with a bright orange bow resting on its hood. The $37,000 dollar car fit the two perfectly in size and performance.

"It's time for a test drive. Come on, Walee!" Spoonie said as she and Tyke trotted down the patio stairs.

Walee and Kahlil stood on the back patio as Naomi, Martha, Samantha, Kimi and Koko walked back into the home while replaying Spoonie and Tyke's reaction to their gift.

"That's a hot car with two hot girls in it, fam," Kahlil remarked as he held his hands behind his back and looked to the ground.

"I know, man," Walee remarked lowly as he headed for the car. "We gone definitely have to watch out for the snakes on campus and put 'em up some game, ya' dig?"

"So long as you know, Playboy," Kahlil stated as he dapped Walee. "Refrigerator raaaaiiiid!" he then sang as he turned and gangster walked towards the French doors. Things returned back to normal inside Ponderosa. It was good times being had by all, but on another portion of the ranch things weren't going so well for one person in particular.

CHAPTER THREE

WEAKNESSES

"So, I'm tellin' the administrator over the athletic department at Mississippi Valley State that if he'd freed up more funds to allow my scouts to travel further, we would've never been stuck with such a sorry bunch of recruits and would've probably had a better shot at the division title," Reynard Jacobs said to Tak as the two sat inside the study on the second floor of the guest house.

"That's how you feel about the kids you recruited?" Takoda asked as he sat on the opposite side of the black marble table that lay in between the two.

"Let's just say I held no punches, Takoda. Football is a man's sport and a man's business," Reynard replied as he sat upright in his chair with a cigar clasped in his left hand. "Now, do you have my money?" he asked sternly.

Takoda clenched his jaws together as he stood up from his seat. "You sure you wanna do this?"

"You sure you want my daughter to remain at your side?" Reynard countered. "You had a month to get me the amount that I asked for. Now, where is it?"

Takoda looked over to one of the bookshelves lining the wall and nodded towards a black satchel. "Twenty thousand," he stated lowly. "And from this point forth? We're even," he ended as he left the room.

Reynard went and stood by the bar counter and watched as the door closed behind Tak. He downed a quick shot of cognac and went over to the bookshelf and grabbed the bag, unzipped it, and pulled out one of the stacks of banded hundreds and fanned the crisp bills. The ease in which he'd extorted Takoda was an act he would repeat again and again was his thinking as he zipped the bag and headed towards the spare bedroom where he was spending nights in order to hide the money. He'd just concealed the extorted loot and was exiting the spare bedroom when he bumped into Mary out in the hallway. He could see that she was holding onto a catalog and flipping through its pages.

"What are you up to?" Reynard asked as he smiled down at Mary.

"I was going into my bedroom to—"

"Great! I'll join you," Reynard interjected through a sly smile as he stroked Mary's arm.

"I don't think so, mister," Mary replied as she blushed. "Remember a couple of months ago I told you I wanted to have a balcony built?"

"Yeah. What about it?"

"I think I found the type of wood to remodel the home's front porch," Mary answered as she continued on up the hall.

Reynard followed and entered Mary's bedroom and leaned against the threshold as he tucked his hands into his silk slacks. He watched her carefully as she stared at the corner on the left side of the pristine room that featured polished white wooden floors, a king-sized white oak sleigh bed with sea foam dressings and matching amenities from nightstands, to desks and armoires. The bed, with its numerous large pillows and chinchilla sea foam comforter, created a vision within Reynard, one of him and Mary tucked under the covers wrapped up in one another's arms. "What're you picturing in that beautiful mind of yours, Mary?" he asked aloud.

"I'm picturing these curved French doors over here in this corner," Mary stated as she pulled the sleeves up on her evergreen wool sweater and walked over towards the left side of the bedroom. "I'm thinking the balcony can run halfway down the left side and half of the front side of the home."

"Can I ask why you're interested in building a balcony? And why in the middle of winter?" Reynard asked curiously.

"I'm doing it in the middle of the winter to keep the men on the ranch working. The family's going through a transition is what Naomi told me. Business is a little slow here now so I decided to start the home renovation project early. As far as the balcony, I'm building it so me, Dimples and Tacoma can sit outside and look at the heavens," Mary answered as she stood staring at the corner, imaging what the newly-remodeled area would look like.

"I never knew you to be interested in astronomy," Reynard remarked as he leaned up from the threshold and walked into the bedroom.

"Your grandson was the one who actually got me and Dimples interested," Mary declared. "Our daughter had bought a coffee table science book for him. Tacoma fell in love with that book. It had pictures of all the different objects in the solar system. One night last summer, Tacoma walked into his mother's bedroom with his favorite book. He'd learn that people on Earth could see other objects in space while reading it and asked his mother to buy him a telescope. Regina ordered one and we sat out on Ne`Ne`s Hill one clear summer night and looked at the rings of Saturn."

"Sounds fun," Reynard chuckled as he rubbed the corners of his eyes.

"Now you're making fun of not only me, but your grandson and your daughter," Mary giggled. "You should sit out with us one night before you leave. Then you'll understand. Looking at stars and planets gives you a sense of awe over God and his creation."

"God does create many things of beauty, Mary. I'm staring at one of his creations right now," Reynard said seriously as he stepped closer.

Mary could suddenly feel her temperature rise as she stood facing away from Reynard. Those old feelings from when she was a seventeen year-old naïve young woman living in Tuscaloosa, Alabama were beginning to resurface. Reynard was a man she'd fallen in love with quickly when she was a teenager, but he'd broken her heart the day he denied that the two of them had sex and the fact that she was carrying his child. Thirty-plus years later, he seemed more refined and mature with a better understanding of what he'd given up on back then in Mary's eyes. He was still handsome to her with his well-built physique, smooth, dark-brown skin, perfectly bald head and distinguished peppered beard and mustache.

"Why did you deny me in Tuscaloosa?" Mary asked as she turned around and looked up into Reynard's eyes.

"I was a scared boy, Mary," Reynard owned up as he raised one of his large hands and touched her chin, gently lifting her head just a little in order to gain deeper access to her brown eyes. She was a stunning woman to him with her pouty lips, high cheekbones and thick, coal black hair, looking years younger than her forty-nine.

Reynard's answer led Mary to believe that he was sincere, but she still harbored resentment over his actions. It was nice to have him around. His subtle flirtations and apologies were welcomed, but he had to do more in order to secure her heart, which was something she found herself wanting to give to this man once more as she was slowly finding it within herself to forgive the father of her daughters for his abandonment thirty-three years prior.

Mary's was an optimistic and forgiving heart, but more so, she was a lonely woman struggling against her own flesh. She told herself she wasn't going to become intimate with Reynard Jacobs just yet, no matter how much she craved to feel his touch once more. If he really wanted to rekindle what had been lost, he would definitely have to earn it was Mary's resolve. She stepped back from Reynard, closed her Home Décor catalog and grabbed his hand. "It's best we make our way to the first floor," she spoke lowly as she let her grip slip while heading for the bedroom's threshold.

Meanwhile, downstairs, thirty-one year-old Regina Kotori-Holland was in the den. Her eight year-old son, Tacoma Kotori, was playing an educational game on the home computer while she read a letter to herself. Tak had made his way into in the kitchen and was quietly blending egg nog daiquiris for him and his wife. It was a concoction Katrina Holland had laid on the family earlier in the day and they were all savoring the milky, ice-laden adult beverage that was laced with brandy.

After pouring the frozen drink into two frosted mugs, Tak sought to join his wife and son. He eyed Regina in shame as he descended the stairs leading into the sunken den, feeling snake ass low over his actions with Siloam Bovina and the situation he now found himself in with Reynard Jacobs.

Tak and Siloam had always gotten along well ever since she'd returned to the ranch after she'd run away for a couple of years. The two enjoyed the acoustic guitar and vinyl albums. Tak often gave Siloam suggestions on songs that she could introduce to Jane Dow. The day he and Siloam had their affair had occurred in late August of 2006, several weeks before Doss was killed. The two's illicit act replayed quickly in his mind as he walked towards his family…

…Siloam had gone to Tak's repair shop to have a new set of tires placed onto one of the family's Suburbans one mid-morning day back in late August of 2006. They soon began talking about classic soundtracks while Tak changed out the tires. In the process, he'd noticed the SUV needed a wheel alignment, a job that would take about ninety minutes. During the waiting period, Tak mentioned to Siloam that he had an album he wanted to play for her and the two could listen to a few cuts over lunch as he and Regina's home was only a ten minute drive from his business, and Siloam innocently agreed.

Tak and Regina's one story home was a luxurious ranch-style home with granite counters in the open area and wooden floors in each of the three bedrooms. The couple had renovated the kitchen with new ceramic flooring a week earlier and it was Siloam's first visit since the home's remodeling—it was also the two's first time ever being alone.

Tak had found the album and put it to a needle before he

went into the kitchen and began pulling out pastrami and salami to make an Italian hoagie for him and Siloam to share. When Siloam heard the opening song to the movie Gone in Sixty Seconds she burst into laughter and walked into the kitchen. "Jane would rock that song to death," she smiled as she snapped her fingers. "We would just have to spice it up a bit because it's one long chorus."

"I knew you'd love it. I can't wait to hear you and the Jane Dow Band perform it." Tak said over the music as he heated a skillet.

"There's a rap group from Memphis that remade that song. Da Headbussaz is what they call themselves. It would be awesome to have all or even one of those rappers perform with us opening night during our performance." Siloam thought aloud.

"That club is going to be hot." Tak stated as he unwrapped the meat and continued moving about inside the kitchen.

"It really will be. I can't wait to record inside that studio. What goes on your classic sandwich again?" Siloam asked.

"Fresh cut salami and pastrami. You can eat it cold, but grilling the meat does wonders for this here sandwich," Tak answered as he began slicing up an onion. "Dimples love when I cook these for dinner."

Siloam leaned against the counter and smiled. "You and Dimples really have a wonderful life, Tak. I'd give anything to find a love of my own," she professed.

"You'll find that special man someday," Tak replied, never looking over to Siloam.

"My biological clock is steadily ticking, Takoda," Siloam chuckled as she bit her bottom lip while bobbing her head to the music. "And there aren't many prospects in Ponca City."

"I understand how you feel. But what I learned is that you have to seize the moment, Siloam!" Tak advised enthusiastically as he sprinkled minced garlic and chopped onions into the hot skillet where the ingredients began to sizzle and smoke. "The first time I saw Regina over to Mary's

produce stand I was struck with Cupid's arrow. The shy man I was at the time prevented me from even asking her out, though. I told myself the next time I see her, I would ask her out. I was afraid to go to that produce stand, though," Takoda admitted as he looked around.

"Why?" Siloam asked as she reached over and handed him a wet towel.

"A woman as beautiful as Dimples? I felt like I was out of my league, actually," Takoda confessed, regretfully shaking his head as his eyes gazed off into nowhere particular. "I thought she'd never date a plain ole country boy like me."

"Plain ole country boy?" Siloam chuckled. "Tak, you're handsome."

"It wasn't my looks I was worried about. It was the fear of her saying no to me. I was lucky to run into her again when she caught a flat tire back in back in September of ninety eight. We've been together ever since. It was like it was meant to be," Takoda stated proudly as he poured olive oil into the skillet.

A flame shooting halfway up to the ceiling erupted from the skillet at that moment, forcing both individuals to jump back from the grill on the island counter. Tak grabbed the wet towel he'd wiped his hands with and began slapping at the blaze, but the fire had latched onto his rag. In the process of trying to dab out the flames by slapping it against the side of the grill, Takoda had knocked the burning skillet onto the ceramic floor. "Dammit!" he said under his breath as he began stomping at the flames.

Water landed onto the fire at that moment courtesy of Siloam, who'd grabbed a sink hose. Tak grabbed three more towels and together, he and Siloam doused the flames.

"Is this how you always prepare your sandwiches?" Siloam chuckled as she placed an innocent hand onto Tak's right shoulder.

"The ceramic floor's ruined in this area," Tak complained. "We just had the floor done and now this!"

"It'll be okay, Takoda," Siloam comforted as she stood

behind Tak rubbing both his shoulders now.

Takoda was a strong, physically fit 5'11" Cherokee Indian in Siloam's eyes. She licked her lips as dirty thoughts of sleeping with a handsome man the same race as she ran through her mind. She briefly fantasized what Takoda would look like naked with his well-toned physique and smooth, baby-faced good looks and long, black hair.

Takoda in turn, was growing an erection over Siloam's gentle touch. "That feels good," he whispered through closed eyes.

"I just wanted to comfort you. Are you better now?" Siloam, relinquishing herself of any inhibition, asked lowly as she pressed her breasts to Takoda's back and slid her hands along his stomach down to his belt.

"Can't you tell?" Takoda asked lowly as Siloam's hand glided over the crotch of his tight-fitting denim jeans.

Siloam had no clue, but she was actually languishing Takoda's resolve by doing just as Regina would do whenever the two were in the beginning stages of their intimacy. "Yes, I can tell," she whispered into Takoda's ear as she reached for his zipper.

"This isn't right, Siloam."

"But only you and I will ever know," Siloam whispered as she unbuckled Takoda's jeans and freed his member. Her soft, warm and cottony fingers wrapped around his thick rod and she began coaxing him to full attention with slow, gentle strokes.

Takoda turned and faced Siloam and pulled her in close, letting lust take control of his psyche rather than common sense.

Siloam continued stroking Takoda as their lips touched briefly. Before long, the two were in each other's arms propelling themselves towards the spare bedroom while kissing one another with deep passion. The thought of having dirty, forbidden sex was a beguiled act too tempting for either party to resist, even though they both knew that what they were about to engage in was one of the most Judas-kissed acts one could ever commit against family.

Takoda kissed and felt on Siloam all the way to the spare bedroom where he laid her on her back atop the queen-sized bed and lowered his jeans. "We got it make it fast," he whispered as he pulled his jockey underwear down.

"I'm ready for you. I want you so bad," Siloam panted as she pulled her shorts and panties down over her sandals and spread her legs.

Takoda leaned into the mattress and placed his hard dick to Siloam's slickened vagina and pushed forth. A sigh of relief emanated from both of their adulterous mouths upon penetration. Siloam absorbed every inch of Regina's husband as he slid into her and thrust hard, taking her breath away before he began stroking her ruthlessly hard and fast. A furious fucking with no strings attached is what a desperate Siloam had been wanting, and it was the very thing she received. She grabbed the backs of her knees and pulled Takoda into her at the same time, opening herself fully as she held him close.

Takoda dug deep into the pussy that was opportunistically offered up to him. Siloam's crevice was hot, soft and silky smooth. She felt good, smelled good and was all-out beautiful in her tan-skinned voluptuousness. The Cherokee Indian's hazel eyes were gazing deep into his eyes as he pounded her relentlessly. "Siloam, baby," he groaned as he kissed her neck and ground down into her with his feet planted to the floor.

"Takoda!" Siloam cried out as Regina's husband picked up the pace, she herself thrusting upwards as the two's pelvises slapped one another angrily.

"God!" Takoda growled as he pulled out and shot his load on the inside of Siloam's thick, quivering thighs. He immediately stood, stepped back from Siloam and stared at her in dismay for several seconds before he took to his knees. "This was so wrong," he confessed pitifully as he planted his hands in his stringy head of hair.

Siloam immediately covered her face as she snapped her legs shut. "What have we done?" she cried repentantly.

"We've made the worst mistake of our lives," Takoda replied as he looked away from Siloam, his heart filled remorse for having grown weak.

What'd gone down between Tak and Siloam was a classic case of lust left unchecked and shocking duplicity. Neither had rhyme nor reason for bestowing Judas' kiss on Regina, but the line had been crossed nonetheless. It was only after their disloyalty that the full impact of their actions had come to be fully recognized. Both were in tears as they began gathering themselves in shameful silence.

Siloam was walking out of the bedroom naked from the waist down, repeatedly apologizing to Takoda when she stepped out into the hall and saw Reynard walking her way toting two suitcases. The two made eye contact briefly just before Siloam hid her lower section with her shorts and hurried off to the bathroom where she slammed the door shut.

Takoda was buckling his pants when Reynard appeared in the threshold. "Mister Jacobs," he remarked stunned. "Is Regina with you?"

"No she isn't," Reynard stated as he eyed Tak with a sly smirk on his face. "What's going on here between you two?"

"This isn't what it seems." Takoda responded embarrassed as he straightened his clothes.

"How do you see it? Because to me it looks as if you two had just gotten through having sex. I wonder how my daughter would feel about this here situation."

"Are you that type of a man? Would you really break your daughter's heart?" Takoda questioned as he straightened the comforter on the bed where he and Siloam lay just minutes ago.

"It wouldn't be of my doing if I were to tell her what I witnessed and she was to confront you and Siloam and ask is it true. You're doing right, Tak. You've just made your own bed," Reynard professed as he set his suitcases down just inside in the spare bedroom's door and walked away from the threshold.

Takoda gathered himself and walked briskly out of the room and caught up to Reynard in the kitchen. "You can't say nothing about this to Regina, Mister Jacobs. Please, man. Siloam and I made a mistake and I promise it won't happen again."

"It's not me you owe the promise to, Takoda," Reynard remarked as he eyed the mess on the kitchen floor. "I'll keep quiet, but it'll cost you. How much remains to be seen. I'm going drop the house keys back off to Regina and visit with her and Mary at the produce stand. In the immediate future, you have some explaining to do on how a fire was started here in the kitchen."

Takoda had no clue what Reynard was going to do exactly. It worried him enough to begin planning on what he would tell Regina should he be confronted with the question as to whether he and Siloam had actually slept together. He was cleaning the wooden floors inside the kitchen when Siloam reappeared.

"I heard you two talking barely. What did Reynard say to you?" Siloam asked as she knelt down and assisted Takoda with cleaning the floor.

"He said nothing. He acted as if he didn't even know what was going on," Takoda replied somberly.

"Are you sure, Takoda?" Siloam asked apprehensively. "Reynard looked me square in the eyes. He saw me."

"Maybe he did, but he didn't say nothing to me about it. Let's just let things be for now. If it comes up? We'll own up to it. As far as the floor it's not the first time I've burned a skillet. I can explain this easily," Takoda remarked as he shoveled wet and burnt food particles into a dust pan with a straw whisk broom.

Tak had all of those things on his mind as he handed his wife a drink. "Baby," Regina said to him as she took the frosty mug and scooted over on the couch. "I have something to tell you."

"What?" Tak asked as he took a seat beside his wife.

"I'm pregnant again!"

"Yayyy! I'm gone have a brother to play with now!" Tacoma

cheered from behind the computer desk.

"Momma might be having a baby girl, son." Regina stated through a smile.

Tacoma swung his chair around, stood up and folded his arms in protest. "That means you're gonna have *two* girls," the muscular eight year-old, who carried his father's physique but had his mother's looks, thick, jet-black hair and tan skin remarked. "They're gonna be bad just like Malaysia and Malara, watch!" he added, bringing light laughter to his parents.

Just then, Mary and Reynard walked into the family room. "What's the happy occasion?" Mary asked.

"I'm pregnant, momma," Regina proudly confessed.

"Pregnant?" Reynard chimed in as he rubbed his chin in deep thought. "Well, this calls for a celebration! Tak? You wanna help me fix a couple of drinks, son?"

"We have our own," Tak spoke through a pretentious smile as he held up his glass. "Thanks anyway, Mister Jacobs."

"No problem, young man." Reynard smiled slyly at Tak as he headed towards the kitchen.

It was as if Takoda could see the thoughts running through Reynard's mind as he left the den with that same conniving smirk on his face he was known to carry. With another baby or babies on the way, he knew sooner or later Reynard would be back to dig into his pockets once more. What to do, however, was a question he had no answer to. Sensing defeat, Takoda had already resovled himself to having to pay Reynard again as he saw no other way to remedy the situation.

CHAPTER FOUR

GREAT ROOM HIJINKS

While Tak was over to the guest house trying to figure out how to deal with Reynard before his and Siloam's secret got out, Ben and Dawk were on the second floor of Ponderosa with their wives and other family members. Katrina had a large pot of gumbo going and was passing out samples of crawfish etouffe` to Oneika and Siloam as the three milled about in the kitchen putting the finishing touches on the mustard greens, baked macaroni and a special-made vegetable couscous for Spoonie and Tyke.

Malaysia, Malara, Baby Ben, Kenyan, Gabby and Tabby were being entertained by Kimi's beau, Udelle Raymond, who was rolling around on the floor and playfully antagonizing two bloodhound puppies that had been given to Malaysia and Malara earlier in the day.

Samantha's husband, Tre` Mitchell, was sitting on one of the sofas before the kids and Udelle sipping a glass of brandy as he texted Lee Sato, Victor Felix, and the rest of the crew from House of I.D.E.A.S. back down in Phoenix. Everything was copasetic on the Arizona home front as the home team entertained their respective families.

Over in the right corner of the Great Room facing the land out back was Jane Dow and the three members of her band. Jane had just received one of the most precious Christmas gifts ever. Her mentor, Siloam Bovina, had gotten her a set of drums, but not just any set of drums. These were Oak drum sets—top of the line instruments used by some of the best drummers from the best rock and roll bands in history. The five thousand dollar equipment was like a dream come true for Jane as she and her band mates quietly set up their instruments to entertain the family.

Meanwhile, Ben had just walked into the kitchen and hugged his wife from behind and snickered in her ear. Dawk was following, but he'd received a phone call. "What up?" he asked as he headed down the back staircase. "Yo, Ben? I gotta take this."

"Alright, we meet back up," Ben replied as he turned to his wife. "You were the shit this morning, girl," he then whispered into Katrina's ear.

"You asked me to find a spot and I did. I had to get some advice from Kimi, but hey, it was fire!" Katrina giggled. Earlier in the day, the two had snuck off to the main barn at Kimi's request to enjoy a romp on the second floor loft and they were still relishing the experience.

"How everything coming with the menu for the club opening night?" Ben asked as he picked up a spoon and stirred the gumbo. "The roux gone stick."

"No it's not," Katrina retorted. "The fire isn't high enough. It's simmering. As far as the menu, I'm practicing now. I got the gumbo, but this couscous for Spoonie and Tyke is the challenge, though, because I can't season it like I want to. All these vegetables and no meat. I can't do anything special with it besides sprinkle salt and pepper and put cheese in it," she sighed.

Katrina Holland was going to be the woman in charge of the family restaurant that sat across from Club Indigo in Saint Charles, Missouri. The club's opening night was also to be the opening night of her third New Orleans Café. The deal she and Naomi had forged had placed her on the road to franchising her business based out of Arizona. A lot was riding on the twenty-eight year-old's ability to offer a world class menu to the Saint

Charles public as she knew Naomi would back out of the deal if the food was in poor taste.

This was a big deal for Katrina. The woman prided herself on her cooking skills, and to fall flat her first time venturing outside of her comfort zone down in Arizona had her somewhat tense. She was the Queen of Cajun Cuisine in Phoenix, but she feared Saint Louis, a city of renowned cuisine from all cultures, would be a much bigger obstacle. "What if I fall short, Ben?" she asked as she brushed a pile of peeled shrimp hulls into a plastic receptacle.

"Say what?" Ben asked through a chuckle as Siloam got up and scraped out a plate of food before walking over to the double door freezer where she grabbed a fresh bag of frozen strawberries. "Naomi wouldna even agreed to give you the first shot at that location in Missouri if she didn't believe in you, baby. It ain't about no couscous, it's about that gumbo right there and those other meals you be hookin' up."

"I have to be on point with everything. Not just the cooking, Ben." Katrina countered. "See? This here," she said as she held up the bag of peeled shrimp husks, "these shrimp shells should've been removed from the counter before I even added the shrimp to the gumbo. And if I don't sanitize," she spoke nervously as she grabbed a bottle of Lysol cleaner with bleach and sprayed the counter down. "If don't sanitize before setting another item down, that's points off. Naomi will have two health inspectors on hand watching how we run the kitchen and they're going to grade me and my staff on the entire cooking processes."

"You mean the cleaning 'process sees' you're doing now?" Siloam, having overheard the tail end of the conversation, asked through a chuckle as she grabbed a bottle of rum off the back counter.

Katrina stopped wiping the island counter mid-swipe and looked to the floor. "I'm over-analyzing, huh, Siloam?" she laughed.

"Yep," Ben chimed in and answered casually as he reached for a bottle opener and popped the top on a bottle of Samuel

Adams beer.

"I agree with your husband, Katrina. You'll be fine. I can't wait to have some more of your gumbo." Siloam spoke humbly as she walked over to the island counter and set the strawberries and rum down.

"I'm gone do good with this," Katrina stated as she nodded he head in confidence. "I can handle it," she assured herself. "I umm, I sometimes wish my mother was around to see me now, you know? I think this would be something she would enjoy doing."

"Faye," Ben said as he sipped his beer, recalling the last day he'd seen the woman, a day in which he and Manny had run her off from in front of a dope house he once ran in New Orleans. "Been twelve, thirteen years since we seen that woman. She might not've even changed."

"Who might not have changed?" Samantha asked as she emerged from the back staircase. "Daiquiris on deck!" she snapped the moment she eyed Siloam setting up the blender.

"They're talkin' about Katrina's mother. Do you know of her, Samantha?" Siloam asked as she walked back over to the freezer and grabbed a bag of ice.

"Only from stories. And from what I know? She was worse than Manhattan." Samantha dragged as she skipped over to the island counter and opened the bag of frozen strawberries.

"Nobody, no parent could be that bad, Samantha." Siloam remarked upon returning to the counter.

"You don't know Faye," Ben chimed in. "The things she did? Hold up. Why we talkin' about this anyway? It's the holiday and y'all dampening the mood."

"That's why me and Tre' hangin' with the little ones," Udelle snapped from the Great Room as he held one of the puppies before Gabby and Tabby. "I ain't with all that drama talk. But, if I was, I'd support Katrina. Mothers are important to daughters."

"Shut up!" three year-old Malara yelled out at Udelle.

Udelle set the puppy down and knelt on his knees before Tiva's daughter. "Who you talkin' to like that, Malara? Say it again! Say it again and watch I do something to ya'!" he stated in mocked anger, holding back his laughter as the rest of the family eyed the scene unfolding.

Malara stepped back and raised her arm as if she was going to hit Udelle in the face. The three year-old suddenly seemed as if she'd sized up the competition and needed back up. She balled up her fist and lowered her blue eyes while walking off. "Come on!" she ordered her twin, Malaysia.

"What?" Malaysia asked she stood up in her red velvet elf outfit.

Malara pointed back at Udelle and said, "Him mean. Going tell," as she grabbed her twin's hand and pulled her towards the kitchen.

Malara and Malaysia had a certain way about themselves; they would sometimes fight one another, but if ever one had a problem, then they both had a problem. Their antics were amusing, but everyone agreed that Tiva would have trouble on her hands as her twins grew older as they could be double trouble at times.

"That's right!" Udelle stated as he and Tre` chuckled. "And you make sure you get all the backup you need for me out that kitchen too, ya' li'l boogers!"

Malara led her twin into the kitchen and walked amongst the big people. She stopped in front of Katrina and looked up at her for a few seconds. "Can I help you, Malara? What you need, baby?" she asked while smiling down at the twins.

"No!" Malaysia snapped as she nudged her sister forward. The twins walked over to a towering figure and looked up at him for a few seconds. "Him!" Malaysia said as she stood before Ben eyeing her twin.

Malara reached out and touched Ben's pant leg and pointed back at Udelle. "Him mean," she remarked softly. "Come on!" she snapped as she reached up and grabbed Ben's hand and tried to lead him to the Great Room.

"I'm sorry, Malara, but I'm off the clock, baby girl." Ben laughed. "No." he then said lowly.

Malara didn't know what the big person said, but she understood the word no. She looked up at the towering figure like, "*You know you can handle that for me,*" before she grabbed her twin's hand and returned to the Great Room. "Heyyyy," she smiled over to Udelle in a friendly tone.

"Now we back potnas," Udelle laughed as he tickled the twins.

Just then, a jazzy keyboard organ was heard over the stereo speakers inside the Great Room. Malaysia and Malara looked at one another and smiled, revealing their identical snagged teething as they tapped their feet in unison and began bouncing up and down to Booker T. & The M.G.s' song *Green Onions* in their red velvet elf outfits and white boots.

"Siloam!" Jane called out from behind her drums as the music took sway over the Great Room.

"They dancing? Are they dancing?" Siloam asked happily as she ran into the Great Room. "Watch this, everybody! I've been practicing with them for like a week!" she added proudly. "I taught them this dance routine! Skip, babies!"

The family watched as Malaysia and Malara skipped to the right three times with Siloam leading them. "Skip!" Siloam yelled aloud again.

The twins then skipped to their left three times as Siloam remained in place this time around. She raised her hand above her head and instinctively, Malaysia and Malara raised their hands and rocked from side to side. "Raid the roof! Raid the roof!" the twins yelled aloud before placing their right hand on their hip and pausing, as if they were frozen stiff.

Siloam touched the tops of the twins' heads with the tips of her fingers and they extended their short arms and twirled around in a circle while laughing before they took off running back towards their puppies.

"Awesome, babies!" Siloam complimented over the music amid claps from the family as the band brought their rendition to a close.

"If you were to see Faye today, what would you say to her, Katrina?" Samantha asked inquisitively as she poured the bag of strawberries into the blender after things had settled back down.

Katrina placed her hands to the counter and thought deeply. "If she were still a junky, Samantha? I would tell her to stay away from me and my family. If she were clean, though," her eyes lit up at the prospect. "If she was clean and sober? I would welcome her back into my life."

"And I would back you on either of those decisions. People can change." Ben replied. "But I wouldn't even bet on Faye like that right about now."

"Look at you!" Samantha chortled as she looked her brother up and down with her hands on her hips. "How many people bet on you not changing, brother? Everybody in this kitchen done been through something and made changes."

"That's right," Siloam added in a serious tone as she poured rum into the blender. "We've all done some things we aren't proud of in life. Things we're sorry for and may not even want to speak on."

Siloam thought back to the day she'd encountered Reynard and was forced into bribery at that moment. For a while now she'd been sleeping with the man in order for him not to reveal the fact that she and Takoda had had an affair to Regina. It was an act she abhorred, but it was the only thing she could do at the time in order to keep the man quiet.

The way in which he now wanted her to act, and the things he wanted her to say and do, were games played that Siloam oddly now looked forward to, however, in spite of its repugnance, as the day Reynard had first approached her replayed in her mind...

...Siloam was inside the main barn on the most northern portion of the ranch tending to a few Clydesdale ponies when Reynard rode up in a golf cart on a cool, cloudless early autumn day in September of 2008.

"Can I help you?" Siloam smiled as she unbaled hay.

"I know I'm out of line here, Siloam," Reynard said as he exited the golf cart. "But I really need to discuss a matter with you."

"Concerning?" Siloam asked anxiously, recalling the day Reynard had seen her naked from the waist down inside of Regina and Takoda's home.

"It's concerning my daughter," Reynard spoke sincerely. "She has a problem and I was wondering if you could help me out?"

Siloam guided a Clydesdale pony back into its stable, closed the door and faced Reynard head on. "What is it that you want to discuss?" she asked as she moved down to the next stable, unlocked it and let another pony walk about freely.

"What are you willing to do in order for me to keep quiet on the affair you had with Takoda?" Reynard asked bluntly as he rubbed the pony's spine.

Siloam played things off by laughing. "What, what are you talkin' about, Reynard?" she asked nervously as she pulled brown hair from her face and began separating hay at a frantic pace with her pitchfork.

"Don't play games with me, Siloam. You and I both know what went down the day Takoda had that small fire inside his kitchen. Now, I don't know how a fire can lead to extra-marital sex, but I know what I stumbled upon."

"You know nothing," Siloam retorted lowly as she let the pitchfork fall from her hands.

"That's where you're wrong. I know everything. We can go back and forth, but I'd rather get straight to the point of my being here."

"Speak your peace." Siloam scoffed as she leaned down and picked up the loose straw and flung it into the stable.

Reynard subtly licked his lips as he eyed Siloam. He tucked his hands into his khaki trousers, his dick hardening as he stepped closer to the full-bloodied Cherokee. She was a beautiful, voluptuous woman with her shapely, curvy legs, wide hips and alluring hazel eyes. "Do I have to spell it out for you? I think you know what is that I want from you, Siloam."

"Mister Jacobs, I have no idea what it is you're referring to." Siloam hissed as she eyed the man.

"Oh yeah?" Reynard asked through a scowl as he checked his watch. "Mary and Regina should be closing their produce store in another thirty minutes or so. Dinner is going to be real interesting tonight."

"You wouldn't." Siloam stated in disbelief.

"I damn sure would if you deny me." Reynard remarked through lustful eyes as he reached out and thumbed Siloam's right nipple. "I think you know what I want from you, little Indian girl," he whispered.

"What about your daughter? What about Mary?" Siloam asked as she backed away from Reynard.

"I'm doing this for Mary and Regina's sake." Reynard said matter-of-factly. "Would you really allow me to break my daughter's heart and unleash you and Tak's betrayal on the family? And so close after Doss having died," he unrepentantly threw in for good measure to further weaken Siloam's resolve.

"What is it that you want?" Siloam asked as her eyes watered in her defeated state.

"Come, come now," Reynard comforted as he stepped closer to Siloam and hugged her gently. "You may get to liking it. A young woman like yourself with no man to call her own? I bet you're in need of a big hard dick to plunder that sweet pussy of yours. Get over there!" Reynard hissed as he shoved Siloam up against one of the horse stables.

Siloam said nothing as Reynard stepped behind her and flung her sundress up over her waist. "Does this make you happy?" she managed to ask over the sounds of Reynard unbuckling his jeans.

"It makes me very happy," Reynard responded as he pressed the head of his dick into the crack of Siloam's exposed ass.

"Wait!" Siloam protested as she turned around. "There're condoms upstairs. And a couch we can lay on."

Reynard pulled his pants up back over his thighs. "Lead the way," he coaxed as he extended his hand. The two adjoined to the second floor of the barn where Reynard did his deed. He'd fucked Siloam twice doggy-style as she stood before him bent over the edge of the couch.

In Siloam's mind, Reynard was right. She did enjoy the fucking he'd given her. She'd even managed to call his name and thrust back on his long, stiff dick while working up a sweat. Deep down inside, she enjoyed being a slut. The entire week Reynard was in town, he and Siloam had hooked up five out the seven days he was in town. By the time Reynard had left to return to his home in Vegas, the two of them had actually begun a secret rapport—one in which they both saw an opportunity...

…"Siloam, I ain't payin' Ben no mind on what he sayin'," Katrina chuckled, shaking Siloam from her thoughts. "And for all I know, Ben might be right. Not knowing is like staring at a blank canvas, though. But still, it's a work of art to be admired. I just miss my momma sometimes, man," she ended somberly as she returned to her duties.

Ben's phone rung at that moment. "Yo?"

"We got a situation, dude. Meet me in my father's room." Dawk requested.

"I'm on my way, fam." Ben stated before he hung up the phone. He turned to Katrina and said, "You know I was just fuckin' with you about Faye. Don't worry about it, Katrina. This restaurant thing? And your mother? Both are good things that's gone happen for you. I feel that coming."

"You right," Katrina agreed. "The answers'll come," she smiled as she kissed Ben's lips before he headed down the backstairs, leaving Samantha, Katrina and Siloam behind in the kitchen just as the blender was clicked on.

CHAPTER FIVE
TOP PRIORITY

Me and Dawk were milling around the bar inside Doss' private room. I cut the ends off a couple of cigars and poured up glasses of brandy for the two of us while he ran down to me everything that DeeDee had told him over a secure line just minutes ago. The two us were the first on the ranch to learn of Mendoza's death. On top of that there, DeeDee had given us the lowdown on Q-Man. Last we'd heard from that dude there was that he was locked up in Cook County after he was snatched up by security in a parking garage not too far from the county courthouse with a concealed weapon. Me and Dawk could've taken care of Q-Man that day had the security not interfered, but looking back on it, it was good he got caught because his murder would've been caught on tape.

DeeDee had people inside the police force up in Cicero who knew all that was going on in Cook County. Word had just come down that Q-Man had talked to a federal agent the day before and he was being moved to Stateville, a maximum security prison located in Joliet, Illinois, in the days following Christmas. I lit my cigar and contemplated the family's next possible move. "Q-Man gone have to go down time he hit Stateville so he won't get at those phones to get back in touch with the feds." I told Dawk.

"You right, fam. We ain't got nobody in Cook County, but we got some people up in Stateville that can do the job," Dawk told me as he dialed a number and paused.

I sat and listened further as Dawk conversed for a minute once the person on the other end picked up.

"What up, Jay-D?" Dawk asked. There was a pause. "Y'all over to Kantrell crib, huh? Tell everybody I said Merry Christmas. That money we dropped off before going to the islands was split up right?"

After a brief pause, Dawk shot back into the phone, "She got you a bracelet, dude? What's up with that?" I heard him ask aloud through a slight chuckle. After several seconds of silence he spoke again. "Okay. That's y'all business—but look here—I need you to relay something to our people on the inside when you go up to Illinois."

There was another pause and Dawk spoke again. "The Somali on his way up there. We need him taken care of ASAP. He been talking to the feds. Tell your people to silence that boy the day he get there. That's top priority as of right now."

After another long pause, I heard Dawk say, "Get at me when it's done." before he ended the call.

"Who you got gone handle that up in Stateville?" I asked.

"Jay-D people up there."

I could only sit and listen as my younger cousin brought me up to date on the plan going down. It would be one of the most dangerous moves ever trying to pull off this hit on Q-Man. And no doubt it would cost a grip.

"You think it's gone work?" I asked Dawk after hearing all the details.

Dawk placed his hands to his lips and shook his head. "I honestly don't know, Ben. It's gutsy, but we gotta get to 'em. Only thing is, whoever do the job gone be looking at more time. Our old Enforcer, Eddie Cottonwood? He only got eight years left on a dime and he looking to get out early so I don't expect him to take the job. I don't know nobody ever killed a man behind bars and got away with it. But it gotta be done because if Q-Man make it inside Stateville he gone no doubt call that agent he been talking to and get moved again."

"If he spoke on the Abbadando hit and told 'em somebody

connected to that hit made Toodie disappear, then he put the feds a step closer to Bay and T-top." I told Dawk.

"The key to the Abbadando hit sit with Asa Spade and his crew," Dawk stated. "They not talking. They looking to get out in a couple of months."

"They wouldn't talk anyway." I spoke confidently.

"You right about Asa Spade and his team," Dawk responded before he took a sip of his brandy. "But a lot of people in Saint Louis know what happened to Toodie, though—namely Pepper."

"That youngster ain't gone talk, fam," I declared as I eyed Dawk.

"She might not, but I know she told her friends what happened. They might not be so loyal."

"They not even on the radar when it come to Toodie, Cuz," I told Dawk. "If they get nabbed on something I don't think they would speak on what happened with Toodie to get off on another charge. That would be hard to prove with no body or evidence. I'd take that to trial any day with O'Malley."

"I would too, but a charge'll put Bay and T-top on the radar and put the feds that much closer to the organization. We gotta off Q-Man to put out the smoke."

"I feel ya' on that. Jay 'nem solid. They get it done. Bay and T-top know about this?" I asked.

"Not yet." Dawk answered as he dialed another number.

"Where they at tonight?"

"Somewhere getting they nerves worked up I bet," Dawk chuckled as he checked his watch and entered another call.

****

"...the yule tide carol...doesn't make it better...knowing that we....won't be...together...a silent night...I know it's gonna be...joy to the world...but it's gonna be sad for me..."

It was approaching 6:30 P.M. in Ponca City, Oklahoma. Bay and T-top were sitting in the front seat of one of the family's

Suburbans parked on the northwest side of town—in AquaNina's parents' subdivision. The windows were rolled down on the SUV as The Emotions' song *What Do the Lonely Do at Christmas* played low on the stereo. From inside the luxurious ride, and over the classic Christmas song, Bay and T-top both could hear glass being broken and doors slamming amidst the angry accusations emanating from within the interior of the one story brick bungalow.

"The children can play...with their new toys...while their little hearts...burst open with joy...and lovers can kiss... beneath the mistletoes...choirs can sing...those glorious songs of old..."

For all Bay knew, AquaNina could've been inside the house getting killed, but at this moment, she didn't care all that much. She'd warned AquaNina that her parents would never agree to having a Christmas dinner with her family before the three of them had left the condo after wrapping gifts for everybody, but AquaNina just had to try and coax her parents into tagging along with her, Bay and T-top back over to Ponderosa.

It took all but a few minutes before Ahiga's angry voice was heard yelling aloud, "Never will I share a meal with those hooligans!"

Bay and T-top heard the man yell mere minutes after AquaNina had entered the home and had sunk back in their seats to see how things would play out.

"You don't even know people, daddy! You and momma don't even try to understand what's going on in my life!" the twins heard AquaNina yell in return. "All you ever do is stay cooped in this house and criticize everybody in town! You ain't no saint! You not shit, daddy!"

A thud was heard at that moment.

T-top looked over to Bay with a concerned expression. "You know he just hit your ole lady, right?" she asked in wonderment.

Bay didn't respond. She sat behind the steering wheel entertaining a box of chocolate-covered almonds that was in the console. She was popping the candy in her mouth like pills and chewing hard while staring straight ahead. "Fuck that shit!" she snapped over the music as she continued chewing. "I told that optimistic bitch this was a fucked up idea! It's always a fucked up idea! She always have a fucked up idea when it come to her people! Fuck 'em!"

Another glass was heard shattering and Lina, AquaNina's mother, could be heard yelling aloud at that moment, "Ahiga, stop it! Stop it now!"

T-top sat up in the seat and scanned the front of the home through the open door and could see Ahiga's shadow in the foyer. She turned to Bay with her eyes wide. "You hear that shit, Bena?" she asked with more concern. "You ain't gone do nothing?" she inquired as she answered her ringing phone. "What's up, Dawk?" Tiva, realizing Bay cared less, asked as she leaned back and shook her head while eyeing the front door.

"Where y'all at?" Dawk asked.

"Over by 'Nina parents' home watching the fireworks," T-top sighed as silhouettes appeared in the foyer of the home through the opened glass door. "You just gone let your boo get beat up on Christmas Eve, Bay. Wow," she stated while shaking her head somberly.

"That's Nina beef!" Bay sneered as she grabbed several more chocolate almonds and popped them into her mouth and licked her fingers. "She make it outta there she did good for herself!" she added while chewing hard and fast.

Dawk merely shook his head over the phone. AquaNina was always trying to get her parents and his family to come together. He, like Bay, knew that that was an impossibility. "I got something to share with y'all when y'all make it back to the ranch. You need me to ride over there, Tiva?"

"Nah, we can handle it." T-top replied just as she witnessed AquaNina being shoved out of the house by her father. She landed on her back in the snow covering the sidewalk leading to the home and hollered out in pain as she grabbed her back.

"Stay the hell from 'round here!" Ahiga yelled towards his daughter before he threw the gifts she'd bought for him and her mother out into the yard before slamming the door and turning off the porch light.

"I hate you both! Never again!" AquaNina cried as she rolled over and picked herself up from the ground and began searching for the rejected gifts.

"That's not right, man," T-top spoke concerned as she eyed AquaNina walking around the yard picking up the gifts her father had discarded. "We gone talk when we get in, Dawk. Let me deal with this here," she remarked saddened as she ended the call. "Why they do her like that, Bay?" she turned to her twin and asked.

"Because she likes it!" Bay snapped as she threw her hands up.

"I think she just wanna be accepted by her parents, Bena. Remember when you came out to the family? How would you feel if we did that to you?"

Bay leaned back in her seat behind the steering wheel and sighed as she eyed her twin. "It would've devastated me, Tiva," she owned up. "I wouldn't even be able to function. But AquaNina carry things too far."

"'Nina just want both families to get along," Tiva said as she opened the door. "I don't think she would be doing this if she didn't really love you, Bay."

"You can't change people that don't wanna change, Tiva." Bay responded as she eyed her twin seriously. "Where're you going?"

"Help her with her gifts," Tiva responded as she watched AquaNina mope about the yard while clutching her back and sniffling back tears.

Bay watched as Tiva climbed out of the SUV and walked through the snow over to where AquaNina was searching. She leaned down and picked up one of the gifts and handed it to her. AquaNina's response, one of appreciativeness and surprise, forced Bay to action. She wasn't going to interfere at first and she'd actually planned on scolding her lover once she made it back to the SUV. Tiva's compassion, however, had illuminated her tender heart as she reflected on the love they shared.

AquaNina's neediness was the thing that excited Bay, but that neediness stirred up resentment at the same time. Having AquaNina crave her at all times was what Bay loved, but AquaNina sometimes carried things too far. She didn't know when to let a matter rest, case in point, the situation with AquaNina and her parents on this night. In her heart, however, and one didn't have to dig deep to find out the truth, Bay loved AquaNina—was in love with the woman in fact—but AquaNina's trying to please her parents and force them to accept her alternative lifestyle was what Bay detested about her love.

While watching AquaNina and T-top search the yard, Bay had the sudden realization that she'd been subconsciously siding with AquaNina's parents all along. She enjoyed going up against Ahiga and Lina Mishaan and simply loved it when AquaNina fought her mother and father. Bay felt that AquaNina would always be at her side so long as her parents rejected their relationship. She never realized, until this day, at this moment, however, that there was much more to AquaNina. The Navajo Indian only wanted nothing more than her parents' approval over what she was choosing to do with her life and the person she loved.

AquaNina had never fully explained to Bay just how much she feared her parents' rejection. And for a while, Bay had been using what she viewed as a half-hearted apology on AquaNina's part as leverage in their relationship. It was a game to Bay in the beginning, a form of one-upmanship on her lover to keep their love going. She now understood, however, that she didn't have to manipulate or fight with AquaNina or take a silent opposition to keep her love because she'd had this woman's heart in the palm of her hands from the very start.

With that understanding now realized, Bay climbed from behind the wheel of the SUV and walked over to AquaNina, who was steadily crying as she dusted snow from the last of the four gifts that had been hurled into the yard.

"You okay, 'Nina?" Bay asked humbly as she wrapped an arm around her lover and pulled her close.

"Do I look okay, Bena?" AquaNina cried as she looked up into Bay's eyes under street lights near the curb that were casting an orange hue over the snow-covered yard. "You were right, okay? This is the last time I ever try to get everybody to get along! They won't accept us!" she yelled as she looked at her parents' darkened porch. "And they hate me for living, for just living my life and I say to hell with them!" AquaNina cried as she turned and faced the front door and bent over at the waist.

"Sometimes the family you were born into isn't your true family," T-top stated as she stood beside AquaNina.

"She's right, you know?" Bay said as she pulled AquaNina up from her bent stance and pressed her forehead to her lover's temple. "Come on home."

"What about the flask and the hand-crafted leather boots? I went to an online auction and bid four hundred dollars for a seventeenth century flask found in a coal mine in South Dakota. Not to mention the silver tray from the Sierra Mountains found on Donner's Pass. The boots I had made special." AquaNina complained.

"Forget all that, AquaNina. Leave the gifts here. Maybe Ahiga and Lina will come around. But I want my gift now."

"Your gift is in the jeep," AquaNina said as she dusted herself.

Bay smiled and leanded down and kissed AquaNina deeply, holding her tight. "You're my gift," she whispered several seconds later. "And you're the best gift I could ever hope to receive on Christmas or any other day." she stated lovingly.

"Umm, could you warn me next time?" T-top snapped as she walked off with her hands at her side. "Get a room or something, dang!"

Bay and AquaNina laughed to themsleves as they grabbed hold of one another's hands and took off running back towards the SUV in order to make their way back to Ponderosa where they would enjoy the remainder of the holiday.

CHAPTER SIX

GET DOWN MOSES

"Tre`, you seen Koko, baby?" Samantha asked as she walked into the Great Room with her cell phone pressed to her ear. "I done searched every room up here looking for that girl."

"She got a glass of daiquiri like five minutes ago and walked down the grand staircase," Tre` answered. "I'm surprised you missed her."

"Now I gotta walk the whole first floor because she's not answering her cell," Samantha complained. "Kimi it's about that time!" she yelled aloud.

"Okay, I'm ready! Where Koko at?" Kimi yelled back from the second floor kitchen.

"I'm going check downstairs! Meet us in the kitchen on the first floor!" Samantha yelled aloud as she trotted down the main staircase.

****

"How did you get my number, Chablis?" Koko scoffed into her cell phone as she stepped off into the family's theater room on the first floor of Ponderosa and shut the door.

"Don't worry 'bout all that. Just know I cared enough to reach out to you and wish you a merry Christmas."

"You don't know how much trouble you causing by calling me, Chablis. We through! I want you to leave me alone, and stop calling me, man!"

"You want me to leave you alone, or your family want me to leave you alone, Koko?"

"I want you—"

"Baby," Chablis interrupted. "I fucked up, alright? How many times I'm gone have to get down on my knees and beg for forgiveness, Koko? Oww," Chablis grimaced over the phone.

"You all right, baby?" Koko asked as she gripped the phone tighter.

"I'm good, baby girl. You can't, you can't see me, but I'm on bended knee in my hospital room, Koko. I can't do it in person, but see me, woman. See me on my knees—bad neck and all— kneeling before this bed begging you again. I'm sorry," Chablis pleaded as he took deep breaths.

Koko sensed tears welling up in Chablis through the phone. She closed her eyes and leaned against the wall inside the theater room. Tears flowed down her cheeks and gathered at the corners of her lips. "You hurt me, Chablis. A woman shouldn't fear her man. You make me afraid," she admitted lowly as she licked the salty liquid from the corners of her mouth.

"I was an arrogant asshole, Koko. I mean, I had scouts looking at me and everything. I had a shot at the NFL, ya' know? I saw, I saw myself able to give you things I knew you could already buy for yourself. That kinda messed with my head, baby. My woman had more money than me, ya' know? I felt inadequate and couldn't deal with the rare oyster I had in the palm of my hands. I didn't love you right, but I'm asking for a second chance. Let me show you how much you mean to me, Koko."

Koko took a sip of her daiquiri and went and sat in one of the theater seats. "How're you gonna do that, Chablis?" she asked curiously as she set her drink down, crossed her legs and rested her head in her hand.

"The new semester start next month," Chablis answered. "If

you find it in your heart to forgive me, baby? Then meet over by the Couch Restaurants first day of classes. We can have breakfast or whatever and sit down and talk about our future. If you don't show, I know I woulda loss the best thing that ever happened to me and I'll lay it to rest. I promise."

Koko wiped the incessant tears from her eyes as she remained silent. Chablis was saying all the right things and had her emotions in a whirlwind. "I need time to think about it," she spoke lowly.

"I can respect that. Take your time. Look, I won't even call you before classes start, alright?"

"Okay," Koko answered meekly. "I just need some time to think about this, Chablis. You'll have your answer first day of classes."

"I hope you give me a second chance, baby. I love you, Koko."

"I love you too, Chablis," Koko replied through heartfelt conviction just as Samantha poked her head into the theater room and called her name. "I have to go, baby," she remarked lowly. "Bye now."

Chablis smiled to himself after hearing Koko speak. That word, 'baby', was music to his ears as he sensed the endearment deriving from within his woman. "See you next year," he stated in a confident tone as he hung up the phone.

"What's up, Samantha?" Koko asked as she pressed the end button on her cell phone.

"Moses! Remember?" Samantha exclaimed.

"Oh, Lord," Koko laughed. "I forgot all about that, girl. You ready now?"

"Hell yeah! I'm gone win this bet!" Samantha sassed.

Naomi's middle daughters were Samantha's unofficial tour guides in Oklahoma. She simply couldn't stay away from the stockyards on the ranch. One animal in particular intrigued her, an eight hundred pound brown and white hog whom Spoonie and Tyke had named Moses. The massive swine was one of two pets Spoonie and Tyke had saved, the other being a calf they'd named Mister Bubbles. Moses and Mister Bubbles got reprieves on the ranch after Spoonie and Tyke had learned the truth behind the livestock on the farm after losing their first pet, a calf named Mister Spots.

What intrigued Samantha about Moses was the animal's relentless appetite and the repugnant routine he would do after eating a meal. She stumbled upon the animal's repulsive performance while helping Kimi, Koko and Martha discard trash the day before. Samantha was headed to the dumpsters with a sack of turkey gizzards when Kimi and Koko stopped her and told her the guts were going to Moses. Samantha had seen the hog during her first visit to the ranch back in October, but she'd never known of his routine until she hopped into one of the family's SUVs with Kimi and Koko where she was driven over to the far east side of the ranch to an area that lay behind the stockyards just the day before…

…*When Samantha eyed the hog, she swore she was looking at a miniature rhinoceros. Moses had a grimacing appeal and was over six times heavier than her one hundred and forty-five pounds at least. Dirty mucous poured from his snout as he grunted and ran from side to side behind the wooden slats that held him captive. He was every bit of a monster to Samantha, but he was a beautiful beast in her eyes.*

Koko threw the entire plastic sack of gizzards into the pen and Moses gobbled up the entire package, plastic included. He was like a living dish disposal to Samantha and she got a real kick out of watching the animal scoop up the turkey remnants, including the ice and mud that lined the floor of his pen. Several seconds later, Moses let out a guttural belch and defecated where he stood before he dropped to the ground and rolled around in the blood and brown muck.

Samantha laughed aloud. "Oh my, God!" she screamed. "He crapped out the raw guts he just ate and rolled around in it!"

"Umm hmm," Koko remarked unraveled. "He do it every time he get fed. Soon as he eat? He shit it right back out and lay in it."

"Moses can't do that every time. He must have a constant case of diarrhea or something." Samantha retorted.

"A diarrhea pig?" Koko laughed as she snorted. *"I hate when I do that goofy ass laugh, man!"* she quickly complained. *"It's embarrassing!"*

"Damn sure is," Kimi said, forcing Koko to shove her playfully. *"Okay, okay!"* she laughed. *"Samantha? You wanna bet on what Moses gone do tomorrow?"* Kimi then suggested.

"If we feed Moses tomorrow, you saying he gone take a crap right after and roll around in it?"

"If he don't? I'll put on one of my most expensive outfits and climb in that pig pen and give him a big hug while you film it." Kimi replied matter-of-factly as she pulled the collar up on her wool coat and tugged down on her cowgirl hat. *"But if he do? You gone have to fly me and Koko back down to Arizona on that private jet you flew in with Ben and my momma from the Cayman Islands and cater to us for a whole week straight before we start classes."*

"Bet on!" Samantha snapped.

Koko eased up from her seat in theater room with thoughts of the day before running through her mind and the bet agreed upon. She readied herself by heading upstairs to grab her wool trench coat, gloves and cowgirl hat and scarf as it was a frigid twenty-one degrees out. The three cousins headed back down to the first floor and hopped into a SUV with all the remnants of the day's meals, including scraps from uneaten portions of meals, more gizzards, raw collard greens and corn husks along with peeled seafood from Katrina's concoctions.

The conversation she'd had with Chablis played over and over again in Koko's mind as she wheeled the Suburban over the land. "Okay here we go, Samantha," she said as she pushed in a CD and skimmed through the songs. A few seconds later, Joe Strummer and The Mescaleros' song *Get Down Moses* came over the speakers.

"What kind of a song is that, Koko?" Samantha laughed upon hearing the song that was a perfect blend of rock and roll, rhythm and blues and a kind of funk that was reminiscent of Parliament and Bootsy Collins.

"Spoonie and Tyke turned us on to this song! They always say it's Moses' theme song! Heyyyy," Kimi sang as she raised her hands and began bouncing to the music...*"Get down Moses...part another sea...carve another tablet out of LSD... get down Moses...out in Tennessee..."*

With the eclectic song blaring inside the Suburban, Koko pulled up to Moses' pen with the headlights aimed at the monstrosity of a hog's wooden fence. The three cousins climbed out of the vehicle, each toting bags of scraps, and hurled them over the fence simultaneously. Moses ran up to the wooden barrier and rammed his head against the wooden slats before disappearing into the darkness of the pig pen.

Kimi, Koko and Samantha all climbed up on the fence where Kimi shined a spotlight down into Moses' pen. The hog was spotted in the center of the enclosure running his head underneath the plastic bags, scattering the contents about as he ran around frantically, gulping up the scraps in the process. Nary had a remnant of the food or the plastic bags that Samantha, Kimi and Koko hurled over into the pen remained several minutes later. Moses began running around the pen going from corner to corner; he was scraping his hooves in the snow-packed dirt and grunting ferociously as he squealed angrily. He stopped all movement a few seconds later and blew a mass of mucous from his nostrils before he turned away.

"Here we go," Kimi said in a sure manner as she smiled to herself.

The three cousins watched as Moses, with his rear end facing them, stiffened, and let out what seemed like a bucket full of manure right where he stood. The animal kicked his hind legs, pushing snow and dirt onto his excrement before he backed up and dropped down belly first into his own manure before flipping over onto his back where he began squealing, seemingly joyful over his antics as he wallowed in his own filth.

Samantha leaned back as she held onto the fence with one

hand. "That is the grossest thing I have ever seen in my life!" she screamed through loud laughter. "How you take a dump and then roll around in the stuff? What's with this hog?" she laughed aloud as she let go of her grip and jumped down from the fence while laughing uncontrollably. "That's sick! I wonder if he would eat a human?"

"I don't know about all that. What I do know is that we on our way to Arizona come next month, Samantha!" Koko yelled loud and proud as she and Kimi high-fived one another.

"After seeing that there? I got the hell outta y'all!" Samantha laughed as she and her cousins broke away from the fence and headed back to the SUV.

"What kind of malls and clubs they have down there, Samantha?" Kimi asked as she backed away from Moses' pen.

"Big malls with all the stores y'all like, and the clubs is always fun. They be packed and you never know who you'll see in there," Samantha replied happily. "I can't wait for y'all to come to Arizona."

The three cousins rode across the darkness of the land and pulled up to the back side of Ponderosa. They were still laughing over Moses' repugnance as they exited the vehicle and climbed the stairs, preplanning an itinerary for the trip as they entered the home. The trio was stunned to see the entire family on the first floor of Ponderosa. And from the looks of things, there was bad news that had been given.

Naomi was hugging a fretful Francine as Martha, Mary, Twiggy, Bay and T-top stood by, leaning against the counter with their heads bowed. The three cousins could see Walee, Kahlil, Spoonie and Tyke sitting inside the dining room off to the left with Ben, Henrietta, Dawk and several more members of the family.

Kimi and Koko had been here before; this time around, everybody was accounted for—everyone except their grandfather DeeDee and Mendoza. Both twins covered their lower faces. They knew DeeDee had been in Chicago for the past few days and their eyes watered over the prospects.

"What happened?" Kimi asked as she walked up to the group with Koko and Samantha trailing closely. "Where's granddad?"

"DeeDee's fine, babies," Naomi replied as let go of Francine. "It was Mendoza. DeeDee informed us a few minutes ago."

"Thank God! I thought something happened to granddad!" Kimi blurted out as she patted her chest.

"Kimi!" Koko scoffed.

Kimi eyed Francine and donned a sorrowful look. "Oh, Misses Cernigliaro! I'm sorry! I'm so sorry! I didn't mean it like that!" she said as she approached the woman and gave her a hug.

"You don't have to apologize for being happy your family is still alive." Francine reassured through a smile as she leaned back and looked into Kimi's brown eyes. "Your father was enough, okay?"

"It doesn't make what I said right, Misses Cernigliaro" Kimi confessed.

"Sure it does," Francine corrected. "Be happy for DeeDee. I'm a big girl, Kimi. I can cope." Francine walked off from Kimi and went into the kitchen and began grabbing plates. "Come on now," she said in a perky tone. "We're, we're supposed to be having a Christmas Eve dinner. I'll have to get ready to go to Chicago soon. Naomi, if you don't mind, this time? We will not have one of those big sendoffs. I want a quiet ceremony. Mendoza always wanted to be cremated."

"You sure that's what you want to do?" Naomi asked as she walked over and nudged Martha, who was still somber over the fact that Mendoza had been killed.

"Yes. And I would like to have his ashes stored here. Whenever I go to the ranch in Montana, I'll take them with me, okay? Come on now, everybody!" Francine yelled aloud. "Let's not let this ruin our Christmas! We have plenty more gifts to open and countless memories to share! If anybody wants to know what happened to my husband they're welcome to read the news article from the Chicago Tribune online."

Seventy-five year-old Francine Cernigliaro did well coping with the pain she was carrying having learned she'd loss her husband. The last thing she wanted to do was bring the family down. Seeing the widow handling the matter with dignity, the rest of the family soon began to liven up again; some went into the library while others went into the observation room to read the online article. By this point in time, everyone on the ranch understood the nature of the business some in the family were involved in; Mendoza's death wasn't as hard to take as the things that'd happened to Doss and Bay. His having terminal cancer had also eased the pain.

Dinner was served after a prayer by Mary, and the family sat inside the large dining room where everybody ate and drank while reminiscing over the life of Mendoza. Francine led the way, telling numerous stories about her husband, the good ones of course, as everybody already knew by now, especially after reading the online article, that Mendoza Cernigliaro was a part of the Italian Mafia.

By dinner's end, it was agreed that only Naomi and Francine would travel to Chicago on New Year's Day to meet with DeeDee and say a final farewell inside The Cicero Hot Dog Deli before returning home with his ashes, where another, bigger ceremony would be held in his honor, which was Francine's final request for her husband.

CHAPTER SEVEN
DIRTY AT DAWN
December 25, 2008

Seventeen year-old Peppi Vargas was sitting on the edge of her bed over to her safe house located in Louisiana, Missouri. She savored the comforts of her domain as she hadn't been to her home in quite a while having been on the move. She'd taken a long, leisurely bath inside her Jacuzzi tub, had eaten a hearty plate of homemade steak burritos and had polished her toe nails while watching a movie in her living room and sipping wine.

Pepper was supposed to have been looking for something inside her bedroom, but she'd become distracted after she'd come across her bible, a book she had to dust off before opening as it had been so long since she'd even touched it. After she read a passage from the book of Revelations, Pepper stood up from her bed and set the book down on her nightstand. She turned to head out of her bedroom, but was greeted by a lone woman standing in her threshold.

Pepper wondered why her two Rottweilers, Hutch and Honey, hadn't barked to alert her that someone was near the home like they always did, which would have put on her on alert.

"I had to finish the job, Peppi," the woman stated coldly as she aimed a gun. When the flash from the gun spilled forth, Pepper woke up screaming in terror and waving her arms in front of her face, trying to shield herself from bullets that weren't flying as music filled her ears.

"...goodbye...this is my second major break up...my first was with a pager, with a groupie, a cook pot and the 'caine......this one's with the school, with the stage...with the fortune...maybe not the fortune...but certainly it's my life...my pain and my struggle...the song that I sing to you is my every...thing..."

Twenty-one year-old Simone Cortez's pristine white H-1 Hummer cruised up Illinois State Highway 57 as Jay-Z's song *My First Song* thumped from the interior of her luxurious ride. In the back seat of the SUV sat the Cruz cousins, twenty-one year-olds Guadalupe 'Loopy' Cruz and Donatella 'Sweet Pea' Cruz. Both had AK-47s laying across their laps as they sat toking blunts.

Pepper's eyes were wide open as she sat upright in the front seat with one of her hands on the dash. She was looking off in every direction while rubbing sweat from her forehead with her forearms.

"What the fuck is your problem?" Simone snapped from the front seat of her Hummer as she stared over at Pepper while bobbing her head to the song's lyrics as she cruised up the dark and void two lane highway.

"I had a bad dream just now," Pepper replied as she began to calm down. "Like, like I saw my own death or something. I had a dream somebody killed me back in Missouri, Louisiana."

"You didn't see your own death. That was just a dream. Where I was at when you was gettin' killed in your dream, though?"

"You was probably dead already, Simone. I don't know. All I know is we woulda died had we gone there like y'all wanted to earlier tonight." Pepper said through heavy breathing as she continued to scan her surroundings.

"Was me and Donatella in your dream, Pepper?" Loopy couldn't help but to ask from the backseat.

"I ain't see y'all," Pepper remarked as she leaned over the

backseat. "Pass that blunt, Loopy," she remarked over the music.

"That dream might be a bad omen or something, Pepper," Loopy stated as she passed the blunt.

Simone sucked her teeth and said, "Nobody don't know about that safe house in Louisiana. Y'all two trippin' right about now."

"My Aunt CeeCee says dreams don't always make sense, but the can deliver a message, Simone. Somebody might be after us, y'all," Sweet Pea spoke hauntingly as she turned and looked out the back window into the pitch darkness.

"She just had bad dream not a bad omen." Simone barked, breaking the silence as she draped her diamond-clad wrist over the steering wheel. "On some other shit, though, you sure this lick we finna pull gone pay off, Pepper? We gone have a hard time pushing meth back down in Saint Louis," she stated as she leaned back in her seat and pushed her knee-length, boot-clad foot harder to the gas pedal and sped up.

"We ain't going in for the meth, we going in for the dough. But if they do have meth in there, we can find somebody to help us off it in Fox Park," Pepper responded as she guided Simone into downtown Quincy, Illinois, a small town that sat on the east bank of the Mississippi River about fifty miles north of Louisiana, and a hundred and ten miles north of Saint Louis.

"Dibble should've been around now. He could've turned us on to some meth users," Sweet Pea remarked.

"Too bad Loopy had to kill him," Simone remarked through a smirk. "How you know they got money in that trap, Pepper?"

"This white boy that broke my virgin took me to this place a bunch of times. He could never keep his mouth shut. Telling me, telling me how much money his boy be makin'," Pepper said as she curled her lips like she knew-it-all. "I used to ride over there from time to time a while back with dude. He wanted to show me off to his white friends and I let 'em so I can see what kind of operation they had."

"Where you meet this guy," Loopy asked as Simone entered the town just after midnight on Christmas Day.

"In Hannibal, Missouri last summer," Pepper answered. "I needed some new Forces and I ain't feel like driving down to Saint Louis so I headed north to see what was popping. Dude was cool and all, but y'all? It's a easy lick where his friends stay. One white dude and his wife sell to everybody in this hick town. They used to count money every night I was there. Right in front my face. How much I don't know, but it's worth takin'. The man that stay there is a friendly and trusting drug dealer." Pepper said as Simone chuckled.

"I'm serious, Simone." Pepper said as she looked down at the chrome Heckler and Koch Uzi resting in between her feet. "He one of the nicest drug dealers I ever met my life. Nice enough to let us in and take all his shit," she added as she leaned back in her seat and got back into focus, watching out for any of the law while Simone roll through several green lights in the small Midwestern town.

"Where we going up here?" Simone asked as she eyed the Christmas lights that lined the small town's downtown area.

Pepper led Simone to the northwest side of town. Which was a rural area near an industrial park and an abandoned high school that sat close to the banks of the Mississippi River. The area was once thriving with printing companies, but the recession had closed many of the factories. What remained was a booming heroin industry fueled by a busted economy.

After riding down a tree-sloped hill, and passing through an abandoned rail yard, Simone came up on the rear of the two story high school Pepper had mentioned. She clicked off the headlights and pulled up beside the high school's main building and parked downhill from a trailer home amongst some tall, lack-luster oak trees. An old pathway that students once used to cut through the woods to get to the high school grounds gave a clear view of the trailer home where the meth was being sold.

"What now?" Loopy asked through sleepy eyes.

"We wait until that porch light go out," Pepper replied

calmly as she watched several cars pulling up to the trailer home.

For six hours Pepper and her crew sat and waited, one or two of them drifting off to sleep on occasion while the other two kept watch. As the sun began to peek over the horizon, Simone shut the engine off on the Hummer and woke Pepper up.

"What you see over there while I nodded off?" Pepper asked as she straightened her clothes.

"They had traffic through that bitch all night, but it's been dead for about an hour since they turned the porch light off."

"Good. That mean they done closed shop," Pepper said through a yawn as she reached down and scooped up her Uzi. "Let's do it," she sighed as she pushed the door open, stepped out and stretched beside the Hummer.

Sweet Pea and Loopy grabbed their AK-47s, and Simone grabbed her automatic twelve gauge. The three eased out of the ride with their weapons draping their sides as they buttoned their hree-quarter length, black leather hooded coats. "Y'all ready?" Simone asked as she rounded the front of her ride while racking her twelve gauge.

"Let's do it," Loopy and Sweet Pea remarked simultaneously as the girls all huddled into a small circlee where they all bumped fists.

Simone, Loopy and Sweet Pea flipped the hood up on their jackets, while Pepper, dressed in a white leather outfit, pink boots and a pink tench coat, led the way.

Together, the four bandits trotted up the trail just as the sun began to break over the horizon through the light-grey clouds. A light snow had begun to fall, dusting the girls' heads and shoulders as they entered the trail with their eyes scanning the entire area up near the hilltop.

"His wife might answer the door." Pepper whispered as the gang of four crept through the wooded trail. "She a real bitch."

"Don't worry about it. I got that hoe," Simone remarked casually as she crept behind Pepper.

"Me and Donnatella will search the house," Loopy stated as she and her cousin followed Simone, the two of them looking back on occasion to make sure no one had approached the Hummer.

"Nobody brought ski masks, so we all know what it is going in. Let's hit this lick as quickly as possible and be on our way," Pepper stated seriously just as she and her crew emerged from the trail. The four casually walked across the snow-covered road with their guns draping their sides and entered the trailer home's unkempt yard that had three foot high snow drifts lining a dirt trail that led up to the front door.

Pepper walked up to the front door while placing a pair of pink leather gloves over her hands. Simone, Looopy and Sweet Pea were constantly scanning the block while she knocked on the door of the small trailer home repeatedly.

"They need to hurry the fuck up." Simone complained as she stood behind Pepper with her head on a swivel.

Just after Siomne had spoken, the wooden door was slowly pulled open. A heavy-set white female in her early twenties answered and stared her down. "Shop's closed, honey. You're gonna have ta' come back ta' night when the sun goes down. Porch light off means shop is closed," she stated in a somewhat condescending tone.

"I'm looking for William. Remember me? I came here about six, eight months ago with William?" Pepper asked as she smiled and rocked slightly while keeping her hands behind her back.

"Willie don't stay here." the female stated in an agitated manner as she curled her lips and stared down at the unknown teenager standing at her door with her hands tucked behind her back.

"Baby, who the fuck is that at the door?" a slender white male in his late twenties asked aloud at that moment as he came to the door shirtless in a pair of dingy white boxer shirts and worn out sandals he was using for slippers.

Pepper recognized the man as the meth dealer. She smiled up

at him and said, "Man, I forgot your name. Remember me? I came here with—"

"You Willie old girl," the man laughed happily as he placed a lit cigarette into his mouth and let it hang from his lips. "He been wondering what happened to you!"

"Yeah, I'm Willie's old girl," Pepper responded with a sly smile on her face as she held her hands behind her back. "Look, it's been a while since I been here. I forgot where Willie stay. We was here more than we was at his house. Can you call Willie and let me talk to him? I'll wait here."

"Nahh, come on in, shit! You Willie girl. He might be gettin' ready for work over to the gas station, but I'm sure he wouldn't mind stoppin' by before he punch in. It's Christmas, hell! Ain't nobody rushing to do nothing! How long you in town for?" the man asked as he grabbed his cell phone off the kitchen counter.

"Just long enough to hit your stash, dude." Pepper replied casually as she removed her hands from behind her back and put her Uzi on display.

The woman broke and ran for the door but she was shoved back into the house by Simone, who'd planted her twelve gauge to her chest.

Loopy and Sweet Pea rushed in behind Simone with their AK-47s locked and loaded and headed down the hall searching for any other occupants while rummaging through the couple's belongings.

"Where you going, mutherfucka? Get your ass over there! You ain't talkin' smart now is ya'?" Simone hissed as she shoved the lady back beside her old man with the tip of her shotgun's barrel.

The woman scurried back and shielded herself behind her husband as he raised his hands in the air. "You know who you robbin', you fuckin' wet back?" he asked through a scowl.

Pepper tilted her head back and eyed the man. "Now I'm a wet back? A minute ago I was Willie's girl!" she stated coldly. "Don't make me waste you and your fat ass wife on Christmas. Where the stash?" she asked through a serious gaze as she racked her Uzi.

The man stood staring at Pepper without responding.

"I'm gone ask you one more time. Where the stash?" Pepper asked as she walked up and grabbed the man's cell phone and tucked it in her pocket.

"Fu—"

Before the man could finish cussing her out, Pepper sprayed his legs with her Uzi. He immediately dropped to the floor screaming in misery as Simone placed her twelve gauge to the woman's face.

The woman quickly shifted her eyes to the freezer, and Pepper, noticing her gaze, went over and checked the refrigerator. "Watch that bitch, Simone," she ordered as she slid pass the man lying screaming on the floor.

Upon opening the freezer door, Pepper laid eyes on stacks of rubber-banded money. "Found it," she stated as she removed a plastic bag from her trench coat and began placing the money inside. After bagging the money Pepper walked back over to the man and aimed her gun at his torso.

"You got what you wanted, let us be!" the man pleaded from the floor as he clutched his bloody knees.

"I would have let you be, but I feel insulted by being called a wet back." Pepper then thought. "Who the fuck am I kidding," she declared through a cold smirk. "I was gone kill your ass anyway," she ended as she opened fire on the man, shredding his chest with bullets from her Uzi.

Simone quickly followed by placing her twelve gauge beneath the woman's chin and pulling the trigger. The woman's face was blown off completely and her reflexes had left both females stunned. They watched in disbelief as the woman's faceless body flailed about against the counter, the stove, and then the refrigerator before it dropped to the floor and began thrashing about like a snake with its head cut off. Blood was everywhere inside the kitchen, some of it splattering onto Pepper and Simone's boots as the woman's body thrashed about sadistically.

"Damn," Simone sighed as she jumped back. "Bitch got blood on me. Let's go. We gone have to clean off before we get back in the ride."

"Peppi?" Loopy suddenly called out as she and Sweet Pea emerged from the hall that led to two bedrooms.

"What's up?" Pepper asked as she stood before the door holding the day's haul.

Loopy was holding onto a Ziploc bag filled with white crystals while flipping it in her hand. "This look like some meth. I wonder how much it's worth on the streets," she pondered out loud.

"We'll find out when we get back to Fox Park! Come on now, y'all!" Pepper hissed as she pulled the front door open.

Pepper, Simone, Loopy, and Sweet Pea were becoming more and more experienced in the art of 'jacking'—a play in which they robbed other dope dealers out of their drugs and money at gun point. Pepper knew well enough not to hit any licks in the Saint Louis area because that would only heat up the streets—something she knew the Holland family would surely disapprove of; but since the day she'd killed Toodie, which was just over five weeks earlier, she and her crew had robbed two other dope houses in rural Missouri—one in the town of Troy and another in the city of Bowling Green.

The licks Pepper and her crew had pulled off in Missouri had only amounted to small stashes of weed, a quarter kilogram of cocaine and around eleven thousand dollars in cash. This lick in Quincy, Illinois, however, was a major score. Pepper and her crew had stolen $35,000 dollars in cash and they now had a new drug to sell in methamphetamine. The gang of four had no clue, however, just how much danger dealing meth would pose for them, neither the calamity that would befall them all.

CHAPTER EIGHT

A MESSAGE FROM THE OUTSIDE

December 29, 2008

The Monday following after Pepper and her crew's lick found a fifty-seven year-old man by the name of Eddie Cottonwood Senior, and his son, thirty-four year-old Eddie Junior in the weight room inside Stateville State Prison, which was located in Joliet, Illinois.

Eddie Senior, or Big Eddie as he was commonly called, had been down for just over twenty years now on a life sentence for first degree murder. He was sentenced back in 1988 after he'd murdered a man on behalf of Doss Dawkins inside the Cabrini Green projects over in Chicago, Illinois. He was an OG in Stateville—a lifer who called shots on all the tiers inside the prison. He could send messages and have men hit in other camps on his word alone.

The Black Peace Stone Nation, Latin Kings, Gangster Disciples and Vice Lords all gave Big Eddie a cut of their drug profits in order to keep the peace inside the facility. He was a man ripped right out of the seventies. Nearing sixty, he still sported a large afro, although it was greying around the edges. He still had the strength and ability to bench press five hundred pounds repetitiously and often bounced five pound dumbbells off his wide, chiseled chest and knotted-up abdomen. He was a one-man-wrecking-crew in his younger years, and he only grew in power when his son, Eddie Cottonwood Junior, was transferred to the prison from a jail in southern Illinois a year earlier.

Eddie Junior, the spitting image of his father, save for his short black hair and more slender physique, still had eight years left on a ten year bid after he was busted with four kilograms of cocaine down in Granite City, Illinois back in August of 2006. Together, he and his father now ran the drug rackets inside Stateville alongside another prisoner who'd been down since the late seventies. Father and son were working up a sweat lifting and spotting one another with their weights when in walked fifty-one year-old Manuel Lawson Taylor Senior, whom everybody simply called Taylor.

Taylor had been down since 1977, serving a sixty year sentence for distribution of marijuana after he was busted down in New Orleans with over one hundred pounds of the drug. He was first shipped to Angola Penitentiary. He was then moved to a federal facility in Illinois before he was shipped to Stateville back in 1997 after filing several petitions.

Taylor was a slender cat, but he was ripped with muscles as he often lifted weights with Big Eddie and Eddie Junior while the three discussed business. Back in the day he sported an afro, thirty-plus years had taken his hair, however; he was now bald with a thick, black mustache, a Rick Ross beard and he wore clear glasses that gave him a rather distinguished appeal.

"'Sup, family," Taylor said in his deep-pitched voice as he approached the men. "Got word from one of the hacks we got visitors comin' in," the convict stated as he dapped Eddie Junior.

"Is that right?" Big Eddie heaved as he thrust his arms upwards and sat the five hundred pound weight back onto the rack. "I know my other two sons and granddaughter comin'," he said as he sat up on the bench. "Who your ugly ass got comin' through for the holidays?"

Taylor chuckled as he dapped Big Eddie. "My son's mother comin' through! She, umm, she a Nurse Practitioner now," Taylor stated proudly. "Before umm, after, I meant *after*, after hurricane Katrina, my son's mother moved back to New

Orleans for a while and got a degree from Tulane University down there. She ran into an old friend, helped her out and the two moved to Chicago. I got you a damn good Christmas gift, brother! You gone like this here!"

"What kind of gift? You gettin' soft on us?" Big Eddie joked in his husky voice.

"Nah, brer! Trust me on this, though! We been down for a while now! Wouldn't it be good to see old faces, man?"

"Anything beats looking at you two ugly mutherfuckas," Eddie Junior quipped.

"Me and Taylor like that wine you be drinking at the end of the month, son," Big Eddie jibed as he stood up and wiped sweat from his arms and temples. "We just keep gettin' better with time."

Taylor slapped his fist into his open palm and said, "We got an hour, fellas. I'm going change up and get ready for this rendezvous and I suggest y'all two do the same."

"I hope you brought me some pussy. That'll be the best Christmas gift ever," Big Eddie spat as the three men left the weight room to prepare for their upcoming visits.

****

Out in the visitors' waiting area, Jay-D sat with Dooney and Nancy Cottonwood. Jay-D had been given a message to relay to his oldest brother by Dawk Holland. He sat in deep thought wondering just how his family was going to pull of what needed to be done behind prison walls as Nancy Cottonwood, the ever-annoying sixteen year-old, dug off into the business of a young woman sitting opposite her.

"Your dude been down for like two years, right?" Nancy asked the twenty year-old female as she leaned forward with her elbows resting on her skinny, dark-skinned kneecaps.

"That's right," the female answered proudly. "And I'm here to show him his baby boy! He be five when my man get out."

"See, that dog right there ain't gone hunt for several obvious reasons," Nancy countered as she ran her hands over her neatly-braided hair.

"Leave people alone, man!" Dooney snapped as he tapped Nancy's thin arm.

"Nahh, brer!" Nancy retorted as she fanned Dooney off. "I'm fucked up over this scenario, son! And I'm tryna save this girl from some drama! Her dude been down for two years is what she said, but she up here at Stateville with this baby that can't even walk and gone tell dude she had his baby while he was locked up? That nigga gone catch another charge time she break the news and that baby gone be like fifteen, not five, when dude get out."

Jay-D sat laughing as he texted on his phone. "Who you talkin' to? Kree ass?" Nancy asked.

"Your skinny ass ain't gettin' in my biz," Jay-D laughed.

"You better not be texting that boy!" Dooney snapped.

"Watch ya' mouth." Jay-D remarked as he texted Kree, thanking her for the bracelet she'd given him on Christmas, which was the least he could do after the way he'd treated her over to Kantrell's house on Christmas Day.

"Back to you, homegirl," Nancy said as she waved Jay-D off. "My advice, because I'm out there in that world, ya' dig? Done seen some shit and done been through some thangs in life! You can't even begin to imagine the shit I done seen out there in that world!"

"This is his baby!" the female retorted. "Mind yours!"

"Okay," Nancy said as she leaned back and threw her hands up in the air. "If I was you—"

"But you not me and you don't know my man!" the female snapped.

"This the problem with you young mutherfuckas now-a-days," sixteen year-old Nancy Cottonwood stated as she crossed her legs and shook her head at the twenty year-old female in disbelief over her stupidity. "Can't tell y'all shit! Tell that nigga that's his baby then! Go 'head! And watch you be callin' for the guards to pull him off ya' ass today. Nigga must got money, though, if you willing to gamble like this here. You tryna get 'em ta' look after somebody else baby, huh? Probably done laid up there and fucked his homeboy while he up here mainlining and done got pregnant for his best friend." Nancy laughed.

The female said nothing in reply. In all actuality, the teenager sitting across from her had her pegged, but she'd come too far to turn back. "Baby ain't even walking and she gone try and tell that man that's his baby," Nancy laughed as she eyed the female. "Seen this shit a hundred times up here at Stateville."

Everyone sitting in the visitor's waiting area knew the skinny, dark-skinned female was making plenty sense, but it was none of their business. Nancy was the only one speaking out, however, saying what others were silently thinking without giving it a second thought. There was no way that a man locked up for two years could have a child that wasn't even capable of walking.

"The li'l nigga might have down syndrome, though, y'all," Nancy started up again as she looked around at other visitors who she knew to be in agreement with her assessment of the situation at hand. "You might wanna run with that lie, sister. But then again, his ass ain't even big enough to pass for two let alone one years old so if he was retarded, that dog ain't gone hunt either. And if ya' able to pull that off, what you gone do if and when he ask for a blood test? 'Cause everybody sitting here today know that ain't your old man baby and it's only gone be a matter of time before your man locked up figure this shit out if he got any sense about himself."

This was Nancy Cottonwood—outspoken, honest to a fault and very condescending towards those she knew to be intellectually inferior. In her eyes, and the world in which she navigated, there were countless dumb individuals. The streets was the very thing that made fools out of so many was what the youngster had observed in her young years while running with her uncles Jay-D and Dooney. She was one who continuously learned from the mistakes of others; couple that with her courageous outspokenness, her arrogant and narcissistic attitude and unwavering confidence, here, you have a bona fide game player in-the-making that would only prove herself to be an asset to the family as time wore on.

"Good luck," Nancy told the female as she let the situation die down and began texting on her phone.

****

Meanwhile, on the opposite side of the bench a ways down from Nancy, sat two dark-skinned women who were waiting to visit inmates as well. One of the women, in her early fifties, appeared to be a professional woman who was well-off given her styled hair, makeup and business suit. The expensive perfume she wore lit up the entire waiting area with a sweet smell as she sat with her legs crossed, popping gum while clutching her expensive leather purse.

The other woman, who was in her early to mid-forties, was dressed in a designer jean outfit, thick wool jacket and new Air Jordan's. She seemed to have come from a hard upbringing, but she was an attractive woman nonetheless, short and on the heavy side with thick thighs and wide hips. Her hair was styled into a French twist and she wore black eye shadow. She had a button nose and slender lips and had a nervous look about herself as she sat shaking her legs rapidly. "You sure this is okay?" she asked the woman sitting beside her. "That man hasn't seen me in over twenty-five years."

"Let me tell you something, girl," the professional woman replied. "Talking to Taylor about Big Eddie? One thing I know about these men is that they care about family. Now, Big Eddie got himself into some shit early on. We all lived a fucked life in the beginning—but this here is all brand new. You'll be fine," the woman assured as she resumed popping her gum and closed her eyes to await the visiting time's arrival.

****

Taylor and both of the Eddies were called down an hour and ten minutes later. Taylor knew what was going down on this day, but Big Eddie and his son hadn't a clue. All they knew was that Jay-D, Dooney and Nancy were in town to visit. After being patted down, the three felons walked through the tunnel leading out into the visitor's room. Eddie Junior spotted his brothers and daughter right away. He smiled as he made his way over to their table.

Big Eddie, meanwhile, was about to follow his son until Taylor tugged on his white turtle neck long-sleeve shirt. "I know you anxious to see your family over there, man, but, take a look over there," he said as he pointed to the opposite side of the room where two dark-skinned women sat. The professionally-dressed woman stood up and placed her hands over her lower face and grew teary-eyed while her friend remained seated.

"My man," Big Eddie quipped as he shoved Taylor's shoulder and looked around for a few hacks he had on the payroll. "You did bring me some pussy. Let me walk over and talk to this hack and tell 'em to clear out the officers' break room so I can have some privacy," he added as he began walking over towards one of the correctional officers.

"Eddie," Taylor said seriously as he pulled his friend back. "The woman standing up is my wife Joyce. Take a closer look, brother. You don't remember that broad sitting beside my son's mother?"

Big Eddie eyed Taylor for a few seconds then turned and looked over to the short, thick-thighed dark-skinned woman and stared hard. He shrugged his shoulders with no clue as he eyed Taylor once more. "Who the fuck is that?" he asked casually.

"That woman there was like a daughter to me and Joyce back in the day," Taylor admitted. "When we first met her, we killed her dog by accident down in the Ninth Ward on the corners of Benefit and Metropolitan Street. Me and this guy Sam Holland buried the dog and took her and bought her a new one. Me and Joyce looked after her right up until I got locked up, ya' dig?"

"What all that gotta do with me?" Big Eddie inquired.

Taylor started walking towards the two women without answering Big Eddie's question. When his road dog didn't follow, he turned back to him and said, "When I got locked up,

Joyce lost contact with that little girl. A few years later, she visited me in Angola and told me that our street adopted daughter, Faye Sanders, had given birth to a baby girl named Katrina Sanders—your daughter, brother."

"Faye?" Big Eddie asked rhetorically as his jaw dropped open. Right away, the fifty-one year-old convict remembered the woman named Faye Sanders. "I have a daughter?" he then asked in wonderment as memories of the first time he and Faye had ever met came screaming back to memory…

CHAPTER NINE

BACK IN THE DAY

March 1980

Fifteen year-old Faye Sanders had just marched nearly four miles from the Garden District, through downtown New Orleans, and over to the Superdome where the Bacchus parade she'd been marching in was scheduled to disband. High school bands and members of the Bacchus Social Club who'd ridden on floats, and numerous police officers, were mingling on the New Orleans Saints' football field. Champagne bottles were being popped and second line music blared loudly over the dome's speaker system. The Bacchus Ball, the huge party thrown at the parade's end, was now underway.

Faye pranced around the field with a group of her majorette friends while still dressed in her green, glittering uniform and white knee-length boots and still wearing her white captain's cap. Orange glitter dotted her smooth, brown skin from head to toe and she was all smiles, thoroughly enjoying the sights and sounds of the parade's participants. After an hour or so, one of the majorettes suggested that the girls all walk through the French Quarters down Bourbon Street. Two bottles of champagne was swiped from one of the large floats and the group of teens began their walk through downtown New Orleans as midnight approached.

Faye Sanders was a spring chicken in all actuality, but she was an adventurous young woman and she loved the French

Quarters. Her grandmother Ora had taken there on several occasions, but that was during the day. She knew night time on Bourbon Street was totally different, however, and being that it was the Sunday before Mardi Gras and the end of the Bacchus parade, she could only imagine how much fun she and her friends were going to have on this night.

Canal Street, the main avenue that cut through the heart of downtown New Orleans and stretched from the Mississippi River all the way to City Park, was littered with Orleanians and tourists from out of town who'd just watched the Bacchus parade roll through. The Bacchus parade was the last of the big parades until Fat Tuesday so many parade attenders were headed to the French Quarters to carry on the revelry. Horns from cars blared loudly as drivers tried to make their way through thousands of partying people, many of them drunk and some literally dancing in the middle of Canal Street while holding onto some form of an adult beverage.

What her eyes were witnessing sent bursts of excitement coursing through Faye's body. She'd been to parades before, but again, that was only during the day time. This was her first year as a majorette and for the first time ever, she was now getting an up-close and personal look at what the New Orleans night life had to offer. The tall stores and hotels lining Canal Street on either side were all lit up and businesses were still open as if it was a Saturday afternoon. The city's street cars and city buses were rolling. Musicians were posted up on just about every corner leading to Bourbon Street. People were bumping into one another, spilling drinks and apologizing through wild laughter. Tourists were walking around with stacks of beads asking women to show their breasts for a pair.

Faye couldn't count the times she'd seen women of all races bare their breasts in the middle of the street to passing cars and along the crowded sidewalk. A couple of majorettes in her bunch had even done so and had even dared her to give it a try. She'd done so briefly, having become a little more uninhibited over the few squibs of champagne she'd guzzled. She'd bared her left breast to an older white man and his wife and earned herself a pair of pearl beads.

This was the most fun fifteen year-old Faye Sanders had ever had in her young life. The sounds of the city, the music blaring from cars, horse and carriages plodding through the streets, the tap dancers and the smells emanating from the many sausage dog vendors and restaurants amid the festive atmosphere was just as intoxicating as the liquor she was consuming.

F.W. Woolworth's store coming into view was the landmark that let Faye know she was now on Bourbon Street. The crowd was so thick on the corners of Canal and Bourbon Street that some of the majorettes had become separated. The group of twenty had dwindled down to Faye and three other majorettes, who began to make their own way through the rollicking crowd as they entered the French Quarters.

Faye now found herself hanging with an eighteen year-old majorette named Fredericka McNeal, whom everybody called Freddie Mac. Freddie Mac, a tall, brown-skinned, statuesque young woman with a large afro, was the lead majorette. She was more like a drill sergeant to many of the majorettes, Faye included, as she often cut into whatever fun the girls tried to have, even during practice after school. With Freddie, everything had to be done a certain way—her way.

"Where everybody else at, Freddie?" Faye asked loudly over the noisy crowd as she tailed the tall teenager.

"Them hoes done left us! They going show they titties I bet! I'm a tell coach Thursday when we get back to school, watch!" Freddie Mac dragged in a slow New Orleans twang.

Faye and the other two majorettes rolled their eyes. Freddie was a stick-in-the-mud to them; they had no champagne bottle and were now walking in a single file line through the masses of people. All the fun they were having had ceased to exist being linked up with Freddie.

Tired of just walking, Faye broke off from her school mates and turned around and began heading back towards Canal Street in order to catch the city bus home. The rest of the majorettes, the ones she really wanted to hang with, had all but disappeared and she knew it would be hard to find them in the crowd. The best thing for her to do was to head back home; besides, her grandmother may have begun to get worried about her.

After fighting her way through the revelers, Faye made it over to a bus stop two blocks down from Bourbon Street closer to the Mississippi River. From here, she figured she would be able to catch a seat on the Desire bus line, the route that would take her back to the Desire project where she lived with her grandmother on Pleasure Street.

Faye could see several buses approaching a few blocks down, but she couldn't make out the name on the lead bus. She'd just stepped off the curb when she bumped into someone. Cold liquid spilled down her right stocking and entered her white, leather knee-length boot, chilling her toes briefly. "Aww, man!" she snapped as she backed up onto the curb.

"Damn, baby! I'm sorry 'bout that," a male voice laughed as he rubbed Faye's thigh.

"Don't rub it! You gone soak it in!" Faye snapped as she moved the guy's hand off her flesh. The fifteen year-old looked up at that moment and was caught off guard.

Faye was expecting to see a guy in jeans, sneakers and t-shirt, the seemingly choice of many of the young men in the city. To the contrary, the guy standing before her wore a pair of brown slacks, a cream-colored shirt and matching pair of cream gators with a cream-colored felt fedora. He appeared to be in his late teens and he was a handsome guy with smooth, dark skin, a neatly-trimmed and tapered afro with long side burns. "That's a cold drink, man." she said as she wiped her leg.

The guy reached into his back pocket and pulled out a cream silk handkerchief and handed it to the young woman. "That was my fault, lady. What's your name?" he asked.

"I'm Faye."

"Nice to meet you, Faye. I'm Eddie Cottonwood from Chicago."

"Chicago? You down for Mardi Gras, huh?" Faye asked while running the rag over her stockings.

"That be true. Came down by myself to see what this city like."

"Well, everything you need is two blocks up. That's the French Quarters."

"I know. That's where I bought my daiquiri. I spilled most of it, so now I need a new one. You wanna go and get one with me?"

"My bus is coming."

"Bus? You going home? You look like you was in the parade! Shiiddd! You know all about the city! Come on and take a walk with me! What time the buses stop runnin'?"

"They run all night." Faye replied as she handed Eddie back his handkerchief.

"You got time, then! Come on!"

Faye really wasn't ready to go home. Eddie was handsome, and seemed to be a nice guy. She took him up on his offer and the two began making their way back to Bourbon Street while conversing. The sounds of trombones, snare drums and trumpets filled the two's ears as they mixed in with the droves of Mardi Gras participants walking up and down Bourbon Street. On the corners of Saint Louis and Bourbon Street, Eddie came across a daiquiri stand that sat across from an A&P Grocery Store. He grabbed Faye's tiny hand and led her over to the window of the small building where the two waited in a long line that was spilling out into the street.

"I'm gone get you a hurricane daiquiri, Faye!" Eddie yelled into Faye's ear over the loud music of a trumpeter and the festive crowd that surrounded the man, many of them throwing loose change and greenbacks into his open trumpet case.

"You tryna get me drunk, Eddie?" Faye asked through laughter over the trumpeter's melodic solo serenade that lit up the corner.

"Nah. Really, you should be paying since you spilled my

drink earlier!" Eddie chided.

"Boy, you bumped into me!"

"We bumped into each other, then!" Eddie laughed as the trumpeter ended his routine and thanked his audience. "You want a daiquiri?" he then asked. Faye nodded in approval before she began bobbing her head to a popular song that began playing on a loudspeaker that sat just below the awning of the daiquiri stand...

"...*Down in New Orleans where the blues was born...it takes a cool cat...to blow a horn...on Lasalle and Rampart Street...the combo's there with a mambo beat...the Mardi Gras mambo, mambo, mambo...Party Gras mambo, mambo, mambo...Mardi Gras mamboooo...down in New Orleans...*"

The Meters' song *Mardi Gras Mambo* was one song Eddie had been hearing over and over again in various locations ever since he'd arrived in New Orleans four days earlier. He and Faye danced alongside the people in the line with them before ordering their daiquiris. They then went on to enjoy the remainder of the night by walking up and down Bourbon Street and hanging out in front of different clubs as Faye was too young to enter. It was nearly four in the morning by the time they'd decided to end their outing.

"My grandmother is going to kill me, man," Faye sighed as she walked beside Eddie, her left arm wrapped around his right arm as she rested her head on his shoulder while clutching her pearl beads in her right hand. "I didn't call her or anything. And I had a midnight curfew."

Eddie slid his arm from Faye's grip and hugged her neck. Both were buzzing from the hurricane daiquiris they'd consumed, but not to the point in which they weren't in control of their actions. "If you want, I'll get you a taxi home, Faye." Eddie suggested.

"Ain't no taxi going into the Desire project this time of morning," Faye laughed. "It's not much different than Cabrini Green where you stay, Eddie. I'll just catch the bus."

"If a grown man riding in a car won't go to your home at this hour, then I can't let you catch the bus by yourself," Eddie spoke through closed eyes as he and Faye strolled up a sparsely-filled Bourbon Street headed back towards Canal Street. "I have a hotel room over to the Howard Johnson's, baby. You can crash there and catch the bus home after you get up."

Faye wrapped her arm around Eddie's waist and drew closer to him. "You want sex," she stated.

Eddie paused at that moment and looked down at Faye. "If sex is what I wanted, I would've asked you for it, Faye," he declared. "Really, that's your decision. I'm just tryna make sure you get home to your grandmother safe, that's all. It's all kinds of crazy people—rapists and kidnappers and shit. You don't need to be out here by yourself tryna catch a bus, baby. You can crash on the bed and I'll sleep on the couch in the room if that'll make you feel better."

Faye accepted Eddie's offer and the two walked over to his hotel room and settled in soon after Faye had called her grandmother and told her she and a few other majorettes were spending the night over to Freddie Mac's home after walking through the French Quarters. She then went into the bathroom to clean up.

When Faye exited the shower, she was wearing one of the complimentary robes the hotel offered with nothing on underneath. She peeked out from the bedroom and saw Eddie sitting on the couch toking on a joint while enjoying the soft sounds of Heatwave's song titled *Always and Forever*. She leaned back on the door's threshold and smiled as she looked down to the floor. The fifteen year-old loved that song a great deal, often fantasizing about walking down the aisle on her wedding day while it played in the background. She parted her lips and sung along with the song lowly as she dreamt of her special day…"*Everyday…love me your own special way…melt all my heart away…with a smile…take time to tell me…you… really care…and we'll share tomorrow…together…*"

"You wanna hit this, baby?" Eddie asked over the music as he held the joint out.

Faye pulled away from dreaming of her future and looked over to Eddie as he sat in the silhouette-lit darkness of the room in his silk wife beater with his fedora still on his head. She'd been checking him out all night, admiring his physique and handsome facial features that complimented his cool demeanor. "No, thank you," she answered softly as she walked over to the couch and sat beside Eddie.

The seventies, to a degree, was the age of innocence—where one could be trusted upon befriending a total stranger. Many people hitchhiked and bunked out in homes of people they'd just met, if only to Laissez les bons temps rouler, or translated from its French origin, Let the Good Times Roll.

After only one night, just a few hours into meeting Eddie Cottonwood, Faye had grown a trusting heart. She was no virgin, having had sex with a member of her high school marching band to satisfy her curiosity, but she was selective in her dealings with the opposite sex. Eddie's kindness and the respectful manner in which he tended to her had given her a fond heart. Still, she wasn't ready to have sex with the guy. The two of them sat up for a couple of more hours talking about everything from Faye's experiences in high school, to Eddie's growing up in Cabrini Green. Just before sunrise, Faye got up and went into the bedroom and put her majorette uniform back on and slid under the covers while Eddie remained on the couch. The night had ended without so much as a kiss between the two, but there was no denying the attraction they held towards one another.

When Faye awoke the following afternoon, Eddie was already up and dressed lavishly in one of his silk outfits and gator shoes. A buffet consisting of turkey club sandwiches, pea soup, french fries and banana pudding was laid out. "I put fresh towels in the bathroom for you to shower, baby. What size you wear?" Eddie asked as he removed lids from the dishes sitting on the cart.

"I'm a four. Why?" Faye asked as she sat up in the bed and stretched.

"You can't go out in that uniform. Get yourself together while I go out and find you an outfit."

Faye blushed as she eased up from the bed in her majorette uniform. It was only then that Eddie got a full glimpse of just how much beauty this fifteen year-old possessed. She'd removed the long gloves she was wearing and had washed the glitter from her hair and face. She was a short and voluptuous dark-skinned beauty with pert breasts, dark eyes and pouty lips. Her jet-black hair hung over down to her shoulders and she had curves on her body that put many a woman years older to shame.

"You like what you see?" Faye asked as she grabbed a towel and wrapped it around her torso.

"Yes indeed, foxy momma," Eddie answered as he stood eyeing Faye from across the room. "You just a young tender right now, though, so I ain't gone even try and shoot game at ya'. I'm gone let you make that decision," he stated as he as he reached into his pocket and pulled out a stack of money and ripped off two twenties and set them down on the dresser. "A li'l somethin' to put in ya' pocket."

Faye eyed the money and looked over to Eddie. "What do you do for a living?" she asked.

"I be back after while," Eddie said in a calm manner as he backed out of the room while stuffing his money back into his slacks, never bothering to answer Faye's question.

Faye watched as Eddie left the hotel room. She began wondering what she was doing exactly with a man seven years her senior who'd she now believed was a hustler. They'd had fun the night before, but it was time to bring things to an end was what she told herself as she entered the bathroom.

Eddie returned just over an hour later with a pair of Chic denim jeans, a blouse and some clods for Faye. She got dressed without saying a word to Eddie, who sat in the living room waiting patiently. "I'm leaving now, Eddie," Faye said timidly as she stepped out of the bedroom several minutes later.

"Cool. Let me call us a taxi." Eddie responded as he reached for the phone resting on the table before the couch.

"I'll, I'll just catch the bus, Eddie. I had fun and all, but I don't know about this."

"Know about what, Faye?" Eddie asked in a surprised manner as he hung the phone up and stood up from the sofa.

Faye's heart began palpating at that moment. The way Eddie looked at her had her frightened. "I just wanna go home," she suddenly cried out.

Eddie sensed Faye's fear so he took a few steps back. With raised hands, he looked the young teenager in the eyes at that moment and said, "Faye? Baby, I ain't out to do you no harm. Shit, we just kickin' it! Didn't we have fun?"

"We did. But, but you being too nice to me, man. No boy— no man has ever been this nice to me."

"Because you been dealin' with the wrong niggas," Eddie stated seriously. "You asked me what I do for a living, you sure ready for me to show you what it is I do?"

"Okay," Faye replied cautiously. "But I have to go home first."

"I can dig it. You want a cab or a bus?"

"Let's take the bus."

"That's not how I like to move, but I'm lettin' you call the shots right now. Lead the way, baby," Eddie replied as he placed his fedora onto his head and stepped aside to let Faye lead the way out of the hotel room.

After a leisurely walk back over to busy Canal Street, Faye and Eddie hopped aboard a city bus on the Desire bus line. Once again, Eddie knew he had won Faye over. He smiled to himself as he thought about how slowly and methodically he was wearing this reluctant young beauty down towards contentedness. During their walk, he'd constantly made her laugh while the two window-shopped along the way. He asked numerous questions about the city, allowing Faye to do most of the talking, which further eased her mind and removed more of the apprehension she held back inside the hotel room.

Faye was chatting away to Eddie about wanting to take a horse and carriage ride through the French Quarters as she sat beside him on the bus. He was taking mental notes of her likes and dislikes as he eyed the scenery along the bus route. The Desire bus line ran along Canal Street for a bit of ways before it made a right turn and left the downtown area. Department stores and theaters soon gave way to homes and small corner stores along the route.

The further the bus got away from downtown, however, Eddie began to notice how the scenery was beginning to change even more as it entered what he knew to be predominately black neighborhoods. This section of New Orleans, an area Faye had told him was called the Ninth Ward, wasn't much different from the area outside of Cabrini Green. He did right packing his jammer was what he'd thought to himself as he eyed a few lounges along the bus line. "What them bars be like, Faye?" he asked as he crossed his legs and placed an arm around her neck.

"Them bars?" Faye sighed. "All the players and gangsters be in there, man. They sell drugs in some of 'em, women be prostituting and stuff. Some of 'em sell good food, though. Like this one place called Persia's around my grandmother house? Man, they got the best po-boys ever!"

"What's a po-boy?"

"You been down here for almost a week and never had a hot sausage sandwich?" Faye asked surprised.

"Nahh. You gone buy me one with your money you got?"

"Yeah," Faye smiled kindly over to Eddie. "Yeah, I can do that. We have to go before five because Persia's don't allow nobody under twenty-one in there after five."

"You gone let me meet your grandmother?" Eddie then asked.

"I don't know, man. She gone fuss if she know how old you are." Faye complained.

"Hell, I look that old?" Eddie asked as he tried to get a glimpse of his reflection in the bus's window.

Faye looked Eddie over again and chuckled. "Not really. If she asks, I'll tell her you're a senior at another school because if I tell her you go to Carver she gone ask who your momma," she said through laughter.

"I can dig it," Eddie laughed as he pulled Faye closer. "You a fun lady to be around, Faye. I like you, baby."

"I like you too, Eddie," Faye responded in a sweet voice as she sunk into Eddie's body and enjoyed the bus ride back to her neighborhood.

The bus neared Faye's stop after another fifteen minute ride as many passengers were off-loading at every stop along the way it seemed. She pulled the line, buzzing her stop, and got up from her seat when the bus approached her block and looked back at Eddie as she walked towards the back door. "You comin'?" she asked through a sexy smile.

"I thought you lived in the projects," Eddie stated as he looked around in wonderment at the two-story light-tan brick apartment complex the bus had entered a few minutes earlier.

"This is it. This is the Desire project," Faye responded as the bus came to a halt on the corners of Pleasure and Desire Street.

Eddie hopped up from his seat and followed Faye off the bus. He laughed aloud as the vehicle pulled off, leaving a cloud of diesel smoke in its wake. "This here is a project?" he asked as he grabbed his knees and continued laughing. "Hell, compared to where I come from this here is Disney World! You and your grandma finally got a piece of the pie like the Jefferson's, Faye!"

"They may not be seventeen stories tall like in Cabrini Green, but don't let these bricks fool you, Eddie," Faye stated seriously. "This ghetto ain't no different from where you come from," she admitted as she started across the street. "They just spaced out a lot."

"I don't know about all that," Eddie stated through laughter as he placed his hands on his hips and looked around at what was to him, nice-looking apartments in a decent neighborhood.

If this was the roughest New Orleans had to offer for Eddie, then he had full confidence that he would be able to put his hustle down. Cabrini Green was like a small city all-to-itself with over seventy-thousand residents and it ran rampant with violence. The Desire project was like a small village of condominiums filled with peaceful residents.

Eddie was going off Faye's gentle nature and the layout of the land. He would've never even known he'd entered into a city dwelling if Faye hadn't alerted him. The Desire project was a place Eddie felt he could run through in a short span of time given first impressions, but he had no idea just how much this seemingly-docile neighborhood would change the course of his Faye's lives forever as he ran and caught up with his newfound lady friend...

...A tap on Big Eddie's shoulder brought him back to the present. He turned and looked over to Taylor with watery eyes. "I owe Faye an apology, man," he spoke lowly.

"Tell her that, brother." Taylor said as patted Big Eddie's back. "She came here for a reason. And after all these years? You still can make it right."

"Yeah," Big Eddie smiled. "I can at least *try* to make it right, Taylor. Thank you for this, man." he ended as he looked over to Faye.

CHAPTER TEN

WHAT THE GHETTO GAVE

Forty-six year-old Faye Sanders locked eyes with Eddie the moment he looked over in her direction. Butterflies quivered in the pit of her stomach as the night they first met flashed through her mind. They'd seemed to be on their way to establishing a romantic rapport the day Eddie had traveled with her into her neighborhood. What she and Eddie shared had become special, but the day he left was a day that always haunted her and left her wondering what if. She stood motionless with her eyes focused on Eddie, her heart palpating as he slowly began walking her way.

"I don't know if I can do this!" Faye exclaimed as tears began rolling from her eyes. "That man!" she yelled as she hid her face and turned towards Ms. Joyce.

The ten year-old little girl Ms. Joyce knew all-too-well had just returned the moment Faye leaned into her and cried on her shoulder. She held onto Faye as she looked upwards towards the ceiling and silently asked for God's guidance in this particular matter. Ms. Joyce had been here before on several occasions, and looking back on the matter, it seemed as if she'd lived life twice with Faye and Katrina. They were one-in-the-same in her mind's eye. She'd met them both when they were nearly the same age.

Faye was ten in 1974, and Katrina was eight back in 1988. Neither had ever really had that strong woman in their life to guide them properly until she came along, but even then, she wasn't able to guide them into womanhood in the appropriate manner given her own demons and life's struggles. In spite of her errors, Ms. Joyce was satisfied with the fact that she'd sincerely tried to have a positive impact on the Sanders females as they'd both made it to maturity. Faye was clean and sober and was supporting herself.

The last Ms. Joyce had heard in regards to Katrina Sanders was that she was attending college down in Arizona after recovering from her gunshot wounds. It was the pain of all that had gone down that had forced the woman to turn her back on the very children she loved and had sworn to protect and uphold. Ben's trial had broken her heart. And the very thing she'd feared most, which was him taking down all those around him, had come to pass and she couldn't bear the pain of having to face her worst nightmare. She hung on from a distance, waiting, praying and hoping that Katrina would survive.

When she got word of Katrina's recovery, Ms. Joyce faded into the background and dove into her medical career. She continued on in the helping of children in need, but only from a medical aspect, because losing a husband, a blood-born son, and a host of youngsters who were like sons and daughters to her in Dirty Red, who'd been imprisoned, Oscar, Jason, Lamont and Jermaine, and another child who was like a daughter to her in Tanaka Romaire, who'd all been killed, had frightened the woman. Her heart couldn't take much more tragedy dealing with youngsters who ran the streets back in the day. She'd tried as best she could to deter those she cared about, but in the end, it proved futile as they'd all perished, or had been sent to jail. The only solace Ms. Joyce took with her back in the day was the fact that Katrina Sanders was now in college living in Arizona, and Dirty Red was still alive behind bars. From there, she let that part of her life relapse as she went forward.

Ten years later, however, Ms. Joyce now found herself back amongst the same people whom she'd once loved and cared about and she was looking to bring some parts of her life to a conclusion and usher in a new start. Faye was around for a reason. She was visiting Taylor for a reason. Ben was still alive behind bars for a reason was her thinking as she held onto Faye while wondering how she would go about reuniting mother and daughter. From there, she had it in her mind to track Ben down behind bars and bring that portion of her life full-circle, if only to be able to move on and close doors to a life that once was.

Ms. Joyce understood Faye's reluctance completely. After all, Eddie had up and disappeared when she was most vulnerable and her life hadn't been the same since. Faye had survived those turbulent times of days long gone, however; and she owed it to herself to at the very least to close this part of her life out completely. "You've come too far to not get the answers you deserve, Faye," Ms. Joyce stated lowly as she rubbed the woman's shoulders softly and stepped back from her. "You've come too, too far to back out, baby."

Faye looked Ms. Joyce in the eyes as tears poured down her cheeks. Her back was still to Big Eddie when his deep, yet gentle voice spoke out and said, "I first wanna apologize for running out on you, Faye."

Faye broke down at that moment. She covered her face in shame and bent over at the waist. "I ruined our daughter!" she admitted. "You—" the overly-emotional woman paused at that moment, righted herself, turned around and placed her hands on her hips. She grimaced as she stared Eddie in the eyes. "I needed you, man!" she screamed, forcing some who were close around the table where the three were standing to look in their direction. "You never came back to let me say what I had to say that day!" she cried.

Eddie swallowed the lump in his throat and coughed briefly. He'd never been one to be at a loss for words, but on the other hand, he knew Faye didn't understand fully the reasons why he'd abandoned her, so he posed a question he already knew the answer to. "Did, did the police come to your home that night?" he asked lowly.

"What that gotta do with anything?" Faye asked through her tears. "You ran out on me!"

"Did the police come that night?" Eddie asked calmly once

more.

"About two hours later," Faye admitted as she looked away from Eddie. "They, they asked if I knew who you were and I said yes, but you'd left earlier. They came back every day for almost two weeks after that looking for you. I was harassed every day at school by this girl named Freddie Mac over that, Eddie."

Big Eddie nodded his head with the understanding that he'd made the right decision that day. "Now you know why I didn't come back, Faye. You knew what'd gone down when I went to get that ice cream. Didn't you?"

"That man was my friend Freddie's brother. She blamed me for what'd happened every day and sometimes she fought me. I was under so much stress. I swear I thought I was gone lose your baby. I waited, hoping you would come back, call or write —but you never did. I gave birth to your daughter Katrina Sanders in February of nineteen eighty-one."

Big Eddie ran his hands over his bearded-face, wiping subtle tears from his eyes. Twenty-nine years and he'd never known for certain whether he had another child floating around or not. Taylor had mentioned some things to him as the two grew closer, but he never believed the guy until he laid eyes on Faye on this day and heard her proclamation. "Had I known, I would've done things differently, Faye—but, baby, believe me when I say I didn't, I never meant to abandon you and my child. Do you know where she is today?" Big Eddie asked as he looked over to Ms. Joyce then back over to Faye.

"Arizona is where she was back in two thousand," Joyce remarked. "She went to Arizona State is all we know. Phoenix would be the most logical place—but then again she may not even be in Arizona now because she been graduated college."

"You mean with all the equipment available there's no way to get an address on our child?" Big Eddie asked in disbelief. "No. We, we can find her and set the matter straight. If I have flesh out there I wanna know who she is and where she's at so she can at least have a choice whether she wants me in her life or not," he stated in an assured tone of voice as he stepped closer to Faye and presented his face. "I wanna hug you, Faye, but I would understand if I was greeted with a slap," he ended as he closed his eyes.

A sting quickly landed across Big Eddie's right cheek. He stumbled back a couple of paces before he felt arms wrapping around his body. "I loved you!" Faye cried as she grabbed the man tightly. "I truly loved you, Eddie!"

"I'm sorry, Faye." Big Eddie said as he gripped the woman tightly. "Forgive me for all I did wrong, baby," he spoke lowly under the realization that other prisoners who revered him were now looking on.

It wasn't a good move on Big Eddie's part to show such emotion given his position inside of Stateville, but it would mean denying the woman that stood before him if he'd done so. He'd wronged her tremendously and was willing to shun pride aside for family's sake. It was the very least thing that Faye Sanders deserved was what he understood to be fact. If anybody had something to say about his showing sentimentalism to his daughter's mother, well, they would get dealt with in a quick and orderly fashion. He'd thought about putting those prisoners who were more attentive to his business rather than their own personal matters in their place, but now wasn't the time and nor did he want to cause a scene. He backed away from Faye slowly and extended his hand, offering her a seat.

Ms. Joyce and Taylor had convened to a table of their own by now. She could only smile as she and Taylor sat down. Bringing Faye along was indeed the right move she now believed. Both of them were doing well in life now. Faye was a manager at a local restaurant in the town of Joliet and Ms. Joyce was a Licensed Nurse Practitioner working at Presence Saint Joseph Medical Center. The two shared a home Ms. Joyce was mortgaging and both had their own late model cars. With so much advancement made in their professional lives, it was now time for Faye to rectify her broken past with Eddie was Ms. Joyce's belief as she watched him and Faye settle into their seats.

"Last time I saw you, you were settin' out your

grandmother's prescriptions and we'd just eaten dinner. What was it?" Big Eddie asked through a smile as he rubbed the side of his face. "What you had a brick in your hand or something, woman?" he then asked as he looked around in search of a brick he knew wasn't there.

Faye smiled. "There isn't a brick, man. That was years of frustration I slapped you with, but you know you got off real easy," she stated. "Dinner that day was pork chops, string beans and mashed potatoes and gravy. It was the only thing I really knew how to cook for a while. Even after Katrina was born."

"So what happened?" Big Eddie asked seriously.

"With what?"

"I was thinking about the day we first set foot on your home turf," Big Eddie replied. "There was this big swimming pool or something in this huge ass courtyard, ya' know? I remember your grandmother singing your name that day," he laughed.

"You remember all that?" Faye asked in appreciative wonderment as she smiled over to Big Eddie.

"I remember everything you told me that day," Eddie smiled back. "About you marching in the parade, and how you and your crew stole those champagne bottles off a float and left the Superdome. I'm glad y'all got split up, though, because we wouldn't have a daughter somewhere out there in the world today."

"That's true," Faye said in a somewhat somber tone of voice.

"Why the sad look?"

Faye looked up to Eddie and sighed. "It's a lot you don't know about me, Eddie," she confessed. "If we ever find our daughter, I may just get slapped way harder than what you got from me. I might even take a couple of slugs, man, because I wasn't a good mother at all."

"Couldn't be no worse than me being a nonexistent daddy," Big Eddie replied as he leaned forward. "I have three sons and a granddaughter, Faye," he admitted. "My oldest son is over there in the corner. He was five when we me and you met, and

I had two more sons by the same woman after I made it back to Chicago when I left New Orleans."

"For a while after we met I felt that you had a family. The day you ran out, I thought you said fuck it. I thought you got the pussy and ran until I heard what happened that day," Faye admitted.

"I did run out—but I never knew you was pregnant. I went back to Chicago and tried to make things work with my sons' mother, you know? This woman, she, she wasn't nothing but a junky, though. Got hooked on crack cocaine, heroin, pills and anything else you can imagine. She ended up dying of a speedball overdose soon after she gave birth to my youngest son Dooney."

"That's the story of my life minus the overdose," Faye sighed as she looked Eddie in the eyes.

Big Eddie leaned back in his chair and eyed Faye in disbelief. "Not you," he hoped.

"Eddie, I did and allowed some things you would never believe, man," Faye spoke as her eyes welled up. "I went to counseling for two years. It took two years of counseling for me to forgive myself, but, but I don't even know if you can forgive me for what I did to Katrina. I been through a lot, man," she stated as she threw her arms up in defeat and bowed her head in shame. "Nothing can justify what wrong I did to myself and our daughter."

Big Eddie didn't have to ask what all Faye had done in life when she became hooked on cocaine and whatever other drugs she was addicted to. He'd seen so many women whore themselves and their children, their own daughters, out to men who willingly took advantage of the situation. He could sense the pain and repentance deriving from within the woman and he began wondering what all had gone down in her life that led her astray. "You know," he said as he scooted his chair closer to the table and placed his arms out before him, opening his hands. "I'm partly to blame for that world of shit you went through, Faye. What's your story, baby? We, we never talked about your family. Who were your people? How did you come about?"

"You really wanna know?" Faye asked as she gazed into Eddie's eyes.

"I have to in order to understand my daughter's mother's family and the reasons why." Big Eddie replied in a tender and sincere manner.

"Well," forty-six year-old Faye sighed as she leaned forward and placed her hands inside of Eddie's hands. "I'll tell you what went through my mind that day you heard my grandmother singing my name beside that swimming pool in the Desire projects. This is what the ghetto gave me and my family, Eddie...."

Eddie nodded as he gripped Faye's hands and pictured in his mind the things she began to relay to him...

March 1980

..."You gone stop making fun of my neighborhood!" fifteen year-old Faye said through laughter as she and twenty-two year-old Eddie crossed the street after jumping off the Desire bus.

"I'm sorry, baby," Eddie laughed as he ran and caught up with Faye. The two walked up a wide driveway lined with cars parked on either side before stepping onto a grassy area. A large courtyard on Pleasure Street was where Faye's grandmother resided.

"Is, is that a swimming pool over there?" Eddie asked in amazement as he and Faye neared the courtyard that was slightly hidden by two long buildings that had a slight gap in the middle that led out into the large open area.

"Yeah," Faye replied casually. "We call it Betty Jean after this girl that drowned in it when it was closed one time. It be live in the summer time, man! It go up to like twelve feet! I be in the deep end all the time, and I'm always the first one in because my grandmother stay right behind it!"

Eddie was truly amazed over the Desire project. It seemed like a really good neighborhood to live and raise a family when compared to Cabrini Green. He had no idea how long he would stay in the city, but he was going to enjoy as much of the town as he could and spend as much time as possible with Faye in the process.

He and Faye walked in between the two story apartments on either side of them as the courtyard came into full view. To Eddie, the courtyard looked larger than Soldier Field. It was covered with lush green grass and several shady oak trees bordered its edges. "This here like paradise," he told Faye.

"Don't let the scenery fool you. This courtyard be full of marijuana and heroin dealers when the sun go down," Faye stated as she and Eddie neared the large swimming pool.

"You gone take me over to that Persia place you was telling me about on the bus or what?"

"Yeah. After I go in and—oh shit!" Faye suddenly exclaimed as she pulled Eddie back behind swimming pool's shelter house. "Eddie, my grandmother's out there!"

"So?"

"I was supposed to be with my friend Freddie Mac! She gone trip if she see me walking up with a boy!"

"See, I would take offense at being called a boy, but I'm cool and all," Eddie chuckled as he removed his fedora. "I'm a friend from another school, remember? Come on, let's go meet grandma," he said as he began walking towards Faye's grandmother, who was standing on the porch with her arms folded as she looked up and down the sidewalk that ran along the back side of the swimming pool.

"Eddie, no," Faye snapped as she pulled him back into the doorway of the swimming pool's shelter house as her grandmother began screaming her name.

"Fayeeeeee?" the older woman sang aloud. "Fayeeeeee!"

"God, I hate when she does that!" Faye sulked. "Eddie, just stay here, and I'm gone go down there and—"

"Never come back," Eddie spoke matter-of-factly as he cut Faye off and looked to the ground. "You got me down here on this unknown turf and 'bouta get punished."

"No," Faye said in a heartfelt manner over her grandmother's incessant singing of her name. She stepped back and placed her hands on her hips as she eyed Eddie. "You wanna meet my grandmother for true?" she finally relented.

"I gotta win her over if I'm gone be your man—I mean boyfriend," Eddie chuckled.

"Fayeeeeee! Where are you child? You know I need my medicine! Fayeeeeeee!" Ora Sanders sung aloud in unintentional harmony.

Faye rolled her eyes over her grandmother's beckoning ghetto serenade. She placed a hand onto Eddie's chest and rubbed lightly. "Okay, come on, man," she sighed. "My grandmother's name is Ora Sanders. And you go to Kennedy Senior High, okay?"

"Like John F. Kennedy? I can dig it!" Eddie quipped as he and Faye resumed their walk.

Fifty-eight year-old Ora Sanders, a short, brown-skinned, voluptuous woman with a head full of long, shiny black hair that was highlighted with streaks of grey, stood out on her front porch in a pair of tight-fitting jean shorts with a pair of black flats on her feet and a large t-shirt covering her ample breasts that hung down to her stomach. She was first generation Sanders to enter the Desire project in 1965. She and her daughter, twenty-one year-old Lorraine Sanders, a stallion of a woman with brown skin, coal black hair and long, shapely legs, was residing in the Lower Ninth Ward section of the city with Lorraine's fiancé, a young man named Otis, before she'd made the move over to the Desire project.

Faye was a newborn all of six months when hurricane Betsy struck in September of 1965. This storm had unknowingly changed the course of her family's history for all times. Her mother, Lorraine, according to her grandmother Ora, had been attending Delgado Community College and was on her way to becoming a dental assistant while her father Otis worked as an X-ray Technician over to Charity Hospital in downtown New Orleans.

The Sanders were poor at their inception, but they were an

upstanding and loving family in spite of their financial woes. Ora Sanders, a lifelong New Orleans native, had very little education. She worked as a maid-servant to many a wealthy white family who owned homes in the Garden District, the wealthiest part of New Orleans with mansions worth upwards of six or seven figures. The then forty-three year-old woman's entire day consisted of cooking, cleaning and tending to children. She was a chef without a degree, a nanny to kids who weren't her own, a humble woman who made beds and picked up the dirty drawers of adults and washed them clean.

Ora wanted better for her daughter Lorraine, however; she'd done right by her only child and her sacrifices had paid off tremendously as she'd saved enough money to pay for Lorraine's entire tuition. Throughout her high school years, Ora, the hardworking maidservant and single mother, made sure that her daughter remained a straight-A student. Her take on the matter was that if she was able to tend to children who weren't her own, then by all means would she do even more for her own flesh and blood.

Tired was Ora Sanders all day every day. Humping city buses and street cars to uptown New Orleans at five in the morning to face what only God knew until five in the evening was taking its toll. She suffered from arthritis and back spasms and had to often deal with scrupulous bill collectors and grocery store cashiers who sometimes took advantage of her inability to read or count properly. She was sometimes cheated out of her earnings by the very people she worked for; people who had the money to pay, but had opted to take advantage of her handicap. The somewhat illiterate woman was sometimes shorted on her change whenever she bought groceries, which caused her to be late with the paying of her rent. Sexual favors to her landlord got her through those bumps in the road, and those would be the times Ora would cry herself to sleep at night over the way her life was playing out.

With Lorraine Sanders came the Sanders family's redemption, however. She'd graduated valedictorian from the inaugural 1962 class of Alfred Lawless High school in June of that year. Soon after, she enrolled into Delgado Community College and pursued a bachelor's degree. She and Otis had met in their second year and had entered into a whirlwind romance that both were certain would last a lifetime. Two years into their relationship, Lorraine became pregnant by Otis. The two were planning on marriage after Lorraine's graduation, and Otis often spent nights over to the Sanders home to be closer to the love of his life.

Lorraine had birthed Faye Sanders in March of 1965 during spring break. She was one semester away from graduating with a bachelor's degree when hurricane Betsy struck in September of 1965. Many of the residents in the lower Ninth Ward opted to take refuge in their homes during the storm, which was a decision that had proved fatal for many as they had no idea just how deadly the cyclone would prove to be. The Sanders family would unwittingly become one amongst dozens of families in the Lower Ninth Ward who would be depleted of membership.

On the evening of hurricane Betsy's arrival, Ora, Lorraine and Otis were tucked away in the Sanders home, having eaten bar-b-cue that was prepared earlier in the day, until their bellies were near bursting. The TV was flickering on and off from the squalls that were beginning to funnel through the city, so Ora had decided to turn it off and turn on the radio and utilize the remaining electricity to keep up-to-date on the storm. Hurricane Betsy was unleashing a torrent of rain upon the city, and as the hours passed, all three adults began to grow nervous. Their brick, one story two bedroom wooden home was rocking slightly and the wind outside was howling like a rabid wolf as the tempests increased in intensity.

Ora had weathered many a hurricane in her time, but this storm was a relentless one. Betsy's brutality went on longer than she had expected, well into the night, and only seemed to intensify as time wore on.

"Momma, I'm a little worried." Lorraine remarked softly as she held six month old Faye in her arms and rocked the baby to and fro.

"We'll be okay, baby," Otis, a short-in-stature muscular brown-skinned twenty-one year-old young man comforted as he went and sat beside Lorraine on the couch and hugged her neck.

Ora looked over to Lorraine and Otis, both of whom were huddled up on the couch shivering in fear while cuddling Faye as Betsy's winds howled, moaned, and growled, bestowing its power and dominance upon Orleanians who dared to wave their fists towards mother nature and say, 'I will not forsake my home.'

Ora had always wanted a son that would protect her in Otis, but he was such a gentle soul. He often avoided conflict. Not the sort of conflict that came with one running the streets, but rather pertaining to speaking up for his woman. Lorraine was a beautiful dark-skinned young woman and she was often hit on by men in the neighborhood—even when Otis was in her presence. Hounding males would sometimes walk right up to the two and step in between them, paying Otis no mind as they tried to get closer to Lorraine. Otis would often stand by quietly while Lorraine handled the matter before grabbing his hand and walking off.

Lorraine often told her mother in secret that she wished for Otis to be more aggressive in protecting her honor, but she loved him so much, it was a weakness she was willing to overlook given Otis's work ethic and ambition.

If her daughter had accepted Otis's shortcomings, Ora herself would not spurn the young man away; but she also understood that she would have to be the protector and leader if the family were to survive, at least until Otis's protective spirit caught up to his enthusiasm for monetary gain. The optimistic woman smiled at the two youngsters as she eased up from her recliner, turned the volume down on the radio, and cleared an area on the couch. She sat down in between Lorraine and Otis, gripped both of their hands and began humming a church hymn.

The three held onto one another as the storm continued to unleash its wrath. Fifteen minutes in, just before ten that night, the lights in the home flickered off briefly, illuminated once more, and went out completely. "Momma!" Lorraine cried aloud.

"Gone be okay, 'Riane," thirty-six year-old Ora remarked calmly through closed eyes as she hugged her daughter and

Otis's neck tightly in the darkness. "Can you believe them white folks uptown asked me to come in tomorrow," she said through laughter, trying to ease the tension rising in the hearts of the two youngsters she now felt the need to protect.

"Momma Sanders," Otis spoke anxiously in the darkness. "Tell me we won't die tonight?"

"Death befalls us all, Otis. Shall we? It be His will and be His will alone. Can't do nothing about that, son, but He gives us strength. I want you, I want you to take that strength. Pray with me now, family," Ora spoke humbly as she bowed her head in the darkness and entered into the Lord's Prayer.

Sitting in total darkness of the home, Ora began relating stories to Lorraine and Otis. She told her child about her high school years and the crush she had on a boy who was on the basketball team who later became her lover before he was shipped off to war and killed in the Pacific Theater during a raid on Okinawa before Lorraine was ever born.

Lorraine in turn, shared with her mother the first boy she ever kissed. Ora cared not to hear about Lorraine's firsts, but if that was what it took to get the three of them through, she would listen. The pitch black darkness was able to hide the look of disappointment on Ora's face as Lorraine shared joyous moments of her high school years. She'd gotten away with a lot in her time it seems, sneaking out after dark and walking to the drive-in with her friends, sipping wine and hanging out in gambling houses, but through it all, she'd managed to remain an A student.

"Otis wasn't my first and he knew that, momma. I experimented, but I was always safe. Just wanted you to know that should this be our last night."

"Lord, I want you to stop thinking death, Lorraine—and I want this one over here to man up!" Ora complained. "I can't do it all by myself, y'all. The three of us gotta be strong for Faye now."

"We are, Momma Sanders," Otis remarked as he laid his head on Ora's shoulder.

Ora flicked her shoulder and shoved Otis's head away from her body. "I keep telling you you're not a baby, man," she grumbled. Ora had a certain disdain for Otis because she felt he was soft. He was a smart man, but he leaned too much on her and Lorraine, literally and figuratively. He was a mother's boy from the good side of town, having grown up near City Park and attended a Catholic school all his life.

Ora had grown up hard and had faced the struggle head on. The silver-spooned Romeo Lorraine had chosen to bring a kid into the world with ailed her to degree, but for her daughter's sake, she'd accepted their rapport. Raising a man wasn't in Ora's make-up, however, and being that her daughter and baby's father were envisioning death, she felt no need to hold her tongue. "When we get through this here, Otis? You best marry my daughter and take her away from this place and start a life of your own. Enough of wanting to be my son. Hell, the way you carrying on I sometimes think you sleeping with your own sister you so up under me and Lorraine. Be a man!" Ora snapped, causing baby Faye to become agitated.

"Now's not the time for this discussion, momma," Lorraine stated in an aggravated manner as she picked Faye up and placed the baby over her shoulders. "Me and Otis will be okay."

"Momma Sand—Ora right, Lorraine. I haven't been that man you need," Otis stated as he got up from the couch. "Where's the flashlight?"

"Otis, sit down," Lorraine snapped.

"Now there you go giving me orders!" Otis defended as he stood up in the darkness. "I see what your mother was talking about now. I'm a man! A man that loves his family! Ora? I take no offense," he admitted.

"And I meant none, sugar. Flashlight's right here," Ora said as she reached down and picked up the flashlight. When Ora grabbed the flashlight, she felt a wetness on her hand. "Lord, sweet Jesus," she gasped. "We got water seeping in, y'all!"

Ora stood up at that moment, but as she clicked on the flashlight, she slipped in the water that was beginning to creep into the home and landed on her back.

Lorraine heard her mother scream and saw her illuminated frame fall to the floor. "I hurt my elbow!"

Otis bent down and helped Ora back onto to her feet. It was at that moment that he noticed the bottoms of his Converse had become soaked. He grabbed the flashlight up off the damp floor and shined it down to the floor and could see a layer of water streaming across the tiles. He then aimed the flashlight towards the front door and could see water streaming into the home through the door's crevices.

Ora sat on the edge of the couch, stared at the front door and was forced to gasp aloud over what she was eyeing. The flood waters were not only seeping through the bottom of the front door, the water was also flowing through the sills of the windows which sat three and a half feet off the floor of the home. "Get to the attic!" she commanded as she stretched out her left arm in order for Otis to help her up to her feet.

Otis helped Ora up and grabbed a medical kit off the coffee table before the three began making their way towards the attic. Lorraine was holding onto baby Faye, trailing her baby's father and mother towards the attic. She was frightened out of her mind over the possibility of losing her baby.

Otis jumped up and pulled the rope that lowered the ladder in the middle of the hall. "Momma, the food!" Lorraine exclaimed as the ladder was lowered.

"I can't carry anything! My elbow!" Ora cried as she began climbing up the ladder with her one good arm while holding onto the flashlight.

Otis stepped up and helped Ora up the ladder where she fell onto the wooden floor of the attic. Lorraine followed with Otis's assistance and laid baby Faye beside her grandmother before she snatched the flashlight from her mother's side and began descending the stairs.

"Lorraine, where're you goin'?" Ora asked while watching her daughter descend the ladder with the flashlight.

"Faye needs her formula and we have no food or water! I'm

going help Otis get the coolers with the food in it! I found another flashlight!" Lorraine screamed as she handed her mother a second, smaller flashlight and disappeared back into the home.

Ora crawled over the attic's opening and pointed the flashlight her daughter had given her out the slats of the home's roof and was left speechless. From what she could see through the torrential downpour and heavy winds, the flood waters had grown to enormous proportions. Not only was the street flooded, the flood waters had now encompassed the entirety of the home's front yard. With the aid of the flashlight, she could see Otis's Pontiac in the driveway just below the slats of the attic to her right. The car was covered up to its windows by the flood waters.

Just then, Lorraine reentered the attic with the portable radio and a gallon of water. "I couldn't find the Pablum! I be back!" Lorraine exclaimed as she descended the ladder once more and disappeared back into the home.

Ora called out for her daughter, but Lorraine had already climbed back down the ladder. She scooted over to the front of the home and aimed the flashlight back out the slats in the attic as she placed an old sheet onto a crying Faye. The water was now halfway covering the windows of Otis's car. "Lorraine! Otis! The water is rising too fast! Get up here!" Ora cried aloud in a panic-stricken state as she crawled back to the attic's ladder and yelled aloud for her daughter and future son-in-law.

Back down the attic inside the home, Otis and Lorraine were now scrambling around the kitchen in waist deep water while gathering fresh formula for baby Faye and food and extra water for themselves. They had no clue, however, just how much danger they were in as water continued seeping into the home through crevices in the windows, doors and walls.

"I found a hammer for us, 'Raine!" Otis yelled aloud in a hurried tone as he grabbed hold of a handle to an ice cooler that he'd packed with bread and bar-b-cue. "I got more water, too!"

"Okay! I got our daughter Pablum!" Let's go, baby!"

Lorraine quickly replied as she and Otis began making their way back to the ladder leading to the attic while wading through the waist-deep water.

The laws of physics would not allow Lorraine and Otis to return to the safety of the home's attic, however; in mere minutes, the water outside had risen to over six feet. In order to save the downtown area of New Orleans and its wealthier citizens, including those who resided in the Garden District where Ora worked, levees south of New Orleans had been dynamited, and the floodwaters from the Mississippi River was allowed to run free in the Lower Ninth Ward.

Pressure from the rushing floodwaters leaning against the Sanders home had shattered all the windows and had knocked the front and back doors off their hinges. Lorraine and Otis were nearing the ladder with the necessities of life for themselves, Ora, and baby Faye, when a wave of cold, murky, debris-filled water rushed down the hallway.

Otis had gone under immediately. He never made a sound as he was swept beneath the rushing waters, leaving behind the ice cooler he was clutching, which remained atop the waters as it rushed down the hall, bouncing off the walls before twirling around violently and being swept into one of the bedrooms and out the window.

Lorraine, however, was able to grab hold of the ladder leading to the attic before she was swept away in the torrent. The dark-skinned beauty's eyes were beyond filled with fear as she looked up at her mother, who was only feet away and had been calling out to her ever since she'd made the decision to go back down into the home a second time and retrieve the things needed in order for her family to survive. She was struggling to hold onto the ladder for dear life as rapid waters filled with debris rushed over her body.

While reaching her one good arm down to help her daughter, Ora saw a pair of hands wrapped around Lorraine's waist. Otis's head came into view momentarily at that moment. "Lorraine! Take the hammer!" he yelled as water swept over his body and covered his head once more.

"Hold on to me, Otis! Momma pull me up!" Lorraine cried desperately as she took the hammer from Otis and placed it over one of the ladder rungs, thereby locking it in place.

Ora extended her right hand down the attic's opening and Lorraine clutched her arm tightly. She'd just begun pulling herself up when Otis's head reemerged from the water where he coughed, spitting out water.

Ora was hoping she was wrong when she witnessed what was to her a body being swept past the ladder, but upon seeing the dark arms disappear from around her daughter's waist, she knew right then and there that Otis was caught up in the floodwaters and had just been swept away. She could only hope that he was able to grab hold of something to keep him afloat as she tried desperately to retrieve her daughter from the rushing waters.

"Momma, take Faye Pablum! Take my baby Pablum and the hammer!" Lorraine yelled over the thunderous sounds of the rushing waters as she unhooked the sack on her shoulder with one hand while gripping her mother's arm with the other.

Ora, through her pain, used her left arm with its sprained elbow to grab hold of the sack and the hammer. She flung the items into the attic before extending both her hands. "Give me both your hands, Lorraine!" she screamed over the storm's torrential chaos. "Lord, spare my pain, please!!" she screamed when the weight of her daughter's body tugged on her injured elbow.

"God, help me save my baby!" Lorraine pleaded aloud as she let go of her mother's arm and began pulling herself a ways up the ladder.

"Where's Otis? What happened to Otis? Did we lose Otis?" Ora asked over the rushing water.

"I don't know! I don't know! Oh my God!" Ora heard her daughter scream aloud as she looked up the hallway to her left. "Momma, pull me up! Pull me up!" Lorraine pleaded hysterically while looking down the hallway in sheer terror.

Ora had forgone the pain in her elbow as she extended both

hands down into the attic's opening once more. She was tugging on Lorraine's arms with all her might trying to pull her up when she felt a sudden jolt. Her body lurched backwards and she landed on her side inside the attic. Her daughter's hands were no longer clinging to her arms, so she quickly rushed back to the attic's opening. What she saw at that moment would forever haunt her.

Lorraine was trying desperately to pull herself up the ladder just before what Ora knew to be the home's front door came rushing down the hallway in violent fashion, bouncing off the walls and leaving holes in the sheetrock along its wake. The horrified mother could only watch helplessly as the home's front door slammed into her daughter's side. The rushing water quickly turned red and Ora could only watch in utter repugnance as the door rolled several times, flinging her daughter's body up against the wall as it banged against the ladder before all remnants of her offspring was washed deeper into the home.

Ora Sanders, at moment, fell back and let out a painful scream inside the darkened attic, having just witnessed the death of her only child as she absorbed the sounds of a crying baby Faye, who was totally oblivious to the tragedy that had just befallen her mother and father.

In spite of witnessing her daughter and future son-in-law's deaths, Ora Sanders' problems had only just begun. While gathering Faye and moving the baby away from the attic, she could now feel water splashing up onto the wooden floor from the opening in the attic. She wrapped Faye up in an old sheet and was able to retrieve the medical kit before it was washed away. She spread the flashlight around until she found the hammer. She then huddled up into a corner of the home with her grandchild in her arms and was left with no other choice but to wait out the storm as the waters from hurricane Betsy continued to rise.

In total darkness, and facing pouring rain and unrelenting winds, Ora was able to wrap her elbow and administer aspirin to help with the pain. She sat huddled with Faye as hurricane Betsy continued to hold sway over not only their home, but the fate of her and her granddaughter's lives as well. The horrified, heartbroken matriarch could only sit and hope that the floodwaters would not rise and cover the home in its entirety, but just in case it did, she decided to bust open the slats on the home's attic. It would be the move that would eventually allow the Sanders family to continue on, despite undergoing such unimaginable tragedy...

CHAPTER ELEVEN

CROSSING PATHS

"I never knew that about your family," Big Eddie told Faye as he watched her wipe tears from her eyes.

"I didn't remember much of what my grandmother told me until I entered counseling. A lot of memories came back during those discussions. I'm lucky to be alive, man." Faye replied humbly. "My grandmother was rescued a day later by the Red Cross and they took us to this elementary school uptown before they moved us to a temporary house. From there, we landed in the Desire project right before Thanksgiving of sixty-five."

"That's heavy, baby. I know your grandmother was fucked up in the head losing her daughter like that."

Faye shook her head somberly. "She told me she never went back to work after that day. They found my momma and daddy's remains like a month later hung up in a fence on side the house. They was almost skeletons. My grandmother loss all the pictures she ever had of my mother and father, photo albums, high school academic trophies—everything. I don't even know how my mother looks," she remarked somberly. "My whole history been erased," she cried lowly through trembling lips.

"Not all of it," Big Eddie remarked as he rubbed Faye's arms. "I'm here now, baby. And we still have a daughter out there somewhere, remember?"

"Yeah," Faye stated dejectedly. "But I fucked that up, Eddie.

149

I let, Katrina was molested and I allowed a man to—"

"Why?" Big Eddie asked, cutting Faye off.

Faye told Big Eddie about the day she was raped and how her life had become the living nightmare that had led to drug addiction. The man had every right to be angry for what Faye had done to his daughter, but he had an understanding over the way things went down when one became hooked on crack cocaine. It did nothing to justify Faye's treatment of their flesh, but it helped him to understand and began to accept the wrong she'd done in times past as he dealt with his own transgressions.

"Whatever happened to that guy that raped you? Was he caught?"

"I don't know," Faye said as she wiped her eyes. "Eddie," she then stated as she looked the man in the eyes. "Say you forgive me. My, my psychiatrist told me that I subconsciously want forgiveness for what I did to Katrina. You're not her, but you are the reason she's here. She's yours as much as she's mine. It'll mean a lot to me if you was—"

"You're forgiven, Faye," Big Eddie comforted seriously. "You're not held in contempt with me, baby."

"Thank you," Faye responded softly through a relieved smile.

Faye had thought about telling Eddie that their daughter had nearly been killed at the age of eighteen at that moment, but she decided against it. She'd just earned a reprieve for all she'd done wrong and didn't want to pile on. Should she and Eddie track down their daughter, then and only then would the rest of the story be told to him. He would be able to hear every detail from the mouth of his daughter herself should the day ever arrive was her reasoning.

"So," Faye spoke coyly, "what happened the day you left exactly?"

Big Eddie leaned back in the chair and opened a bag of corn chips, popped the can on his strawberry Fanta soda and said, "After I met your grandmother, you took me over to Persia's, remember?"

"Yeah, but that was like two months before everything happened."

"Well, that day kinda led up to it," Big Eddie replied. "We walked in and this dude met us over by the bar. I remember him coming over and..."

Faye leaned back and reflected on the day she and Eddie went to Persia's for the first time. He'd learned more about her that day, and she him, namely, what he did for a living...

****

..."Welcome to Persia's. I'm the owner here. Sam Holland. What you and the young lady having?" twenty-three year-old Sam Holland asked as he stood behind the counter of he and his wife's sparsely-filled night club.

"Hey, man," Eddie stated through a smile as he extended his hand and shook Sam's hand. "I come down for Mardi Gras to see what the city be like. I met this young lady Faye last night in the French Quarters and she told me about a po-boy sandwich?"

"Yeah, yeah, we got 'em, brother. Where you from?"

"Chicago." Eddie responded while scanning the club.

"Chi-town!" Sam snapped. "That might be a first for Persia's. Baby," he smiled as he looked over to his right towards a woman placing money into a register.

"One minute, Sam," the woman remarked politely.

Eddie watched as the woman near the register placed what was to him, at least a hundred dollars in cash into the register before closing it. He had his jammer on him at that time and had briefly contemplated robbing the joint as there wasn't anyone around to witness the play except for Faye. He held back on those urges, however, as the guy before him seemed to be a laidback brother that was only trying to run a legit business. He looked over to Faye, who was reading a paper menu. Her lips were moving as she read and Eddie could hear her trying to pronounce some of the words. "You know what you reading, girl?" he joked.

Faye shoved the menu away from her. "I don't have to know what it says to know what I wanna eat!" she snapped as she cut her eyes at Eddie.

Sam and Eddie both noticed Faye's change in demeanor when questioned about her reading ability. "Hey," Eddie said seriously. "I didn't know about that, alright?"

"It's nothing. I get by," Faye replied slightly embarrassed.

Just then, the woman behind the counter walked over to the group. She sensed some agitation and couldn't help but to ask, "Is everything okay here, guys? Something wrong?"

"No, Gabriella. It's cool. Right, Eddie?" Sam inquired.

Eddie was dumbfounded over learning Faye could barely read. '*How did she ever make it to the tenth grade.*' he wondered silently. Not wanting to bring about an awkward moment, Eddie looked over to Sam and said, "Yeah, brother, it's cool. Say, I notice you got some pool tables over there. You shoot, Sam?"

"I do okay."

"Alright, then." Eddie chuckled as he went into his pocket and pulled out his grip. He peeled off a twenty dollar bill and laid it flat on the counter. "Now, me and Faye want two of those hot sausage po-boys she been telling me about, and two cold beers."

"The sandwiches I can do," Sam remarked. "But Faye can't be no older than seventeen. Now we do throw a mean party, Eddie, but she not allowed to drink in here because of her age."

"The extra beer not for Faye. It's for you, Sam," Eddie laughed.

Sam dapped Eddie. "Okay," he said while nodding his head. "You wanna a piece of me?"

"Before I start runnin' that table over there?" Eddie said as he pointed towards the pool tables on the left side of Persia's. "Before I start winning? I wanna be able to brag that I beat the owner of this bar, who said he did alright on the table. But here's the catch, Sam—if I win? The beers and sandwiches is on the house,"

"You hear this man talking smack, Gabriella?" Sam asked as he smiled back at his wife. "You got yourself a game, brer."

"Brer?" Eddie laughed. "I been hearing that word for the longest! What that mean?"

"It means 'brother'. It's New Orleans slang," Gabriella chimed in. "Sam? Take him down." she cheered.

Sam turned his black Kangol around and ran his hands over his neatly trimmed beard and goatee as he stepped back from the counter in his gold silk shirt and black slacks. "I got this, baby," he remarked as he grabbed his pool stick case and pecked his wife on the lips. "But, Eddie? Here's my counter bet—if I win? I get the twenty dollars—and you still have to pay full price on the sandwiches and the beers."

"That's like eleven extra dollars!" Faye quickly exclaimed as she looked down at the menu.

"You count good," Eddie smiled.

"What's that supposed to mean? Don't you be mean to her, Eddie," Gabriella respectfully admonished while noticing the dejected look on Faye's face.

"I didn't mean it as an insult, Faye. It was a compliment, baby," Eddie admitted to his honey. "Look, me and Sam gone shoot a game of pool and I be back. I don't know who cooking? But I do know we ain't paying," he said in assurance of himself as he climbed down from his stool and followed Sam over to the pool tables.

Gabriella, meanwhile, had turned her attention to the teenager before her. "Was he implying that you couldn't read, Faye?" she asked meekly.

Faye began bouncing her right leg anxiously as she curled her lips. This was a secret she didn't want to get out that she couldn't read too well. "He don't know what he talking about," she stated in a defensive manner.

Gabriella didn't believe Faye. "It's okay, baby," she said in a comforting tone. "If you want? I'll help you learn. I have a son that's five and I read to him every chance I get. It's easy if you're taught right."

"They just kept passing me in school. I didn't learn right, but they just kept passing me. My grandmother not too smart. She can barely help."

"Well, do you want me to help?"

"I guess."

"Good," Gabriella yelped as she reached down underneath the counter and came up with one of the many Doctor Suess books she often read to her son whenever he was inside the club during its non-busy hours.

Nearly an hour later, Sam and Eddie made their way back over to the bar. "Baby," Sam spoke meekly as he approached the counter while scratching the side of his nose. "Could, could you, umm, could you get another twenty out the register while I hook these two up with a couple hot sausage sandwiches?"

"You loss?" Gabriella asked in wonderment as she looked up from the book she and Faye were reading.

"Hey, this guy's good. I mean, trick shots, combinations, jumping the eight ball," Sam rattled off while shaking his head in amazement over Eddie's skills. "He'll give the guys who play on a regular basis a run for their money. I better stock up on beers. Remember what I said, though, Eddie. We close at five—that's about thirty minutes from now. I got enough time to make y'all sandwiches, but Faye can't come in once we open at eight."

"It's cool," Eddie replied. "We gone take our money you owe us, take our food back over to the Desire, eat, nap, and then I'm gone come back and run me a table. Let everybody know I ain't a shark, I just got game when it comes to working that cue stick."

"You got it, brother," Sam said as he shook Eddie's hand.

"And, Faye? Remember, whenever you feel the need? I'm here to help," Gabriella added as she and Sam returned to their duties inside of Persia's.

CHAPTER TWELVE

SILHOUETTES

"I kicked Sam's ass that day, Faye," Eddie laughed as he clutched Faye's hand tightly. "Wow, baby. That brought back some memories let me tell ya'."

"You shoulda let me sneak in with you when you back that night," Faye smiled. "I was your good luck charm that day."

"Well, I hope that good luck you carry is still in effect once we start looking for our daughter," Eddie remarked through a slight smile as he looked to the floor and entered into a brief moment of deep thought. He snapped his fingers several seconds later after recalling another conversation that had taken place the day he'd whipped up on Sam Holland on the pool table. "That night, I never told you, Faye! I was around some, Sam 'nem knew Taylor back then!" he snapped.

"What?" Faye snapped as she waved Eddie off through unbelievable laughter. "Man, Taylor was locked up around that time. That was like nineteen seventy-nine or eighty when you and me first met. Taylor went to jail in seventy-seven."

"Right, right," Eddie agreed as he rubbed his chin. "You had tried to sneak into Persia's that night but—"

"That ole chubby dude ran me off," Faye laughed as she reached out and grabbed a few of Eddie's corn chips. "I was hanging out in front of Persia's for a while when you was in there, but that man ran me off, talkin' 'bout the police was gone take me down because I was out past my curfew."

"He was right, though," Eddie stated. "Wasn't he?" he then asked to confirm.

"Man, it was only like nine 'o' clock and school wasn't even in session because of Mardi Gras. That was the night I ran into Freddie and her brother 'rounding the corner while I was on my way back home to wait on you."

"The boy that fucked it up for us," Big Eddie declared as he nodded his head.

"Umm hmm," Faye nodded. "Freddie tried to stayed out there, but we ended up going back to my grandma house and played cards with her. I never knew she would become one of my worse enemies," she added. "So, what was that conversation all about? And how you and Freddie brother fell out?" Faye then asked.

Eddie grabbed a few corn chips and threw them into his mouth. He pointed to Faye as he chewed slowly and said, "That chubby dude you talkin' about was Alfred. He was placing bets all night with me on the pool table. You must've just left or something, because him and Sam came over with a couple of beers to check in on the games, you know? The pool table was crowded. Hell, the whole club was packed. I was handling my business when Sam and Alfred walked over talking about the young girl that was hanging outside the club. That young girl was you."

Faye, at that moment, began imagining in her mind what Eddie began relaying to her concerning the happenings that had unfolded that night inside of Persia's and shortly thereafter as she knew they were events that had altered the course of not only their budding relationship, but the sequences of their lives altogether...

"Have you ever went over a friend's house ta' eat and the food just ain't no good...I mean the macaroni's soggy, the peas are all mushed and the chicken taste like wood...so you tryda play it off like you think you can by sayin' that you're full...and then ya' friend says momma he's just being polite he ain't finish uh, uh that's bull..."

The Sugarhill Gang's hit rap song *Rapper's Delight* was

blaring over the speakers inside a crowded Persia's on Lundi Gras, which was the Monday before Fat Tuesday, in March of 1980. The dancefloor was filled to capacity as partiers showed off their skills, the men doing the robot in one place while performing tricks with their fedoras as the women they danced with snapped their fingers and dropped to the floor before bringing it back up.

Neatly-styled afros in shades of tan, brown and black were bouncing, hands were clapping in unison to the hot song and clods and gators were leaving impressions in the wood. A thick cloud of cigarette smoke lingered in the air and a tinge of marijuana that was emanating from the sitting tables to the left of the dancefloor whiffed through the nostrils of some out on the dancefloor on occasion. The bar on the opposite side of the club was lined with women gyrating their hips as they sat atop stools sipping from clear plastic cups laced with either dark-brown or clear liquor cut with either Coca-Cola or 7UP.

While the dancefloor and bar held down the people who were out to have a good time and nothing more, over on the far left side of Persia's, behind the tables where scores of people were being served home cooked New Orleans cuisine ranging from red beans and rice, shrimp creole and signature po-boys, sat the pool tables. Young Eddie Cottonwood was striding along the side of a pool table in his red silk slacks and black gators. His red, fish-tailed silk shirt was unbuttoned, showing off the black silk wife beater and the gold chain that draped his neck.

To say he was running things on the pool tables would be speaking humbly of twenty-two year-old Eddie Cottonwood at this point in time. Persia's had four tables laid out in a square, two each side by side. Eddie was going from table to table, taking on all comers, and earning money for those who were betting with him. The game being played was eight ball; one in which one white cue ball and fifteen color balls were racked and broken. Each ball sunk was worth fifty dollars, and whoever came up short had to cough over fifteen hundred dollars and another fifty dollars for each ball the winner had sunk on the table. The side bets ran as high as a $1000 dollars on either shooter. Young Eddie had won three games and

$3200 dollars since he'd returned to Persia's a couple of hours earlier, and he'd earned many of the other players that had bet on him hundreds of dollars in the process.

"Game shot!" Eddie yelled out over the music as he removed his silk shirt and chalked his cue stick. "This here gone be thirteen balls in, my man," he reminded his opponent as he walked backwards around the table trying to figure out the best angle to sink his winning shot.

While walking backwards, Eddie bumped into a chubby guy who he knew to be named Alfred. "You still bettin' with a winner?" he asked.

"As long as the man playing," Alfred stated through laughter as he handed Eddie a beer.

Sam was standing beside Eddie taking bets when he eyed his friend Alfred. "You got them youngsters from in front the club?" he asked as he rearranged a stack of twenty dollar bills.

"Yeah, I did," Alfred replied. "Say, Sam," he added as he rubbed his chin. "You remember that dark-skinned girl from back in the day? The one Gabriella was helping teach how to read earlier?"

"Should I?" Sam asked as he righted the money, never looking back over to Alfred.

"She the one got hit that day, umm, her dog. Remember Taylor and Joyce hit that dog that day we was on our way to Biloxi?"

"L'il Faye?" Sam asked as he eyed Alfred.

"What about my baby?" Eddie asked, overhearing the conversation as he was standing right beside Sam.

"Eh, man! You gone take the shot or what?" a twenty year-old young man by the name of Lawrence McNeal asked Eddie disgustedly from across the table.

"Faye went home, Alfred?" Eddie asked as he eyed Lawrence with disdain before he took a sip of his beer.

"Yeah," Alfred replied as he pulled out a wad of cash. "Her and this other chick stabbed out a few minutes ago."

"Eh, that's my sister. Her name Freddie Mac. You better not had let her in, Al!" Lawrence snapped. "Lotta snakes in this place."

"Don't we know it," Alfred replied as he eyed Lawrence with contempt.

"Fuck that supposed to mean?" Lawrence scoffed as he stared back at Alfred and sniffed his nose.

"Relax, brothers," Eddie said confidently as he sat his beer on the edge of the table. "He ain't got no more money after this game here, Al. My second time beatin' this chump tonight. Bank shot in the top right pocket for a extra three hundred dollars on top of what I win!"

"Bet! But you ain't gone make it, sucka!" Lawrence quipped. "Your luck finna run out, sissy!"

Eddie shook his head as he prepared to take his final shot. Lawrence McNeal had been nothing short of rude the entire game in not only his eyes, but in the eyes of all the other players gathered around the pool table as well. He'd entered Persia's bragging on how he was gone take all the money on the pool tables. He often hovered over Eddie whenever he was taking a crucial shot, and had even bumped him on one occasion.

Lawrence McNeal was a tall, wide-bodied youngster with an afro the size of a twelve inch record. He seemed to be an intimidator to many on the pool tables, Eddie quickly discerned. Some of the men around the tables walked off when he began placing bets while others put him in his place, albeit in a joking manner because the last thing they wanted to do was offend the volatile gangster. Eddie liked nothing about Lawrence, however, but he was willing to take all of his money, if only to get him to shut his fat mouth.

Everyone around the table grew quiet as Eddie leaned down and took his final shot. His cue stick connected with the cue ball with a loud clack, forcing it into the left bumper of the pool table where it bounced off the border and hit the bumper on the far end of the table before making a beeline back towards Eddie where it connected with the last ball and sent it into a slow roll as it headed towards the corner pocket. Eddie, Sam, Alfred and everyone else placing bets, leaned back collectively, trying to will the ball into the hole.

"Come on, come on!" Eddie yelled as he began jumping up and down in place as the ball slowed. "No!" he pleaded.

"You ain't put enough English on it, Eddie!" Alfred complained as he threw up his hands.

"Pull up! Pull back, mutherfucka!" Lawrence laughed as he balled his fists, tucked them against his chest and raised his right leg. "And don't 'ner one of y'all mutherfuckas fan it!" he commanded.

Eddie anxiously ran his hands over his face as he watched the ball roll to the edge of the right corner pocket and pause.

"Pay up!" Lawrence stated happily as he jumped up and down.

Just then, the ball dropped into the pocket. Lawrence saw it and immediately announced that the game had already ended. "Game was over!" he yelled. "Shit was over!" he snapped as he waved his hands.

"How you get ta' call that?" Eddie complained. "Game don't stop 'til the ball stop rollin'! It stopped rollin' when it fell into the pocket! The pocket I called, brother!"

"Nah, fuck that! Fuck that!" Lawrence scowled as he snatched his silk jacket up off one of the coat racks. "Your Chicago ass come down here and try and hustle a nigga!"

"I won the game fair and square, mutherfucka!" Eddie complained as he threw his pool stick onto the table and started towards Lawrence.

"Fuck that! You gone make me pay, nigga?" Lawrence countered as he charged at Eddie.

"Not in here! Not in here!" Sam defended as he got in between Eddie and Lawrence, holding Eddie back while Alfred shoved Lawrence back up against the wall.

"Sam? Sam, are you okay?" Sam's sister-in-law, Henrietta Jenkins, spoke aloud as she walked from behind the counter upon noticing the ruckus unfolding.

Janice, Charmaine, Yvonne and Gabriella made their way over to the pool tables as Clyde, the original owner of Persia's, commanded the Dee-Jay to turn off the music before he calmly made his way over to the pool area.

Lawrence, meanwhile, was eyeing the crowd surrounding him as he stood with his back to the paneling behind him and immediately felt threatened. He was without backup inside of Persia's and he knew everyone supported Sam. "Yo, Clyde?" he called out upon noticing the elderly man making his way over to the table through the gathering crowd. "Clyde, work it out, man!"

"I been watchin' you all night, young man. You been being disrespectful the whole time ya' been in here," Clyde stated as he went into his dark green silk slacks and pulled out a wad of cash. "Now, I know your family and all—respectable people. Smart people. Your sister has a level head, your mother is a hardworking woman. You should be more like your family instead of playing gangster—something you ain't. You ain't scaring nobody, son. You just a sore loser. How much money you got and how much you owe this young man?" he asked as he nodded over to Eddie.

"I got two grand on me, but I owe twenty-nine," Lawrence replied in an embarrassed tone.

Clyde raised his finger and pointed over to Eddie. "This guy here ain't no chump, Lawrence," he let it be known. "I'm gone cover this bet. But you are no longer allowed to shoot pool in my—"

"I want it from him!" Eddie interjected. "You ain't covering this man debt, old man! He came in knowing what it was!" he added as he looked over to Lawrence. "This how you get down, man? You got a old man covering your losses, Lawrence?"

"Eddie, take the money." Alfred pressed.

"Fuck that!" Eddie refused as he backed away from the table. "*He* gone pay me!" he declared as he pointed over to

Lawrence. "We don't do business like that where I'm from! Where I'm from a man pays what he owes and don't lean on the leg of another man!"

"You take my nine," Clyde bargained as he walked over to Eddie and began peeling off crisp bills. "You take my nine, and this young man will owe me and not you."

Eddie shook his head to say no and followed with, "You can't be nice to a fuckin' bully, Clyde!" He then pointed over to Lawrence and said, "Empty your pockets!"

"You robbin' me?" Lawrence asked in disbelief as he moved off the wall and stepped to the edge of the table.

"I can't rob a man that owe me money!" Eddie barked. "You got two thousand on you right now? I wants all of that! *And* you got all but a week to get the rest of the money that you owe me!"

"It mean that much to you, boy?" Lawrence asked as he placed his hands into his pockets.

Eddie pulled out a .32 snub nose at that moment, believing Lawrence was going for a gun. Those who saw the play scattered way from the pool area.

Sam grabbed Eddie's arms and Alfred moved and snatched Lawrence up once more at that moment.

"It's money! It's money!" Lawrence yelled aloud while being pinned up against the wall by Alfred.

"I ain't gone shoot 'em, Sam!" Eddie assured as he lowered the gun. "But he gone pay me all what he owe me in full before I leave this town!"

"Lord, you youngsters is gonna be the death of me," Clyde professed as he rested his hands against the pool table and shook his head somberly. "Eddie?" he stated as he eyed the twenty-two year-old Chicagoan, "you was all right with me just a few minutes ago, but this is not the legacy I wanna leave behind for Persia's and you just lost favor. Whatever gripes you and Lawrence care to carry on? It won't be settled in *here*!" he emphasized as he tapped the edge of the pool table with his right index finger. "Take that shit to the streets! I want the both of y'all to never show your faces in here *again*! And if I see either of you two again? I just may be hauled off to jail because I'll been done killed both of you *hotheads*! At least in jail I'll have peace of god-be-damned mind! Lawrence? Pay what you can and leave!"

"Place wasn't never all that anyway," Lawrence huffed as he came up with two thick wads of twenties and hundred dollar bills and slammed them down onto pool table. He then raised his flabby left leg and planted it on the edge of pool table, his white ostrich skin shoes shining under the club's strobe lights. "Got the rest here," he stated as he slowly reached down into his white knee-length silk sock and came up with a solid stack of hundred dollar bills. "That's everything." You happy now, mutherfucka?" he asked Eddie as he threw the last of his money onto the table.

"Not until I get the rest that you owe me! It's nine hundred dollars. And this better be a solid two grand, chump!" Eddie scolded as he tucked his revolver back into his back waistband and stepped up to the pool table where he began counting his earnings.

Lawrence was escorted out of Persia's by Alfred and Sam where he met up with his sister, Freddie Mac. Back inside Persia's, Janice and Gabriella had just guided Eddie back over to bar to serve him a drink on the house in order to allow Lawrence enough time to cool down and vacate the area. Henrietta, Yvonne and Charmaine, meanwhile, had begun to reassure the crowd that the misunderstanding had been rectified and the party would resume shortly.

About an hour later, Eddie donned his silk suit jacket, placed his fedora onto his head and called out for Alfred in order to alert the man of his departure. "You want me to drop you off, man?" Alfred asked as he walked from behind the counter.

"Nah, brer, that dude don't scare me." Eddie remarked as he and Alfred made their way over to the front door.

"Brer? You catchin' on," Alfred chided as he and Eddie stepped out onto the sidewalk amid a darkened sky and claps of thunder.

Eddie laughed himself as he rubbed his chin. "You all right, Al," he admitted. "Sam, Gabriella, Clyde, y'all some real down-to-earth people. Thanks for everything, man," he stated as he and Alfred dapped as rain drops began to fall from the sky.

"Look," Alfred then said as he wiped raindrops from his chubby face. "Clyde can go overboard sometimes, man. You did nothing wrong, brother. If you wanna come back inside Persia's? You welcome. I can vouch for you with Clyde."

"That's cool and all, Al," Eddie spoke appreciatively as he buttoned up his silk suit jacket. "But I'm done hustlin' in there after tonight. People don't play by the rules," he stated as he looked up and down the dark, lonely block. "It was a legit hustle and Lawrence done took it to whole other level. I come across that dude and he don't have my money I'm gone have to hurt that boy."

"Lawrence ain't worth it. None of it worth it, Eddie."

"It's worth my pride, Alfred," Eddie replied as he pulled down on his fedora and trotted off into the rain that had begun to fall.

Eddie made his way through the isolated streets of the Ninth Ward under the pouring rain with his hands tucked inside his slacks, his right hand clutching his revolver as he was anticipating running up on Lawrence once more. The walk back to the Desire proved uneventful, however, as Eddie entered the complex. He paused as he came upon the large courtyard that reminded him of Soldier Field and then took off running under the falling rain, headed towards the swimming pool that blocked the path to his love. The nearer Eddie grew to the swimming pool, the more he could hear music playing. He could see the portable radio situated in the side window of Faye's bedroom window as the sounds of Harold Melvin and Bluenotes' song *I Miss You* caressed his ears.

Eddie made it over to the edge of the building underneath the now pouring rain and tapped on the screen-covered window. He'd knocked a little too hard and the portable Panasonic radio was knocked off the sill. The music stop playing and only the raindrops were heard as that sweet, comforting face Eddie had been accustomed to seeing appeared soon after, albeit a little altered.

"Eddie?" Faye called out lowly as she picked up her radio.

"Yeah, baby. Can you let me in?" Eddie asked in a pleading tone as he pulled himself up onto the window's edge and eyed Faye, who had a head full of pink rollers in her hair and a face full of Noxzema plastered across her face.

"My grandmother gone fuss if she know you was here overnight, boy!" Faye whispered.

"Baby, I ain't got nowhere else to go," Eddie countered. "You already said taxis don't come back here after dark. You want me to stand at that bus stop by myself in the pouring rain?"

Faye wasn't in agreement with Eddie coming into her home, but he'd been so nice to her. To see him stranded in a neighborhood unknown to him, one in which she'd taken him to, didn't sit right in her heart. "Go to the back door," she whispered as she set her radio back into the window sill and pulled it down halfway.

Eddie trotted around to the back of the apartment, jumped up the stairs and entered a hallway with two doors on either side with a wooden grey staircase before him that led up to apartments on the second floor. Several seconds later, the door on his right eased opened and he was immediately encompassed in warm air and an aroma reminiscent of that of a place he'd visited back in the French Quarters in an area called Jackson Square where the French Market lay.

"You hungry?" Faye asked as she pulled the door open and stepped back, allowing Eddie to enter the kitchen. "I was warming a snack in the oven."

"I'm hungry and I need to get out these wet clothes," Eddie replied as he walked into apartment, gently brushing past Faye.

The spark was undeniable as the two brushed bodies briefly. "Them those fancy doughnuts I'm smelling?" Eddie asked as he turned back to Faye.

"They called beignets." Faye answered as she closed and locked the backdoor. "Come on to my room before my grandmother wakes up," she added as she slid past Eddie and tip-toed him to her bedroom.

Faye entered the room first. She had no idea what she was doing exactly with Eddie, but she was trying her best to help him out. "What now?" she asked meekly as she sat on her twin bed and stared over to Eddie through the darkness, giving him the lead.

"I'm tired, baby," Eddie remarked as he closed the bedroom door and removed his suit jacket.

"My grandmother is in the bedroom right on the other side of the hall across from this room," Faye let it be known.

"There you go again worrying," Eddie stated lowly. "I'm, I don't know how many times I have to say it, but I'll keep saying it until you understand, Faye. I'm not gonna hurt you."

"All your clothes wet?" Faye asked as she removed her radio and pulled her window shut completely.

"Soak and wet."

"We have a washer," fifteen year-old Faye remarked lowly in the darkness as she got up from the bed and handed Eddie a large towel from her clean clothes basket. "I'll leave so you can take them off and come back in like five minutes so I can clean them for you. My grandmother sleeps hard, but you still gone have to be quiet."

"I hear ya'," Eddie replied low and casual as he opened the door for Faye in order to allow her exit the room.

The twenty-two year-old was sitting on Faye's bed with the towel wrapped around his waist when Faye returned. To his delight, she held a plate of food and a soda. "This some beignets me and my grandmother made while she was washing my hair and the last half of my hot sausage sandwich we had earlier with a pineapple soda," she spoke lowly in the darkness as she held onto the items.

"Damn, Faye," Eddie stated in an appreciative tone. "I love this New Orleans food, baby," he laughed as he picked up one of the beignets, which was a deep-fried pillow-shaped ball of dough covered in white powdered-sugar. The pastry treat was complimented perfectly with the spices from the remnants of the hot sausage po-boy, which had instantaneously become one of Eddie's favorite delicatessens down in the Crescent City.

Eddie had met Ora Sanders briefly when he and Faye made their way over the apartment shortly after Persia's five 'o' clock closing. Under the guise of being a high school student that had met Faye during the Bacchus parade, a rapport was quickly established where Eddie learned Ora was suffering from high blood pressure and required daily medication three times a day. He'd left an impression on the woman right away as the three sat at the kitchen table inside the pristine apartment. Neither he nor Faye was certain how Ora would take to the seven year discrepancy in age, so neither brought age into the discussion, and Ora never bothered asking.

"My grandmother usually gets up around six," Faye told Eddie as he chomped down on the food. "She knocks on my door and call for her medication before she go in the bathroom. I'll go out in the living room and come back in here before she gets up to wake you up so you can leave."

Eddie wasn't in agreement with Faye's plan, but he understood. The youngster was frightened over her grandmother's reaction should she find him sleeping in her home. "Make sure you come and get me," he stated, holding back his reluctance as he continued to nip at the food handed to him on a wooden block.

Faye left the room without saying a word and pulled the door shut before returning to the living room where she laid down on the couch on her back with a pillow over her chest, subconsciously shielding her heart as thoughts of being with Eddie encompassed her psyche.

Eddie, meanwhile, had finished up his food and had lain down to fall asleep. He wasn't sure how much time had passed, but it was still dark out when he sensed the bedroom door being opened. Believing it was Ora, he turned and faced the wall, pulled the covers over his head and said in a high-pitched voice, "Grandma, you up early."

"You not my granddaughter. And she can't give you want I can give you," a woman's voice scoffed as she eased into the room and closed the door.

Eddie was at a loss for words upon hearing what he believed to be that of Ora Sanders' voice just before the bedroom door was closed. *This old woman tryna fuck me,* he said to himself through wide eyes before he turned over and pulled the covers off his body while struggling to rewrap the towel around his genitals. "Miss Sanders," the baffled and shamed young man stated as he stood up from the bed with the towel dangling from his waist. "I swear, ma'am! I was cold and it was raining outside! Faye, Faye was, she was somewhere else in the house, Miss Sanders! I only wanted—"

"A place where you felt safe," Faye spoke through naughty laughter as she walked over to Eddie and ran her hands across his firm biceps.

Eddie flopped down onto the bed and looked up at Faye. His heart was pounding as he was certain he was about the face the wrath of a horny grandmother that had stumbled upon her granddaughter's smuggling a male into her home. "Why you playing?" he asked as he fell back onto the bed and breathed a sigh of relief.

Faye walked over to Eddie and placed her hands onto his knees as he lay back on her twin-sized bed. She'd removed the pasty white cream from her face, yet the pink rollers remained, complimenting her slender, dark eyes and creamy, milk chocolate skin while simultaneously displaying an alluring elixir of loved hoped for that radiated unhindered inside the darkened room.

Eddie could sense Faye's longing heart. She was young, yet willing to learn. Naïve, yet eager to experience true love. He grabbed the fifteen year-old's wrists, removing them from his knee caps and allowing her body to fall flat against his own as he lay on his back.

"Eddie? I want you to make love to me," Faye moaned as she wrapped her arms around her true love's neck and pressed one side of her cheek to his and gently moved it up and down against his rugged skin.

"You sure you wanna do this, baby?" Eddie asked as his hands subtly moved down to Faye's curvy waistline where he gripped her tightly.

Tears filled Faye's eyes as she raised her hips slightly and reached down.

Eddie was in tune with his lover's motions. He reached down and unhooked the towel from his waist, springing forth his hardened rod as he rolled Faye over onto her back. "You're amazing," he professed before leaning in and kissing Faye deeply as he tugged down on her loose-fitting cotton shorts.

CHAPTER THIRTEEN

THAT DAY

Faye leaned back in her chair and crossed her legs as she smiled over to Eddie. The first night the two had shared together was so fresh in her mind it might as well have happened only seconds ago. "I couldn't take all of you," she admitted coyly. "But it was the best I've ever had 'til this day, Eddie."

"Is that so?" Big Eddie blushed, enjoying having his ego stroked by Faye. "You had me thinking your grandmother was sneaking into the room that night."

"To do what?" Faye asked curiously, raising her eyebrows.

Big Eddie laughed. "Not even gone get into that," he chuckled.

"Eddie, no," Faye scowled playfully. "Now, they did have families that got down like that, but not mine. Not my grandmother," she stated proudly.

Big Eddie laughed inwardly. *"If only you knew,"* he said to himself as he recalled the day vividly...

Fat Tuesday 1980

...A tender, yet deep-pitched hymn graced Eddie's ears as he rose up from his slumber. The sun was shining bright on this warm spring morning as he looked over to Faye's radio sitting in the window facing the apartment's backyard. She was supposed to have awakened him long before, but he now found himself still holed up inside her bedroom. He peeked out the window over the radio's top and saw her and Ora hanging clothes on a clothesline behind the home. *"Damn,"* he said to himself as he looked around the room.

Resting in a chair beside Faye's closet, he spotted the clothes he'd worn the day before. He scooted over Faye's twin bed and sat before his items and noticed a tooth brush and a white sheet of paper lying on top of his freshly laundered clothes. He picked up the paper as he held onto the toothbrush. w*oked up late this mourning and not had time to woke you. me and granma go hang clothes then go to the grosary store. you can leeve out the front dor call me 949-7329,* it read.

Eddie stared at the letter, noticing Faye's poor spelling. Yet despite her weakness, she cared enough to let him know what was going on by writing him a letter. He smiled over her consideration and initiative as the hymn he listened to coated his ears with a certain form of tranquility he hadn't experienced in quite some time as he began to dress himself. After creeping into the bathroom to wash his face and brush his teeth, Eddie eased out into the hall. The smell of bacon and biscuits graced his nostrils as he neared the living room. In the darkness of the previous night, Eddie couldn't see how neat the apartment was, but he was pleased what his eyes were witnessing this morning.

Many of the apartments he entered in Cabrini Green were littered with trash and had a foul odor that seemed permanently fixated into the home's interior. Faye's home was neat and tidy with polished furniture and floors waxed to where he could see his reflection in the tiles beneath his feet. Eddie grabbed a biscuit and two slices of bacon and shoved the items into his mouth as he made his way towards the front door. He was wiping the remnants of the quick meal from his lips as he approached the edge of building and leaned in for a peek while appreciating the harmony that he now could see was deriving from within the mouth of Ora Sanders as she sung Mahalia Jackson's song, *Precious Lord.*

"When my way grows drear…precious Lord linger near… and when my light is almost gone…hear my cry hear my call…

hold my hand lest I fall...take my hand precious Lord...lead me home..."

Eddie leaned his right shoulder up against the building and listened in amazement as Ora sung while slowly moving down the clothesline with Faye at her side under the bright morning sun. "It'll be okay for us, grandma," he heard Faye speak humbly.

"Child, I don't see how," Ora replied as she ended her song. "I used everything I had to pay the rent this month," she said with a tinge of despair. "No matter what, Faye, I don't want you get it in your head that you have go out and make a way for me. I'll be okay without it, just have to, just have to watch what I eat the rest of the month to keep my pressure down."

Faye's eyes began to water over the circumstances. Her grandmother had a heart condition that required a daily dose of blood pressure pills to prevent her from having a heart attack. Dieting would only stave off the ailment for a little while. The woman's monthly medication had run out and she had no resources on tap into in order to attain another prescription. "Maybe we can borrow the money from the community center?"

"Already asked, Faye. All they have is emergency food stamps. Can't do anything by way of money. This is my issue anyhow." Ora then paused and looked over to Faye as she clamped a pair of jean shorts to the clothesline. "Aren't you marching today?"

"I'd rather stay here with you, grandma. I had fun Sunday night anyway. My missing this day won't count against me."

Eddie, having a slight understanding of Faye and Ora's plight, stepped out from the side of the building at that moment. "Morning," he spoke with a smile on his face.

Faye turned and eyed Eddie with wonderment as she grew nervous. *"What you still doing here?"* she mouthed.

"Well, now! Eddie, how you doing?" Ora remarked as she removed several clothespins from her apron.

"I'm fine, Miss Sanders. I caught the Desire bus back down

here this morning because I knew Faye wasn't going to any parades today. Thought I'd hang out with y'all for the day if it's okay?"

"That's fine, sugar. We ain't got nothin' planned, though. Just gonna be a day spent around the house doing much of nothing."

"Not on Fat Tuesday!" Eddie stated lively. "Do they have a grocery store around here somewhere?"

"Sure is," Ora replied. "There's a few corner stores upfront on Louisa Street and we got a big Schwegmann's market out front in Gentilly."

"Can I get a taxi back here over to that Squigaman's?"

"That's Schwegmann's," Faye corrected through light laughter. "I'll go and call a cab, but you gone have to ride there and back here to get a ride because almost every cab is downtown today."

"Tell 'em I'm tipping big," Eddie said as he smiled over to Faye.

"How you like your stay down in New Orleans, Eddie?" Ora asked as Faye made her way back into the apartment.

"Loving it, ma'am. Would've like to have seen the parades today, but this, this is cool. I feel like steak today—on a grill."

"Well, I can't afford those items, Eddie. I have a few food stamps left over for some chicken, but not steak," Ora remarked as she resumed hanging clothes.

"It's on me, Miss Sanders. Whatever you want, I'll get it. You have some things in mind? You need anything?"

Ora looked over to Eddie and swallowed the lump in her throat. "Food doesn't matter to me, Eddie. That I can provide, young man. But if, if you're willing to buy my medication it'll be of great help."

"How, Miss Sanders?"

"My prescription needs fillng. I feel ashamed, Eddie." Ora admitted as she choked back tears of pride. "But, God I have no one. No one. And I don't want Faye worrying about me."

"What you need me to do, Miss Sanders?"

"If you could be so kind, Eddie? There's a pharmacy inside of Schwegmann's where I get my, my blood pressure pills," she responded as she ran her hands over her slightly-greying black hair while shifting her weight and extending her hips outwards towards Eddie. She looked Eddie up and down and licked her lips before saying, "If you do that for me? I'll be more than grateful."

"I'll be glad to do that free of charge, Miss Sanders," Eddie stated, ignoring Ora's sexual advances.

"You sure?" Ora asked in a surprised manner. "You want nothing in return?"

"You don't owe me anything in return, Miss Sanders," Eddie told the woman. "I'm doing what I'm doing because I wanna help. Nothing's behind it. I want nothing from you."

Ora pressed her lips together at that moment and held back tears of shame. She placed a hand on Eddie's shoulder, closed her eyes and said, "You don't know all what I've done in my past. I, I fear for Faye. To me it's like the only way she'll be okay is if I was to be here until she becomes a woman and I'll do anything to stay alive. Anything, Eddie."

The sincerity deriving from within Ora Sanders had touched Eddie. He somewhat understood the woman's plight. Her motives did nothing to justify her means, however, but he understood. "I can look after you and Faye," he said as he reached into his black silk slacks and ripped off fifteen twenty dollar bills and handed it to the woman. "Take these three hundred dollars and take care of you and Faye."

A taxi's horn blew from the driveway at that moment, getting Eddie's attention as Faye ran down the stairs while placing a scarf over her head. "Come on, Eddie!" she said happily.

"Girl? You can't go out in the public with your head looking like that!" Ora snapped as she stuffed the money down into her apron. "Go back in there and get my hot comb and put it on the stove!"

"Grandma, it's Mardi Gras day! Ain't nobody even around! Look!" Faye retorted as she extended her hands outwards to the empty complex that was void of patrons save for the three of them standing out amongst the clotheslines.

"I guess," Ora relented as she eyed Eddie. "Look after my baby, Eddie. And Faye? It's the hot comb for you when you get back here."

"God, just don't burn my scalp again!" Faye said as she stomped off towards the taxi behind Eddie.

Eddie and Faye returned with a trunk full of groceries a couple of hours later. The young man had also taken it upon himself to fulfill three month's worth of prescriptions for Ora to go along with the three hundred dollars he'd given her earlier in the morning. A delectable meal of broiled steak and baked macaroni with string beans and mashed potatoes was prepared and the three spent the remainder of the day lounging around the house watching television.

CHAPTER FOURTEEN

THEIR LAST DAY

"Our life was boring, man," Faye laughed as she reflected on the days long gone.

"You think so?" Eddie smiled. "I learned what it took to be a family man the short time me, you and Ora spent together, Faye. I mean, I didn't admit to some things concerning me and my boys' mother back in the day, but it helped. They did alright because of what I saw go down between you and Ora. Y'all was the first family I ever knew and I never forgot that."

"My grandmother did the best she could," Faye remarked. "That illness, though," she said somberly. "She died early, man. And in the end? I became her."

"Ora was a woman trying to survive the best way she knew how, Faye. And you yourself could be understood if not forgiven. Just like Ora. Stop carrying that guilt, baby. Because to the people that matter? You're forgiven."

Faye nodded in silence. "You and I may have forgiven one another, but the reconciliation that matters most still lies ahead. What will Katrina's point of view be, Eddie?"

"That remains to be seen, Faye." Eddie replied.

"So, what happened the day you went over to the corner store that night?" Faye then asked. "Because that was the last time I ever saw or heard from you."

"Well, you know I was going up in Uptown New Orleans by

this cat Damon's spot called the Beanstalk to put my hustle down, right?" Eddie disclosed. "See, the cats up there was more adhering to the rules of the game and paid what they owed. I was able to mail money back home to my son's Eddie's mother to take care of home and me, you, and Ora was doing okay. I respected her for not lettin' me stay nights in y'all apartment by the way."

"Didn't stop you from sneaking and doing that, Eddie," Faye laughed.

"Them was the nights I could no longer stand being away from you, Faye. God, we had chemistry!" Eddie reflected as he licked his lips. "You tasted good, woman."

"It's still sweet with a clean bill of health," Faye replied as she went into the inside pocket of her denim jacket and handed Eddie her most recent medical exam test results dating back to the previous month of November 2008. "I haven't been touched since November of nineteen ninety-five, Eddie—the month I entered rehab. You making it breathe again, baby," she added as she reached out and grabbed Eddie's hands. "You were the only man I ever loved in life. The day you left? My world came to an end. Took nearly twenty years to recover, but it wasn't your fault. You already know about my rape in April of eighty-two. I just, I just felt had you still been in the city, it would've never happened because you would've moved in with me after my grandmother passed away."

"I most certainly would've been there. And whoever that rapist was would've never came at you like that, baby." Eddie said as he eyed Faye's test results.

"I know," Faye remarked as she crossed her tingling, thick thighs. "We have so much to forgive, Eddie. Am I wrong to say that we have much to look forward to?" she asked as she placed her hands beneath her pointed chin and stared the man in the eyes.

Two things were on Eddie's mind. First was his daughter, Katrina Sanders and how she would receive her rehabilitated mother and the father she'd never known. Second was the fact that Faye had been celibate for fourteen years and was now sitting before him with a clean bill of health. If only he could sample the goods was his thinking as he held onto the woman's hands.

Big Eddie wasn't out for just another shot of pussy, however; just to be able to lay next to Faye Sanders once more, something he hadn't done in nearly thirty years, would supersede any fleeting moments of pleasure he had access to inside of Stateville with a couple of female hacks. "If I clear a path for you and I to be together, would you accept it?" he asked Faye.

"I would welcome it, Eddie," Faye assured. "But that's neither here nor there right now. Make it happen if you can, because we both want it—but not today. Today? We let go of the past. The streets talked back in the day, but I wanna hear from you what happened that day between you and Freddie Mac's brother."

"This is what went down," Eddie replied as relayed to Faye the day that had shattered their lives...

****

August 1980

"...Isn't it funny...how time can change...all the things you want...to believe...but time won't change...the way I feel...'cause in my mind(in my mind)...it's you and me...you and meeee...Gloria...my Gloria...yeah...things ain't been the same...since you went away..."

The sweet sounds of Enchantment's song *Gloria* graced Eddie's ears as he walked up the driveway leading to Faye's apartment on a hot mid-summer afternoon. For the last five months he'd been back and forth from New Orleans to Chicago, visiting his son's Eddie's mother to make sure his firstborn was okay, while at the same time, returning to the city in the bayou where his pool hustle was earning him enough money to support two households.

The more Eddie traveled back and forth to Chicago, the more he began to believe that New Orleans was where he belonged. Call it coincidence or God's fate for him and Faye, but whenever Eddie returned to the apartment that lay beside the large swimming pool inside the Desire project, it always seemed as if he was being beckoned towards a cradling nest where true love lay—as if he belonged there. Faye's radio was always in the window, and a song that triggered his emotions and encompassed his mind's heart was always playing whenever he stepped off into the driveway.

Smiling as his eyes focused in on Faye's bedroom window, Eddie began jogging over to Faye's apartment in his grey and white silk jogging suit and fresh white leather Nike's with the grey suede swoosh on the side. "Hey, Eddie!" "There go Faye boyfriend, everybody!" Eddie you got a quarter?" kids yelled at random upon noticing Eddie's presence. He took the time to pass out dollar bills to the dozen or so kids that were around before making his way over to Faye's apartment where he tapped on the back door.

Ora answered a minute or so later and an unfamiliar aroma greeted Eddie's nose through the opened door. "Hey, boy," Ora smiled as she widened the door and stepped aside to let Eddie in. "Ain't seen you in a couple of months almost!" she added as she walked back over to the stove and picked up a large spoon.

"Been busy, Miss Sanders," Eddie remarked as he locked the door and removed his white Kangol.

"Faye has been, too," Ora replied as she stirred the contents inside the pot. She then looked over to Eddie and said, "Look, the way I came at you on Mardi Gras? I was, I was out of line asking you to pay for my prescription. How I go from church songs to propositioning you made no sense. If I could take it back I would."

"That was nothing, Miss Sanders. I was glad to be able to do it. It's all behind us. Did that money help?"

"Still is, son," Ora replied. "You hungry? I got some pork chops, string beans and mashed potatoes that'll be ready shortly. Faye actually made it, but she went to bathe so I'm just tending to it."

"I would love that, Miss Sanders," Eddie remarked just as

Faye, dressed in a pair of thigh-high, loose-fitting dark green shorts and orange tank top, her high school colors, timidly walked into the kitchen.

"Hey, Eddie," she said through a welcoming smile and eyes that silently confessed, *I've been missing you.*

Eddie held his breath momentarily as the epitome of beauty stood before him with a look of love undeniable in her dark eyes. For the past two months, he and Faye had been making love repetitiously. The pay-by-week motel out near New Orleans' International Airport where he stayed whenever he was in town was their rendezvous point. Faye would sometimes skip majorette practice and catch a cab from Carver High School on Eddie's dime in order for the two of them to be together. Their moments were fleeting because Eddie was always on the go, back and forth to Chicago, but the time spent was all-so-intense.

"How long you in—how long you staying today," Faye asked after catching herself and nearly giving up Eddie's secret lifestyle.

"We'll talk later, baby. I don't plan on going away for college, though. I plan on staying here in the city now." Eddie stated, helping Faye along.

Faye grew flushed at that moment. What Eddie had told her was such soothing words as she had so much she wanted to share with him on this day.

"Faye, can you make a picture of Kool-Aid for me, baby" Ora asked, breaking the sweet silence between Faye and Eddie, who'd been eyeing one another seductively.

"Okay, grandma," Faye replied as she eased past Eddie, the two of them feeling the heat emanating from one another without their bodies ever touching.

"Eddie, make yourself comfortable in the living room and me and Faye will let you know when dinner's ready," Ora offered kindly. Eddie smiled and walked into the living room and turned on the evening news and sat and waited for dinner to be prepared.

After eating dinner, Ora, Eddie and Faye sat around in the living room watching evening soaps on this muggy August night. Faye was sitting atop a folded blanket on the floor underneath a hair dryer having just gotten her hair washed, and Ora was sitting on the sofa nodding off on occasion.

"All in the Family be on after while, grandma. Know what that mean." Faye laughed.

Ora stirred awake and looked at the clock on the wall and saw that it was ten minutes to eight, "Lord, it sure will be."

"We out." Faye sulked.

"You ate all the ice cream, girl?" Ora asked as she eyed Faye through sleepy eyes. "That's the best part of the show, honey— the ice cream!" she said as she tilted her head back and sighed.

"What kinda ice cream y'all talking 'bout?" Eddie asked.

"Brown Velvet chocolate!" Faye answered as she laughed aloud. "It's like a tradition on Thursday nights around here, man." she added as she picked up a deck of cards and shuffled them. "You can only get it from the corner store at the end of the courtyard on the other side the swimming pool, but they close in like ten minutes and my hair ain't even ready," she let it be known.

"No problem. I'll run over there and get some," Eddie remarked as he eased up from the couch.

"Grandma? Eddie? I got something to tell y'all," Faye professed at that moment as she raised the head of the hair dryer and smiled at the two.

"Hold up, baby," Eddie replied as he ran to the back of the home. "I need to use the bathroom."

Faye watched as Eddie walked down the hall, but she noticed that he hadn't gone into the bathroom. Instead, he entered her bedroom and returned several seconds later and headed for the front door. The wary fifteen year-old never asked why Eddie had gone into her room as she eyed him walking up the hallway. "Eddie I gotta tell you something, man," she remarked lowly as he stepped over her legs.

"When I get back, Faye. I need to catch this store and make it back in time for the start of the show," Eddie replied as he rushed out the door.

Faye sighed as she watched the front door being pulled closed. In her mind, she'd just told Eddie she was pregnant with his child. She'd actually wanted the ice cream to be a celebration. Earlier in the week, she'd gone to the neighborhood clinic earlier after missing two menstrual cycles. The fact that she was now pregnant for Eddie was a secret she'd been from both Ora and Eddie and on this day, she'd wanted to share her joy.

Thursdays was always a good day around the Sanders home and Faye was going to use her grandmother's usually jolly demeanor over watching her favorite TV show and Eddie's presence to break the news. With Eddie around, the blow to her grandmother wouldn't be as hard a pill to swallow was Faye's thinking, but things hadn't going according to plan. Ora seemed too tired and Eddie's mind seemed to be elsewhere.

"I don't even know my baby daddy's last name, grandma," Faye stated as she shuffled the cards, her way of putting it out in the open that she was pregnant for Eddie in order to get the scorn she was sure to follow over and done with.

Only the sounds of the laugh tracks erupting from The Jefferson's comedy show was heard by Faye as she looked over to Ora, who was now slumped over on her right aside. She threw the hair dresser off her head and scurried across the floor and cradled her grandmother's head in her hands. "Grandma?" she asked confused as she shook her unresponsive grandmother. "Grandma!" she cried. "Grandma!" she repeated, getting no response.

Ora's eyes were wide open and saliva was dripping from the corners of her mouth. Right away, Faye had an idea what was happening. She ran to the bathroom and checked the sink and saw that two doses of blood pressure pills remained. Ora was prescribed to take three pills every day—one in the morning around six, another between two and three, and the third before bedtime around ten at night. With the understanding that her grandmother was having a stroke having missed one of her doses, and coupled with the fact that she'd had a high-caloric meal consisting of pork chops and mash potatoes, Faye ran to her bedroom and called for an ambulance.

Meanwhile, on the other side of Betty Jean swimming pool near the edge of the courtyard, Eddie was crossing Piety Street after emerging from in between two long apartment complexes when a burgundy two door 1979 Ford Thunderbird with a white rag top sped towards him. He jumped back into the grass beside the sidewalk as the car came to a screeching halt.

"Better stay your ass out the street before you get ran over, punk!" Lawrence McNeal growled as he eyed Eddie with contempt over War's song *Four Cornered Room* that blared over his cassette deck. "Fuck you doing back in my neighborhood anyway?" he asked as he patted his large afro while looking into his side mirror.

"Eh, nigga! Where my fuckin' nine hundred dollars?" Eddie asked over the loud music. "I been looking for your chump ass!"

"Fuck you and them nine hundred dollars, boy!" Lawrence countered as he slammed his car in park and opened the door.

Eddie wasted no time. He rushed Lawrence before he could clear the driver's side door of his car and began unleashing a flurry of blows. The chubby young man fell back into his driver's seat after suffering several strong punches to the face.

After stunning Lawrence, Eddie leaned down into his car and ripped off the gold Rolex he was sporting. He then went into his front pockets and pulled out two wads of cash. He was breathing hard as he stared at Lawrence, who was splayed out over the front seat of his car with his legs dangling from the Thunderbird and his front pockets turned inside out.

"We even, mutherfucka!" Eddie remarked coldly as he ushered past onlookers and walked off, headed towards the corner store to retrieve Faye and Ora's ice cream.

People were staring at Eddie as if he were possessed as he walked around the rear of Lawrence's car with a carefree attitude. "The hell you think you doing, man?" the owner of the small corner store asked in disbelief over what he'd just witnessed as he eyed Eddie walking his way.

"I want some ice cream! Chocolate! Brown Velvet! Fuck that boy out there!" Eddie snapped as he walked through the door leading into the small, dark-brown bricked store where he quickly spotted the ice cream cooler resting beneath the counter that held the register.

The glass top on the cooler was slammed open by Eddie and he reached down and grabbed two pints of Brown Velvet chocolate ice cream and threw them up onto the counter just as screams began to emanate from the people who'd witnessed the fight between him and Lawrence.

'I knew he was gone make me do this shit!' Eddie said to himself as he went up under his lime green and white stripped Gator shirt and pulled out the .32 revolver he'd gotten out of a secret stash spot in Faye's bedroom. He leaned over the ice cream cooler and could see Lawrence rounding the front end of his Thunderbird with a nickel-plated .44 magnum in his left hand, the interior of his car lit up, and War's song steadily blaring as he crossed the street.

At that moment, Eddie ran out the store with his gun aimed on Lawrence, who was also brandishing his gun now. The two were no more than thirty feet away from one another when they entered into a rapid and violent exchange of gunfire out in the open. A scene reminiscent of the O.K. Corral played out on Piety Street as both gangsters pulled their triggers.

Eddie was dumping rounds and moving from side as bullets whizzed by him.

Lawrence was mere feet away, skipping around while firing off shots at Eddie and dodging bullets himself.

People began screaming and running off in all directions as bullets bounced off the store's wall behind Eddie and the concrete beneath Lawrence's ostrich skin shoes.

Eddie fell to the ground and fired a round that hit Lawrence in the knee. He leaned forward as he aimed his gun once more while wincing in pain, but Eddie had quickly fired the last shot from his six shot revolver. Everything then went silent at that moment. Only the sounds of War's song *Four Cornered Room* lingered in the air, ironically, in odd contrast to what'd just gone down…*"I knew we met each other for a reason… thinking…talking…we worked out our problems…look like we should have better days in front…just because we took our time to think and talk…for a much better understanding…"*

Eddie watched as Lawrence continued walking forward with the gun extended while squeezing the trigger of a weapon that no longer fired rounds as blood began to spurt out from a hole above his right eye. The dead-man-walking had a look of surprise planted on his face as momentum lured him forward. His head turned slowly and he and Eddie were staring one another directly in the eyes as he fell face first onto the concrete in a bloody, mangled mass of lifeless flesh.

Eddie picked himself up from the ground and was hit with a slight sting on his right side. He looked down and saw a hole in his shirt that had been singed by a bullet that had ripped through the cloth. People were calling Lawrence's name and pointing over to him while yelling aloud and at random, "He shot Law!" "That man shot Freddie brother!" "Fuck you doing, man?"

Eddie was certain henchmen belonging to Lawrence were lurking amongst the dozen or more people on hand, so he waved his gun at the crowd, dispersing people who were walking up on him as he made his way over to Lawrence's idling Thunderbird, where he jumped behind the wheel and sped off from the murder scene.

****

"Where'd you go after you took Lawrence car, Eddie?" Faye asked after digesting the events that had led up to that day back in August of 1980, events in which she knew to be true after encountering Lawrence's sister, Freddie Mac several days after the drama had unfolded.

"I knew people knew my first name so I couldn't head back to the airport where I was flyin' out from," Big Eddie responded matter-of-factly. "So I took Lawrence ride, dumped it on the Lakefront, and walked over to the Louisa Street bus line and caught it up to the Broad bus and made it over to Canal Street. I walked the rest of the way to the Greyhound bus station not too far from that Howard Johnson's hotel we stayed the night we first met. From there, I caught the first bus out. I ended up in Dallas and I caught the train from there back to Chicago two days later."

"Us riding around on the city buses when you came back in town got you through," Faye smiled proudly.

"It did, baby," Big Eddie replied seriously as he stroked Faye's arm. "But had I known you were pregnant? I would've at the very least came back to say goodbye—if only for a little while until I could've made it back. I had no number, and no way of knowing what all you were going through so I returned to what was familiar to me. I'm sorry for running out on you."

"It's not your fault, Eddie. I had all day to tell you, but I waited until the last minute. You went and got that gun out my bedroom didn't you?"

Big Eddie bowed his head in slight shame. "I had it my mind to go look for Lawrence that night, Faye. That ice cream was the hand I fanned with," he admitted. "I never meant to kill dude, just wanted my money, you know? I was a hot head. Just like Clyde said that night in that club. I was a hot head. Whatever happened to those people in that joint anyway?"

"Persia's closed down a few years later. I think Sam and Gabriella got killed. Umm, Clyde caught a stroke and died— the same thing that happened to my grandmother. She caught a stoke the night you killed Lawrence and she died two months later when she didn't wake up from her coma."

"Wow, sorry to hear that, baby. All those good people died like that?" Big Eddie asked rhetorically.

"It's all in the past, Eddie. Let's move forward, baby," Faye replied as she eyed Big Eddie with a look of love expected.

"Yeah," Big Eddie responded as he smiled over to Faye. "So, you comin' here regular now that you know where I'm at?"

"I don't plan on losing you again, Eddie," Faye stated with

conviction as she stroked Big Eddie's arm tenderly. "I haven't a man in my life. Who else visits you?"

Big Eddie looked over to his two youngest sons, Jay-D and Dooney, and his granddaughter Nancy Cottonwood and nodded in their direction. "They the only ones, baby. Now, we have business with our daughter Katrina if nothing else, but I would like more—if it's what you want for us."

"I want it, Eddie." Faye stated seriously.

"Give me time to make some arrangements. In the meantime, we need to figure out how we gone track our daughter down," Big Eddie replied as he looked over to Eddie Junior, who'd just stood up and escorted Jay-D to a private corner inside the visiting room. Big Eddie knew that move. His sons Eddie and Jay-D were discussing the streets now. What it pertained to he hadn't a clue, but he knew Eddie would fill him on things once visiting hours were over.

****

"So, what's happening out there?" Eddie asked Jay-D as the two stood in an isolated corner staring out a window that faced the prison's entrance.

"Got word from Dawk that the nigga that was in on the hit against Doss might be being moved here today or tomorrow," Jay-D remarked lowly.

"The Somali." Eddie stated as he looked to the floor and rubbed his chin.

"When he make it here, the Boss say he gotta be taken out the day he get in," Jay-D replied calmly as he shifted his $2,400 dollar cuff-link bracelet.

"Why so quick?"

"Nigga been running his mouth to the feds, ya' dig? Mendoza took care of Chloe before he checked out to keep from going in front of a grand jury, but Q-Man done spoke on some things—told the feds that the same people that killed Desiree back in Denver was behind the hit on Toodie and made her disappear."

"Any idea who this agent is?"

"Nahh," Jay-D said as his nostrils flared. He was incensed that Q-Man had bitched up and turned state when everything between the Holland family and Carmella's organization had been playing out on the streets and he wanted nothing more than to get the call that would let it be known that Bahdoon 'Q-Man' LuQman had been sent on his way.

"If he get in here, he a dead man. How Dooney coming along out there?" Eddie asked.

"His murder game a beast. Done racked up two bodies in the Lou and sent another one to the hospital. He solid. Steady learning. It's all good."

"And Nancy?" Eddie asked as he tucked his hands into his jeans and looked over to Jay-D.

"I remember how Bay 'nem was at sixteen. That's not Nancy, Eddie. She a dealer first, executioner second."

"Well, put her up on the cocaine side of things, brother," Eddie stated nonchalantly. "You out there and see way more than what I can see up in here. Think she got it in her to take a life, though?"

"Given what all she done seen rolling with me and Dooney? It ain't a doubt—but like I say—she got the gift of gab and would make a better earner in my eyes. She still got a lotta play in her."

"School her on that playing around and shit. She always been happy-go-lucky, but this ain't a happy-go-lucky business and she gone have ta' learn that there in order to get down." Eddie said as he gazed out the window and nodded in agreement with his younger brother.

Just like Doss had done with his oldest daughters, Eddie Cottonwood Junior wanted nothing more than to see his own daughter walk in the footsteps of not only himself, but that of Jay-D and Dooney. He knew with Jay-D and Malik being bumped up to Enforcers, the family would need more Lieutenants. On his word alone he could've gotten Nancy rank within the family that garnered her privilege based on the work he'd put in, but it wasn't how he was taught the game from Doss Dawkins. Everyone in the Holland family had earned their position. Nancy Cottonwood's rise to power would be no different from the ones who'd preceded her and had earned their stripes by getting their hands dirty.

"Okay," Eddie remarked, breaking the silence. "I want you to keep an eye and an ear to the streets for any feds in the area. Watch for anything suspicious on the block. See if they on to us or not. While you doing that? See if you can find a spot for Nancy in one of the traps for a while. Run that by Dawk before you do anything in order to get the go 'head."

"The only spot open is with this Lieutenant named Pepper over to Wimmer Place. Only thing is, Dooney killed this chick Noodles that was working for Toodie. The chick that survived the hit named Jada Murdella. She ain't been heard from since she checked outta Mercy Hospital, so Pepper may be up against some shit pretty soon."

"Let Nancy know all that, Jay. I know about Pepper and that bounty from what you told me a while back. You know who behind it?"

"Tito and Toine put it out there, but they got wasted. Jada the only one left that might be able to put it back on."

"Hold off from introducing Nancy to Pepper until you get more info on that situation," Eddie replied. "Ain't no need in putting her off in the middle of an unresolved issue with another click."

"I have a feeling this thing with Ya Murder gone end bad." Jay-D pondered. "That might kick off another war."

"That won't be good. And the product be in soon, right?"

"Be in some time next month maybe." Jay-D stated. "Pepper already looking out for Jada so she ready. At least she better be," he pondered.

"That's the game for ya', young brother. " Eddie replied as he looked over to Jay-D. "You take care of things on the outside? And me and dad gone handle things on the inside. Q-Man dead man walking now—and his legs 'bout to get cut off," Eddie replied as he and Jay-D dapped and hugged briefly. The two then walked over towards the table where Nancy and Dooney sat in order to enjoy the remainder of their visit.

CHAPTER FIFTEEN

HARSH REALITIES

December 30, 2008

The day after the Cottonwoods, Faye and Miss Joyce had visited Stateville Prison found Q-Man eyeing the same facility that lay off in the distance from the back of a van. He was thinking he should've known better than to trust the feds. Special Agent Laddy Norcross had told him he was going to be moved to Rockland State Prison. Problem for Q-Man was the fact that there wasn't a Rockland State Prison in the state of Illinois. When the guard announced that he was headed to Stateville, his heart sunk to the pit of his stomach. Stateville was no man's land. Q-Man wasn't sure if he would survive his stay. He began struggling with the guards as he was being guided to the prison bus. *"C'est un ensemble! Je préfère mourir ici!"* (This is a set up! I'd rather die here!) he yelled aloud in his native French tongue.

The lifelong gangster could feel the walls closing in and vultures circling, and in his mind's eye, Illinois was slowly becoming the place where he would die—behind bars to add insult to injury. The Holland family was onto him was what his gut was telling him, and he was helpless to stave off the grim reaper. Guards cornered a handcuffed Q-Man, pinned him up against the wall and sprayed him with mace, incapacitating him briefly before throwing him into the back of prison van. Now fully awake, he sat rigid in the seat with intense uneasiness filling his psyche as the van rolled onto the prison grounds.

****

Back inside Stateville, Eddie had just walked into his father's cell, rattling the cage before he entered. "Hacks on the payroll say Q-Man rolling in as we speak," he said as he walked into the cell.

Big Eddie threw his King Magazine down on his mattress and rose from his bottom bunk, placing his feet to the concrete floor. "We don't have a way to get to 'em right now," he pondered as he rubbed his chin.

"Not without catching a murder charge. They gone put him in gen pop for now."

"Where he have access to those phones. That's not where we want him," Big Eddie said as he stood up and paced the cell. He paused with his back to his son and said, "Run back and tell that hack to run that boy through the infirmary for a TB test. That'll give us some time to figure out how we gone get at him."

Eddie left the cell to talk to the paid hack and Big Eddie followed, headed in the opposite direction. He walked along the slender corridor with the jail cells on his left until he reached Taylor's cell, which was locked up as he'd had his free time earlier in the day.

"Yo," Big Eddie called out as he leaned against Taylor's cell and tucked his hands inside his denim jeans. He chuckled to himself and looked down at the floor the moment he noticed Taylor's hand moving up and down underneath his blanket as he held onto a picture with his free hand. "Yo, Taylor," he called out again while staring down at his black jack boots.

Taylor eased up and stretched. "Can a man get some privacy? Shit!" he scoffed as he stood, turned his back to Taylor and slid on a pair of jeans. "What's up, man?" he asked as he leaned over to the sink and rinsed his hands.

"We got a situation with the Somali. Hacks was gone place him in gen pop, but I got Eddie moving him through the infirmary."

"That'll keep him off the phones for like another hour,"

Taylor said as he walked to the front of the cell and grabbed hold of the bars.

"Who you got over in gen pop that can get to him?"

"Princess been moved back to the main floor," Taylor thought. "She could do it, but she just got out the hole for fucking in the shower and she damn near went crazy. She gotta make up for lost time with them punk-loving mutherfuckas anyway."

Besides controlling the drug rackets, Taylor had a half dozen homosexuals that he was pimping inside the facility. He was forcing them to sell themselves to other inmates for profit. Many a young, so-called gangster with notorious reps on the streets had been hit with a heavy dose of harsh reality when confronted by Taylor—a real gangster from back in the day. They hadn't the guns to use whenever they felt disrespected in prison like they had on the streets, nor did they have their clicks with them for backup. When forced to fight hand to hand, or use a shank in one on one combat, they simply bowed down. Prison wasn't a fairy tale, neither a kiddie camp. Taylor had never slept with another man in his life, nor would he ever, but it didn't prevent him from sending many a new age gangster out on the stroll.

Even though they were behind bars, Big Eddie, Eddie and Taylor were doing the same things on the inside that they had been doing on the outside, which was hustling and getting money anyway they could and for as long as they could get away with it; the three had several lucrative rackets going from pimping to drug dealing. Their latest job, however, was causing problems because murder behind bars was nearly impossible to commit without being caught.

"Family paying good on the job if it get done," Big Eddie remarked. "I'm thinking I could do it myself. I ain't got nothing but a life sentence left to serve."

"I be seventy-three before they even consider me for parole, man. I can't even file for another appeal." Taylor followed.

"Seventy-three? At least you get a chance ta' get out." Eddie stated. "I'm looking to die in this joint."

"I'm not getting paroled." Taylor stated seriously. "I be eighty when I get out this mutherfucka. Lettin' me out seven years early ain't gone do me no damn good, Big Eddie. What I'm gone do when I get out? Go to a old folk's home and play pinochle with a bunch of elderly folk that done worked all their life? I be outta place in the free world. I rather stay here where everything make sense to me."

After a brief lull in the conversation, Taylor reran in his mind what Eddie had said about the family paying good for the job on Q-Man. "What the going rate on this guy?" he asked Big Eddie.

"Fifty stacks," Big Eddie replied.

"Okay," Taylor remarked lowly as he rubbed his chin. "I'll do the hit," he said seriously as he stared Big Eddie in the eyes.

"You'll do it? Why? You know ain't no coming back from that shit, Taylor."

"I'm in here, man. In here until I die maybe," Taylor remarked somberly. "I been gone from the streets since seventy-seven and all I ever did was leave my woman behind to struggle. I loss a son to the streets in Manny—some shit I didn't even know until me and Joyce reconnected a few years back after hurricane Katrina."

"Yeah, I know all that, but why you jump on it so quick?"

Taylor walked off from the cell bars. He clicked on a lamp in his cell, placed his glasses on his face and began shuffling through stacks of manila folders on the floor beside his bed. The convict knew the law inside out having been down for so long and he'd actually helped a few lifers give back their time to the state and the feds after filing several appeals on their behalf. He was working to get Eddie Junior out on early release, but that case was still pending.

Big Eddie watched as his friend went through stack after stack of thick folders with documents hanging out the sides. "Here we go," Taylor finally said as he pulled a thick folder from the huge pile and walked back to the front of the cell. "Grab that drawing," he told Big Eddie just as the Isley

Brothers' song, *For The Love of You* came over the radio.

Big Eddie grabbed a white sheet of paper that had a picture of a tan, one story office building drawn on it. "What's this, brother?" he asked Taylor.

"I been telling you that Joyce was a Licensed Nurse Practitioner for the longest, man," Taylor stated proudly. "She do okay at the hospital she working at down in Joliet, but she always talk about opening her own practice over the phone and in letters, ya' dig?"

"Okay," Big Eddie stated as he nodded his head to the music.

"Yo, Taylor, turn them Isley Brothers up, Boss Man! Remind me when I was in the free world laying my Mack game down in west Chicago back in seventy-nine!" a prisoner called out from his cell.

Taylor reached over and turned the radio up as Big Eddie, getting a feel for the reason why Taylor was so quick to take the hit on Q-Man, smiled and said, "This here like a sketch of what could be."

"Right, brother. An architect designed it. I got," Taylor fumbled with the folder, excited to share the news with his partner. "I got a copy of the blueprints and everything, man," he said as he flipped through the folder and pulled out the blueprints to his woman's dream.

"You got a few racks put back, right? How much we talkin'?" Big Eddie asked.

"Ninety thousand to get the ball rolling," Taylor told Big Eddie. "Joyce got like twenty put away, I got about thirty myself. The payoff on the hit would put us over. With that much collateral the architect say he could get her in on a small business loan up to a half million dollars. She make that back in the two years with her own practice."

"You sure this the route you wanna take, Taylor? I give you this job, man, the family gone be expecting results tonight." Big Eddie said seriously.

"Keep him in the infirmary," Taylor spoke as he stared into

Big Eddie's eyes. "Joyce deserves this after the way I left her stuck out, brother. I ain't got shit to lose back here. They done ended the death penalty, so it's nothing but more time on a long time already being served," he declared as he extended his hands through the bars where he and Big Eddie shook hands, thereby sealing the deal.

****

Q-Man had been on the prison grounds for nearly thirty minutes now. He'd been registered and had received his inmate package, which consisted of a thin mattress, a small blanket, a fresh bar of soap, short toothbrush and small tube of toothpaste. He'd changed out into a yellow jumper and was being escorted to his cell. "I need to use the phone, man," he told the correctional officer that was escorting him to his cell as the two walked down an isolated corridor. "I'm in a one man cell, right? Ain't nobody speak on my behalf and let y'all know I was coming here?"

"What is this right here? A fuckin' Sixty Minutes interview?" the correctional officer asked in an aggravated tone as he walked behind Q-Man, eyeing him harshly. "Just keep walking!" he snapped as he shoved him forward.

Q-Man could feel his heart pounding through his chest as he walked towards a solid steel door at the end of the corridor. He could only imagine entering an open tier filled with prisoners who may very well be enemies of his. Word had a way of traveling fast through the prison system and Q-Man wasn't sure whether or not the Latin Kings or the Somalis back in Cook County hadn't put some of their boys in Stateville on alert of his arrival.

"I need to make a phone call!" Q-Man snapped as he looked back at the guard while walking up the corridor holding onto his prison-issued garments and hygienic items.

"When you get to where you're going, I'll let you settle in and take you to a phone," the correctional officer stated. "Just keep walking."

A quick peek through the small window when he reached the steel door let Q-Man know he was going onto an open tier with at least seventy inmates. A few Italians hung out on the stairwell straight ahead. Latinos were on one side and the blacks were on another side while the whites sat in the middle of the room at several tables. "Welcome home, Bahdoon," the guard said as he stuck a key into the steel the door. Just before the guard entered a key code, however, a whistle was heard from the opposite end of the corridor. "The fuck is it?" the correctional asked as he turned back to look up the corridor.

"TB test for that man!" another correctional officer called out from up the hall.

"I already had a TB test over to Cook County!" Q-Man yelled back. "Just get me to my cell and over to the phones!"

"Captain says you need another TB test you need another TB test. There's phones in the infirmary," the officer beside Q-Man stated.

"This here some bullshit," Q-Man mumbled as he was led back up the hall.

****

Back on his tier, Taylor had just stuck two fingers into his mouth as he sat on his bed. He was a healthy man, so it was hard to go through with the act. Repeatedly, he shoved fingers into his throat, forcing himself to gag. After several tries, he puked onto the cell's floor and fell down screaming. "Some, somebody get me some fuckin' help!" he screamed. "Don't take me, Father! Don't take me like this!" he screamed.

"Yo! We got a man sick in my next cell!" a prisoner in the next cell up yelled. "Get this man some help!"

"Man need help!" a prisoner yelled.

"Sick man! We got a man down!" another followed.

The message shot all the way up to the front of the tier within seconds. Taylor leapt up and grabbed a mirror on a stick and stuck it out the cell to get a bead on the door leading to the tier. When he saw the door open and two guards rushing in, he snapped the mirror off the wooden stake and hid it behind the sink in his cell and stuffed the sharp object in his front waistband. He then laid back down in his own vomit and started yelling again. "Food poison! Food! Food poison!" as he hunched over pretending to be in pain.

Two guards, one of whom was on Taylor and the Cottonwoods' payroll, ran up to the cell. "What the fuck is your problem?" the correctional officer not in on the scheme asked aloud as he shined a flashlight into Taylor's cell.

"I don't know, man!" Taylor said as he squirmed about on the floor. "We had tuna for lunch! I let my sandwich set out all day! Shit went bad!"

"Stomach pump for this guy," the guard in on the plan said as he unlocked the cell. "Can you walk?"

"Look like I can walk, man?" Taylor winced. "At least help me to the infirmary!"

The guards pulled Taylor out by his feet and helped him up by the arm pits. On weak legs, he shuffled in between the men, headed towards the prison infirmary.

****

Q-Man, meanwhile, had just closed his arm to secure the small gauze pad that was in the crease of his right arm after having blood drawn to be tested for tuberculosis. "While I'm in here you think you can change these bandages for me, nurse? And can I please make a phone call?" he asked.

The nurse secured Bahdoon's blood sample and walked back over to him and checked his bandages. "They really worked you over didn't they? I'll see what I can do."

"What about the phone call?"

"Follow me," the woman said as she began to guide Q-Man to a small office.

At that moment, two correctional officers rushed in with a screaming prisoner. Q-Man paid it no mind as he could see the phone just ahead inside the office. He knew once he talked to Laddy Norcross, he would have things rectified as the agent could verify that he was a key witness to an on-going federal investigation and have him moved to solitary confinement where he would be safe.

Taylor was continuing on with his act as he was being led into the infirmary. He could see the bandaged prisoner walking towards him. "Q-Man," he stated through gasped breaths as the guards drug him towards the beds inside the prison hospital.

"Who the fuck are you?" Q-Man asked as he walked past the prisoner who'd called his street name. The correctional officer in on the scheme patted Taylor's side, inconspicuously letting him know he had the right target.

Taylor broke free of the guards' grip with a loud roar as he went up under his shirt and came out with a wooden shank. "Die, mutherfucka!" he screamed vehemently.

Q-Man began swinging his arms to defend himself as the nurse scrambled out of the way. The unknown prisoner was slicing at him with a wooden shank and he was doing all he could to prevent from getting stabbed. A powerful punch to the inmate's face forced him to stumble back. He landed over against the opposite wall grimacing as he slid down the wall.

Q-Man ran over to his attacker, attempting to grabbed the shank and use it against him.

Taylor, however, was only feigning. He righted himself and lunged forth at that moment, catching Q-Man off guard and driving the stake into the pit of his stomach. Q-Man squealed like a stuck pig through wide eyes as the foreign object pierced deep into his torso.

"Doss Dawkins sends his regards!" Taylor hissed as he pulled up on the stake, forcing the wood to crack Q-Man's sternum at the base as he and Q-Man fell off inside a small office.

The fight had unfolded in a matter of seconds. Guards on the scene and had little time to react. One sounded the hospital alarm as the other two guards rushed into the office. Taylor was now hovering over Q-Man. He'd pulled the wooden shank from his victim's body and had just slammed it down a second time right before he was hit across the head with a black jack.

When Taylor rolled off of Q-Man, all the guards could see was his body laid out on the floor trembling violently with a wooden stake planted in his right eye. When the Somali turned his head, the guards could see the pointed tip of the wooden shank protruding from the side of his skull.

"What the fuck?" the correctional officer not in on the plot exclaimed as he backed away from the gory scene.

Several more officers in S.W.A.T. gear rushed into the office at that moment along with several doctors as Taylor was beaten while being dragged from the infirmary. Prison medical staff, meanwhile, had tried to save the life of the prisoner who'd been attacked. All was in vain, however, as Q-Man had already checked out. The stake through the eye was too much to overcome. He died on the floor of the prison infirmary's office as the jagged, wooden stake had gone through a large portion of his brain and had damaged it beyond repair.

Big Eddie had gotten the word and a call went out to Jay-D within the hour via Eddie Junior. Taylor would be compensated for the hit on Q-Man, but he now faced another murder charge. The man had been given up hope of being freed from prison; and being that the state of Illinois had done away with the death penalty, the most he could get was a life sentence, something he'd always felt he'd serve anyway. Taylor had sacrificed his own life for the sake of his son's mother. At least Joyce would have a chance. He'd done something good on behalf of his wife was his reasoning as he lay on the floor of a cell in solitary confinement, where he would remain for an unspecified amount of time.

Bahdoon 'Q-Man' LuQman's run had started in August of 2001 when he'd linked up with Carmella Lapiente` down in East Saint Louis. Seven years and four months later, he was the last of that bunch to be eradicated by the Holland family. His death would only pave the road for a new cast of gangsters who were just as ruthless as he and his crew once were, however; and once again, the Holland family would find themslves facing another adversary—one of their biggest adversaries to date.

CHAPTER SIXTEEN

THEY GET THE JOB DONE

"...*He thinkin' about comin' up a lick to get it quick and it involves that local corner store...I overheard him say he knew who work there...and whatever they do don't let the owner know...I hope he come back with enough to let me borrow some change at least for the summer...and if he don't let me borrow nothing but ask me what I want I'm a tell 'em I want a...diamond in the back...I wanna(sunroof top)....I wanna(dig in the scene with a gangster lean)...*"

It was the following night after Taylor had taken out Q-Man. New Year's Eve across the country. While Taylor lay in solitary confinement up in Stateville, back down in Saint Louis in a world far apart, Ludacris' song *Diamond in the Back* was blaring loudly behind the tinted windows of a lime green 1976 Caprice Classic as it made its way over the Mississippi River bridge about a quarter past eleven. The gangster whip's twenty-seven inch chrome Sprewell rims glided over the snow-plowed westbound lanes of I-70 as it and its passengers slid into downtown Saint Louis, Missouri.

Behind the Caprice's wheel sat twenty-four year-old Helen Weinberger, Under Boss of the Weinberger family, a group of Germans from Cincinnati, Ohio who fullfiled murder contracts, distributed heroin and pushed a few kilograms of cocaine. Helen, who was better known as Boogie, was a 5'9" slender German-Jew with a nappy, tan afro and sleeve-tattooed arms.

Fluent in both German and English, and an elegant dancer and masterful piano player, Boogie had grown up in the heart of New Orleans inside the French Quarters. She spent many a day in her youth dancing on corners up and down Bourbon Street and hanging with countless musicians. She was educated, having earned a college degree in Choreography from the University of New Orleans. When she wasn't pushing weight or fulfilling contracts, Boogie spent her time inside her personal dancehall where she taught ballet and gave piano lessons to many of the youth in the rundown section of Cincinnati known as Over the Rhine, which was where her mother's organization was now headquartered.

Sitting beside Boogie was twenty-six year-old William Slack, known to most as Popeye, because of his thick, veiny forearms. Popeye was a 6'1" physically fit high-yellow-skinned muscular African-American/Sioux Indian with a head full of jet black zig-zag braids and pearl white teeth.

Like Boogie, Popeye was an educated individual, and he, too, was fluent in German. His mother had paid out-of-pocket for him to attend Georgetown University where he'd earned a degree in Foreign Affairs. When he wasn't conducting business on the streets he could be found aiding his mother in her political endeavors over in Washington D.C.

The Weinberger family was a highly-technological criminal organization whose tentacles crossed over into the legitimate corporate and political worlds. College degrees and powerful political connections often kept them several steps ahead of the law and their competition. Their history of violence afforded them the strength they needed to control the underworld they navigated. Indeed, they were a force to be reckoned with in any given city and against any crew.

Boogie picked up her cell phone and dialed a number. "The Millennium Hotel," she said in her trademark slow-paced, pedantic drawl when the person on the other end picked up. "Where is this Millennium Hotel where my sister is staying?"

"It's like three exits up," Ya Murder replied from behind the wheel of Toodie's black, four door, old school Cadillac Deville as she eyed Saint Louis' skyline under the bright moonlit sky.

"Your people back in Naptown gone put me back in the game once we done here, right?" she asked.

"I will take you to see RJ after we are done with the job here in Saint Louis. Pass us and take us to this Millennium Hotel," Boogie commanded just before she ended the call. Ya Murder eased past Boogie and Popeye and guided them to their preordained location.

While the crew was pulling up under the hotel's canopy, Boogie texted her sister from another mother. *We just touched down. Where are you?*

1808 was quickly messaged back as the two luxurious rides were greeted by valet. Boogie, Popeye and Ya Murder quickly made their way into the hotel where they caught an elevator up to the eighteenth floor. A quick tap on room 1808 forced the door to slowly open several seconds later. Twenty-eight year-old Maggie McPherson stepped aside to let Boogie and Popeye, and a woman she'd never seen before into the room.

Boogie couldn't help but to smile at the young woman who'd been her sister for as long she could remember. *"Wie ist das alles in Cherryvale, Maggie?"* (How's everything in Cherryvale, Maggie?) she asked as she gave her best friend a tight hug.

"Toll! Meine Mutter denkt, ich bin eine Geschichte Vortrag über die UC Berkeley für den Monat Januar so meine Zeit ist begrenzt hier in Saint Louis." (Great! My mother thinks I'm giving a history lecture over to UC Berkeley for the month of January so my time is limited here in Saint Louis.)

"We gone get it done quicker than that," Popeye chimed in as he closed the luxurious suite's door and locked it. "You got the toys?" he asked as he walked over and hugged Maggie tightly, rocking her body to and fro slightly and forcing her to emanate a girly giggle as his hands slid down to her wide, soft rear end.

"Beginnen Sie nicht nichts kann man nicht fertig stellen, William." (Don't start nothing you can't finish, William.) Maggie laughed as she backed away from her first while tightening the black silk robe that shielded her naked,

voluptuous body.

Twenty-eight Maggie McPherson was a full-bloodied six-foot tall, wide-hipped, thick-boned, hazel-eyed pale-skinned German with a head full of red hair. She was born in Pittsburgh, Pennsylvania, but now resided on a farm in Cherryvale, Kansas.

Like her friends, Maggie was college educated; having graduated Suma Cum Laude from Brown University where she'd majored in World History. She and her mother were arms dealers for the Weinberger family and also specialized in taking down international targets. In between those times, the Junior Professor could be found giving lectures on prestigous collegiate campuses around the country and throughout the world.

Maggie had gone on a couple of hits in times past with Boogie with her mother's approval. Those jobs paid top dollar, but this job in Saint Louis was unsanctioned by Maggie's mother as she felt it would lead to another war. Yet, she still chose to join her friends without her mother knowing as committing murder was a turn on for her. She got off on knowing she was killing people and getting away with it while giving lectures on World History, Strategic Medieval War Tactics and Culture being her experise.

"Come and see for yourself what kind of toys I have, Popeye," Maggie smiled slyly as she backed into the open area of suite and extended her hands towards her bed, where an assortment of high-powered artillery lay.

Boogie walked over to the bed after introducing Ya Murder to Maggie and eyed the assortment of weapons Maggie had brought down to Saint Louis. "What's this?" she asked as she ran her hands over a black steel assault rifle.

Maggie walked over and stood beside Boogie and picked the weapon up and stated proudly, "This is a Heckler and Koch G36 assault rifle. The G thirty-six is a German-made assault rifle accurate up to eight hundred meters and comes with a thirty round clip."

"Nice," Boogie said as she took the gun from Maggie and

ran her hands over the gun. She held onto the weapon, caressing it as if she were holding a newborn baby while eyeing another weapon. "What's that one?" she nodded towards another gun lying on the bed.

Maggie picked up the second weapon and clicked on an infrared beam and aimed it at Ya Murder with a smile on her face. She looked the Mexican square in the eyes and said, "This is the Tavor, Ya Murder. It is an Israeli gun that fires nine hundred rounds a minute and like the G thirty-six, it comes with a thirty round clip. Ya Murder? You may like it," she chuckled as she held the gun out. "See how it feels in your hands."

Ya took the gun from Maggie and was surprised over its light-weightiness. "I can get down with this," she said while nodding her head up and down.

While Boogie and Ya Murder became acquainted with their toys, Maggie turned to Popeye and smiled into his eyes as she ran her hands over his silk suit jacket. "I used to sneak and watch you masturbate when we were younger," she giggled. "Didn't take long for me to realize you were left-handed. For you I have the Australian-made Steyr Aug. Thirty round clip, six hundred and sixty rounds a minute and effective up to three hundred meters."

"Not really my style," Popeye remarked as he held onto the gun.

"I know," Maggie replied as her heart rate increased. "I brought it to use myself because I just want to kill someone again," she panted as her nipples grew erect.

"What else you have?" Boogie asked.

"An M four Carbine and two AK forty-sevens RJ wanted dropped off in Indianapolis when you two head back to Cincinnati." Maggie replied as she fanned herself, having grown horny over the thought of murdering someone. "I have the ammo here," she said as she grabbed a leather duffle bag.

"This is all we'll need," Boogie replied as she sat her weapon of choice down. She then turned to Ya Murder and said, "Jada? Tomorrow night we begin our hunt for this Peppi Vargas."

"Where should we start looking, Ya Murder?" Maggie chimed in as she dumped clips and boxes of shells onto the mattress.

"At her trap house over in East Saint Louis at this spot called Wimmer Place," Ya Murder answered as she picked up one of the clips to see if it fit her gun.

"Okay," Boogie stated. "That we will do, but not tonight," she added as she walked over to the bar. "I would like to propose a toast on this New Year's Eve to a successful job," she ended as the group all gathered around her inside the pristine suite just as fireworks sponsored by several casinos began to erupt over the Mississippi River, signaling the start of a New Year.

CHAPTER SEVENTEEN

NEW YEAR, SAME CHABLIS

The following morning after the Germans' arrival in Saint Louis found Chablis lying on a bench inside of OU Medical Center's rehabilitation ward in downtown Oklahoma City. On this New Year's Day, he was lifting leg weights with his legs while reflecting on the play and the hit that put his football career on pause. *"I told you I was gone fuck you up today, mutherfucka. That's for Koko!* The sound of his neck snapping and Kahlil's laughter echoed in Chablis' mind as the images he'd watched of what had gone down that day replayed over and over in his mind. Seeing Kahlil run off the field unscathed while he lay helpless left him angered every time he thought about the matter, which was every waking moment.

Determined to put the past behind him, Chablis continued kicking the weights up into the air with his muscular legs. Just five days ago, he was laid up in his bed barely able to move. Now, he was fully mobile having spent over a month confined to his bed. His neck brace had been removed a couple of days earlier and there was no pain whenever he twisted his head in either direction. Doctors said he may never play again, but they had it wrong in Chablis' eyes. He was now well on his way back to returning to doing what he loved most, which was playing football. His plan was to obtain a sports agent while going into his junior year and give Oklahoma University his all in order to have a shot at the NFL.

While working up an intense sweat inside the rehabilitation

ward, Chablis' on-duty doctor approached him. He spotted the woman and sat up on the bench in his Adidas jogging shorts and silk wife beater as sweat streamed down his ripped biceps and temples. "What's the word, girl?" he smiled.

"It's Doctor Duchene," the surgeon remarked as she stood before Chablis with her arms resting against her scrubs while holding onto a manila folder.

"Okay, Doctor Duchene," Chablis chuckled. "What my original doctor come up with? What he say?"

"Nothing has changed, Chablis," Doctor Duchene remarked calmly. "I know you were expecting better news, but as of now, you can't be cleared to play football."

"What?" Chablis asked in dismay as he stood up from the bench. "Look at my fuckin' neck!" he scoffed lowly as he whipped his neck to and fro.

"I would advise you not to do that, Chablis." Doctor Duchene stated seriously.

"Why not? My neck is fine! Where's my real doctor? I can't trust what this woman sayin' to me!" Chablis complained as he stormed past Doctor Duchene.

"Your prescribed surgeon is off for a week to play Pebble Beach for the holidays, sir!" Doctor Duchene remarked as she turned and faced Chablis' backside.

Chablis paused at that moment and turned around in disbelief. "He left me with you to go play golf in San Diego? Fuck he was thinking? You don't know what you talkin' about!"

"Is that so?" Doctor Duchene said as she removed her eyeglasses. "Let me break it down to you in medical terms to get you understand me," the thirty-three year-old African American woman sassed, having been forced out of proper doctor-patient etiquette over Chablis' chauvinistic demeanor while managing to hold onto a slight manner of professionalism. "You've suffered a fracture to your neck. Your youthful strength has allowed the fracture to heal quickly, but you now suffer from cervical stenosis, which is a narrowing of the spinal canal in your neck. At any given time, should you sustain any trauma to your neck from sustained kinetic force of any kind, you'll know the true meaning of pain. You run the risk of being paralyzed for the rest of your life, Chablis. If you were to keep going like you're going you'll find yourself attached to a breathing machine and confined to wheel chair for the rest of your natural life. You'll be unable to control your bodily functions from the neck down."

"I don't feel no pain in my neck! You lying to me!" Chablis screamed as he charged at Doctor Duchene.

Several male physical education instructors stepped in and blocked Chablis before he reached Doctor Duchene, but the enraged twenty year-old charged on. Medical staff had to lift him off his feet and pin him up against a treadmill momentarily while keeping in mind his fragile neck. He was sedated and taken back to his room where he lay for several hours. When he awoke, Doctor Duchene was there inside his suite sitting in a chair beside his bed.

Chablis tried to move again, but quickly discovered that he was shackled to the bedrails. "I've requested that you be treated as a hostile patient," Doctor Duchene remarked calmly. "I'm also transferring you to a male doctor until your assigned physician returns," she added.

"Good. Because a man would understand what I'm going through."

"As if a woman doctor wouldn't," Doctor Duchene replied as she squint her eyes. "I know your kind," she stated matter-of-factly as she patted Chablis' file in her hands. "This is off the record, sir," she said as she stood up beside Chablis. "In my book? You deserve everything that's happening to you."

"Fuck you, lady! You don't know me!"

"I know what you're about, Chablis. And that tells me all I need to know about you, young man," Doctor Duchene replied casually as she began to breakdown Chablis' inner being. "You have the physical talents axiomatic to that of the mythological Hercules, but the mindset analogous to that of a ten year-old boy. You feel threatened by a woman similar to your masculine physiognomies from an academic standpoint and the only way for you to assert your position during an intimate liaison is to use somatic force."

"Fuck you, lady!" Chablis scoffed as he eyed the woman while trying to decipher what all she'd said to him.

"Am I speaking over your head, young man?" Doctor Duchene smiled. "Let me break it down further for you then. Chablis? You're an abuser. A womanizer. If you don't change? Football will not be the only thing you will have depraved yourself of in life because you will never know the love of a real woman. Good luck, sir," she ended as she backed away from Chablis' bed and headed for the door.

The good doctor was reaching for the door handle when the door was pushed open slightly. She stepped back as a tall, muscular, tan-skinned young man with short dreads and a platinum grill in his mouth eased into the room. "I'm sorry, doctor," the young man spoke politely as he removed his dark blue Dallas Cowboys skull cap. "Can, can Chablis have visitors now?"

"Help yourself," Doctor Duchene replied as she looked back at Chablis and curled her lips up in disdain. "I'm surprised someone's even bothering to show up," she ended as she walked out of the room.

Twenty-four year-old Tonto Jamison closed the door behind the doctor and thumbed his nose as he smiled over towards Chablis. "You damn sure have a way with women, boy," the 6'3" two hundred and twenty-five pound twenty-four year-old stated through a chuckle as he walked over and stood at the foot of Chablis' bed and tucked his hands into his dark blue, sagging Gucci jeans.

Silence encompassed the room as Tonto raised his leg and planted his Gucci shoes on the wood at the foot of Chablis' bed. He and Chablis stared at one another for several seconds before Chablis looked off in the distance. "I can't play ball no more, man," Chablis managed to admit, although pained over the realization.

"Fuck you gone do now?" Tonto asked as he knocked

slushes of snow from the sides of his $1,100 dollar black leather Gucci sneakers.

"Hopefully, the college won't cut my scholarship. Guess I'll go on with my major in sports management and become an agent."

"Who in the fuck gone sign with you, dude?" Tonto asked as he laughed lightly. "Two years in the game on the college level with no professional career and no contacts. How that's gone work out?"

"You always downing shit." Chablis complained.

"I call it how I see it, Chablis," Tonto replied sternly. "Look at you, dude. Laid up shackled to a hospital bed with a fucked up neck, empty pockets and a future that's uncertain? You locked up and don't even know it. I don't understand y'all catching-feelings-for-a-bitch-type-of dudes, man," Tonto stated through a sigh as he dropped his foot from the edge of the bed and walked around and sat in the chair Doctor Duchene had vacated.

"This don't have nothing to do with Koko, Tonto."

"How you know I was talkin' 'bout you and that bitch right there?" Tonto countered in his slow, country drawl as he leaned back in the chair and crossed his legs. "How that phone call you told me you was gone make to Ponderosa on Christmas day go?"

A smile crept across Chablis' face at that moment as he looked up to the ceiling. "I laid it out for her. Apologized to her and told her I'm gone change. She gone meet me on the campus first day of classes."

"That's what she said?"

"She actually said she was gone think about it," Chablis admitted. His eyes were lit up when he turned towards Tonto and said, "But, but before we hung up? She called me baby. Just like old times."

"Just like a placating bitch you mean," Tonto laughed. "She playin' you, son. That bitch ain't comin' back to you ever!" he stated aggressively as he flashed his platinum grill.

"You half-crazy, man. Fuck that shit you talkin'," Chablis replied through light laughter as he fanned his handcuffed hands in the air, waving Tonto off as best he could.

Tonto wrinkled his face and suddenly rushed from the chair and clasped his hands around Chablis' neck. "'I only want the one who put the money up!' Ain't that what you told me five days ago about Walee, mutherfucka?" he whispered angrily as he tightened his grip on Chablis' neck.

The pain Doctor Duchene had warned Chablis about had just been made known courtesy of Tonto Jamison. It was as if flames shooting up from a charcoal grill were engulfing his esophagus as Tonto's hands clung to his neck. "My cervix! My cervix! Fuck you doing?" Chablis cried lowly as he stared Tonto in the eyes fearfully.

"Your cervix? You sound like the bitch from Ponca City you in love with, boy! I'm tryna put you up on game because your career in sports is all but over! Over!" Tonto hissed as he shook Chablis' neck violently, offering up no concern towards the young man's vulnerable state-of-being.

"Give me 'til opening day! Opening day!" Chablis bargained as he shut his eyes and let tears flow over the pain Tonto was inflicting upon his neck.

"Opening day then what?" Tonto asked as he relaxed his grip on Chablis' neck.

"If Koko don't show we go after Walee and Kahlil! We go after Walee and Kahlil!" Chablis offered up as he gasped for air while grimacing in agony.

Tonto nodded his head in silent agreement as he let go of Chablis' neck while stepping back from his bedside. "If you bitch up on me and go to the police, or let the Holland family know what the deal is? I'm gone kill you. Point blank and done deal on what I just said." Tonto declared as he reached for his dark blue Dallas Cowboys skull cap and placed it onto his head. "See you first day of school, homie," he ended while eyeing Chablis in a cold-hearted manner as he made his way over to the suite's door and quietly left the room.

CHAPTER EIGHTEEN

THE PACT

Shortly after Tonto and Chablis' encounter down in Oklahoma City, eighty miles up the road in Ponca City, on the west side of town, Siloam had just kicked the front door of Jane Dow's trailer home open and was walking out of the dump into the cold air toting a pair of drumsticks and a sneer drum. "Come on, Jane!" she screamed angrily.

"She's not going anywhere!" Jane's mother, a skinny, knock-kneed, 5' tall Lakota Indian yelled as she ran and pushed the door open once more, the black eye she'd sustained from a weekend brawl clearly visible under the clear blue sky.

Siloam had gotten her protégé a new set of custom made Oak drums for Christmas, but barely a week later, the drum set had been stolen, save for one drum, the set's cymbals and the hand-carved drum sticks. Jane was heartbroken over the loss of her instruments and she blamed no one but her parents. She'd been forced to stay in her bedroom the entire weekend, but was finally able to sneak and call Siloam and tell her what had gone down once her cell phone had charged.

Siloam had had it up to her neck with Jane's living situation. Jane's parents' meth addiction was now beyond out of control. The trailer home the eighteen year-old lived in was littered with trash a foot high in some places. One could barely breathe as the seven cats that inhabited the single-wide, rusty structure shed hair constantly. The smell of cat urine was permanent, fixated into the clothes and carpet, and that of Jane and her parents' skin. Sickening wasn't a strong enough word to use in describing the home in which Jane Dow resided.

Jane's father had gotten locked up over the weekend after he and his wife had gotten into a brutal fight that left him with a gash over his right eye after Jane's mother hit him across the head with a beer bottle to defend herself from his punches after the two had gotten high off the methamphetamine they'd purchased after selling portions of Jane's new drum set.

Siloam knew she couldn't handle them both, but upon learning that the man of the house had been locked up, she felt now was the perfect time to remove her protégé from a hostile environment. "Jane, I said come on!" Siloam yelled as she sloshed through the packed snow covering the ground.

"I said Jane isn't going anywhere!" Jane's mother sassed as she held the front door open while wobbling her head.

"You're gonna ruin her *life* if she stays here! She can't live out her dreams because you two keep screwin' with her! How can you steal from your own child?" Siloam stormed as she threw the instruments in the back seat of one of the family's Suburbans. "Jane, come on out of there!"

Jane walked to the front door and her mother turned and pushed her back into the home. "Get your ass back in that room and stay there!" the woman yelled. "I told you not to call no fuckin' body, but you never listen!"

Siloam ran up to the front of the home and dragged Jane's mother outside and down the three wooden stairs. The two fell over into the snow wrestling, but Siloam was much stronger than Jane's mother. She pushed the woman over onto her back and straddled her, placing a hand to her neck as she balled up her left fist. The Cherokee Indian's eyes were filled with rage as she let go with a powerful punch to Jane's mother's face. She purposely hit the woman in her sore eye one time, knocking her stitches loose before jumping back up on her feet. "You stay, stay away from her, until you get yourself some help!" she scoffed as Jane stepped from the dilapidated home. She was crying incessantly as she walked over and hopped into the Suburban.

Siloam left Jane's mother rolling around in the snow with a bloody face as she walked off. The thirty-four year-old woman was slow to anger, but she was a very vindictive and dangerous female at her core. There was a dormant dark side to Siloam that none in the family had ever witnessed, but slowly, given the pressure in her life, that dark side was beginning to manifest itself. And for those enraging her, it would only mean wretchedness—deadly wretchedness.

"Where're we going?" Jane asked meekly with her head bowed.

"I have a studio apartment near where Bay and 'Nina stays. I leased it last year not too long after Doss was killed. I rarely stay there, but if you want a new home now's your chance. I advise you to take this opportunity."

"I do. I will," Jane said as she sniffled her nose.

Siloam looked over to Jane pitifully. For a while now, she'd known that she could've been much more to the teenager than just a music tutor. She'd never had a child of her own, and although Jane was eighteen, to thirty-four year-old Siloam, she was a baby still. Hugging Jane and pulling her close, Siloam rubbed her shoulder and said, "I won't let anything happen to you from here on out."

"You've always been like a mother to me," Jane admitted through her tears.

"And I'll be that for as long as you need me. Even if it's forever." Siloam replied lovingly as she pulled down on the front of her sombrero and continued driving.

Siloam had a lot on her mind. Going after Jane's mother was more of her lashing out at the world as she could've easily taken Jane without the fisticuffs. She was a nervous wreck; had been ever since she'd entered into an alliance with Reynard. It was the ultimate betrayal, but Siloam had her reasons. Reasons she could share with no one at the time, if only to have her plan succeed. She'd resolved one situation with Jane, now the culminating of a much bigger matter she had to resolve was before her as the day for her and Reynard to execute their plan was drawing close.

Siloam held on to Jane as the two rode through downtown Ponca City. She was overcome with watery eyes, realizing that she really was no better than Jane's mother given her actions. She'd told the woman that she was going to ruin her daughter's life, but yet and still, she was on the verge of destroying an entire family.

It's fair to say that Siloam's own demons were propelling her to do better by Jane, if only to even the scales of morality out a little more while she manipulated some down on the ranch. The things she had to do, the lies she had to tell and the games she had to play, left her heart in shambles each and every time she engaged Reynard, but it was what needed doing in order for the truth to be laid bare concerning Reynard Jacobs while sparing Dimples the pain of knowing she and Takoda had had an affair.

****

After stopping at Walmart to pick up new clothes and toiletries for Jane, Siloam dropped her off at her two bedroom studio apartment. She then left the apartment and headed back to the ranch. Upon reaching the property, she rode over to the main barn and sat out behind the building in the SUV for a few minutes with the vehicle idling. A plan was formulating in her mind. One, should it succeed, would solve all of her problems. She opened the SUV's door, climbed out and walked over the snow-covered ground towards the barn and pulled one of the large doors open and crept inside. The family's dozen Clydesdale horses were all inside their stables resting comfortably under the heating system that hummed lightly.

Siloam tightened her wool trench coat and climbed up the stairs leading to the human quarters inside the barn. The loft overlooked the first floor and six of the stables. There was a fully-equipped kitchen, a comfortable sofa set and a TV. No one in the family hung out there really, it was an area mainly used whenever the animals were being treated with medications on the main floor of the barn. The loft was also the place where medications for the horses were kept behind lock and key inside a safe. Only Naomi, Mary, Siloam, Flacco and the big three had access to the medications. Each time the safe was unlocked, the time and by whom would be catalogued as each person with access had their own key code.

Siloam punched in her key code and pulled the safe open. It was about the size of a sixty-inch flat screen TV and had three shelves filled with small jars of liquid medications. The Cherokee picked up vials of horse tranquilizers and read the labels. The family only had Ketamine and Xylazine tranquilizers on hand, she noticed. *"They have the Revivon, but not the etorphine. Neither of these will stop the heart from beating. I need the etorphine."* Siloam said to herself as she closed the safe and reset the passcode.

After securing the safe, Siloam headed back downstairs as she contemplated on what would need to be done once she'd completed her task. She needed the help of a man with her plan. Takoda hadn't the heart. Dawk had too much going on and there was no way she would even dare ask Walee. *"Who else in the family could help me with this problem and say nothing about it,"* she wondered to herself as she descended the stairs.

"Senorita Bovina!" Flacco stated through a smile, startling Siloam in the process as he stepped into the barn gripping a small cardboard box. "You're treating the horses today?" the Mexican asked as he closed the barn door.

"No, Flacco," Siloam smiled. She then eyed the box he was holding and asked, "Is that etorphine by chance?"

"It most certainly is. Why?" Flacco asked as he set the box at the foot of the stairs.

"If I share something with you, Flacco, will you hold it secret?"

"Is this pertaining to the family, Senorita Bovina?"

"It's a matter of life and death," Siloam said frustrated as she sat down on the stairs.

Flacco could tell right away that Siloam was troubled. Over what he hadn't a clue. He listened intently beside the stairs as she shared with him her problems. When she was done, the two had entered into a pact.

"If you do it," Flacco stated as he bent down and picked up the box of medicine. "If you do this thing, Senorita Bovina? There's no turning back. You will have to live with it forever. And in order for me to help you out, you'll have to show me proof. I will also have to notify Senorita Dawkins. If Naomi says no, you will have to find another way."

"I've been trying to get proof, Flacco. I'm constantly sleeping with guy to earn his trust," Siloam remarked as she leaned forward and rested her arms on her knees. "I know he's up to something. I just don't know what. I don't know how long I can go on sleeping with him."

"He's a slick one. Mary and Dimples adore the guy, but no one in the family likes him," Flacco admitted. "Which means if he were to disappear, no one would ever miss him around here or even much care," he declared as he began walking up the stairs.

"I'll see what I can find out. And I think I can lure the guy. I just have to come up with a way to kill him before I do so," Siloam stated as she eyed the box Flacco was holding on to and followed him back up the stairs.

"I think I know a way to do it," Flacco said as he walked over and unlocked the safe.

"Me too," Siloam stated through fixated eyes as she grabbed a vial of Revivon off the shelf's safe the time Flacco pulled the door open. "Revivon is etorphine's antidote, correct?" she asked.

Flacco paused mid-motion as he held onto a tube of etorphine. He looked over to Siloam with a serious look on his face. "Revivon is etorphine's antidote correct. This is your plan?" he asked curiously.

"I don't know," Siloam sighed as she set the Revivon back onto a shelf inside the safe. "Etorphine is a pretty dangerous drug. Three drops can kill a man. And it can't get on your skin. I'm afraid to handle it. Maybe there's another way."

"What if I were to leave a small semi-automatic pistol here in the safe for you should you lure him here," Flacco said as he resumed stocking the shelves with etorphine.

"Where will I shoot him?"

"In the head twice. The gun will be a twenty-two. It's small enough to do the job not, but not big enough to exit the skull." Flacco remarked as he closed the safe's door. "There will be no blood to worry about."

I know where. I mean, where?"

"In the car I will supply to you to drive him here in on the night of the murder." Flacco responded as he stared Siloam in the eyes. "From there? You leave his body in the car and I'll take care of the rest."

"I'll let you know when," Siloam whispered as she shook Flacco's hand. "Thank you for this."

"Don't thank me," Flacco remarked as he stared Siloam in the eyes. "Had you not done what you did to Dimples you wouldn't be in this situation, Senorita Bovina. You have work to do now. Be careful."

Siloam nodded and headed for the stairs. She climbed back into the SUV and made her way over to the guest house where she saw two dozen or so carpenters erecting the pilings around the front of the home. A few men were setting up scaffolding on the home's northern corner and Mary was out front with Takoda and Regina at her side overseeing the project. She climbed from the SUV and casually sloshed through the snow, feeling like a pile of dung as she eyed Dimples, unable to believe what she'd gotten herself and Tak caught up in, all over a mere moment of envy towards another woman's status in life, a family member at that. "How's it going, guys?" she asked as she put on a smile.

"Better than expected," Mary smiled as she extended her hand.

Siloam scooted over and gripped Mary's outstretched hand. "How long before they finish?"

"They talking two weeks at latest if the weather holds up. I thought it wouldn't be ready until spring," Mary quipped happily.

"Looking at space forecasts already, huh, Mary?" Siloam smiled.

"I even got Udelle watching out for some stuff, Siloam," Mary giggled.

"Who wants coffee? Fresh french vanilla coffee here!" Reynard called out from the front porch over the power saws, drills and clinging of metal.

"I'll have a cup," Mary replied as she let go of Siloam's hand and traveled up the front porch where Reynard stood with a kettle and wearing an apron. She leaned up against his body and took a mug and held it out with both hands as she smiled up at the man while he poured.

Dimples trotted over to her father asking about the apron he was wearing. "Thought I'd whip up a quick lunch," Reynard said as he smiled over to Siloam and Tak. "I'm making Italian hoagies!" he yelled out at the two, barely able to hold back his laughter. "You want me to fix enough for you all as well?"

Tak looked away in shame. Siloam, however, kept things on an even keel. "I would love a sandwich, Mister Jacobs! Thanks!"

"Got you covered, young lady. Come on in!"

Siloam watched as Mary and Dimples walked into the home behind Reynard. "How long has he been here?" she asked Takoda.

"Since this morning. He flew in from Vegas. I came to the ranch and went up on Ne`Ne`s Hill with Tacoma. When we came back down he was here." Takoda said as he shook his head somberly. "I'm thinking about telling Dimples what happened."

"Why?" Siloam asked. "What would be the point in telling your wife if he doesn't know what happened between us?" Siloam probed.

"Never mind," Takoda replied glumly, too embarrassed to

tell Siloam that Reynard was bribing him in order to keep quiet on their fling. "That was the same sandwich we had the day he spotted us. It's like he's toying with us mentioning that sandwich or something."

"Is he doing something to you? Did he tell you anything about that day?" Siloam inquired.

"No," Takoda answered as he looked to the ground. "He said nothing to me about seeing us two together, but what can we do from preventing him from telling if he wants to?" he asked as he cut his eyes over to Siloam.

Siloam thought deeply at that moment. She remembered Takoda telling her the day they were caught that Reynard hadn't seen the two of them, but he'd just told her the two of them had been seen by the man. She knew it was a lie as it was impossible for Reynard to not have seen her and Takoda had only affirmed her beliefs.

Siloam wasn't sure where Takoda was in his thinking, but she had way too much at stake to risk being placed on the outs with the family. Naomi had taken her in and trusted her to the fullest. The entire family viewed her as blood. If Siloam were to lose her esteemed position within the family her world would come crashing down. The people she loved, all of her dreams, and the dreams of Jane Dow would falter and the only family she'd ever known would be taken away from her. What she was now contemplating on doing to save her future was a risk she was willing to take, because if the truth ever came out about her and Reynard, her life would be ruined anyways.

"It'll work itself out, Tak," Siloam said as she patted the man's back. "I just have to figure out what I'm gonna do."

"What are you planning on doing? What do you mean by 'do'?" Takoda quoted.

"It's just a saying," Siloam uttered wryly as she pulled down on her sombrero and walked towards the home's front porch and entered the house.

While walking up the aisle leading to the stairs that led up to the kitchen, Siloam could hear Regina laughing loudly as the smell of grilled pastrami and pepperoni filled the air. "I would love to take a trip to Vegas, dad! When?"

"At the end of this month! We'll leave out together," Reynard answered over the sizzling meat that lay on the island counter grill. "Mary? You wanna join me and Dimples?" he asked as he smiled sexily at his child's mother.

"I wouldn't mind," Mary smiled. "I haven't taken a trip out of state in so long, Reynard," she stated enthusiastically as she nodded her head, realizing just how drab her life had become. "I look forward to that trip and I'll hold you to your word. Me and Dimples both."

"We're on, then, baby," Reynard stated through a smile as he reached out and gently touched Mary's cheek with the back of his hand.

"Vegas is awesome, you guys," Siloam smiled as she eased up to the island counter, took a seat and smiled over to Reynard.

Reynard noticed Siloam's subtle smile and couldn't help but to ask, "What you know about Vegas?"

"I spent some time there some years ago," Siloam replied as she rested her elbows on the counter. "It is indeed Sin City. Mary, you better be careful going west with this man," she said jokingly.

Reynard licked his thumbs and backed away from the grill and reached down to grab his vibrating phone from his silk trousers at that moment. He walked off without saying a word as he pressed the phone to his ear.

"Where're you going?" Mary sassed playfully. "You're preparing lunch for your family."

"Oh, I'm sorry, Mary," Reynard laughed incredulously. "I'm, I'm up for another coaching job in Nevada. This is a call I have to take."

Mary smiled in appreciation. "You're getting back on your feet I see?"

"Yeah," Reynard responded as he pressed the phone to his

ear and walked down the stairs leading into the den where he closed the door. "Sorry for the delay, Bianca. How everything going, baby?" he immediately asked after locking the door.

"I'm fine. How are you, Mister Jacobs?" the woman on the other end stated perkily.

"Fine. Did everything go through?"

"Everything checks out. I have received the signed copies and the insurance policies you have on your family have been renewed, sir."

"Great, that's great, baby. I was worried they were going to lapse."

"Nearly did, but we have Mary's signature so all is in order. Thank you for doing continued business with Prudential Life Insurance. Can I help you with anything else?"

"No," Reynard smiled. "You've been more than helpful. Now, I'll receive those copies in the mail over to my home, right?"

"I'll have them mailed out to Las Vegas in three business days, Mister Jacobs."

Reynard smiled to himself as he clicked his phone off. His plan was slowly coming together, and he'd been having help the entire time. He thought about his partner in this most diabolical scheme and grew an erection as he reflected on the time they'd spent together a week or so after Doss had been killed. If all went well, the two would be able to cash in on the downfall of others and remain free. In other words, the two of them would get away with cold-bloodied murder.

CHAPTER NINETEEN

THE COLDEST IN THE GAME

January 5, 2009

It was the Monday after New Year's. Fifty-four year-old Naomi Holland-Dawkins, with the aide of Martha Holland and her middle daughters, twenty year-olds Kimi and Koko Dawkins, the family's matriarch was preparing to officially open the doors to Holland-Dawkins Enterprises (HDE) on this cold, snowy winter day.

While in Chicago attending Mendoza's farewell, Naomi had met Sharona Benson and DeeDee's son. She was surprised to learn she had a brother-in-law age seven and thought it to be amusing. When she questioned DeeDee about his relationship with Twiggy and introducing the child to the family, DeeDee told her to remain silent and he would introduce the boy in a few weeks or so after he'd spent time with him up in Chicago. His date of return was unknown at present. Naomi wondered how Twiggy, let alone the rest of the family would react to DeeDee having a child as her thoughts drifted over into the situation at hand.

The family now had twenty-four trucks and thirty-four trailers in total situated at their warehouse just outside of Oklahoma City, not including the six trucks and nine trailers that ran livestock and hauled Mary's produce to market back up in Ponca City. With a fleet of that size, Naomi knew she needed a new warehouse and terminal space as the ranch's warehouse could only accommodate five trucks at a time, not to mention the family needed a place to breakdown cocaine shipments coming in from Rafael Gacha.

Under the guise of running a legitimate trucking company, Naomi had decided to move the family's headquarters from Ponca City down to Oklahoma City. Their new base of operations now lay on the major crossroads of two main highways in the mid-west, I-40 which stretched all the way from Wilmington, North Carolina on the Atlantic coast to Barstow, California, and I-35, which spanned north and south from Laredo, Texas up to the Canadian border.

Naomi brushed lint from her periwinkle cashmere trench coat as she rode in the front seat of her bulletproof Phantom with Flacco sitting behind the wheel. Kimi and Koko was in the rear seat of the car, the both of them sitting quietly with a briefcase resting in their lap as the luxurious vehicle cruised south on I-35 headed into downtown Oklahoma City.

Trailing Naomi's Phantom, in one of the family's black, dark-tinted and bulletproof Suburbans, was Dawk and Martha. Dawk was behind the wheel with Martha on his side. The two of them were headed over to the family's 100,000 square foot warehouse to meet up with Twiggy, Bay and T-top in order to lay out their plans for shipping cocaine while Martha and Twiggy held orientation for the drivers the two had hired over the past several months.

This day was one of the most important days of the Holland family's storied history, and Kimi and Koko were going to be intricate in the big scheme of things. Naomi had caught wind through insider business reports that Tropicana was being squeezed out in Venezuela, so-to-speak, due to high transportation tariffs deriving from the Venezuelan government. Her angle was to offer a deal to the produce company by guaranteeing them a set rate on three thousand acres of land that was owned by Holland-Dawkins Enterprises, an American company that would operate under the laws of the United States of America, thereby off-setting the high tariffs placed on Tropicana by the Venezuelan government. The only problem was the fact that Naomi hadn't secured the land as of yet; but it was a mere bump in the road for the business savvy woman as she'd already given Flacco and his family the job of acquisitioning the needed land as the deal with Tropicana forged on.

"How's everything going on the real estate deal with the orange groves down in Brazil?" Naomi asked thirty-seven year-old Flacco.

"Negotiations are still on-going between the Deveraux family in Sao Paolo. They've placed an offer on the table, Senorita Dawkins," Flacco replied as he sat behind the wheel of Naomi's Phantom. "The price per acre in the city of Boa Vista is now eight thousand dollars per acre for three thousand acres."

"Twenty-four million dollars cash," Koko quickly calculated as she jotted down notes. "That's nearly a third of the family's net worth with no guarantee from the New York Stock Exchange that we would even be able obtain licensing to distribute orange harvests on the international market let alone transport the produce across the Venezuelan border safely. Too big a risk given the finances we would have to put up from the deal's inception."

Flacco countered with, "The Devereaux family guarantees that the appropriate licensing from within the Tropicana Corporation in South America is all but a certainty, Senorita Dawkins. Included in the deal is their supplying us with truck transportation from Boa Vista, Brazil one hundred and seventy miles north into the city of Santa Elena de Uiren."

"That'll spare the family the expense of having to finance transportation, momma," Koko stated as she nodded her head in approval, albeit with slight reluctance over Flacco's given numbers as she had the full rundown on the Deveraux family from a business aspect sitting in her lap.

The Devereauxs were coffee bean dealers who'd emerged onto the NYSE a few years earlier with a public offering of $77 dollars per share based upon on 750,000 shares for a net worth of $57.7 million dollars. The Deverauxs had a gross worth of just over a quarter billion dollars. Big time indeed, but the family's stocks had dwindled from an Initial Public Offering of $77 dollars per share to $53.40 per share, nearly a thirty percent drop from their IPO back in 2005.

Kimi and Koko believed that the offer was a bad deal given the numbers and future speculations. Given those facts, the family now had leverage against the Devereaux family given the depleting stock price shares that were now being offered. The Brazilians were hemorrhaging money and needed an infusion of cash to keep their doors open. The twins had not the final say so in the matter, however; but they continued on breaking down the intricacies of the potential deal at hand.

"The Deveraux family has a long history with the Brazilian government," Kimi related to her mother. "But their power and influence is waning because of budding coffee bean harvests from Africa entering the stock exchange and it has brought about a thirty percent decrease per share nearly and according to speculations, they're facing another double digit downturn. The Deverauxs may be on their way out. Eight thousand per acre is not a good price. A lower offer less than half would be in the family's best interest. Given their current financial situation? The Devereauxs will be willing to discuss lower terms."

"Counter offer for the Devereaux family, Flacco," Naomi declared after hearing Kimi's assessment. "Thirty-five hundred on each acre, for a net total of ten and a half million dollars. We will supply our own trucks and security. On top of that? We'll offer to transport the Devereaux family's coffee beans to Puerto de Dos Bocas for half the tariffs Folgers is offering and ship the product on our own freighters."

"We can supply our own trucks and security, but where will we obtain cargo ships, Senorita Dawkins?" Flacco asked.

"The Asians still control a couple of ships left over from Maruyama's downfall. Those were left off the books. They moved them down to San Francisco and they're just sitting idle now. We can put those ships to work and ship coffee beans to the ports of New Orleans."

"Why not ship the rest of the product with the coffee

beans?" Flacco inquired.

"I'm not sure about New Orleans just yet. Our port of entry will be Laredo via rail initially. Martha has everything set up and ready to go there."

"When Gacha finds out he's been undercut he may not take kindly to it, Senorita Dawkins." Flacco remarked as he exited the highway.

"Gacha has guaranteed delivery from Venezuela to the United States border on *his* product," Naomi countered as her eyes gazed upon downtown Oklahoma City. "We will honor the deal my nephew forged last month on Little Cayman Island on behalf of the family—but I'm not purchasing three thousand acres of land to continue on doing business with Gacha—I'm looking to build a cocoa plant factory for the family when it's all said and done."

"We're going to need numbers on how much revenue will be coming in from Brazil in order to move the money around, momma," Koko remarked. "This is going to be a huge undertaking."

"One step at a time, Koko. No need to worry about that now." Naomi replied. "You and Kimi just focus on Tropicana for now until the deal in Brazil is secured."

Flacco looked over to Naomi. "You think of starting your own cartel," he smiled slyly. "For so long, my family in Mexico has awaited the day that an American family with enough heart and muscle would arrive."

"What is it that keeps you loyal to this family?" Naomi asked as she eyed Flacco.

"I've loved this family from the very first day Doss gave me a job, Senorita Dawkins. Your children were mere babies when I first arrived and I've watched them grew into strong people to be respected," he stated seriously as his eyes drifted nowhere in particular as he drove. "If any American family can move south of the border and set up their own operation it is this family."

Naomi could see the love and pride Flacco carried in his

heart for her family as she watched the twinkle in his reminiscing eyes. The man was, by all accounts, Doss's most trusted man. No one inside the organization, neither she, DeeDee, Mendoza, nor Eddie Cottonwood, had ever known just how close Doss and Flacco were until Doss's death. It was as if her husband had looked years into the future and had foreseen that the family would need a loyal ally with Mexican roots in order to start their own cartel. Whether that was true or not, Naomi could appreciate the fact that she had a trusted man in Flacco Ramirez, a man who would indelibly become more valuable to the family than he could ever imagine.

Naomi smiled to herself as she reflected on Flacco's admiration of her family and Doss's decision to hire the guy early on; but in spite of it all, the question she'd asked warranted more depth of answer. "Outside of family," she said. "What else is there, Flacco?"

Flacco knew Naomi wanted more insight to his reasons, but he was actually being respectful of Kimi and Koko. "Can I speak frankly, Senorita Dawkins? I mean, real frank? In front of your daughters?" he asked.

Naomi crossed her legs, looked straight ahead and said, "Flacco, the four of us will be spending a lot of time together in the upcoming months and years in order to get this business running on all cylinders so it's nothing we can't speak on when in one another's presence."

"Si, Senorita," Flacco replied. "Truth is, for my family? The cartels we've been dealing with in Mexico don't last long. One day the Ramirez family is guarding this cartel, the next day we guard another one because the other family's boss has been taken out. There's no consistency south of the border for us, no?" he admitted. The tall, slender Mexican then pointed to his temple and said, "I always told my cousins that one day, 'one day familia'. I always used to say to them, 'one day a strong, smart family will come along and lead us to paradise'. They laughed at me, Senorita Dawkins, but after the trip to Little Cayman where we supplied the security? And for what we was paid for that detail? They laugh no more."

"If this deal with the Devereaux family goes through,

Flacco," Naomi said as she looked him in the eyes. "If this deal goes through? I will need you and your family to run our operation in Brazil. Are they capable?"

"They are, Senorita Dawkins. My family specializes in cartel security and organized hits south of the border. I've waited so long for this day. You have no idea, Senorita, how long I've waited." Flacco spoke in a serious tone.

Naomi said nothing as she reflected on Flacco Ramirez's background. His family was from the city of Paraiso, in the state of Tabasco, Mexico. Paraiso was located in the southern portion of Mexico and bordered the country of Guatemala to the south and east. The town was just ten miles south of Puerto de Dos Bocas, a major Mexican port sitting on the Gulf of Mexico.

Naomi had plans for Flacco as the state of Tabasco was ripe for growing orange groves, amongst other things, but with the Mexican drug cartels in a constant state of flux and waging battle with one another, and an unstable government coupled with a police force and a military that went to the highest bidder, she dare not place the family in harm's way.

As of now, the safest place to build the family's self-sustaining cocaine empire lay further south in the docile country of Brazil where business could be conducted without interference. The only problem would be transporting the product into Venezuela for shipment—Rafael Gacha's territory —but by then, Naomi was gambling on the fact that the family would be too powerful for Gacha to wage battle let alone win the war—a war in which she knew Flacco and his family was willing to wage should the occasion arise.

"You spoke on paradise," Naomi said to Flacco as he pulled up in front of the Kerr-McGhee Building, which held the offices of Holland-Dawkins Enterprises. "My vision is to see that we all succeed, but remember, Flacco, Jesus promised a dying man that he, too, would be in paradise. A dying man," she reiterated.

"I'm a spiritual man, Senorita Dawkins. "I understand your point fully." Flacco smiled. "Let's not hope we all don't end up on the stake trying to accomplish our goals," he ended before he climbed out of the $400,000 dollar ride and helped Naomi, Kimi and Koko from their seats and escorted them towards the high rise.

The entire ninth floor of the Kerr-McGhee Building was leased by HDE in order for the Holland family to run their business. The structure at 101 Park Avenue, located in the heart of downtown Oklahoma City adjacent to Kerr Park, and directly across the street from Santa Fe Plaza, an old railroad depot that had been converted into a retail center, was a twelve story, steel and glass sqaure configuration that featured vaulted ceilings, black marble columns and white marble floors. The offices were luxurious suites that featured soft brown leather furniture and wood-stained marble top desks.

Naomi was in superb company. The Kerr-McGee Corporation, and Hadson Petroleum, two of HDE's neighboring tenants, were billion dollar companies specializing in oil and pharmaceuticals. Naomi had done her homework on these two companies and was making good headway in the family's corporate law division. She was in talks with the Kerr-McGee company, who'd recently settled an eighteen million dollar law dispute for violating the Clean Air Act, on representation for pending lawsuits filed by the Environmental Protection Agency (EPA) for further violations. She was also scheduled to close the deal on becoming one of several retained lawyers that would assist Hadson Petroleum in acquiring new land for drilling oil in North Africa. In just her first year of opening Holland-Dawkins Enterprises (HDE), Naomi was in a position to make over three-quarters of a million dollars on retainer fees alone. She was truly an ambitious and savvy business woman with a knack for forging new business deals.

"There, Senorita Dawkins," Flacco remarked as he pointed towards a tall, slender Caucasian woman with a prefect tan and a well-toned body wearing a bright orange business suit, brown cashmere coat and brown eel skin stilettos. The older-appearing woman, given her sagging chin, greying brown hair and the wrinkles on the corners of her lips and eyes, was smiling and waving as she held onto a brown eel skin briefcase inside the building's lobby.

Beside the woman stood an elderly-looking, bald Caucasian male decked out in a white and black pin-striped white silk suit and black shoes and he was gripping a black briefcase. "Here they are!" the man quipped as he eyed what was to him a quartet of novices approaching him and his colleague.

Naomi was sizing up the two business professionals as she approached them. The woman she could see herself getting along with without much fanfare as she gave off positive vibes and had a radiant persona.

The man standing beside her, however, left some things to be desired in Naomi's mind as he had a slick appeal about himself given his demeanor. He looked the part of a man of persuasion to Naomi—a man who was only interested in what was best for him and the company he worked for, but so was she for that matter, so the contemptuous feeling the two held towards one another upon their inception was mutual.

"Miss Ernestine Maxwell. Mister Iiayahd (Eyeyaad) Sheinheimer. It's nice to meet you both," Naomi put on as she walked towards the marketing reps. "You know, I would've gladly taken a flight out to California to hold these meetings?"

"Nice to meet you, Misses Dawkins," seventy-seven year-old Ernestine Maxwell responded kindly as she extended a kind hand. "It is me and Iiayad's pleasure to travel here on behalf of Tropicana. We actually wanted to see firsthand the organization you run here. I have to say we're both pleased so far."

"Well, thank you now," Naomi stated politely. "Let us please you even more with our proposal after I introduce my family," she added as she shook the woman's hand extended her hands towards Flacco, Kimi and Koko.

After the introductions were completed, Naomi turned to the rigid man that was accompanying Miss Maxwell. "Iiayad," she nodded while eyeing the man without smiling and never bothering to extend her hand as she walked past him.

"Naomi," Sheinheimer remarked dryly. "Shall we?" he

added as he stepped aside and motioned towards the elevator. Light talk was made about the cold winter weather in Oklahoma as the group rode up to the ninth floor and entered the pristine offices of HDE and took seats at a large, circular, dark-brown marble table to begin negotiations.

Flacco closed the bulletproof steel doors and set the alarm. He took a seat out in the hall with a hot cup of coffee in his hands and a loaded Uzi tucked inside of his wool trench coat while watching the elevators.

****

As the first round of negotiations got underway inside the Kerr-McGhee building, several miles to the west of Oklahoma City, in the town of Valley Brook, Dawk and Martha had just pulled through the security guard shack and rode onto HDE's trucking terminal's property. On their left was a long, two story white stucco and steel building with twenty-three dock doors on the lower level. The dock doors were void of trailers as the family hadn't any freight to haul as of yet, but there was still activity on the two plus acres of land.

A few trucks were going through the detail shop on the far right and some were having amenities placed inside, including CB radios, refrigerators and televisions. The mechanic shop to the far north was teeming with activity as several trailers were having new tires put on.

Reaching the edge of the building's north side, Dawk and Martha came up on Twiggy, who was holding a clipboard as she watched a driver back down in between two cones inside the facility's large asphalt-covered drop yard.

This was not a rag-tag outfit the Holland family was putting together. Serious money was on the line and all federal laws were being adhered to; drivers had to have their blood taken in order to have drug tests run and they also had to pass a physical examination. Moving violations were grounds for immediate disqualification from consideration of hiring and every driver had to pass an extensive background check.

"My girl know she be working her ass off," Martha said to Dawk, letting the window down as the two of them pulled up alongside Twiggy. "Irene, you 'bout done with the road tests?" she asked aloud.

Twiggy turned to Martha and threw her hands up in frustration as she walked over to the Suburban. "Try ta' help folk out and they don't do right, Mar!" she complained.

"What happened?"

"This here dude, young black dude—he just graduated trucking school, right? I told him we might be able to get him on some local stuff being he from OKC. Now, he done went through the entire process, but just laid up there and told me he got a DUI last month!"

"You gone have to let him go, then," Martha stated matter-of-factly.

"He got a forklift license so we might can get him in the warehouse. At least he was honest about it. His background check out and all and he got a li'l girl he tryna look after. I'm just tryna help him out."

"What's his name?" Dawk leaned over and asked.

"Terrence Mays with his plain ass," Twiggy ridiculed.

"You makin' fun of that man name," Martha chuckled.

"I mean, he cool. He just got a old ass name, Mar. What?"

"Irene ain't too up to date either, yeh?" Martha teased.

"Neither is Martha!" Twiggy snapped as she poked out her tongue. "I'm gone put him in the warehouse. But if he get a DUI on one those I'm gonna have to let him go for real," she added as she looked back at the young man with concern.

"Let him sit in on orientation and see how he do for the ninety day probation period. In the meantime, find another driver to hire using the rest of the applications we have. All of 'em checked out so it's your call," Martha stated to Twiggy before she and Dawk pulled off.

****

Inside the massive HDE warehouse, Bay and T-top were riding one of the warehouse's forklifts along the docks. Tiva was behind the wheel and Bena was standing on the two protruding steel forks with her back against the steel grates. Both twins were dressed in identical tight-fitting stonewashed Burberry jean outfits wearing a three-quarter length dark-tan leather Burberry jacket and matching dark tan boots. Dark tan, suede skull caps covered the twins' short jet-black hair as they rode over the premises.

Bay was holding onto a blue print map of the warehouse. Together, she and Tiva were studying the layout and laying out their portion of the family business, which was to oversee the transport of the cocaine from dock to storage on the day of its arrival. From there they would break it down and have it ready to be shipped within an eight hour shift to one of the organization's remixing facilities further east where Dawk would oversee things.

Bay and T-top had at minimum, two hours to break down just under a half of ton of cocaine. Every eight hours, there was a shift change inside the twenty-four hour facility. The twins were going to use the shift change to load the broken down cocaine in order to personally make sure it got done correctly.

They cruised through the freezer, up and down each aisle, getting a feel for their cocaine's first transfer while imaging in their minds the hustle and bustle that would surely dominate the environment once things got up and running in another week or so. The family had hired a dozen forklift operators along with twenty-four warehousemen who pulled orders. Everyone that worked the docks was out-of-loop when it came to the family business of drug smuggling.

Sixty thousand square feet of the building was one giant freezer that would keep a core temperature of thirty-three degrees. Wide aisles with steel shelves on either side stretching midway up to the ceiling allowed for palletized frozen goods to be stored while awaiting transport. The entire building could only be accessed through a key code held by the supervisors, which were Martha, Irene, Dawk, Bay and T-top. Everyone else had to be buzzed in, including drivers and dock workers.

Motion cameras were engaged each and every time a person or object entered an aisle, and every time a freezer was opened, it was electronically logged and videoed. There were five large coolers inside the main freezer to the rear of the building. Naomi, Martha, Irene, Dawk, Bay and T-top were the only ones who knew the access code. Here, the family's cocaine would be stored amid high quality steaks and be broken down for shipment. With confidence that things were in line inside the family's warehouse, Bay and T-top left the main freezer and met up with Dawk and Martha in order to set up the warehouse's break room for the upcoming orientation as newly-hired drivers and dock workers began arriving on the premises.

****

Back inside the Kerr-McGhee building, negotiations were under way. Things were going good for the family right about now albeit it tense. The family had done their homework on Tropicana, but Mister Sheinheimer was a relentless soul. He was constantly searching for a reason to say no to the deal, but each time, he was rebuffed with cold hard facts.

"Three thousand acres of oranges is good for a start-up company, Misses Dawkins," Mister Sheinheimer stated. "But for a company of Tropicana's caliber? It's a very small percentage."

"Let's check the numbers before you jump to a conclusion. You may be surprised, Mister Sheinheimer." Naomi replied in an assured tone of voice.

"Okay, let's do it," Mister Sheinheimer replied. "A typical acre may contain somewhere around one hundred and fifteen orange trees," the man stated as he opened his briefcase and pulled out a calculator. "Say you have an average of forty-five oranges per tree on each of those acres—which is a bushel."

"We're very aware of what constitutes a bushel," Naomi smiled as she poured herself a caramel latte.

"Just making certain," Mister Sheinheimer let it be known. "With three thousand acres, you would have," he paused as he ran the numbers.

Kimi and Koko, meanwhile, fully aware of the numbers,

were running the figures inside their heads right along with Mister Sheinheimer and his handy calculator.

"With three thousand acres you would have just over thirty five thousand orange trees on your grove. A typical tree would yield maybe forty fruit thereby equaling a bushel," the man stated as he clicked away on his calculator. "With thirty-five thousand trees each producing one bushel, you would have a net gross of one point three, closer to one point four million dollars wholesale. You factor in shipping costs from south of the equator? Export tariffs? Stateside taxes on imports of said product? Processing? It may not be cost efficient for Tropicana to do business with such a small grove."

"I think you ran the numbers wrong, Mister Sheinheimer," Kimi interjected.

"Have I? I've been in this business for nearly three decades. My numbers are accurate, young lady."

Kimi had sense enough to know that Mister Sheinheimer was viewing her and Koko as light-weights, but she was prepared to deal with the man in a professional manner. "Hear me out, Mister Sheinheimer," she remarked as she pushed her chair back from the table. "I think you're off by a tenth," she added as she rose from her seat and walked around to the opposite side of the table and stood beside the man.

Kimi picked up Mister Sheinheimer's calculator, cleared it and spoke calmly, "Maybe it's your device, or better yet, your input. A calculator can only compute what you've put into it."

"Show me where I'm wrong," Mister Sheinheimer said as he shrugged his shoulders.

"I will," Kimi replied in a confident tone. "You were right about trees per acreage. But *three thousand* times one fifteen, not times *three hundred*, equals three hundred and forty-five thousand trees, not thirty-five thousand."

Mister Sheinheimer reran the numbers on his calculator and saw that Kimi was correct. "Well, it was just a simple mis—"

"Calculation on your part, Mister Sheinheimer," Kimi finished as she walked back around the table and sat in her seat once more. "Now that we're on the same page and past your attempt to deprave us a fair chance, follow me now, if you will, sir," she requested as she stared the man in the eyes.

"Thirty-five thousand, correction, ladies, *three hundred and forty-five thousand* trees. I follow you, Miss Dawkins."

"At forty dollars a bushel per tree, and with three hundred and forty-five thousand trees sitting on three thousand acres, were talking thirteen point eight million dollars per harvest, not one point three million dollars. With those many bushels? I think Tropicana would lend us an ear," she ended.

Miss Maxwell intervened with, "The numbers are strong. With that amount of capital, Naomi? Your family could negotiate a lower tariff. It'll be beneficial for all involved if the company agrees. I'll put in a good word, but I haven't the final say in the matter because we're talking international commerce here. With that aside, our main point of agreeing to this meeting in the first place was to discuss shipping arrangements from our processing plant down in Bradenton, Florida by unit rail to your facilities here in Oklahoma. Where do we stand on that proposal today?"

Kimi and Koko rose from their seats simultaneously and began going back and forth in their presentation as they stood side by side before the group.

"We're emphasizing and specializing in expedience from rail to market at this point and time. International commerce, although being our ultimate goal, can be set aside for now with a promise of future negotiations based on our initial performance," Kimi stated as she held a pointer to a chart that broke down the family's shipping process.

Koko followed with, "Our hundred thousand square foot warehouse in Valley Brook has sixty thousand square feet of refrigerated space and our docks are able to accommodate five specialized refrigerated rail boxcars. From there, work orders submitted by Tropicana will be processed, sorted by locale and routed throughout the Midwest to grocery-chain warehouses for distribution on our semis."

"What is your company's safety record, Miss Dawkins?"

Miss Maxwell asked as she stirred her coffee. "And you two have my word that we'll discuss further the matter of international commerce at a later date," she told Kimi and Koko.

"And we'll be ready. Thank you for considering," Koko replied as she walked over to her seat and picked up a printed out copy of the family's trucking company's Department of Transportation (DOT) report and handed a copy to Miss Maxwell. It was a short, single page with little wording as the family hadn't had a driver that had so much as gotten a speeding ticket in the nearly twenty years Naomi had been in the trucking business.

Miss Maxwell slid the document to Mister Sheinheimer. "Impressive," she told the man. "Of course you ladies know that hauling for Tropicana requires more than just a safety record that's outstanding. Facilities, damage reports, weather delays. The company pays no per diem on late loads or delays due to weather."

"We'll eat the cost," Kimi stated. "I know freshness is of concern. We have very capable drivers that have flawless track records and our company prides itself on safety as you've seen in our DOT report."

Koko then chimed in. "We know we're an upstart company, Miss Maxwell, Mister Sheinheimer, but we offer the lowest shipping rate of any other trucking company in the Midwest. People here in Oklahoma know our brand," she said confidently as she flipped the page on the stand she stood beside.

A layout of Mary's Produce then came into view. "From this small building in Ponca City, and from this farm on our ranch, comes some of the best onions and tomatoes." Kimi stated. "Mary's Produce is our brand. It is a brand popular with Piggly Wiggly, Kroger, Safeway and Albertson's. Now, I'm not saying Tropicana needs our little ole brand to boost its long established brand?" she quipped, bringing about a slight smile from Miss Maxwell. "But here at Holland Dawkins Enterprises? Tropicana's product will be treated as if it were our own brand. You're in good hands, if I may borrow from All

State Insurance."

Miss Maxwell chuckled slightly. "I like the numbers. And the attitude!" the increasingly-convinced woman stated. "Your daughters know their profession, Naomi," the woman complimented. "If you had a slogan, Naomi? What would your slogan for Holland Dawkins Enterprises be?" she asked off-the-cuff.

Naomi leaned forward in her seat, looked over to Miss Maxwell and Mister Sheinheimer, smiled, and stated bluntly, "We're the coldest in the game."

Kimi and Koko, knowing exactly what their mother meant, were hit with immediate headaches. They held their composures as the meeting room went ear-deafening silent. Their brown eyes focused in on their mother, who was still leaning forward with her elbows on the table while staring at Miss Maxwell and Mister Sheinheimer, who only stared back blankly. Several lingering seconds passed by as the five all eyed one another at random.

Just before the mood grew tense, Miss Maxwell's body began to heave. Her small breasts bounced up and down as she removed her glasses and parted her lips. She rubbed her eyes as she let go with a belly laugh. "I fuckin' love it!" she laughed aloud. "The coldest in the game! It applies to so much when it comes to business! Any business!"

"That it does," Mister Sheinheimer smiled as he stood up from his chair. "Misses Dawkins? Protégés?" the man said as he nodded to Kimi and Koko, who could only sigh in silent relief. "The preliminary deal put forth for four rail cars per week to be shipped to your company's warehouse in Valley Brook for distribution to various grocers has been accepted should we find your warehouse facility up to our standards."

Kimi and Koko, as excited as they were, practically bursting with joy on the inside, remained professional. They walked around the table as their mother stood and shook the hands of Miss Maxwell and Mister Sheinheimer respectively.

"Let's get ready to tour the facilities," Kimi stated proudly as the group entered into a relaxed state.

"We're sure it'll be just a formality," Miss Maxwell remarked as she walked over and shook Naomi's hand, still tickled over her 'The Coldest in the Game' slogan.

HDE's inaugural day would be viewed as a complete success by the family over dinner in downtown Oklahoma City later on that night. Miss Maxwell and Mister Sheinheimer had toured the family's warehouse during the time Twiggy and Martha were conducting orientations and were impressed with the orderliness of their new shippers.

Freight was scheduled to be picked up and delivered the following week, and Tropicana had entered a preliminary deal with HDE to allow them to transport oranges from Brazil to America on their behalf midway through the year. The only thing remaining was for Flacco to secure the land down in Brazil in order for the family to begin harvesting their own oranges and processing cocoa leaves.

With business in order, Kimi and Koko prepared themselves for a trip out to Arizona to collect on their winning bet against Samantha that'd been won on Christmas night concerning Moses and his actions. The twins had in mind to go down and kick it with their cousin before their classes started in just over a week, but what would come out of it, would eventually leave a trail of tragedy unexpected in its wake.

CHAPTER TWENTY

GETTING AWAY

January 6, 2009

The side door of a luxurious snow white 2008 Gulfstream G550 sixteen seat corporate jet slowly opened as the plane rolled to a halt before the rented hangar where Samantha kept the plane parked when not in use. "Welcome to my stomping ground," she smiled as she and Amber emerged from the jet's cockpit.

Kimi and Koko both held on to digital cameras as they filmed their cousin and her co-pilot walking up the aisle towards the exit the day after their meeting. "Show us how you get down in southwest!" Kimi laughed as the four young women began descending the stairs as music began to fill their ears.

Identically dressed in all white leather pant suits and black leather boots and adorned in diamond earrings with wrists glittering under the seventy-one degree sun, Kimi and Koko looked like royalty as they stepped onto the runway and eyed their cousin, Ben, dressed in a pair of black Girbaud's and white t-shirt and fresh white sneakers, standing before a 2009 black and red H-1 Hummer with thirty inch black steel wheels. A muscular Mexican around the same height as Ben, dressed in a grey Dickies outfit and black suede shoes with a black bandanna tied around his head stood beside him.

Victor Felix stood beside Ben watching his boss' family

emerge from the plane. The young Mexican knew Samantha and Amber well, but the two stallions walking on either side of the two holding digital cameras on he and Ben warranted second and third looks. "Yo, Ben? Who that?" he asked.

"That's my people, fam," Ben replied. "They down for a few days to kick it with Samantha, ya' dig?"

"Yeah, yeah—Kimberly and Coo-Coo!"

"That's Kimi and Koko, brer. K-I-M-I and K-O-K-O." Ben corrected through a chuckle as he eyed Victor. "They only here for a few days so don't make no long term plans."

"Nahh, it ain't like that, fam," Victor said seriously as he eyed the twins walking his way. "How many twins in your family, though?" he asked as he rubbed his chin.

"You eyeing my people, boy?" Ben asked as he cut his eyes at Victor.

Victor laughed and said, "Never, dude. I just remember those other two twins we met in OKC and over in Saint Louis after we did that job on them Charles brothers. Kimi and Koko get down like Bay and T-top?"

"Nahh, fam. They all about business from a legitimate standpoint," Ben replied as he stepped up and welcomed Kimi and Koko to his home town with open arms.

"Ben?" Kimi said as she hugged her cousin. "Me and Koko saved our appetites because we wanna go straight to Katrina café and get some more of that gumbo!"

"I already know," Ben laughed as he bumped fists with Samantha and Amber. "She got the whole staff waiting so let's get to it," he ended as the group of six climbed into the Hummer and made their way over to Katrina's downtown café to have lunch.

The New Orleans Café was teeming with business as Ben and company walked around to the front of the restaurant. Through the large windows, they all could see that most of the tables inside the eatery were filled with at least three or four people. Waitresses rushed about with serving trays while bussers cleared vacant tables to prepare them for waiting customers. Ben led his family past the long line of customers standing on the sidewalk and entered the restaurant.

"Unt, unt! Y'all better get back to the end of the line, Ben!" JoAnne Clemmons, the café's manager joked. "How everybody?" she then asked as she grabbed a stack of menus.

"We good, we good," Ben answered. "Katrina around?"

"In the back office," JoAnne answered as Ben eased past her. "Let me get y'all a booth and have her come out while y'all look things over," she told Samantha and company.

Kimi and Koko enjoyed seafood platters and gumbo as they sat and chatted with Katrina and on occasion, JoAnne, who would join in whenever she caught a break. Much of the day was spent over to the Mansion in Mesa with Ben and Henrietta where the family mostly kicked back while talking and cooking dinner and sipping wine.

The following morning, Samantha took Kimi and Koko to Scottsdale Fashion Square, one of the city's most upscale malls that featured all the stores Kimi and Koko loved from Barney's of New York to Tiffany and Co. and Prada. Everything from business suits to suede attaché briefcases and high-heeled shoes were purchased by the twins during their mini shopping spree. Upwards of $12,000 dollars was spent by each twin and they'd dropped another $4,000 dollars on Samantha for new outdoor apparel. The cousins left the mall several hours later with over half the back seat and the trunk of Samantha's Caprice loaded down as they had bought so many items.

"Where're we going now, Samantha?" Koko asked as she slid a fresh pair of $1,000 dollar Gucci shades over her brown eyes and leaned the front seat back.

"Since Henrietta keeping the babies, we going offload these bags at my house and then hit up Ben over to his shop so his crew can put some new tires on the Caprice."

"I'm hungry," Kimi quipped from the backseat as she texted Udelle. *How your day going, love?* "What's a good spot to eat besides Katrina place?" she asked aloud.

"For real, for real," Koko chimed in.

"Y'all two been eating since you stepped off the plane!" Samantha laughed.

"Me and Kimi came down here to have fun, Samantha," Koko responded as she smiled over to Samantha while kicking back in the front passenger seat. "Once classes start and we start heading to the offices in Oklahoma City, we won't see each other until the club open in Saint Louis unless you come to the ranch. It's gone be a busy time the next couple of months or so helpin' our momma get this company up and running."

Just then, Kimi got a text back from Udelle. *I'm good, baby. Chablis came back over to the apartment. He asked about Koko. I told him I didn't know where she was.*

How he acting?

Foul. They let 'em keep his scholarship, but he can't play ball no more and he upset about that walkin round slamming things. I'm going up to Bay condo til u get back. I can't deal with this dude. Call me later up there in the OKC

K, love u

Love u 2, baby.

Kimi laid her phone in her lap and stared out the back passenger side window in deep thought as she crossed her legs. Chablis' return to he and Udelle's dorm apartment was the last thing she wanted to hear on this day, or any other day for that matter. His keeping his scholarship allowed him to have access to the apartment as it was part of his scholarship. With him and Koko being done and over with, she felt it would be awkward spending nights with Udelle inside the apartment he shared with Chablis knowing the guy was on the outs with her twin. She kept quiet on the matter, opting to not tell Koko the news and ruin the trip, while at the same time, deciding that she and Udelle should begin looking for their own place in the upcoming months while they moved into Bay's condo with Koko for the foreseeable future.

Samantha, meanwhile, had pulled up to her neighborhood and entered the code leading into the subdivision and eased through the gate. Kimi and Koko had seen their cousin's home the day before, but they could never grow tired of looking at the Swedish-style split-level home. Samantha had a small stream running across her front lawn that flowed to the back of the house and emptied into a pond filled with Japanese koi fish. There was a wooden bridge near the front door that crossed the stream and several palm trees dotted the land, which had an oasis theme.

Kimi and Koko were eyeing the homes, checking messages and whatnot when the Caprice suddenly lifted up in the front and sped up. The twins looked up and over towards Samantha as she floored the car down her block, their backs pressed against their seats.

"What's wrong with you, Samantha?" Koko asked from the passenger seat as she grabbed the seat belt and clicked it.

"I done told this woman that stay next door to me three times not to let her dog shit in my lawn and he out there again shitting on my lawn!" Samantha snapped as she let her window while approaching her neighbor's home.

Kimi and Koko looked at one another and laughed to themselves. "This should be interesting," Koko remarked as she and Kimi eyed the woman Samantha was referring to as the car swerved to the left.

The mid-fifties woman was standing in her driveway watching her dog, a medium-sized tan Border Collie, do his thing in her neighbor's lawn when what she called 'that gangster family's car' pulled up.

"Eh!" Samantha yelled out to the woman as she sat behind the steering wheel of the Donk. "The fuck I told you about letting that dog take craps on my property?"

"The vulgarity," the woman sighed. "He's a dog for Christ's sake! He doesn't know any better!" the woman reasoned as she stood in her driveway with her arms extended.

"I don't give one good fuck if it was the goose that lay golden eggs! Keep that mutt out my yard! Your old ass know better than ta' let him do what he doing in my yard! Now, I'm a give you today! But this the last day! If I catch that mangy mutt back on my side it'll be the last time he take a shit over there!" Samantha ended as she mashed the gas pedal and sped up into her driveway, which sat off to the left of the cul de sac she'd entered.

Kimi and Koko were laughing to themselves as they climbed from the vehicle and began unloading their bags. They'd never heard Samantha use such language. She was indeed fun to be around. These three cousins had been close since day one. Their bond was instantaneous, having been solidified the time Samantha had walked out of the main entrance of Will Rogers International Airport the day the family had been reunited.

Kimi and Koko began unloading their bags as Samantha ran inside her gate and reemerged with a pooper scoop. "Tired of this!" she snapped as she scooped up the dung and slid it inside a plastic bag.

"Why she do that?" Kimi asked as she carried bags into the house.

"She president of the homeowner's association," Samantha replied as she tied the bag of manure. "She act like she have the right to whatever she wanna do around here."

"Don't they vote on that every year?" Koko asked.

Samantha scratched her forehead in frustration and said, "That heifer won twice. She, she be campaigning like she running for Senator or something 'round here. Garbage can gotta be three feet from the curb! Block letters on all the mailboxes! All deliveries at the main office and picked up by five! I don't even be here at five in the evening sometime! How she know I don't be needing my toys and shit?"

"Toys and shit?" Kimi and Koko asked simultaneously through laughter.

"What? Yeah, what? I gets my freak on, okay?" Samantha chuckled. She then looked over to her neighbor's home and donned a serious look. "I'm gone steal her job is what I'm gonna do. I'm gone run for president of the homeowner's association this upcoming year."

"You 'bout as suburban as they come," Koko laughed.

"Ain't she?" Kimi followed.

Samantha Holland-Mitchell, although an adventurous woman, lived a simple life when it got down to it. She sky-dived and hiked, and flew around with her brother on occasion, but for the most part, she was a suburban wife. Problems that many across the country would never even entertain were big deals in her world: a dog pooping in her yard, she couldn't grow certain plants during certain times of the year. She had to water lawns on odd number days. Samantha was tired of it all —plain and simple— and she was now adamant on changing things in her subdivision.

The only problem with Samantha, however, was the fact that she'd grown up around gangsters. She'd also been in the military, an experience that lended her to over aggression at times. Her thinking was far different from many a civilian and she often operated under her own umbrella. She would indeed run for president of the homeowner's association, but hers would become a crusade to remember for all times given her background once she began campaigning.

****

Once Samantha had removed the dog feces, and after Kimi and Koko had unloaded their shopping bags, the three cousins climbed back into the Caprice and headed over to The House of I.D.E.A.S. in order for Samantha to have new tires placed on her ride.

Ben's detail shop was an immaculate, spacious building that took up half a block just outside of downtown Phoenix on East Buckeye Road on the west side of town near Seventh Street in a highly-congested area that featured several trucking terminals and numerous smaller businesses.

The lounge area inside The House of I.D.E.A.S. was laid out like a bar. It featured four fifty-two inch wall mounted plasma TV's and three plush leather C-sectional sofas. Two pool tables were in the center of the room and Ben and Tre` had even placed a stripper pole in the back corner of the lounge in complete defiance of Katrina's protests.

Ben had never put the stripper pole to use though; it was

more of a prop and a conversation starter. Many well-known people, including football, baseball, and basketball players, rappers, actors and pop stars, often came through to have their rides go through the shop and Ben wanted his high-end customers to feel at ease and loose.

Male customers often dared their girls to get up on the small stage and dance while they looked over rims and described what they wanted done to their rides. A few female reality show stars and pop singers had even danced for Ben and the boys and a few lucky customers that were on hand to witness those events during those times. The lounge was often filled with customers, some famous, some not so famous, just hanging out with their crew and kicking it. Ben didn't mind. Most of the customers that came through always spent plenty of money and often brought in new customers.

The next room over from the lounge was the showroom. Up to four completed cars were always kept on display here; the showroom's huge vestibule window gave a clear view of the newly detailed cars from the street in this area. Today, Ben had a powder blue 1999 Big Body four door Cadillac Deville with 26" chrome Giovanna rims on display beside a black on black 2008 Range Rover on 26" Dub Nasty 6 black chrome wheels. Next to the Range Rover was a 2009 ocean green Porsche Cayenne with chrome 22" Victor Muslanne rims underneath, and next to the Porsche was a tangelo 1975 four door Jaguar with 22" Foose Nitrous Chrome rims and all white interior.

The showroom was a teaser that led into the huge sales room. Here, customers looked through catalogues and wall-mounted photos of the shop's previous work and read over a long list of distinguished customers who'd had whips laced out in the very building in which they were standing. Next to the sales room, through a set of steel double doors, lay the detail shop itself. The work area could hold up to eight cars. Everything was done here, the sound systems and alarms, the painting, and the changing of rims and tires. Ben also had a body repair shop which was in another building beside the detail shop.

Samantha made it over to East Buckeye Road and wheeled

her Caprice around back and parked before one of the open garage doors where several mechanics could be seen up under the hoods of cars while others knelt down beside some of the luxurious vehicles going through transformation. The females exited the car amid the loud whizzing sounds of hydraulic drills and diesel generators powering spray guns as they made their way over to Ben's office.

"Do they have somewhere we can go and eat around here while they change the tires?" Koko asked as the females bypassed the shop's floor and entered the sales room.

"We'll see. Let me check in with Ben first," Samantha replied as the cousins covered their noses to ward off the pungent smell of paint.

Back out on the shop's floor, Lee Sato was overseeing a paint job being placed on a 2009 four door Bentley Flying Continental Spur valued at $175,000 dollars. He'd just signed for a shipment of tires and was reading the packing slip when he walked into the work area. His eyes widened upon seeing what he perceived to be a major mistake being made by one of the workers. "Yo!" he exclaimed as he threw the clipboard down and rushed over to the Bentley Spur. "What the fuck color is this?" he asked in dismay as he unplugged the generator powering the spray gun.

The guy kneeling down beside the four door Bentley removed his face mask and said, "Turquoise blue! Just like it called for, Lee!"

"No, man!" Lee corrected loudly. "This the Bentley Spur! Turquoise blue was for the two door Bentley Continental GT and *navy blue* was for the four door right here! Eh, who the fuck loaded the paint guns this morning?" he asked aloud as he looked around.

"Ya' man, Victor!" another worker yelled aloud as he ceased painting the two door Rolls he was kneeling before.

"Hold everything in the paint shop! No more painting right now! Tire man? Take that Caprice out back and pull it in and change out the tires!" Lee ordered as he walked into the main building, heading towards Ben's office.

****

"My rich cousins bought me some new canyon equipment and flying gear, brother," Samantha joked with Ben as he sat behind his desk inside his office.

"You takin' Kimi and Koko skydiving and hiking, Samantha?" Ben chided. "'Cause I damn sure ain't doing none of that there with ya' ass ever again."

"If they got a buffet on the plane or the hiking trail we can go right now," Koko stated as she and Kimi giggled.

"I don't know about hiking and skydiving, brother, but they may be willing to sign up for the mile high club with their respective men someday." Samantha replied through a smile as she sat atop the pool table and swung her legs.

"Kimi maybe. Not me," Koko sighed as she rolled her eyes. "I have no love life."

Just then, the double door to Ben's office was pushed open. "Where he at? Where's Victor?" Lee asked sternly as he walked up to his boss's desk.

"What's the problem?" Victor asked as he turned and looked back at Lee.

"You loaded the wrong guns this mornin', man! The paint jobs got mixed up and it's gone cost thousands on a delay because the cars won't ship on time!"

"The Bentleys?" Vic asked surprised.

"Yeah! The Continental GT was supposed to get the turquoise blue and the Flying Spur ordered the navy blue!"

Victor looked over to Ben and the two burst into laughter. "He must've ate some bad pussy last night, boss," Victor joked as Samantha, Kimi and Koko chuckled. "Oh snap!" Victor quickly followed when he remembered the females were in the office. "My fault, fam. But this dude here be like half-right sometimes," he sighed as he leaned back in his chair and shook his head.

"Check the work order, dude! You wrong this time!" Lee retorted as he approached Ben's desk.

"He gone learn us Mexicans be up on our shit, Boss," Victor sighed as he grabbed his work order off Ben's desk and handed it to Lee without making eye contact.

"Always fuckin' up!" Lee complained as he snatched the clipboard from Victor and read the work order. "Bentley Flying Spur, metallic turquoise blue. Continental GT Bentley, navy blue with six clear coats. Gee, dude!" he laughed as he slapped the clipboard in the palm of hands.

"What you gotta say now, mutherfucka?" Victor chuckled as he looked over to Lee while rubbing his stubble beard.

Lee stood dumbfounded for a few seconds, realizing his mistake. "Umm, well, it's lunch time for the fellas," he remarked as he checked his watch. "I'll let the crew go eat. I'm going get some hot wings from up the block, though. Anybody want something?"

"Yes!" Kimi and Koko replied simultaneously.

Lee eyed the twins standing before him and subconsciously licked his lips. He knew of Bay and T-top and had never forgotten the twins he'd met in Oklahoma City as he'd actually had a thing for one of them back then. What stood before him on this day, however, was beauty personified—two voluptuous caramel-skinned sisters with flowing brown hair and dreamy brown eyes with distinguishable birthmarks under their left eye. "The wing shop within walking distance," he said in a polite manner as he eyed Ben's cousins. "I'll be glad to take y'all over there. My treat?"

Kimi and Koko were tickled by this young Asian. He was cute and all with his slender physique, standing around six feet or so with spiked jet-black hair. His eyes were dark and mysterious, naturally slanted given his race, yet sexy and alluring at the same time. The platinum and diamond grill he sported made his mouth look heavy. One would think he would have a hard time talking given the precious stones that coated his teeth, but he spoke with rapid ease.

"You just gone act like what just happened didn't happen, huh?" Ben asked as she shook his head while smiling, knowingly stirring Kimi and Koko from their subconscious trance.

"My bad, Boss," Lee remarked as he extended his hands towards the office's exit. "I'll paint both cars when I get back to make it up to ya', Victor. Right now? I'm going cater to the family," he ended as he eased out the door behind Kimi and Koko, leaving Ben, Samantha and Victor behind to play a game of pool.

CHAPTER TWENTY-ONE

SIMPLY BEAUTIFUL

"How long y'all ladies down here for?" Lee asked as he walked in between Kimi and Koko, the three of them headed west.

"Another four days or so," Kimi replied as she and her twin eyed the sights and sounds lining East Buckeye Road leading to the wing shack.

"You two gone have to let me take y'all out on the town. I know this city like the back of my hand. All the hot spots."

"We supposed to be going out to Myst night club tonight with Samantha," Koko remarked.

"Cool. Mind if I meet y'all there and buy you two beauties a round of drinks?"

"I wonder if Udelle made it up to the condo back home," Kimi said aloud as she went into her purse and grabbed her cellphone.

Lee laughed and said, "You tryna let me know you got a ole man or somethin', Kimi?"

"Yep!" Kimi snapped through a friendly smile.

"What about you, Koko?" Lee asked as the three approached the busy Seventh Street and East Buckeye Road intersection.

"Nope! And ain't lookin' for one either," Koko stated as she pressed a button to hurry the cross signal.

"I'm a mind-changer, yeah?" Lee smiled. "Everybody needs somebody in this crazy world."

"Maybe so, but it's too much heartache and pain dealing with men." Koko replied as the light changed.

"Dealing with the wrong men can bring about that attitude, but all of us aren't the same." Lee said as he stepped off the curb behind the twins. "See, you can't give up 'cause times are hard, Koko. It's just that old devil tryna tear you apart. Say devil? You ain't got nothing here and show no fear when it comes to getting that man you—"

"I know you're not reciting Betty Wright song No Pain No Gain," Koko interjected as she laughed aloud while staring back at Lee.

"Oh you know that one?" Lee smiled brightly, flashing his platinum grill.

"Yes I do. Me and my sister love old school music. Surprised you know about that there, boy. Thought you'd be into Metallica or AC/DC or something."

"Why? Because I'm Asian?"

"Yep!" Koko replied with a sly smile. "You just earned yourself some cool points, though," she added as she leaned into to Koko and whispered into her ear.

Lee smiled to himself as he looked to the ground while trailing the twins with his hands tucked behind his back. His eyes couldn't help but to glide up to their rear ends. The all-in-one off-white suede dresses they wore hugged their hips and exposed their smooth, shapely calves, and their wide, shapely derrieres seemed to be moving in slow-motion as their cheeks bounced up and down with each stride of the black, leather three-inch-heeled stilettoes adorning their feet. Both females had a sweet aroma flowing in the air that was all-so intoxicating to Lee.

Smitten wouldn't be a strong enough word to describe the emotions flowing through Lee Sato as he eyed the twins from behind. Kimi was taken, but Koko was available, he now knew. He found himself wanting to know more about the woman walking a few paces ahead of him, and for the first time in his life, he found himself with sweaty palms.

"Here's the place," Lee said as the three walked under a green and white canopy attached to a single story white-stone building.

"This place?" Kimi asked as she eyed the small structure. "We didn't even smell no food cooking."

"They cook to order, Kimi." Lee replied. "They usually a little slow on weekdays when it's early, too," he added as he stepped up and held the door open for the twins.

A female of cashier of Jamaican descent greeted the three as they walked up to the wooden counter and began eyeing the overhead menu behind the counter. "Lee? One isn't enough, no?" the dark-brown-skinned woman with long, thick brownish-grey dreads smiled.

"We're not together," Lee replied. "At least not yet," he added as he eyed Koko, who could only blush in return.

"What ya' want?" the cashier laughed.

"Let my friend Kimi here get the medium hot lemon pepper wings and for Koko? She would like to have the triple spicy garlic wings with extra sauce. Fries, garlic toast and drinks with both and make it for here," Lee remarked as Kimi and Koko eyed him with surprised expressions.

"How you know what I want?" Kimi asked curiously. "You don't have to order for me, man."

"Trust me," Lee smiled. "If you don't like my selection? I'll get you whatever you want on the menu."

"I'm fine with my order, Miss," Koko chimed in as she walked over to a booth near the front window.

The cashier looked over to Kimi, who threw her arms up. "Whatever, can I have a cup for a drink, Miss?"

Lee smiled at Kimi as he walked off and joined Koko, sliding into one of the chairs before the booth. "What's wrong with your sister, Koko? She stuck up or something?" he asked.

"Nah, man. She just don't get too friendly with other men outside her man Udelle so they won't get the wrong impression. She in love and talking marriage."

"I see. How you get single? You just as beautiful."

"I'm really not single, just taking a break from my current relationship more or less."

"Y'all serious?"

"Could be, but not if I don't want us to be serious." Koko stated dejectedly as she gazed out the window at the flowing traffic.

"You in the give-me-time-to-think-about-it stage," Lee chuckled as he leaned back in his chair and crossed his legs.

"You think you know women, huh?" Koko asked through a smile, vibing with Lee on a friendly level while finding him rather intriguing.

"I know some things." Lee admitted. "But it's much more I have to learn about the beautiful ones worthy of a good man."

"You have to be a good man to get a good woman."

"Good women like the bad boys."

"So you a bad boy? You get down like my cousin Ben?"

"What if I said yes?"

"I would say just—" Koko went silent as Kimi approached the table with her soda.

"Now it's starting to smell like a kitchen in here with them wings going," Kimi said as she slid into the booth beside Koko. "These wings better be good, Lee," she added as she removed her purse.

"You'll love them bad boys," Lee said as he smiled over to Koko.

****

"For real," Lee laughed. "I say to this guy, 'I didn't order raw sushi! I ordered cooked shrimp wrapped in seaweed.' And for the second time, he laid up there and called me Wang

Chung! 'Wang Chung say he want cooked shrimp in seaweed!' He called back. To this day I fuckin' hate Wang Chung!"

Kimi and Koko were both laughing lowly as they ate their hot wings while listening to Lee describe the day he received a citation for disorderly conduct after being disrespected by a Japanese chef with poor customer service when he first touched down in Phoenix. The ice had been broken between him and Kimi, something he knew was key to him getting closer to Koko. The females were pleased with the food, enjoyed the conversation and had invited him to join them later on that night when the girls all went out.

****

"...If you with a girl...get it poppin'...roll with me...ain't no stoppin'...so get it shawty...we parking lot pimping in my dorm...she want that lovey dovey...that kiss kiss...in her mind she fantasize 'bout(getting with me)...they hatin' on me...they wanna diss diss...'cause she mine and so fine...)* The dance floor inside Myst night club was filled to capacity as a host Dee-Jay spun records. Chris Brown and T-Pain's hit song *Kiss Kiss* filled the ears of all inside the darkened club as spotlights of various colors rained down on the massive dance floor.

Koko and Lee had been in their own little world ever since Lee's arrival an hour earlier. Koko hadn't really awakened until the slender, debonair young man walked into the club and found her, Kimi, Samantha and Amber's V.I.P. booth. He'd approached with two bottles of champagne and poured the ladies a drink as he and Koko began to converse.

Samantha and company had quickly noticed the spark emerging between Lee and Koko as the two were solely into one another, talking it up and laughing aloud while subconsciously rubbing one another and gazing into each other's eyes.

For Koko Dawkins, Lee Sato was a stress reliever. He was fun to be around and always made her laugh. He got along with everybody, and Samantha and Kimi had nothing bad to say about the guy, actions that only spurred her on and made her more receptive to his subtle hints at the two of them maybe blowing the club to spend time alone. The two had shared several dances as Lee showed off his skills proudly by holding down his and Koko's area.

Lee had even caused a small crowd to surround him and Koko as the two blended perfectly to the music. This was the most fun Koko had had in such a while. Chablis was never this entertaining. He had to be hard at all times, rarely being spontaneous and often stopping her from having any fun. To dance with another man was a definite no-no whenever the two went out, which was a rare occasion, even though Koko loved to just go out and have a drink and a dance or two. The song ended and Lee led Koko off the dance floor back to the V.I.P. booth amid the hoot, hollers and claps of fellow patrons.

"What that boy about, Samantha?" Kimi asked over the music as she eyed her twin walking back to booth with Lee leading the way.

"Lee cool, Kimi." Samantha said as she poured glasses of champagne for her and Amber. "He got a few women he deal with, but nothing serious."

"So he a player." Kimi said as she sipped her champagne.

"Somewhat, but I think he could be faithful."

Kimi looked over to Samantha and said, "Well, if he do that, he might get his feelings hurt. Koko ain't looking for nothing serious."

"Don't have to be serious, girl," Amber chimed in. "Sometimes a woman just want that one man she can call on to make her feel special."

"And Lee can definitely do that," Samantha replied through a smile as Amber looked her up and down with a dead stare.

"Hold up," Samantha said as she waved her hands. "Trust me? That ain't and won't ever happen, Amber? Lee? You just have to be around him enough to know how much he talk about his sexual conquests. He knows how to treat a woman, though. And if Koko only out for a good time then she picked the right one is all I'm sayin'."

"Why Amber checkin' for you like that, Samantha?" Kimi

asked through raised eyebrows.

"What?" Samantha smiled as she leaned into Amber while staring back at Koko as she leaned up and pecked Amber's chin.

"Lord," Kimi sang as she crossed her legs and reached for the champagne bottle. "Tre` know 'bout y'all two?" she asked as she topped off her glass.

"Been tryna put him on but he not takin' the hints. I wanna make a video with us three just one time so we can save it and look back on it when we get old," Samantha admitted.

"We got a female Walee in the family!" Kimi laughed.

Samantha tapped Kimi's arm, smiled and said, "I asked Tre` what his fantasy was not too long after we got married and he told me a threesome with another woman. He know about me and Trudy and all, but I know he was just talkin' out the side of his neck that night because he don't think it'll ever happen, but I want the same fantasy."

"Udelle better not *ever!*" Kimi avowed loudly as she tapped the table. "Samantha, I am shocked and appalled!" she then said in a royal manner.

"Really," Samantha asked anxiously as she eased off of Amber. "Kimi, I'm sorry. I just thought I could share this with you."

"Girl, I have a sister that's married to a woman," Kimi snickered. "You in the no judgement zone, cousin. At least you tryna bring your man in on your thing. What you gone do if Tre` ain't with it, though? Some men don't like sharing at all."

"Not my husband. When the light clicks on in his head? The one on his neck? He'll get into the groove."

"You know best, Samantha," Kimi answered as she eyed Lee and Koko walking towards the table.

"Keep quiet on that with the family, though." Samantha quickly added.

Kimi took her fingers and made a zipping motion across her lips as Koko and Lee flopped down in the booth out of breath.

"We, we fixing to go and get something eat y'all," Koko said through elated gasps of breaths. "What y'all finna do?"

Samantha, Kimi and Amber smiled at one another like, *'Whaaaat?'*

"Since we're not invited to a late night dinner with y'all I guess we'll stay here and get drunk and catch us a limousine ride back home," Samantha chuckled.

"You okay with me taking off with your sister, Kimi?" Lee asked with a hoping spirit.

Kimi eyed Lee, her eyes scanning him up and down briefly as she curled her lips. "I don't know," she dragged.

Koko, at the same time, sat beside Lee eyeing her sister anxiously, wanting her approval, as Kimi's word meant the world to her. She wouldn't dare leave with Lee unless her sister gave the okay. "Come on, Kimi. Don't be like that," she pleaded.

Kimi and Koko's relationship was truly that of a big sister looking out for the younger sister as if they were years apart. The oldest twin by mere minutes had the power to shut her sister down completely on any given matter if she wanted to. Kimi was by no means a hater, however; and if anybody deserved to just let her hair down, it was her twin given all she'd been through with Chablis. This was the happiest Kimi had seen her twin in a long time. She'd gotten the low down on Lee from Samantha and Amber as all she'd done was ask questions about the guy the entire time she sat inside the booth while texting Ben back and forth concerning the matter.

The look in Koko's eyes, that of, *'just for tonight'*, was a look Kimi couldn't refuse even if she'd wanted to. Lee was Ben's boy; he could be trusted to a certain extent was something Kimi felt to be true. Ben even knew about the attraction the two had towards one another and had no problems with it. Going off of Samantha's giddiness, and Ben's assessment of the situation via text, Kimi nodded as she went into her purse and picked up her phone. "It'll be on all night, Koko," she smiled. "Lee? Take care my sister."

"If she with me?" Lee said as he pointed to himself. "If she with me she gone be taken care of like the secret service guard the first lady," he said confidently as he stood from the booth and held his hand out to assist Koko.

"This here trip? Is a trip!" Kimi laughed. "All y'all wild," she added as she popped another bottle of champagne and topped of Amber and Samantha's glasses.

****

The wing shop over on East Buckeye Road had a crowd of people hanging out front and the inside was filled with patrons as Lee pulled up in front of the building in his yellow Nissan 350ZX with the sunroof open and Koko at his side. "Lee," she groaned as she eyed all the people out on the sidewalk. "We gone be here a while waiting on some food, man."

"Not even," Lee retorted as he climbed out of the car and walked around and opened the door for Koko and escorted her towards the curb.

"How you say that? And why you leaving your car running?" Koko asked as she looked back at Lee's idling car that was double parked.

"Yo, Lee?" "My dude, what's happenin', player?" "Big Dog on set!" several young men called out at random as Lee made his way towards the sidewalk, leading Koko by the hand.

The crowd of people parted as Lee stepped up onto the curb and dapped a few people he knew right off the back. The door was held open for him as he and Koko walked inside the crowded building where loud conversations were being held as customers waited on orders.

"A lot of people know me around here!" Lee spoke loudly into Koko's ear over the crowd's noise. "And trust me, a lot of people know who that car belongs to and wouldn't dare fuck with it!"

Being with Lee offered Koko a sense of security. She felt comfortable around the guy, adored his style, and respected the reverence that he was given on the streets. Everyone spoke to him and treated him kindly, allowing him to make his way up to the front counter where he was quickly handed two orders of wings and two sodas as he slid the cashier a hundred dollar bill. The two vacated the area and jumped onto I-10 headed west.

Koko had eaten some of her food as she and Lee conversed during their ride. Forty minutes in, the Asian exited off the highway. Koko was wiping her hands with a couple of wet towels as she began to take notice of her surroundings. There wasn't a street light or man-made structure in sight she'd observed. Lee had taken an exit onto a road that seemed to be in the middle of nowhere out in the desert. "Where are we?" she asked in an apprehensive manner.

"Scared?" Lee chuckled as he made a left turn and crossed under the interstate and rode across land that was high, hilly and rocky.

Koko didn't know what to expect. Silhouettes of eight foot tall cacti were on either side of the road and countless stars lit up the sky to the south and west. Wind poured in through the sunroof of the car, sending her hair whipping about her face as Lee shifted the gears and sped up, the car zooming over hills and around sharp curves.

Koko was beginning to wonder where Lee was taking her. "Where the hell we at, man?" she asked aloud as she unbuckled her seat belt.

"Don't be nervous," Lee stated as he smiled over to Koko.

"I wanna know where we're going!"

"Me too," Lee replied as he slowed the car and grabbed Koko's hand. "Ben showed me this place some time ago. He say whenever him and Katrina have a lover's spat or something? They would always meet up over here after dark and make up. He said this place is like a natural aphrodisiac or something."

"I, I don't think this is a good idea, Lee."

"If you think I'm going to hurt you," Lee said as he went into his back waistband and pulled out a .380 pistol. "Here's something to protect you."

Kimi knew guns. She reached down and picked the gun up, racked it, and fired a round off into the desert through the sunroof to make sure it was actually loaded before she and aimed it at Lee's right side.

The car swerved to the left at that moment. "The fuck you doing! That's a loaded pistol, Koko!" Lee snapped.

Koko merely chuckled at Lee. If he was acting, then he was damn good. The metal slingshot had a way of getting one's mind right and she knew the real thing when she saw it. She'd frightened Lee and she herself now felt as if the two were now on an even playing field. "You're trying to seduce me," she said to Lee as she lowered the gun and crossed her legs while staring the man in the eyes.

Lee ran his hands through his hair as he looked straight ahead. Never in his life had he'd done such a thing; but he knew he'd been loyal to Ben and his family and they had no reason to harm him. He was only trying to make Koko, a woman he was crushing on, feel at ease as he had no intentions of harming her whatsoever.

"Seduce you? Yes. Harm you? Never," Lee said as he looked over to Koko. "Never have I allowed a woman to touch any weapon I own. I only want to show you something beautiful, like yourself. Can I do that?"

"I suppose," Koko answered sweetly as she chuckled slightly. "Sorry if I made you afraid. You took me off in the middle of nowhere without warning."

Lee widened his eyes as he sat up in his seat and cupped the steering wheel. "We was riding for like forty miles!" he snapped. "You think of that now?" he added as he shook his head.

"You have a charming way about yourself, man," Koko responded softly as she smiled over to Lee, still holding onto the gun.

"Was it my dance skills back at the club? Nah, it was the wings wasn't it? Those, them wings is what got you. You a woman that love to eat. I love to eat too, and I'm being subjective," Lee stated as he nodded his head while pointing towards the windshield.

Koko let a goofy snort rip from her nostrils and quickly grew embarrassed. "Oh my God," she sighed as she covered her lower face and eyed Lee. "That was gross, man. I'm, I'm sorry."

Lee laid his head back and laughed to himself as he neared the entrance to Ben and Katrina's secret spot. This young woman he loved everything about. She was a good-hearted person who loved to laugh and have fun. She had some gangster in her, and could be a little goofy at times, but those contrasting characteristics made her all-the-more adorable. She was a woman Lee could see himself loving and protecting as she held many of the qualities he was looking for in a potential love interest.

Thoughts of a future with Koko flooded Lee's mind as he rode up to the entrance leading to the secret spot, which was on his left tucked in between two tall, rocky hills. He hadn't been to the area all but one time, and last he remembered, the place had free access. As he pulled up to the entrance, on this night, however, he noticed a chain draped across the road with a No Trespassing sign hanging from the steel rope.

"Aww no! What the hell is this!" Lee scoffed as he climbed out of his Nissan and trotted over to the barricade.

Koko watched as her new man friend walked back over to the rear of his car and opened the trunk. He reappeared on the driver's side, his lanky body skipping over to the gate as he clutched a small mallet. The wonder-filled female watched as Lee made his way over to the chain and pounded the post repeatedly until the link fell to the ground. After knocking the chain loose on the other side, Lee casually walked back to the rear of his car and set the mallet down, the car vibrated slightly as he slammed the trunk before climbing back into the driver's seat.

"Are we gonna be okay back here?" Koko asked as Lee pulled forward.

"I don't know," Lee shrugged casually. "But no little chain is going to stop me from showing you what I want to show you, Koko."

There wasn't much to it really, but Koko imagined her and Lee traveling into an unknown place of uncertainty and great risk. She admired his cavalier attitude at that moment as the car crept over the rocky road bordered by steep, rocky hills on either side. After a mile or so of creeping uphill through the small canyon, a small opening appeared on the horizon under the dark sky. The hue of a bright, white light came into view and Koko eased up into her seat to get a better view as Lee drove up to the crest of the hill.

Koko watched in wonderment as Lee exited the car, walked around, opened her door and helped her from the ride. "Close your eyes for me, Koko," he requested as he helped her to her feet.

Koko closed her eyes as Lee led her by the hand. Last she'd seen was the edge of a cliff and she knew she was being guided in that direction. Her heart began to pound with each step she took as she knew not how close she was to the cliff's edge. "What are you doing?" she asked while being guided forward.

When Lee eased behind her and placed his hands on her waist and said, "Keep your eyes closed," Koko grew tense. She could sense the vastness of the valley below as the wind picked up, sending her long brown hair into a whirlwind as she sensed herself nearing the cliff's edge. Her heart pounding against her chest, but the mystery of it all was intoxicating to her. Knowing she could easily be pushed off a cliff ran through her mind, but the senseless why of such an act led her to believe she was on the verge of having a greater surprise. One far sweeter than being murdered by a man she'd met only hours earlier.

"*'Cause you are my sister...my strength and my pride...only God knows why...*" Brandy, Gladys Knight, Tamia and Chaka Kahn's voices erupted in the air as their vocals to the song *Missing You* played over Koko's ringtone, letting her know Kimi was calling to check on her.

At that moment, Lee lowered Koko's hands. "What you

think?" he asked over Koko's ringtone as he hugged her from behind.

Koko's eyes hung low and she licked her lips as her eyes gazed upon the entirety of the city of Phoenix. From over thirty miles away, the downtown area could be seen. An array of colors on the spectrum was on display under the star-lit sky and it felt as if the world was at her fingertips.

Koko now found herself standing at the edge of a steep cliff eyeing a perfect sculpture of human ingenuity set against the backdrop of God's heavenly creations. "It's beautiful, Lee," she remarked in amazement over one of the most beautiful sights her eyes had ever witnessed.

Lee had been touching Koko in intimate manner for a while now. He knew at this stage of their rapport that he could do just about anything he wanted to do as he stood behind her; but this was no mere sexual conquest for Lee Sato. The manner in which he wanted to be with this particular young woman was prompting him to be courteous and careful with what he perceived as that of a delicate woman worthy of respect. To ask for the things he knew he need not ask set right with him, made him feel like the descent man he was capable of being when confronted with what he could only describe to himself as 'the one'.

Lee moved his hand around the front side of Koko's midsection, gently nudging her around. "At this moment, and forgive me if I'm out of order here, Koko—but I want nothing more to than to hold you tight in my arms and just, to just kiss you. Can I?"

Koko bothered not to answer as she wrapped her arms around Lee's back. She closed her eyes and leaned into him. Lee reached up and cupped Koko's tender jawline in his hands as he leaned his head forward. The emotions that had emerged from their first kiss were so intense, immediate and deep, that the tips of their extremities tingled briefly. Lee became immediately aroused and Koko moistened between her thighs as their tongues intertwined. Heavy breathing ensued as the two new lovers stood on the edge of the cliff wrapped in one another's arms and experiencing heavenly bliss.

"You wanna go to my place?" Lee asked a minute or so later, having come up for air.

"Take me," Koko responded through closed eyes as she held onto Lee and planted her head in his chest as her arms held him close.

"Come on then," Lee said in a seductive manner as he grabbed Koko's hand and led her back to his car.

I'm okay. Spending the night with Lee. Koko texted Kimi as she and Lee left the secret spot.

LOL! Love you, sis! Have fun! See you tomorrow. Kimi texted back several seconds later.

****

The Orpheum Lofts, located on Adams Street in downtown Phoenix was where Lee Sato laid his head. His eleven hundred square foot one bedroom two bath $300,000 dollar condo, which featured a master chef's kitchen, had been erected in the 1930s. Some of the original brick still remained, exposed and inculcated into the newly-renovated condo's art deco. Lacquered wood floors inside the condo of this gated community served to enhance the architectural design that was based on sharp, ninety-degree angles.

Koko was in appreciation of Lee's living quarters at first sight. Unbeknownst to her, she was the first female ever to grace his domain besides his mother. The only other woman Lee had ever even considered bringing into his home was a woman he'd had to kill after she'd tried to set him to get robbed out of a kilogram of cocaine. Koko, however, was his boss's cousin. She would pose no threat; and Lee had already made up his mind that if things didn't work out between him and Koko, he would let her go on with her life, if only to keep the peace between him and Ben, the man he was loyal to; but on the flip side, if he and Koko were to hit it off, how much more so would he gain favor with the family and show his loyalty was his reasoning.

Lee wasn't dealing with Koko in order to earn brownie points with Ben. To the contrary, she was a woman who'd simply captured his heart upon first sight. The need to protect and adore her was his driving force. For all the wrong he'd done in life, and may have to do in the future given his occupation, Koko Dawkins gave Lee Sato life. A newfound something to live for—if only she would accept him for the man he was.

"You care for a drink or something?" Lee asked as he clicked on the low-hanging lights above his island counter.

"A glass of wine would be okay," Koko responded as she walked over and sat at the counter before Lee and watched him move about in the kitchen.

"I got a bottle of Chablis but that shit there fake," Lee chuckled as he pulled a bottle of vintage merlot from his chilled wine rack.

"You might be right," Koko smiled, knowing Lee was referencing her ex.

Lee grabbed two glasses, uncorked the wine and poured. "I just want you to know I don't expect nothing to happen tonight," he stated as he raised the glass. "A toast to a beautiful, classy woman," he said.

"And to an interesting man," Koko followed as the two touched rims.

Lee walked out into his living room and picked up a remote control and turned on his surround sound. The smooth sounds of Johnny Gill's song *There You Go* came over the speakers.

"I haven't heard that song in so long," Koko stated as she rocked slightly in her seat.

"Care to dance?" Lee asked as he walked over and extended a hand.

Koko set her glass down and accepted the offer. She was led to the center of the floor and immediately wrapped up in Lee's arms. The two danced together in perfect rhythm. Before long, they were kissing passionately in the center of the room.

By all measures, Lee was making strides with his newfound love from Oklahoma. Thirty minutes after entering his condo found him and Koko taking a steaming hot shower as a soft, soulful voice crept over the waterproof speakers lining the shower's ceiling...

"...If I gave you my love...I tell you what I'd do...I'd expect a whole lot of love outta you...umm hmmm....you gotta be good to me...I'm gonna be good to you...there's a whole lot of things you and I could do..."

Queen Latifah and Al Green's song titled *Simply Beautiful* dominated the stall. Steam rose up from the shower's marble floor as water cascaded down on the two's naked flesh. Standing behind Koko was something Lee could never grow tired of, despite its newness. She and Kimi both had a few love handles, but it did nothing to detract their beauty given the manner in which they carried themselves; not to mention they had curves in all the right places and looks that would crush many a woman weighing pounds less than their one hundred and sixty-five pounds.

Koko had the type of build that allowed Lee full access to all of her intimate parts. They'd been playing in the shower while enjoying Queen Latifah's *The Dana Owens Album*. One sight Lee would never forget was when Koko rested her back against the marble tile of the shower and raised her leg and planted it against the wall while smiling at him seductively where she asked him, *"What are you doing to me?"* just before she bit her bottom lip and looked him in the eyes.

Koko's body, her entire being, was one of perfect sculpture to Lee. Her spirit compensated for what many a shallow person would view as a physical flaw given her being slightly overweight; but in Lee's eyes, he couldn't picture Koko Dawkins no different than what his eyes were witnessing.

Right there, in the shower, under the streams of hot water, Lee leaned into Koko and kissed her neck. He worked his way down to her shoulder blades, slowly flicking his tongue down in between her erect, dark brown nipples, tweaking and sucking on each one repetitiously as he palmed her rear end with one hand and massaged her clitoris with his other hand. Chablis used to do it, but Lee's lips on Koko's midsection, the part of her body she felt she needed to tone up, made her feel as if his actions were genuine and not just token service given before he went further south and did what he really wanted to do to her. It was the attentiveness Lee gave to Koko's body in areas where she felt insecure that forced her to let go of a moan of appreciativeness. "Lee," she called out as the man's tongue flickered over her soft midsection.

Firm hands on the inner side of her thighs forced Koko to spread her legs open in anticipation as she slid a ways down the shower's marble wall, the cascading water matting her hair to her head as she placed a fingertip in between her teeth and tentatively palmed the back of Lee's jet-black matted head of hair. "Can I?" she asked as she stared down at her lover.

"Where you want me, baby?" Lee asked as he placed his other hand around Koko's backside, both his hands now palming her soft rear end.

Over the sensual sounds of Queen Latifah and Al Green, Koko Dawkins guided the second lover in her young life's head to her clitoris. She could only lean her head back against the shower's wall as Lee's warm tongue connected with her center of pleasure. Desire forced her turn her head to the side as she gripped Lee's head tighter and pulled his skull deeper into her fleshy thighs as her jaw slowly lowered. "Oh my," she moaned over the sensation of her lover's sharp tongue massaging her bud. "Do it, Lee," she groaned in ecstasy.

Lee pulled Koko closer to his face, pressing her pussy against his lips as his tongue lay firmly planted on her clitoris. Koko's eyes widened, water streaming down into her eyes as stupefied tears of pleasure incomparable to any other sensation took over her body. She had to place a hand on the shower's ledge to sturdy herself as she began to thrust her hips forward, gapping her legs wide to allow Lee's probing tongue full access to her opening.

A lone finger soon ran up and down Koko's spine and neared her crack, pausing at the base of her spine as the fingertip pressed harder and slid down into her crack. Wanting it all, she grabbed hold of the gold shower handles on either side of her and planted her legs on the marble ledge surrounding the shower and exposed herself fully for Lee, planting her drenching wet pussy onto his face as his finger slid down to her anus. Moist all over in her pleasure zone, Koko easily accepted Lee's exploratory finger into an area on her body that had never been touched by another. She gasped as Lee's finger slid into her rectum amid strong sucking motions that had her clitoris throbbing and on fire. Back and forth she went on Lee's tongue and finger as he poked, sucked and licked, practically worshipping her body and taking her to heights unexpected.

"No, boy!" Koko grunted as her gyrations increased. "Yes, Lee!" she called out as she face-fucked her lover as he held a finger deep inside her ass while sucking her clitoris with lustful abandonment. "You finna make me come!" she let it be known as she held onto the shower handles.

"You like that shit, huh?" Lee asked as he came up for air.

"Fuckin' love it, baby! I love it!" Koko cried aloud.

A deeper finger and harder sucking was too much for Koko to bear. She began panting through wide open eyes as she stared down at the top of Lee's head, unable to comprehend what was happening to her twenty year-old body as convulsions uncontrollable took over. And for the first time in her life, Koko squirted. Clear fluid gushed forth from her vagina and her body immediately went limp, but not before Lee, recognizing her moment, rose up and placed his hands in the pits of her under arms to hold her up as he drove his tongue deep into her mouth.

After a lingering shower, Koko soon found herself on her back resting atop Lee's king-sized bed with her knees nearly touching her ears as his hands rested under the backside of her knees. Her body bounced in a furious, wanton manner as she was being ravished by a rugged, firm-bodied man with a long, veiny dick that was hitting spots she never knew existed inside her own core. Lee's condom-covered dick was constantly caressing the sides of her tight walls and rubbing up her against her clitoris as he hovered over her voluptuous frame, his hands pinning her legs back as he stood up in it like a man possessed.

"Fuck me!" Koko cried aloud as she stared up at Lee with love-struck eyes. She couldn't help but to tilt her head to the side and close her eyes and mutter, "You're the best!"

Lee hadn't spoken much ever since he and Koko had entered his condo. He was bent on delivering nothing but his A-game to this woman, if only to show her that he was serious about what the two of them had agreed upon, which was to be there for one another no matter the circumstances.

Koko could feel Lee growing ever more rigid inside her, if it was even possible. She felt his body tense as he began moaning loud. "You finna come?" she asked her man in a submissive, lovingly manner, wanting to see him become just as satisfied as she herself had been inside the shower stall.

"Baby!" Lee groaned.

"Lee?" Koko paused at that moment. *Too soon.* She thought to herself and held back on the three words that were at the tip of her tongue.

"Koko!" Lee called out as he let go off her legs and wrapped his arms around his lover's neck and kissed her deeply as he continued driving into her.

Koko was expecting Lee to arrive within minutes of their verbal exchange; but to the contrary, he continued on, bringing her to another intense orgasm where she squirted again. She could only lay flat on her back while being taken six ways from Sunday in the famed missionary position. She reached her hands out on occasion to stoke her lover's arms as he slowed his rhythm and lay flat atop her body where he cupped her face and kissed her deeply with his rigid pole planted deep within her love. With their faces meshed together, Lee looked Koko in the eyes and said, "I'm there, baby."

Koko kissed Lee at that moment and reciprocated by thrusting her hips upwards. "You make me feel so good," she confessed. "Whenever you ready, daddy!"

Lee tilted his back and let go with several powerful jolts, his thighs slapping up against Koko's thighs as he erupted into the condom. His throbbing dick pushed Koko over the edge once more as the two climaxed together while gripping one another tightly. "Damn," was all Lee could manage to say as he held onto Koko, the two of them now laying side by side nuzzling noses in total silence through heavy gasps of breath.

"Do it again," Koko requested.

"You beat me to it," Lee laughed. "You wanna smoke a blunt first?"

"Bring it on," Koko responded as she nuzzled up against Lee.

For the remaining four days, Koko's every waking moment was spent with Lee. She was either hanging around the shop with him and Ben, or over to his place after work where she spent nights. Lee hung out with the family the few days Koko had left and made nothing but lasting impressions on everyone.

The day of Kimi and Koko's flight back to Oklahoma City on a scheduled flight, it was Lee who'd driven the two to Phoenix International with Ben and Katrina. He and Koko sat alone in the lobby talking about their future. "So, how will this work?" Koko asked as she held Lee's hand and laid her head on his shoulder.

Lee wrapped and arm around Koko and pulled her close. "We can see each other whenever you want. I can get Samantha to fly me there, or you can catch a flight here on weekends if you're not busy. There's spring break and holidays, too."

"I'd like that, Lee." Koko raised her head at that moment and looked her new love in the eyes. "Can you be faithful? Will you be faithful?"

"I can be with the right one. And as of now? You're the right one. I have a lot of work to do down here every day. You see how I move from day-to-day."

"I really like you, man. I just don't wanna get my feelings hurt—again."

"I'm not like that guy." Lee replied, in reference to Chablis, whose history he'd learned through several conversations with Koko. "I'm a man with mines. If you're worrying about me playing games, you have no worries. I promise."

Koko didn't reply. In her heart she really wanted to believe Lee; but a long distance relationship was something she wasn't sure she would be able to deal with knowing Lee came into their newly-formed love being that of a player. Thoughts of meeting Chablis on the first day of classes crept into her mind. At least there, she would have access to her man on a daily basis and not have to wonder of he was several states away cheating on her, which could become the case with Lee in her mind's eye. Once she and Kimi's flight was called, Koko stood and kissed Lee deeply before the two parted ways. Lee left floating on clouds. Koko, however, left Phoenix pondering whether or not she would just meet up with Chablis and try and work things out with her first love.

CHAPTER TWENTY-TWO

ALWAYS INTO SOMETHING

January 8, 2009

It was now the night of Kimi and Koko's return flight to Oklahoma City. From the interior of her trap house over in Fox Park, seventeen year-old Peppi Vargas could hear the crystal clear lyrics of Juvenile's song, *Numb Numb* thumping in Simone's H-1 Hummer that was parked out front on Saint Louis Street as she mixed up her first batch of methamphetamine inside the trap's kitchen while Loopy and Sweet Pea made sales on the batch of meth the crew had jacked from a husband and wife team up in Quincy, Illinois two weeks earlier.

It had taken a little over a week for Pepper's crew to let it be known they had meth for sale before the drug caught on; but two and a half weeks in, shop was now bumping. Pepper remembered asking the woman Simone had killed how much they made and the woman telling her that she and her husband made fifteen thousand dollars a day, which in Pepper's mind, added up to a half pound of meth per day at seventy-five dollars per gram once she'd run the numbers repeatedly in her head.

The meth market in Fox Park had been tested and proved profitable over time for Pepper. At the outset, her crew was only making four or five hundred dollars a day with their stolen meth. Barely twenty days in, they were nearing the end of their stolen stash and were on the verge of reaping just over $25,000 dollars in tax-free money, the bulk of the money being made over the last three days as clientele had increased once the drug took hold in Fox Park.

Loopy stood beside the table in the kitchen with an AK-47 in her arms as her cousin Sweet Pea made sales in the threshold of the kitchen and living room. The crew was accepting all buyers who came correct with either cash or merchandise of value. Seventy-five dollars was the going rate on a gram of meth, but negotiations were allowed. Brand new plasma TVs, stolen lap tops and home surround systems were some of the items accepted in exchange for the potent synthetic drug Pepper and her crew was putting down in Fox Park.

There was a lot of traffic inside the trap house, and the constant noise was making it hard for Pepper to concentrate as she mixed her first batch of methamphetamine per the library books she'd been studying on the history and processing of the drug. Several users had scored and went and sat down in the living room in order to prep their hit, but turning her trap into a drug gallery was not Pepper's intent. Users had to score and immediately vacate the premises.

With Simone out front in a jovial mood with the music blaring, Pepper soon realized that her money-making-set was slowly being transformed into a shooting gallery and party spot on this cold early January night. From what she'd witnessed, users felt as if they could just hang out in the living room or out on the block and snort or shoot their drugs, but Pepper was in total disagreement.

Upon noticing several users making themselves at home in her living room over her counter, Pepper left the kitchen, storming past Loopy and Sweet Pea and entered the open area of her trap where she confronted the three meth heads who'd spread their paraphernalia out onto her coffee table. "Y'all gettin' the fuck outta here with that bullshit!" she yelled as she reached down and scooted the lumps of crystals into a single pile.

"The fuck you doing?" one of the junkies cried aloud as she reached for her portion of the drug she'd spread out onto the glass table.

"I'm rushin' y'all up out my shit!" Pepper exclaimed as the two Rottweiler pit bulls, named Hutch and Honey, that she'd placed in the backyard began to bark ferociously. Paranoid, the seventeen year-old drew down with a Glock .9 and waved it in front of the now frightened junkies, the gun's barrel repeatedly being drawn towards the front door. "Outside! Shop closed!" she spat aloud.

The three meth users swept their crystals into their palms and scurried towards the front door with Pepper trailing them out into the darkness with Sweet Pea on her heels. "Simone, turn that shit off!" she yelled aloud over the music as she emerged from the trap house and stood on the sidewalk leading up to the apartment. Simone powered down her Hummer with her remote control kill switch and the entire block was brick-walled with silence, save for the two barking Rottweiler pit bulls on the backside of the trap house.

Pepper stood on the sidewalk eyeing the entire block carefully. For a while she'd been having the feeling as if she was being by watched by someone, but she hadn't a clue as to who or why. Over her dogs' incessant barking, she made her way to the end of the building and peeked down the dark alley. The search lights she'd placed in the rear of the home were on, she noticed, and Hutch and Honey could be seen barking over towards the back alley on the next set of apartments. The canines ran as far their leashes would allow them before they were snapped back.

Curious, Pepper headed down the alleyway as she racked her Glock .9mm. The dogs' barking grew louder and wilder the nearer she grew to the end of the building. Just feet away from her Rottweilers, Pepper paused and looked over towards the edge of the building on her right and suddenly felt like a fox being led into a trap. She had a feeling that she would encounter sheer terror should she emerge into the back alleyway. It was as if someone, or something, was waiting for her to show herself.

Pepper backed up the alleyway as her dogs continued barking. She reached the front side of the building and whistled for Sweet Pea, who quickly trotted over. "Go upstairs in the bedroom on the backside and see what Hutch and Honey barking at," she requested. "Simone? Let's move everything inside for now."

The block had been cleared out in a matter of minutes as Pepper returned to her task of cooking up her first batch of meth. She was in the kitchen melting hydrochloric acid in the sink when Sweet Pea jumped down the stairs. "Them dogs was barking at some cats or something back there," she said nonchalantly. "I saw nothing."

Things soon returned to normal inside the trap house. Pepper and her crew were counting money and looking over the electronics they'd traded some meth for as she stood over the sink rolling a blunt. She sat the blunt down and picked up a two liter bottle and poured the hydrochloric mash she'd melted through a strainer as a pungent odor began to dominate the kitchen. Having just rolled a fresh blunt, the young hustler had decided to take a break from the cooking process for a minute. She went into her baggy jeans and pulled out a lighter and scooped the blunt up just as Loopy returned to the kitchen in order to finish rubber-banding the few remaining thousands that lay on the table. "We're nearly done with the shit we stole. How long before you have that first cook done?" she asked.

Pepper looked back at the sink as she held onto the blunt and lighter. "Maybe an hour, but it'll be another two days before it's ready."

"Who knew meth was worth this much money?" Loopy stated seriously as she continued stacking money.

"I know, right? We on to something here, homegirl," Pepper quipped as she placed the blunt to her lips and flicked the lighter.

The moment Pepper clicked her lighter a large fireball erupted inside the kitchen. Orange and yellow flames quickly spread all along the kitchen counter and engulfed the sink and the wall behind it as the kitchen window shattered. The ceiling was covered in thick orange flames that dripped down onto the floors and table. Some of the money Loopy was counting had also caught fire.

"¿Qué diablos pasó?" (What the fuck happened?) Loopy asked in a panicked state as she began slapping the flames off the money. She looked around and grabbed a duffle bag off a chair and began shoving meth and cash into the sack as droplets of fire landed in her hair and on the back of her leather, hooded bomber jacket. With cash and drugs in hand, Loopy made a beeline out the kitchen towards the front door while fanning flames from her clothes and hair. *"Mierda va a volar! Vete de aquí!"* (Shit's going to blow up! Get the fuck out of here!) the twenty-one year-old slender Uruguayan yelled as she ran to the front door, pulled it open and ran out the smoldering apartment.

Pepper, meanwhile, was leaning against the refrigerator fanning flames from her sweatshirt and jeans amidst the wild fire. *"Yo estoy en fuego! I'm fucking de fuego! Help me! Simone!"* (I'm on fire! I'm fucking on fire! Help me! Simone!) she yelled out loud as she pulled her hooded sweatshirt over her head. The startled seventeen year-old was stumbling around the kitchen and knocking the table aside as she came up out her sweatshirt and bra. The fire was spreading rapidly out into the living room where the carpet was now smoldering as flames latched onto the living room curtains. Pepper had begun coughing over the fumes and was taking a knee, no longer able to sustain air in her lungs when a hand grabbed her upper arm and pulled her up from the floor.

"Esta manera, Peppi! Que te conseguí, hermana! Venga, fuck!" (This way, Peppi! I got you, sister! Come on, fuck!) Simone had made it out the apartment, but when she heard her friend calling for help she'd dared to run back into the burning building to pull her out.

Loopy and Sweet Pea, meanwhile, were running around the living room picking up a few laptops and PlayStation systems and whatever else they could carry before they made their way to the front door a second time, as they too, had followed Simone back inside. Together, the four friends emerged from the burning apartment just as the first floor became completely engulfed in flames. A large fireball shot out from the front door and all the windows on the front side of the two story apartment shattered over a small, but powerful explosion that vibrated the ground slightly.

"*¿Qué diablos pasó?*" (What the fuck happened?) Simone asked as she, Loopy and Sweet Pea ran to her Hummer and jumped inside.

Pepper, meanwhile, had broken off from her crew and ran to the back of the burning building where her two dogs were steadily barking. She freed the canines from their iron posts and led them back up to the front of the apartment. She was planning on alerting other tenants, but sirens off in the distance forced her to turn and run back to Simone's Hummer and jump inside with her dogs where Simone burned rubber over emerging tenants' loud screams and cuss words.

Pepper was shaken as she looked back at the flames pouring from the windows of what was once her trap house as she contemplated the mistake she'd made that nearly cost her and her girls their lives. The flame from her lighter had ignited the fumes coming off the melted hydrochloric acid and sparked a fire that had spread quickly. She knew she and her crew was lucky the meth lab didn't explode instantly. She also knew she could've died as she was on the verge of passing out just before Simone saved her. "*Eso, que fue un gran fuck por mi parte, todo el mundo. Lo siento.*" (That, that was a major fuck up on my part, everybody. I'm sorry.) she said somberly as she turned around and slumped down in the front seat dejectedly.

"*Lo hemos hecho, está bien. Pregunta es, ¿qué chingados tenemos que hacer ahora?*" (We made it out okay. Question is, what the fuck we do now?) Simone asked.

"*Doble a la derecha en Ohio Street,*" (Turn right on Ohio Street) Pepper said as she sat upright in her seat and got back into focus. "*Tengo que ver Malik.*" (I have to see Malik.)

The crew made their way over to Malik's trap house and was lucky to find him out there. He'd seen the orange flames from the opposite end of Fox Park, and when Pepper hopped out the Hummer bare-chested and covered in ash, he could only look back at his crew and solemnly shake his head. It was always something with Pepper in his eyes. He knew about her trying to cook meth and it was obvious the plan she had put together to get money while waiting on the Holland family's first cocaine shipment had gone amuck. *"El fuck que hacer ahora?"* (The fuck you do now?) he asked Pepper.

"La joda, hombre?" (The fuck it look like, man?) Pepper said out of breath as she slapped her baggy jeans pockets and wiped ash from her face. *"ME tocã³ mi fucking shit! Usted debe de me detuvo. El fuck me estaba pensando cocinar esa mierda?"* (I fucking blew my shit up! You should of stopped me! The fuck I was thinking cooking that shit?) she asked aloud as she placed her hands on her hips and looked back across the large park where the three fire engines were out in front her trap house. The entire block was roped off. Red and white bright lights were off in the distance lighting up the street as orange flames poured into the dark, cold night sky.

Malik couldn't help but to chuckle as he eyed Pepper with her breasts hanging out. The way she looked back over to her trap house, pathetically, like that of child having lost her favorite toy, had tickled him briefly, but through it all, he was downright pissed off with his protégé as he watched her approaching him while standing on the sidewalk. "Get her a shirt and jacket to cover up with," he told one of his soldiers as he looked over to a rental car one of his soldiers had gotten from a crack head earlier in the day, anticipating Pepper's next move. "The fuck are you gonna do now?" he asked.

"Tenemos metanfetamina, perros salvajes, las armas y el dinero. Usted tiene un coche que pueda utilizar?" (We got meth, wild dogs, guns and money. You have a car I can use?)

"I do this? You have to get in line, no?" Malik stated seriously as he wrapped one of his arms around Pepper and walked her up the sidewalk. "I told you if you were going to hustle until the cocaine to sell weed. We had pounds you could've bought and broken down—but this," Malik said as he pointed to the burning trap house across the way. "This methamphetamine experiment? It ends!" he hissed into her ear. *"Usted tiene a personas con usted, Peppi! Eres un cocaína!"* (You have people counting on you, Peppi! You're a cocaine dealer!) he affirmed through a harsh whisper and clasped teeth as he shoved a t-shirt and jean jacket into Pepper's arms. "I can't keep covering for you, no? First the bounty with Tito and Toine. Now this? As a Lieutenant you have to do better because this family isn't fuckin' around."

"I know, man," Pepper sighed. *"Estoy hecho hasta que la familia obtenga en línea."* (I'm done until the family get on line.)

"You have two months to get your act right, Peppi. Try to stay out of trouble!" Malik admonished as he nodded towards a four door grey 2000 Grand Prix he and his crew had been using to move around in while they sold pounds of marijuana. Malik and his team had rented the car from a crack head and had free reign over it for the foreseeable future. "Where're you headed now?" he asked Pepper as he handed her the keys.

"To my safe house in Louisiana," Pepper replied as she took the keys.

"You call me when you get there or if you need anything else. You have meth left? You get rid of it. No more hustling for you until the first shipment."

"Si. Gracias, Malik," Pepper replied as she hugged him briefly and trotted back over to her girls.

The four females transferred the dogs, their electronics, drugs, guns and money to the Grand Prix and left Simone's Hummer on the block and rode out of Fox Park, planning on headed over to Pepper's safe house in Louisiana, Missouri, an hour's drive north on State Highway 79. They'd stopped briefly over to the McDonald's on Jefferson Avenue and hit the drive-thru and ordered food and drink. When Simone pulled back out onto Jefferson Avenue and headed towards I-44, Pepper spotted a dual pair of light blue headlights in the side view mirror coming up quick on the passenger side. "Eh, get in the right lane and go east on forty-four," she told Simone.

"That ain't the way to Louisiana," Simone said as she slid a few fries into her mouth.

"I wanna see something," Pepper replied as Simone moved

over to the right lane and jumped onto I-44 east. "Y'all see them light blue headlights about five cars back?" she asked as Simone merged in with the flowing traffic.

Simone looked through the Grand Prix's rearview and Loopy and Sweat Pea looked over the backseat, the three of them quickly spotting the light blue headlights on a car that had a wide front grill and sat high up off the ground.

"You think it's the police tailing us over the fire back in Fox Park?" Simone asked as she moved over to the left lane and slowed a bit while eyeing the suspicious car through the rearview mirror.

"*No creo que la policía.*" (I don't think that's the police.) Loopy said as she reached down and grabbed her AK-47. "Could be somebody we robbed outta town comin' back on us," she guessed as she racked her assault rifle and let the window down.

Pepper had already had her Heckler and Koch Uzi locked and loaded as she let her window down. She and her crew had robbed several dope houses and dealers out of town. Paranoia hit them often and tonight was another one of those nights it seems. Simone eased off the gas pedal. Cars trailing the Grand Prix moved over to the middle right lane and sped by, several drivers blowing their horns and flashing their headlights as the car was traveling just that slow in the fast lane.

The car the crew had been watching eased over into the middle right lane, sliding past a slow-moving eighteen wheeler as it began easing up on the passenger side of the Grand Prix with the tinted driver's side window and back passenger window rolled halfway down.

The barrels of Loopy and Pepper's semi-automatics were resting on the edge of the passenger side windows as the car, which they could all now tell was a lime green old school Caprice sitting on big, chrome rims, neared the Grand Prix's bumper. Hard bass and the lyrics to Houston rapper Ganksta Nip's song titled *Get Out of the Game* could be heard jumping from the gangster whip, strong enough to vibrate the crew's ride as the car rode nearly side-by side with the Grand

Prix…"…*keep my finger on the trigger steady watching my stash cash…gotta move fast 'cause cops be watchin' my black ass…see I ain't got a pity on another brother…I'll kill your bitch ass…and I'm serious than a mutherfucka…*"

Pepper and company watched in silence as the Caprice slowly cruised by, its passengers unable to be seen as the interior was pitch black and the car sat a couple feet higher than the Grand Prix they were riding in.

Loopy analyzed the license plate on the Caprice. *"B-O-O-G-I-E. Boogie,"* she said to herself as she took a mental snapshot of the mysterious car's license plate while watching it merge over into the right lane and take an off ramp.

"That's probably some of them dudes that be over to Bangin' Heads who know the car," Simone remarked as she eyed the car disappearing onto the off-ramp.

"I don't know," Loopy remarked in an unsure tone as she repeated the license plate over and over in her head. "That was weird. Like they was sending us a message or something."

"Say, y'all," Pepper remarked. "I know I told Malik we was going to Louisiana, but, umm, let's head over to the other trap in East Saint Louis on Wimmer Place."

"Why?" Loopy asked curiously. "We should just get a hotel room or go over to my Aunt CeeCee's in Saint Charles if we not going to the safe house."

"I just don't wanna go home tonight," Pepper replied as she set her Uzi down on the floorboard. "Y'all don't feel this shit, man?" she reasoned as she eyed her friends. "It's like a bad omen in the air or something. Remember that dream I had Christmas night? The best thing to do is to keep moving. We got more meth to sell. Let's just go and kick it over there for a while."

Pepper, although admitting she felt as if she was being watched, would not admit the fact that she was afraid to go home to her own safe house. Louisiana was close to where she and her crew had robbed several dealers in towns north and also over in Illinois. She now felt that one of those crews was now onto her team. Louisiana would only be their downfall should she ever travel there with her crew in the near future was her belief.

Loopy, meanwhile, had never let go of her chopper. She sat in the backseat of the Grand Prix in deep thought. As of lately, she hadn't been feeling Pepper's moves. First the double murder in Quincy, and now this thing with a burned out trap house. On top of that, they were now headed to another trap house after having a strange encounter, an encounter that now left her wondering if the crew was actually being hunted. Everything about the night was wrong in her eyes; but Pepper had been in the game. She'd been taught by Carmella Lapiente` and the Perez sisters, and had been pushing weight long before she and Sweet Pea decided to get down. Loopy said nothing, uttering not a word of protest as Simone merged onto I-55 and headed towards East Saint Louis.

Pepper, meanwhile, was still feeling as if she was being followed. She was looking around in all directions when she spotted another pair of headlights, brighter than the light blue dual headlights that had rode up on her and her crew earlier, speeding up behind the car as the Grand Prix approached the Mississippi River Bridge leading to East Saint Louis. "Here they come!" she exclaimed loudly as she reached for Uzi once more, preparing herself for a rolling shootout.

Blue flashing lights soon lit up the rear of the Grand Prix. *"La fucking policia? El puto estado en nuestra policia ass todo este tiempo?"* (The fucking police? The fucking police been on our ass all this time?) Pepper in asked in a high-pitched rhetorical voice of disbelief as Simone, needing no instruction, floored the car over the Mississippi River Bridge.

Hutch and Honey, who'd been quietly licking themselves, rose up and stuck their heads out of either side of the back passenger widows of the Grand Prix as Simone floored the car up to the crest of the bridge. The Grand Prix skidded briefly over a patch of ice and Simone screamed aloud while correcting the car as it briefly skidded along the south rail of the bridge, the only thing blocking it from going off the side and plunging into the ice cold murky waters of the Mississippi

River.

"Obtener derecho! Obtener derecho, mutherfucka!" (Get right! Get right, mutherfucka!) Simone yelled aloud as sparks shot up on the car's passenger side as it ran along the steel rails.

Hutch and Honey were going berserk. Honey was now standing in Sweet Pea's lap barking at the sparks. Drool was splashing in her face as Hutch jumped into the front seat where Simone was struggling to get the car off the side rail.

"Bájese del lado antes de ir!" (Get off the side before we go over!) Sweet Pea yelled as she shoved Honey off her lap.

Simone corrected the car with Hutch still in her lap. She elbowed the dog over onto Pepper right before she grabbed the steering tightly and floored the Grand Prix once more as she moved to the center lane, just missing the front end of what she could now see was a Missouri State Trooper.

While flooring the car over into the down slope of the bridge, Simone spotted three East Saint Louis police cars coming up quick on the ramp to her right as she was passing by at over one hundred miles an hour. With four cars now on their tail, Pepper, Loopy and Sweet Pea began unloading everything. A few cars could see the high speed chase coming up on them, so they quickly moved over to the right lane and slowed. All they could see was a car speeding by with what appeared to be trash flying from its interior.

The lone Missouri State Trooper and the three East Saint Louis squad cars soon found themselves dodging items being flung from the car they were pursuing. The dash cam on the State Trooper's car was recording everything in black and white. The camera clearly showed three pairs of arms repeatedly popping out of the Grand Prix as laptops, video game consoles, boxes of shoes and silhouettes of three assault rifles crashed down onto the highway from the speeding car.

Inside the Grand Prix it was total chaos. Pepper and Loopy were now wrestling with Hutch and Honey respectively as the dogs had suddenly turned on them; the beasts were now barking and nipping at their arms and trying to bite their faces.

"*¿Qué chingados está mal con este perro? ¿Qué hay de malo con tu perro, Peppi?*" (What the fuck is wrong with this dog? What's wrong with your dog, Peppi?) Loopy fretted as she began throwing punches at Honey, knocking the dog upside the head.

"*Que miedo!*" (They just scared!) Pepper screamed over the car's roaring engine as she stuffed her jean jacket-clad arm into Hutch's mouth to keep him busy while dangling a plastic bag out the window with her free hand where she began running it up and down the door handle frantically.

"*Todos tenemos miedo! Pero esta perra no tenga que comer yo!*" (We all scared! But this bitch don't have to eat me!) Loopy retorted from the backseat as she grabbed Honey and placed the dog in the headlock and fell over onto Sweet Pea.

From the dash cam, the State Trooper's patrol car recorded a lone hand extending from the front passenger side window. Soon, what looked like large droplets of salt began to spread out onto the highway from the speeding car. The white crystals bounced across the road like broken Mardi Gras beads as the car sped up.

"There go the drugs! They're offing the drugs!" the Missouri State Trooper called over the radio.

Back inside the Grand Prix, Simone was repeatedly asking where to go as Sweet Pea continued unloading any and everything she could get her hands on to slow the police down. "*Bájese en Saint Clair para que podamos ir a correr!*" (Get off on Saint Clair so we can jump out and run!) Sweet Pea yelled as she threw a set of computer speakers out the window.

Loopy, meanwhile, was still wrestling with Honey, she and the dog in a battle for position.

"*Joder esta mierda! Donatella, ayuda para lanzar este mutherfucka!*" (Fuck this shit! Donatella, help me throw this mutherfucka out!) Loopy, tired of fighting with a dog off its marbles, yelled aloud as she leaned over, pushed the back door open and leaned back into Sweet Pea, holding the back door open against the pushing wind with left foot.

"No el perro! No el perro!" (Not the dog! Not the dog!) Pepper screamed as she continued warding off Hutch.

"Esta puta Mierda!" (Fuck this bitch!) *"Fuck este estúpido perro!"* (Fuck this stupid dog!) *"Vete de aquí!"* (Get the fuck outta here!) Loopy and Sweet Pea yelled out loud and in random as they clutched the dog tightly.

The Missouri State Trooper's patrol car was still recording when what appeared to be a small, black calf fell from the car she was pursuing. Honey yelped aloud as her body twirled violently over the concrete. The trooper swerved her car after realizing a live dog had been flung from the speeding car, but the animal rolled in her direction nonetheless, slamming into her front bumper and shattering her right headlight and flattening her right tire. "I'm out! I'm out of commission!" she quickly radioed as the three remaining squad cars shot by her and continued on with the chase.

Simone and company, meanwhile, had exited onto Saint Clair Avenue where Simone made a sharp left turn and entered a rundown warehouse district. She made another sharp left turn as the flashing lights of the remaining police cars appeared off in the distance. The warehouse district just off Saint Clair Avenue was nothing more than a dumping ground. Loopy and Sweet Pea, when they were boosting furniture stores in Granite City, Illinois, often used the place to offload stolen merchandise from their heists back in the spring of 2007. Nearly two years later, the place was even more desolate than previous times.

Large, three story, red-bricked warehouses with hollowed out windows and rusted smoke stacks stood like ancient remnants of the Roman Empire under the dark sky. This area once teemed with heavy tractor-trailer and railroad traffic as goods were shipped, received and transferred from rail to truck and vice versa. In January of 2009, however, creepy, could best describe this urban wasteland whose roads were now littered with junked-out cars, discarded furniture, and weathered concrete docks that contained immovable, rusted-out railroad cars that would have to be shredded where they sat parked on brittle steel rails.

With the law still hot on her and her girls' tail, Simone moved from under the pylons and turned off into an entrance that was surrounded by three story warehouses, two short ones that lay on either side, and one long building that lay straight ahead. She rode in between the two short buildings and entered a wide open area and slammed the Grand Prix into park in the middle of what was once a semi-trailer drop yard that was now covered in grass and gravel.

All four doors on the Grand Prix opened simultaneously and the four outlaws jumped from the car and scattered in all directions, headed towards the long building directly in front of them as flashing lights lit up the bottom side of the elevated freeway. *"Vaya hacia el norte. Vaya hacia el norte a National City!"* (Go north! Go north to National City!) Pepper yelled over the approaching sirens as she tucked the duffle bag of money underneath her arms as she and her girls scattered off into the darkness.

The three East Saint Louis police cars rounded the corner and rushed into the complex. Six officers hopped out and were immediately greeted by an idling Grand Prix and a barking Rottweiler that was charging at them; all six officers pulled out their service pistols and gunned Hutch down where he stood barking. They'd dumped over eighteen rounds into to the frightened dog before jumping up on the docks of the short warehouses that lay to their left and right with guns and flashlights drawn while radioing for backup.

Two officers were approaching what was once a warehouse office. They leaned up against the outside of the building where one called out, "East Saint Louis police department! Show yourselves! Show yourselves or we fire on sight!"

A rustling sound was heard inside the small office as the patrolmen eyed one another and nodded in unison. The officer who'd given the command pointed his pistol and nodded over to his partner, who quickly shined his flashlight into the room. The officer entered the room and opened fire, spraying the room as he moved his Glock .9 mm from side to side. With the aid of the flashlight, he could see a gang of hybrid rats scurrying off into the darkness of the warehouse's main floor.

The area was too dark and vast to enter without backup, so he held his position as he reloaded his pistol. "Sweet Jesus," he heard his partner remark as he held his flashlight on an object lying over in the left corner of the room.

"The fuck is that?" the first officer asked as he leaned down for a closer look.

"It's a dead body. A federal agent looks like," the officer's partner let it be known as he eyed a mummified skeleton with long black hair that was partially dressed in what appeared to be an all-black FBI uniform. "Forget about the thieves. This is a murder scene—one involving an officer, man," he ended as he radioed for more backup. The search for what the female Missouri State Trooper had radioed in as being that of thieves was called off at that moment by the East Saint Louis Police Department as a bigger issue now lay in the laps of law enforcement—that of a possible murdered person-of-the-law.

CHAPTER TWENTY-THREE

IF IT AIN'T ONE THING IT'S ANOTHER

"Jason! Daddy, make love to me. Make love to me," Kree Devereaux pleaded as she lay beneath Jay-D in her bedroom inside her home over in Saint Charles.

Making love to Jason David was like a dream come true for Kree. For so long she'd wanted this man-of-a-thug to take her in anyway his heart desired. The bracelet she'd given him on Christmas Day over to Kantrell's home was the start of something beautiful. He'd accepted the gift in front of everybody before telling them that he was interested in being with Kree openly. Over the stunned eyes of their friends, the two had left Kantrell's home hand in hand to adjoin to Kree's home to be alone.

Kree had no clue as to when or how Jay-D had obtained her car keys, let alone why he drove home in her car in total reverse, but none of that mattered as she was where she wanted to be in life—under Jay-D, kissing him deeply as he made sweet love to her. "I make you feel good, Jason?" she moaned as she wrapped her arms around her lover's back.

There was no reply as a loud ringing entered Kree's ears. Jay-D's image started fading and his weight grew lighter. Kree reached out for the man as the ringing phone grew louder in her ears. She awoke from her dream with her legs spread and her arms clutching her lonely body as reality hit her. She'd never been with Jay-D save for the dream she'd had that was all-so-real. Disappointed, she reached over onto her night stand and grabbed her cellphone and answered the call. "Hello?"

"Yo!"

Kree sat up her bed upon hearing the voice. "Pepper?" she asked as she looked around her room dejectedly, yet and still smiling over her sweet dream.

"You busy? You got company?"

"Me? Company? I who have nothing?" Kree laughed sleepily. "I could only wish. What's up, girl?"

Pepper had just fucked up big time and she knew it. She'd lost over ten thousand dollars in stolen goods and meth, had lost the rock rental Malik had let her use to get up to Louisiana and was now stuck out in the middle of nowhere with her crew. She knew not to call Malik after all that had gone down. Jessie didn't have a car. The only person left was Kree. She explained as much as she could, leaving out the high speed chase and her burning down her trap house and was able to persuade Kree into driving fifty miles in the dark, cold night over to what was basically a no man's land in order to pick her and her crew up.

Kree eased out of her bed after hanging up her phone and moped around the room as she dressed up in a velvet, tight-fitting jogging suit and grabbed her clutch purse. She stepped out into the cold night air with Luther Vandross on her mind as she climbed into her car and backed out of her driveway. She drove the whole way to National City replaying her dream. It seemed so real to her, except for Jay-D driving to her home in reverse. She did give him a bracelet, and he'd accepted it before everybody before giving her a brief hug, a hug that brought about 'uh ohh's' from his brother Dooney, his niece Nancy, Kantrell, Malik and Jessie.

Although Jay-D had reiterated that he and Kree were nothing more than friends, and had even offered to give the gift back, Kree refused politely and reiterated the same statement Jay-D had made seconds earlier, that the two of them were nothing more than friends. Kree, however, had subconsciously viewed Jay-D's accepting of her gift as segue that could possibly lead to something bigger.

The love-longing transsexual's heart pounded with unwavering hope as her white Maxima on chrome wheels cruised up a desolate, snow-lined I-70 headed east towards East Saint Louis. Alone in her thoughts, Kree picked up her phone. She hadn't talked to Jay-D since he and his family had left for their trip to Stateville, Illinois to visit his father and brother. She wasn't sure if he'd even made it back into town or not as it had been nearly two weeks since they'd last spoken or seen one another. Her fingers glided over the touch screen of her phone, prepared to text.

Are you ok? Was the message Kree had wanted to send, but given the hour of the night, she opted not to, if only to stave off the awkwardness of it all.

As orange lights hanging over the freeway lit up her solitary path into downtown Saint Louis, Kree set her phone in her Maxima's console and pushed in her Luther Vandross Greatest Hits Cd and selected *I Who Have Nothing*, a song that had become her favorite song ever since she'd found herself having a heart fond of Jason David Cottonwood. The smooth saxophone and piano coated her ears as she removed some her curly black hair from her face and eyed Embassy Suites off in the distance. Curtis Morrow should've been the end of her search for love was her reasoning as she reflected on a love lost. On the other end of the spectrum, Jay-D offered so much promise. He accepted her and was friends with her. He was comfortable in the person she was whenever he was around. Yet, he didn't love her—maybe not—maybe so. A definite answer was what Kree wanted, yet she was afraid to ask for fear that she would ruin what little rapport she had with Jay-D, a rapport that allowed her to sleep at night and gave her something to look forward to when she awoke the following day to go through the rigors of life while searching for that special one.

"I don't want a knight in shining armor," Kree spoke softly from behind her steering wheel as her eyes welled up. "*I just want him to love me. Why won't he love me? I can be a good woman to him if he gave me the chance,*" she reasoned to herself.

Kree leaned back in her leather seat with a hand over her forehead in frustration as she drove. She had no clue as to why Jay-D was in her system so heavy, but his stake was planted in her heart nonetheless. She had no control over her love; and truth be told, she wanted no governance over her emotions when it came to Jason David Cottonwood for the simple fact that she loved the responsive torture he dished out. She would forever combat what she felt was an emotional tug-of-war with kindness for as long as the two kept up their empathy towards one another.

Like rushing water over granite, slowly was Kree's hope to break Jay-D's resistance, thereby making love's conquest all-the-more praise-worthy and life-everlasting. She would await, for all times, if that's what it took, the day, should it ever arrive, the day that Jay-D said to her—'yes'—which was the magic word, the answer to the one specific question she knew would usher the two of them into a life of love-fulfilled.

Crossing over the Mississippi River Bridge in the still of the night, Kree entered East Saint Louis, Illinois while steadily enjoying the sweet sounds of Luther Vandross as she rode along the elevated freeway. Numerous flashing lights up in the distance soon caught her attention and she slowed her car as she approached orange cones that narrowed the multi-lane expressway down to one single lane. Fire crews were out sweeping up debris and a bloody sheet covered what appeared to be that of a hit deer, or God-forbid a small child in Kree's mind. Hers was the only car out on the highway as she rode into the roadblock where Illinois State Troopers shined bright lights into the interior of her Maxima.

"You the first car besides a bunch of tractor trailers come through here. Where're ya' going?" a pudgy State Trooper in his mid-thirties asked as he shined the light directly into Kree's face.

"I'm on my way to a hair convention in Chicago, officer," Kree responded unnerved. "You need to see my driver's license?" she asked respectfully.

"Damn right I do!" the trooper snapped as he shined the light into the occupant's backseat, which was filled with store-bought hair weave in assorted colors, high-end shampoos and conditioners, and an array of hair dryers and curling irons, new items she'd bought to take over to Bangin' Heads later in the morning. "Step out the car for me would ya', ma'am?" the officer requested.

Kree stepped out of her car in her tight-fitting fuchsia velvet jogging suit and white Ugg boots with a white fur top hat on her head and the officer smiled, admiring her physique. "Well, now, lady," he said in appreciation as he tugged down on his hat. "I'm just gonna run a quick check, and if all comes back clean you'll be on your way."

"Fine," Kree sulked as she folded her arms and leaned against her car in anticipation of what was to come. She watched as the trooper walked back to his patrol car while looking over her driver's license. When he paused briefly, Kree knew what was going down. She could only watch in silence as the State Trooper turned around and looked her up and down as he held onto the license while radioing for backup.

Several officers stationed further up the roadblock ran in Kree's direction as she raised her hands in silence. The State Trooper who'd obtained her license stood beside his car and yelled aloud, "License says Kareem Devereaux! But you don't look like a fuckin' Kareem to me! Fuck's going on here?"

"Kareem is my government name." Kree stated calmly.

"Place your hands behind your back for me please, sir," an East Saint Louis police officer requested.

"For what?" Kree asked through teary eyes. "What did I do, officer?"

"You're under suspicion."

"Suspicion of what? Suspicion of being human?" Kree asked as she was shoved around to face her car while her wrists were being grabbed.

"We don't know who you are exactly! Until we do we have the right to take you into custody!" the trooper who'd pulled Kree over yelled aloud from his patrol car.

"I'm, my name is Kareem Deveraux! It's on my license!"

Kree retorted as she struggled to free herself.

"Stop resisting!" an East Saint Louis police officer countered as he hit Kree in the back of the head with a powerful elbow that forced her head up against the side of her car's roof.

Twenty-five year-old Kree Deveraux grew weak knees after having her face slammed against the fiber glass of her car's roof. She was dropping to her knees in between her open driver's side door in total defeat and surrenderance when another East Saint Louis officer forced her to the ground completely.

"I can't breathe!" Kree muttered weakly while lying on her stomach as another officer placed a knee to her back and hovered over her body, pinning her face first to the frozen freeway in between her car and the open driver's side door of her Maxima. "Please! I can't breathe!" Kree whimpered.

"Alright, alright," the officer who held Kree's license stated as he walked back over to her car after completing a background check.

The officers eased back from Kree as the State Trooper who'd pulled her license helped her up from the ground. "Sorry for the misunderstanding, Mister Devereaux," he said seriously. "Identity theft is all-too-common nowadays. Be careful on your journey to Chicago," he ended as he handed Kree back her driver's license.

Humiliated, yet relieved she hadn't been done further harm, Kree climbed back into her car after wiping what grime she could from her clothes and continued on her journey. The exit to Saint Clair Avenue was marked on her GPS, but when she noticed numerous police cars at the bottom of the off ramp and numerous flashing lights and two circling helicopters shining lights over the entirety of the warehouse district she had to pass by in order to get to National City, she continued north on I-55.

Recalculating she heard her GPS remark.

After traveling several miles out of route, Kree finally made her way over to the location where Pepper and her crew were waiting. She pulled up to an abandoned steel pipe fabricating plant in National City just off Industrial Avenue as the hour neared two in the morning.

Pepper and her girls were hiding in various parts of the plant. When they spotted the white Maxima rolling through the yard, they began emerging from four different locales. They all reached the car at the same time as Kree climbed from behind her steering wheel to further clean herself off. Her outfit and hat were ruined and her face was covered in mud.

Despite their own troubles, and all they'd been through earlier in the night, Pepper, Simone, Loopy and Sweet Pea all eyed Kree with worried looks.

"What the hell happened to you?" Pepper asked befuddled as she stared Kree up and down.

Kree popped the trunk on her car and stormed off to its rear end while sliding into a rant in her native tongue. "*Estúpido policía me llevó después de leer mi licencia de conducir y ver el nombre Kareem Devereaux. Que se quedaron en mí y me tiró al suelo como si fuera un delincuente común.*"(Stupid police took me down after reading my driver's license and seeing the name Kareem Devereaux. They ran up on me and threw me to the ground like I was a common criminal!)

Pepper and company began sniggling while watching Kree search her trunk in her soiled outfit as she continuing to argue aloud with herself while shoving items around. "*Su fat ass iba a pedirme una fecha hasta que vio mi nombre! Quiero cambiar mi nombre para bien! No te puedo ayudar, si yo soy hermosa en la vida y él un fat bastard! I love me un hombre. Pero aun tengo las normas! Era una chapuza de futuro a rancio, suelta ropa de vestir jelly-barriga hijo de puta!*" (His fat ass was probably going to ask me for a date until he saw my name! I should change my name for good! I can't help it if I'm beautiful in life and he a fat bastard! I love me a man. But even I have standards! Sloppy-looking musty, sloppy clothes-wearing jelly-belly son-of-a-bitch!)

"That thang is going *off!*" Pepper laughed as she and her girls stood by watching Kree.

"And I thought we was having a bad night," Loopy

remarked.

"You should sue their asses, Kareem! I mean Kree!" Simone joked.

"Nada soleado, Simone! Me podría haber ido a la cárcel!" (Nothing's funny, Simone! I could've gone to jail!) Kree snapped as she came up with a towel and a gallon of water she used to wash her face and arms.

Once Kree cleaned herself, the gang of five climbed into the Maxima and began making their way home. They had to travel over forty miles north to the town of Alton, Illinois and cross back over into Missouri in order to dodge roadblocks. By the time they arrived over to Kree's home in Saint Charles, it was approaching five in the morning.

"Make yourselves at home," Kree welcomed. "Nobody said nothing about what happened the whole ride, but I know you four have troubles. I just hope y'all make it through this one here," she ended before adjoining to her bedroom to gather clothes for a shower.

Pepper and Sweet Pea went into the kitchen to search for food while Loopy and Simone flopped down on the sofa dead tired. The TV was turned on the morning news and a live broadcast was airing. A reporter was stationed out in front of an obvious crime scene given the yellow tape and officers behind her as she related details.

"In what has left the East Saint Louis authorities in a state of confusion, a budding mystery has landed in their laps. A high speed chase last night ended here," the female reporter said as she pointed to a warehouse door that was roped off with yellow tape. "Officers involved in the chase tailed what has been reported as being a stolen Grand Prix into this abandoned warehouse complex just off interstate fifty-five and Saint Clair Avenue. The suspects fled, but officers stumbled upon something far more pressing. I'm here live with Illinois State Trooper Sandra Cordova, the lead lawwoman in the chase," the reporter said as a heavy-set, blonde-haired Hispanic woman in her late-thirties came into view.

"Morning," Sandra said as she removed her state trooper's

hat and tucked it under her arms.

"Sergeant Cordova, why is this case more important to the state of Missouri than East Saint Louis, Illinois?" the reported asked.

"We did a preliminary search of the remains found in the office behind us and found an identification card and a damaged cell phone. The cell phone has to be examined, but identification listed the victim as one Xanthipian Zamora. Zamora was reported missing by her mother back in September of two thousand and two."

"It's my understanding that Zamora was wearing an FBI uniform. What's the significance?"

"It's an ongoing case over in Saint Charles so I can't comment. Let's just say the case has been given new life and I'll be leading the investigation. Anybody with information is asked to call the Missouri State Patrol's headquarters in Saint Louis, or my former partner, Lieutenant Darby Jones, down in robbery homicide at Saint Louis Police Headquarters." Sandra ended.

"Yo! Xanthipian! That's that bitch Carmella killed the day she robbed the Holland family!" Simone snapped as she laughed aloud. "That was like Fox Park biggest mystery and we just solved that shit with our high speed chase!"

"That pretty much took Carmella and her crew down. Xanthipian was Maximillian's sister." Loopy remarked somberly.

"We chose the right side, homegirl," Simone said seriously. "They looking into that shit but they ain't gone find nothing. Everybody in on that lick dead and done with," she added as she yawned. "I'm going take a shower and take my fat ass to sleep for a couple of hours. Gotta hit the DMV later for a new tag on my ride."

The girls all turned in an hour or so later after eating and showering and woke up several hours later in the late afternoon. Kree had taken the day off in order to take them where they needed to go. After a quick breakfast and a changing into clothes they'd had stored in Kree's home, the four climbed back into the Maxima with Kree and made their way over to Fox Park.

Kree was cruising down Saint Louis Street and had just passed *Kirk's Corner Store*. Fox Park was a place that held many a memory for her. This was where her transformation began. Where she first met Alonzo Milton, and where she'd come into her own as a transgender. She smiled as she thought of the apartment where she'd lost her virginity to Alonzo lay, but she had to do a double take when her brown eyes fell upon a burned out slab of concrete. "When did this happen?" she asked in a high-pitched voice.

"You ain't hear?" Loopy asked from the backseat as she shook her head with a slight smile on her face. "Pepper burned this place down last night tryna cook meth."

"Meth," Kree stated as she shook her head. "Pepper, what is it with you, girl?"

"Tellin' ya'," Simone quipped. "Ya' lie, ya' cheat, ya' steal—sell drugs and kill people. The fuck we doing here, man?" she chuckled as Kree's Maxima eased past the burned out hull of what was once a fun place to hang out for Kree.

"Simone, you playin', girl," Pepper laughed as she looked back at the burned-out structure. "All our asses could've went up in flames last night."

"That was some wild shit," Simone chuckled. "I ain't never move that fast, homegirl."

The conversation continued on as Kree drove over to Ohio Street and pulled up in front of Malik's trap house. Her heart fluttered when she saw Jay-D's navy blue, dark-tinted Navigator parked out front. The SUV's driver's side was facing her car's driver's side as the ride sat idling in front of Simone's Hummer that was parked behind it. *"There my baby,"* Kree smiled to herself.

Kree pulled up alongside of the pristine SUV on thirty-inch chrome rims and smiled sweetly, the reflection of her white teeth clearly on display in the Navigator's dark tint. She waved a friendly wave and was all smiles as the window slowly lowered.

"Who the fuck you smiling at?" Dooney asked as he mean-mugged Kree.

A red fat bastard, Kree thought to herself. "I'm sorry," she said aloud as she dropped her smile. "I though you was—"

"Yeah, Jay-D ain't 'round here!" Dooney snapped as he raised the window.

"Damn, you thought that was your l'il boo, huh?" Simone joked as Pepper, Loopy and Sweet Pea sniggled.

"You'll get him one day, Kree," Sweet Pea said in a believing tone. "Don't give up."

"Jay-D kill her before he fuck with her on that level." Simone said as she opened the back door on Kree's Maxima and planted a foot to the ground. "She thought the police last night hemmed her ass up—let her keep playin' with Jay-D like that," she chided.

"He wouldn't dare," Kree smiled. "Go on and handle your business at the DMV. You be there all day 'cause it's a Friday."

"Nah. I'm just gettin' a new tag. I be in and out," Simone snapped as she eased out of Kree's Maxima.

"Alright then," Kree responded. "I'm going drop Pepper off by Malik's Grill before I head over to Bangin' Heads. I see y'all later," she ended as she pulled off with Pepper, Loopy and Sweet Pea in tow.

Simone turned her attention to Dooney at that moment. He lowered the window once more as she approached. "What's up, homegirl," he asked as he smiled, revealing his platinum teeth.

"Chillin'," Simone said in a sexy voice as she looked over into the passenger seat and nodded at Nancy Cottonwood briefly. "The fuck y'all doing 'round here?" she asked, turning her attention back to Dooney.

"Malik and some of the crew over to the club in Saint Charles putting the finishing touches on the joint, ya' smell me? He ain't won't leave your ride, so me and Nancy been riding through keepin' a eye on it." Dooney answered. "You still taste like raspberries, girl?" he asked seductively as he licked his lips.

Simone blushed at that moment. She and Dooney had hooked up not too long after Bay, T-top and Pepper had killed Toodie. They were the unspoken fuck buddies inside the click and did well keeping their rapport on the low. "You can find out tonight, homeboy," Simone smiled as she pressed her tongue to her cheek and eyed Dooney through her sexy, slender dark eyes.

Dooney looked Simone up and down proudly as she stood before him dressed in a baggy pair of khaki capris, white knee-length boots and a white leather mid-quarter hooded jacket. She was a thick woman who wore her hair styled in a neatly trimmed flat top. She was thick-thighed, wide-hipped and had a small pair of pert breasts. She was a wild one in the bed despite her size, able to grab her ankles and pull them back behind her head.

"You know we on, baby," Dooney spoke in a sexy voice while biting his lower lip and imagining how he was going to take Simone on this night.

"Alright," Simone smiled. "I'll call you later. Tell Malik thanks if you see him before I do. He looked out."

"Yeah he did, yeah he did," Dooney smiled. "But he heard about that shit last night," he followed in a serious tone. "Y'all burned down a money-making set on the other side Fox Park, got in a high speed chase and got a rock rental confiscated."

"We can pay to have the car released, man." Simone said nonchalantly.

"Say what?" Dooney exclaimed as he sat up in the seat and hugged the steering wheel. "Police trashed the hell outta that car this morning! Dude who own it say he want a brand new used joint after he reported it stolen!"

"See, we ain't know all that," Simone said as she rubbed her chin.

"You know now," Dooney quipped. "Pepper gotta pay that

man at least eight thousand dollars! And Malik gone let it be known that this shit ain't going down like with what Loopy ass did to that boy Dibble for Jessie bullshit back in two thousand seven!"

"Whatever, man! We got that!" Simone retorted. "Let me get outta here. I catch up with you later."

"Where you going now?"

"To the DMV." Simone answered as she headed for her Hummer.

Dooney looked over to Nancy and the two laughed. "On a Friday? Your ass have fun," he ended as he put the Navigator in drive and pulled off.

****

Simone was certain she wouldn't be at the DMV long in spite of her friends' clowning on her. All she had to do was go in and show her registration, pay the fee and be out. When she pulled up to the DMV, however, she was hit with a rude awakening. The line leading into the building was out the door and around the corner. It seemed as if there were nearly a hundred people waiting to get inside the building, and they were only letting a few people in at a time.

"Awwww, hell nawww! What the fuck, man?" Simone asked aloud in disbelief as she searched for a parking spot.

It took nearly five minutes to find parking, but during that time, Simone had come up with a plan. Pepper had split fifteen thousand dollars with her, Loopy and Sweet Pea before the crew left Kree's home. They each had a little under four grand after breaking Kree off for picking them up in National City.

After parking, Simone grabbed her registration and headed towards the front door of the DMV and entered the building, bypassing waiting customers. She pretended to be filling out a slip as she eyed the counter. When an opening came, she darted up to the window with her registration in one hand, and five one hundred dollar bills in the other. "I just need a tag right quick, Miss," she told the bi-focal-wearing elderly woman as she held onto the money. "My tag like two hundred and thirty dollars. You can keep the change," she slyly smiled as she slid the five one hundred dollar bills across the counter.

The woman shifted her glasses and curled her lips up at the youngster standing before her. "What makes you think I want that?" she asked matter-of-factly. "I been an employee for the state of Missouri for over forty years and I be damned if I fuck up my pension for a little over two hundred dollars. What you will do, young lady, is take your ass to the back of the line outside and wait in line like everyone else. Next customer!" the woman yelled as she fanned Simone off.

"Wait! I'm just sayin', Miss! I'm only here for a —"

"Security!" the woman yelled.

"You gone do me like that, old lady?" Simone asked in dismay as a stout security guard approached.

"She's tryna skip the line!" the old woman snapped.

"Come on with me, ma'am," the security stated as he nudged Simone towards the exit.

"You ain't have to do me like that with your old ass!" Simone barked while being ushered away from the counter.

Once she was escorted outside, Simone quickly came up with another plan. She walked a few paces down from the DMV's entrance, looking for someone she could make an offer to. About seven paces down from the entrance, she eyed a young Hispanic female texting on her phone. "*Yo! Homegirl? ¿Quieres hacer un extra de dos cientos de dólares?*" (Yo! Homegirl? You wanna make a extra two hundred dollars?) she asked, careful to use Spanish so those around wouldn't pick up on the conversation.

"*Cómo?*" (How?) the young Hispanic asked as she eyed the female standing before her.

"*Permítame su lugar en la cola y en mi lugar al final*".(Let me have your spot in line and you take my place at the end.)

"*Trescientos.*" (Three hundred.) the female countered.

"*Muy bien. Estoy en la final ahora?*" (Fine. I'm all the way at the end now?)

"I know," the female replied as she took Simone's money and left the line.

Simone was all smiles now as she waited in line. It took all but ten minutes for her to near the counter once more. As luck would have it, she encountered the same clerk whose window she'd approached on her arrival. Simone eyed the woman and could tell right away that things weren't going to go according to plan by the way the old woman was shaking her head. "What did I tell you barely ten minutes ago?" the woman scoffed. "I know damn well we ain't moving that fast!"

"Somebody fell out the line!" Simone reasoned in frustration.

"No they didn't! You bribed them the same way you tried to bribe me with your two hundred dollars! Maybe more! But it ain't gonna work with me! You get your ass in line and play by the rules!"

"Fuck the rules!" Simone yelled as she shoved the woman's calendar off the counter.

"Security!" the old woman yelled aloud for a second time.

"Follow me, ma'am," the same security guard who'd approached Simone the first time said as he approached her once more.

"*Este mierda!*" (This some bullshit!) Simone snapped as she was guided to exit once more.

Simone had tried to skip the line in DMV, but it didn't work. She then tried to bribe her way into the DMV, but in the end, she found herself right behind the female whose spot she'd paid to take. She thought about asking for her money back, but she knew the female would refuse and she would have to knock her out cold given her frustration, so she calmed herself and went with the flow.

Two hours later, Simone was back inside the building. Call it fate, or mere circumstance, whatever it was, she now found herself before the same clerk she'd encountered the previous two times. "How can I help you?" the old woman smiled.

"You know what I'm here for!" Simone snapped as she slid

her registration across the counter while holding onto her money, preparing to pay her vehicle tax and receive her tag.

The woman grabbed Simone's registration and peered over her glasses as she read in silence. Several seconds later, she looked up and said, "Miss Cortez, you're looking to get a new tag for a registered vehicle. Here we only do title transfers and issue new driver's licenses. You're in the wrong place. Here's the address where you need to go to get your tag," the woman said as she slid Simone a card.

Simone's eyes widen and her jaw dropped as she tilted her head to the side, looking at the lady like she was mentally challenged. "You knew what fuck I was here for the whole time and you had me wait in line all this time, bitch?"

"Security!" the old woman said as she walked off from the counter.

Simone threw her hands up in defeat as security guards approached. *"Mierda no me toque! Sé que el camino de esta perra!"* (Don't fucking touch me! I know the way out this bitch!) she bellowed as she threw her hands up in defeat and headed over to another DMV, where she encountered another long line and wait.

****

While Simone stood in line frustrated waiting to obtain her license, Pepper, Loopy and Sweet Pea, meanwhile, had been sitting inside Malik's grill for nearly three hours waiting his arrival. Two of his soldiers, twenty year-olds DeMarco Covas and Maximillian 'Max' Zamora, had been entertaining the three in between making food and weed sales inside the grill.

DeMarco and Max had teamed up with Malik back in two thousand five, shortly after Max had learned that Carmella Lapiente' had killed his older sister Xanthipian Zamora the day she'd robbed Connections over in Saint Charles. During that time, the Hispanics in Fox Park were being forced to choose sides by Carmella and the Perez sisters.

DeMarco, a 5'7", one hundred fifty pound frail-looking, dark-eyed Mexican with a bald faded haircut, had jumped on

Malik's bandwagon early as a foot soldier at the tender age of sixteen. As of 2009, he now oversaw the trap over on Ohio Street with his best friend from elementary school, Maximillian Zamora.

Maximillian was a husky, one hundred and eighty-five pound 5'8" Mexican with a black, curly head of hair and brown eyes. At age twenty, he and DeMarco were deep into trapping and rapping. They were next in line behind Malik to be bumped up to Lieutenant if ever an opening arose. Their statures and innocent looks often left them taken for granted, but when it got down to it, DeMarco and Max were the two soldiers Malik could rely on whenever gunplay was called upon. They hadn't any bodies under their belts to date, but they were more than up to the task and weren't to be taken lightly in spite of their fun-loving demeanors.

One couldn't tell DeMarco and Max they weren't the next Tupacs. Ever since DeMarco had bought a home studio, the two had been practicing rapping while getting high together. From time to time, they would spit rhymes for Pepper, Loopy and Sweet Pea while looking out for them inside Malik's diner. The only problem was that every rap DeMarco and Max spit was a song Tupac had recorded.

Pepper and company thought the two had a good flow, however; before long, they were requesting some of Tupac's music. "Eh," Loopy called out as she sat in the booth with Sweet Pea and Pepper. "You know that song Until the End of Time? That's my favorite by Tupac."

DeMarco and Max tucked their hands to their chests and hopped over to the booth side by side where the girls were sitting enjoying foot long hot dogs and fries. "Let's go with the second verse, Max," DeMarco said as he dropped his arms and came with…. *"So you know…I don't hang around the house much…this all night money making got me outta touch…"*

Max followed with…*"Shit…ain't flashed a smile in a long while…an unexpected birth…worst of the ghetto childs…my attitude got me walking solo…while I'm alone in my lo-lo…"*

"Watching the whole world move in slow mo!" Pepper,

Sweet Pea and Loopy yelled out in unison as they all rocked inside the booth with their arms in the air, raising the roof, Sweet Pea pounding the table to provide a baseline.

DeMarco and Max went back and forth with the lyrics as they danced in unison before the booth in their black Dickies outfits and white Chuck Taylors. Loopy was blown away by the two as Max flipped the lyrics back to DeMarco... *"Who can I trust in this cold world...my phony homie had a baby by my old girl..."*

"But I ain't trippin'...I'm a player I sweatin' him...I sexed his sister had her mumbling like a Mexican..." Max rapped as he pounded his chest and laughed aloud. *"Besides rappin' the only thing I do good is trappin'!"* he ended, changing the last words of the verse as he and DeMarco dapped and spun around in place.

"Glad to see everybody enjoying themselves," twenty-three year-old Malik Gomez said casually as he entered the diner decked out in a dark grey silk suit, black wing tips and a black wool trench coat with three more of his henchmen following.

DeMarco and Max walked off from the booth in silence as they returned to their duties behind the counter. Malik looked his empty diner over. *"Le he dicho dos a mantener un ojo sobre ellos no arrojar un concierto aquí."* (I told you two to keep an eye on them not throw a concert in here.) he reprimanded. He then looked over to the booth where Pepper, Loopy and Sweet Pea were sitting as he held his hands inside his trench coat.

Pepper, knowing she was in the wrong over the things that had gone down the night before, grabbed a brown paper bag, stood up and eyed Malik from across the floor. "Lo siento," she said humbly.

"Siempre siento mucho después de los hechos." (Always sorry after the fact.) Malik remarked in disappointment as he eyed Pepper. *"El ochenta y cinco cientos de dólares es lo que se le debe ese chico de mierda de su coche. ¿Lo tiene?"* (Eighty-five hundred dollars is what you owe that guy for fucking up his car. Do you have it?)

"He aquí nueve mil." (Here's nine thousand.) Pepper remarked as she held out the bag.

Malik looked to the floor beneath his feet, silently signaling for one of his henchmen to retrieve the money. One of his goons went and grabbed the bag and had pulled some of the money out and was flipping through the stacks. *"Todos cientos, Jefe."* (All hundreds, Boss.)

Malik nodded and said, *"Asegúrese de que guy obtiene su dinero. Tenemos que hacer frente en línea recta. Peppi?"* (Make sure that guy gets his money. We straight on that deal. Peppi?) Malik said as he nodded towards his office.

Pepper turned and headed for the office as Malik walked past Sweet Pea and Loopy. He eyed them harshly as he strode by without saying a word as they looked off in different directions, avoiding eye contact. He rounded the corner of his diner and could see Pepper facing him inside his office as he approached. The Mexican gangster had every intention on scolding his hand-picked Lieutenant, but the look on her face, that of a little girl who'd upset her father, had knocked down fortified walls of angry reprisal.

"Ella tiene un gran potencial." (She has so much potential.) Malik thought to himself as he stepped into his office and eyed Pepper for several lingering seconds before gently closing and locking the door. *"Tienes la capacidad de ser un ejecutor de esta familia algún día, Peppi."* (You have it in you to be an Enforcer in this family someday, Peppi.) he said as he turned and faced the youngster. *"Su temeraria forma es lo que obstaculiza. El dinero vendrá si siguen siendo paciente."* (Your reckless ways is what's hindering you. The money will come if you remain patient.)

"Esto no estaba en mí, Malik. Asumo la responsabilidad por la destrucción de la trampa, pero no me refiero a la pérdida de ese coche." (This wasn't on me, Malik. I take responsibility for destroying the trap house, but I didn't mean to lose that car.)

"Usted me dijo que se iba a Louisiana ayer por la noche. ¿Cómo se le terminan en East Saint Louis?" (You told me you were going to Louisiana last night. How did you end up in East

Saint Louis?)

"Este Capricho, como un verde lima Capricho estaba haciendo los mismos movimientos de Simone. Ellos nos seguían de Fox aparcar justo antes de que nos estaba a punto de llegar al lado de la autopista interestatal, he cambiado la ruta." (This Caprice, like a lime green Caprice was making the same moves as Simone. They followed us out of Fox Park right before we was about to get on the interstate so I changed the route.) Pepper defended as she ran her hands through her thick, black head of hair in frustration. *"Pensé yo y mis niñas son seguidos, pero al final resultó ser la policía. Nos metimos en una persecución y flotó en Oriente a Saint Louis y el coche. YO no que eso ocurra, Malik."* (I thought me and my girls was being followed, but it turned out to be the police. We got into a chase and floated over to East Saint Louis and dumped the car. I didn't plan on that happening, Malik.)

Malik eyed Pepper as he walked behind his desk and remained standing. *"Quiero que a mi lado en todo momento hasta la familia de New Holland primer envío. Hay que aprender a moverse cuando usted no tiene que vender cocaína. Esto no es un sprint de fortuna. Se trata de un maratón de la riqueza. Legit. ¿Qué es lo que quiere hacer con tu vida?"* (I want you by my side at all times until the Holland family's first shipment. You need to learn how to move when you have no cocaine to sell. This is not a sprint to fortune. It is a marathon to riches. Legit business. What is it you want to do with your life?)

Pepper merely shrugged. She had no clue what she wanted to with her life exactly. For as long she could remember, she'd been hustling. She'd never even considered life outside of running the streets until Malik posed this question this very day.

"Think about a legit business. Something you would love to do. Something you wouldn't mind getting up in the morning and doing outside of hustling the game," Malik suggested.

"Maybe I could help Loopy and Sweet Pea get their Aunt CeeCee a restaurant or something. I don't know," Pepper sighed. As much as she respected Malik's counsel, Pepper really wasn't feeling his guidance. Going legit was the furthest thing from her mind.

"We'll talk about it later," Malik replied, interrupting Pepper's thoughts. "I'm gone set you and your crew up at the Millennium Hotel tomorrow morning. No movement until you get the go ahead from me, understand?"

"Si," Pepper replied.

"You meet me here in the morning at nine and we'll get everything set up," Malik ended as he extended his hands, allowing Pepper to leave his presence.

"I need a ride over to Bangin' Heads to meet up with Simone," Pepper let it be known.

"I'll drop you and your girls off," Malik ended as he grabbed the keys to his four door white on white 2008 Mercedes GL 450 SUV.

CHAPTER TWENTY-FOUR
THEY CAME FROM THE NORTH

"What Malik say to you, Pepper?" Sweet Pea asked the moment Malik pulled away from Bangin' Heads.

"He gone set us up at the Millennium Hotel tomorrow," Pepper answered as she and her girls walked into the nearly empty salon. "Before we do that, though, I gotta go up to Louisiana and pick up some more money and guns. All we have is Loopy Mac-10 stashed in Simone's Hummer and a nine millimeter. We gone need some paper while we over to the hotel."

"If we going to the hotel tomorrow we should just chill here in Saint Louis until the morning. Malik can give us some more guns and me and Sweet Pea have enough money," Loopy reasoned.

"Y'all got money but I don't. I gave up all my loot paying for that car we lost last night," Pepper retorted. "I got money stashed up there and I need to get it anyway."

"Well, well, well! The dirty trio has arrived," Kantrell dragged as she eyed her friends walking into the building.

"The fuck y'all been all day?" Simone asked as she sat in Jessie's chair getting her fade tightened up.

"She was gettin' scolded by her father," Sweet Pea joked while pointing to Pepper.

"Malik ain't for playin' games," Kantrell chimed in as she

cleaned her station. "Y'all work for my man y'all gone have to do away with all that foolishness. The game ain't nothing to joke around with trust me."

"We know," Pepper sighed as she sat in an empty salon chair.

"We was talkin' about going to the inauguration to see Barack get sworn in," Kree remarked as she straightened her work station. "Y'all should take the trip and see history."

"Presidents get sworn in every four years," Loopy remarked.

"Not a black one, though," Jessie smiled proudly. "Me and Kantrell the only ones can feel that right there. Y'all Mexican mutherfuckas don't know how good this shit feel."

"Barack's cool," Loopy chimed in. "Tell him I wish him all the best when you get to the inauguration."

"Now ya' being facetious and shit!" Kantrell laughed. "I bet you voted for McCain old ass, huh?"

"I ain't vote for nobody." Loopy retorted. "Makes no difference to me. They all some crooks."

"See? I don't like your attitude. You gone respect my President," Jessie chimed in while lining Simone.

"None of y'all was into politics until Barack got in the race. Now y'all jocking," Sweet Pea laughed.

"Well, we going see history," Kree remarked. "I know they gone hate that black man, though. They is gone hate his guts."

"They better not harm one hair on his head!" Kantrell snapped. "I got his back! Y'all coming to DC or not?"

"If it ain't nothing going on we'll go," Pepper replied. "I never been to the capital city."

"We can have like a Obama bash!" Kantrell snapped, happy her girls were joining her Kree and Jessie. "We have a suite at the Ritz Carlton. We gone stay the whole weekend and go see him get sworn in. We can tour the city and everything. It's gone be so much fun, watch."

"Kree you think you can do my hair tonight? You know that

style I like with the curly locks on the side and the spider arms at the top?"

"That'll take a couple of hours, Pepper. We're closing early tonight. It's been slow all day. See me tomorrow. I got you."

"Cool," Pepper remarked. "We 'bout ready to ride out anyway soon as Jessie finish lining Simone big head," she ended.

****

Later that night, after hanging over to Bangin' Heads, Pepper and her crew climbed into Simone's Hummer and began heading north to Pepper's safe house in Louisiana, Missouri. It was still early for the crew at eight 'o' clock, but it was dark and bitterly cold out. The streets of Saint Louis were void of vehicles, save for straight-laced citizens trying to make it home after completing a second, or headed in for a third shift amid the lightly-falling snow.

Loopy sat in the backseat of Simone's Hummer behind the driver's seat in deep thought. After leaving Malik's place, she and Sweet Pea had plans on going seeing their Aunt CeeCee to let the woman know the two of them were okay as it had been nearly two weeks since they'd seen the woman. Both were calling on a regular basis, but their aunt only reprimanded them, telling them they should be home and not out running the streets playing gangster.

Loopy's Aunt CeeCee's words, *"Ain't nothing out there but death,"* words that had been quoted to her during each and every call she'd made to her aunt, rang aloud in her ears ominously as Simone entered the town of Saint Peters and exited off of I-270 onto Salt Lick Road, which was Highway 79—the road that led north to Pepper's safe house in Louisiana, Missouri.

Loopy looked over to Sweet Pea as dread overtook her psyche. Her cousin was on the phone ordering several pairs of suede and fur Ugg boots she'd mentioned earlier inside of Bangin' Heads. Her eyes then honed in on the front seat. Simone and Pepper were passing a blunt back and forth while laughing to themselves. Pepper had her seat laid back with one of her legs posted up on the front of the dashboard as she and Simone went back and forth, running down episodes of the crazy day they'd both had dealing with the DMV and Malik.

"I wasted three hundred dollars tryna jump the line. I swear I ever see that old ass lady on the streets I'm a hit her ass in the head with a brick! Them new bricks with the sharp ass corners, ya' smell me?" Simone assured as she passed the blunt to Pepper, who was laughing at Simone's remark.

Loopy leaned back in her seat and placed her hand underneath her chin, eyeing her surroundings as the Hummer cruised up the four-lane highway. Businesses were open, and the highway was lit up, offering up a sense of security, but the slender Uruguayan simply couldn't shake the feeling that the ride to Louisiana was a mistake in the making.

"Boots be in next week!" Sweet Pea exclaimed delightfully as she set her phone in the back console.

"You shoulda waited until the club in Saint Charles open up in March, girl," Pepper snapped. "Malik gone have our asses hemmed up come tomorrow morning."

"That's only for a little while," Sweet Pea shot back. "And I'll have way more money to order more boots and clothes by then."

"Yo," Simone chimed in. "I was supposed to hook up with Dooney tonight, right? But you can believe he gone be in the suite tomorrow night so y'all gone have to find something to do for a couple of hours."

"Whaaattt?" Pepper and Sweet Pea sang.

"When, how long y'all two been fuckin', bitch?" Pepper asked in wonderment as she passed the blunt back to Simone.

"'Bout a week after that shit went down with Toodie," Simone replied as she took a quick toke and stretched her arm over the backseat.

Loopy turned away, but Sweet Pea grabbed the blunt and began toking. She passed the blunt to her cousin a couple of minutes later, but Loopy fanned it off. *"No me siento como el fumar esta noche."* (I don't feel like smoking tonight.) Loopy said as her eyes continued scanning the road.

"You okay?" Sweet Pea asked as she passed the blunt over the front seat to Pepper.

"*No deberíamos estar aquí, Donatella.*" Loopy sulked.

"The fuck you mean we shouldn't be here?" Simone booted as she eyed Loopy through the rearview mirror.

"That's that paranoid shit hittin' again," Pepper laughed, buzzed from the potent marijuana she'd been toking.

Loopy said nothing as the four-lane road narrowed up into a two lane highway. Soon, the numerous businesses that dotted the Saint Louis suburb of Saint Peters faded into the background and the dense darkness of State Highway 79 began to dominate the area. The inside of the Hummer grew dark as dense woods on either side began to dominate the scenery. For a good portion of the ride, the four remained silent, absorbed in their own individual thoughts, Pepper thinking about what Malik had said to her about opening a legit business someday. Simone was anticipating on hooking up with Dooney the following day and Sweet Pea was hoping UPS didn't fuck her order up. Loopy, meanwhile, was carrying with her the feeling that tomorrow was not going to come.

Several cars had approached from the north and Loopy took notice each and every time. The journey to Louisiana seemed possible after a fifty mile trek, but just ten miles outside of town, Loopy saw it—that same lime green Caprice with the white rag top that had ridden up on the side of the Grand Prix she and her crew were riding in the night before. She sat up in her seat and watched in seemingly slow motion as the old school Caprice glided by the Hummer headed south as she and her girls headed north. "*Que ellos!*"(That's them!) she yelled as she looked over the back seat at the backlights on the car. The car was braking as it rounded a sharp curve Loopy noticed, so she leaned down and grabbed the thirty-two shot Mac-10 resting in between her feet.

Back inside the Caprice, two miles south, Boogie, Ya Murder and Maggie McPherson were already locking and loading their assault weapons as William 'Popeye' Slack slowed the car and entered into a three point turnaround while lowering the white rag top on the gangster ride. The trunk was popped on the ride as the assassins from Cincinnati, Ohio righted the car and headed back north, hell bent on catching up to the pristine white Hummer they knew belonged to Simone Cortez after spying the ride over in Fox Park the night Pepper had burned down her trap house.

Two miles to the north, confusion ruled the interior of the Hummer as headlights rapidly approached the rear of Simone's ride. Pepper was looking around, having not a clue what was about to go down as she was high out of her mind.

Sweet Pea had gripped the nickel-plated nine millimeter Beretta she was toting as she and Loopy eyed the car speeding up on them.

"Que eso? Quien carajos es, Loopy?" (Who that? Who the fuck is it, Loopy?) Pepper asked while looking over the back seat as her heart raced.

Before Loopy could answer, a volley of bullets cut loose from the Caprice that was now on the bumper of the Hummer. Loopy grabbed Sweet Pea and pulled her down as the front and rear driver's side window on Simone's ride shattered. Flesh and blood splattered onto the shattered front windshield as Simone Cortez let go of the steering wheel and slumped over into Pepper's lap. The massive SUV swerved to the right, headed towards a steep drop off that was filled with trees. Pepper screamed aloud and grabbed the steering wheel and tried to right the SUV.

Loopy and Sweet Pea rose up and opened fire at that moment, their bullets shattering the back window of the Hummer as it fell off into the trench bordering the highway.

Simone had checked out early. She was shot in the neck and the back of head, her face blown off completely. Pepper continued struggling with the steering wheel trying to bring the SUV back onto the road, but she couldn't control it; the Hummer rolled over onto its passenger side and slid down the slope for several feet before rolling over onto its top and slamming into a thick grove of trees nose first.

Sweet Pea was unhurt in the crash. She could see the headlights on the car the people who'd fired upon her crew slowly approaching. The car braked hard and three silhouettes jumped from the interior of the convertible with long, shiny objects that looked like baseball bats in their hands. She was still clutching the nine millimeter as she crept to the rear of the Hummer across the upside down SUV's roof.

Loopy, meanwhile, was unable to move as she lay dangled over the collapsed backseat in suspended animation. She was looking up at the hit squad as they crept to the edge of the highway.

"Donatella, no se mueven!" (Donatella, don't move!) Loopy pleaded, unable to control her arms and legs as she coughed up blood.

Sweet Pea ignored her cousin's request as she emerged from the rear window of the smoking Hummer while blasting her weapon, doing the best she could to stave off an unknown enemy. Bullets from her .9mm fired off into the night uphill and Loopy could only watch in futility as the silhouettes of her crew's attackers casually scattered amid Sweet Pea's gunshots while firing back at random.

Loopy heard a yelp spill forth from one of the gunmen as her cousin continued dumping off rounds as she stood outside the fallen Hummer. She could see the figure, who she believed was a female, given her scream, lunge up against the front of the Caprice while clutching her leg before she scurried off to the driver's side, her chrome rifle draping her side as she shielded herself.

Everything went silent at that moment as both parties had run out of bullets and had to reload. Sweet Pea threw the .9mm aside and knelt down at that moment. *"Guadalupe, donde el Mac diez?"* (Guadalupe, where's the Mac ten?)

Loopy tried to answer, but she now found herself unable to speak. She had wanted to tell her cousin to just lie down and play dead, but she couldn't utter a word. Blood continue dripping from her mouth, and now her nose. She tried to move her arms and reach out to Donatella, but she simply couldn't as she'd lost all control of her movements below her neck.

Sweet Pea, meanwhile, was crawling around in the back end of the Hummer. Loopy knew where the gun lay, just beneath her dangling arms, but she was hoping Donatella didn't find it, if only to allow her to remain still. Her eyes filled with tears as she watched her cousin find the Mac-10 and slide back out of the jeep. Seconds later, Sweet Pea stood up and opened fire.

Loopy could see her crew's attackers preparing to leave, but when Sweet Pea opened fire, it spurred them on once more. *"Diese hacken will einfach nicht sterben!"* (These hoes won't die!)

Loopy didn't know what language was being spoken, but she knew it wasn't of any solace as she watched another female run to the back of the Caprice. "Ya, help Maggie!" she heard the female scream aloud as she raised the trunk.

"Jada," Loopy said to herself as she watched helplessly.

Amid Sweet Pea's gunfire, Loopy could only watch as her cousin waged battle. Silently, she was calling out for Sweet Pea to just fall and play dead because what she now knew to be Ya Murder's team wasn't going to stop shooting until all movement ceased.

Sweet Pea lit up the night with the Mac-10 as the Caprice backed up a ways. Loopy watched in silence with tears streaming from her face as the female who'd jogged to the car's trunk caught up with the car, disappeared briefly, and reemerged with what seemed like a Gatling gun in her hands.

Flames from the gun the woman welded shot out at least three feet from the gun's barrel in rapid succession and it sounded like a hundred bowling balls landing on empty steel trash cans. Sweet Pea's Mac-10 could no longer be heard over the thunderous gunfire, even though Loopy knew her cousin was still waging battle. Bullets began landing all around the wrecked SUV. Simone's Hummer vibrated from the shells lodging into the ride.

Loopy was hit in her side with only God knows what, the shell slicing through the seat she was dangling from and forcing her to the ground. The last thing she saw before everything went black was the backside Donatella's body dropping to the ground, her entire back covered in a dark reddish hue as blood spurted from her back and the top of her head as she lay convulsing on the snow-covered ground that had been dyed red with her spurting blood.

CHAPTER TWENTY-FIVE

ON BORROWED TIME

Pepper coughed into the cold night air as she lay on her back in the snow. Last she remembered was trying to brace herself as Simone's Hummer slid across the ground while approaching a bunch of trees. The impact had thrown her from the SUV. She was lucky not to slam up against a rock while in the air. She'd landed in a thick snow bank, which had knocked her out cold momentarily. Grabbing her head and rising up slowly while looking around, Pepper spotted Simone's Hummer, the once pristine vehicle now unrecognizable in the silent darkness. Two of the rims were bent, the front end was smashed and all the windows were shattered.

"Simone?" Pepper called out weakly, breaking the silence as she crawled over to the wreck where she saw her friend lying on the roof of the up-ended SUV.

Pepper was hoping what she last remembered wasn't what she'd seen as she crawled over to her best friend while repeatedly moaning her name. Simone made not a sound, however, as Pepper neared her and reached out to her. Wetness coated her fingertips when she reached out and touched Simone's shoulder. She leaned in and saw her friend's mangled face with what looked like bloody ground meat lying beside her open skull and grew horrified.

"Simone, no te puedes ir! No se puede dejar. No me dejar, Simone!" (Simone, you can't leave me! You can't leave me!

Don't leave me, Simone!) she cried. Not wanting to believe her best friend had been killed, Pepper broke down into tears, shaking her friend repeatedly. *"Simone, wake up! Wake up tenemos que—"* (Simone, wake up! Wake up we have to—) reality finally hit Pepper and she stopped speaking. She lay on her stomach crying her heart out as she stared at the one person in life who mattered most to her. Flashes of the day she'd first met Simone over on Ann Avenue back in Fox Park ran through her mind. For as long as she could remember, and for every important event in her young life, for Pepper, Simone had always been the one that was able to share in her joy, what little she had throughout her young life. She'd shed many tears with Pepper, backed her faithfully on the streets and had become more than a sister to her throughout the course of their friendship. In a matter of seconds, Pepper's life had been forever altered with the death of twenty-one year-old Simone Cortez.

While lying on her stomach in a state of disbelief, Pepper caught sight of Loopy staring at her as she, too, lay on the roof of the Hummer. She could tell Loopy was still alive given her neck movement, so she backed out of the SUV and headed towards the back of the vehicle to try and help. She remembered the cell phone in her pocket at that moment and pulled it out to call 911 as she rounded the rear end of the ride. The phone flew from her hands when she tripped over what she thought was a fallen log. The taillights on the Hummer lit up a small area behind the ride, enabling Pepper to find her phone quickly. She turned and knelt down near the Hummer's shattered back window and came face to face with Sweet Pea and was struck with another round of horrification.

Like, Simone, Pepper could tell another one her friends had been killed. Sweet Pea lay with her eyes open, a single bullet hole was clearly seen in her face, the shell having ripped off her top lip and shattering her nose. Sweet Pea's chest was stained in red and the snow around her body was iced over in red as well. She'd bled out and died minutes after being ripped to shreds. Pepper could go no further. She sat communal style in the snow and frantically dialed 911 while staring at Loopy, who was able to twist her neck around and make eye contact with her once more, yet and still, unable to speak. The two had no choice but to sit and wait on help.

****

Malik was over to Kantrell's house sound asleep when his phone rang. He stirred awake and removed Kantrell's arm from his chest as he reached for his cell phone. *"¿Hola?"*

"Esta noche nos golpeó en la Autopista setenta y nueve. Simone y Donatella están muertos y Chiflados no pueden sobrevivir." (We got hit tonight on Highway seventy-nine. Simone and Donatella are dead and Loopy may not survive.) Pepper said in disbelief as she walked up the sidewalk leading to her safe house in Louisiana after being dropped off by a Louisiana sheriff's deputy.

Malik removed the phone from his ear and stared at it for several seconds. Pepper's words hadn't sunk in fully just yet. Just hours ago he was in their presence, now two of her crew were dead and another's fate was uncertain. *"¿Dónde están ahora?"* (Where are you now?) he asked as he nudged Kantrell awake and grabbed his Glock .45 off the nightstand.

"Estoy en el estado de Louisiana. VOY cambiar y volver a Mercy Hospital. Loopy era la vida de empate se hace una hora para la cirugía." (I'm in Louisiana. I'm going change and head back to Mercy Hospital. Loopy was life-flighted there an hour ago for surgery.)

"Me reuniré allí con vosotros!" (I'll meet you there!) Malik snapped before he and Pepper ended the call.

"What happened?" Kantrell asked as she sat up in the bed and stretched.

Malik looked over to his woman and right away she knew something was wrong. "Who was it?" she asked somberly.

"Everybody in Pepper's crew besides her," Malik answered, somewhat shocked as he dialed another number.

****

"...Nah, I never gave a fuck about got damn a bitch... because when it comes Z-Max...you know all about flippin'

bricks...never gave fuck about a snitch because to me that mean drama...take out your whole click come back and murder ya' momma...yeah them Gomez boys....you know we keepin' 'shit in order...been about that murder game ever since we came across the border..."

The home studio inside of DeMarco's pad was dark and smoky as he and Max freestyled over the instrumental of Birdman and T-Pain's song *Know What I'm Doing*. Max, who'd come up with the name Z-Max while spitting the verse, was dumping lyrics as he vibed inside the makeshift recording booth DeMarco had built inside his closet using old egg shell containers and insulation.

DeMarco dubbed Max's voice and deepened the base in the microphone and it was on from that point forth. "Use that hook over and over again on the break down!" he yelled into Max's headphones as his cell phone vibrated.

DeMarco answered and Malik ran down what had briefly gone down with Pepper's crew and ordered him over to Mercy Hospital. He powered down the keyboard and everything went silent. Max was still spitting lyrics, but had stopped when the music cut off. "What the fuck, dude?" he asked as he pushed the closet door open.

"We have to go, man. I'll tell you about it on the way." DeMarco stated as he looked around for the keys to his Escalade.

****

Kree was in tears as she ran around her room trying to dress herself. The news Kantrell had given her sent shockwaves through her body. Sweet Pea and Simone? Dead? She couldn't believe it. Just hours ago she was kicking it with her friends and they were all alive, healthy and happy and talking about going to the Presidential inauguration. Now, two were gone, one was barely hanging on and the other had to be in a total state of flux from an emotional standpoint. She was worried to death about Pepper, having called her friend repeatedly and leaving messages as she wasn't picking up. She ran out of her house with her phone pressed to ear as she dialed the Cruz cousins' Aunt CeeCee's number to learn whether the woman had heard the news or not.

The entire crew from Saint Charles was converging on Mercy Hospital. Whether they knew it or not, Pepper and her girls had mad love in Fox Park. Malik and his crew vouched for them, backed them and aided them for the simple fact that they were thorough. Everybody that spoke Spanish knew about the murder Loopy had committed against Dibble in order to keep Jessie from going to jail. They also knew about the snitch Pepper and Simone had bodied when they were under Toodie Perez, and they all had a gut feeling that Pepper was involved in the disappearance of Toodie as well. The numerous licks Pepper and her crew had pulled off, namely the one against Tito and Toine Charles was gutsy to say the least. She and her crew had a reputation to be respected in Fox Park, and when word spread that they'd suffered a crushing blow, everyone close to them came out to show love and support.

Pepper pulled into the parking lot of Mercy Hospital feeling numb. She'd cried the whole way down to Saint Charles. She'd tried to travel back down Highway 79 in order to check on the crime scene where she knew Simone and Sweet Pea lay, but the highway had been shut down completely at the town's edge. She rerouted down U.S. Highway 61 and had arrived nearly two hours later after calling Malik.

With her shoulders drooping, Pepper, dressed in a long, olive green suede trench coat and matching knee-length boots and her thick, black hair hanging wild over her head, somewhat shielding her pained, redden eyes, walked into the emergency room with tears dripping from her pointed chin.

"*¿Le parece bien, la pimienta? Dios, no se puede estar bien después de pasar por esto.*" (Are you okay, Pepper? God, you can't be okay after going through this.) Kree spoke through compassionate tears as she, Jessie and Kantrell flanked Pepper and gave her hugs.

Seeing her friends in the emergency room moved Pepper deeply. No longer able to bear the pain, she heaved and dropped to one knee as Kantrell and Jessie held her up by the arms. "*Simone Cortez y Donatella Cruz! Que mi familia! He perdido a mi familia! Mis hermanas, hombre! Mis hermanas!"* (Simone Cortez and Donatella Cruz! They my family! I lost my family! My sisters, man! My sisters!) Pepper cried aloud, her mouth wide open and her eyes wide, still unable to comprehend what tragedy had befallen the only family she had left in the world.

Kantrell and Jessie tried get Pepper to stand, but she hadn't the strength in her legs as her heart was too pained. They guided the emotionally-wounded seventeen year-old over to a row of chairs and sat her down. Pepper hid her head in her lap as her friends rubbed her back. "Guadalupe?" she asked as she heaved.

"She's, she's in surgery," Kantrell spoke softly. "She has a spinal fracture and a collapsed lung. A bullet pierced her liver, too, that's the major injury," she ended through tears.

Malik walked up at that moment. He looked down on his protégé and could only imagine the pain she was in. Pepper had a lot to bear in her young age. Most would crack, but here she was, where she needed to be, amongst family who cared. *"Todo, todo lo que ha ocurrido es que no fallo, Peppi Vargas."* (Everything, everything that has happened to you is not fault, Peppi Vargas.) he spoke out in a comforting tone as he tucked his hands into his trench coat pockets.

Pepper raised her head slowly and eyed Malik from her seated position. *"Usted no está loco de mí? Creí que me culpan por ello."* (You're not mad at me? I thought you would blame me for this.) she stated through tears.

Malik eyed Kantrell, Jessie and Kree, silently requesting with his eyes that he and Pepper be left alone. When the three cleared out, Malik occupied an empty seat beside Pepper, placed an arm around her neck and pulled her close. He kissed her thick head of hair as he held her tightly and whispered in her ear, *"Quién le hizo esto a tu tripulación? Quién estaba detrás de todo esto?"* (Who did this to your crew? Who was behind it?)

Pepper rested her elbows on her knees inside the emergency room and looked to the floor. She hadn't a clue as to who was behind the hit because she and her crew had done so much dirt on the streets. For all she knew, it could've been some dealers out of Troy, Missouri, or maybe a crew from Quincy, Illinois where they'd killed two people after robbing their meth lab. *"No sé, hombre."* (I don't know, man.) Pepper groaned as she clutched her stomach and continued to agonize over her friends' demise. *"Nos fue tan en mierda podría haber sido cualquiera. Todo lo que sé es que vinieron desde el norte, hizo un giro en forma de U y montó en nosotros y que suelta."* (We was into so much shit it could've been anybody. All I know is that they came from the north, made a U-turn and rode up on us and let loose.)

Malik sat back and ran his hand over his neatly trimmed beard as he entered into deep thought. Pepper had mentioned to him about being paranoid of a Caprice that was tailing her crew the day before and he began to wonder if there was a connection to be made.

"Loopy vimos todo." (Loopy saw it all.) Pepper stated, interrupting Malik's thoughts. *"Yo recuerdo que ella diciendo que ellos antes de que todo se vino a pique. No sé que son."* (I remember her saying that's them before everything went down. I just don't know who them are.)

"Si tuviera que adivinar." (If you had to guess.) Malik whispered as he leaned into Pepper. *"Si tuviera que adivinar? Que diría usted estaba detrás de todo esto?"* (If you had to guess? Who would you say was behind it?)

"Jada Murdella." Pepper replied somewhat unsure. *"Ella ha sido un hecho real tranquilo desde que salió de su mismo hospital. Pero si es ella? Ella no lo hizo por sí mismo."* (She been real quiet ever since she left this same hospital. But if it was her? She didn't do it by herself.)

"Me han puesto algunos oídos en las calles." (I'm gone put some ears on the streets.) Malik replied. *"Mañana, yo te daré esa habitación en el Hotel Millennium."* (Tomorrow, I'll get you that room over to the Millennium Hotel.)

"No se preocupe por ello." (Don't worry about it.) Pepper countered. *"Me ha saltado al Kree, pero ahora, quiero ver*

cómo unos iluminados." (I'm gone chill by Kree house, but right now, I just wanna see how Loopy doing.)

Malik and Pepper left the emergency room and traveled up to the floor where Loopy was undergoing surgery. Wails from her Aunt CeeCee let them know that the situation hadn't improved. Malik threw his arms up as he stared at DeMarco and Max. His soldiers walked over to him with their heads bowed where DeMarco let it be known that Loopy had slipped into a coma. The only person in Pepper's crew who knew exactly what'd gone down had been silenced for time unknown. Malik was now left without any solid confirmation as to who exactly was behind the hit on his protégé. All he could do was hope for Loopy's recovery so he and Pepper could maybe learn what had gone down exactly and take their revenge.

CHAPTER TWENTY-SIX

SWALLOWED UP

January 10, 2009

Dawk had just pulled up to the warehouse in Valley Brook in Bay's Continental where a flurry of activity was underway. Many of the docks held trucks waiting to load and unload this early, cold but sunny winter day. The sky was clear blue and there was a crispness in the air this early Saturday morning, one that created a certain tranquility that made one appreciate life.

Dawk looked up to the sky towards the east and stared at the bright sun through his sunshade covered eyes. Somber was his mood having learned what had happened to Pepper's crew. She hadn't even gotten her feet wet in the family business and had been dealt a blow that would be hard to recover from, if ever at all. He climbed from the car and walked over to the security doors and let himself in with his key card. Amid the whizzing forklifts and other dock workers, he made his way to the second floor office where he saw Martha, Bay and T-top sitting behind a long desk that faced the office's door. He stepped in, closed the door and locked it as he removed his black skull cap.

Bay looked over to him and knew something was wrong right away. "What happened?" she asked as she stood up from her seat.

"One of our crews got hit last night," he spoke somberly.

"Who?" Bay asked.

"Pepper's crew."

Bay stepped back and ran her hands through her hair as T-top leaned back in her chair. "Dammit, man!" she scoffed.

Twiggy had a pair of earbuds in her ear jamming Beyonce`. When she heard Dawk speak, she raised the volume to drown out the conversation as she wanted to know nothing about the family's illegal activities.

"Was it over that Tito and Toine deal?" T-top asked Dawk.

"Nobody not sure. Pepper survived, but two of her crew dead and the other one in a coma—don't look good for her."

"What's the plan?" Bay asked. "They at least know who did it, right?"

Dawk shook his head to say no. "The Mexicans think Ya Murder had something to do with it, but they not sure. We gone have to get to the bottom of it quick-like because Malik say his crew ready to kill any and everybody over this one," he answered as he eyed Martha. "Can you cover for us why we head over to Saint Louis to keep order over there?"

"Yeah," Martha assured. "Me and Irene can handle it."

"Whenever y'all ready," Dawk told Bay and T-top before he turned and left the office. Within minutes, the big three were on the road with nothing but the clothes on their backs.

****

Doctors were only allowing one visitor at a time to sit with Loopy inside the ICU over to Mercy Hospital. Her Aunt CeeCee had sat with her for several hours after she'd come out of surgery, but she soon had to leave to identify Sweet Pea's body and make funeral arrangements for her niece. The woman had cried so much in the early morning hours, a nurse had to come in and mop the floor beneath the chair she sat in.

When CeeCee left, Pepper went in and sat with Loopy. The youngster was no stranger to death, but what lay before her eyes was carnage unparalleled. Loopy lay on her back with a breathing tube inserted into her mouth as she couldn't breathe on her own. Her neck was in this thick plaster cast to keep her stabilized. A large gauze pad covered her midsection where doctors had cut her open to remove the bullet fragment lodged in her liver. There were so many instruments surrounding her friend, Pepper felt as if she had enough machinery to guide her beyond the stars all the way to heaven. Doctors said Loopy may not survive because her immune system was too weak to recover. If her wounds didn't heal, her aunt would have to make the decision on whether or not to pull the plug as the breathing machine was the only thing keeping her alive at this point.

Pepper sat with her right hand balled up and her left fist to her lips as she eyed her friend with tears streaming down her face. *"Todo lo que tienes que hacer es vivir. Simplemente vivir, Loopy. Lo siento por todo. Tiene usted razón. No deberíamos haber estado allí por la noche."* (All you have to do is live. Just live, Loopy. I'm sorry for everything. You were right. We shouldn't have been there last night.) Pepper admitted as she wiped tears from her face and leaned back in the chair.

Pepper placed her hands atop her head and bit her bottom lip as she continued eyeing Loopy. How she herself survived that crash, she had no answer, but she couldn't help but to feel as if it should be her and not Loopy on the verge of death. The future was now a veil over her eyes as she wasn't sure how things would play out from this point forth. The world now seemed empty to the bewildered seventeen year-old. Never had she felt so alone. *"Tal vez mañana será un día major."* (Maybe tomorrow will be a better day.) she spoke lowly as she reached out and touched Loopy's arm.

Pepper checked the time on her cell phone and saw that it was nearing four 'o' clock in the evening. If she left now, she could beat the traffic and be in Louisiana before six. She'd told Malik she was going to stay with Kree, but the youngster simply wanted to get away from everything to be able to clear her mind and accept the fact that her friends weren't going to be around any longer. Two funerals, funerals of two of her best friends would have to be attended in the upcoming days and she wasn't sure if she was up to saying a final farewell. On top of that, it wasn't a certainty that Loopy would even pull through. She eased up from the chair and stepped closer to her comatose friend, leaned over and kissed her forehead tenderly. *"Te amo, Loopy. Cuando se despierta, todo será mejor para nosotros."* (I love you, Loopy. When you wake up, everything will be better for us.)

Pepper backed away from her friend and grabbed her hand and squeezed tight. She was hoping Loopy would respond, to at least tremble or flinch her eyes, but there was nothing. She remained where she lay without budging. She let go of her friend's hand, backed away with tears steadily running down her face, turned, and silently walked out of the room where she was met in the hallway by DeMarco and Max, who were assigned to guard duty by Malik.

"Did she move?" DeMarco asked as he looked down at Pepper.

"Nothing yet. She, I hope when I come back tomorrow she's still here, man!" she cried aloud.

DeMarco and Max hugged Pepper. "Get some rest, Peppi," Max whispered.

"Yo soy. Si alguien me busca, estaré en Louisiana." (I am. If anybody looking for me, I'll be in Louisiana.) Pepper said as she dropped her head and walked out of the intensive care unit in a state of intense depression.

The walk through the parking lot was a slow, lonely walk for Pepper. It had been a bright sunny day, but her heart was poisoned. God's sun did nothing to make the day bright in her eyes. She was feeling as if she had nothing left in life without her friends. She kept replaying the good times she and her girls had shared. All the laughter—the wild times they'd had committing crimes—it was all fun and games for them not too long ago, but on this day, the life she and her girls were living was brought home in a heavy dose of reality that had her drunk on regret, and not knowing which way to turn, so she headed to the only place that now offered solace—her home in Louisiana, Missouri.

Pepper climbed behind the wheel of her 2005 four door black Mazda RX-8 on chrome wheels, a car she hadn't driven in months until the night before as she'd been riding around with Simone since the fall, and pulled out of her parking spot with a wet, red face. The ride to Louisiana was a smooth, carefree one for Pepper. She'd ridden up Highway 61, afraid to have to past the scene where she'd lost two of her best friends. She made it to her safe house in Louisiana just before six P.M. and pulled her RX-8 into her driveway and up under her canopy. Hers was a newly-built three bedroom HUD house that sat in a cul de sac on the west side of Louisiana, Missouri just off U.S. Highway 54. Louisiana sat right on the Mississippi River to the east and only had a population of 3,300. It was a small town in the middle of nowhere, and here, Pepper felt safe as only Malik's crew knew where she resided.

The neighborhood was dark and void as Pepper climbed from her car. A few dogs off in the distance barked and she couldn't help but to think about Hutch and Honey. She chuckled to herself while climbing the stairs and fumbling with her keys, reminiscing on the high speed chase through East Saint Louis where Loopy and Sweet Pea flung Hutch from the speeding car. She unlocked her door, paying no mind that her alarm hadn't gone off, as she turned and locked herself inside her home and immediately removed her coat.

Pepper was preparing to call Kree to let her know she wasn't going to spend the night, but the battery on her cell phone had just died. She made her way through her home, clicking on the hall lights as she headed for her bedroom to search for her phone charger. Unable to find it, Pepper hung her coat in her closet and headed back to the kitchen to search out something to cook for dinner.

She pulled her freezer open and reached for a pack of ground meat to make beef tacos, but opted for a pack of sirloin strips in order to make steak enchiladas instead. While the meat thawed out in the microwave, she went and drew herself a bath inside her Jacuzzi. She returned to her bedroom to search for her charger once more, but still couldn't find the plug. She really needed to call Kree to let her know she was safe at home, and she also knew Malik would be calling to check on her pretty soon. Knowing she needed her phone charged, the youngster donned a cotton robe and stepped out into the cold with her phone where she unlocked her car and placed her phone on her car charger to charge it up while she bathed and fixed dinner for herself.

After a long bath that lasted nearly an hour, Pepper climbed from her Jacuzzi and dried herself. She was drying her hair when a feeling as if she was being watched entered her mind. Slowly, she removed the towel from her face and was greeted with the wall out in the hallway. She exhaled deeply as she looked around the bathroom relieved as she was expecting to see someone standing before her.

Donning a pair of powder blue silk sleeping shorts and matching tank top and white fur slippers, Pepper walked up the hall towards the kitchen. The sirloin strips had been thawed completely and she set about seasoning the meat in the sink. Before long, the steak was sizzling in the skillet and the tortillas were warming in the oven. The movie Takers, with stars Idris Elba, Michael Ely, T.I. and Chris Brown, was a movie Pepper had never seen since it'd come out back in 2008. Simone had given her a burnt copy, but she'd never gotten the chance to watch the movie. Tonight, she would treat herself. She sat in front of the TV eating her steak enchiladas while polishing her toe nails and enjoying a glass of wine. From time to time, she would reflect on her friends and simply break down in tears, other times, she would laugh aloud.

A rollercoaster of emotions filled Pepper's psyche, but just being in the comfort of her own home brought about a sense of relief for the time being. She was on the edge of her seat watching the movie, fantasizing over the movie stars as she sat on her comfy couch with her legs tucked underneath her body sipping glasses of wine. When the movie ended, Pepper remembered she had to call Kree to let her know she wasn't spending the night at her home. She checked her wall clock and saw that it was nearing nine 'o' clock. Kree had gotten off at eight and Pepper just knew her friend was wondering where she was as she was supposed to had met at her home at that exact hour. Buzzing off the wine she'd been sipping on, she rose from her sofa and began searching for her cell phone inside her home.

****

Sixty miles down the road, Malik had just entered the ICU of Mercy Hospital, having closed his diner early. For the past hour he'd been calling Pepper and had been getting nothing but her voice mail. He tried again as he walked into the hospital lobby. *This ya' girl Pep! If ya' got this ya' ain't got me! Say something and I'll hit ya' back!* Malik snapped his phone shut, believing Pepper was still sitting with Loopy as he made his way up to the ICU. He stepped off the elevator and eyed a sleeping DeMarco as Max sat in the waiting area watching an NBA game while sipping coffee.

"Pepper still in there with Loopy?" Malik asked as he walked into the waiting area.

"She was in bad shape, Boss," Max answered. "She went home to Louisiana. Said she'll be back in the morning."

"No, No, No! Es una sesión de pato!" (No, No, No! She's a sitting duck up there!" Malik yelled as he punched the wall repeatedly. Security rushed the gangster. *"El fuck lejos de mí!"* (The fuck away from me!) he yelled as he threw his hands up and backed away from the two guards as he turned and ran from the ICU. *"Max, hombre! Tenemos que llegar a Peppi!"* (Max come on, man! We have to get to Pepper!) Malik commanded as he ran towards the elevators.

Max shook DeMarco awoke before he took off after Malik. He'd missed the elevator, so he took the stairs, jumping down over a half dozen flights where he met Malik out in front of the hospital's main entrance. "What the fuck, Boss?" he asked as he jumped into the passenger seat of Malik's Mercedes GL 450.

Malik didn't answer Max right away. He was hoping he was wrong in his assumptions, and at the very least, Pepper was over to Kree's house. He dialed Kree's number as he sped out the hospital parking lot. When Kree picked up, Malik said right away, "Kree, tell me Pepper with you!"

"I been calling her for the past hour and she not answering. She was supposed to meet me here at my house after I got off work. Is she still at the hospital with Loopy?"

Malik snapped his phone shut and pounded the steering wheel. *"El fuck you doing, niña? Ellos vinieron del norte, Peppi! Saben dónde está el fuck su estancia!"* (The fuck you doing, baby girl? They came from the north, Peppi! They know where the fuck you stay!) he cried as he ran a red-light at a busy intersection, repeating the process over and over again until he made it over to Salt Lick Road and headed north on State Highway 79. The fretful man remembered Pepper telling him that whoever hit her and her crew had come from the north. In his mind, they had to have known where Pepper lived to be coming from Louisiana. It was a good chance they had already been to her home to look for her and just happened to run up on Pepper and her crew returning to Saint Louis the night they killed Simone and Sweet Pea.

****

Pepper, meanwhile, was still searching for her cell phone. She'd searched the kitchen, the cushions on her sofa, and was now searching her bedroom. She was looking up under her bed for her phone when she stumbled upon a bible lying in between her bed and nightstand. She picked it up and dusted the cover off as she sat on the edge of her mattress. It had been so long since she'd picked up the bible. She remember knocking it off her nightstand some months ago and had never even bothered to pick it up because she was so much in a hurry to leave home and get down to Saint Louis and kick it with her girls. She looked to the ceiling and closed her eyes and prayed in silence. *"God, show me something,"* she requested as she flipped the Good Book open.

The bible opened up to the book of Revelations and Pepper's eyes, for some unknown reason, focused in on Chapter 21:4, which read, *"And He will wipe out every tear from their eyes, and death will be no more, neither will mourning nor outcry nor pain be anymore. The former things have passed away."*

No more death. No more mourning and pain. The words were comforting to Pepper. *"I wonder what that kind of world would be like,"* she wondered silently as she stood up from her bed, faced her nightstand and set the bible beside her lamp.

It was at that moment Pepper remembered she'd placed her

phone on her car charger. She turned towards her door to go and retrieve her phone and was startled by what she saw. A slender pale-skinned woman wearing a black trench coat with a nappy, tan afro stood in her bedroom's doorway welding a chrome handgun with a plastic bottle and duct tape wrapped around the barrel.

Pepper quickly remembered having this scenario play out in a dream she'd had on Christmas Day, only this was a dream she could not wake up from. Her knees gave out and she braced herself against her nightstand as a single gunshot landed in her chest. She fell over onto her closet door, her back against the wood as she slowly slid down the doors while watching the woman slowly approaching her with the gun now aimed at her head. The assassin stood over her and squeezed the trigger a second time, but the gun didn't fire.

Pepper watched helplessly as the intruder pulled the gun back and stared at it in wonderment before racking the weapon and aiming it back at her face. She raised her eyes from her slumped position and could see her killer walking towards her with the gun pointed at her once more as she sat on the carpeted floor of her bedroom, too wounded to defend herself.

The intruder pulled the trigger, but again the gun didn't fire. She cussed aloud as she ran out the bedroom.

Pepper could faintly hear metal sliding against metal several seconds later. Everything went silent at that moment. Blood spurted from her chest with each beat of her dying heart. Suddenly, the footsteps of stilettoes were heard pressing into the wooden floor out in the hall. When the woman reappeared, she was holding onto a thick butcher's knife.

Pepper's eyes crossed as she looked up at the woman. In her weakened state, she mustered up enough strength to spit blood in the woman's face the moment she knelt down before her brandishing the knife. *"Deseo que tenía SIDA, perra. Kill me, puta!"* (I wish I had AIDS, bitch. Kill me, whore!)

Pepper had a mean scowl on her face as she watched her killer jump back in surprise and stand to her feet where she wiped her face free of blood. A loud, agonizing scream erupted from her, however, when the woman hauled off and kicked her in the stomach. She fell over onto her side as the unknown slayer knelt down and grabbed her thick head of hair with one of her glove-clad hands. She pulled Pepper's head back and said, "If I had the time I would torture you."

"Igual que hicimos Toodie? Te contaré Asesinato ME dice chupar mi coño y sangrienta que veré su en el infierno." (Like we did Toodie? Tell Ya Murder I said suck my bloody pussy and I'll see her in hell.) Pepper said in a near whisper while staring the woman in the eyes as blood continued to trickle from her mouth and the bullet wound in her chest.

A jolt of electricity quickly shot through Pepper's body. Her trembling hands instinctively reached up and grabbed hold of the knife that had been plunged into her chest all the way up to its wooden handle. The blade was so long it'd traveled through the seventeen year-old's back and had impaled her to her closet door. She tried pulling the knife from her chest, but she hadn't the strength as she held onto the blade.

In mere seconds, Pepper's life flashed before her eyes. The day her mother died. The day she met Carmella. She saw herself at age ten dancing in a mansion in Colorado as Carmella and Desiree egged her on. She saw herself visiting her mother's grave at age thirteen. The last day she talked to Carmella before she was killed in Mexico ran through her mind. Simone's smiling face. Sweet Pea and Loopy's antics. She saw her hands whipping up cocaine and the many gun blasts she'd dished out to her victims echoed on her mind, right along with their dead expressions. Piles of money. A high speed chase, and a wrecked Hummer. Malik's voice echoed in her mind, telling her to slow down. The premonition she'd had the night she and her crew had killed two people crept into her mind.

Pepper's legs began kicking and she entered into a seizure. She would swallow hard three times, pause, exhale rapidly several times and repeat the process. "Momma!" she called out before she swallowed hard three times and exhaled. *"ESTOY libre! Mamá, soy libre!"* (I'm free! Momma, I'm free!) the seventeen year-old cried out weakly.

Less than ten seconds later, seventeen year-old Peppi 'Pepper' Vargas breathed her last breath. She died slumped over on her left side with her eyes half-closed and covered in blood on January 10, 2009.

CHAPTER TWENTY-SEVEN

THE AFTERMATH

It had taken longer than expected for Helen 'Boogie' Weinberger and her crew to take Peppi Vargas down. She had been the intended target all along as the contract brought down by Ya Murder would not have been considered fulfilled had Pepper not been killed despite Boogie and her team having taken out Simone and Sweet Pea. The Germans prided themselves on fulfilling each and every contract and would settle for nothing less.

Boogie had never anticipated on the make-shift silencer malfunctioning on her gun, let alone the gun jamming in the process. The first shot startled her as she never meant for the blasts to be heard. She knew she was lucky the gun didn't backfire on her, but the time it took to kill Peppi Vargas was enough time to alert nosey neighbors. She'd fled the scene out the front door and ran underneath Pepper's canopy and hopped the fence leading to the backyard where she hopped a second fence and ran through the woods to her car parked in the next cul de sac inside the same neighborhood and crept away.

Boogie had been onto Pepper and her crew ever since the after day she and her rode into Saint Louis on New Year's Eve. They were outside of her home the day Pepper set her trap house ablaze and had to abort the job. They later caught up with Pepper and her crew on I-44 after she'd left Malik's trap house and were about to open fire until Maggie McPherson spotted a Missouri State Patrol car tailing their Caprice, so again, they had to call the job off.

Ya Murder had known all along where Pepper ducked off to courtesy of Toodie Perez, a fact that went unbeknownst to Pepper. And it had never entered Pepper's mind that because of the fact that the hit came from the north, whoever was gunning for her the night Simone and Sweet Pea where killed, had to have known where she lived.

Malik knew that angle, but he was too little too late as he wasn't able to reach Pepper via cell phone to warn her. The crew from Cincinnati had been to Pepper's house everyday trying to catch her there; it was only by sheer fate that they'd crossed paths with her on Highway 79 and was able to attempt the hit.

Knowing Pepper had survived the hit on Highway 79, Boogie, operating on a hunch, had decided to travel from Barry, Illinois, where Maggie McPherson was receiving treatment for a bullet wound to her leg, back into the town of Louisiana just to see if she could catch Pepper slipping—and she did.

The night Simone and Sweet Pea were killed, Popeye had disabled Pepper's alarm. The seventeen year-old was so distraught over the tragedy that had befallen her friends she'd paid it no mind. Boogie was able to slip in without Pepper being alerted; and because Hutch and Honey had been killed, the last warning system she had left was no more. Inattentiveness to detail had ultimately led to Peppi Vargas' downfall.

Boogie, meanwhile, had a new set of problems to deal with. She was certain the Caprice could be easily identified. She'd removed the tag on the car before setting out on her solo mission, but she knew it stood out. She was now making a beeline back to Illinois. Law figures on the other side of the Mississippi River would be far behind on the carnage she'd left behind in Missouri was her assumption. She drove casually towards the U.S. Highway 54 Mississippi River Bridge. This was a dangerous time for Boogie. Reason being was because the bridge was so narrow and infrequently traveled, that a red-light on either side regulated the flow of traffic. Her heart sunk to her stomach as she approached the bridge where she saw a red-light, signaling that a vehicle was traveling west from Illinois over into Missouri. She had no choice but to wait as headlights on a massive vehicle off in the darkness came into view halfway over the Mississippi River.

Once the eighteen wheeler cleared, Boogie sped onto the bridge as she let the passenger window down on the Caprice. While over the middle of the river, she slowed the car and threw her handgun and the knife she'd used to stab Pepper with out the window, watching as the metal objects floated over the low railing and plummeted into the muddy waters below the bridge before she mashed the gas pedal and headed back to Barry, Illinois.

****

Meanwhile, back in the town of Louisiana, Malik had just pulled into Pepper's cul de sac. The sight his eyes bore witness to let him know his young protégé was no more. Her home was taped off and there was at least a half dozen police cars on the scene along with a coroner's van. His eyes watered as he sped up the street and braked a ways down from the crime scene. Climbing from his car, he ran towards Pepper's yard just as two deputies were emerging with a black body bag.

An officer, having spotted the man running up to the crime scene, stopped him in the front yard. "Are you a relative of the deceased?" the man asked.

"Peppi Vargas was a close friend! I been, I been trying to call her, but she never answered!" Malik snapped in frustration. "What happened to her?"

"Peppi was the victim of a homicide, sir. Neighbors heard a gunshot and saw a slender figure running from the house. Whoever it was disappeared into the woods behind the home. There's a neighborhood on the other side of that small forest behind the house. A man coming in from work mentioned a light green four door car unknown to the neighborhood parked over on the next block. We're searching, but the suspect appears to have left the area. Any idea who would want to hurt your friend or do you know of anybody driving a light green car that maybe knew her?"

"No, sir," Malik answered somberly as he watched Pepper's body being placed in the back of the coroner's van.

"Well, does she any family for us to notify?"

"I was her family."

"She's going to have to be identified and we'll need a name to release the body. You are?"

"Malik Gomez."

"Okay, Mister Gomez. She'll be autopsied back down in Saint Louis. Should be done in couple of days. I'll need a number on you so I can make sure the Medical Examiner can contact you. If you have any information," the officer said as he reached into his top jacket pocket and pulled out a card and handed it to Malik. "If you have any information, please, don't hesitate to call. Sorry for your loss," he ended as he turned and reentered the yard.

Malik looked on somberly as the doors to the van that held Pepper's body was closed. It was a hard pill to have to swallow —a heavy dose of reality. Pepper was on her way to becoming one of the best, a boss in the making, but she was cut down before she'd even reached midstride. Her death would haunt Malik for a while and be used as a cautionary tale to those coming up behind him. He balled up the card the detective handed to him and headed back to his SUV and told Max what Max already knew as he climbed inside.

Just like Malik, Max was heartbroken. "Who did this to her, man?" he asked somberly.

Malik pulled off from the curb, not answering Max just as his phone vibrated. He recognized the number right away and quickly answered. "Boss," he sighed.

"We in the Lou over by Jay-D. Where you at?" Dawk asked as he, Bay, T-top and the Cottonwood family sat inside the den of the pristine two-story Victorian home with an arsenal of weapons spread out on the carpeted floor.

Malik broke the news that Pepper was dead and Dawk was

stunned. "Come straight here, dude," he spoke in a solemn tone before ending the call.

Another shockwave over Pepper's demise hit members of the family when Dawk broke the news to his sisters and the Cottonwoods. Everybody was stunned beyond words. They all sat in silence for over an hour, digesting the fact that Pepper's crew had been wiped out. It was a scary prospect, but a reality of the business they were involved in. It could happen to anyone of them at any time, they knew and understood.

What bothered everybody involved was the fact that such a strong crew was taken out in mere days. And truth be told, it didn't sit well with no one. They had to get to the bottom of things and prevent another war like the one that had gone down with Carmella Lapiente`, and later Toodie Perez. With the night club and restaurant opening in a couple of months or so, and having just gotten things in order with Gacha and the Asians, the last thing the big three needed was another long, bloody feud in the midst of their first cocaine shipment and first legitimate endeavor.

Just before two A.M., Malik and Max arrived over to Jay-D's home in Saint Charles, which was down the street from the family's nightclub. He and Max were let in and hugs and condolences went around as everyone knew how close he and Pepper were.

"What do we know?" Dawk asked as the crew adjoined to the den of the home.

Malik ran his hands through his thick, black head of hair and said, "Pepper had been having a feeling someone was following her, homes. She got into a high speed chase a few days ago and mentioned something about a Caprice, a lime green Caprice she believed was following her and her girls. I talk to a detective, because I had to give a name so somebody could claim Pepper's body. He told me a light green four door car was seen leaving the area in the next neighborhood shortly after a gun shot was heard. It's no coincidence."

"Pepper didn't who they were, though, right?" Bay remarked.

"Nahh," Malik responded as he rubbed his chin. "All we know is the car. Pepper, Peppi did a long of wrong, no? She burned down her trap house trying to cook meth, I vouched for her on the hit against Tito and Toine—"

"And we made her a Lieutenant and gave her a cash bonus not even a month ago," Dawk chimed in.

"I know, Boss. I feel at fault here. It's my fault and I take full responsibility for what happened."

Dawk nodded as he stood and extended his hand, offering Malik and Max a seat on the couch where he once sat. He walked over to the bar in the den and pointed to a bottle of brandy as he eyed Jay-D.

"Help yourself, Boss," Jay-D remarked. "Let me wipe out those shot glasses for ya', though, fam."

Dawk removed his ten gallon cowboy hat and tucked his hands in his jeans as Jay-D set out several shot glasses and poured a round of drinks. He took a quick shot, grabbed two glasses and walked over to Malik and Max and handed them each a glass while contemplating on how he was going to give counsel.

Lesser men in positions of power would've made a mistake at this juncture having loss an entire crew. Dawk had every right to go off on Malik for allowing Pepper to run wild and not reporting back to him her actions, but he had the capacity to understand that his trusted Enforcer had simply made a mistake and nothing more. He understood the fondness Malik had for Pepper, and for that, he knew she got leeway—only there was too much leeway given to the youngster this time around and it'd cost the family dearly as it was enough leeway to cost Pepper and two members of her crew their lives in a most unforgiving and dangerous vocation.

Dawk knew what he was up against in handling Malik. Slapping a man of honor and respect upside the head and/or shouting him down like he was a mere child was not how he was going to handle the matter as he was taught way better by his father. To scold a man in front of others would definitely create an enemy. Everything would be kept in-house with the ones seated at the top, but it would unfold out in the open in order to allow others to learn. Whenever problems were able to be rectified cordially, diplomacy would be the first form of reprimand, and it was always done with respect as it was the way Dawk had been taught.

"Jay-D remember the day Carmella hit our spot right up the street and killed Lucky, Coban and Gaggi," Dawk began as he grabbed the bottle of brandy and poured Max and Malik another shot of liquor.

"That I do," Jay-D nodded as he stood in a corner bumping his fists.

"You remember what Eddie said to my father when he visited?" Dawk asked as he looked back at Jay-D.

"He said it was his fault and he took full responsibility for it."

Dawk looked back over to Malik and said, "*Cuando usted compra los errores, la familia toma nota, amigo. Usted puede permanecer en gracia, pero tenemos un problema que merece toda nuestra atención.*" (When you own up to your mistakes, the family takes notice, amigo. You remain in good graces, but we have a problem that warrants our undivided attention.)

Si, Boss," Malik responded as he sighed a sigh of relief as he believed Dawk and his sisters were going to explode in anger over his handling of Pepper.

"If you had to guess? Who you think hit Pepper? Who was driving that light green car?" Dawk asked, realizing he'd relieved Malik's anxiety.

"Pepper mentioned Ya Murder maybe going after her, but, I never knew Ya Murder to drive a light green car."

"Ya Murder. That's the chick I ordered Jay-D to bust at a while back and her friend Noodles." Dawk said as he looked to the floor and rubbed his chin. "I ordered the hit, but not the deaths of those two because I was just trying to get at Toodie and shake her up a little bit. So, I'm partly to blame for this if Ya Murder was behind the hit."

"It's not your fault, Boss," Malik retorted. "Toodie was the main target."

"We got Toodie out the way," Dawk stated. "But we didn't close all the doors look like, fam. So, we owe you one. What's going on in Indianapolis?"

"This guy RJ," Malik answered. "He runs things over there. If you moving in? He's the one to take down."

"And Cincinnati?"

"All we know is this area called Over the Rhine. No names behind it, though." Malik answered.

"Okay," Dawk remarked. "What you know about RJ?"

"I used to score a few kilograms from the guy—even turned Pepper on for a minute. A few times we made deals at a Pacers game. He has season tickets and told me he never misses a game."

Dawk entered into deep thought. His gut was telling him that an organization based in Cincinnati was pulling the strings. He didn't know if this RJ guy was connected to Ohio, nor did he care. The only thing that mattered was the family going on the offense to rid themselves of any and all potential enemies.

"No more playing around," Dawk declared. "Malik? What I want you to do is track down Ya Murder. Jay-D? You keep an ear to the streets and watch out for the feds like Eddie said. That's my order as it stands."

"Done deal." Jay-D replied.

"Si, Boss. I'm on it," Malik stated. "How you plan on getting to RJ?" he then asked. "He always in public."

Dawk looked over to Bay and T-top, and without speaking a word, everyone, including the twins, knew they'd been given the task of taking down RJ.

"We'll take care of it," Bay remarked casually.

"How you two plan on getting close to that guy over in Indianapolis?" Malik asked curiously.

"Via the long shot," T-top replied as she looked to the ceiling. "How much tickets to a Pacers game cost?" she wondered aloud. "Somebody get me a lap top or something so I can look that up."

"We got our best on RJ. Malik? You just search out Ya Murder. Jay?" Dawk stated as he pointed to Jay-D.

"I'm fed-watching. Boss," Jay-D responded.

"Okay, we set," Dawk stated. "Now, let's get ready to send some of our crew home righteous-like," he ended.

CHAPTER TWENTY-EIGHT

THE GERMAN CUT OFF

January 12, 2009

Boogie and Popeye had just eased out of the old school Caprice. It was two nights after Boogie had killed Peppi Vargas. After setting Ya Murder up with their cocaine connect over in Indianapolis, where she'd left her with her partner RJ, she and Popeye had returned to the Rhine over in Cincinnati, Ohio. Under the darkness of night, Boogie and Popeye made their way to the entrance of 3600 Mulberry Street, the night club she ran with her mother, and entered.

Like many a weeknight, 3600 Mulberry Street was sparsely-filled, save for a few locals who perused the neighborhood club on a daily basis to share drinks and discuss the ever-disappointing Cincinnati Bengals and whatever problems they had at home with their wives or on their jobs. Boogie eyed her mother, who was behind the counter talking on her cell phone, and slowly made her way over to the counter.

"They've just arrived. I'll have her call to talk with Maggie when I'm done with her," forty-four year-old Tanya Weinberger remarked, ending her call as Boogie approached. *"Warum haben Sie rekrutieren Maggie, Boogie? Sie wissen, dass ihre Mutter ist sauer, richtig?"* (Why did you recruit Maggie, Boogie? You know her mother is pissed, right?) she spoke in fluent German the moment her daughter made her way over to the counter.

"*Maggie hatte die Waffen brauchten wir in Indianapolis für RJ. Sie bestand auf der Hit.*" (Maggie had the guns we needed shipped to Indianapolis for RJ. She insisted on going on the hit.) Boogie responded as she pulled the hood of her leather trench coat from her head, bringing her full, nappy tan afro into view.

"*Es kostet uns tausende von Dollar, um das medizinische Personal in Barry, Illinois von Reporting Maggie's Wunde an ihrem Bein, die Polizei. Sie und Popeye hat Recht mit ihren über staatliche Linien, sondern wir haben Geld verloren in diesem Job. Haben Sie mindestens das tun, was sie zu tun?*" (It cost us thousands of dollars to keep the medical staff in Barry, Illinois from reporting Maggie's wound to her leg to the police. You and Popeye did right taking her across state lines, but we've lost money on this job. Did you at least do what you set out to do?) Tanya asked as she pointed to her office, signaling for Boogie to enter as the two left Popeye behind to watch the floor.

Boogie entered the office and turned and faced her tall, blonde-haired mother. Tanya closed the door and stood before her daughter and stared her down through her brown eyes. "*Haben Sie den Job abzuschließen?*" (Did you finish the job?) she asked again.

"*Nahm drei von ihnen heraus. Pfeffer enthalten. Ich musste doppelt zurück, um Ihre. Wie die Maggie? Wo ist sie?*" (Took three of them out. Pepper included. I had to double back to get her. How's Maggie? Where is she?)

"She's home with her mother recovering," Tanya replied as she walked behind her desk. "Did you leave any witnesses?"

"No. Well—"

The moment Boogie said 'well' Tanya paused and stared at her from behind her black ivory desk. "Well what?" she scoffed.

"*Es gibt eine noch lebendig, aber sie ist in ein Koma. Sie ist bewacht von zwei Wachleute und zwei Männer angehören, Malik Gomez. Er war Pepper's Chef. Arbeitet für die Holland Familie.*" (There's one still alive, but she's in a coma. She's being guarded by two security guards and two men who belong to a Malik Gomez. He was Pepper's boss. Works for the Holland family.)

Tanya placed her hands on her hips and entered a deep thought as she paced the floor behind her desk. "I could very well order a hit on this Malik Gomez, but there's no need just yet," she told her daughter.

"You sure, momma?" Boogie questioned. "*Was ist Ihre Argumentation?*" (What's your reasoning?)

"*Zu gehen, nachdem Gomez kann nur weg geben den Vorteil. Wenn ich vermute Rechts, die einzige Person, die sich auf der Front dieser Deal, sie leiden unter den Fallout wäre Ya Mord.*" (To go after Gomez may just give away the advantage. If I'm guessing right, the only person out on the front lines of this deal that'll suffer the fallout would be Ya Murder.)

Boogie folded her arms and eyed her mother, who'd donned a sly smile. "*Sie weiß nicht, wie ernst dieses Business ist hat sie?*" (She doesn't know how serious this business is does she?) Boogie asked in a serious tone.

"You said the day she arrived last December that she was a fuck up," Tanya remarked. "But now you and RJ are, or rather Ya Murder is into you and RJ for four kilograms of cocaine."

"She bought two stones with the money she had left over from the hit," Boogie corrected.

"Okay, she's into you for two kilograms of coke instead of four. At least you have that going for you," Tanya remarked as she shook her head in disbelief. "But if this thing with Peppi Vargas gets answered like I know it will? Ya Murder will not last long. I'd be surprised if you get any money back off the two kilograms you and RJ are fronting that woman."

Boogie looked to the floor as she placed her hands behind her back. "I moved too quickly," she told her mother.

"You went against your own word, Boogie. Ya Murder is an earner, never a boss. She's going to go back to Saint Louis feeling like a queen pin after helping take Peppi Vargas down and fall flat on her face."

"Should we step in on her behalf?"

"Not even," Tanya remarked casually as she stared her daughter down with her hands clasped behind her back. "I don't give a damn about a Ya Murder. And I refuse to engage this Holland family and start another war. Natalia the third wouldn't take the hit anyway. What's happening in Saint Louis is between the Mexicans now. We operate in different markets. I warned you about Saint Louis, Helen."

"You did."

Tanya eased from behind the desk and stood before her daughter and looked down her nose at Boogie. "*Sie sind mehr ein Killer als ein Händler, weil sie noch nicht die Weitsicht noch. Sie nehmen den Verlust auf zwei Kilogramm Kokain und vergessen Ya Mord. Verlieren Ihre Nummer ist mein Vorschlag.*" (You're more a killer than a dealer because you haven't the foresight—yet. You will take the loss on two kilograms of cocaine and forget about Ya Murder. Lose her number is my suggestion.) Tanya remarked as she held out her left hand.

"I'll let RJ know," Boogie stated humbly as she gazed up into her mother's eyes while grabbing her cell phone from her trench coat and placing it into her mother's palm.

"Good," Tanya remarked as she walked behind her desk and snapped the phone in half. "Next order of business is this situation in Philadelphia. I found out who was behind this thing with Brenda."

"Speak," Boogie said as she stepped closer to her mother's desk with her head tilted slightly as this was a situation dear to the family's heart and far more important than Ya Murder.

"An Asian woman by the name of Tammy Moto took Brenda down. She's a federal agent. Dirty cop," Tanya remarked as she eyed her daughter seriously. "We're not welcomed in Philadelphia because this, this Tammy Moto has a heroin network set up coming in from Seattle according to Willameena."

"We stepped on some toes," Boogie responded. "Who else is

with her?"

"Don't know," Tanya replied. "But she's acting on orders from a higher source. Her superior is like a ghost to us right now, but it does nothing to stop us from getting to Tammy."

"You're thinking of killing a federal agent, momma?"

"No, Boogie. We need, we need someone, a crew maybe, a crew crazy enough to go after this Tammy Moto for high dollar and with nothing lose in this business."

"You have someone in mind?"

"Not right now," Tanya admitted. "But I believe the best way, with Tammy being Asian? Is to get her own kind to go after her. It'll take some time for me to find those capable, but eventually? Miss Moto will have to answer for what she's done to our sister Brenda Marshall."

"I'll keep my ears to the street as well." Boogie replied.

"Good. Now go and check on Maggie," Tanya ordered as she extended her hand, allowing her daughter to leave her presence. "Boogie!" she suddenly called out as she walked behind her desk and removed her fur hat.

"Yeah, momma?" Boogie inquired as she stuck her head back inside the office while holding the door open.

"*Laden Sie so viele Gäste, wie sie an den Ort, wo Sie sie legen ihren Kopf zum Abendessen, aber es diejenigen, die bleiben, um den Tisch und stellen Sie sicher, dass das Haus sicher ist, bevor Sie ihn verlassen, was wirklich wichtig ist.*" (You can invite as many guests as you want to the place where you lay your head for dinner, but it is those who stay to help clear the table and make sure the house is secure before they leave that truly matter.)

"Wer sie zitiere? Julius Caesar? Kennedy?" (Who're you quoting now? Julius Caesar? Kennedy?) Boogie asked as she pressed her forehead to the door's edge and smiled. Her and Maggie's mother was always quoting some historical figure to get their points across during counsel and it often left the younger ones tickled.

"I just made that up," Tanya chuckled as she sat down behind her desk. "You like it?"

"The point is understood clearly. I would've never guessed it came from you," Boogie remarked as she smiled over to her mother.

"Are you implying that I haven't a philosophical viewpoint on life and the business?" Tanya smirked. "Hell, I done wrote speeches for our beloved Senator."

"I didn't mean it like that, momma," Boogie smiled. "It was just profound to me. Something I envision a historical figure saying."

"*I'm* a historical figure," Tanya boasted. "Ya Murder wouldn't even get up to clean her own plate, let alone help with the dishes," she then said seriously. "That Mexican has no place inside of our family. Not because she's Mexican? But because of the fact that she doesn't know what she's doing on the streets. She has no table manners. No street etiquette," Tanya stated seriously. "Forget about her, Helen. This thing with Tammy Moto in Philadelphia is our top priority."

"*Ihr Wasser ist vollständig abgeschnitten werden.*" (Her water's been cut off completely.) Boogie ended before she left the office to call and check on Maggie.

CHAPTER TWENTY-NINE
YA'S ASCENSION

"...But I ain't gone play with 'em...uh uh...rather let the AK hit 'em...tough niggas get fucked up...and put on ice for the rest the rest of they life...I'm straight out the hoods bruh...see that's who I do it for...my low class ghetto ass...just renewed my ghetto pass...I'm so hood..."

The hunch in twenty-five year-old RJ's back was clearly visible as he deep-stroked Ya Murder hard and fast as DJ Khaled's song *I'm So Hood* blasted loud on his surround sound inside the Conrad Indianapolis located in downtown Indianapolis. Rapper Trick Daddy was ripping the verse as he and Ya Murder worked up a sweat inside the extravagant suite that overlooked downtown Indianapolis.

"Papi, give me that long black dick! Fuck me hard! Fuck me!" Ya Murder screamed as she held the back of her legs up.

RJ bit his bottom lip and thrust hard, knocking the slender Mexican's head up against the thick wooden head board. "God, yes!" Ya Murder yelled.

"That's how you want it, bitch? Yea, you like that rough shit." RJ groaned in a raspy voice as he ground down into Ya Murder's sloppy wet vagina. He stirred it up like coffee, his rigid pole forcing Ya's pussy to make slushing sounds as she began trembling.

"Usted está golpeando mi spot, niño! Ricky!" (You hitting my spot, boy. Ricky!) Ya moaned as she clasped her hands to

RJ's face and looked up into his dark eyes.

Five hours earlier, Ya Murder had been dropped off by Boogie and Popeye. She was only supposed to hang around until her Greyhound bus arrived and head back to Saint Louis, in which she did, but during the seven hour delay, RJ began flirting with her. She was already feeling the men inside the German crew the day she'd met them back in December and was hoping one of them, either Popeye or RJ, or maybe both even, made a move on her. Popeye wasn't vibing like that with Ya Murder, but when he and Boogie met up with RJ in a Kentucky Fried Chicken parking lot near downtown, Popeye put RJ up on some game. He told RJ he could get some easy pussy if he wanted it.

Ricky 'RJ' Gross Junior could've done himself a service by investing stock in Magnum Trojans Condoms as the list of women he'd run through stretched coast to coast. The 6'5" one hundred and eighty-five dark chocolate tatted-up gangster with thick dreadlocks that flowed to the center of his back had a body most women found themselves eyeing without even trying. Handsome features, a slender face with thick eyebrows and smooth, dark chocolate skin complimented a pristine set of white teeth. RJ had a killer smile as his mother had spent nearly five thousand dollars on bracelets to straighten out his crooked teeth when he was a mere boy. He was blessed above and below the neck with a killer gift of gab and length and girth that touched many a spot inside a woman that they'd never even known existed.

An access of money from heroin and cocaine sales, style of dress and his rugged demeanor attracted females from all walks of life to the lifelong gangster from New Orleans, Louisiana. Married women his age, cougars tired of their limp-dick lazy old men and even a few models in the greater Indianapolis area had gotten a taste of what RJ had to offer; and even though they knew he was a man of many women, it bothered none of them. He could pick up the phone at any hour and attain companionship whenever his heart desired.

Ya Murder was his latest conquest. When she'd stepped out of the back of the Caprice a few hours earlier, the first thing that caught his attention was Jada's pretty, freckled face. She was a slender female with light-tan skin and shiny black hair she'd cut into a crop. Her eyes were hallucinogenic. Brown and slender, like her 5'10" frame, and glinted, even under the darkness of night; just staring at her had aroused him from a physical aspect.

It didn't take long for the two to hit off. Now, several hours later, Ya Murder was being taken to new heights of pleasure. Rock hard nipples and a throbbing pussy that was stretched open like never before had her speaking in tongues almost as inch upon inch of rock hard black dick pleasurably stabbed deep into her inner walls. She'd come minutes ago, but only craved more as she lay beneath RJ with her head tilted to the side and her eyes closed. If Ya Murder had her way, and if it was at all possible, she'd lay there beneath RJ for the next twenty-four hours absorbing his dick. *"Maldita sea, esta dick es maravilloso, bebé."* (Damn, this dick is wonderful, baby.)

Ya Murder's raspy moans was the ultimate turn on for RJ. She was delicate to him, but he was allowed to handle her roughly as that is what she craved. He placed his hands to the back of her knees and dug deep. Her pussy walls began convulsing uncontrollably as she screamed aloud in pleasure, *"En este coño! Entran en esta mutherfuckin' coño, RJ!"* (Come in this pussy! Come in this mutherfuckin' pussy, RJ!)

"Ohh!" RJ groaned as he thrust deep into Ya Murder, their pelvises pressing against one another, bone against bone. With each word that followed, RJ thrust into Ya Murder hard. "You —good—pussy—having—Mexican—bitch! Umph!" he grunted as his pole twitched deep inside Ya's quivering vagina.

Sensing her RJ's arrival, Ya nudged him off her body and grabbed hold of the condom on his dick.

RJ leaned back and smiled. He'd been here before more times than he could count. He loved when the married ones did it, but took delight in each explosive episode. He rested back on his hands as Ya's hands rolled the condom off his throbbing dick and was replaced with her mouth. It was the warmth and the feel of her tongue and hands sliding over the base of his pole that forced an eruption from within RJ. He grabbed the back of Ya Murder's head.

The horny, lust-filled woman gagged as semen splashed her mouth. She moved her head away and continued her stroking motions as sperm coated her lips and closed eyes. She then took the tip of RJ's shaft and rubbed it on her cheeks before taking him back into her mouth and sucking him clean.

The two collapsed down onto the king-sized mattress a couple of minutes later, laughing aloud and panting as they gasped for breath. "The fuck was that?" Ya laughed.

"Got hit with a snow blizzard," RJ laughed as his chest heaved up and down.

"My shit gone be sore in the morning. It's sore right now." Ya said as she wiped semen from her face and licked her fingertips.

"I did my job then," RJ said through heavy breaths as he rolled over and sat up on the edge of the bed.

The clock on the nightstand came into view at that moment and Ya saw that she only had ninety minutes to make it to the bus station. "I can't miss the Greyhound!" she complained as she eased up from the bed.

RJ smiled at Ya as she pranced into the bathroom. He wasn't going to let her miss her bus by a long shot. He'd gotten what he wanted and now it was time to send her on her way. Popeye had texted him while he and Ya were sitting in the living room toking blunts. The message was that all ties were to be cut off with Ya Murder per order of Tanya Weinberger. The Boss had spoken and the order would be respected.

When Ya came out dressed ten minutes later, she saw that RJ was up and about in a pair of silk boxers. He'd lit a blunt and was sitting at the mini bar inside the suite with a duffle bag on the counter. "That's the work?" she asked as she sashayed over and placed her chin to his slender shoulder and sniffed his hair.

"Four bricks. Two on consignment," RJ said as he looked back at Ya. "You better get going before you miss your bus."

"You're not taking me? I wanna ride the Ferrari," Ya Murder sulked playfully as she folded her arms and tucked in her chin.

RJ laughed lowly as he knocked ashes from the tip of his blunt. "My black ass ain't going nowhere with that amount of work. You want me to ride in a Ferrari with you and four bricks? Where they do that shit at? I'll call you a cab."

"Man, I was hoping you see me off, RJ. We had fun, man," Ya smiled as she rubbed RJ's back.

RJ leaned back and eyed Ya Murder. "Oh, you—you thought we was hooking up on some man and woman-type-shit?" he asked, speaking with his hands. "We cool and all, but, nahh. This here all about business now. What we did off the clock was for fun. You gotta handle your business," he let it be known as he eyed Ya Murder seriously.

Ya dropped her comforting smile and removed her hand from RJ's back. She scratched her head in confusion for a few seconds upon realizing she'd gotten caught up in her feelings. "You right," she admitted somberly. "It's business. And this," she said as she extended her hands outwards towards the suite and eyed the tangled silk sheets on the king-sized bed. "This was just a moment in time," she ended as RJ picked up his phone and dialed a taxi.

****

Ya Murder arrived back in Saint Louis the following morning after a six hour ride via Greyhound. She'd ridden the whole way with a duffle bag containing four kilograms of cocaine tucked in between her feet without giving it a second thought. She exited the bus and headed for a side entrance where she saw Toodie's black four door 1976 Cadillac Coup de Ville parked, the car vibrating slightly as bass thumped from the trunk. She walked over and tapped the window and the door was unlocked.

"*¿Qué casa, chica?*" (What's up homegirl?) Ya asked a female Mexican as she climbed into the front passenger seat and threw the white powder on the back seat.

"*Ain't shit. Eh, Fox Parque se estremeció el fuck sobre lo que sucedió a Peppi Vargas y su tripulación.*" (Ain't shit. Eh, Fox Park is shook the fuck over what happened to Peppi Vargas and her crew.) the female, named Julietta Juarez, whom everybody called 'Juggie'(Juggy), answered with a slight grin on her face. *"Han distribuir volantes hablando de los funerales y mierda."* (They been passing out flyers talking about the funeral and shit.)

"Is that right?" Ya Murder sighed as Juggie pulled out of the parking lot. *"Cuando es?"* (When is it?")

"Mañana." (Tomorrow.)

Ya Murder nodded her head as she lay back in the seat. "Fuck that hoe Pepper. We're back in power," she told Juggie.

"Where you going first, Boss?" Juggie asked as she wheeled the dark-tinted old school whip on 28" inch chrome rims out of downtown Saint Louis.

"You let our girls know what the deal was, right?"

"Yeah, but they asses went out last night to celebrate what happened with Peppi, no?"

Ya Murder chuckled, extended a balled-up fist and said, "Yeah, that shit was worth celebrating, homegirl," as she gave Juggie a fist pound. "But on the real, though, we gone get them up and head back over to Ann Avenue and let everybody know we got shop," she remarked as Juggie nodded in agreement.

Juggie was a 5'5" vanilla-skinned, one hundred and sixty pound blonde-haired Mexican. She wasn't the most attractive female around with a long, wide forehead, high cheek bones and slender, brown eyes. She had lived a hard life on the streets of Piedras Nagras, Mexico before she crossed the American border near Eagle Pass, Texas for the final time.

Juggie started out as a mule for a local marijuana cartel in her home city back in 2006. She carried fifty pound backpacks of weed across the border for two hundred dollars a trip. After numerous successful runs, she'd made a last run to the city of Del Rio, Texas and paid $5,000 dollars to be taken from there to the city of Saint Louis. Being a criminal since the age of ten, it didn't take long for Juggie to return to a life of crime once she'd landed in Fox Park. Recruited by Toodie Perez as a foot soldier, she began running with Ya Murder and her dead friend Angelica Arnaz and had worked her way up to dealer inside the trap house on Ann Avenue.

Ya Murder, with Toodie being dead, was next in line to take control of the profitable set. She knew Malik had no cocaine to sell, so for her, it was nothing to go right back to where she knew she could off the product quickly. After picking up two more soldiers from the apartment she and Juggie now shared, Ya and her newly-formed crew of four went and got a hotel room south of Saint Louis where they cooked and re-bagged the cocaine before they parlayed the rest of the day. Once the sun had gone down, the gang of four made their way back over to Ann Avenue with their rocked up product and four AK-47s.

****

Ann Avenue. Some who live in Fox Park call it Little Saigon because of the constant violence, but it had become known to most as Scarface Alley ever since Toodie had disappeared from the scene because it seemed as if whoever ran it, gained the world, but the ones who wore the crown never lasted long and died hard, just like the American icon Tony Montana.

Legends were made and people's bodies were riddled with bullets on this one, long, u-shaped block in the heart of Fox Park, where the scepter of power changed hands as rapidly as a chameleon walking across a multi-colored canvas. Ann Avenue had seen so much bloodshed and violence over the past seven years that bloodstains where some had died months and years ago still remained in the concrete, the winter's rain and snow unable to remove the plasma of those who'd perished in this man-made hell fueled by a lust for power, money and street fame.

Bullet holes in brick and wood, scars from gun battles from days long passed still remained. Junked out cars lined the street and there were a couple of empty duplexes with busted out windows and doors missing from the hinges. Off in the distance, directly to the south, one could see the burned out quad-plex that was once Peppi Vargas' trap house, where another brief reign had come to a violent end. Even in its dilapidated state, however, Ann Avenue and Fox Park itself, was still a dope dealer's paradise. And as the neighborhood's violent history rolled on, Ya Murder and her crew, after the demise of Carmella Lapiente`, Phoebe Perez, Toodie Perez, and a brief stint by Peppi Vargas, now held the reins of power on the west side of the neighborhood.

It was as if she was riding atop a white horse, given the adulation she received, when Ya Murder rolled up on Ann Avenue in Toodie's Cadillac. Fiends seemed to come to life, running up to her car asking if she was selling as she and her girls climbed from the ride with satchels of rocked up cocaine.

Right away, at least a dozen of the Mexican teenagers who'd been foot soldiers for Toodie asked for jobs. Ya Murder hired them right away as lookouts and soldiers. Lookouts got on just for the sake of numbers, soldiers were hired on the spot if they showed her that they had their own weapon as she hadn't many guns to pass around. Within an hour, under the darkness of night, Ya Murder had Ann Avenue pumping once more. And with the Germans backing her now, there was no telling just how far she would rise in the game. She was now poised to take control of the entire neighborhood.

CHAPTER THIRTY

NO TABLE MANNERS

January 13, 2009

Saint Cecilia, the red-bricked high-steeple Catholic Church located on Louisiana Avenue, which sat tucked in between interstates 64 and 44 and just west of Fox Park, was where seventeen year-old Peppi Vargas, and twenty-one year-olds Simone Cortez and Donatella 'Sweet Pea' Cruz were being sent home on this snowy day of January 12, 2009.

Ceilings three stories high and art deco reminiscent of the Grecian Empire with its turquoise and white marble columns and arches adorned the sides, bordered three rows of pews that led to a black and white marble-floored stage that held a magnificent white stone sculpture of a crucified Jesus on the cross on its back wall.

Saint Cecilia was a cavernous, colorful house of worship meant for celebration, but this was by far one of the saddest days ever for many of the Mexicans in Fox Park who attended the church every week. Theatrical stairs led up to three large double doors, all of which were wide open as throngs of people filed into the building. Cars were pulling up constantly, dropping off loads of people of Hispanic descent and heading back to Fox Park to pick up more individuals who hadn't a ride. Not even Carmella, nor Phoebe when she'd been killed, had such a large turnout as Pepper, Simone and Sweet Pea's funeral had garnered.

Dawk, Bay and T-top had arrived a couple of hours early and were on hand when the coffins were wheeled inside through the church's rear entrance in the early morning hours. They stood in somber silence before the coffins dressed in all black. Contemplation over the lives lost filled the big three's mind as they eyed three members of their crew lying at rest. The one that stung the most was the sight of Peppi Vargas in her open casket. She wore a pink dress and had a pink flower nestled in her thick, black hair as she lay in eternal sleep. As violent a person as she was when she was alive, Pepper looked like the little girl she really was on the inside as she lay in her coffin with her hands over her chest.

"She was just a baby," Bay remarked somberly as her eyes watered. The day she, Pepper and T-top had killed Toodie came back to memory as she stared at the body in the casket. "She would've been a good one," she stated somberly.

T-top, meanwhile, was thinking about Spoonie and Tyke. They were the same age as Pepper, but they were worlds apart. Her youngest sisters were on their way to college and were star athletes in only their freshman year of college. T-top said nothing in reply to Bay; she only felt pity for Peppi Vargas, a youngster who'd gotten caught up in the streets and paid the game's ultimate price.

Dawk, on the other hand, was thinking about the fallout. The Mexicans were crying for blood, and he was worried the family could fall into chaos over this treacherous deed. The mistake he'd made, which was telling Jay-D to only bust shots at Ya Murder and Noodles when they'd left Toodie's house, had come back ten times harder. Dawk told no one, but inside, he felt responsible for what'd happened to Pepper and her crew. Discussing the matter would do him no good as he was convinced this entire day would've never happened had he ordered a hit instead of a drive-by shooting. No one could change his mind about that matter, and Dawk was intent on answering on behalf of Pepper, if only to even things within the Mexican faction of the family, all of whom were on the verge of going on a bloody rampage.

While the big three milled about in the church, outside, a

black, stretched BMW limousine, followed by two black H-1 Hummers, pulled up and double parked. From the custom chrome wheels, many from the streets knew that these weren't rental cars. Whoever sat behind the mirror tint were obviously people of importance. The funeral attendees watched in silence as a slender Hispanic man opened the passenger door of the limousine, stepped out, and walked to the rear of the vehicle and opened the passenger side door.

Before she'd even emerged completely, people began cheering for the famed R&B singer Narshea. *"No hay imágenes. Después de la ceremonia."* (No pictures right now. After the ceremony!) the Grand Diva yelled as funeral attendees ran towards her holding cameras. She repeated the saying again as she was flanked by three more security team members and ushered up the stairs into the massive church.

"Did I say that right?" Narshea asked her tutor as she walked up the aisle leading to the front row of pews.

"You did, ma'am," the man replied.

For the sake of Ben Holland, who'd requested that she do him a favor if she could, Narshea had agreed to help a man she admired based on one meeting she'd had with the man back down in Phoenix, Arizona the day after his release from federal prison back in August of 2005. Ben and his team couldn't make the funeral, but he'd wanted to send his love to the Mexicans in Saint Louis to let them know that not just the big three, but the entire Holland family felt their loss, so he requested Narshea do a special performance.

When she walked into the building and began walking up the empty church's middle aisle, Narshea spotted three people standing in front of the coffins. She slowly walked up the aisle and approached the three individuals. "Ben sent me," she spoke softly.

Dawk extended his hand and welcomed Narshea. "That's my cousin. We wanna thank you for coming on short notice."

"Anything for that man. I know real when I see it," Narshea remarked as she walked up and eyed the coffins. "She was just a baby," she added as she eyed the young female in the pink dress resting inside the coffin.

"She was," Bay remarked. "These three females were loved by a lot of people."

"The game," Narshea remarked somberly. "We humans are the cause of our own troubles sometimes," she said as she walked over to the open casket and stared down at the young woman. "What are their names?"

T-top gave the names and a brief rundown on what had gone down to Narshea. Seconds after she'd stopped speaking, a woman's incessant cry was heard. Dawk, Bay, T-top and Narshea all turned simultaneously and saw a middle-aged Hispanic woman walking up onto the stage.

"Was this your family?" Narshea asked the middle-aged woman.

The woman looked at Narshea, her eyes asking was it okay to approach. "Come," Narshea invited softly as she motioned the woman over.

"Thank you. I am Cecilia Cruz."

"Cecilia? The same as the church," Dawk remarked as he looked down at the sorrowful woman.

"Yes. But this is not my church. Everyone knows me as CeeCee. This one here," the woman said as she pointed to the middle coffin. "This is my niece Donatella Cruz. The one on the right is her friend, Simone Cortez, they were only twenty-one. The one who remains with the open casket is their friend Peppi Vargas, and she was just seventeen. We celebrate not how they lived, but the loss we all suffer."

"We're sorry for your loss, Cecilia," Dawk spoke somberly as he grabbed the woman's hands tenderly.

Just then a loud sound was heard. The group all looked towards the front of the church and saw that the crowd outside was all standing at the entrance together with Malik in out front. "Cecilia?" Malik said aloud, his voice echoing through the cavernous house of worship. "*Queremos que ustedes nos guía a la vista. Nos llevan!*" (We want you to guide us to the viewing. Lead us!)

Cecilia walked amongst the coffins as Narshea went and took her place on stage beside the Mexican band Malik had supplied her with. The big three took seats on the third row in the middle, a gesture that would allow the leaders of their Mexican crews to sit front and center.

The bishop of the church emerged from a rear door with a handwoven basket filled with carnations and went and stood beside Cecilia. She grabbed a rose, walked over to Simone's coffin and laid one on top of her coffin. With the bishop following her, she walked over to her niece Donatella's coffin and reached down into the basket, her hands trembling and her eyes filled with tears as she grabbed a carnation. *"Se le ha llamado Sweet Pea por una razón, mi niño. Usted era el azúcar en mi té. Todo lo que tenía que hacer era colocar el dedo dentro de mi té y sería dulce, Donatella."* (We called you Sweet Pea for a reason, my child. You were the sugar in my tea. All you had to do was place your finger inside of my tea and it would be sweet, Donatella.) the woman spoke softly through her tears. *"Mi té dulce no más, mi amor."* (My tea will be sweet no more, my love.)

Cecilia then walked over to Pepper's coffin. As wrong as it was, she wanted to spit on the youngster for leading her niece down the road to destruction—literally and figuratively—as she felt had her nieces not joined forces with her they would've never been inside that car the night they were attacked while heading to Pepper's home in Louisiana.

Guadalupe still had a chance of living, however; and the last thing Cecilia wanted to do was block a potential blessing from God by cursing a dead soul. *"Mi corazón pecador quiere convertir al diablo. Pero usted ha sufrido bastante el poco tiempo que estuvo aquí. Ruego por misericordia de tu alma, niña."* (My sinful heart wants to cast you to the devil. But you've suffered enough the short time you were here. I pray for mercy on your soul, little girl.) Cecilia said as she slid a carnation in between Pepper's hands resting atop her chest and walked away, clutching her rosary beads and mumbling a prayer as she went and stood in the center of the aisle. When she was done praying, Cecilia looked up and nodded towards the rear of the church.

At that moment, over the harmonious piano, Narshea walked out to the middle of the stage and opened with… *"Late at night when all the world…is sleeping…I stay up and think of you… and I wish on a star…that somewhere you are…thinking of me too…"*

Malik, and the scores of people behind him, began walking up the aisle as Narshea sung a soulful rendition Mexican singer Selena's song titled *Dreaming of You.*

Malik walked up to Cecilia and kissed both her cheeks before placing flowers onto each of the coffins as Narshea sung on. He then guided the grieving woman to the front row as the entire crew from Fox Park sat in the middle pews, encompassing the two front rows as those in attendance continued filing by the coffins as Narshea slid into the song's chorus…*"I'll be dreaming…of you tonight…till tomorrow…I'll be holding you tight…"*

Narshea ended the song as the last of the visitors walked by the coffins. Near the end of the line, Ya Murder and her crew of three came into view, much to the dismay of the Mexicans sitting on the two front middle rows. With a smirk on her face, Ya eyed Malik and waved a friendly wave towards a crying CeeCee.

Malik, DeMarco and Max stood up and rushed her before Dawk, Bay and T-top could even react. Malik ran and grabbed Ya around the hood of her bubble jacket and began shoving her away from the coffins.

"El fuck you doing? Yo la conocía!" (The fuck you doing? I knew her!) Ya Murder scoffed as she broke free and ran and stood before Pepper's coffin.

"Deje que su niño le diga su despedida, Malik." (Let her say her farewell, Malik.) CeeCee interjected. *"Este es un lugar de paz."* (This is a place of peace.)

Malik kept it street by not telling CeeCee that he believed Ya Murder was in on the hit against her niece and her friends. He eyed Ya coldly and said, *"Que no era un amigo de nadie en ninguna de los ataúdes. Dejar!"* (You was not a friend to no one in either of those coffins! Leave!)

Ya Murder stretched her arms as she stood before Pepper's coffin. *"Usted escuchó CeeCee! Permítanme decir adiós! Y yo lo deje una vez que he hablado de mi paz!"* (You heard CeeCee! Let me say farewell! And I'll leave once I have spoken my peace!) she scoffed at Malik while staring him in the eyes.

CeeCee grabbed Malik's arm to pull him down in his seat, but he snatched away from the woman. "I want to stand!" he stated, never taking his eyes off Ya Murder, who'd turned to face Pepper.

Ya Murder was bursting with joy on the inside as she stared down at Pepper. She wasn't in Louisiana to see her foe die at the hands of Boogie, but she did have a part in taking down Sweet Pea on Highway 79. The way Donatella's body had twisted when she pumped shells into her body had become one of her most cherished memories. The entire hit, from the time Maggie had dumped rounds into Simone and sent her Hummer into a violent rollover, to the sight of Boogie lighting up the interior of the upturned SUV, was exhilarating. Never had murder felt so, so liberating.

"Lo siento por lo que le ha ocurrido a usted." (I'm sorry for what happened to you.) Ya said in mocked reverence as she looked down on Pepper with Juggie and her two other girls at her side. She then smiled over to Malik at that moment and said, *"Lo siento, no estaba allí para ver a su muerte!"* (I'm sorry I wasn't there to see her die!) right before she turned and hawked a wad of phlegm right into Pepper's face as she lay in her coffin.

Malik had seen and heard the whole play, as did all of the crew. A dozen or more of his soldiers rushed Ya Murder and her crew, but they were quickly blocked by church parishioners.

Malik pulled a chrome .357 automatic as funeral attendees began scattering from the pews while screaming aloud. Bishops inside the church had rushed over and stood in between Malik and Ya Murder's team. *"El señor Gómez? Si no el arma lejos tendrá que elogiaban sus amigos en algún otro lugar hoy mismo!"* (Mister Gomez? If you don't put the gun away you will have to eulogize your friends somewhere else today!)

Cecilia had fainted on sight. DeMarco and Max had run to her aide as the drama unfolded inside the church.

Malik was still holding on to the gun when Dawk walked up to him and gently placed his hand on his wrist. *"No, aquí no."* (Not here.) he whispered lowly.

"Peppi, así que quieren que yo haga esto, Jefe!" (Peppi would so want this, Boss!) Malik said through tears as one of the bishops placed a hand on Ya Murder's shoulder to protect her.

Dawk leaned closer to Malik and whispered into his ear. *"Ella no lo hizo. Ella quiere que lo haga con y sin que nadie se entere. Dejar que se vaya por el momento, Malik."* (No she wouldn't. She would want you to do it and get away with it. Let it go for now, Malik.) he said as he applied pressure to Malik's wrist, signaling for him to lower the gun.

Bay and T-top walked up at that moment with a few members of Malik's crew and stood on other side of him and Dawk as they eyed the female intruder with cold stares.

Ya Murder eyed the identical twins, not knowing who they were in return. "What? You two bitches gotta a problem with me too? I'm saying fuck Peppi Vargas!"

"Cuide su boca, niña. Respecto al obispo la iglesia antes de hacer que llueva en el ass de aquí." (Watch your mouth, little girl. Respect the bishop's church before we make it rain on your ass in here.) T-top remarked, never taking her eyes off the female.

"Excusa de mi hermana francesa, obispo. Ella tiene una cierta forma de narrar invitados no deseados a abandonar." (Excuse my sister's French, bishop. She has a certain way of telling unwanted guests to leave.) Bay quickly followed as she, too, held her eyes on her enemy.

Ya Murder was hit with a sudden jolt of reluctance. She'd never expected the two black women to speak Spanish at all, let alone so fluently. Wondering who they were, she backed away from Pepper's coffin while nodding her head up and down. *"Me fuera en ese mundo."* (See me outside in that world.) she boldly stated as several bishops escorted her and her girls from the church.

"Lo voy a dejar para que ahora, ¿sí?" (I'm gone hold you to that now, yeah?) T-top stated through a smile as order was slowly restored.

"No hacer nada al respecto." (Do nothing about it.) Bay whispered to Malik. *"Este es para nosotros."* (This one is on us.) she ended just before the ceremony resumed.

CHAPTER THIRTY-ONE

NOBODY LEFT

The ceremony had just ended minutes earlier and Pepper, Sweet Pea and Simone's coffins were now being wheeled from the church towards the hearses. What'd happened with Ya Murder had some people spooked. Many had left early, Narshea included, having sensed more animosity on the horizon.

The Mexican band Malik had hired was playing Eric Clapton's song titled *Layla*, which the instrumental from the movie Goodfellas. Their violins and guitars created a relaxing atmosphere as members of the crew toted the coffins down the church stairs. The big three, Malik and the Cottonwoods followed with Kantrell and the crew from Bangin' Heads. All were somber watching the coffins being toted towards three separate hearses in order to be taken to their final resting place.

Just when the crowd was beginning to settle down and prepare for the final farewell, gunshots erupted over the Mexican band's harmony. The music ceased and everyone hit the ground. Malik's team had the decency, however, to not drop the coffins. Instead, they eased them down and laid flat on the ground in their suits as gunfire continued to erupt.

From atop the stairs, Dawk could see Ya Murder off to his right across the street standing before a black four door Cadillac firing off an AK-47 into the air as he ducked behind the church doors, shielding his sisters and the Cottonwoods.

Several seconds later, he watched as Ya and her three goons hopped into the Caddy and backed away from the scene before spinning around and peeling out while steadily blasting off rounds into the air.

Saint Louis police had to come and restore order and guide the caravan to the cemetery. Amid falling snow, final farewells were said at Pepper and her girls' gravesite and everybody then convened over to Malik's diner for the repass once the three were lowered into their graves.

Inside Malik's Diner, the big three sat in Malik's office eating hot beef tamales and baked ziti as they strategized over glasses of sangria. Ya Murder had crossed the line earlier in the day and she now had to answer for disrespecting a well-liked team.

Dawk, Bay and T-top weren't going to drag this thing out with their latest foe off Ann Avenue for no longer than necessary. With their own shipment of cocaine arriving in less than two months, they could ill-afford to sit by and let Ya Murder build rank and power only to be dragged into another long, bloody feud.

The battles they'd fought with Carmella and Toodie had given the big three enough foresight to understand that this go around, they would have to make quick work of their competition in order to put things back on an even keel. While the siblings were eating, Jay-D, Dooney, and Nancy Cottonwood walked into Malik's office.

"What y'all find out?" Dawk asked as he bit into a hot beef tamale.

"They over in Fox Park on Ann Avenue like you said, Boss." Jay-D answered. "You want us to go handle that?"

"Not right now," Dawk replied as he set the tamale down, dusted his hands and stood up. "We gone head out together and take care of this business on behalf of the Mexicans."

"What you want us to do?" Dooney asked.

Tiva chimed in by saying, "We gone need y'all to go and sit on Juggie crib while we handle this thing in Fox Park after we tool up."

"Let's let everybody out there know what the deal is," Dawk stated as Nancy turned and opened the office door.

Dawk led the way out of the office with Bay and T-top following. Malik's diner was filled with at least a score or more of Mexicans, all loyal to the Holland family. Tejano music from the band Malik had hired was going, and many were dancing and laughing as they reminisced over their fallen comrades. The music ceased and everyone inside the diner grew quiet, however, when they caught site of the leaders of the organization making their way through the crowd. It was rare that the Bosses were on hand. They were spoken of often, yet rarely seen. But on this day, many who'd never laid eyes on the Bosses, knew exactly who they were just by their sheer presence and statuesque, silent power. And if they were in town, then what had gone down with Pepper and her crew had to be a big deal.

Dawk, standing 6'4", commanded attention as he made his way through the crowd in his black silk suit, his hair braided into a single ponytail with a pair of clear glasses covering his eyes. Bay and T-top followed in their black business suits, the shoulder holsters of their .45 calibers clearly visible. Jay-D, Dooney and Nancy followed the twins, all dressed in black. If it wasn't known before, now, all those affiliated with the game had come to understand that the Holland family, an African-American family, not a Carmella Lapiente`, not a fucking Toodie Perez, and damn sure not a Ya Murder, was the ones who truly ran the streets of Saint Louis.

From his father, Dawk had learned not to give a long speech on reprisal before a large crowd. Malik, DeMarco and Max were trusted; as were Jay-D, Dooney and Nancy, the rest were foot soldiers who need not know every single detail as there was no telling who would be stupid enough to record the scenario and post it online. With those thoughts in mind, Dawk stood in the center of the diner and said, "I know everybody hurting over what happened. I'm sorry for the loss. Enjoy yourselves, but do nothing about it."

Everyone remained silent as they watched Dawk and

company exit the diner without uttering another word. The big three climbed into Bay's Lincoln and Jay-D followed in his Navigator, the six of them heading back to Saint Charles. The big three, although running things, knew just how crucial the Mexican faction of their organization was to the overall scheme of things. To keep them loyal, they'd decided to bear the burden and the risk of going after Ya Murder in order to prevent anarchy.

Malik Gomez had been on the frontlines from day one, and the big three felt that if they were to place the job of going after Pepper and her crew's killers in that of his lap and the foot soldiers he controlled, it would only open a door that would possibly tip the scales in the Mexicans' favor.

Some of the foot soldiers may begin to think that Malik should be the one to run the organization instead of a bunch of African-Americans who only passed down orders. The events that had unfolded with Junior Cernigliaro, however, had schooled the big three on the importance of preventing racial tension. They were always several steps ahead of those around them. And what was about to go down on this night, would only serve to confirm to all involved that the right ones were in charge of the rising juggernaut known on the streets as The Holland Family.

Back inside the diner, several foot soldiers had approached Malik and asked him what was going on once Dawk and company had vacated the premises. He responded by telling them to ask him that same question come morning as he carried on with the festivities, satisfied that The Holland Family would bear the weight of the pain he carried in his heart over losing his protégé, Peppi Vargas.

It's fair to say that Malik Gomez had not the capacity to go against the family in spite of having the complete understanding that he had the muscle to stage an uprising if that is what he chose to do. Loyalty. It was the glue to The Holland Family's survival. And Malik Gomez was one who wore that badge with honor. He went on, leading the celebration for his fallen comrades while hoping for a favorable turnout for the Bosses of the family, who were putting it all on the line on behalf of the crew he controlled.

****

Once they'd made it back over to Saint Charles, the big three and the Cottonwoods climbed out of their cars under the darkness of night and convened to the home's den where Jay-D began pulling out an assortment of weapons consisting of two Browning .226 assault rifles, an AR-15, two Mac-10s, and the family's most cherished weapon of choice—the famed Chicago Piano—A.K.A. the Tommy gun.

Clothes worn to the funeral, that of silk, formal, black attire, was changed out into black street gear. Gloves and masks were selected and weapons had freshly-loaded magazines stuffed into their chamber before The Holland Family and the Cottonwoods left the Victorian-style two-story home that lay just up the street from the soon-to-be-opened Club Indigo and New Orleans Café.

The big three climbed into Bay's Lincoln while Jay-D and his family climbed into one of Malik's white cargo vans. All six knew that they were about to take a big risk, but the preventing of another budding war superseded all caution.

Dawk pulled up the corner where the family's future club and restaurant lay and waved Jay-D forward. The van pulled up alongside the old school Lincoln where Dooney rolled the passenger side window down on the van and made eye contact with Dawk.

"Once we done, get on the line with Malik and tell 'em meet us over on Ann Street at ten tomorrow morning. And this time," Dawk added. "Make sure everybody that pull up to that house check out."

"Gotcha, Boss," Dooney replied as he reached down and bumped fists with Dawk before the group separated.

****

Back over in Fox Park, Ya Murder was feeling as if she was sitting on top of the world as she and her crew prepared to close shop for the night. "I can't believe you got away with spitting in Pepper's face!" Juggie laughed as she sat at a table with Ya Murder and two more soldiers.

"That was a slap to Malik's face." Ya laughed as she ate a bowl of nachos. "We gone do what Toodie couldn't do! We gone run Ann Street again! Fox Park again!" she ended as she and her girls left their trap house and climbed into Toodie's old school, black Cadillac de' Ville with dark-tinted windows.

Juggie cranked the engine and right away, a new radio show was announcing an upcoming event. "Saint Louis? We, we on in Saint Louis now, Sister Spanks?" a female Dee-jay's voice was heard over the radio air waves.

"And you knoowww ittttttt!" Sister Spanks quipped. "If ya' ain't knowwww now ya' knowwww, pimpin'!"

"Gateway city to the west? Umm, the hottest club in the Midwest is opening come March! Y'all need to be on the lookout for this one! Indigo! Club Indigo is opening in Saint Charles and they got an all-star line up! Non-Stop! The platinum selling artist from Atlanta G-A will be in the house along with the crew of The Fantastic Four! But we ain't even done! The Grand Diva herself—Narshea gone be in the house! And a special performance by up and coming artist Jane Dow will go down—and trust—y'all don't wanna miss the Jane Dow Band because I seen these Lakota Indians perform live? And they just may outdo the ones y'all already know!"

"Who that?" Ya Murder asked as she looked down at the radio.

"That's the Fantastic Four," Juggie answered. "They talkin' about that new club the Holland family opening in Saint Charles."

"Guess who crashing the party at Indigo?" Ya Murder said as she stuffed several nacho cheese covered tortilla chips into her mouth. "Damn, these jalapeno peppers hot as the fuck!"

Juggie laughed at her friend's remark as she steered the Cadillac onto Saint Louis Street while listening to the radio.

"Sister Spanks? I—Misses Jones—is calling for this power mix! Indigo is gone be on fire, sister! Ain't nothin' but what gone be in that piece?"

"Rock star, baby!" Sister Spanks, A.K.A. Tracey Sanchez laughed as she stood before her turntables inside WKLV studios back in Las Vegas, Nevada. She then let the turntables rotate and let loose with…"*…Hey…you's a rock star, baby… up in the building makin' the club go crazy…hey….you's a rock star baby…throwin' ass like that you must be a rock star, baby…"*

Ya and her girls had covered their mouths in appreciation as R Kelly, Kid Rock and Ludacris' song titled *Rock Star* thumped over the Cadillac's system. "That's my shit!" Ya laughed aloud as she turned up the volume and vibed to the music. "I ain't heard that song in a while!"

"Hotter than tamales…you probably should be my wild thang…tell them other chicks mind they own business…and let us do our own thang…" Ludacris rapped as Ya and her crew cruised down Saint Louis Street, raising the roof inside the pristine Cadillac while making their way out of Fox Park.

"Eh, stop up to Kirk's so we can get some wraps for this bud I got from this fiend!" Ya Murder yelled from the front passenger seat as she continued to stuff nachos into her mouth.

The move she'd made over to Saint Cecilia had Ya feeling as if she was indeed running Fox Park. And with the Germans backing her, there was no stopping her was her thinking as Juggie pulled the Cadillac up in front of *Kirk's Corner Store* so the crew could grab a few blunts before striking out over to Juggie's apartment.

Ya Murder handed Juggie a twenty dollar bill before she climbed out of the Caddy with her girls. She remained in the front passenger seat rocking with the music as she continued eating her nachos.

Meanwhile, Bay's Lincoln was parked at the back end of Fox Park facing away from Kirk's, which was just up the street, and shielded by the darkness of night.

"They just rode up there," Bay said as she looked out the back window of her car and saw Toodie's Cadillac ride by slowly just before the brake lights lit up and the car came to a halt. She lowered the Michael Myers mask she'd gotten from

Jay-D over her head and racked her Mac-10.

"Just like we knew they would," T-top followed as she racked the chrome Tommy gun she was clutching and pulled down on her own Michael Myers mask.

A false sense of security was the allure of Fox Park for many of the hustlers. Here, they all felt at home, as if they could travel wherever they wanted to inside the neighborhood because no one would dare hit them on her home turf. Many had it wrong, however; and Ya Murder was no different. A simple stop for blunt wraps would turn into a night of sheer terror that would leave a lasting impression on any and everybody who dared to step off into *Kirk's* from this night forward.

"Let's move," Dawk stated calmly from behind the steering wheel as he pulled down his black ski mask and eased from behind the steering wheel of the Lincoln with his Browning . 226 rifle locked and loaded.

Bay and T-top pushed their doors open and eased from the car simultaneously with their weapons draping their sides. Together, dressed in all black, the big three entered Fox Park from the rear and began trotting through the darkness, headed towards the corner store. They crossed the isolated basketball court with weapons locked and loaded, peeking through the tree trunks as flashes of the lone street light emanating from Kirk's, which was on their left, gave glimpses of the black Cadillac that was facing away from them. They neared the park's front entrance and all three raised their weapons as they stepped off the curb and crept out of the darkness into the middle of the street that ran alongside of Kirk's.

Juggie and her two girls were emerging from Kirk's, the three of them dancing in a single-file line and singing along with R Kelly. "...*smoke what you want...Kell's about ta' give you what you need...up in my room you screaming Hercules, Hercules...*"

Ya was in the passenger seat rocking with her girls when three people, dressed in all black, two wearing Michael Myers Halloween masks and toting rifles, ran out from the entrance to the park directly across the street from the corner store.

Juggie was backing it up with her hands in the air when she saw the play about to go down. She tapped both her girls and frightfully yelled aloud, "It's a hit!" before she broke out running.

Ya saw her girls running up the street and turned around to look out the back window of the car. Semi-automatic gunfire erupted into the night air at that moment and the back window evaporated seconds after she'd laid down on the front seat. She grabbed her Glock .40 and opened the passenger side door on the Cadillac and was emerging when she saw two gunmen rounding the rear of the Caddy.

Ya Murder opened fire right away, dumping off rounds from her Glock as she stood outside the Caddy hunched over with the music blasting. One of the shooters, who wore a black ski mask, screamed aloud and clutched his stomach as he fell back behind the Cadillac.

Ya Murder dodged the bullets from the remaining shooter and returned fire once more, forcing the second shooter in the Michael Myers mask to take cover. She'd just turned around to flee the scene when the third shooter rounded the front of the car. The two met eye-to-eye, but the gunner on Ya had the ups as she held a chrome Tommy gun on her. Yellow flames immediately erupted into the air. Ya's body thrashed about furiously as she let go of a terrifying and blood-curdling scream of agony as shell after shell ripped through the passenger side door, shattering the window and lodging in her torso.

Adrenaline kept Ya Murder going as she stumbled along the side of the Caddy, leaving a trail of blood on the car's rear passenger side window and its white interior as the gun she was firing slipped from her hands. The gunner on Ya ceased firing and ran around to the side of the car and stood before her. "You told me to see you in that world, huh, bitch?" she asked before she let loose with a torrent of bullets.

The bullets going into Ya Murder's torso had forced her up against the side of the car. The rear passenger window shattered and the tires flattened amid the thunderously-violent gunfire. Ya's body was actually trying to collapse, but the repeated shells crashing into her torso were holding her up against the side of the car as she screamed to the top of her lungs like a cat set afire. Through her screams, Ya crossed her arms over her chest, instinctively trying to shield her vital organs as she slowly began to slide down the side of the car as bullet after bullet continued shredding her body and tearing the Cadillac apart at the same time.

T-top was holding the Tommy gun level, swaying it side to side gently as she ripped the car apart, shutting down the stereo and forcing smoke to erupt inside the Cadillac's interior in the process. The further Ya's body slid to the ground, the closer the bullets grew to her skull.

Things seemed to play out in slow motion as blood-stained cotton and flesh jumped from Ya Murder's arms and breasts, then her neck, and finally, her face and the top of her skull once they became level with the assassin's weapon. When she came to rest, Ya Murder's jacket had been shredded and her intestines were dangling from her back. The nachos she'd been eating only minutes before were oozing from her stomach. The jalapeno peppers she'd eaten were still green, and the cheese she'd sucked down was still yellow as it dripped down onto her jeans and the concrete beneath her body.

Jada 'Ya Murder' Murdella's death would become one of the most infamous homicides to unfold under the lone street light out in front of *Kirk's Corner Store* and Fox Park itself given the way everything had played out. Her reign had lasted all but a couple of weeks, and had come to an abrupt and violent end at the hands of Tiva 'T-top' Holland, who'd left her leaning up against the passenger side of the once-extravagant Cadillac frozen stiff on her knees with her mouth wide open looking up at the dark night's sky. Ironically, she lay dead with her hands crisscrossing her chest—the same manner in which she'd witnessed Peppi Vargas lying in her casket only hours earlier.

****

While T-top was in the process of killing Ya Murder, Bay was standing over Dawk with the Mac-10. She was looking around for the rest of Ya's crew as her brother knelt down on one knee behind the trunk of the Cadillac trying to catch his breath.

"We fuckin' missed three of 'em!" T-top complained as she and Bay helped Dawk up from the ground and led him back to the Lincoln.

"You know that was on purpose," Bay responded as she and T-top hurried Dawk back to the car. "You okay, Dawk?" she asked anxiously.

"I think I got a bruise on my ribs," Dawk grimaced as he and his sisters neared the Lincoln.

"You need us to call Doctor Wickenstaff?" T-top asked as she opened the back door and eased Dawk into the backseat before she and Bay jumped into the front seat.

"Nah," Dawk exhaled as he pulled off his sweatshirt and removed his bulletproof vest as Bay pulled off and rounded the curb to head out of Fox Park.

While heading back to Saint Charles, Dawk grabbed his cell phone and called Jay-D as he lay slumped over in the backseat. "You watching that spot?" he scowled once Jay-D picked up.

"We on it, Boss. Ain't nothin'. You all right, fam?"

"Slug hit my vest, gangster. I'm good. Time they, time they show? You know what to do." Dawk ordered painfully before he ended the call as Bay merged onto I-44 and headed west back to Saint Charles. "Fuck!" he yelled out in frustration as he punched the roof of Bay's car, pissed that he'd taken a slug on the job, yet all-the-while knowing he was lucky to have worn a bulletproof vest.

****

Juggie and her two girls, meanwhile, had met up back over on Ann Avenue. Off in the distance through the burned-out hull of what was once Pepper's trap house, the three could see red lights blaring. This was bad news for Juggie. When she and her girls walked into the store, they'd left their guns behind on the seats. They'd also left two kilograms of cocaine and all of their earnings in the trunk of the Cadillac.

Juggie knew Ya hadn't gotten away; she couldn't have escaped all the bullets unleashed. Besides, she'd seen the first shot that hit Ya and heard her scream just before she ducked off into an alleyway. The police were sure to find the guns and cocaine and that would leave her assed out as she and Ya were into the Germans for those two bricks.

With Ya Murder now out of the equation, Juggie knew she would now owe the Germans; on top of that, they were into it with the Holland family—and that in itself posed a major threat to their lives. She and her girls had lost their guns fleeing the scene; so even if she wanted to, Juggie couldn't wage a battle because she had no guns to fight with. Compounding the problem was the fact that she hadn't the dough to pay back what was owed to their connect. "Let's go home," she told her two girls. "I need to make a phone call to Indianapolis and get some help down here."

A few miles north of Fox Park, Jay-D and Nancy were sitting inside their traditional white cargo murder van waiting patiently. Anticipation and patience was what was required on this particular job. The big three had gone after Ya specifically, purposely letting Juggie and her crew slip away. They'd made a statement by gunning Ya down in such horrifying fashion: this our set.

Outside of Ya Murder, the rest of her crew was such nonfactors, they warranted no true plan of action. They were merely being manipulated to their own deaths and had no idea as to what was going down.

While riding with a dope fiend who was willing to take her home after offering him the change from the twenty dollar bill Ya had given her to purchase the blunt wraps, Juggie used her cell phone to call RJ back over in Naptown as she needed more guns to get back at The Holland Family. Her first plan of action was to push the re-up date to RJ back by at least a month in order to recoup the losses. During that time, she would retool and go after Malik Gomez.

Juggie went through her phone and dialed a number Ya had keyed in as the fiend drove out of Fox Park. The phone rang two times before a dial tone was heard. *"The number you've dialed is no longer in service. If you feel this message is in error, please hang up and try your call again."*

"The fuck?" Juggie asked perplexed as she hung up the phone and dialed the number a second time, only to hear the same message.

Juggie leaned back in the passenger seat of the fiend's Chrysler 200 in frustration. She then scrolled through her phone and came up on another number Ya had given her that had a Kansas area code. She dialed the number, and much to her relief, someone on the other end picked up. "Who this?" a female asked.

"This Juggie!"

"Who?" the female snapped.

"Juggie! I'm a friend of Ya Murder! She got killed tonight and I was—"

The call ended abruptly so Juggie dialed the number again, believing she was disconnected by mistake. When the phone's voicemail picked up, she was hit with an ominous feeling in the pit of her stomach, one that told her that none of the people affiliated with Ya Murder was going to come to her aide. She was now on her own, she knew, as anxiety filled her psyche.

****

Over to the state of Kansas, Maggie McPherson had just finished sending Juggie's second call to voice mail. She eased up from the recliner in the den of her and her mother's sprawling, immaculate ranch-style home and grabbed her empty bowl of chili to retrieve a second helping from the mansion's front kitchen.

"Who was that?" Maggie's mother asked as she flipped through the channels on the wall-mounted TV.

"Those stupid Mexicans from Saint Louis. Ya Murder was killed tonight." Maggie answered as she threw her phone into the fireplace.

"Tanya was right. That brings an end to whatever business you, RJ, Popeye and Boogie had with that crew." Maggie's mother stated nonchalantly as she laid her head back in the chair she was resting in and went on watching TV in peace.

The Germans were loyal to no one but themselves at this present day and time. When Toodie disappeared, the crew from Cincinnati had all but given up on Saint Louis as they knew there was no one left to keep their cocaine profits coming in on a steady and even keel. They could've retaliated on behalf of Toodie, but they'd opted not to do so as they had bigger issues to deal with in Philadelphia with a federal agent by the name of Tammy Moto, who'd taken down one of their own in Brenda Marshall.

The Germans didn't give up on Saint Louis, however; they'd merely conceded the market to a strong opponent, one in which they felt they had no animosity towards. And going further, they weren't willing to risk dealing with inexperienced dealers like Ya Murder and Juggie, both of whom had a serious lack of discipline while trying to take down a federal agent, one in whom they knew was getting her hands dirty on the streets of Philadelphia.

****

Back down south over in Saint Louis, meanwhile, Jay-D sat and watched as Juggie and her two girls climbed out of a four door Chrysler 200. He looked over the back seat at his niece Nancy Cottonwood, who was clutching a Mac-10 semi-automatic. "You know what to do?" he asked lowly as he eyed the headlights on the car facing him.

"Point and shoot," Nancy replied calmly as she racked the weapon and unlatched the cargo van's side door.

Sixteen year-old Nancy Cottonwood was set to be initiated into The Holland Family via a hit on this night. The AK-47, which was the Cottonwood's usual weapon of choice, was too powerful for the skinny teenager at this point and time. The gun often got away from her during practice because of its recoil, but she was an expert with the Mac-10.

Nancy eased the van's cargo door open just as Jay-D began easing the van forward. The Chrysler was still in front of the apartment, and Juggie and her girls were crossing the front lawn to her apartment when the van pulled up. Nancy, dressed in all black and wearing a ski mask, kneeled in the van's cargo bay, the same as she'd seen her uncle Dooney do on several occasions, and let loose.

Juggie and her girls screamed aloud and took off running in all directions when what sounded like firecrackers began erupting from a van in the middle of the street.

Nancy had a bead on Juggie. Bullets nipped at her feet and soon lodged into her legs, forcing her to fall to the ground.

Dooney emerged from behind a parked car at that moment with an AR-15 and ran up on Juggie's two friends as they ran in his direction. They were gunned down where they stood, falling face first onto the sidewalk, dying there on the scene in pools of their own blood. Dooney then aimed the gun at the terrified dope fiend and stared him down for several seconds. Not this time. No one was to get away was the Boss' order. He let loose, ripping the man's body apart in the front seat of the car before running back towards the van.

Jay-D flipped a hoody over his head and hopped out at that moment and racked the .45 caliber he was toting. Casually, he walked over to Juggie, who was writhing about over the snow-covered lawn as she clutched her legs and screamed aloud in pain.

Juggie knew about the white van and the killers it carried. Dooney was a fat, red gangster. The guy walking up on her, however, was slender, dark-skinned and had long braids. She recognized him right away. "Jay-D, go easy, man!" she pleaded. The thought of dying had forced Juggie to defecate in her jeans as she continued pleading for mercy. "Come on, Jay-D!" she cried and begged. "Please don't kill me! I wasn't even down with Ya like that! I was going inside! I was going in—"

Jay-D fired three rounds into Juggie's skull, ceasing her pleas and movements without uttering a response, as monologue before murder wasn't his motus operandus.

Juggie's head swelled to nearly twice its size and brain matter seeped from her ears and the top of her blown open cranium as Jay-D turned and trotted back to the van. He was bending the corner inside the van when he called Dawk and let him know everything had gone according to plan.

"Y'all house locked up," Dawk responded as he drove Bay's Lincoln over to the Millennium Hotel. "I want y'all to go on and get out of town until this here blow over."

"Where to?"

"I got you and your family set up in a suite out in Vegas at the Bellagio under your name, dude. I be out there in a couple of days."

"Good looking out, fam." Jay-D said as he wheeled the van back over to Malik's home in Maplewood.

"We talk," Dawk stated before ending the call.

****

The morning after Pepper and her crew's burial and the hits on Ya Murder and Juggie found Malik, De Marco and Max parked on Ann Avenue as ten 'o' clock approached. The neighborhood was unusually quiet on this morning. It hadn't been this peaceful in quite some time. Word had spread on Ya Murder being killed, but Malik was steadily wondering why Dawk wanted to meet him at this specific location as he sat in the backseat of his Mercedes jeep.

Several minutes in, Bay's old school Lincoln rounded the corner onto Ann Avenue and pulled up alongside of Malik's SUV facing the opposite direction. The driver's side window rolled down slowly and Dawk came into view. "You heard what happened last night, right?" he asked casually.

"Si, homes. What now?" Malik asked as he watched the block ahead.

Dawk looked the block over briefly in the opposite direction and said, "They got a few empty apartments on this block. I want you to rent 'em out, ya' dig? Change the windows out and put some burglar bar doors on the downstairs windows and the front and back doors. This here our block now."

"Si, Boss."

"Give your people some work on those houses. We gone try

and expedite the product. In the meantime? No cocaine. Y'all can hustle weed, but lay off that powder. Jay-D and his family headed out to Vegas for a while until the heat die down so you got the power while me and my sisters fall back."

"Si, Boss. And if anybody else try and sell cocaine?"

Dawk stared at Malik, and without him having to speak on it, Malik knew the play coming from Dawk: no one was allowed to sell cocaine in Fox Park from this day forth.

"What about Juggie?" Malik then asked.

Dawk looked over to Bay and then back at T-top, who was in the backseat, and chuckled. "You ain't heard? We wiped Ya whole crew out last night, dude," he let it be known. "Nobody left."

Malik laughed from the backseat of his SUV as he stared down at Dawk. The war between Carmella's crew had been brought to a complete and utter end he now understood. There was no one on Carmella's side left to wage battle. The one sitting at the very top, Carmella Lapiente`, had been killed down in Mexico. Phoebe Perez followed, having been gunned down at the McDonald's on Jefferson Avenue. Toodie Perez had all but disappeared. Q-Man was annihilated behind bars. Ya Murder was taken out in extravagant fashion in front of *Kirk's Corner Store* and Juggie had been gunned down in front of her apartment in Saint Louis. Anyone and everyone affiliated with Carmella's click since her demise back in January of 2004 had been wasted. Finally, after a five-year-long violent street campaign on the streets of Saint Louis and elsewhere that left countless bodies in its wake, The Holland Family had seized control of Fox Park entirely.

With the renting of two apartments that were to become strongholds, Ann Avenue now belonged to the next drug organization that was now pulling the strings. Through a campaign of merciless violence, The Holland Family had taken over the biggest money-making set in the city of Saint Louis. And because of their actions, namely taking the lead to go after Ya and her crew and killing all four in quick fashion, the Mexicans would fall in line with Malik Gomez, the family's trusted and loyal Enforcer and prepare themselves for a cocaine blizzard due to come in the near future.

With their base of operations now in complete order, the next job for the big three lay over in Indianapolis. It would be a job that would fall into the laps of Bay and T-top, who were now on their way to Nap Town to takedown a man known on the streets as RJ after checking out the hotel just before noon.

Dawk, meanwhile, was on his way back to Oklahoma City where he would book a flight to Vegas later on in the night. He was planning to meet up with Phillip Tran and Grover Kobayashi the following day in order to put a rush on the cocaine shipments coming in from Rafael Gacha. The streets of the Midwest were soon to experience a severe cocaine drought once the Naptown connect fell, and that's the way Dawk Holland wanted things once the family's cocaine hit the streets in order to keep the prices high during the family's first run.

CHAPTER THIRTY-TWO
SOME DOWN TIME
January 14, 2009

Dawk arrived back in Ponca City just before six in the evening. He'd stopped at several truck stops along the way and had picked up a new supply of Tracfones for the family back in Oklahoma. He rode through the front entrance of the gated neighborhood where Bay and Walee's condo lay and backed the Lincoln up into Walee's driveway when he saw that his brother's Dodge was not in the slot. He exited the car and let himself into Walee's condo with a spare key his brother had given him with the intentions of using the bathroom before he walked around the corner to Bay's apartment.

When Dawk entered the condo, he was immediately hit the aroma of marijuana and the sounds of Too Short's song *Freaky Tales*. The house was completely dark as music coming from the bedroom at the end of the hall to his right thumped throughout with a tinge of moaning mixed in. He pulled out his handgun, clicked on the kitchen counter light and walked down the hall in silence as the moaning sounds grew louder. When he reached the bedroom, he peeked inside and saw Jordan lying on her back atop the king-sized mattress with a black female draped over her body. The two were naked and locked into a sixty-nine with their faces planted in between one another's legs as *Freaky Tales* played on. "*...I said I don't pimp...or* *gigolo...I havin' so much money I don't need a hoe...you can break yourself...but you can't break me...you never met a player like short ba-bee..."*

Dawk tucked his gun inside his denim jeans and stood in the doorway eyeing his ex-lover getting down with another woman. A camera was set up on a tripod at the foot of the bed, and a lesbian porno flick was playing on the wall-mounted flat-screen TV. The two were sliding their pussies back and forth over one another faces. The brown-skinned female on top of Jordan's face couldn't be seen as her hair covered the entirety of her head. From the looks of things, the two were enjoying themselves.

Dawk tapped the wooden double door leading to the bedroom at that moment. The female atop Jordan looked up. She had a smile on her face and was licking her lips happily until she saw the stranger standing the threshold.

"Oh shit!" Anquette yelped as she jumped off Jordan and covered herself with the bed's silk sheet. "Jordan? What the fuck? Walee sent you, man? He didn't—he didn't say we had an appoint—"

"Chill the fuck out, Anquette!" Jordan laughed as she remained on the bed with her legs spread wide. "That's Walee brother, girl. What's up, Dawk?" she asked as she picked up a remote and paused the camera.

"Ain't nothin'," Dawk chuckled as his eyes scanned both females.

"You want some of this?" Jordan asked as she rubbed her slick pussy. "She'll do whatever I tell her to do," she added as she nodded over to Anquette.

Dawk looked over to Anquette, who was standing in obvious fright as she removed hair from her face while looking down at the floor in shame. *"Hood rat move right there,"* he smiled to his self. "You'll never click that camera on on me. Not that I would do it anyway," Dawk stated seriously as he walked away from the threshold. "I'm just here to take a whiz. Handle your biz with your fuck buddy."

"Let me hold that fat dick for ya', man!" Jordan blurted out through laughter as she watched Dawk's shadow disappear from sight while getting no response from her ex-lover.

After using the bathroom and washing his hands, Dawk opened his leather jacket, raised his pull over sweater and checked his bruise. The gun shot that'd crashed into his vest stung and left a purple and black mark, but he was able to deal with the pain without any medication. He straightened his clothes and walked into the kitchen to search the refrigerator for a cold beer. Walee had Heineken on deck so he grabbed one. He was popping the top when Jordan walked into the room butt naked. "You think real low of me now, huh?" she asked.

"You right where you wanna be, girl. I can't judge you, Jordan. That ain't me anyway. Tell me this, though—are you happy?"

"I am," Jordan confessed. "Look at my life, man!" she quipped as she spread her arms outwards.

"You got what you were seeking from the family then." Dawk said as he took a swig of his beer. "So long as you okay then we good. But we could never go back to what it was back in the day."

"I know," Jordan smiled as she touched Dawk's hand lightly. "But if ever? You know I'm game."

"I know," Dawk responded as he let out a low belch. "Where my brother?"

"He up in Stillwater with Spoonie and Tyke. Classes start tomorrow."

"I was hoping to catch him before I leave out." Dawk said as he moved for the door.

"Where you going?"

Dawk looked back at Jordan blankly before he walked off without answering her question. "My fault for dipping!" she snapped as she backed up a few paces with hands raised. "Tell Oneika I said hello."

"Gotcha," Dawk replied. "I'm gone."

Jordan followed Dawk to the door and closed and locked it behind him. Anquette emerged from the hall at that moment. "What was that all about?" she asked curiously.

"That was an old flame, girl. Nothing there 'cause he a faithful man."

"He fine, though," Anquette sassed.

"Aint he?" Jordan agreed happily as she walked back into the kitchen. "You hungry, girlfriend?" she asked Anquette.

"Hook something up, chick!"

The institution that Walee had forged between Anquette and Jordan on Christmas Eve had gotten off to a rocky start at its inception. Not even a month later, however, the two had become Walee's top recruiters and faithful allies. They'd bonded so quickly because of the tactics Walee had used on the both of them: time and freedom. It was understood that Anquette had to play her position, which was third behind Jordan Whispers. It was only an illusion, however; both females received the same treatment, albeit from different aspects.

Walee understood the fact that Jordan felt she should be the one to drive his Dodge at all times whenever she an Anquette had the car so he gave her that privilege. Anquette on the other hand, was given the privilege of accepting or rejecting females for the movies she and Jordan were recruiting.

Walee knew Anquette wanted a say-so in whatever decision Jordan made and he gave her that right. And truth be told, she knew more people in the OKC than Jordan, so she was allowed to make suggestions on where to go to recruit. She was right more times than not, and that held favor with Jordan. The more time they spent together, the two highly-sexual females began to enjoy what they were doing and eventually began messing around with one another inside the condo a couple of weeks back while lounging and getting high.

As of now, Jordan and Anquette were only recruiting women for lesbian porn because Walee wasn't ready to film his self just yet and take it public, but when he was ready, he was expecting his top women to have nothing but tens lined up and they were on the job something fierce.

Walee was also more than generous with the profits. DVDs went for ten dollars each, or three for twenty. A lot of hustlers in the sex game sold their movies for three dollars a pop, but they were using chicks that were busted up and trashy-looking.

Walee, however, had what was called the *What's Good in the Hood* series going. No models were used ever—just your everyday street dimes. For fifteen hundred dollars a shoot, any female willing to get down on camera was offered the opportunity, so long as they had the looks and a clean bill of health.

Jordan and Anquette had some of the most fun times of their young lives running game on females eighteen years of age and older who were looking to earn a quick payday via lesbian porn. They'd pulled in clothing sales clerks from several malls, gas station and grocery store cashiers and even daycare workers—innocent-looking females who did the raunchiest of things after consuming a couple of shots of liquor and a few tokes off a blunt. The Skirvin Hilton was where they filmed. The clients were taken to dinner first, and then out to a club where Jordan and Anquette comped them out in V.I.P. while explaining what was expected of them later on in the night.

Jordan and Anquette both loved clubbing, riding in fancy cars and sleeping inside a plush condo. To add to that, Walee was breaking them off proper through the sales they made. They each received fifteen percent of the $1500 dollars Walee put up for each client they recruited and two dollars off each ten dollar DVD sale.

The *What's Good in the Hood Series* was extraordinarily popular throughout Oklahoma as many watched to see if they recognized someone they knew on film. Needless to say, many faces were recognized, and for those who'd gone before the camera that were willing, they were able to make money on the side by getting paid for a one-on-one session with many a woman on the down low who sought discretion.

The *What's Good in the Hood* series DVDs were also sold in bulk to bootleggers from Texas and Kansas, who only served to hype up the series in those states. Walee, Jordan and Anquette were sitting on a budding gold mine in the Midwest, earning thousands of dollars a week, but with success comes jealousy. And sooner rather than later, Walee and company would eventually come to learn that the sex game was no different than the dope game.

****

As Jordan and Anquette set about preparing themselves dinner, Dawk, meanwhile, had rounded the corner and was walking up the sidewalk leading to Bay's condo. He'd grabbed two duffle bags full of Tracfones out of Bay's Lincoln and was thinking about his brother and youngest sisters as he neared the condo. He was a little upset he wasn't gone be on hand to wish Walee, Spoonie and Tyke well their first day of classes, but when he saw Spoonie and Tyke's Infinite out in front the home along with his mother's Phantom, his heart grew warm. He rang the doorbell, as he had no key to Bay's apartment, and Flacco opened the door a minute or so later.

"Senor Dawkins. I take your being here as confirmation that all went well in Saint Louis," Flacco smiled as he stepped aside and let Dawk in while giving the area a quick scan before locking the door.

Dawk stood in the foyer and nodded. "We straight over there. Got some new phones for everybody," he told Flacco as he handed him the two duffle bags.

"I'll put the list of numbers together, Senor." Flacco remarked as he led Dawk into the home.

Dawk walked into the sprawling 5,500 square foot single-story three bedroom condominium and was hit with and immediate sense of home. It was cold out, but inside Bay's condo, it was all hearth. His mother was in the kitchen tending to something sizzling in the grill. The aroma let him know it was blackened salmon and grilled shrimp. He walked into the kitchen and rinsed his hands in the sink.

Naomi had seen her son enter the area out the corner of her

eye. She flipped the four salmon fillets over in the skillet and wiped her hands as she turned to him. "Did we do right by Pepper?" she asked.

Dawk turned from the sink. "Took the whole click out," he let it be known. "Malik saying it might be more to it, but Loopy in a coma and can't fill us in. We took care of what we could."

"And Indianapolis?" Naomi asked casually as he grabbed a cutting block, a lemon and a knife.

"Bay and T-top on that job. While they doing that, I'm gone book a flight tonight to Las Vegas to talk to the Asians about speeding up the shipments." Dawk spoke lowly.

"Martha has everything set up with customs down in Laredo so it's definitely a go on this end."

"Me and Ben gone work it, momma," Dawk remarked. "You need help with dinner?"

"No," Naomi smiled as she began slicing the lemon. "This is my domain, son," she ended as she leaned over and kissed his cheek.

Dawk touched his mother's face with the back of his hand before walking out into the open area of the condo. There was more than enough room for the family to hold their own private spot, but on days like this, when it was cold out and their mother was around, Naomi's children loved being not only her presence, but within eyesight of her.

"We heard you come in and it took you like five minutes before you even made your way over here to see us while we packing the last of our stuff to drive to Stillwater, Dawk, you gone be up there for our first day of classes tomorrow with Walee?" Spoonie asked in one breath as she sat on the carpeted floor of the living room pulling plastic off her textbooks.

"He gone say no, watch!" Tyke chided as she sat beside her sister pulling tags off brand new sweatshirts.

Dawk eyed his youngest sisters with appreciation as they rose from the floor and ran over and hugged him. "Where Bay and T-top?" Spoonie asked.

"They be back in a few days. I stopped around the corner. Jordan said y'all was up in Stillwater."

"We been supposed to left with Walee and Kahlil," Spoonie confirmed. "But momma say she and Flacco gone follow us in the morning. We leaving early like around six."

"I'm gone miss that, but we on for dinner. How that sound?" Dawk asked he hugged his sisters and kissed them each on the forehead.

"I guess," Spoonie sassed as she and Tyke returned to their duties of preparing for their first day of class.

Being close to Spoonie and Tyke on this day meant more than ever to Dawk on this particular night. The night before, he and his sisters along, with the Cottonwood family, had put in major work on the streets of Saint Louis; but the bigger picture, the one that stuck with him the most was the sight of seventeen year-old Peppi Vargas lying inside that coffin inside Saint Cecilia Church. The way Ya Murder had clowned during the funeral coupled with the manner in which T-top had cut her down in the middle of the street was something he could never imagine having happen to Spoonie and Tyke. He was glad his youngest sisters were being placed on a path far different than the life Pepper had lived.

Dawk then turned his attention to Kimi. She was on the oversized plush leather couch nuzzled up with Udelle. If there ever was a couple in love, these two were the epitome of such an emotion. Kimi lay up against Udelle's right side with a wool blanket covering her legs, the two of them watching the weather report on the six 'o' clock news. He couldn't help but to eavesdrop in on their conversation as he neared the two.

"It's a high pressure system over the Midwest, baby," Udelle told Kimi as he sat smiling, imitating the meteorologists' movements as he held onto a toy clicker while staring at the screen in amazement over the weather patterns.

"Okay. That mean clear skies and cold temperature," Kimi spoke through closed eyes while nuzzled up against her true love. "Hey, Dawk," she added softly as she yawned and stretched out her left hand in order to flash the diamond engagement ring she sported. "You like it?"

"Y'all getting married," Dawk stated as he smiled down upon his sister and her fiancé.

"In October of this year," Kimi responded matter-of-factly. "So you have to find us an island in the Pacific because I want you to give me away."

"And Walee gone the best man, homie! But he don't know it yet!" Udelle laughed as Dawk walked over and shook his hand.

"Wow," Dawk remarked through a smile as he rubbed his chin. "Congratulations, y'all. But this comes as no surprise to the family."

"We told her grandpa gone be upset he not walking her down the aisle and she should let him be the one but she ain't listening to me and Tyke!" Spoonie chimed in.

"Just because grandpa the oldest in the family don't mean he have to be the one do it, Shima!" Kimi sassed. "This my wedding and I wants what I want! So there!" she added as she rolled her neck and stuck out her tongue at her baby sister.

"Doss the third can be the ring bear—who ready for grilled fish?" Naomi asked, having realized she'd mentioned the name of DeeDee's second son aloud. *"Don't ask me. Don't ask me. Please, don't ask me about it,"* she repeatedly said to herself.

"Who is Doss the third, momma?" Tyke asked as she stood up from the floor and stretched.

"What?" Naomi asked through light laughter. "I meant to say Tacoma. Tacoma for the ring bearer."

Spoonie stood up beside Tyke and both twins smiled at their mother while shaking their heads in disapproval as they grabbed their jump ropes.

"You said Doss the third, momma!" Tyke corrected as she let her jump rope fall at her feet. "So, if daddy was a junior," she continued as she began jumping rope in place, "for a Doss the third to be here, that means—"

"Lord, that old man got another child walking around out there!" Kimi snapped as she stood up from the couch and raised her hands to the ceiling with her head bowed. "Seventy-five! He seventy-five, momma!" she huffed as she shook her head in mocked disbelief. "Who grandpa got pregnant, man?"

"And how old is our uncle?" Tyke asked aloud through laughter as she joined Spoonie, the two of them now jumping rope side by side.

"He better be older than everybody in here outside of momma and Flacco," Dawk let it be known. "Last thing we need is a young buck running around Ponderosa tryna flex 'cause of his title."

"I bet he's a young boy." Kimi surmised. "I'm tryna think." She went further in her thoughts as she looked up to the ceiling and contemplated. Unable to decipher the scenario, she let loose with, "But, damn, granddad been live since like the sixties. This Doss the third fella could be in his forties, or close to it. Ugh!"

"See, that ain't gone work, momma." Tyke chimed in as she and Spoonie jumped rope in unison. "Ain't no way a forty year-old man can be a ring bearer in a wedding. Can somebody be that old and be a ring bearer?"

"Ring bearer?" Dawk spoke calmly as he eyed Tyke. "If he that high in age we have bigger problems. Grandpa better not bring no old dude 'round this camp talkin' 'bout he family."

"Dawk?" Naomi said as she eyed her son with a smirk. Naomi knew exactly what her oldest son was getting at. DeeDee's son, if he were an adult, would enter into a world of wealth, but his ties would lay with DeeDee and DeeDee only, which was different from Ben's circumstances and past history.

Given what all the family was involved in, this person, DeeDee's second son, who'd been on the outside for so long, would have to undergo unprecedented surveillance just to be able to have a meeting with the family in Chicago, let alone set foot on Ponderosa. It was bad enough Mary had Reynard milling about, even though he was out-of-the-loop when it came to the family business. The bottom line was the fact that another straggler would not be accepted by the family in the same manner in which Reynard had been, not accepted, but merely tolerated. Reynard held no favor with the family whatsoever as everyone outside of Mary and Dimples disliked the guy given his shady disposition.

"Okay," Naomi said, breaking up the discussion of protests being held amongst Dawk, Kimi, Spoonie and Tyke as she emerged from the kitchen. "Here's the deal—but not a word to your grandfather or anyone else in the family," she admonished. "DeeDee wants the arrival of his seven year-old son to be a welcomed surprise for the family. As of now? Everyone here, and Francine, are the only ones who knows of this. Let's keep this to ourselves and let things unfold naturally when the time arises."

Kimi and Dawk fanned their mother off at that moment as they walked away. "Seven? This gone be Walee young self all over again," Kimi mumbled as she walked over to the couch and plopped down beside Udelle. "I want Tacoma to be my ring bearer!" she declared aloud.

"Where Koko at?" Dawk asked he entered the hallway leading to the rest of the condo. After giving the matter further thought, however, he walked back into the living room and said to his mother with a smirk on his face, "I ain't—this here? I so hope I'm still able to pop out some critters in my sixties like grandpa. Dude a Mack in his old age."

"Not a word to no one!" Naomi reiterated as she walked back into the kitchen where she removed the first batch of salmon fillets just before they began to scorch.

****

"*...everybody have fun tonight...everybody Wang Chung tonight...everybody have fun tonight...everybody Wang Chung tonight...everybody have fun...*"

Koko was lying across a king-sized bed in one of the condo's suites as her cell phone screen lit up. Wang Chung's song *Everybody Have Fun Tonight* played as glimpses of the text she'd just received flashed over the top of her phone. *You ready for classes tomorrow?*

Yes. Woulda been better if you were here.

Wang Chung played again and Koko couldn't help but to giggle like a middle school preteen talking to her first boy ever as she read the text...*Woulda loved to do that. Too early for us. IMO*

I know. I have something I want to show you later. A way of welcoming you into the family.

What's that?

Wang Chung started to play again, but Koko cut it short. Her body temperature rose as she was about to take a gamble on love for the second time in her life. *A special place far way. I'll put it together just give me a few months.*

I don't have a passport.

Koko laughed and texted back...*You don't always need a passport to get to paradise.*

Gotcha, Paradise.

A perceptive man. More points for you. Gotta go for now. It was good talking to you, Lee. K.I.T. Later, babe.

As one we be

Koko sat her phone down beside her and picked up the remote control and scrolled the cable guide until she came across an old episode of *The Fresh Prince of Bel Aire*. She rested her head inside her hand as she let out a deep sigh, wondering what it was she was doing exactly. Men—they were a complication for Koko at this stage of her life. On one end, she had a man who'd wronged her in Chablis, but found herself still in love with. One the other end, there was Lee Sato, a man who'd moved her briefly, yet left her with a feeling of uncertainty given the distance between the two cities in which they resided.

Koko felt as if she had no one to talk to concerning her heart's matter. And even if she did feel differently, she felt that whatever decision she made concerning her and the two men she was contemplating should be her decision and her decision alone. She'd just grown comfortable and was weighing her options when a soft tap came across the door. "It's open!" she called out.

Dawk eased the door and poked his head inside. "What's happening, sis?" he smiled.

"Hey, man. Bay and Tiva out there?"

"Nah, they out right now. How you?" Dawk asked as he walked into the room.

"I'm good," Koko smiled pretentiously, steadily thinking about Chablis and Lee and the ultimate decision that lay ahead the next morning. "What's up?"

"Chillin'," Dawk remarked as he sat down in a chair before a desk situated beside the bed and powered up Koko's lap top. "You ready for class tomorrow?" he asked as he logged onto Hotwire.com.

"As ready as I'll ever be," Koko smiled.

"That's what's up," Dawk said as he eyed the computer screen and checked for flights headed to Vegas. "Eight hundred dollars," he said lowly after the prices came up on the screen.

"Eight hundred for what?"

"Gotta meet up with Ben tomorrow."

Koko smiled to herself as thoughts of Lee Sato crept into her mind.

"What's funny?" Dawk asked as he went into his back pocket and pulled out his wallet.

"Nothing," Koko said as she smirked, replaying the time she'd spent with Lee over and over again in her head. "Tell Ben I said hello."

Dawk eyed Koko with a look of apprehension. "What happened out there when you and Kimi went to Phoenix?" he asked as he slid a credit card from his billfold.

"Why you ask that?" Koko chuckled as she licked her lips.

"Nah, you all giddy and carrying on." Dawk said as he eyed the numbers on the credit card.

"Because I said tell Ben hello?" Koko laughed. "We just went shopping and stuff with Samantha that's all."

"Yeah? You shoulda found yourself a new boyfriend while you was out there instead that chump Chablis. Ole fake ass tough guy," Dawk remarked, his words wiping the smile off Koko's face.

"What you think about Lee, Dawk?"

Dawk looked over to Koko in wonderment. "You fucking with Lee?" he asked.

"I just asked what you thought about the dude. We went to lunch and hung out at a club," Koko replied, making sure to leave out the fact that she and Lee had hooked up.

"Yeah? I think he have a thing for Tiva, though," Dawk remarked, totally unaware that Koko had hooked up with Lee down in Phoenix.

Koko's heart dropped to the pit of her stomach after hearing her brother speak. She picked up her phone and texted Tiva. After the text went through, she climbed out of the bed and clicked on several lights and began grabbing clothes that were scattered about the room in order to hang them up.

"Didn't wanna hear that," Dawk spoke through low laughter as he typed in his credit card number in order to book a flight to Vegas.

"You don't even know what you talkin' about," Koko sassed as she placed her fur coat onto a hangar and pulled the doors open on the walk-in closet. "I just asked what you thought about Lee because I thought he was cute."

"You fucked him, though?" Dawk asked as he looked over his shoulder. "You better find out where Tiva stand with that dude. But on the real? I don't think Lee play no games like that. What y'all do down there exactly?"

Koko emerged from the large closet and said, "Trust me, Dawk. You don't wanna know," as she looked over to her brother with her lips curled.

"Yea, you right about that," Dawk stated seriously as he turned around in the chair and faced Koko. "I never asked Tiva if they hooked up or not, but it's something that need to be made clear before—"

"We end up sleeping with the same man," Koko cut in as she picked up her knee-length leather boots and placed them on a low-lying shelf inside the closet.

"You fucked 'em," Dawk said matter-of-factly as he threw his hands up and shook his head from side to side.

"I didn't say that, Dawk!" Koko scowled as she reappeared. "I just asked what you thought of him, man!"

"Lee real," Dawk admitted as he turned and faced the lap top one more and printed out a flight ticket. "But I can only speak on the street level. How he do with his women I don't know."

"You think he do something like what Junior did?" Koko asked as she walked over and sat beside her brother.

"I don't sense that from dude," Dawk admitted as he stared Koko in the eyes. "But nobody saw what Junior did coming either."

"What you think I should do?"

"You talked to Ben?"

"Yeah. Ben was the one that said it was all right. I spent four days with Lee, Dawk," Koko confessed as she reached out and touched her brother's arm. "Never once was I afraid with him. The only thing I'm worried about, well, now that this thing with Tiva is known, besides that? I just wonder if he a player or not."

"You really like this dude, huh?" Dawk remarked seriously.

"I do," Koko responded warmly. In spite of the happy feelings, she also wanted to add the fact that she wasn't sure if she was going to give Chablis another chance.

Neither Dawk, nor Bay and T-top knew what had gone down with Chablis and Koko as they were out of town killing Q-Man's brother, Daneel LuQman, when Chablis had assaulted Koko. Koko, in turn, had never revealed the fact that Chablis had taken her against her will to no one in the family. She herself, while being as open as she could with her brother, was still harboring a secret: the fact that she still loved Chablis.

As far as the family was concerned, Naomi included, Koko

413

had gotten over Chablis. He hadn't been heard from since he'd been knocked out of the football game back in November and Koko had the ones who were holding what had gone down secret from the big three under the impression that she was done dealing with the guy.

"Better check with Tiva," Dawk let it be known, shaking Koko from her thoughts. "As far as I know? Lee and T-top ain't never got down, but he went at her first and if she feelin' him? We got a problem with Lee."

"If that's what it is, then I'll let it rest," Koko told Dawk. "But say nothing about it, man. Whatever happen? I'll be sure to let you know," she added as she went and checked her phone to see if Tiva had texted her back. "Where T-top and Bay?" she asked.

"They going to a ball game out of state," Dawk said as he powered down the lap top. "Before you do anything, Koko? You need talk to Tiva. We don't sleep with each other men and women in this family. That's that bullshit," Dawk admonished as he left the room.

"Why Walee sleeping with Jordan then?" Koko chuckled.

"That hood rat?" Dawk scoffed as he pulled the door open while shaking his head. "Come and have dinner, girl."

"I be out in a minute," Koko said as she ran up and hugged her brother and kissed his cheek. She wiped gloss from his face before walking off and headed for her cell phone. Still no message. "Come on, Tiva. Where you at on this, sister," she said to herself as she began to hang up her remaining clothes.

CHAPTER THIRTY-THREE

KOKO'S DECISION

January 15, 2009

It was the following morning after Dawk and Koko's talk. The family had sat at the dining room the night before and enjoyed a hearty seafood dinner. Conversation was upbeat, and laughter abounded. Many a family night in Ponca City had been replicated by some of the family down in Oklahoma City inside of Bay's condo, a city and place where some in the family, namely Kimi and Koko, were beginning to spend more and more time ever since Naomi had opened the doors on Holland-Dawkins Enterprises inside the Kerr-McGhee building in downtown Oklahoma City.

Dawk had been dropped off at Will Rogers International Airport by Udelle around four that morning and was on a flight headed to Vegas in order to meet up with Phillip Tran and Grover Kobayashi where discussions would be held on the expediting of cocaine being shipped in by Rafael Gacha.

Naomi, Flacco, Spoonie and Tyke had left the home around six in the morning. The four of them were headed up to Stillwater in order to have breakfast with Walee and Kahlil before their classes started up for the day. From there, Naomi and Flacco would travel back to Oklahoma City to begin day's business over to HDE.

Kimi, Koko and Udelle, meanwhile, had left Bay's condo and drove south on I-35 in the twins' Maserati. They'd just landed on the Sooner Campus in Norman around 8:45 A.M.

"Koko," Kimi spoke as Udelle backed the candy apple red, four door red Maserati into a parking spot near the college's Accounting building, "I think I forgot my Accounting text book, girl," she said as she rummaged through her Australian handcrafted white ostrich skin handbag.

Koko eyed her twin searching the $3,000 dollar leather bag. She reached down into her identical bag and pulled her text book. "Here," she remarked as she handed Kimi her own textbook. "Save me a seat in the lecture hall. I'm going get breakfast. You want something?"

"Kimi ain't the only one here, no?" Udelle chimed in as he peeled a banana.

"Chiquita got you," Koko chuckled as she climbed from the backseat. "You want something, Kimi?"

"A bacon cheese sandwich and cheese-smothered hash browns with a milk to feed my baby," Kimi snickered as she eyed Udelle.

Udelle eyed Kimi with wide eyes. "For real?" he asked happily.

"No, boy," Kimi remarked as she snorted. "Oh no!" she exclaimed as she covered her nose. "I sound like—"

"Get down Moses...part another sea..." Koko sang as she backed away from the Maserati and pulled down on the grey fur hat she was sporting.

Kimi sulked as she climbed from the passenger seat of the Maserati. She poked her tongue at her sister as snowflakes landed on her lips. "Umm, remind me of you, baby," she said as she closed the door and eyed Udelle.

"You tasted his babies?" Koko remarked in bewilderment as she stepped back and raised her hands even with her shoulders while looking up at the grey clouds.

"Hey, that ain't right!" "The hell you mean!" What's wrong with your fam, Kimi?" "Koko, you ain't even have to take it there!" Udelle and Kimi blurted out at random.

"Don't worry about her, Udelle," Kimi finally sassed. "She done pissed out Lee babies days back!" she clapped back as she eyed her twin with a slick smirk.

"Who Lee, Koko?" Udelle asked with a smirk. "Never mind. You ain't gotta answer that. I'm glad you through with that fuck boy Chablis—even if you is swallowing babies!" he mocked.

"Bacon cheese, hash browns and milk—got it." Koko replied, refusing to engage her twin and Udelle in further sexually explicit talk. "Just to let you know, Kimi, I didn't swallow. Didn't even taste it."

"Not yet!" Kimi laughed as she, Udelle and Koko separated, Udelle headed to his Geography class while Kimi headed to the Accounting hall to reserve seat for her and Koko.

Koko snapped her fingers at her twin. "Whatever, cow!" she snapped as she began walking across Oklahoma University's campus headed towards the Couch Restaurants, which was the college's large cafeteria area, and the place where she was scheduled to meet up with Chablis on this day.

****

Meanwhile, out in front of the cafeteria area, Chablis stood bundled up in a hooded leather jacket. The bitter cold weather had his neck aching something fierce, but he was bearing the pain if only to see the woman he love approach the building. He looked around, getting excited every now and then whenever a woman resembling Koko by figure approached, only to grow sad once he realized his eyes were fooling him. *"Where you at, baby?"* he said to himself as he waited patiently.

Koko, meanwhile, had neared the Couch Restaurants. She knew her man right away the time she'd eyed his tall, muscular frame off in the distance as she stood behind a large statue that hid her from sight. Chablis had a look of want on his face to Koko, coupled with a look of hope and sincerity in his eyes. What to do now was the question she asked herself as she eyed Chablis. She loved the guy no doubt, but she was more afraid of him given all he'd done in the past.

Confused, Koko turned around, leaned up against the statue and sighed as she peeked around the figurine, contemplating on whether she should give Chablis another chance, or just walk away. She stared at him unnoticed for nearly a minute as the day he'd manhandled her ran through her mind. If she went back to Chablis, she knew she would have to keep everything under wraps as Kimi and Walee would no doubt come down on her for making such a stupid decision.

Stupid. Decision. Those two words shot through Koko's mind as she rested against the statue underneath the falling snow. Thoughts of Lee Sato soon crept into her mind. In the beginning, the Asian had been nothing more than some rebound dick for her, but she couldn't deny she had developed feelings for the guy during the time they'd spent together. They'd had a good time, and had even discussed having a relationship.

Potential lay with Lee for Koko. And the more she thought about it, it would've been a step back to get involved with Chablis once more. Should he ever so much as raise his voice at her once again, all the fear she carried towards him would resurface. She didn't want to have to go through life being a man's appeaser and having to suppress her own thoughts for fear of him shouting her down for just being herself.

A relationship would have disagreements Koko knew; but she was no longer trusting in Chablis' ability to handle adversity should it arise as his relationship resume` had now been tainted. He'd taken advantage of her after she'd uttered the word 'no' and had acted as if her body was his to do as he pleased. The possibility of having to go through a battle for her own dignity and the right to do as she pleased was the very thing that had forced Koko Dawkins to walk away on this day. She gave one last look back at Chablis before she walked off in silence as the snow began to fall a little harder, never bothering to say goodbye as she headed towards her Accounting class.

Just mere seconds after Koko had walked away from Chablis, her cell phone began to chime. She pulled her phone from her coat and read the text. *Lee? Girl, please I ain't gone get with that dude. Go for it! He cool, sis!*

Koko let loose with a sigh and an involuntary pump of her fist as she walked under the falling snow while repeatedly reading the text Tiva had sent her. *I am. Thank you Tiva. Love you.*

Love you back.

Koko joined Kimi in the lecture hall, telling her that the lines in the Couch Restaurants were too long to wait in. She sat down with her head in the clouds and her heart fluttering with joy, knowing she'd made the right decision concerning Chablis and Lee.

****

Chablis, meanwhile, had remained out in the cold for over an hour. When he realized Koko had stood him up, he walked back to the parking lot in a downtrodden manner and climbed into the backseat of Tonto Jamison's alabaster white, four door S-class Mercedes.

"So what happened out there?" Tonto asked as he chomped down a double cheeseburger.

"What it look like? She ain't show," Chablis spoke lowly.

"So that mean we get to do what we shoulda been doing from jump," Tonto said as he removed foil from his half-eaten burger.

"I guess, man. But I ain't really feeling this here, Tonto. I should call Koko. Maybe she got sick or something and couldn't make it."

Tonto was about to bite into his hamburger one more time until he heard Chablis speak pathetically. "You sounding like a bitch right now!" he scoffed as he looked over into the backseat. "What the fuck you gone do is get us in inside that house so we can get paid!"

Chablis leaned back in the seat meekly. "I'm just sayin', man. Something coulda happened to her. At least let me call and check on her."

"You don't need to call her," Tonto's accomplice retorted from the front passenger seat. "We gone find out who in that house where she at. When it's clear? We gone run in there, snatch her up and take her somewhere and hold her for ransom until we get paid."

"Y'all niggas wild," Chablis laughed nervously, trying to keep his composure.

Tonto calmly set his burger on the car's dash and casually pulled out a .9mm. "You think this a game, boy!" he asked matter-of-factly as he leaned over the backseat and placed the barrel of his gun to Chablis' forehead. "You in way deep now, son, and you can't *even* back out!"

"You said we was gone after Walee!" Chablis retorted in fright. "What about Walee?"

"That boy ready, already. The way in is with Koko," Tonto hissed. "It's easier because she ain't 'bout that gunplay."

"This shit ain't right, man," Chablis whined as tears filled his eyes.

"Wasn't meant to be right, son." Tonto spoke lowly as he pressed the barrel deeper into Chablis' head, the front of the gun now pressing into his skin to the near point of drawing blood. "Now say you ain't gone do it. Say it!"

Chablis was now in fear for his life as he knew Tonto wasn't bullshitting. Dead was not where he wanted to be. "I'll do it," he stated in compliance. "Just, just don't kill her, man. Let's get paid and, and let her go on her way."

Tonto eased the .9mm back from Chablis' forehead and sat back down in the driver's seat. "These lames be falling for some hoes quick-like, yeh?" he complained as he eyed his right hand man, who was sitting beside him in the front seat.

Tonto's goon, a Caucasian male named Chauncey Gainey, laughed lowly as he rubbed his pointed chin beard while toking on a blunt. "Guess we gone have ta' take the show on the road," he said just before he coughed and passed the blunt to Tonto. "His ole lady said fuck him and he don't even see that shit!" he laughed through harsh coughs of the potent marijuana.

Chauncey Gainey was a twenty-seven year-old lifelong

resident of Oklahoma City. The pale-skinned tatted-up 6' rebel-of-sorts was a notorious kidnapper that wreaked havoc in Oklahoma, namely the city of Tulsa. Chauncey could best be described as a modern day hippy. He always wore baggy cargo jeans, toboggan hats and canvas sneakers. He idolized serial killers Charles Manson and Ted Bundy. He was a heavy metal enthusiast. Bands like Kiss, and musicians like Marilyn Manson and Ozzy Osbourne were gods to him.

Chauncey had served four years in state prison for armed robbery. He'd been back on the streets for the past two years and had only gotten worse. His saying, 'Take the show on the road', meant he was prepared to snatch up another victim for rape, ransom and murder.

Having given up robbing what he deemed as being that of civilians, Chauncey now made his living by kidnapping major players' innocent family members and holding them for ransom. In his mind, snatching up those who had no criminal ties to the streets, but were kin to a family known to get their hands dirty was an easy way to get paid, as crime families tended to pay high dollar for their innocent ones without notifying the law.

Kidnappings didn't always go right for Chauncey during an abduction, however; and for that given fact, a few of those that the stringy black-haired outlaw with the long, black beard had kidnapped and didn't receive ransom, had to be disposed of in order to keep his identity hidden.

As of date, Chauncey Gainey had wasted three innocent lives—a twelve year-old boy belonging to a meth dealer down in Ardmore, Oklahoma who hadn't the ransom money, the nineteen year-old sister of a night club owner in Kansas City who'd called his bluff, and the last was just a month earlier over in Tulsa. The father of a young player, who Chauncey had actually let go on a preliminary deal that the guy's son would pay a $100,000 dollar ransom a week later, had to be taken out when the guy was arrested in a sting with several of his women.

The guy had called Chauncey from jail and told him of the delay, but Chauncey felt the guy was going to speak on the kidnapping in order to get his time cut. Not willing to take the risk, Chauncey went back and killed the guy's father while the guy was still locked up, never giving him the chance to make good on the ransom. To put it plain and simple, Chauncey Gainey was a cold-hearted, senseless killer. And now that Koko had shunned Chablis, the door was now open for him and Tonto to go after one of the princesses in the Holland family in order to earn a large payday.

"We gone lay low for a minute and map things out," Tonto told Chablis as he placed his Mercedes in drive.

"I need to call my momma, man." Chablis spoke humbly.

"You call your momma when I say you can call," Tonto retorted. "You got business to take care of first," he ended as he made his way of out of the campus' parking lot.

CHAPTER THIRTY-FOUR

SILOAM'S MANIPULATION

It was now mid-afternoon, a few hours after Chablis' encounter with Tonto down in Oklahoma. Thirty-four year-old Siloam Bovina was inside her studio apartment on the south side of Ponca City that she shared with Jane Dow. Jane was over to The Holland Family's multi-plex preparing for a performance inside the bowling alley later on in the night so Siloam was home alone.

Siloam was standing in the center of the unfurnished living room, which had been converted into a home studio, strumming her guitar and going over a song she and Jane were planning on singing for the club's opening night come March, when loud, repeated taps on the door caught her ear. She leaned her guitar up against Jane's brand new replaced $5,000 dollar drum set, wiped her forehead with a clean white towel and laid it over Jane's sneer drum. She walked over to the door while going over the song's lyrics in her head. When she pulled it open, she eyed Reynard standing in the threshold.

"Can I help you?" Siloam asked dryly while sliding into the routine she knew to be appreciated by the man.

"I know I'm out of line here, Siloam. But I really need to discuss a matter with you." Reynard smiled.

"Concerning?"

"It's concerning my daughter," Reynard spoke in mocked sincerity. "She has a problem and I was wondering if you could help me out?"

Siloam pulled the door open and let Reynard into her apartment. She offered him a drink, but he'd declined. "What is it that you want to discuss?" she asked as she poured herself a shot of tequila to soothe her nerves for what she knew was to come.

"What are you willing to do in order for me to keep quiet on the affair you had with Takoda?" Reynard asked bluntly.

Siloam played things off by laughing. "What, what are you talkin' about, Reynard?" she asked as she pulled brown hair from her face and backed away from the kitchen counter.

"Don't play games with me, Siloam. You and I both know what went down the day Takoda had that small fire inside his kitchen. Now, I don't know how a fire can lead to extra-marital sex, but I know what I stumbled upon."

"You know nothing," Siloam retorted lowly as she folded her arms in a coy, playful manner.

"That's where you're wrong. I know everything. We can go back and forth, but I'd rather get straight to the point of my being here."

"Speak your peace."

Reynard subtly licked his lips as he eyed Siloam. He tucked his hands into his trousers, his dick hardening as he stepped closer to the full-bloodied Cherokee. "Do I have to spell it out for you? I think you know what is that I want from you, little Indian girl."

"Mister Jacobs, I have no idea what it is you're referring to." Siloam chuckled playfully.

Reynard remained serious as he stepped closer to Siloam and ripped the front of her dress open, sending the buttons flying every which-a-way. "You role play very well, young lady. Very well," he smiled. "Plan's going smoothly. Are you still with me?" he added as he leaned down and kissed Siloam's lips.

"I'm with you, Mister Jacobs. I've been nothing more than a helper to this family my whole time being here. They live in that big home and look what I have," Siloam complained as she stretched her arms forth. "No one even cared to ask how me and Jane were and are doing. They know what I want to do with my music, but do they ask or offer? No?"

"Well, all that will be behind us in the near future," Reynard remarked as he walked into the kitchen and grabbed a beer from the refrigerator.

"I agree." Siloam confessed. "If they won't give what I need, I'll take what I want and so much more."

"This scheme is turning you on, huh, girl?" Reynard asked through a sly, appreciative smile. "Get over there!" he suddenly commanded as he pushed Siloam into the living room and unzipped his pants while taking several deep gulps of his can of beer.

Siloam panted like a pathetic whore as she pretended to let Reynard's momentum push her into Jane's drum set. She placed her hands onto the instruments and leaned forward and readied herself. "It is turning me on. Mary knows the combination to the safe," Siloam panted as she raised her all-in-one skirt above her waist.

Reynard let his silk trousers fall to floor when he walked up behind Siloam. He ripped off her panties and turned her around and the two kissed passionately as Siloam guided him behind the drum set, ripping his silk shirt open in the process in order to rub his broad, masculine, chest.

Jane had a leather-back swivel seat to accommodate her movements when playing, and it was there that Siloam had planted herself. She swung the chair around and placed her feet on the window sill behind the instruments and spread her legs. "She knows the combination," Siloam reiterated. "When are you going to do it?"

"In time. In time," Reynard stated seriously. "Can you get a hold of a gun?"

"Yeah," Siloam moaned as she began stroking herself. "Eat me. Come and eat me, Reynard," she pleaded through lustful eyes.

Reynard stared at Siloam, his eyes glazed over with desire unmeasurable. Her fat, bald-shaven vagina with its thin, tan outer lips made his mouth water. He'd been making love to her since September of 2008 and it had become the best sex ever. Hers was tight, a hot pussy. He'd been lusting after Mary, but when Siloam came along, not only his focus, but his plans had been shifted.

Siloam Bovina had unleashed the malice that had been seething within Reynard's heart shortly after he'd extorted her out of sex. Together, they began to conspire against the family by plotting against Mary in order to cash in their tickets. Theirs had become a world filled with malevolent sex, uncontrollable greed and an unexpected betrayal that would have deadly consequences.

Reynard undressed and wasted no time. He dropped to his knees and dove head first into Siloam's pussy. The way he sucked and licked was a severe turn on for the woman; and when she raised her legs higher and exposed her anus, Reynard didn't hesitate. He flicked his tongue over her exposed anus before assaulting her clitoris once more while sliding a condom over his hardened member. "I'm coming!" Siloam groaned several minutes later as she tilted her head back and shuddered in the seat.

Reynard stood just as Siloam leaned forward and give him a few quick sucks of his rod to keep him hard. She stood and turned around, exposing herself for penetration. "Fuck me," she panted.

Reynard smacked Siloam's wide ass several times before gripping her hips and easing into her opening. Both moaned over the sensation, Siloam letting her head drop into her arms, and Reynard tilting his head back as he slid into a fast-paced pounding. The two rocked together, moaning aloud in their own worlds of lust until Reynard filled Siloam to hilt and erupted inside the condom.

"Oh dear God," Reynard panted as he slid from behind Siloam and flopped down into the leather-back chair. "No amount of money could offset the jewel you possess," he told Siloam as he reached out and stroked her back tenderly.

"And you're special to me as well," Siloam remarked casually as she walked from behind the drum set and picked up her torn dress and panties. She also grabbed Reynard's slacks and threw them to the man. She laughed to herself as the pants landed in his face.

When Reynard removed the clothing from his head, Siloam was standing before him with her hands behind her back staring down at him coldly as she rocked back and forth on her heels. "How was it?" Siloam asked as she came from behind her back with the clean white towel she'd placed on the drum set before she'd went and opened the door.

A chill shot through Reynard's body and he froze up in the chair momentarily. He'd actually thought Siloam was going to shoot him for a few seconds. "It's the best I ever had," he professed as he reached out and grabbed ahold of the voluptuous naked woman's hand. "Come here, girl," he said as he pulled her close.

Siloam went willingly, falling over into Reynard's lap. "We are so bad," she said seductively as her fleshy breasts pressed into Reynard's face.

"But we're damn good together," Reynard responded as he flicked his tongue over Siloam's erect nipples.

"How far are you willing to go with me?" Siloam asked as she stroked Reynard's beard gently.

"I think the real question is, how far are you willing to go to with me and how much would you risk?" Reynard countered.

"I've agreed to keep quiet on us," Siloam replied as she smiled down at Reynard and planted a kiss on his bald head. "Isn't that enough loyalty?"

"It is. It is. And there's much to be gained by it, baby."

"And they'll never see it coming," Siloam responded as she leaned down and kissed Reynard's lips. "How will you handle things with Mary?" Siloam asked as she wrapped her arms around Reynard's waist and held him close.

"You just let me take care of that thing with Mary," Reynard stated. "Just be ready when I call and give you my return flight's arrival time."

Siloam said nothing as she backed away from Reynard and headed towards the half-bath inside the two bedroom studio apartment. "There's a bath inside the master bedroom down the hall. You know where it's at," she stated while disappearing from sight. "I have to do a number so I'll use this one."

When she was certain Reynard was off in the shower, Siloam opened the bathroom door and tip-toed into the living room, grabbed his phone from his trousers and scanned the numbers he'd called. She was able to send his most recent numbers incoming and outgoing calls to her own cell phone via text. She then deleted the texts she'd sent to herself and placed Reynard's phone back into his pants, making sure to leave them disheveled as she scurried back off to the second bathroom.

Siloam was wiping down the drum set and straightening the instruments when Reynard returned to the living room after his shower. She handed him his trousers and his torn shirt while kissing his chest gently.

"Guess I'll have to stop and grab another shirt before heading back to Ponderosa," Reynard chuckled as he began to redress himself.

"I was headed there myself. It may look suspicious if we were to arrive at the same time. You should go first," Siloam remarked.

Reynard walked over and grabbed a hold of Siloam. "You're magical," he said. "I never expected to develop feelings for no one here. I only wanted to be a part of my daughter's life. And then you came along with your scheme."

"Seems as if it was to meant to be," Siloam said seriously as she stared up into Reynard's eyes.

"I wouldn't change a thing about you, baby. See you back over to ranch, Siloam." Reynard spoke tenderly as he kissed her lips tenderly.

"This thing with Mary? Where will you do it? Over to Regina's house?"

"That won't work," Reynard responded as he rubbed his chin. "Mary is the one we're after. We'll have to make it look like a robbery. I'm thinking the barn where we take her?"

"I was hoping you would say that," Siloam smiled. "I'll be waiting for your call," she ended as she escorted Reynard to the front door.

CHAPTER THIRTY-FIVE

PUSHER MEN

Dawk had called me yesterday from Saint Louis and told me he was on his way up to Vegas to meet up with Grover Kobayashi and Philip Tran. He wanted me to pick him up from the airport and had requested that I sit in on the meeting this morning. I knew from what had gone down with Pepper that something serious had jumped off in Saint Louis. I was expecting the family to retaliate, but damn, they'd worked this li'l chick Ya Murder and her crew over something crucial the same night of the funeral. I was clued in on all the details after picking Dawk up from the airport as we made our way over to the town of Paradise where Grover and Phil's mansion lay.

"Where Bay and T-top?" I asked Dawk as we rode down I-15 in a brand new black and black 2009 S-Class Mercedes my wife had given me for Christmas.

"They over in Naptown taking care of some business," Dawk said as he leaned the seat back

"They on to that dude RJ you was telling me about?" I asked as I drove.

"Yeah, they gone handle that. I'm gone fall back on Kansas City right now, though."

"Why?"

"I'm not saying we giving it up. I'm just gone give that job to Natalia the third next month," Dawk responded casually as he sat upright in the seat.

"Who Natalia the third?" I asked.

"That's our Italian connect up in Chicago. He the one made Toodie disappear. He find out who the dealer is in Kansas City and take 'em out, he be in charge of Chicago, Kansas City and Minneapolis."

"That's what it is, then," I replied casually. "What about Indianapolis, though? Who gone run that camp?"

"I'm gone bump DeMarco and Max up to Enforcers and move them over to Naptown. Jay-D and Malik gone stay running Saint Louis. Me, Bay and T-top be there when the first shipment come in to lay down how we want this here weight moved."

"So Saint Charles gone be the headquarters," I said as I exited the freeway.

"We gone use the restaurant to discuss business through the week and do our pickups inside Indigo on Saturday nights once the club up and running," Dawk said to me. "In the meantime, we gone have to use the warehouse in Oklahoma to break the shipments down until we lease a place. My momma told me before I left you got the deal closed on some property in Flagstaff so we should be good here in Vegas."

What Dawk was speaking on was something that was agreed upon during the flight back to Cayman Island after the family's meeting with Rafael Gacha on Little Cayman Island. What was understood was that the family needed land and privacy to run this part of the business. Naomi had come through major with the leasing of a brand new warehouse over in Valley Brook and a deal forged with Tropicana Produce here in America. All was left was for me to bring the west coast faction of the family on line by setting up a drop-off point.

This is where Samantha, and her friend, Amber Slovak fit into the equation. I knew the woman who owned the property wasn't going to sell me the land without doing a background check because it was stipulated in the ad I'd read on line. To get around that, I sent Samantha and Amber up there to

Flagstaff. The two of them had pretended to be life partners, which was something that I knew wouldn't be too far-fetched for those two having observed how they interact. Blonde, innocent-looking-girl-next-door-type Amber Slovak and her go-with-the-flow partner Samantha had closed the deal on the $375,000 dollar vineyard the same day.

Slovak Vineyards was the company I'd started in Flagstaff, thereby keeping me and Samantha's name off any legal documents. Her and Amber now had a business to run, but whenever we roll through with that white powder, the two of them weren't going to be around was how I was going to run this leg of the operation.

"Drop-off spot set up in Flagstaff, Cuz." I told Dawk after reflecting on the set up I'd established. "The only thing you gotta do is get that Levamisole over to the warehouse I got set up down there so my crew can remix and repack it. I'll give you the address before we split."

"Done deal," Dawk nodded. "We gone send one trailer your way first shipment," he told me as I nodded my head in approval.

As we continued riding down the freeway headed towards the Asians' home, Dawk ran down to me how he, Bay and T-top had delivered Asa Spade's brother Alvin Spencer to the same house I was heading to as I traveled the same route he, Doss, Bay and T-top had traveled just over two and a half years ago back in August of 2006.

T-top had ran things down to me briefly on the day of my arrival to the ranch back in October, but Dawk brought it home. Several of the most devious murder tactics, from the use of the female lure, the buddy-buddy play, and the-officer-of-the-law had been used over a period of days to murder four people and deliver another to his death.

"In August of two thousand six I was into chopping up cars, fam," I told Dawk.

"Yeah?" Dawk asked as he smiled over to me.

"I met Lee and Vic at a auto show, brer. We was walking

around this fifty-five maroon Thunderbird on chrome mag rims. This old white man was playing, he was playing House of the Rising Sun on his stereo, ya' dig? That was the next to the last song that my mother sung inside the club she and my daddy owned before Manhattan killed them."

"Never knew that," Dawk shot back. "The exit coming up, Cuz."

I laughed to myself as I reflected on that day as I clicked on the blinker and moved over to the right lane. "It wasn't the song, though, Cuz." I told Dawk. "What me, Lee and Vic was tripping off was the fact that this old man had a forty-five disc player in his ride and he was playing The Animals song on a forty-five record."

"A forty-five in a disc?" Dawk asked amazed.

"That old man told us CDs wasn't new, brer," I stated as I exited the freeway. "We all learned that CDs been out and got to talking about that there while looking the car over."

"So from that one car came all this?" Dawk chuckled. "When I met Malik I had to make sure he wasn't gone put a bullet in my back. I wish it was that was easy to find people you could trust, Ben."

"That's how it was in the Ninth Ward, brer. But let me say this—a lotta dudes clicked up? But a lot of them boys ended up turning on one another. I was fortunate to run into some real gangsters that was true to the streets. My boys was solid, that thing with Damenga took us down." I told Dawk as I exited the freeway.

"We got 'em back for ya' down in Mexico and we ain't even know, Cuz," Dawk smiled as he licked his lips while extending his hand. "This here was meant to happen. Take a left," he added.

I crossed under the freeway and Dawk guided me over to what I knew to be 533 Middle Valley Lane in the town of Paradise. We exited the Benz, walked up to the door and was greeted by Phillip Tran, who was wearing a dark grey silk suit and black wing tips. "Dawk? Ben? Glad to see you again.

Enter," he said to us he held the door open.

Phil closed the door and walked over to us and stood facing me and Dawk. "The line is all set up." he said as he extended his hand towards a lounge area on the first floor of the three story mansion where we were joined by Grover.

"I know its short notice, but we really need to get word to Rafael that the family ready." Dawk told Phillip.

"He knows per your request," Phillip replied as he walked from behind the bar and went over to a shelf and pulled down a black leather bag. "All's needed is confirmation, which is why you're here."

I watched as Grover reached underneath the bar counter and came up with a lap top and a router. He pulled the lap top open, powered it up and ran a wire from the router to the computer. Together, the two Asians placed headphones onto their heads. "Come and check this out," Grover beckoned.

Me and Dawk walked over and looked down at the computer. There was a series of numbers running across the screen too fast to recognize. "What's this here?" I asked.

"We were able to use some of the money from our pay out on the negotiations with Rafael to find a computer tech who was able to secure a line between here and Venezuela," Phillip stated. "Cost us ten thousand dollars. One call is all we get, my friends. Afterwards? We destroy the line. Each time we need a shipment or to contact Gacha for whatever reason? It will cost us ten thousand dollars."

Me and Dawk eyed one another. "That's an extra added expense," I remarked.

"Gacha isn't taking any chances," Phillip reasoned. "The only time he will agree to meet face to face is to renegotiate. Everything was agreed upon during the meeting on Little Cayman so there's no need to keep running down there," he added as the numbers on the computer screen stopped moving and locked in on an international number beginning with zero, followed by ten more digits.

"Dial 'em up," Dawk remarked as I stood beside him

memorizing the number.

"That's his home number?" I asked.

"Not sure," Grover remarked as he pulled out one of those old school cell phones, the big ones with the long, thick antenna. "This is the same number my Godfather used to dial, so it's a good chance it is his home number," he ended as a ringing sound came over the lap top's built-in speaker.

****

"You are such a doll, Bridgette!" Rafael Gacha laughed as he nuzzled his wife's neck. The married couple was sitting out underneath their custom-built white marble gazebo situated near the edge of a cliff that overlooked the Caribbean Sea, which lay four hundred feet below.

Rafael's wife stood up and pulled open her silk robe and put her bikini-clad body on display. "I want tan pon it lang, bwoy. (I want sex for a long time, bad man) Take me now, Rafael! Yah champion in tha' bed!" the vanilla-toned, blonde-haired Jamaican spoke in her heavy Jamaican accent as she faced Rafael with the waters of the Caribbean Sea at her back.

"Yah wanna jook? (have sex) Rafael laughed as he sat watching his wife.

"Yah sah!" the woman smiled as she removed her bikini top.

Just then, Rafael's secure line rung. He looked over to the phone lying on the table beside him and answered. "I have to take this," he said. "Sorry, dear."

"Feel no way about it," Bridgette said as she picked up her straw hat and snapped her fingers. The guitarists ceased playing and guided her over to a golf cart where she was driven home after she'd kissed her husbandl's lips.

"Such an understanding and loyal woman," Gacha said to himself. "Hello?"

"Mister Gacha?"

"Tran? How's everything?"

"We have the leaders of the family wanting to talk to you."

"Put them on."

"Evening, Mister Gacha. Dawk."

"Si."

"We're requesting a move up on the first shipment. The sooner the better."

"Well," Gacha smiled as he leaned forward and gazed out into the open sea. "How's next week sound? It'll be your way in say…ten days? But that is on a contingency, my friend, not consignment. You have to make payment…in order to receive…payment?"

"The day of. Cayman. Send your people." Dawk remarked.

"They'll be there at the place we've prearranged during our previous meeting," Gacha replied. "Looks like where're back in business," he added before he ended the call.

Rafael Gacha was the Boss of Bosses in the big scheme of things. He lived the life of a king untouchable in the land of Venezuela. He was a man hard to get next to living on the Margarita Islands. His was a fortress, and he had minions of men on the island protecting him and his family.

While families like the Holland family fought battle after battle for turf on American soil, Rafael Gacha spent his days parlaying with his wife, enjoying the Venezuelan night life, and making millions of dollars by simply answering phone calls and giving the go ahead on large transactions of the cocaine the he manufactured. He supplied three other organizations, but they weren't as violent as The Holland Family.

The man had watched The Holland Family from afar as they conquered every obstacle thrown their way. The Lapiente` family. The feds, where their leader had taken a five decade plus sentence rather than roll over. Even the Enforcers were facing thirty years in Asa Spade and his crew. Yet they remain. If ever they were to manufacture their own cocaine, they would be a force to reckon with; with that aside, Rafael was looking at the bottom line. And the bottom line was that The Holland Family was now back at full operating capacity. Still, they were an organization to be watched being they had Mexican connections, the people who he feared the most as he knew they were the ones who could topple his kingdom.

****

"We back in power before month's end," Dawk told me and the Asians as he set the phone down on the counter.

"And it's coming at the right time." Phillip remarked. "Now," he said as he looked down at his watch. "We have a clear schedule. You guys play poker? We have a private room over at the Trump Towers were we can get comped out fully on food, cigars and drinks and umm, maid service—if you know what I mean?"

"I play no limit from time to time with my sister," I stated. "I'm bout that there. I have a friend that's gone meet us. I flew him in town last night," I remarked as I sent a text. "Trump Towers you say?"

"Yes. We'll have a limousine come and pick us up," Grover answered.

Me and Dawk went on to kick it with Phil and Grover. We were both feeling good over having the product coming in early. With other crews around us toppling over, now was the time to move ahead in order to prevent new clicks from gaining power while we sat idle waiting on our first drop. Ten days was no time. After picking up Jay-D, the five of us went out on the town and discussed further business inside a private room inside the Trump Towers while playing a leisurely game of poker and sipping cognac inside a private room. We'd all put up twenty grand of our own money to make things a little more interesting while we discussed business.

"What's up with Asa Spade?" I asked as I shuffled chips in my right hand with a cigar in the other as music played in the background.

"Trial's on schedule as of right now. It's in the hands of your lawyer, Ben," Phil replied.

"My sister looking forward to seeing him and his team back on the streets," I remarked. "What's up with Lisa Vanguard, Laddy Norcross and Tammy Moto?" I asked. The Asians knew more about Lisa and her movements than anyone in the family being they'd had previous encounters with the woman. Phil and Grover were our ears when it came to the feds and their movements.

"Laddy hasn't been on the scene. Lisa's been going back and forth between Denver and Philadelphia right now with Tammy. She may be working another case, but she's into something off the books."

"You think she dirty?" Jay-D asked as he dealt out the next hand.

Phil and Grover looked over to one another and laughed. "Of course she's dirty, Jason David." Grover replied. "We visited JunJie up in Florence and he—"

"Florence?" I asked, cutting Grover off momentarily. "He in ADX?"

"Yeah, that's right," Grover replied as he puffed on his cigar.

"I'm gone have to make a trip up there, fellas. Next time y'all talk to JunJie, tell 'em I said get in touch with a man named Yiska Hoka. He a good man. A friend of mine."

"I'll be sure to contact my father and let him know, Ben. If you want? I'll also have you added to his visitor's list," he added as he threw two thousand dollar chips into the center of the table.

"That's what's up." I remarked as I set my chips aside. "So what JunJie saying about Lisa, Grover?"

"My Godfather knows many men, Ben," Grover replied as he threw in two thousand dollar chips. "Word on the streets is that Lisa Vanguard and Tammy Moto drove to Salem, Oregon and ripped a guy out of four kilograms of heroin the day after Asa Spade obtained a new lawyer on your family's behalf. Killed the guy and his wife in the process."

"If she did that to a dealer, then she definitely in the game one hundred," Dawk replied.

"You thinkin' about going up against Lisa Vanguard, fam?" Jay-D asked Phillip as he placed chips onto the table.

"Why not?" Grover chimed in. "She's no different from any other dealer on the streets. There's no telling how much dirt this woman has hidden and she's worthy of being touched just like any other criminal against the organization."

"If we can uncover some past crimes she committed? That might be a better way to get to Lisa," I remarked. "A woman like that has a big ego. If she were to be humiliated in public? She'd never live it down."

"We want that bitch dead." Grover swiftly followed. The way he spoke let me know the man was dead serious about going after this federal agent and prosecutor. I have to give the Asians credit, though. They were the only ones willing to go after Lisa Vanguard on the streets. It was to be respected. How they fared, though, remains to be seen.

Just then, there was a repeated tap on the door. Grover got up and answered. When he pulled the door open, Dante` O'Malley walked into the room with his east coast swag as the song *Full of Smoke* came over the speakers… "*But let us leave these two young men…to sit and reflect on the fate of the world…while life as we know it my brother must go on…and so the hustlers continue to hustle…and the players continue to play…*"

"Evening, gentlemen," the counselor spoke over the music as he walked into the room with a stack of chips and a Japanese female following him with a silver tray containing a bottle of cognac and two cigars. "Sorry I'm late, but the maid service here is outstanding," he smiled as he bit his bottom lip while taking a seat at the table. "Got umm, got tied up for a minute, literally speaking."

Dante` was one to readily admit that he cheated on his wife Olivia. Tonight was no different I knew given his remark. Phil and Grover had a half dozen Asian women hanging out in the lounge area outside the private room. We'd all been offered their services. Me and Dawk declined, but Jay-D had disappeared for about fifteen minutes into the bathroom with one of the Japanese women and had sampled some international pussy.

O'Malley's arrival livened up the party. Everybody was surprised to see the guy. He sat down and was poured a glass of yak and had his cigar lit by the voluptuous Japanese female accompanying him. "Is there anything else you require, Mister O'Malley," she asked politely.

"I think I've been satisfied, young lady," Dante` smiled as he placed three hundred dollar bills onto the tray.

The game resumed and all eyes were on Dante`. "What's going on with the case?" I asked as I eyed one of the coldest defense attorneys in America.

"Lisa Vanguard is going to throw the case, gentlemen," Dante` let it be known.

"Throw the case? How? Why?" Phillip inquired.

"The why I don't know," Dante` answered. "My best guess is that she wants your man Asa Spade on the streets for whatever reason. The how is that she's going to withhold evidence. One witness was killed, but Lisa could have very well placed the second witness into witness protection and take Asa Spade down. Yet, she refuses to bring the guy forth."

"What if she hit us with a surprise witness?" I asked.

"Lisa can't come with a surprise witness without letting me cross examine the guy. I'll simply ask for a delay. If she does bring a surprise witness and he takes the stand I'll shred his ass apart." Dante` took a sip of his cognac and sighed. "Ben? I appreciate you flying me into town, but our being in the same presence can greatly hinder this case," he remarked. "Now, I have some valuable information that can be of use if I were to play these pair of queens out fully."

I watched as Dante` placed $10,000 dollars in chips into the center of the table. "Anybody care to risk their hard earned dollars?"

This here was the beginning of the payoff to Dante` for his providing us with inside information on Lisa Vanguard. "I'm in," I declared as I pushed $27,000 dollars into the center of the table.

"I call," Dawk followed as he slid $25,000 dollars into the

center of the table.

"Bet," Jay-D joined in as he slid his $15,000 dollars worth of chips into the table's center.

"Call," Grover and Phil replied in unison as they slid a total of $60,000 dollars worth of chips into the pile.

"Give us a turn card," Dante` smiled as he eyed Jay-D.

The turn card was flipped over and Dante` bet again. "Ten thousand. All in," he said as he pushed the remaining ten grand into the center of the table.

"Fold," Phil and Grover remarked as they threw their cards in.

"Fold," Jay-D followed as he threw his cards aside.

"Too big a bet for me," Dawk stated as he slid his cards into the slush pile.

"I call," I chuckled as I slid an extra ten grand into the pot. Everybody looked at me like my face was melting or something. There was $152,000 dollars on the line and Dante` stood to walk away with said cash in under five minutes. I only had a deuce of heart and a three of clubs. On the board was a queen of diamond, eight of heart, a six of club and a jack of diamond. I had no chance of winning this hand, but Dante` and company didn't know that.

Jay-D shook his head and flipped the river card and a deuce of club hit the board, giving me a pair of deuces. I looked over to Dante` and could see sweat forming at his temples. He'd called a pair of queens, but the look on his face told me he had nothing. Being that he was out of chips, he had no choice but to tap his finger onto the soft, green felt. "Check," he said while eyeing me in wonderment.

"Check," I quickly followed.

Dante` flipped his cards over. "Queen high," he stated as he eyed me anxiously.

I had Dante` beat with a simple pair of deuces, but I chucked my cards aside. "Your pot," I said as I poured another glass of cognac while nodding my head to Christion's song... "...*cause*

I'm too cool...and what they say is true...oooh...I'm fulla smoke...'cause I'm too cool...and what they say is true(straight player)...oooh...I'm fulla smoke...watchin' my life go down...watchin' my life go down..."

Dante` pulled his chips down while pointing a finger at me. "You live on the edge, Ben," he chuckled. "Are you a traveling man?"

"I've been around," I stated as I leaned back in my seat and crossed my legs. "What you got?"

"If ever you make your way over to the city of Baltimore? Be sure and check out this spot called Jonas' over in the Highlandtown section."

I looked over to Grover at that moment and could see his mind working. Dante` had just given us the location to where Lisa Vanguard could be found. I then eyed Dawk and could tell right away that he wasn't ready to give the order on Lisa Vanguard. My gut was telling me that he, too, was thinking that it was too much swirling around Asa Spade and his crew's trial to hit the woman.

"What you think, Cuz?" I asked.

"If Vanguard gone let Ace walk, we gone allow that to happen," Dawk told me, confirming my beliefs.

"Once he's free," Dante` chimed in as he stacked his chips to have them cashed in. "Once Asa Spade and his crew are free, they'll all be kicked out of Colorado. The man can't come back here to Nevada either because he's been blacklisted."

"He gone need a job if he wants one," I let it be known. "What we gone do with dude?"

"I got a spot for him," Dawk stated. "I'll look out for Asa Spade. In the meantime, I think me and Ben on the same page when I say nothing happens to Lisa Vanguard and Tammy Moto until Ace and his crew touch down."

I nodded in agreement. "That's our order," I said while eyeing Phillip and Grover. "Let Lisa be until Asa back on the streets. We gone from there." I could sense the disappointment deriving from within Phillip and Grover, but they'd given my family control. And as of now, our word was law. "We all on the same page?" I asked as I eyed the two Asians.

"We want first shot at Lisa once Asa is reestablished," Grover stated. "We wait based on the order," he ended.

With business in order, me and Dawk checked out the game early and went and sat up inside one of our suites over to the Bellagio and further strategized on the things to come. We both knew about Naomi's plan to purchase 3,000 acres of land down in Brazil and we wondered what would come of it if and when Rafael caught wind of the situation. Neither of us was blind to the fact that the man loved complete control. He was just a stepping stone for us, though; the last obstacle standing in the way of our family becoming international players. Why stop at the threshold? We'd come this far, might as well go for it all was me and Dawk's thinking.

"The family gone have to take a flight down to Cayman Islands in ten days and do the drop," Dawk said to me as we sat at a bar inside the luxurious suite sipping brandy.

"That's nothing, fam. Samantha be ready." I replied.

Dawk looked over to me with a serious look on his face. "This here gone be the run of a lifetime, Ben."

"Everything has a beginning and an ending, Dawk." I said as I poured another shot of liquor. "I don't think your momma plan on making a career out of this here thing of ours."

Dawk laughed as he reached for the bottle and poured himself another shot. "We in it for life, Cuz! It's a Holland thang," he said to me as we bumped fists.

Dawk's phone began sliding across the counter at that moment. "That's Bay texting, fam," he said as he checked the message.

****

We at the game with dude. Bay texted Dawk as T-top sat beside her with a pair of binoculars, scanning the crowd behind the Indiana Pacers' bench as the two set up in the nose bleed sections on the Detroit Pistons' side of the basketball court inside Market Square Arena in downtown Indianapolis.

Handle that when you can. See you at home. Dawk texted back.

The meeting? Bay texted.

We in. Dawk texted back.

Cool. Later.

"Dawk got in touch with Rafael," Bay whispered into T-top's ear.

"Good, won't be too long now," T-top replied as she continued scanning the crowd on the opposite side of the court, looking for one person in particular.

By halftime, the twins still hadn't laid eyes on their mark. They knew the man to be a slender, dark-skinned brother with long dreads and sunken eyes. Malik said he always sat behind the Pacers' bench alone and always wore a dark blue silk suit. The platinum grill he wore was supposed to make him easily distinguishable from the rest of the men sitting behind the Pacers' bench who fit his description, but the man they were looking for hadn't been spotted as of yet.

As the halftime show was nearing completion, the teams began walking out onto the court for warmups. A few of the Pacers' players were standing beside the bench removing their t-shirts and warmup pants when a slender, dark-skinned man walked down onto the court and shook hands with a couple of players. The guy was tall himself, but when standing next to 7'1" Roy Hibbert, backup center for the Pacers, he held the statue of a midget.

T-top bumped elbows with Bay and handed her the binoculars. "Down on the floor in front Indiana bench," she said.

Bay placed the binoculars to her eyes and honed in on the young man. He was smiling from time to time while talking to a couple of players. When he smiled while looking out to the court and pointing to the basketball rim, Bay caught sight of the platinum grill he sported. It took confirmation from both twins before they would move on to the next phase of the hit, and Bay had just jumped onto the same page as T-top.

The twins sat and shared the binoculars throughout the second half of the game, which had gone into overtime. The overtime afforded the twins the time to travel around to the Pacers' side of the court where they continued spying their mark. By game's end, he was up out of his seat milling about with assistant coaches before he disappeared into the hall leading to the Pacers' locker room.

Bay and T-top had been expecting this move. A guy of RJ's caliber didn't walk out of the front doors of a public building too often. Before the game, they'd spied the area where players parked their cars during a home game. Some teams would meet up at a hotel and travel by bus, but the Pacers allowed their players to drive up to the arena in their own rides.

Bay and T-top had watched a couple of tricked-out Escalades, a Bentley Rose Royce and a few Mercedes Benzes and a Ferrari enter the arena's underground parking area that was reserved for players. They knew not their mark's real name, only the name of RJ, but they'd surmised that the guy was driving one of the cars that had entered the underground garage, namely the yellow Ferrari, as it was the style of car they knew the man to be driving courtesy of Malik. The tinted windows had prevented them from figuring the guy for certain, and security in the parking garage was extra heavy before the game's start. In spite of the snafus the twins had encountered, they'd fingered their mark and were now going into the second phase of their plan.

Arena staff wore blue and yellow uniforms. When RJ disappeared into the aisle leading to the locker room, Bay and T-top headed back to Jay-D's Navigator and changed into identical uniforms and were out near the guard shack leading to the underground garage with trash bags and pickers, pretending to be part of the cleanup crew. From their vantage points, both twins could see the players emerging from the player access door and heading towards their rides.

NBA games were sometimes a show all to themselves; although security was always on hand, some could be paid off to the look the other way in order to let a few reporters and more importantly, club promoters and groupies through so they could proposition players. The groupies were out heavy on this night, and the numerous women dressed in skimpy outfits, some being led by men who were obviously setting them out for sex, were providing the perfect cover for Bay and T-top as many on the security team had their attention focused elsewhere.

Players were emerging at random, and each time, they were approached by groups of women who wanted to take a picture. Some were complementing them on their win while others asked what club they were going to on this night. It was a festival of debauchery as players worth millions of dollars exited the player's entrance on this frigid night in Indianapolis. A couple of players left with two or more women while a few took selfies with several groupies, smiling into their phone cameras while copping a feel.

When RJ emerged with two of the Pacers' players, Bay and T-top, who'd worked their way into the parking lot, quickly took notice. T-top went about picking up small pieces of paper and cigarette butts while eyeing the man out the corners of her eyes as Bay headed back outside. When RJ hopped into the yellow Ferrari, T-top went and stood at the edge of the drive leading to the guard shack. With her face hidden from sight, she eyed the tag on the Ferrari as it slowed before the guard shack and waited for the gate to rise.

Once the car disappeared from sight, T-top called Bay. "Yellow Ferrari B MARSH tag," she remarked.

"Gotcha," Bay remarked lowly just as the yellow Ferrari slid past the dark brown Ford Focus rental she was sitting in. Bena tailed the Ferrari while Tiva made her way back to the Navigator. Once behind the wheel, T-top called Bay and her twin began guiding her along way as she trailed the Ferrari.

Tiva met up with Bay over to the Ice Ultra Lounge, a nightclub within walking distance of Conseco Fieldhouse. Even thought it was cold out, many where still out on the street celebrating the Pacers' win over the Pistons. Tiva rode past the rental car and parked the Navigator a ways down facing the opposite direction. She shut the engine down and she and Bay waited in silence while texting one another back and forth on occasion while patiently awaiting their next move.

Many people have images of grandiosity in their minds when they think of one being a contract killer. Like an old western or mafia movie, the image of a hired killer walking up on a mark and gunning that mark, or marks down in cold blood and running off into the night and getting away scot-free was what many believed.

Admittedly, for Bay and T-top, some jobs came about easily, like the hit on Desiree Abbadando, Daneel LuQman, and Ya Murder, but for the most part, it took time, tactic and above all else, patience, for a hit to be pulled off and to keep the law's tentacles from connecting the dots—and even then it wasn't a guarantee that the job would go unhinged, i.e. what had happened to Dawk while the big three where in the process of executing Ya Murder, and what had gone down with Doss and Bay the night the family were fulfilling a contract on the Onishi brothers up in Seattle where Bay had to take down a police officer in order to prevent the hit from being disclosed. There was nothing glamourous about the life being led by some in the Holland family as theirs was a serious business that only a few were capable of comprehending fully, let alone live.

After sitting out in the cold in downtown Indianapolis for nearly three hours, Bay and T-top's mark emerged from the club. They'd texted one another simultaneously, receiving the same message: *He moving*, as they started their ignitions. The yellow Ferrari was driven up to the front of the club and the twins' mark climbed behind the wheel and eased off.

Less experienced killers would've made their move when the Ferrari slowed to enter an on ramp leading to I-74, but Bay and T-top both recognized that a lime green Caprice was tailing RJ to wherever he was headed. The twins would not be able to pull off the job on this night, but Bay, as Tiva peeled off, was able to follow the Ferrari and the Caprice, tailing the cars back to the Conrad Indianapolis. She made it back to the hotel on the outskirts of the city and met up with T-top an hour or so later and shared what she'd witnessed as the two of them set about with their plan to take down their last mark before returning home to Oklahoma.

CHAPTER THIRTY-SIX

THE NAPTOWN HIT

January 16, 2009

"Yeah, that bitch wanted me to drop her off with work on her, Boogie," RJ laughed as he dressed inside his suite over to the Conrad Indianapolis.

"My mother was right about her," Boogie replied in reference to Ya Murder as she rolled a blunt for RJ, she herself still naked after going a couple of rounds with him atop the ruffled silk sheets. "I'm sorry we even agreed to do that job. We only broke even in Saint Louis."

"That right. But Natalia got us on fire with that work coming from the Chi so it's nothing. I'm headed down to Nashville to bust things open after the game tomorrow." RJ said as he tucked his silk shirt inside his silk slacks.

"Cool beans. We still trying to track down this Asian in Philly. You know somebody who'd be willing to do that job?" Boogie asked as she got up, walked over to RJ and placed the blunt to his lips and flicked a lighter.

"Not off hand," RJ replied as he shook his head slightly. "I'll ask around. I doubt we find somebody willing to take down a fed, though," he said before taking several pulls on the blunt to get it going.

"This thing is really getting to my mother. I have to do something about Philadelphia," Boogie said dejectedly. "But how?" she questioned as she plopped down on the bed's edge.

"It'll be all right, baby girl," RJ stated as he took several deep tokes off the blunt and handed it to Boogie.

"Go to your game. I'll see you when you get back here," Boogie snapped as she lay back on the bed and took a toke off the blunt and began choking and coughing. She was in state of flux over the conundrum her family was up against trying to go after Special Agent Tammy Moto and she hadn't the answer as to how to resolve the issue at the present time.

RJ went and grabbed his silk suit jacket off the back of a velvet chair and donned it and a leather trench coat. Grabbing his Ruger Blackhawk .41 magnum off the bar counter, the self-proclaimed king of Naptown checked the chamber on a revolver powerful enough to take down a moose with its velocity, making sure six rounds were loaded into it before he tucked it in his back waistband and walked out of his suite.

Ricky 'RJ' Gross Junior was a man hard to get next to. The Conrad Indianapolis had security cameras throughout; the hotel had no self-parking so he and everyone else who either lived or stayed overnight, had to use the valet parking, which suited a man of RJ's caliber perfectly because he didn't have to worry about being hit in any parking garage. One had to spend top dollar in order to camp out inside this particular establishment. No one would dare attack him where he lay his head was RJ's belief each and every time he left the Conrad as everything was out in the open on busy South Meridian Street.

****

Bay and T-top, meanwhile, were parked across the street from the Conrad Indianapolis in the packed parking lot of the Hard Rock Café Indianapolis. Game night in downtown Indianapolis was a big event. The basketball game was ninety minutes away and many future attendees were out on the town having dinner before start time.

The twins were posted up in their rented Ford Focus that was parked at the rear of the Hard Rock in the second slot. From their vantage point, Bay and T-top had a bead on the Conrad Indianapolis' main entrance. Numerous luxurious cars were being driven up to the front of the hotel, which was illuminated brilliantly as those with wealth stood out underneath the canopy in pristine furs, and silk and leather attire worth several months of mortgages to the average Joe.

"I thought he woulda been down to Conseco Field by now," Bay remarked as she looked through the night vision goggles while sitting in the backseat of the Ford Focus with an SR-25 ten shot sniper rifle resting in her lap.

"Who dat?" T-top asked.

"Reggie Miller," Bay replied as she held the binoculars to her eyes. "He call their games, remember?"

"He shoulda beat Jordan 'nem that year," T-top remarked as she eyed the main entrance.

"If Lucky were alive to hear you say that, girl," Bay laughed as she continued peering through the binoculars.

"Just kicking the real," T-top retorted through a sly smirk.

"I don't know about all that there, sister. Thing got me is what dude see in the Pacers right about now. They ain't hittin' on nothing this year."

"Malik say he be brokering deals at these games. From what we know, RJ the one supplying this whole town," she added as the guy Bay knew to be RJ emerged from the Conrad Indianapolis' main entrance.

"Maybe we should rethink this," Bay remarked somewhat uncertain.

T-top looked over the backseat at Bay in surprise. "Why?"

"RJ could be like the middle man. For all we know, he could be working for that white chick driving that Caprice last night. We do this, ain't no telling what gone come of it."

T-top, like Bay, had never considered the prospect. The white, tatted-up female did appear to have clout, but on the other end, RJ was the known distributor in Naptown. "Whether he working for somebody or not, we got the go ahead on RJ. It's your call, though. Your kill," she remarked as she looked over to the Conrad where heavy activity was unfolding.

"Whatever come of it so be it," Bay remarked as she picked up her rifle, stuck it out the window and looked through the scope, quickly focusing in on RJ.

RJ had just tipped the valet and was climbing into his Ferrari when something sharp and hot sliced through the side of his head just behind his left ear and shattered the right side of his face. Shocked and in intense pain, he leaned up against the side of his Ferrari trying to balance himself as another bullet entered the left side of his back and ripped through his heart. The last thing he saw was the image of his wide open, stunned eyes imaging back at him through the bloodstained driver's side mirror as he fell over onto the floorboard of his $250,000 dollar car. He died mere seconds later amid the screams of only a few horrified citizens who were able to comprehend his sudden change of fate.

T-top pulled away from the scene calmly, tailing a couple of cars, whose drivers were unaware of the assassination that had taken place directly across the street, out of the Hard Rock Café's parking lot. The two quickly blended in with the flow of traffic and disappeared from the scene undetected as chaos began to unfold underneath the canopy of the Conrad Indianapolis as they vacated the area and prepared to head back to Ponca City.

CHAPTER THIRTY-SEVEN

SILOAM AND THE BIG CAHOOTS

While Bay and T-top were making their way back to Ponca City, Naomi was sitting in her office inside her suite inside Ponderosa reading over documents that had been faxed to her the day before. She couldn't believe what her eyes were gazing upon as she read the data, but she wasn't all that surprised. A soft tap on her door forced her to look up from the paper she held. "It's open," she spoke calmly.

Flacco opened the door and peeked in. "Senorita Dawkins? I have Senorita Bovina."

"Send her in," Naomi replied as she stood up from her high-back leather chair.

Siloam eased past Flacco and walked over to Naomi with her hands clasped before her trench coat. She stood staring at the woman who'd taken her in as Flacco stepped into the room and closed and locked the door. "I guess I don't have to explain how you not letting the family know about Reynard has landed us in a most precarious position," Naomi stated as she eyed Siloam.

"I have no words for my actions, Naomi. I thought I could handle the situation on my own—I was wrong."

"You weren't wrong, just in over your head. You did right sharing things with Flacco," Naomi said as she walked from

455

behind her desk and stood before Siloam. "Because of that, we have the upper hand in this matter."

"I never wanted this to happen," Siloam replied anxiously as she stared Naomi in the eyes.

Naomi reached up and touched Siloam's face. "I always knew you had it in you, child. And whether you wanted this to happen or not, the die has been cast."

"I understand, Naomi." Siloam replied lowly as she bowed her head.

"You'll do just fine, Siloam. Just do as Flacco instructed and we'll take care of the rest. What time does the flight arrive?"

"In two hours. I'll be heading out shortly."

"I'll be right behind you. I'm going over to the guest house to get things set up with Mary."

"Okay," Siloam spoke meekly as she headed for the door.

Flacco stepped aside and pulled the door open. "No matter what, Senorita Bovina, continue to be the woman you were and everything will fall into place."

"I understand, Flacco," Siloam replied as she left the suite.

Flacco was about to leave the room when Naomi called out to him. "Senorita?" he asked.

Naomi walked over to Flacco. "I see potential with Siloam. Would you like an assistant? One you can train to do certain jobs here in America should the occasion rise?"

"Senorita Bovina would make a deadly lure if she's taught right, Senorita Dawkins. A very tempting woman she is."

"I know," Naomi replied. "Bring her along slowly. We'll see what becomes of it."

"Si, Senorita Dawkins. Now, I have a task to perform myself down in the stockyards."

"Call me if you need anything," Naomi replied as she watched Flacco exit her suite.

The family's matriarch walked over to her walk-in closet the size of a small apartment and set up like a clothing boutique where she selected one of her black wool trench coats, a matching sombrero and a black scarf. She grabbed the folder containing the documents she'd been reading off her desk and left her suite to head over to Mary's home on the west side of the ranch. Martha, Twiggy and Francine were all in the theater room with Malaysia and Malara and were unaware of the on-going plot.

Naomi climbed into one the family's Suburbans and drove over to the guest house. The home was dark, but she could see Mary's balcony lit up and the telescope she often used to watch the stars situated on a tripod that pointed south. She exited the SUV and let herself into the home after deactivating the alarm. "Mary?" she called out.

Mary had just trotted down the stairs. "I saw you pull up," she smiled. "I was sitting on the balcony when I saw you headed this way."

"Star gazing are you?" Naomi asked as she held onto the folder.

"Yeah," Mary laughed. "The whole point of me building this deck was to spend more quality time with Tacoma and Dimples, but since it's been up they've been here only three times. I enjoy it more than they do now."

"It's wonderful fun," Naomi smiled. "Mind if I join you?"

"Really?" Mary asked surprised. "I, I would love that, Naomi. I have a heater on the balcony and coffee and Kahlua upstairs!" she spoke as if it were a naughty saying.

"Lead the way," Naomi smiled. Together, the sisters headed to the second floor and began setting up to watch the night's sky.

****

Ninety minutes later, Siloam was headed back to Ponca City with Reynard in tow. The ride was going smooth. Siloam did well hiding her anxiety outwardly, but on the inside she was a nervous wreck. She knew what lay ahead, and it was hard for her not to imagine that the man next to her would no longer be the animated individual he was at this moment.

"No one knows I'm in town, right?" Reynard asked.

"You've asked me that four times, Reynard," Siloam sighed as she drove. "I told you I made sure Mary was alone before I left. If someone's there at the guest house you can hide over to my place until the time is right."

"I'm just making sure, Siloam. This plan is a risky one. If we fail, we're looking at jail or worse if the family was to find out."

"No one knows." Siloam reiterated. "It's after eleven. The family is all settled in. You'll surprise Mary by telling her you're back in town for a few days to celebrate getting the coaching job at Nevada. I'll start talking to her to distract her and you'll use the gun I give you to take control of the situation. We'll take her to the barn and take all the drugs out the safe. From there we'll set it up to look like a robbery. One of the ranch hands will find her body in the morning."

"I'll wait a month or so after the funeral to file a claim," Reynard remarked. "From there, you and I can go wherever we want to in the world."

The nonchalant attitude displayed by Reynard was sickening to Siloam. She was repulsed over this man's deviousness and how far he was willing to go for the sake of a dollar. Looking back on it, his stumbling upon her and Takoda had actually been a good thing. She reflected on Reynard telling Mary about taking her to Nevada and it was her belief that Mary would've never made it back from Vegas alive. Reynard could've very well have the woman killed in his hometown and come up with some excuse to cover his own tracks and still cash in, leaving the family heartbroken over the loss of Mary.

"We're coming into town," Siloam remarked as she entered downtown Ponca City and made a right turn, headed towards Kaw Lake Bridge. "Let's get ready. I have to go to the barn first to pick up the gun."

"You're in control," Reynard replied, somewhat distrusting as thoughts of what he was going to do on this night entered his mind.

****

Mary Holland, meanwhile, was sitting before her telescope with Naomi. The two of them were watching the stars to the north east when an unfamiliar car traveled onto the land. Mary was paying it no mind as she was too preoccupied with gazing up at the stars.

Naomi had been eyeing the car the entire time, however; "Who's that turning onto the property?" she asked as she got up and turned off Mary's lamp light, darkening the entire balcony.

"I don't know," Mary said as she aimed the telescope at the car riding onto the property.

****

Siloam, meanwhile, was riding over the land. "She's home alone. Just like I told you," she told Reynard as she headed towards the main barn.

"Why not drive over to where she's at right away?" Reynard asked as he pulled a mask from the inside of his trench coat. "I'm not even supposed to be in town. You know this to be true, Siloam."

"I told you I had to get the gun," Siloam replied nervously as she pulled up to the barn.

"You should've had it on you!" Reynard scoffed.

"I'm sorry, baby," Siloam cooed as she leaned over and stroked Reynard's bald head while kissing his lips. "This is what we've been planning. I didn't want to take any chances on riding down to Oklahoma City and back here with a gun. I'll go in and get it and be right back. You'll have to drive this car over to Mary's home. She'll think it's someone in the family and will open the door."

"Where will you be?"

"There's golf carts in the barn," Siloam whispered. "I'll take one and ride over there. Mary will be surprised to see you, but she loves you, man. I'll ride over there and distract her and all you'll have to do is put the gun to her back like we planned."

"Then what?"

"We'll take her back here to the barn and make her open the safe."

"Then," Reynard raised his hand and configured his right hand into a gun. "Pow!" he smirked. "Let's do it, baby."

"Be right back," Siloam responded lovingly, kissing Reynard one more time before she exited the car and let herself into the barn.

Siloam ran up to the loft, unlocked the safe, pulled out the gun and walked around in a circle for several minutes before trotting back down the stairs. "*I don't know if can do this,*" she said to herself as she trotted back up the wooden staircase and unlocked the safe once more and placed the gun back inside. A minute later, she reemerged and climbed back behind the steering wheel. She looked straight ahead and said nothing as she started the engine.

"Okay, so where's the gun?" Reynard asked.

Siloam said nothing as she came up with a syringe filled with etorphine. Reynard, already uneasy over the entire scenario, as Siloam had taken longer than necessary to retrieve the gun, lunged over with his forearm and elbowed her in the face just as he was pricked in the arm with the needle.

Siloam dropped the syringe and it poked her thigh before bouncing off her leg and landing on the floorboard. Her chest immediately began to tighten, depriving her of oxygen as she leaned over onto the steering wheel.

Reynard was preparing to lean over and strangle Siloam, but he could no longer move and was now finding it difficult to breathe. He eyed her stunned. "You fuckin' bitch," he hissed through wide eyes just before he fell over onto Siloam.

Before Reynard's head landed in her lap, Siloam had pushed her coat pocket forward and poked herself in the thigh with a second needle containing Revivon, the antidote to the powerful tranquilizer etorphine. Within seconds, her lungs relaxed and oxygen began to enter her system once more. She reached for the door handle while gasping for air.

When the door opened, the car's interior and immediate surrounding area became illuminated in the night. Mary, who'd been watching the car from her balcony through her telescope, caught sight of Reynard slumped over in the front seat. A wobbly Siloam soon came into view and the shocked woman watched in horror as she fell over onto the trunk of the car while clutching her chest.

"Are you okay, Mary?" Naomi asked as she sat beside her sister sipping on coffee.

"I'm fine," Mary smiled pretentiously as she moved the telescope from before her face.

"You sure? You look sort of flustered," Naomi remarked as she stared Mary in the eyes.

"It's nothing," Mary stated as she jumped up from her chair and walked into her and turned on her lamp light. Mary wasn't sure she'd witnessed what she'd just seen. Reynard looked as if he was dead lying across the front seat, or badly injured at best. The ringing of her phone startled Mary; she screamed aloud and dropped it before scrambling to pick it up. "Regina!" she sighed as she walked over and closed the doors, leaving Naomi behind on the balcony. "Regina where are you?"

"I'm over to Bay's condo in Oklahoma City. Takoda had a stalled car to pick up in the morning down here so I came down early. I'm just kickin' back with Kimi, Koko and Udelle. Me and Takoda going shopping tomorrow for some clothes to wear out to Vegas with daddy next month. Everything okay up there?"

"Everything is fine," Mary responded as she stared off into space. "Just, you all stay there. I'll be down in the morning and we can all go out to breakfast."

"Cool. I love you, momma."

"I love you too, sweetheart," Mary replied before ending the call.

Mary clutched her phone and began rubbing her shoulders as tears began to fill her eyes. It was no secret that she wanted no part of the violent lifestyle some in the family lived; but in a flash, she now find herself witness to a possible murder perpetrated by Siloam Bovina. "This family is rife with evil," she said lowly as she looked down at her cell phone and pressed 911. Her finger hovered over the call button as she practiced what she was going to say to the person on the other end. "I can't do it!" she then blurted out.

"Can't do what?" a voice called out to Mary.

"God! You scared me, Naomi!" Mary gasped aloud.

"What are you doing? Who were you about to call?" Naomi glared as she walked off the balcony and entered Mary's bedroom with her hands clasped behind her back.

Mary looked at the cell phone in her hand, then back over to Naomi. "I wasn't going to do it," she confessed through her tears.

"Do what?" Naomi asked casually as she walked towards Mary and began circling her slowly.

"Don't make me say it, Naomi!" Mary pleaded as she watched her sister circle her in her black cashmere trench coat and matching leather sombrero and leather boots.

"Say what?" Naomi screamed as her nostrils flared while circling around Mary, her hands being steadily being held behind her back.

"I saw it, alright?" Mary whispered through tears. "I saw what Siloam did!"

"And I saw you watching her, Mary!" Naomi admitted. "You did good, sister," she added matter-of-factly as she looked off nowhere in particular.

"How could I have done good? How? When I didn't want any of this to happen ever? What did Reynard do to deserve such treatment?"

"What he did was try to set you up to be killed here on the ranch." Naomi let it be known as she threw the manila folder at Mary's feet. "That is a life insurance policy worth five hundred thousand dollars upon your death and Reynard Jacobs was listed as the beneficiary."

"Reynard would never do something like that to me," Mary spoke humbly as she shook her head in disbelief. "He wouldn't dare bring that much pain into Regina's life."

"Aww, Mary," Naomi sighed. "Are you that susceptible and incredulous? Reynard doesn't give one rat's fat ass about you, Dimples or Tacoma. And he certainly doesn't care for Takoda," she declared as she removed her hands from behind her back.

Mary flinched at that moment, believing her sister was about to brandish a weapon.

Naomi sensed Mary's reasoning. She could only stare at her sister as she removed the black leather gloves from her hands. "Really, Mary?" she asked disappointedly. "You really thought I came here to kill you tonight?"

"Business comes first for you." Mary whispered in fright.

"Family comes first, dammit!" Naomi yelled through wet eyes. "Everybody is doing what they're doing tonight on behalf of you! I'm not gone sugar coat anything with you tonight, Mary, because you need to hear it straight!"

"Hear what?" Mary yelled as she stomped her boot-clad foot to the wooden floor. "That this family kills people and sells drugs? That we, that we live a lie here?"

"A lie we live?" Naomi frowned. "The only ones we lie to are the ones you contemplated on calling a minute ago because they are the only ones who can stop us! You and the ones who think like you are the only ones who could stop us tonight after witnessing Reynard's death!"

"Why put me in the middle of everything, Naomi? Why?" Mary cried as she stared her sister in the eyes.

"Because you had to see it to believe it, Mary. I gave it to you up close and raw, sister."

"I didn't have to know what—"

"I prevented you from embarking on some self-righteous meaningless crusade to find out exactly what happened to the worthless piece of shit of a man you were beginning to fall in love with all over again before he killed you tonight and took you away from us!" Naomi interjected, screaming to the top of her lungs as she stared Mary in the eyes coldly with tears streaming down her face. "Call me whatever you like, but it was your life on the line or his life, Mary! And I chose to put your life first!"

"You could've let me talk to him, Naomi. Killing people isn't always the answer!"

"In my world it's what brings about contentment and secures the future survival of this family!" Naomi countered as she walked over to Mary's coffee maker and poured herself a cup of coffee. "Reynard was a gambler. A degenerate. He was in debt to some bookies in Vegas. If it wasn't you, it would've been somebody else in the family. Maybe Dimples. People like Reynard can't be reasoned with because of their habit. The family is better off without him around trust me."

"I, how, what can I tell Regina? She's gonna be looking forward to this trip to Vegas next month. She'll be expecting to hear from Reynard long before then, Naomi."

"Vegas is no longer feasible, Mary." Naomi replied calmly as she knelt down and picked up the folder and removed the policy and showed it to her. She stroked her sister's jet black hair and ran her hand along Mary's arm tenderly.

Naomi knew about the affair Siloam and Takoda had, but she felt it wasn't her place to disclose such information. While holding back on that knowledge, she stepped back from Mary and said, "I know you don't agree with none of this, but Reynard was going to ruin lives here."

Mary's eyes were filled with tears as her brown eyes focused in on Reynard's name to a life insurance policy that also bore her signature. She would've never agreed to such a thing and knew full well she hadn't signed any sort of document handed to her by Reynard. While she was contemplating on rekindling lost love, he'd snuck into town and was preparing to take her life she now understood.

"He really did come here to kill you tonight, Mary," Naomi stated, shaking Mary from her thoughts. "He may have gotten away with it, but he would've been the number one suspect."

"How?" Mary asked as she held onto the document.

"Reynard caught a flight here to Oklahoma under his name. His plan was to sneak into town, but had he not shown his face and you ended up dead he would've have some explaining to do. It may have ended up being circumstantial in the court, but there was no way he was going to get away with harming you or anyone else in this family. We would've figured it out real quick."

"What's going to happen to Reynard now?"

Naomi took another sip of her coffee and said, "I think this is where you get off, Mary. Let your imagination run wild if you want, but just know Reynard will no longer be around to pose a threat. Remember, that man tried to kill you and abandon your daughter again. Remember that."

"What role did Siloam, why was Siloam involved?"

"Siloam set the whole thing up, Mary. You want the answers as to why she did what she did to Reynard? Ask her," Naomi said as she eased out of Mary's bedroom.

"Naomi!" Mary called out.

Naomi walked back into the threshold and eyed her sister with her chin held up high and her head slightly rocking with a sly smile on her face. "Yes?"

"I'm scared to be alone. But I wanna stay here tonight." Mary said.

"What do you have to eat downstairs, Mary?" Naomi asked as she walked off. "And do you have liquor here? I think we both need a shot of something strong," she ended.

Mary threw her phone aside and ran out of the room. "Tell me more about this thing with Reynard and his plan to kill me at least!" she said aloud as she caught to Naomi and wrapped her arms around her sister as the two walked down the hallway side by side.

The sisters were in the kitchen pulling out leftover lasagna and pouring up wine when Siloam entered the home. Mary eyed her and donned a stoic look. She looked over to Naomi, fearful at that moment.

"No one is going to hurt you, Mary," Naomi said as she poured two glasses of wine. "I think dirty laundry has to be aired out tonight. Can you handle it?"

"I'll manage. Whatever I'm told will never be spoken on outside of these doors. But I have to know what role Siloam played in all of this." Mary remarked lowly as she eyed Siloam walking her way.

Siloam walked over and sat at a stool before the island counter. There was a brief moment of silence before she spoke, her eyes watering in the process. "Me and Takoda had a, we had an affair, Mary," she admitted. "But it only happened one time! Reynard was bribing me for sex and wanted me to help set you up. I did a good thing!" she defended.

Mary said nothing as she stared at Siloam. After several seconds, she lunged out and slapped her face as tears flooded her eyes. "Are you serious?" she screamed as she ran up on the Cherokee Indian and began beating her furiously. "Look at all the damage you've done!"

"He was going to kill you, Mary!" Siloam cried as she shielded herself.

"You got me acting crazy now! Violence isn't always the answer," Mary reasoned as she backed away from Siloam. "Had you two been stronger at the time, this would've never happened!"

Naomi walked over and stood before Mary. "You think their having an affair led to Reynard's death?" she asked as she eyed her sister unwavering. "Had Siloam not done what she done, you would be dead. Reynard had it set up to look like a robbery. He was going to drag you over to the barn and force you to open up the safe and steal the veterinarian drugs we use for horses and bulls. People get high off those drugs. That's why we have the safe, Mary. Because it didn't happen, doesn't mean it wasn't going to happen. You should be thankful we cared enough to see it through."

"This is going to crush Dimples," Mary stated through her tears.

"Dimples doesn't have to know, Mary." Siloam cried as she righted herself. "We've won," she declared as she wiped her bloody nose. "Just let it rest. Please?" she begged through clasped hands. "Dimples doesn't need to know about this at all."

"What will I tell her when she asks?" Mary inquired as she looked over to Naomi, the one person she knew who would offer up a precise and sensible answer.

Naomi sipped her wine and said, "When Dimples asks? Tell her you gave her father ten thousand dollars for a medical bill and haven't heard from him since. He left two weeks ago and snuck back into town so she doesn't even know he was here. Tell her that—and I'm sure you'll learn more about this man that you're feeling so sorry for," she declared, leaving Mary to marinate in her thoughts as she set about warming up some leftovers.

****

Back near the stockyards, Flacco was powering up a chainsaw inside the family's slaughterhouse. He and Siloam had dragged Reynard's corpse into the medium-sized wooden structure and laid him atop a large sheet of plastic poly wrap. The walls inside the slaughterhouse had been lined with plastic as well, and the steel cutting table in the room's center had a large black tarp covering the table saws. Siloam offered to stay, but Flacco sent her on her way.

Flacco was wearing a leather apron caked in flesh and goggles specked with droplets of blood. The plastic covering the floor was filled with body parts belonging to Reynard Jacobs that were no bigger than a foot in length. A wheelbarrow was filled with some of his remains and Flacco wheeled them down to Moses' pen.

The wild hog could be heard grunting by Flacco as he neared the animal. A section of the wooden fence poked out as the hog rammed his head repeatedly against the barrier. Flacco threw what body parts he had inside the wheelbarrow over the fence and returned to the slaughterhouse for a second load. A third load was given to the hog, and this time, Flacco climbed up onto the fence and shined a flashlight down into Moses' pen to check for remnants. The snow was red in some areas, but Flacco had a cure for that; he watched as the hog used his snout to roll around Reynard's skull, trying to grasp it in his mouth. After several failed attempts to eat the awkward meal, Moses began trampling the lumpy, meaty object into a mush that was more easily consumable.

Flacco stood on the fence stone-faced as he watched the hog gulp down brain matter, eye sockets and teeth. Nothing was left of Reynard, save for the blood and some flesh on the snow-covered ground some fifty minutes later. He was prepared to jump down from the fence and power up the generator that powered the one of the disinfectant tanks that was nearby Moses' pen. The hog's loud squealing kept him in place, however; Flacco had never really dealt with Moses. For all he knew, the animal was no more than a living garbage disposal. Naomi was the one who'd told him about the animal and what to do with Reynard's remains, but he hadn't a clue as to what he was about to witness.

Flacco watched as Moses blew mucous from his nostrils. A gurgling sound was then heard, but it wasn't coming from the hog's mouth. Flacco leaned over the fence and could see a waterfall of manure spilling from Moses' rear end. He looked on in silence as the animal let out what seemed like gallons of feces before he dropped flat on his stomach and rolled over onto his back, withering around happily in the dung of the human he'd unknowingly ate until his belly was full.

Flacco pulled down on his cowboy hat and choked back bile in silence. It was the grossest thing he'd ever witnessed—a human being eaten by a hog, only to be defecated right back out and have the animal cover its body in its own excrement. "Couldn't have happened to a better man," he spoke lowly as he jumped down from the fence and powered up the disinfectant hose, where he washed Moses and the entire pen free of blood, manure and flesh.

The liquid flowed downhill into a large hog waste receptacle tank situated underground at the base of the hill. Although foul-smelling, the pig sty was in complete compliance with government regulations, which stipulated that all animal waste had to be contained to prevent groundwater contamination. What was left of Reynard Jacobs, now lay inside a steel tank filled with hog manure that was scheduled to be pumped out in under a week's time. And if the law had even the slightest inkling of what had happened to the man, there was no DNA left behind on the ranch to lead to suspicion of murder, let alone prove it.

Reynard Jacobs was a man that had becomne consumed by greed, envy and lust to the point in which he was willing to kill the mother of his only living daughter by Mary Holland in order to collect on a $500,000 dollar life insurance policy. His fantasy of murdering an innocent woman and running off with another woman nearly the same age as his daughter had been all but thwarted; he would simply vanish into thin air and become part of Holland folklore for all times.

CHAPTER THIRTY-EIGHT

SAVE MY SISTER

January 17, 2009

"I see your li'l fifty thousand dollar raise and raise you another fifty thousand dollars! What's happenin'?" Udelle said as he threw five twenty-thousand dollar poker chips into the center of the poker table.

It was a clear, but cold Saturday night, the day after Siloam had killed Reynard. Udelle, Koko and Kimi were setting up for a poker game. The trio had mixed drinks flowing, a large pot of beef chili and tortilla chips, melted cheese and taco salad on hand to eat and the Colts and Ravens playoff game was playing in the background. A box of cigars was on hand as well. It was a Vegas feel inside Bay's playroom down in Oklahoma City. Although playing with authentic casino chips, neither of the three had real money to bet; they were actually setting up for a $1,000 dollar winner take all tournament while waiting on Walee, and his crew to make it over so the festivities could begin.

"You called Walee, Koko?" Kimi asked as she scooped up some chili with a tortilla chip and folded her cards.

"He had to stop at the liquor store so Jordan could get some more tequila." Kimi replied. "He should be here in a little bit."

Koko folded her hand as well and stood up from her seat. "Let's sort out the chips for everybody so we can get straight to it when they get here. Everybody get twenty-five thousand worth of chips."

While Kimi, Koko and Udelle were setting up for the game, out on the streets of Oklahoma City, Walee and company had just pulled up to a liquor store near downtown. "Get that uh, get that Patrón, ya' dig? Big bottle," Walee told Jordan. "Spoonie? Tyke? Watch y'all drinkin' tonight?"

"Gatorade!" the twins stated in unison as they laughed at their brother's remark.

Spoonie and Tyke were more than overjoyed on this night. For the past couple of weeks they'd been trying to hang out with Walee. They would see him around campus, but that was about all. After classes, the two had softball practice indoors then studies inside their on-campus dorm. The one day a week and weekends when they free, they sought out Walee, who usually had a quick meal with them as he was busy with not only classes, but something more important in the filming of his *What's Good in the Hood* series.

Walee didn't want Spoonie and Tyke hanging nowhere near him when he and Kahlil were filming. The twins knew what their brother was into, but they didn't care. All they wanted to do was be up under Walee. The youngest of Naomi's eight had been their younger brother's shadow since the day they'd started walking and wouldn't have had it any other way.

Times had changed, however; Walee was no longer the prank-pulling, instigator of mischief he once was as a mere boy. Naked women and fast money through the selling of sex videos had taken center stage of his life and Spoonie and Tyke knew it all-too-well. They stayed away from their brother whenever he was conducting business so a night like tonight, one in which they were afforded the time to spend the entire day with Walee, was deeply cherished.

Walee and Kahlil exited his burnt orange Dodge Charger and Spoonie and Tyke followed. The eighteen year-old could only chuckle to himself; every move he'd made throughout the day, either Spoonie or Tyke, or sometimes both, was on his heels. The twins leaned against the car just out of ear shot of Walee as he talked to Kahlil in the sparsely-filled parking lot. "I ain't won't say nothing in front of my sisters, homeboy, but Anquette got a couple of chicks off the Cowboy campus that wanna get down with you on camera."

"For real?" Kahlil asked as he looked over to Walee. "I don't know about that, fam," he said as he rubbed his chin and looked to the snow-covered ground in deep thought.

"I already know, dude. You got your football career to worry about, ya' dig? I cancelled that there, but they still wanna get down," Walee replied casually. "They bad, man. Couple of white girls from Texas."

"Shiddd, run that, fam. When they wanna hook up?"

"I told 'em tomorrow night since we got late classes on Monday, ya' feel? And while we makin' it do what it do, we can try and get 'em to get down with Anquette and Jordan on camera."

"Cool. Cool," Kahlil answered as he tucked his hands inside his leather, hooded jacket. "Cold than a mutherfucka out here. Spoonie and Tyke? Why y'all out her being nosey?" he chided.

"We stretching!" Tyke responded as she looked around. "Hey, while Jordan in the store me and Spoonie gone run to that gas station and grab us some Gatorade."

"Hurry back!" Walee yelled as he watched his sisters running off to the gas station, which sat the next parking lot over.

****

While Walee and company were purchasing drinks, Mary and Dimples were over in a part of the city known as Bricktown, looking over menus as they sat inside Mickey Mantle's Steakhouse discussing their plans for the following day. Mary had just hung up with Naomi, who was back in Ponca City enjoying some time alone inside Ponderosa as she sipped wine and looked at homes for sale down in Oklahoma City.

After getting Mary to calm down over Reynard's murder, Naomi had given her an assignment: that of purchasing of another mansion for the family. It was her way of asking for

473

forgiveness from Mary, who'd come to understand her sister's reasoning, and somewhat condoning it to an extent given Reynard's plans. Although the hideous act perpetrated against him still weighed on her, Mary felt little concern for Reynard. Her key anxiety was that of Dimples, who had no clue her father was dead nor was she aware of the fact that Siloam and Takoda were behind it and had had an affair. There were some dark secrets Mary was holding on to for family's sake. Getting away from Ponca City did her some good, but on this night, Mary was about to have her resolve tested.

"Momma, you heard anything from my daddy," Dimples asked as she scanned the menu.

Mary resumed reading the menu and said, "Ever since I gave him ten thousand dollars to pay what he told me was a medical bill a couple of weeks ago I haven't heard a thing, Regina. I wouldn't be surprised if I never hear from him again. It was the first time I'd given him money. Seems as if that's what he was after all along."

"He took money from me, too, momma," Dimples admitted as she scanned the menu while shaking her head.

Mary looked up at that moment. "When was this?" she asked curiously, recalling Naomi's words..."*Tell her that—and I'm sure you'll learn more about this man that you're feeling so sorry for.*"

"During the summer. He told me he needed ten thousand dollars to pay off some debt. I been knew about his gambling, but I thought I could help him. That's why I never said anything."

"You know," Mary said as she set her menu aside. "When your father first returned? I was so upset with you for doing what you did. But then I realized it wasn't my decision to make. I, like yourself, had to accept the man for what he was and take him at face value."

"He seemed so sincere, momma," Dimples replied as she laid her menu flat on the table. "There were signs, though. He used to get online at our house and check results for all kinds of sporting events—horse racing, NBA and NFL playoff games, soccer, whatever big game or event was current he had to know the score."

"Sometimes we get so blinded by a person because our heart wants what it wants, Dimples. It wants to believe. It wants to love. It hopes and holds onto a certain kind of faith that we ourselves don't understand at times because it wants to love a certain someone so badly."

"I hoped for my father to be sincere, but deep inside I always had this lingering doubt that he was hiding something. Like he wasn't being honest all the time and had ulterior motives."

"If you were to see your father again, what would you do or say, Regina?" Mary asked as she picked up a glass of ice water and took a sip.

Dimples' eyes watered at that moment. "I still love him, momma," she admitted. "As dishonest as he was? I'm not mad at him. He had a disease that's all."

Mary wanted so badly to tell her daughter the truth about Reynard. The man didn't have a disease in her eyes. He was nothing more than a con artist looking for an easy pay day to support his lifestyle and it didn't matter to what or at whose expense the succeeding of his plans came to fruition. On top of that, he'd gone so far as to try and kill her for monetary gain. Had Siloam been sincere in her endeavors with Reynard, Mary knew she would've been killed the night before. She'd started fifty-fifty on her feelings towards what Naomi had done, but she was now resolved to the fact that Reynard, plain and simple, had it coming because of his treachery. The conversation she'd just had with her daughter had basically sealed the deal for Mary and let it be known that Naomi was right all along.

"You're right, Dimples," Mary said seriously, withholding the truth from her daughter concerning her father. "You've enjoyed two plus years with Reynard. And if he returns and welcoming him is the thing you want to do? Then you have my support, baby."

Dimples looked over to her mother and smiled. "Thanks for understanding a daughter's love towards her father," she said through heartfelt conviction.

"Umm, hmm," Mary replied as she sipped her water as she looked off into nowhere particular.

Dimples couldn't see it because her mother was sipping her drink at the time, but Mary was actually smiling while she sipped. She knew Reynard was never coming back. Her daughter may have still been carrying a hopeful heart, but Mary carried the truth. And the truth was, Reynard Jacobs had gotten exactly what he deserved in her mind's eye. A waiter came over to the table several seconds later and mother and daughter began asking questions concerning the ordering of their entrees, basically casting Reynard off to the annals of history and going on with their lives.

****

"What time you got, Chauncey?" Tonto asked cooly as he sat behind the wheel of his S-class alabaster white four door Mercedes.

"Eight fifty-five, dude. Five before nine." Chauncey said before downing a cup of cognac and pulling down on his black toboggan.

"Cool. Now what you gone do is go up there and knock on that door. Time it open, me and Chauncey rushing in," Tonto told Chablis as he looked back at him before placing the car in drive.

For the past week or so, Tonto and his crew had been watching the condo inside the complex where Bay's condo lay. Chablis had pointed the place out the day Koko had stood him up and had never bothered calling, an act which left her under the impression that he'd went on with his life after she'd left him standing outside of the Couch Restaurants.

Most days, the house was filled with family. Tonto knew everybody that went to and from the house being that he himself was from Ponca City and grew up around the family. Martha and Twiggy had been there, Dawk, Bay and T-top had spent nights and Naomi had spent several days inside the condo. There was always heavy traffic, but on this night, the trio knew none of the family was around except for Kimi, Koko and Udelle. They'd been scoping the place something fierce the entire day, and the only ones who'd emerged was Udelle, Koko and Kimi, who'd gone to the store earlier and returned with a few bags of groceries.

"What if they don't open the door?" Chablis asked nervously as he placed a ski mask onto his head and rolled it up.

"We kick that bad boy down," Chauncey said as he tied a bandanna around his lower face.

"You heard the man," Tonto said as he brought the car to a halt just down from Bay's condo where the three exited the car.

Back inside the unit, Udelle, Kimi and Koko were still setting up the poker table when the doorbell rang. "Udelle, let Walee and 'nem in, baby," Kimi remarked.

Udelle downed the remainder of his margarita and set the glass down. "Don't short me on my chips," he joked.

"Boy, you could have twice as many chips and we'll still beat you out," Koko laughed.

"We gone see about that, sister-in-law," Udelle quipped as he left the room.

Back outside, Chablis could hear someone approaching. He pulled down his ski mask and bowed his head as locks on the door began to rattle.

Udelle, under the impression that it was Walee and his bunch, never even bothered checking the peep hole before pulling the door open. He was stunned when the door was shoved open completely as three men in ski masks rushed in toting handguns.

"The fuck y'all doing?" Udelle screamed aloud.

Tonto wasted no time. He grabbed Udelle around the rim of his t-shirt and hit him over the head with his .44 automatic, sending him to the floor where he lay knocked out cold with blood spurting from the left side of forehead just above the left eye.

Kimi and Koko heard Udelle scream. They thought it was

Walee fooling around so they both trotted out of the room with smiles on their faces. "You got the tequila, Walee?" Kimi asked as she led the way up the hall.

When Kimi entered the living room and looked to her right, she saw three men creeping past the kitchen. "Koko, run!" she screamed aloud as she turned and shoved her twin back down the hall. Kimi didn't know where Koko's mind was, but she was going for a .45 caliber Bay had stashed in her closet.

Koko, however, was terrified. Even through the masks and handkerchief she knew one of the men chasing her and Kimi was Chablis. She was deathly afraid of her ex-boyfriend and actually thought he was there to kill her. Fearing for her and Kimi's lives, she, too, remembered the gun in Bay's closet. Both twins were just outside of the bedroom when they were snatched up from behind by Chablis and Chauncey. They were grabbed by their necks and dragged back into the living room where they were shoved down flat on their stomachs.

"Don't kill us!" Koko begged.

"None of that screaming," Chauncey said nonchalantly as he stood behind the twins and pulled out a black. 44 handgun and racked it. "Which one of y'all Kimi?" he asked as he aimed the gun at the backs of the twins as they lay face down on the wooden floor.

"Please, don't do this! Take whatever you want!" Kimi cried lowly.

Chablis knew right then and there that Chauncey was going to kill Kimi. To slow him down, he picked Koko up and stood over her twin. "This just supposed to be a kidnapping. I'm not agreeing to anything else. You shoot Kimi you gone have to shoot to me," he told Chauncey.

"The fuck you care?" Chauncey scoffed through his handkerchief as he eyed Chablis coldly.

"You kill her you think the police not gone get involved? The shit ain't necessary."

Tonto, having searched the home briefly, walked back into the living room at that moment. He eyed Chablis holding on to

Koko. "I thought y'all woulda had the bitch in the car by now. Let's be out," he remarked as he headed for the front door.

"Tonto, don't do this!" Kimi pleaded as she lay on her stomach. "Chablis?" she called out.

"Stay put for me, Kimi," Tonto turned and remarked as he eyed Kimi lying on her stomach. "You move or call the police we gone have to kill Koko. This only a kidnap, don't make it a homicide."

Koko was so terrified she couldn't utter a sound while being led out of her home.

"Just be calm," Chablis whispered into her ear.

"Shut up and get on out the door!" Chauncey snapped as he shoved Chablis and Koko forward. "Ole save-a-hoe ass boy!"

"Mister, no!" Koko managed to beg through her tears as Chauncey shoved out into the cold darkness.

Chauncey batted Koko across the back of her head with his freehand and shoved her harder, nearly knocking her free of Chablis' grip. "I said move! And shut the fuck up!" he hissed as he planted his gun to Koko's back.

Chablis rushed Koko back to Tonto's Mercedes under the darkness of night. He was about to climb into the backseat himself, but Chauncey stopped him. "Get in the front! I got her," he spoke lowly as he climbed into the car and pulled a struggling Koko inside.

Chablis was covering Koko's mouth to keep from screaming. She was struggling to get free until Tonto punched her in the side, knocking the wind from her momentarily as he pushed her into the backseat of his Mercedes and closed the door. "Get in the front so we can stab out and make the call, homie," he told Chablis as he hopped behind the steering wheel.

Chablis ran around the rear of the Benz and hopped into the front passenger seat just as Tonto was pulling off.

Back inside the condo, Kimi had hopped up the time Koko's kidnappers had left the home. She'd run into Bay's room and grabbed the .45 caliber off the shelf, racked it and took off running towards the poker room where she grabbed her cell phone and headed for the front door. Running past an unconscious Udelle, she stepped out into the cold night's air in time to see the taillights of a car heading up the block. She quickly recognized Tonto's Mercedes and ran back into the home and grabbed the car keys to the Maserati. "Somebody call nine-one-one! My sister been kidnapped! Help me! Call nine-one-one!" she screamed aloud as she ran towards her and Koko's ride and jumped behind the wheel.

Kimi was scared out of her mind over the thought of losing Koko. She was also enraged at Chablis for helping Tonto get her sister kidnapped. She backed the car out of the driveway and peeled out behind her sister and her captors while dialing 911.

Not even two miles way, Walee had just entered the large condominium complex when he received a text from Anquette. *Pick me up before you go around the corner. I made some couscous for Spoonie and Tyke!*

Your ass can't cook! LOL! Walee shot back.

Whatever man come get me frfr

I'm pulling up now. Come on out.

Back inside Tonto's Benz, Chablis, still wearing his ski mask, listened to the pitiful pleas of a terrified Koko as Tonto wheeled his ride to the front of the complex. He was wondering how he'd ever allowed Tonto and Chauncey to manipulate him into this ultimate act of betrayal. Koko could've easily let Dawk know what he'd been doing and had him harmed or worse, but she'd forgiven him because she really did love him, even if she wanted to no longer be his woman.

"I'm not gone say nothing! Just let me go! Don't do this! Please!" Koko pleaded as the car eased through the complex.

Hearing his former lover plead had softened Chablis' resolve. Even if he was mad at Walee for putting a bounty on him, he now realized, as Doctor Duchene had told him when she'd read him his rights, that he deserved everything he'd received. Kidnapping Koko had only compounded his problems, and the chance of her ever loving him again had been all but ruined. On top of that, there was no guarantee that Tonto and Chauncey wouldn't just do him and Koko in if and when the $500,000 dollar ransom they were going to seek was ever paid.

Chablis had no loyalty to the two men he was riding with; all-of-a-sudden, everything about this night was wrong—sinister in fact. He no longer wanted a part of the matter at hand. What to do now was the question he now found himself asking in silence as the car neared an intersection.

Walee had just pulled up to his condo and was climbing out his ride when a car rounded the corner. He wasn't paying the approaching vehicle any mind until he recognized it as being that of Tonto's. "Fuck that boy doing back here?" he asked himself lowly as he stood at the front of his Dodge Charger eyeing Tonto's ride.

Back inside the Benz, everybody inside had spotted Walee. "Everybody just be cool, we gone roll by like ain't nothing happenin'. He can't see behind the tint." Tonto schemed as he watched the rear driver's side door open on Walee's Dodge Charger.

Koko started pounding on the driver's side rear window and yelling Walee's name aloud at that moment. "Walee, they takin' me! They takin' me! Walee, this Koko! This—"

Chauncey scrambled and wrapped his hand around Koko's mouth to muffle her cries for help. Through the brief seconds of distraction, Chablis took advantage. He lunged out in between the front seats and grabbed Chauncey's gun, pinning the pistol to the seat in between his legs. "Koko, open the door and fall out, baby! Run, Koko! Koko, run!" he screamed as he and Chauncey began struggling over the pistol.

Walee was still trying to figure out what Tonto's car was doing in the neighborhood when the back door flew open. At the same time, Spoonie had just hopped out the car. She and Walee both heard Koko yell aloud, "Walee, help me!" as she rolled out of the car.

The rear wheel of Tonto's Benz rolled over Koko's left foot and she let go of a blood-curdling scream.

Just then, Kimi rounded the corner in the Maserati. When she spotted Koko lying on the ground clutching her foot and screaming aloud in agony, she slammed the car in park in the middle of the street and hopped out. "Koko, you, okay? Walee, Tonto tried to Kidnap Koko just now!" she yelled as she ran and knelt down beside her screaming twin.

Chauncey was still struggling with Chablis inside the Benz. Because of his awkward positioning, Chablis was at a disadvantage. Chauncey was able to get the better of the weapon after several seconds that seemed to last an eternity. He turned the barrel upwards and pumped two slugs into Chablis' chest before aiming his weapon out the back door.

Tonto's Benz was passing the front end of Walee's car when Chauncey began shooting. "The fuck you doing?" Tonto asked hysterically over the thunderous gunshots as he sped up.

Walee dropped to one knee, and Kimi was shielding Koko. As gunshots continued ringing out into the night, Kahlil emerged from the passenger side of the Charger with a tech nine and opened fire on his brother's car as he sped by.

Tonto sped away from the scene with the back driver's side door of his Benz wide open. The car spun out of control, running over a mailbox before returning to the road where it rounded the corner and hurried out of the complex.

"You all right, Koko?" Walee asked as he ran towards his sister. "Where everybody else at? Everybody okay?" he then asked aloud.

"Dog!" Kahlil called out as he rounded the front side of Walee's car.

Walee looked back at Kahlil and his eyes focused in something he'd never even imagined. He was frozen stiff with shock.

Kimi was still tending to Koko at the time. "You all right, Koko?" she asked as she removed her twin's hands and eyed her foot.

"I'm okay, Kimi! I'm okay! I think it's a fractured foot," Koko hissed as she laid her back onto the concrete. "We gotta go help Udelle."

"On my daddy no!" Koko and Kimi heard Walee cry aloud.

The way their brother screamed reminded both twins of the day they'd loss their father. Slowly, they looked over in Walee's direction. What they both witnessed left them horrified. There, in the middle of the street, stood Spoonie. She was gagging and spitting up blood as she hobbled around in a daze.

"Is Koko all right? What happened, y'all?" Spoonie asked weakly as she let the Gatorade she was sipping on slip from her hands. "Walee?" she cried softly as she fell up against the hood of the Charger, trying desperately to catch her breath and balance herself. "What happened?" she asked again as she began to fall to the concrete.

Walee's entire body grew numb. He stood in a state of shock, watching through a fog as Kahlil ran and caught Spoonie before she fell face first onto the cold concrete.

Kimi left Koko behind and ran to her sister's side and knelt down. Kahlil rose at that moment, his shirt covered in blood.

"She not breathing, Kimi!" Kahlil cried aloud as he began pumping Spoonie's chest. "Come on, Shima!" he pleaded as he pumped several more times as tears ran down his face. "No, man!" he pleaded. "One time, God! Just one time, Man! I'm gone do right I promise! I promise on all I love!" he prayed aloud as he continued pumping Spoonie's chest.

Anquette ran out of Walee's condo at that moment. "Everybody all right? Oh my God!" The twenty-one year-old gasped when she saw Spoonie lying before Walee's car with Kahlil leaning over her giving her CPR.

"We gotta go!" Kahlil snapped as he lifted Spoonie's head, noticing she'd parted her lips slightly. Blood and small bits of flesh spilled forth from her slightly-opened mouth as she lay with her eyes closed. "We gotta go! Help me get her in the car!"

Walee said nothing as he knelt down beside Spoonie and stared at his sister, who lay motionless with her eyes closed.

"She hurt bad, fam!" Kahlil cried aloud. "We only four miles from the hospital!"

Koko had managed to crawl over to her siblings and their friends at that moment. "Is she dead? Nobody say nothing to me if she dead! Chablis, you mutherfuckin' bitch! You fuckin' bitch!" she scream aloud in anguish as she lay on her back slamming her fists against the concrete.

"Listen to Kahlil!" Tyke, who'd been hiding in the backseat the entire time said upon emerging from the car. Without giving it a second thought, she ran and grabbed her sister's legs. "Shima, hold on we takin' you to a doctor!" she cried through her tears.

"Y'all go ahead, Walee!" Kimi yelled. "Go ahead!"

Walee, Kahlil and Tyke carried Spoonie to the Charger while Kimi, Jordan and Anquette assisted Koko to the ride. Once Spoonie and Koko were placed into the car, Walee climbed behind the wheel with Kahlil and Tyke and sped off, leaving Kimi, Jordan and Anquette behind.

"We gotta go help Udelle and get to Spoonie!" Kimi told Anquette and Jordan as she ran back to the Maserati. Kimi turned the car around the time Jordan and Anquette climbed inside and she sped back to Bay's condo while dialing her mother's number.

CHAPTER THIRTY-NINE

FOURTEEN HANDS

Naomi was walking up the grand staircase in Ponderosa with a glass of wine, preparing to turn in for the night inside her suite and read a novel when her cell phone rang. She answered and heard nothing but chaos coming from Kimi. "Calm down, Kimi! I can't, I can't understand you."

There was a mass amount of screaming and wind blowing into the phone, but Naomi thought she'd heard the words 'Shima' and 'shot.'

"What did you say?" Naomi asked as her heart rate accelerated.

"Momma! Momma, where you at?" Naomi heard Tiva screaming aloud.

"The house phone rang at that moment. Several seconds later, Naomi heard Martha scream aloud from the Great Room, "Lord, somebody done shot Spoonie!"

Naomi dropped the phone and the wine she was holding onto and her face contorted. "Not one of my angels," she spoke though a whisper while shaking her head in disbelief. "Not my blameless child, God!" she declared.

Tiva ran up the stairs at that moment with a .226 semi-automatic rifle in her hand. "Spoonie got shot in Bay complex, momma! We gotta go! We gotta go!" she stated frantically as she hurried up the stairs. "I'm going get Malaysia and Malara coats!"

Francine was donning her trench coat when she rounded the bend leading to the stairs with Malaysia and Malara in tow. She saw Naomi on her knees on the stairs' mid drift and her heart went out to the woman that had become a daughter to her years ago. "It's gonna be okay, Naomi," she comforted as she climbed the stairs.

"When Kevin and Serena died I asked God why He allowed that to happen," Naomi stated. "This time, I refuse to ask why —because God couldn't that cruel of a person."

Francine looked Naomi in the eyes. "This is not of God's doing, Naomi," she stated lovingly. "Spoonie's gonna be okay. Let's go. I'm sure she's waiting to see you," she ended as she helped Naomi up from the floor and returned to the twins at the foot of the stairs.

Tiva, Martha and Irene rushed back down the staircase just then.

"Who did it?" Naomi asked Martha as she was handed her coat.

"Walee said it was Tonto Jamison and another guy."

"Koko's ex," Naomi said in a drab tone of voice. "I'm not going to ask for forgiveness for what I want to happen to Tonto and his associate," she stated coldly as her eyes flooded with tears of anger.

"They tried to kidnap Koko. She has a fractured foot," Tiva said as she placed coats and hats on her daughters.

With little of nothing, Naomi, Francine, Martha, Twiggy and Tiva, with the baby twins in tow, hurried out of Ponderosa, jumped in two of the family's Suburbans and headed down to Oklahoma City.

****

"How was Vegas, baby?" Oneika asked Dawk as the two sat inside Oneika's parents' home enjoying dinner with her parents. She was all smiles as she looked at her brand new two and a half karat diamond engagement ring.

"Vegas was cool. Played a li'l poker and what not. Nothing major. I picked up the ring while I was out there."

"Kimi 'nem was playing poker tonight. We shoulda went down there. I can't wait until we tell your family," Oneika remarked happily as she scooped green beans onto Dawk's plate.

"We'll catch 'em next time."

"They don't play often do they?" Oneika's father asked as he passed a plate of bar-b-cue brisket to his wife. "If ever you guys get another chance be sure and let an old man know. I'd love to play."

"Tell, you what, Mister Brackens? After Oneika have you and Misses Brackens' grandchild? We'll take a trip to Vegas and play at a real table in a real game. I know a private room where we can play."

"When's the wedding?" Oneika's mother inquired.

"Kimi and Udelle getting married at the end of the year. She wanna have her ceremony on an island in the Pacific."

"I really don't want anything that extravagant," Oneika remarked. "A late spring wedding on the ranch would is something I've always dreamed."

"Let's make it happen," Dawk remarked as he leaned over and kissed Oneika's lips."

"I love you," Oneika professed lovingly as she leaned over and kissed Dawk's cheek.

Just then, Dawk's phone vibrated. He pulled it out and recognized Bay's number and answered. "Yo?"

"Where you at?" Bay asked calmly as AquaNina placed a trench coat onto her trembling body. She stood shaking in the darkened foyer with a face full of tears, staring blankly at the front door of her condo while preparing to head down to Oklahoma City.

"I'm having dinner with my future wife and in-laws. How you makin' out?" Dawk asked as he chuckled, believing Bay and AquaNina were arguing again and she needed to vent.

487

"Dawk," Bay said sniffling her nose. "I just talked to Jordan. She just told me Spoonie got shot tonight."

Dawk wasn't sure he'd heard Bay right. "Say again?"

"You heard me right." Bay responded as she sniffled once more and wiped tears from her eyes. "Spoonie got shot, Dawk."

"Where? Who did it? She alive?"

"She hurt bad, man. Me and 'Nina on our way to OU Hospital."

"I'm right behind you!" Dawk said as he jumped up from the table amid a stunned Oneika and her parents.

"Dawk," Bay called out over the phone.

"What, Bay? I'm on my down there right now!"

"I know. You asked who did it. It was Tonto. Him and some other dude set Koko up to get kidnapped. "Shit went bad. Koko got away. They started shooting all wild and hit Shima."

"We talk about it when I get down there," Dawk replied matter-of-factly before ending the call.

"Is everything all right, Dawk?" Oneika inquired.

Neither of the Brackens family members had ever seen Dawk so flustered. Oneika swore she saw tears, but even if that was not the case, she knew something terrible had gone down. "Dawk," she said lowly as she got up and followed her man around the table.

"Are you okay, son?" Mister Brackens asked as he himself stood up and followed Dawk through the home.

"I'm good!" Dawk grimaced as he snatched his suit jacket off the coat hanger in the foyer.

"Dawk, tell me what's wrong!" Oneika pleaded as she grabbed her fur coat. "Where're you going, baby? What happened?"

Dawk paused at the front door. "Shima was shot down in Oklahoma City. She hurt pretty bad."

Oneika gasped. "We have to get down there! Momma, Dawk's sister Spoonie was shot tonight!"

"Dear God. We, we have to get you down there," Mister Brackens stated. "Honey, grab your coat. I'll make sure everything is secure in the home."

"I can handle it, everybody." Dawk stated as he pulled the door open. *"I'm gone kill 'em,"* he thought to himself in reference to Tonto.

"Dawk," Oneika spoke softly as she gently closed the door. "We're not going to let you drive down there by yourself under these circumstances. We're coming, baby. Let's just, give us a few seconds to get our things."

Dawk looked down at Oneika and thanked her softly. "Somebody hurt my baby."

"It'll be okay, Dawk. I'm asking God as we speak," Oneika responded lovingly just as her parents rushed back into the living room while donning coats, scarfs and hats.

Together, Dawk and his future in-laws left the Brackens' home with Mister Brackens behind the wheel of the family's Cadillac STS. Dawk was enraged on the inside. He refused to call anyone, except for Ben. After a brief conversation, he clicked off his cell phone as he didn't want to know Shima's fate until he reached the hospital. Silently, he was preparing for the worse, all-the-while silently praying for the best as he sat beside a crying Oneika.

****

"Oooh, you good-dick man you!" Sharona Benson moaned as she lay with her face planted to DeeDee's mattress inside his Chicago condo on Lake Shore Drive while thrusting her ass back and squeezing her vaginal muscles. The forty year-old woman was milking her man and herself to climax as the two rocked in unison.

DeeDee had the classic hump in his back as he gripped Sharona's hips and drove deep inside, squeezing his ass cheeks tight to pump his long, veiny organ. "Give me this pussy, woman," he grunted.

"I feel that shit!" Sharona moaned. "Yes, daddy! Fuck it! Fuck your pussy like you mean it, Doss!"

DeeDee's phone rung, but he didn't bother answering as he was busy with his head thrown back, his eyes closed with his mouth agape and his dick deep off in some tantalizing pussy. It was hades hot inside the bedroom suite as the two lovers rocked in unison, their bodies covered in sweat, champagne glasses half full on the night stand with Stevie Wonder's song *Knocks Me off My Feet* playing low in the background.

"Doss," Sharona groaned in a hoarse voice as she dropped her mouth open and rose up on all fours. "I can't, I can't take no more, baby!"

DeeDee slammed deep into Sharona and she gripped the silk sheets tightly, nearly breaking her manicured nails. Both lovers soon exhaled as DeeDee slid out, leaving just the tip inside as he tickled Sharona's outer lips. "Don't run from the sensation, now," he said as he shifted onto one knee and continued massaging Sharona's clitoris with the head of his dick.

"Too much!" Sharona cried aloud as she slammed back and climaxed all over her lover's stiff rod.

DeeDee, at the same time, spread Sharona's ass cheeks and filled her with a load that began to drip down her inner thighs. The two collapsed onto the bed panting heavily as DeeDee's home phone rang.

"That was amazing," Sharona stated through heavy panting as she lay flat on her stomach beneath DeeDee.

DeeDee eased off Sharona and answered his ringing home phone. "Yeah? Doss here," he stated while breathing hard.

Sharona was lying on her side smiling over to DeeDee as she stroked his arm tenderly. When he stood up and said, "Tell me this isn't happenin'!" she sat up.

"Is everything okay, Doss?"

DeeDee shushed Sharona and returned to the call. "No. Everything is okay here, Irene. That was the TV. I'm, I'll be there on the first available flight. Let the family know for me, please," he stated before ending the call.

"Are you okay, Doss?"

"My niece, Spoonie," DeeDee said in disbelief as he looked over his shoulder towards Sharona while standing naked. "She, she was shot tonight down in Oklahoma City."

"Oh no," Sharona sighed somberly.

"We have to get there." DeeDee said as he began gathering under clothes to take a shower.

"We?" Sharona asked curiously.

"Yes. We were going to introduce little Doss to the family, remember?"

"I know, but, under these circumstances, Doss?"

"The family will be all together. They may need some uplifting, good news if Spoonie were to..." DeeDee's voice trailed off as his eyes watered. "Not my grandchild. My *innocent* grandchild," he cried as he bit his bottom lip and walked into the bathroom. "Get yourself and my boy ready, Sharona!" he snapped as he walked into his bathroom and slammed the door shut.

****

"For real, though, momma," Dimples laughed as she and her mother enjoyed their stuffed pork chops and crab legs as they sat inside Mickey Mantle's Steakhouse in downtown Oklahoma City. "Tacoma be like, 'well, if Jesus is God's son, then who God daddy? Like, Jesus got a grandpa, right, momma?'"

"That is something problematic for some adults to comprehend let alone a child, Regina." Mary chuckled as she used a fork to scoop up some of her baked potato inside the crowded restaurant.

"Tell me about it. Tak asked the same thing a while back," Dimples laughed. "But he gets it. I tell Tacoma, I say, 'son, God is the beginning and the end. He always was and always will be. He had no start.'"

"What he do?"

"He runs his hands over his face and say, 'Everything has a beginning and will have an ending. How God pull that off? What's His secret?'"

"Then you're stumped because only He and Jesus knows that secret." Mary replied as her phone vibrated across the table. She checked her watch and saw that it was nine 'o' clock. "Naomi must be calling to say good night," she told Dimples as she answered the phone. "Yes, Naomi?"

"Mary, where are you?" Naomi asked anxiously.

Mary could hear the distress in her sister's voice. "I'm, I'm downtown having dinner with Regina. Why?" she asked nervously as her nerves frayed.

"Sister, I need you to get over to OU Medical Center and head straight to the emergency room."

"For what?" Mary asked as she sighed. "Who's hurt, Naomi?"

Naomi placed a balled fist to her mouth and leaned forward. She was about to utter words she'd never imagined she would have to speak ever. "Spoonie was shot tonight, Mary," she said as she heaved and placed a hand to her forehead.

In a flash, the night she'd loss Ne`Ne` flooded Mary's mind. "Is she alive?" she asked as she stood up and grabbed her jacket and keys.

"Is who alive, momma?" Dimples asked puzzled.

"Walee driving her and Kahlil's giving CPR. Just get there, please. The rest of the family is enroute from Ponca City. Get to my baby, Mary. Please," Naomi pleaded softly.

"I'm on my way, Naomi! I'm on my way!" Mary reassured. She hung up the phone and sat back down briefly to regain her composure. The thought of losing Spoonie was too incomprehensible for all inside the family, but no one more than Mary, who'd been here before when she'd loss her own daughter. She began to cry aloud as she leapt from the booth and took off running through the crowded restaurant, knocking over a couple of trays of food being carried by two waiters.

Dimples took off after her mother, screaming aloud and repeatedly asking her what was wrong as scores of patrons inside the restaurant looked on stunned silence. "Shima's been shot!" Mary yelled as she looked back at Dimples briefly. Another waiter was knocked down as Mary neared the front door.

"It's a family emergency! My cousin's been shot!" Dimples told a couple of hostesses as she ran out the door.

"You have a tab, ma'am!" one of the hostesses yelled aloud unconcerned.

Dimples let the door close behind her without responding as she and her mother ran towards the Suburban they were riding in. The manager had met the two as they passed the front of the restaurant. Mary was about to the run the guy over, but she caught herself. She slammed on the brakes and pulled a credit card from her purse as the manager scrambled around to the driver's side of the SUV. "Take it!" she screamed through her tears before she sped off.

It had taken all of three minutes for the entire family to come to learn of Spoonie's fate. Now, they were all converging on Oklahoma City from various parts of the city itself and across the country.

****

Back inside the complex, Kimi, Jordan and Anquette had helped Udelle into the Maserati and were speeding out of the units. Udelle was in the backseat leaning up against the back door with a towel of ice covering his busted forehead and could barely remain conscious as he groaned lowly.

Kimi rounded the corner and sped past Walee's condo, noticing the bottle of Gatorade Spoonie had dropped into the street and the bloodstain where she once lay. She rounded the curve leading out of the complex with a face full of tears. The Maserati bounced into the air two times on its right side just as she'd straightened the car out.

"That was a body in the road!" Anquette snapped as she looked out the Maserati's rear window.

Kimi stopped the car and climbed out with her .45 caliber and Jordan hopped out the passenger side with the tech nine Kahlil had used minutes earlier. The two ran to the rear of the car and saw a man lying in the middle of the street, his body twisted and his midsection crushed.

Kimi stepped closer and saw that it was Chablis. She'd run him over on her way out of the complex. Whether Chablis was alive or not before she'd run him over, Kimi didn't know, but from the guts and unrecognizable organs that were spilling from his mouth and the way his eyes had popped out his head, it was obvious that he was beyond help. She felt nothing for the guy as she and Jordan ran back to the Maserati where Kimi hopped behind the wheel and sped off again, neither she, Jordan or Anquette ever even bothering to dial 911 for Chablis.

****

Walee and company, meanwhile, had just pulled up to OU Medical Center. It took all of five minutes to make the drive to the trauma center. Doctors were aware of the situation via calls from Walee and they were waiting at the entrance. Before the car could even come to a halt, three surgeons, three nurses and three medical assistants were rolling a gurney out under the canopy.

Walee climbed from behind the wheel and leaned back against the car as he watched his sister being pulled from the backseat. He hadn't the strength to continue on.

Koko had turned and placed her wounded foot on the outside of the car. She was attempting to stand when she was assisted by a doctor. "You're the one with the fractured foot, ma'am?" the doctor asked as she knelt down and began inspecting the patient.

"Yes." Koko's eyes widened as she stared down at the woman, realizing she knew her personally. "Doctor Duchene! Go help my sister! I'm fine!" she declared just as Spoonie was placed onto the gurney.

"Your sister? What's her name?" Doctor Duchene asked as she looked back at the young girl who was having her clothes cut off while being wheeled into the trauma center.

"Shima Dawkins, but we call her Spoonie," Koko grimaced. "Please, Doctor Duchene," she cried through pleading eyes.

"Doctor?" This is a fractured foot! Switch with me and give me the lead!" Doctor Duchene ordered.

The undergrad ran over to Kimi as Doctor Duchene took off running behind her staff. Kahlil and Tyke were running behind the medical staff, both pleading for the doctors to save Spoonie's life. They were held back by a security team and could only watch through pitiful, worried eyes as Shima was carted through a set of double doors.

Doctor Duchene had a full view of the damage Koko's sister had sustained after all of her clothes had been removed. "Okay. Can someone give me a preliminary prognosis on Shima 'Spoonie' Dawkins?" she asked as she donned a pair of latex gloves while trotting beside the gurney.

"She's sustained a gunshot wound to the pelvis and another wound through the left side of the abdomen that exited the front right side!" the second surgeon remarked as he jogged beside the gurney while sliding a surgical mask onto his face.

"The through and through damaged her small intestine. Exit wound on the front right side ruptured her stomach," a third surgeon remarked calmly as she began setting up an IV for morphine.

The doors leading into a cold, sanitized room that had one long light resting over an operating table boomed opened as Spoonie was wheeled into the operating room with three surgeons, two medical assistants, a Registered Nurse and a surgeon's assistant.

It was organized chaos as Doctor Duchene led the way. She stared at the pristine table—that one, long, lonely bed that had been her and her rookie staff's stage for only a short period of time. She asked God to guide her and her staff's hands over the musical cacophony of medical terms that were being used by her inexperienced staff: "Duchene doesn't want the morphine until we get a second reading on her pressure!" "...sure the EKG monitor is set up so we can get a precise read on her heart rate." "...gauze pads and scissors for this surgical procedure on her pelvis and several change of clothes for everyone because this may take hours." "...with the right amount of electrical sockets for the monitors and defibrillators."

Amid the medical lingo, the gurney paused before the operating table and the two medical assistants lifted Spoonie, laid her down gently, and Doctor Duchene and her crew of six went to work.

Spoonie was hooked up to a heart monitor and right away Doctor Duchene saw just how weak the child was. "No morphine. We have to stop the bleeding and get her stabilized. The bullet in her pelvis is lodged in the bone and it's sticking out. Remove it, please, and staple it close after administering a local anesthetic. The through and through is where the real damage lies. She's suffering heavy internal bleeding," she spoke calmly as she numbed Spoonie's chest with an amphetamine topical. The doctor then grabbed a small saw and cut into Spoonie's chest, performing a thoracotomy. "We're going to need a bag valve mask and a thoracostomy tube because she's going to go into cardiac arrest soon after I cut her open," she stated serenely as she cut into Spoonie's chest in a relaxed manner.

"She didn't flinch when you cut her, Doctor Duchene," another surgeon stated.

"That's not a good sign. What's my EKG monitor saying? I can't hear anything, guys." Doctor Duchene stated calmly as she stuck two fingers from her left hand into the slit and pushed the skin back on Spoonie chest cavity, creating a two-inch circular opening.

The volume on the EKG monitor was turned up and all Doctor Duchene heard was a flat line. "Where's my thoracostomy tube, people? Did I not say she was going to go into cardiac arrest time I cut her open?"

The second surgeon grabbed an oxygen bag just as a thoracostomy tube was placed into Doctor Duchene's right hand. She gently inserted it into Spoonie's opening. "Okay. Give her the bag valve mask and administer oxygen," the good doctor requested as she looked over to the heart monitor and waited several seconds. "No response," she remarked lowly. "Shima Dawkins, I need you to fight with me, baby. I need your help, Spoonie. Spoonie?" Doctor Duchene called out again. The heart monitor beeped briefly but flat-lined after only several seconds.

"We're losing her," the second surgeon remarked calmly as she squeezed the oxygen bag covering Spoonie's mouth and nose harder and faster. "Come on, young sister. Fight with us," she remarked lowly as she continued pumping oxygen into Spoonie.

"Just keep bagging her, I'm clearing her cavity," Doctor Duchene stated calmly as blood and flesh began to flow through the thoracostomy tube she'd inserted into Spoonie's chest. "Her airway is clogged. It should be cleared momentarily."

What Doctor Duchene was doing at this moment was removing excess blood and flesh from Spoonie's chest cavity in order to prevent her from drowning in her own blood while pumping pure oxygen into her lungs at the same time. She and her medical staff, in effect, were using life-saving instruments to breathe on behalf of Spoonie and filter her body free of loose debris from the gunshot wound that had traveled through and through until they could stabilize the badly wounded seventeen year-old before operating further.

"Okay, she has a heartbeat," Doctor Duchene remarked lowly upon eyeing the heart monitor. "That's enough oxygen," she said as all movement ceased inside the operating room. "Come on, Spoonie. We need you to breathe on your own for just a few seconds."

As the medical staff went about their duties, for a second time, the heart monitor flat lined.

"Not again. Doctor Duchene?" the third surgeon asked anxiously through her mask as she eyed her from across the operating table.

"It's only momentarily, everybody," Doctor Duchene remarked calmly as she began counting backwards. "Ten... Nine...eight..."

Doctor Duchene and the rest of the medical staff held their positions. Seven pairs of eyes were on the heart monitor, and fourteen hands remained frozen for the moment, which seemed like an eternity as they hovered over Spoonie's wounded body. The long beep seemed to last an eternity as Doctor Duchene continued counting down…"…four…three…two…one…"

The heart monitor kicked up again and the choreographed medical symphony began once more as fourteen hands went to work in an all-out-attempt to save Spoonie's life.

"…opening a three inch slit on her left side." "Scissors!" "…stomach has a rupture on the back side." "…to remove most of the small intestine to get to the stomach wound." "…gauzes after I remove the bullet from the pelvis." "...readministering oxygen throughout the procedure."

"Shima, don't you stop fighting!" a woman's voice, that of Mary Holland, yelled aloud as she ran into the operating room while warding off two security guards.

"Get that woman out of here!" Doctor Duchene remarked though her surgical mask as she kept her eyes focused on the heart monitor while removing debris from Spoonie's opening.

"I'm her aunt!"

"I don't care who you are!" Doctor Duchene yelled. "You're not allowed here!"

"Shima, go back!" Spoonie heard a voice echoing.

"Ne`Ne`!" Spoonie called out as her eyes opened then quickly closed.

"Who's Ne`Ne`?" the second surgeon asked.

"She's rambling," Doctor Duchene remarked lowly as she continued to work on Spoonie.

"Spoonie, I'm here, baby! The whole family is here!" Spoonie heard Mary yell aloud before everything went silent once more.

"Debris clear, heart rate has stabilized. I'm going to open her completely." Doctor Duchene remarked lowly as she set the tube aside and picked up a scalpel. "Hang in there, Spoonie," she sighed. "You're doing just fine, sweetie. Just fine," she comforted as she slowly began to extend the incision she'd made just mere minutes ago.

"You have the hands of an angel, Doctor Duchene," the nurse remarked as she smiled through her surgical mask, realizing Spoonie had been stabilized completely.

"Thank me in the morning if God allows it. We're only just beginning," Doctor Duchene remarked somberly as she and her staff set about repairing the damage done to seventeen year-old Shima 'Spoonie' Dawkins.

CHAPTER FORTY

A MIRACLE AND A BLESSING

January 18, 2009

Me, Samantha, Henrietta, Lee and Victor had just walked through the entrance of OU Medical Center in downtown Oklahoma City. When Dawk called me and told me Spoonie had been shot, I just had to get there. I had Samantha get her leased jet ready, and against protocol, she flew alone to Oklahoma City without her co-pilot Amber. It was that serious.

Spoonie and Tyke were the innocent ones in the family, ya' dig? Neither of them deserved this here. I sometimes think that God be repaying us outlaws back for the wrong we do by allowing things to happen to those, who if they were ever to be taken away, would devastate us. But from what I know about the Man upstairs, He don't search out and seek revenge in that manner. At least that's my belief about the Big Guy. But this here was no doubt a wakeup call.

Given the fact that the work was coming in soon, the family had to beef up security for those not affiliated with the business so situations like this wouldn't arise again. My end was secure. I had Tre` and two of my boys from the shop over to the house with my wife and children. Katrina was already about that life, and JoAnn, who was gangster as well, was spending the night. They were all locked up in the mansion on the second floor, with Tre` and his boys holding down the first floor.

This here, what happened to Spoonie was played out at the

hands of some dude named Tonto Jamison, Walee homeboy Kahlil brother. Dawk had called me mid-flight once he made it over to the hospital. He'd gotten the lowdown from Koko. Her ex old man was in on it too. He'd been toe-tagged, though. Whoever it was that was riding with Tonto shot him and he was thrown out the car before they left the neighborhood and Kimi had finished him off when she ran him over while transporting Udelle to the hospital.

I was glad I'd brought Lee and Victor along. They knew Dawk and had put in work for the family. They was in now on the strength of their work, my word and Dawk's approval. They were the only ones outside of Tre` as of now that will learn my family, know where some reside and come to know those I cherish the most. I know this here a risky business. Backstabbers come in all forms, but I got the right ones in Lee, Vic and Tre` and the rest of my team from House of I.D.E.A.S. and can't nobody tell me different. They fam. Trusted fam.

We made our way up to the floor where Spoonie was located and stepped into the waiting room. T-top had told me how when Bay was shot how the family had taken over the waiting room inside Mercy Hospital. I imagined it, but now I knew what she was speaking on. The entire family was there; from Naomi to Jane Doe and everybody in between, except for Mary, Reynard and DeeDee. Some were nodding off in chairs and others were lying on blankets on the floor, but most were wide awake sitting in silence with sad faces.

"Ben here, y'all!" Tyke said aloud as she got up and ran over to me and my boys upon our walking into the room.

"How you makin' out, cousin?" I asked tenderly as I hugged Tyke tightly.

"Spoonie still in surgery, man. Mary ran in there but the doctors ordered her out. They won't let nobody back there— not even my momma. All we can do is wait. I'm glad you're here," she said to me as she hid her face in my chest and heaved.

"Thanks for coming, fam," Dawk said as he walked up and shook my hand while I held onto Tyke. He then nodded to Lee and Victor as he moved to hug Henrietta and Samantha. "Glad you came, auntie. Thanks for comin', cousin."

"No doubt. Shima didn't deserve this. How's your mother, Dawk?" Samantha asked through concerned tears as she took hold of Tyke.

"I'm doing as well as a mother could be under the circumstances." Naomi remarked somberly as she approached Samantha and Henrietta with two steaming cups of hot coffee and handed one to each of them. "Thanks for coming, Ben." Naomi then eyed Lee and Victor and then eyed me as she nodded her head in approval. "Welcome to the family, guys. Thanks for being there for my nephew in our family's time of need. Naomi Holland," she said as she shook my boys' hands.

"Lee Sato."

"Victor Felix, ma'am."

Naomi gave a polite nod then said, "Henrietta? Samantha? Join me, please? Come on, Tyke." The four of them went and sat in corner and began talking as Dawk answered his ringing cell phone and walked out of the waiting room without saying a word.

I could see the pain in Naomi's face and it pained me to see my aunt have to go through this here. Lee tapped my arm at that moment. I looked over to him and followed his nod. Over in the last row sat Koko and Kimi. Kimi was opening up a bottle of pills and had handed a few to Udelle, who sat beside her with his head bandaged. I saw that Koko was staring my boy in the eyes, offering up an unspoken request for him to join her as she removed the crutches from the empty seat beside her.

Lee looked back at me awaiting the word. "Go 'head, fam. I'm sure she glad to see you, dude." I told him.

"Thanks, Ben. You know I got her, right?"

"Without a doubt. Look out for her, brer. Naomi would love that."

"Nuff said, Boss." Lee ended as he walked over and sat beside Koko.

I looked over to Victor and followed his eyes. He was focused in on Martha as she slept upright in a chair in her tight jean outfit. Her legs were slightly parted with her hands in between her thighs. It's a odd time to mention it, but Mary and Martha some stallions. They be fifty in March, but man, you couldn't even tell. Some women look years younger, Mary and Martha looked half their age, though. It was their smooth, tan skin, flowing jet-black hair and brown eyes and those curvy legs that caught many a man's attention. I was actually glad my aunt was asleep, because if Vic had caught a glimpse of those brown eyes, he probably woulda started drooling. "You doing it again, brer." I told him.

"What?" Victor asked me.

"You eyeing my people."

Victor laughed it off. "We here on business, man. Can't blame a man, though, Ben," he said to me as he smiled and shook his head like, *"Boy, you got some fine ass women in your family, yeh?"*

Just then, Dawk poked his head in the door. "Ben? Vic? Check this out."

Me and Vic stepped out the room before I had a chance to talk to the rest of the family. "What's happening?" I asked.

"Just got word from Malik over in Saint Louis—Loopy just come out her coma." Dawk said lowly as we stood outside the waiting room.

"That's the chick who survived the hit the night Simone Cortez and Sweet Pea went down, right?" I asked to confirm.

"Right, fam. DeMarco and Max was up there when she pulled through. They say she tryna talk, but she too doped up. Got word from Doctor Wickenstaff that the drugs gone wear off in about eight hours," Dawk said as he stared me in the eyes.

When ya' been in the game long enough, and involved with men of honor, real gangsters I mean, you come to understand a man's thoughts without him even speaking. Me and my family vets to this game. We not no block-hugging, on-the-corner, saggy-jean-wearing, loud-talking, I-love-my-old-lady-but-I'm-a-fuck this hoe anyway type of dudes, ya' feel? Ours is a business. Serious business. Blunt smoking, club banging and whip-riding has its place, but dudes who floss and keep a line of women all up in their business on a daily basis don't last long. That's not how we roll.

Dawk wanted me to fly over to Saint Louis to talk with Loopy was what his eyes told me as me, him and Vic stood in a small circle in our silk suits and leather shoes. "What you think she know, fam?" I asked Dawk.

"Pepper mentioned a lime green Caprice following her the night she burned her trap down. Hold up," Dawk said as he stuck his head back in the door. "Yo!" I heard him call out.

Several seconds later, Bay and T-top walked out of the room. "What's up," Bay asked dryly, her face still wet with tears.

"Loopy out her coma." Dawk stated.

"She said something about the car over in Naptown?" Bay asked.

"She medicated big time. Be like eight hours before the affects wear off. What's the name on the plate of that Caprice y'all saw up in Naptown?" Dawk asked as he rubbed his chin.

"B-O-O-G-I-E. Boogie," T-top answered.

Dawk looked over to me and Vic and said, "It's a long shot, but I'm hoping Loopy remember the tag if she even saw it the night Pepper burned her shit down. At worse, she might be able to describe the car, ya' dig?"

"If that's what it is, then that mean that the people who killed Pepper and the people running Naptown is the same click." Bay reasoned as she rubbed her chin.

"And we bodied one of their key players in RJ," T-top added as she ran her hands through her short, black hair. "We still in the shit, man." she sighed in frustration.

"Way deeper than before." Dawk mumbled as he shook his head somberly.

"We gotta find out who pulling the strings in Naptown," I

stated. "RJ wasn't the end of it, fam, he was only the beginning of who knows what's to come."

Just then, the doors leading to the operating rooms was pushed open and an African American female surgeon around Dimples' age led a team of surgeons. The group of seven, all wearing light green scrubs, white hair nets and white sneakers, seemed to be walking in slow motion as the doctor out in front made slicing motions with her hands with a serious look planted on her face before she reached up and removed her surgical mask, revealing what was to me, a proud smile.

I saw Mary run from behind the doctors at that moment. She paused when she eyed me and the rest of the family. "Oh my God!" she cried aloud as she covered her lower face and bent over at the waist.

We all rushed to Mary's side. "What happened?" Dawk asked.

"She's gonna be okay! Shima's gonna be okay!" Mary screamed aloud as she fell over into Dawk's arms. "She's gonna be all right!"

I walked over to the doctor who'd led the group out of the operating room and extended my hand. When the woman's hands touched mine, a warm feeling encompassed me. This woman had hands that were baby-skin-soft. Delicate. I felt as if I were to squeeze them I would crack her knuckles.

"I'm Doctor Heidi Duchene."

"Ben Holland. Spoonie my cousin," I said as the rest of the family rushed out of the waiting room and surrounded the doctors.

Numerous questions were being thrown at Doctor Duchene concerning Spoonie. She had to quiet everybody down. I watched as she caught sight of Koko and grabbed her hand just as Naomi approached her. "How's my daughter?" Naomi asked.

"She'll survive, Misses Dawkins."

"We owe this doctor! She saved Spoonie life! I waited outside the doors leading to the operating room and was on my knees praying off and on," Mary spoke through tears of joy.

"I cannot and will not take all the credit. It was a group effort on behalf of me and my experienced staff. We've induced a forty-eight hour coma to allow Spoonie's body to adjust to the medications and surgical procedures." Doctor Duchene remarked humbly. "We learned more than you all could ever know treating Shima. It was nothing but a pure joy to be able to soothe your souls."

"What happened to her, Doctor Duchene?" Koko asked.

"Spoonie suffered a bullet that entered here," Doctor Duchene said as she raised her left arm and pointed to her midsection. The slug exited the front of her stomach here," she then said as she pointed to the right front side of her stomach. Her intestines were shredded in some parts and she suffered heavy internal bleeding. She went into cardiac arrest and had to be revived on the operating table. A wound to her pelvis required a dozen staples. The bullet fragment barely penetrated the bone, but it's going to be a nagging injury. Mary says she plays softball. I think it's safe to assume that Shima will be sitting on the sidelines this upcoming season, but she'll be ready for her sophomore season and I would just love to see her play."

"I owe you," Naomi professed through tears of joy. "If there's anything I could ever do for you, Doctor Duchene, don't you dare hesitate to call," she stated as she pulled a card from her clutch purse and handed it to the doctor.

"Thanks, Naomi. But I was only doing my job. I was wondering if you all could answer one question for me?"

"What's that?" Naomi asked.

"Is there a Nay, a Ne`Ne`? Spoonie called her name. "Is Ne`Ne` here?"

"Ne`Ne` is my deceased daughter," Mary spoke through trembling lips. "She was shot and died on the operating table just under fourteen years ago in Jackson, Mississippi. She was the same age as Spoonie when she passed away."

"There's your angel, you guys," I heard Doctor Duchene

remark as she smiled back at her team.

Everyone was left speechless after hearing Doctor Duchene speak. Death is a mysterious thing to mankind in my opinion. When Manhattan shot me I had a vision—one that I believe had showed me Lubby's fate. My beliefs were confirmed the day Rolanda and company visited me and Katrina's home October of last year. I knew it was no coming back for Ne`Ne`, but Spoonie had called her name. Why? Nobody knows. Maybe Rene was there, maybe not. All I know is that it helped. Whatever Spoonie saw or heard, it helped. I know I wasn't alone when I thanked Ne`Ne` in silent prayer.

The entire family went down to the cafeteria and had an early breakfast with the medical staff. I have to say, if there were ever rock stars in life, I'd just met seven this morning. Doctor Duchene broke down to the entire family, at all of our request, how she had actually cut Spoonie's chest open and lifted her rib cage to repair the damage done to my cousin. She told us how two of her staff had lifted some of Spoonie's intestines from her stomach and set them aside to operate on the back side of her stomach.

In my eyes, Doctor Duchene, after hearing her speak, had taken Spoonie apart the way me and my boys break down cars and had put her back together. And the worse to come of it would be that she would miss her freshman year of college softball. It was indeed a miracle and a blessing for the family.

CHAPTER FORTY-ONE

A MESSAGE TO WALEE AND KAHLIL

The majority of the family was asleep inside the waiting room the evening after Spoonie's surgeries. Only Walee, Kahlil, Tiva, Malaysia, Malara, Martha, Victor and Ben were up. Some, like the Brackens family, Mary and her family, and Ben and his family, had gone to hotels to rest. The family was now in 'round-the-clock shifts, taking turns on guard awaiting Spoonie's awakening.

Lee and Koko had had a long conversation the night before; he was now officially her man. They sat in a corner planning on making things official, but that was a ways off as Spoonie was everyone's main concern.

Kahlil, who sat by his lonesome in one of the room's corners, had just changed the channel on the wall-mounted flat screen in order to watch ESPN. He'd just caught the opening broadcast and leaned back in his seat and crossed his legs.

"What it is, Home Skillets? Stuart Scott and Scott Van Pelt here to kick off your NFL Playoff Sunday on this presidential inaugural eve, eve! Props to Barack Obama, the nation's first black President...and believe me when I tell you that that man is...as cool as the other side of the pillow," ESPN Sports Broadcaster Stuart Scott stated through a smile.

"That's right, Stuart," Scott Van Pelt chimed in. "And just like Barack's landslide victory back in November, it was a one-sided affair last night as the New Orleans Saints *trounced* Kurt

Warner and the Arizona Cardinals down in the Superdome in old Nawlin's."

"This here Barack," Stuart Scott said as he coughed, sat up straight in his chair and set out to imitate Barack Obama. "Scott Van Pelt, you, sir, speak the truth about the Saints. I would like to thank the New Orleans Saints for their excellent performance on the football field."

"What was that? You're going off kilter!" Scott Van Pelt stated as he looked over to Stuart Scott and laughed while shuffling papers.

"Okay, that wasn't a good impression nor a good segue. Not to mention Obama is a Bear's fan," Stuart Scott smiled out into the camera. "But what is a good impression and segue is how the Saints manhandled the Arizona Cardinals last night down in the dirty, dirty and as they say…it was a party in the bayou! Let's get to the highlights from last night's first playoff game!"

Kahlil was up early this Sunday morning watching the sports news. He was worried that what had gone down the night before would be mentioned on ESPN and was certain it would be the header, but because it was the playoffs, he realized what had gone down the night before, should it even be mentioned, would be at the bottom of the news because the juggernaut known as the NFL had every sports fan's undivided attention.

Kahlil and Walee, along with Spoonie and Tyke, and a few of Spoonie and Tyke's friends had watched the Saints game inside Spoonie and Tyke's dorm room the previous night. So much fun had been just the day before, and the party was going to continue over to Bay's condo where Kahlil, Walee and the twins, along with Jordan and Anquette, were going to hold a poker game with Kimi, Koko and Udelle while watching the Indianapolis Colts and Baltimore Ravens playoff game. The Saints had the game sewed up early, so Kahlil, Walee, Spoonie and Tyke set out early for Oklahoma City.

Kahlil was thinking had they all stayed up in Stillwater until the end of the Saints game, Spoonie wouldn't have been shot, but on the other hand, had they not left early, his brother Tonto would've succeeded in kidnapping Koko, and had that happened, things could've ended far more tragic.

"Saints deserve to win after last night, dog," Walee said, breaking Kahlil's chain of thoughts as he walked over and sat beside his best friend.

"Had they not had that big lead Tonto woulda pulled that shit off, fam," Kahlil said as he rested his hands beneath his chin. "What the police saying?"

"Jordan told 'em she bust the shots, just like we talked about on the way to the hospital last night, ya' dig?" Walee remarked lowly. "The tech nine registered to her. Tonto and whoever else was in the car ain't turn up hurt nowhere as far as I know. So you either missed or they got help somewhere else. We in the clear."

"They lookin' for 'em? My brother, I mean?"

"Koko told 'em everything, dog. I ain't mad at her, though. She did right. Because if I ever catch up with that boy he gone wish the law caught up with 'em, ya' feel?" Walee said as he looked Kahlil in the eyes.

"He better hope I don't get to 'em first, fam."

Kahlil then leaned back in his seat and folded his arms. "We do this thing with Tonto, man, I, I'm gone focus on my career. Last night showed me how fragile life is."

"It showed me how serious the streets are, Kahlil. You know we always kept it real. Kept to ourselves, but no matter how hard you try to avoid shit, it just happens, man." Walee wiped tears from his eyes at that moment. "I bitched up last night, fam," he cried lowly as he bowed his head.

"What?" Kahlil asked as his face wrinkled while staring at the side of Walee's face.

"When Spoonie got shot I froze up, man. That there fucked with my head, ya' know?" Walee said as he raised his head and wiped his tears before looking down at the floor in shame. "I saw my sister walking around shot! She was bleeding and shit asking was Koko all right when she was, she was fucked up! And I ain't do shit! I ain't do shit but cry like a fuckin' bitch!" Walee screamed aloud as he leaned back in the chair and broke down completely.

"We all cried, Walee," Naomi stated as her son's cries stirred her from her slumber.

"Ain't no bitches in this family, my G." Kahlil remarked lowly as he hugged his boy, he himself shedding tears upon reflecting on the way Spoonie walked around confused after being shot through the body. "We was there, dog. Nobody hollered 'cut'. It wasn't a movie. The shit just kept," Kahlil broke down himself right beside Walee. "It just kept going on and fuckin' on, man! And it wouldn't stop! I'm a kill that boy for you *and* Spoonie, fam!" he screamed as he lay back in the chair and covered his eyes with his large, rugged hands.

"What you gone do is keep yourself in college and let things work they self out, Kahlil!" T-top snapped as she and Naomi approached Walee and Kahlil and stood before the two.

Naomi picked up the remote and turned the volume down on the wall-mounted flat screen and knelt before her youngest sons in Walee, her blood, and Kahlil, who'd been her son for years now. "This is not on you two," she said lowly as she placed a gentle hand on their knees. "You both have good hearts. Good and strong hearts! I know y'all some players—using the lingo of the day—but don't let this thing with Spoonie and Koko change who you are as men."

"Tragedy," T-top chimed in as she stood behind Naomi. "Tragedy brings out the best and the worst in people. A bitch, Walee?" Nahh, brother. You drove Spoonie here under the most trying time of your life. You got her here. You stepped up like a man. Daddy would be proud. Proud of you and Kahlil both."

"You think so?" Walee asked humbly as he looked up at T-top.

"When daddy got killed? Dawk cried, man. That's what love does to you when you see the ones you love hurt. People talk about what they would do in this situation and that situation, but until it happens? Nobody knows. But you reacted. Everybody that was out there that night reacted and did the right thing. Ain't nothing bitch about what you did. And I don't wanna ever hear you refer to yourself in that manner ever again or else you gone have to fight this bitch. And believe me when I say I'm a bad one."

"Bye, Tiva," Naomi stated seriously, all-the-while smiling on the inside.

Tiva didn't budge, however; she only kept staring at Walee over her mother's back as she stood with her hands inside her sweat pants, speaking with her eyes.

Walee nodded towards Tiva as she walked over to him and leaned down and kissed his cheek. "Thanks, sis. I see what ya' gettin' at."

Tiva then eyed Kahlil, who was leaning forward with his elbows on his knees. He looked up at her and merely nodded, speaking with eyes, and giving affirmation. "Ain't no bitches nowhere in this family."

Tiva pointed at Walee and Kahlil before she walked off and tended to her daughters, never uttering another word about the matter.

The Holland family had their own way of showing love and support. Gangster ran throughout the bloodline, but some veins carried it more fluently than others. Counsel was given by the strongest on certain matters when needed and everybody had a specific strength. Walee knew what Tiva was about, and to have her admonish and praise him all-at-once had set his heart right; he'd done his part, just as Kahlil had done, and wasn't held in contempt by anyone in the family, which was his belief ever since he'd arrived over to the hospital.

Naomi nudged her hands against Walee and Kahlil's knees and they slid over, allowing her to sit in between them. All three were staring at the TV when a picture of Kahlil was suddenly broadcast across the screen. "What's this about?" she asked as she picked up the remote and turned up the volume.

"Turning away from the NFL for a sec," Stuart Scott spoke. "Unnamed sources have confirmed that Oklahoma State's star sophomore defensive back Kahlil Jamison was reportedly involved in an overnight shooting that left one person from Oklahoma State's softball team injured and one Sooner player dead. We go live to Kirk Herbstreit to get the details. Kirk, what's the latest? Good morning, by the way."

"Morning, Stuart. The latest is that Cowboy defensive back Kahlil Jamison was present at the time of the shooting, but was not involved in the overnight shooting and is unharmed. Oklahoma State's athletic department isn't commenting on the circumstances surrounding this on-going story as none of the coaches had contacted Jamison or the injured softball player's family just yet."

"Now," Scott Van Pelt chimed in. "Now, we're hearing that the guy that was killed was a Sooner. A guy named Chablis Marcus who was a projected third round wide receiver pick at some point and time is that correct, Kirk?"

"That's accurate, Van Pelt. Marcus, if you go back to the Bedlam game down in Norman last November, Chablis Marcus was the guy Kahlil Jamison had knocked out of that game with a vicious hit in which Marcus had to be carted off the field. As a consequence, the hit Jamison placed on Marcus earned him a suspension from Oklahoma State's bowl game earlier this year —a game in which they loss by the way."

"Are these two incidents connected? The on field and off field incidents?" Van Pelt asked.

"Sources are saying they aren't connected. Jamison hasn't been charged and is only scheduled to be interviewed as a witness in the upcoming days. This looks like a case of domestic violence that simply got out of control according to unnamed sources."

"Wow," Stuart Scott said as he turned back to the camera. "Just goes to show that one needs to be careful with the company one keeps. On to the next. Later today, Brett Farve and the Minnesota Vikings—"

"Let me just interject here, if I may, Scott?" Kirk cut in.

"Knock yourself out, man. In the famous words of Busta Rhymes...Give me some more."

Kirk shifted in his seat, and it seemed as if he was staring Kahlil directly in the eyes when he said, "I don't know if

Jamison is even listening or even watching this morning. But what I wanna, and this goes out to all young men with potential to do whatever it is that they dream of doing in life…so long as it doesn't involve the streets. Jamison? Son? I've seen this way too many times to count! You have the world at your fingertips! Unlimited and untapped potential you haven't even discovered! Skills you don't even know you possess! Scouts? NFL scouts from numerous of NFL teams are already talking about you and you're just a sophomore! Just a sophomore, Jamison! Go your butt to class! Keep your head in the books and out the streets and you can live a life that thousands of college players dream but never realize! It's not about being 'hard' or 'keeping it real'. You kids with talent don't owe nobody but yourselves and your families! I don't, I don't wanna hear about you gettin' into another situation like *this*, Kahlil Jamison! You're an NFL prospect early, and you're on the verge of blowing it! Blowing it! Straighten up and fly right, son! That's all, Scott!"

"Wise words spoken from one of college's best quarterbacks ever. Jamison? If you're listening, my friend…if you listen to no one else? Listen to Kirk Herbstreit because he's in your corner, bug guy. Stuart Scott and Scott Van Pelt…back in…two and two…" Stuart Scott ended as he stared out at the camera.

Naomi placed an arm around Kahlil and Walee at that moment. "From miles away, wise words are spoken. "Take heed, young men. Take heed."

Kirk Herbstreit's words had really hit home for Kahlil. There were millions of people in the United States, but he'd been singled out on national TV on NFL Sunday. He saw his future flash before him and it was all good.

Not many could relate to Kahlil Jamison's life. His world was sports. He was a sought-after athlete that was talked about by prominent figures in coaching, sports analytics and broadcasting. The world was indeed his. After hearing Kirk Herbstreit speak, Kahlil had resolved himself; he knew exactly what he was going to do with his life. He only hoped that Walee wouldn't be disappointed in the decision he'd just made about the direction in which he wanted his life to go.

As far as Walee, he himself would slow down, but he would always be on guard, watching and waiting for the time, should it arise, to get back at Tonto as he moved forward with the business he had going with his DVD series. The streets was Walee, through and through now. What had gone down with Spoonie had changed him to a degree. He now saw the world as a cold and unforgiving place. Can't be cool with everybody and smile up in their faces. Haters lurked, he knew, but he couldn't and refused to become a sheep amongst wolves. He had a strong team behind him in Kahlil, Jordan and Anquette. His plan was to stick close to those he trusted without fail and do his own thing while staying ready for whatever.

After a while, things had settled down and the morning wore on. The rest of the family was awakening and those who'd spent the night at the hotel had all returned. The waiting room was filled to capacity once more just after noon when DeeDee walked into the room with a stunning woman at his side who was gripping the hand of a boy that appeared to be around the same age as Tacoma.

"Hello, everybody," DeeDee remarked lowly as the family looked on in wonderment, many silently asking who were the people accompanying the family's patriarch.

CHAPTER FORTY-TWO

TAGGED

January 19, 2009

Tired, me, Bay, T-top and Victor made it over to Saint Charles the following day after Spoonie's successful surgery. We'd spent the entire day over to OU and let me tell ya', when I say somebody grew hot? I ain't even much bullshittin'. We was all sitting in the visiting room when DeeDee walked in with this li'l boy around Tacoma's age.

"The hell on going here? Ain't nobody glad to see me?" the little boy yelled out as he stood before the entire family with his hands on his hips and a frown on his face. "I'm somebody uncle and what I say goes!"

This one here looked every bit like Naomi husband to me. He was a short, brown-skinned muscular fellow with a short haircut. "I'm Doss Dawkins the third! I'm Doss Dawkins the third and I'm seven years old!" he kept yelling as he walked up and hugged some in the family. "How everybody? I'm Doss Dawkins the third!"

Naomi was the first to stand up. Watching her? I could tell she already knew DeeDee had a son. She was all rattled as she eyed Tyke, Kimi, Udelle and Koko subtly. They knew about it too I quickly picked up on. I was sitting in between Samantha and Martha laughing like a mutherfucka to myself as I stared at a nervous DeeDee. He was scratching his forehead and swallowing hard as Twiggy walked up to him with a smile on her face.

I could tell Twiggy had picked up on the play the time the tip of DeeDee's gator shoe broke through the threshold. She was ready for some fuck shit to jump off early because when she learned what time DeeDee's flight was landing, she'd offered to pick him up from Will Rogers International. When DeeDee declined and said he would just catch a cab and had something to tell her, Twiggy went and told Martha that she felt DeeDee was hiding something.

According to Martha, Irene's words were, "He talking about it was the TV I heard in the background last night, Mar. Do I look stupid?"

So we all sitting watching Twiggy and DeeDee talk by the doors leading to the waiting room after Doss Dawkins the third made his presence known. "Who's his mother, Doss?" Twiggy asked in front of everybody. "You just pop up with a child seven years old and expect me to be cool with it, man?"

DeeDee came prepared, though. He had DNA results and everything. That was all cool and all—until this woman named Sharona Benson walked into the room fully.

Twiggy stared the woman down. She looked a little younger than her, but Twiggy had a youthful appeal herself. She looked the woman up and down. If she wanted to, Twiggy couldn't find fault with Sharona in my opinion, except for her having flown into town with DeeDee, because she was a knock out. The woman tried to introduce herself by extending her hand, but Twiggy up and walked out the room. "I'm not dealing with this shit!" was what she said.

"I told you this was a bad idea, DeeDee," Sharona remarked. "I'm sorry everybody. I'll just leave."

At Naomi's request, Sharona was welcomed to stay. DeeDee was tripping. I don't know if it was old age or what that had him off base, but I picked up right away that he and Sharona had been together before they made it over to the hospital. It wasn't a certainty, but being that DeeDee had been up in Chi-town with his son and baby's mother since before Christmas, and had only returned when he'd learned Spoonie had gotten shot? And knowing him and how he was with women? Come on, man!

Twiggy was no fool. She didn't take kindly to what DeeDee had done and how he tried to play her in front the family. Those in the family, who didn't know, which was damn near everybody in the beginning, now knew that Twiggy and DeeDee were intimate. But for how much longer remains to be seen because me, Bay, T-top and Vic had headed out before we could get the full scoop and learned how DeeDee would handle the matter. Baby momma drama was minuscule compared to what lay on our plates at this point and time. The situation with DeeDee would be clarified later on down the road.

Arriving over to the Cottonwoods' home in Saint Charles, we exited Kimi and Koko's Maserati and walked up on the stairs. Jay-D heard us coming and welcomed us in. "'Sup, fam," he spoke as he held the door open.

"What's the word on Loopy?" I asked the time the door was closed.

"Malik over there now. I think you gotta hear it for yourself, though, fam."

The Cottonwoods was where we exchanged guns and phones. I'd picked up a fresh batch of Tracfones to pass out to the crew at Dawk's suggestion. Me and my team was all handed a Glock .40 before heading over to Mercy Hospital.

Leaving the guns behind inside the car, we all walked into the hospital and made our way up to Loopy's room. She was sitting up in her bed eating Jell-O pudding when me, Bay, T-top and Victor walked in, much to Malik's surprise and relief.

"Homes," he smiled enthusiastically as he rose from his seat and gave me handshake and a brief hug. "How that bullet wound, amigo?" he then asked Victor.

"It's all good, fam. Small thang to a chicken wang. What your people saying, though?" Victor asked, getting down to business.

Malik looked back at Loopy. "Tell them," he said as he turned and faced his soldier.

"The car, the Caprice? It was the same one that we saw the night Pepper set her trap on fire."

"You seen, did you get a look at the tag?" I asked.

"Si," Loopy replied. "It was the letters, B-O-O-G-I-E."

"Boogie," I remarked.

"I have more," Loopy said to me.

"I'm listening."

"Before my cousin Sweet Pea was killed she shot one of them. It was a female. They were speaking some language not Spanish. Whoever they was they spoke another language."

"You don't know the language?"

Loopy shook her head to say no at me. "But the tag was from Ohio," she noted.

"Cincinnati, maybe," Malik remarked.

"There that city again." Bay stated as she shook her head somberly. "There's the missing link."

"It ain't a doubt in my mind they connected," T-top followed.

"I don't doubt it either, fam," I stated. "I think I know a way to find out who it was that was in that car, at least one of 'em."

"How?" Malik asked.

"If Loopy shot one of 'em, it's a good chance they had to take this person to a hospital. What me and Vic gone do is double back to Louisiana and check all the hospitals in the surrounding towns. What you and Bay could do, T-top, is search the hospitals here in Saint Louis and see if anybody was shot the night Simone and Sweet Pea got killed and learn their names." I let it be known.

T-top nodded and said, "We can hit the DMV, too. Maybe there we might be able to match the name to the Ohio tag."

"A Caprice registered under the tag Boogie is who we're looking for." I declared, more than sure that we were all on the right track. "How long before you well, Loopy?"

"A month or so. I'll need a cane for a while, but I'll be back at full strength."

"Tu tía CeeCee?" I heard Bay ask Loopy.

"She asked her about her aunt CeeCee," Victor told me as I listened in on the conversation.

"I have to see her, Bena." Loopy remarked in English.

"Take your time recovering, Loopy," Bay replied. "You want a job when you get better you got it. The family could use you. You've earned your rank as a Lieutenant if you want it, homegirl."

"Si. I'm still down," Loopy said as she extended her hand towards Bay and myself.

I looked over to Bay at that moment after shaking Loopy's hand. "We'll be okay here, Ben," Bay said to me.

I nodded to Vic as I tucked my hands into my silk slacks. "We gone take the Maserati."

"We got Jay-D Navigator to ride in. We'll make our own way back," Bay replied, sure to leave out our base camp down in the state of Oklahoma.

"Let's get to it, fam," I said as I made my way out the room with Victor following my lead.

CHAPTER FORTY-THREE

THE CALCULATED RISK

January 20, 2009

Me and Vic rested up the remainder of the day and got up mid-morning and traveled up to Louisiana, Missouri. Along the way, we'd stopped at the scene where Simone Cortez and Donatella 'Sweet Pea' Cruz had been taken out. We pulled over as close to the edge of the road as we could and I climbed out of the Maserati under the falling snow. I stood at the road's edge with my hands tucked in my maroon trench coat as I stared downhill at the carnage left behind. There was still recognizable damage left from where Simone's Hummer had crashed into some trees about twelve feet below the road's surface. Worn yellow tape was hanging from a couple of tree trunks, but what tape lay on the ground had been covered over with snow.

I couldn't help but to feel for what had gone down with Pepper's crew as this here was where two good ones had perished in Simone and Sweet Pea. Peppi Vargas, at the same time, had entered into her time of dying and had gotten swallowed up by the streets only days later. That there outcome coulda *been* in making for Pepper. On the other hand, though, I can't help but to feel as if she'd checked out way too early. Streets ain't no fairy tale was what I knew. Pepper had come up against a team too strong for her to handle. They ran through her crew like a hot buzz saw cutting through soft butter and had danced circles around 'em.

The family had indirectly gotten even when Bay took down this dude RJ in Naptown, but I had this deep, nagging feeling that I was on the verge of uncovering something way bigger than what the rest of the family was expecting. I never told Naomi or Dawk, don't even know if they recognize the fact that we'd been warring with the same click for years now. This here shit go way back to Damenga Lapiente` and my crew.

Killing RJ was a bad move in my eyes. Bay should've waited when she and Tiva spotted that Caprice over in Indianapolis based on what Pepper had told Malik the day before she was killed. Everybody knew about this fuckin' Caprice, but kept lettin' the shit slide. And this is where we end up—me staring down at the scene where two of our crew had gotten wiped out.

It took nine years for things to die down with the Lapiente` family. I wasn't sure that we could survive another decade war. Who would go down during this next campaign? Me? Dawk? Bay or T-top? Martha? Naomi? Even the innocent ones in the family could get it. Spoonie a testament to that fact. We had to get back to making money—which was the only reason we'd all agreed to continue on in this God-forsaken business and make that final run once we were all reunited and everyone's resume` was laid bare.

The family been stagnant for over two years now—ever since Doss got killed. We can't keep running around in circles killing those who kill us while spending money on mansions, cars, college tuitions and buying land without benefitting from it all. I don't want another war. Not that I'm scared or anything like that because I'm about that life. I just been around long enough and seen so much that I can see what lay ahead in this business should the family stay the course.

My gut telling me that should we wage battle with the people backing this guy RJ, it'll be so much carnage sustained it would destroy both organizations. This shit here has to end. I now find myself thinking that it's time to do something I never even considered doing for as long I've been in the business and would hold any and everybody that I once ran with in contempt for having even considered bringing the shit to the table—that of negotiating a truce.

"Can you believe this shit?" I heard Victor laugh aloud as he leaned up against Kimi and Koko's Maserati.

"What's that, fam?" I ask as I return to the car.

"I thought I wasn't gone be able to find it. Obama inauguration on the radio."

"That's right. He get sworn in today," I spoke lowly as I climbed back into the passenger seat. "New man taking charge," I smiled as I rub my chin and listen to the introduction.

"It is my great, personal honor...to introduce...the forty-fourth President...of these United States...Barack Obama."

As Victor pulled off, thunderous roars and claps vibrated over the Bose system. I hear so many people yelling, "Obama! Obama! Obama! Obama!" over and over again.

The scene where I viewed as that of my family embarking on that of a new journey faded off in the rearview mirror as President Obama's voice came over the speakers inside the pristine vehicle that had silenced the outside world and set me off into a deep reflection of where my family stood as of January 2009, and where we were possibly headed as time wore on...

"...My fellow citizens...I stand here today...humbled...by the task before us....grateful...for the trust you've bestowed... mindful...of the sacrifices born by our ancestors..."

This guy's opening words stirred me, let me tell ya'. 'Sacrifices born by our ancestors'. I reflect on my family and all we've been through. Many that'd come before us would not be proud, but we didn't choose this life, we were forced into it. I make no excuses. We a crime family. But I'm to the point to where I feel it's time we use our intellectual power instead of our muscle to accomplish our goals.

We made it up to Louisiana and found the town's small hospital. The small building, no bigger than a post office, was more like a neighborhood clinic. It had no emergency room, but I went in anyway and asked did a shot gun victim arrive on the night of January 9, 2009. The woman behind the small registration desk told me that the hospital in Louisiana didn't have the capabilities to handle gunshot victims and told me I should travel eleven miles west to the town of Bowling Green.

Fifteen minutes later, me and Vic had come up empty in Bowling Green. One thing I was glad to see was that the people were willing to cooperate. I had assumed that I would've needed some kind of an official document to get the answer to my question. That wasn't the case, though. I was able to stand by and watch as a nurse went through the data base and answered my question with ease.

After leaving the hospital in Bowling Green, Victor pulled into a gas station. "We should get a map, Boss. That way we could see all the towns around here and decide our next move."

"Good idea," I said as I stepped out the car and stretched my legs.

Vic went in and came out a few minutes later with a map and a pack of Newport cigarettes.

"When you gone kick that habit, brer?"

"When they diagnose my ass with a disease," Victor told me as he chuckled. "My nerves gettin' bad, Boss. We could be out for a while and this shit working my nerves early," he then said as he unfolded the map and laid it out on the hood of the Maserati.

We found the town of Louisiana and a thought crossed my mind as I looked at the town's location. Louisiana sat right on the Mississippi River and had a bridge that crossed over into Illinois. The hospital in Bowling Green hadn't received a gunshot victim on the ninth or tenth of January. The next big towns were Troy to the south, and Hannibal to the north. Whoever hit Pepper's crew would have a ways to travel to either town. Bowling Green was the closest place to get help, but according to medical reports, no gunshot victims had been registered. I walked back inside the store and went over to the magazine rack and found a map of Illinois. After paying for it, I returned to the car and laid the Illinois map beside the Missouri map atop the hood while explaining to Vic my hunch.

"What if whoever got at Pepper crew on highway seventy-nine played it out and was thinking ahead that ahead that night, Vic? What if they crossed over into Illinois to receive help for a gunshot wound? That would throw the law back over in Missouri off their tail, ya' dig?"

"That make sense, Boss," Victor realized, nodding his head with understanding as we both eyed the conjoined maps.

My fingers trailed the Missouri map across the bridge leading out of Louisiana, Missouri and me and Vic both eyed two towns that had an 'H' beside them: Barry and Quincy. Barry was the closest, so me and Victor gathered up the maps and drove back through the town of Louisiana and headed towards the Mississippi River Bridge. When we got there, we came up on this narrow ass bridge wide enough for only one car to cross at a time. A small traffic signal was at the bridge's foot and the light was lit up red.

Victor had ignored the light and jumped onto the bridge. I looked back at the light for a second, "Yo, Vic? I think you was suppose—"

Just then, Victor slammed on the brakes. "That's a fucking dump truck!" he yelled out as he sped back down the bridge in reverse. "I can't get around that shit!"

Victor backed the car down the bridge and placed the car in park. The dump truck lumbered towards us and descended the incline, the driver laying down on his horn as he thundered by mouthing a slew of cuss words.

"I guess that traffic signal mean something," I said to Victor as I chuckled.

The light remained red and we waited. Several seconds later, another dump truck and three cars rolled down the incline. As soon as the last car cleared the bridge, the light on the right side of the Maserati turned green and Victor rolled up onto the narrow channel.

It was frigid out this morning. Clouds covered the sky and wind whipped about. The car was rocking as it approached the middle of the river. I imagined Pepper's killer or killers traveling this same bridge with their wounded soldier as I looked out at the swift moving, white-capped waters of the mighty Mississippi. They might've even tossed some guns and shit over the side. I would've done it myself. The river was moving tree stumps, chunks of dirty ice, and looked like a body of liquid mud. Whatever lay down on its bed would remain hidden for all times because it was no way one could enter and find shit.

We made the hour or so drive northeast over to the town of Barry, which sat along I-72, and found the hospital. I donned my trench coat and put on a pair of clear glasses to give myself a distinguished appearance and walked into the medium-sized building's emergency room. There was an elderly, skinny white woman sitting at the desk and several adults and a couple of sick-looking children sitting in the three rows of chairs that was on my left.

"Can I help you, sir?" the woman asked me in a friendly manner.

"Yes, ma'am," I responded politely. "I was wondering if you could help me out? Did this hospital receive a gunshot victim on January ninth or tenth?"

"Well, this hospital receives a lot of accident victims being we're the only trauma center along this stretch of interstate. Lots of truckers and people traveling through the state seek aide. But a gunshot victim? I would remember that. Give me a sec," the woman responded as she walked into an office. I heard her speaking a few words to someone before she and another younger white woman approached.

"Can I help you?" the younger woman asked.

"I was wondering if you could tell me if a gunshot victim was treated here on the ninth or tenth of this month?"

The woman waved me over and led me to a small office on the opposite side of the emergency room. "Are you the police?" she asked me as she closed the door.

"No. Just a man looking for answers concerning my missing family."

The woman stared at me for several seconds. "If you are the police then it means you're a dirty cop," she said as she grabbed a purse and unzipped it. I laughed to myself while wondering what this woman was getting at. I offered no reply as I watched her pull out a white sheet of paper. "I'm so glad to be over this," she sighed as she handed me the slip of paper.

"What's this?" I asked puzzled.

"The woman who came here the night her daughter was shot in the leg told me to not mention to no one inside the law that her daughter was ever treated here. I had to clear medical reports and go on as if this woman and her daughter were never here. I told her if the police ever came, all bets were off and she agreed."

"Did the police ever come here?" I asked.

"Never. Thank God!" the woman sighed as she shifted her weight.

I looked down at the sheet of paper I'd been handed and saw a phone number starting with a 620 area code. I wasn't familiar with location. "Do you know this area code?" I asked the young woman.

"What?" she scoffed under her breath. "Mister?," she whispered. "I was given enough money to pay off my mortgage and put money aside to send my son to college when he graduates high school in ten years. This," she said as she pointed to the sheet of paper she'd handed me, "this has nothing to do with me and I don't wanna know what it is you and this, this woman and child have going on. It's none of my business. I don't know the area code, don't want to know who you are, and I ask that you forget me and this conversation. I can't help you anymore. I was told to give the number to anyone not the law looking for someone shot on the ninth of January. We're done," she ended as she walked over and held the door open.

"Thank you," was all I could say as I walked out of the office with phone number in hand.

"She said to call immediately," the woman whispered lowly

as I passed by.

I walked back to the car and grabbed my cell phone and dialed the number: 620-457-4433. The phone rang several times and a female answered. "This phone hasn't rung ever. Who am I talking to?"

"I'd like to ask the same?"

"Where are you? Did you do what was instructed?"

"To call immediately?" I inquired somewhat nonchalantly, but I was really wanting to know who this woman was and what this here was all about.

"Yes. Where are you?"

"Barry, Illinois."

"Your name?"

I wasn't about to divulge too much just yet. I'm tryna find this chick's angle and get a better feel for her, ya' dig? "What is it that you want from me?" I asked.

"Reluctance on your part will only hinder progress, sir. But if you must know? What I want is to negotiate with you on behalf of my family in Cincinnati, Ohio. I will trust you no more than you're willing to trust me, but I invite you to my home in order to make peace before we both annihilate one another. As a token of my sincerity, I will extend the first olive branch."

The woman gave me an address and I was instructed to meet her there.

"I'll call when I'm close." I told her.

"Sunset's no good. Make it eight in the morning tomorrow just to be safe. I believe you to be a man of honor. And you appear to be a reasonable man. If something were to happen to me? Then the streets of Saint Louis and beyond will run red. I put trust in you that you're willing to act civil first rather than bring your hit team to my home. Death holds no sway over me. It'll only serve its purpose, which is to free me from this god-forsaken life I've chosen to continue living."

I could relate to the woman's words, but I had no idea what I was getting myself into right about now as it was a calculated risk. "Death holds no control over my life either," I truthfully admitted. "Can't say it's something I welcome, though. But I'm willing to talk face to face with you if that's what it is."

"It is what it is. Let us never negotiate out of fear, but never let us fear to negotiate."

"Famous words quoted by the late President John F. Kennedy," I responded while nodding my head in admiration of the woman's historical reference.

"You're a knowledgeable man of history I see," the unknown woman replied. I could tell she was smiling through the phone, ya' dig? "Come, sir. I welcome you to my home. Names need not be spoken until we meet face to face. I will roll out the red carpet for you so that we can discuss matters in the morning."

"I'm on my way." I replied before ending the call and instructing Victor to jump back onto I-72 and head west while pulling out the Missouri map once more.

CHAPTER FORTY-FOUR

A COMMON GOAL AND ENEMY

It was a six hour drive over to our rendezvous with this mysterious woman, but me and Vic had broken it up by camping out over in Jefferson City, Missouri the night before. We came in on U.S. Highway 169 from the north. Following the directions, we made our way through this small town, traveling down Main Street, and headed to the north east side of town. This place here was flat and dead looking. I counted four red lights before we left the little downtown area that was nothing more than a bank, lawyer's office, post office and a gas station.

Before long, me and Vic were back out on the open plain riding down a narrow two lane road with snow-covered fields on either side. This place here way different from Arizona with its mountains, canyons and gulches. This was the Wild West personified. I knew the state's history through reading books while locked up in ADX. The pictures did the place no justice, however; and as barren a place as the area was, it was beautiful. The sky was clear blue, contrasting perfectly with the pure white snow. Wide open is how I would describe it. The blue sky touched the snow-covered land on the horizon.

Three, shiny silver grains silo on my left five miles outside of town was the landmark I'd been given. "This it here," I told Victor.

Victor slowed the Maserati and made a left turn onto a

plowed asphalt road that was bordered by a black, three-railed fence on either side. We traveled for another mile or so and cows resting in the snow soon came into view. Far off in the distance to the north east I could see a two story white wooden home with three large square-shaped columns, one in the center, and one on either end.

Off to the left on the opposite side of the road was a large red barn, the kind with the tall double doors that had the slats lying across the front in an X pattern. One of those green and yellow tractors with the blades across the whole front was parked beside the barn along with two eighteen wheeler dump trucks I knew were used to haul wheat were parked side by side along with one of those cattle trucks like Naomi had. Whoever this woman was, she had a set up similar to my aunt, only she had no trees and the land was a little smaller.

"Yo, Ben," Victor called out to me as he tapped my shoulder and nodded straight ahead.

I looked through the windshield and saw a black Crown Victoria with Montgomery County Sheriff splayed across the side. The car was parked sideways, blocking the road and a black Chevy Silverado 3500 Crew Cab was parked behind it facing us. Right away I grew uneasy and pulled out my Glock. 40. "Slow down, Vic," I said as I racked the gun.

Through the side view mirror I quickly spotted the fender of another car. I looked around and saw three more black Crown Victorias coming up behind us.

"What's going on, Boss?" Victor asked a little uneasy as he pulled out his Glock .40 and racked it.

I was looking back at the Crown Vics trailing me and Vic, while at the same time trying to watch this car and the Silverado in front of us that was blocking the road. "It's at least five of 'em, fam," I spoke calmly. "I know this woman ain't playing no games like this here. I sent Dawk the info so he know where we at if something fucked up go down."

"We ain't gone make it outta here, man," Victor spoke somberly as he shook his head.

"We ain't got nowhere to hide and can't turn around, brer," I remarked as I leaned back in the seat with the gun in my hand. "Just ride up on 'em. If this day we check out, we go down bussin'."

"Like a man," Victor said to me as we bumped fists.

With three dark tinted Crown Vics on our tail and two more rides blocking the road ahead, me and Vic rode on, headed towards this Montgomery County Sheriff's patrol car as we held onto our loaded handguns. We was maybe thirty feet away when the driver's side door on the Sheriff's car up ahead opened and this short and petite grey-haired white woman who looked to be in her fifties stepped out with a twelve gauge and racked it. She was dressed in all black leather wearing a black fur toboggan with ear flaps. Being that she kept the gun at her side, me and Vic kept our guns in our lap.

Behind me, the driver's side door opened on the lead Crown Vic tailing the Maserati. A voluptuous white woman with long brown hair emerged. She looked to be in her late thirties or so and her green eyes looked as if she'd been to hell and back and she had wrecked shop while she was down there. She approached us wearing a white trench coat, white knee-length boots and a chrome Uzi draping her left side, an outfit and a gun I knew no legitimate cop would ever wear or possess while on duty.

"I'm gone ease the door open," I told Victor. "You already know what to do, fam."

"They bust we dump 'til we can't dump no more, fam," he said to me as he leaned back with his finger on the trigger. "I'm watching the bitch with the twelve gauge."

I climbed from the Maserati slowly as the woman in all white kept walking towards me in seemingly slow motion, never dropping her gaze as she kept her Uzi at her side while eyeing me harshly. "You made the call from what city?" she asked me as she strode past Victor.

"Barry, Illinois," I responded as I stood beside the Maserati to shield myself as best I could should the gunplay go down.

"Your name?"

"Ben Holland."

"Holland," the woman responded as she nodded while passing the front of the Maserati and walked over to the Sheriff's car. The two spoke a few words amongst themselves before she turned back to me and Vic. "Tell your friend to get out!" she called back.

Victor heard the woman and he looked over to me. I nodded my approval and he eased from the car and straightened his suit while holding onto his pistol. The older woman spoke into a CB radio before climbing back into her car and righting it on the road, facing the land straight ahead. The female in all white walked over to the 3500 HD and opened the passenger side door. I watched as a young female with a thick head of red hair emerged on crutches. She was helped by the woman in all white and began limping towards the front of the truck on the wooden sticks.

The driver's side door on the Silverado opened and a slender, brown-haired woman with green eyes who resembled the voluptuous white woman dressed in all white appeared. She was dressed the same as the woman who I believed was a family member in all white, only she wore a white leather cowgirl hat. The woman stretched, I'm guessing it was her way of letting me know she held no weapon as she rounded the front of her Silverado and approached me with a serious stare planted on her face.

"Mister Ben Holland. It's nice to meet you. I'm Faye Bender," the woman said to me as she extended her hand.

Right away the name was familiar to me, the last name I mean. "I see you're a woman who takes full precautions, Miss Bender," I replied as I shook the woman's hand.

"One could never be too careful in this business, Mister Holland," Faye said to me. "No need to be anxious if you are. I'm a woman of my word. This is a negotiation, nothing more," she said to me as she extended her hand outwards towards her Silverado. "Let's walk, you and I. Your friend will be fine I assure you. Keep your gun if that makes you comfortable. I have no weapon on me."

I looked back at Victor and nodded my head towards the road behind me. He nodded and pulled out a cigarette. The woman with the chrome Uzi walked over and offered him a light. "Where're you from?" I heard her ask while flicking the lighter with a smile on her face.

This could very well be that buddy-buddy play I was familiar with—when your killers make you feel comfortable right before taking your life. It was the same move I'd done to this dude Rico right after I linked up with Damenga Lapiente` back ninety-nine. Meetings of this sort could descend into madness in a split second. There was always an underlying feeling of distrust initially because both parties had a lot to lose by exposing their hand. One had to have an open mind going in unless all possibilities would diminish and the gunplay would ensue.

Faye and her click had more than one chance to annihilate me and Victor. No way could we ever make it out this situation alive if she had plans on killing us. The area was out in the open. The only thing we had to protect ourselves was the Maserati and two Glock .40s. We had nowhere to run and were outgunned. My life and that of Victor's was in possible danger, but I had no choice but to follow through as I'd agreed to this meeting without knowing what I was getting into exactly—it was a claculated risk I'd chosen to take.

"I'm glad you were willing to follow through on this, Mister Holland," Faye said to me as we began walking side by side with our hands behind our backs while looking to the ground in deep thought.

"I'd been having this feeling for a while now that it was a bigger picture on the horizon," I told the woman.

"Is that so? How big? If I may ask?"

"Whoever it was that got shot on highway seventy-nine that night is what led me here. You had to have spent plenty of money to keep the staff over in Barry, Illinois quiet. So it means something you."

"It does, Mister Holland."

"Your last name is Bender. As in the Bloody Benders?" I asked.

Faye looked over to me befuddled. "What do you about the Bloody Benders, Mister Holland?" she asked inquisitively as we continued our stroll in the cold winter's air.

"Only that they were viewed as America's first serial killer family."

"Do you believe it?" Faye asked me as she looked directly into my eyes without smiling.

"I do believe that there. I tend to believe certain matters pertaining to history when I can corroborate and research accordingly."

"It is true," Faye stated while looking to the ground. "My family was and is serial killers. As well as yours by all accounts. Our families sail the same waters."

"The reason you called me here?"

"In order to prevent a blood bath, Mister Holland," Faye answered as she paused and stared me in the eyes. "Had you not come by winter's end there would be nothing I could've done to prevent both of our families from going to war."

"Why me?"

"I wasn't searching for you exactly," Faye remarked as we resumed walking. "I don't even know you personally. I was just awaiting someone from your side with enough balls and intellect to follow through on the clue I left behind."

"What's your angle?"

"RJ is my angle. He meant a lot to my family. He come up dead after this female Jade Murdella, known on the streets as Ya Murder, was killed in Fox Park in a guy by the name of Malik Gomez's neighborhood. We know Malik works for the Holland family—your family—but he also did business with RJ."

I knew Bay and T-top had killed RJ back over in Naptown. I

wasn't going to give them up ever, but I was willing to compromise as Faye seemed to be the type of person willing to negotiate before resorting to one of the most expensive campaigns a crime family could ever undertake in this business: that of going to war. To lie to her at this point and time would do nothing more than damage the rapport we were beginning to establish. I had to use diplomacy to get the truth across about what had gone down with RJ.

"Blood and treasure takes its toll on a family," I told Faye. "In times like these, a family has to consider how much they're willing to risk in lives and finance to come out on the winning side."

"We'll be living on a meat farm, Mister Holland. Bloodshed is an expensive undertaking. I try to avoid war all costs. But if we're going to bring about the peace between our families I can't have you lie to me today. Now, is your family responsible for killing RJ?"

"For me to admit to you that my family was responsible for killing RJ it would give you leverage. But I have a question myself that I already know the answer to. I'm expecting you to do the same as pertaining to the question that I will ask." I told Faye as the two of us walked side by side, now looking deep into one another's eyes to dissect truthfulness.

"That I can agree upon, Mister Holland," Faye said to me, never dropping her gaze.

Just then, the horn on the Sheriff's car blew. Faye turned and beckoned the car forward.

"He's about to speak!" the old white woman said as she pulled the car forth, stepped out and turned the volume up on the radio. "It's on AM," she said while adjusting the dial.

A local news report came over the speakers. There was a bunch of static and the radio popped before this old man sounding as if he was about to take a permanent nap came over the airwaves. "This, this is Sheriff Frederick Cooper with your morning news," the voice spoke slowly. "The mayor, the mayor is having a celebratory breakfast at the town hall. Our candidate, Mitt Romney, didn't win the presidency, but our beloved mayor Faye Bender's campaign has left me holding onto my seat as town Sheriff. Now, we'll be down at the town hall breakfast, and I expect, my family would hope, would like to see many of our friends there was well to see me get sworn in for a record twentieth time," the old man said happily as static came across the radio once more.

If I'd just heard correct over the radio, Faye was mayor of this town. It was right then and there that I realized that this woman had invited me to her fortress.

"Sheriff Cooper has been Sheriff of this town for over forty years," Faye stated to me, shaking me from my thoughts. "He was old when me and my sister Bonita learned who he was and he's even older now. I make sure Frederick is elected Sheriff every year, but—"

"You and your family actually run the town," I remarked through an understanding nod.

"You're a very brave young man to come here under the circumstances, Mister Holland." Faye said to me as she waved the Crown Victoria off. "If I had intentions on killing you, you would've never made it into my town. I run Cherryvale, Kansas. This is my homeland and I do well to protect it. I've lured men here before to their death and have protected my homeland more than once. It's only twenty-three hundred people here and they all love me and my family. I know what everybody here in town is doing when it comes to the law so they fear me as well—more than they love me, but it doesn't matter so long as they stay in line and keep their mouths shut on what goes on here."

"It was my family—the Holland family who killed RJ." I let it be known to Faye as we resumed walking.

"You owe us compensation for killing RJ, Mister Holland. This is where our negotiating begins."

I was expecting Faye to feel as if she had the upper hand on these negotiations once I admitted my family's guilt, but I also a trunk card to play. "My family killed RJ, but I now have a question I need answered." I told her as we continued our leisurely stroll side by side.

"I'm listening," Faye said as she pulled down on her cowgirl hat and looked out over her land.

"Somebody driving a lime green Caprice with an Ohio tag with the name Boogie on the back was seen with RJ the night he was killed down in Indianapolis. That same car was fingered by one of our members. She survived the hit on Pepper that night on highway seventy-nine. Pepper wasn't so lucky. Now, I'm not saying your family was responsible for killing two of our soldiers on highway seventy-nine just outside of Louisiana, Missouri and killing our newly-appointed lieutenant Peppi Vargas, but it's a certain possibility given what we now know."

"My adopted daughter Maggie, the one on the crutches back there? She supplied the guns for that hit on highway seventy-nine. Boogie killed Pepper in her home a day or so after the hit on highway seventy-nine. Peppi Vargas was the contract Ya Murder had paid for and my family had to fulfill it. Nothing personal against your family or Peppi—it's just how we do our business."

"RJ was standing in the way of my family's expansion into the market down in Indianapolis. Nothing personal against RJ —it's just how my family conducts business." I replied cooly.

"I understand your leverage, Mister Holland—three of your soldiers for one of mine. I'm willing to institute the peace between our families given the losses we've both suffered. RJ is worth three of your crew. But further negotiation is in order," Faye said as she looked me in the eyes. "Indianapolis still belongs to my family. To sell there requires a five percent street tax on the gross."

Faye's words let me know that her family wanted in on the profits my family would reap once we set up in Indianapolis. That there was a no go. It was bad enough we were paying nineteen thousand a kilogram. To share a percentage of what we brought in with another family without them having to take partial risk wasn't going to work. When our cocaine hit Naptown every dollar we brought in was going back to the family. A cut of Indianapolis was off table. The Holland family was about to take that city. But what I could do was offer Faye and her family another city—one more suitable to their market. "You give us Indianapolis, and I guarantee that my family will dispose of any crew east of Cincinnati. Indianapolis will be as far as we would go."

"You offer a contract?" Faye asked.

"Your family's market is heroin is what I know. My gut telling me your family is looking for a bigger market, otherwise, you all wouldn't be dabbling in cocaine, which isn't your organization's main hustle. You give us the cocaine, we'll help you get reestablished with heroin."

"Malik," Faye stated. "Had we not met, your guy would've been killed."

"Same could be said about Boogie," I countered.

"In this business it's always someone somebody wants dead if only to even a score," Faye said to me. "A contract put out on the caliber of person in which I'm considering having killed is what's known as a million dollar hit, Mister Holland."

"My family has been known to take on such hits. What's his name?" I asked.

"Not him. Her. Her name is Tammy Moto. She's an Asian woman who distributes heroin in the city of Philadelphia."

"Tammy Moto a federal agent." I stated.

"How'd you know she was a federal agent?" Faye asked as she eyed me curiously.

"Her and her superior, Lisa Vanguard, is prosecuting a case on four of our crew. Word according to the lawyer working the case is that both of 'em is dirty."

"What did she do this time?" Faye asked me.

"Lisa Vanguard and her assistant Tammy Moto took two hundred and thirty kilograms from evidence over in Seattle, Washington and brought 'em down to Philadelphia and sold it to a crew for ninety-five hundred a brick. Problem was, Tammy Moto came back with the FBI. The product she sold was repossessed and some inside that family were sent to jail. You know that family?"

"You've really done your homework," Faye spoke as she looked over to me without smiling. "We were that family, Mister Holland. She ripped us out of three million dollars and did damage to our ranks. Lisa Vanguard is worth much more than just a million dollars. I'd go broke trying to kill that woman after what she's done to me."

The day me and Dawk had met up with Phillip Tran, Grover Kobayashi, and later Dante' O'Malley over in Vegas, the Asians and the lawyer had laid down some information on us concerning Lisa Vanguard that I could now use on behalf of the family after hearing Faye speak.

The information I had was enough to catch Lisa and Tammy off guard and possibly pull off a hit—but it would cost because we talking about killing federal agents. Whoever took the job would have to leave the country until things blew over and may not ever be able to return.

Faye said she was willing to go broke, I wondered just how much she was willing to pay to have two federal agents killed, because I knew for certain that there were some in our organization that would go after Lisa and Tammy for free, but in order to sweeten the deal, I wanted to give them an incentive.

"For ten million dollars my family will kill Lisa Vanguard and Tammy Moto." I told Faye.

Faye looked over to me and then turned and stared out into the desolate, snow-covered land. "The money doesn't matter. This thing with Lisa has gotten personal—it has been personal."

"Why?"

"Lisa killed my best friend's parents up in Kanas City, Kansas—Maggie's mother," Faye stated. "She caused the deaths of my husband, my son and my best friend Gayle McPherson on a farm in Patterson, Iowa in nineteen eighty-three."

I really had no beef against Lisa Vanguard. When she was on my retrial, she was only doing her job is how I saw it. She'd gotten Samantha off on killing Manhattan down in Wichita, Kansas also; but the bottom line now was that all of that had nothing to do with what was going down at the present day and time. Lisa was a dirty cop. She was killing people and selling drugs the same as me and Faye's families so she was fair game like all the rest of us.

"What was the deal behind Lisa killing your family? Family supposed to be off limits." I stated.

"Lisa did those things to the people I loved for no good reason other than for the sake of getting back at me for killing her father Ivan Vanguard five years earlier over in West Virginia when he tried to raid me and my friend Gayle's moonshine operation."

"Never mind the robbery. All she saw was the fact that you killed her father." I told Faye.

"And she went psychotic in its wake."

"Lisa and Tammy's downfall will benefit us both." I remarked.

"You've given me valuable information, Mister Holland. Let me do you a solid in return."

"I'm listening."

"When RJ went down? His connect from Chicago was left on the outside. He's good earner that is of value to you. An Italian guy named Natalia the third."

"Natalia is our Italian connect in Chicago," I let it be known to Faye.

"That explains why he refused to take the hit on Malik Gomez. You have a very loyal organization, Mister Holland. More loyal than you could imagine. I think your family and my family can do business together, if only to see a common goal obtained."

"Which will maintain the peace between our respective families," I replied.

"My advice," Faye said to me as she grabbed my hand and held on tight. "For the sake of your family and my family as well? My advice is to make things right with your Italian connect in Cicero. Natalia the third is basically fending for himself up there. The guy is hungry and feels as if your family is ignoring him. Bring him on board and that will solidify your family—just some friendly advice."

"Advice heeded," I responded. "Now, what about the ten million dollars?"

"Ten million is no good. This is my counter offer—if you kill Lisa and Tammy, we'll return the favor. We will kill up to six individuals on your behalf. It'll be our way of returning the favor for your family going after Tammy Moto and Lisa Vanguard."

"Philadelphia means that much to you and your family." I stated. "Three lives for each agent."

"Three lives per agent. And it doesn't matter who so long as it is on American soil and within reason. For an International hit? We'll give you only two. No politicians whatsoever, though."

"I understand. You'll do six hits on American streets on our behalf, and go international for two."

"That is the deal. If my family were to get Philly, we'll be one step closer to New York, which is our ultimate goal, Ben. You and you're family are invited to join us. Our move will open up a cocaine market in the financial capital of the world." Faye said to me. "All that stands in our way is these two dirty federal agents."

"What's in it for my family should I agree?" I asked.

"What's in it for your family, Mister Holland, is that we'll concede Indianapolis. In return, you will help my family take Philadelphia by eliminating Tammy Moto and Lisa Vanguard. Together? We go after New York, but you're not obligated to join us in taking New York since we're only after the heroin racket. But should you join us and we succeed? We'll have a network set up running coast to coast. We'll be unstoppable."

I knew what I was entering into would contradict my entire thought process before I'd ever met Faye Bender. While listening to Barack's inaugural speech, I spoke on using intellect rather than muscle. But drastic times call for drastic measures. The Germans were willing to kill on our behalf, and we on their behalf. I had only one peron in mind off the top of my head whose named needed to be crossed out.

To add to that, we'd get the Naptown market. I already felt three hundred and fifty kilograms was a bit more than the family could handle at this point and time, but this deal would all but guarantee a lucrative market, plus we'd have our Italian connect back in pocket by bringing Natalia the third back into the fold. It was a deal too sweet to pass up.

"We got us a deal. ," I told Faye. "Tic for Tac. We get Lisa and Tammy and give you Philly. I only want one person taken care of—an international hit—but now isn't the time. Once my family eliminate Lisa and Tammy, your family will give us Naptown and everything west of the Mississippi River tax free with the promise that you won't move in our market." I stated as I shook Faye's hand.

"We have ourselves a deal, Mister Holland," Faye remarked as she smiled up at me while holding on to my hand. "Just give us a fair amount of time for the job. International hits aren't easy."

I knew I'd just placed my family under the gun by agreeing to do business with the Germans. Once again we were about to undertake another deadly campaign, but this time, everybody involved was going to take great risks. Should we succeed, the only person standing in our way would be Rafael Gacha. But if we were to rid the world of Lisa Vanguard and Tammy Moto, the Germans would owe us a huge favor in return. Only time will tell if I'd made the right move this time around.

CHAPTER FORTY-FIVE
THE FORGOTTEN ONES

While Ben was discussing business over to Cherryvale, Kansas, three hundred and fifty miles or so to the south in the city of Saint Louis, Special Agent Laddy Norcross sat at a table inside a break room at the Missouri State Highway Patrol Headquarters. Struggling through a severe cold that kept his head stuffy and his throat sore, the more-than-capable agent poured steaming hot water into a styrofoam cup and sprinkled it with Theraflu. He popped two Daytime Nyquil pills into his mouth and washed them down with a cup of room temperature water as he stirred the powdered medication.

After swallowing the pills, Laddy took a sip of the Theraflu and tilted his head back as he sat in a hard back chair. "You could've, you could've given me this cold before I left for Chicago, yeah, God?" he declared as he looked up to the ceiling while wiping sweat from his forehead with a silk handkerchief. "My dog sneezed on me and gave me his cold? You, you are such a funny, Man." he nagged as he pointed upwards.

"Agent Norcross?" a female called out, redirecting Laddy's attention.

"Yeah, who's asking?"

"Sandra Cordova. My former partner Darby Jones down in robbery-homicide referred you here to my office?"

"Yes," Laddy said through a hacking cough as he rose from

his seat and extended his hand.

Thirty-eight year-old Sandra Cordova looked down at Laddy's hand and brushed her blonde hair away from her face as she stood before him smiling.

"I'm sorry," Laddy remarked, removing his hand. "Bad cold."

"I know. I heard you blaming your dog and God," Sandra chuckled. "What can I do you for, agent?"

"I umm, I come down after receiving information from a Bahdoon LuQman."

"LuQman? Doesn't ring a bell," Sandra replied as she made her way over to the coffee pots on the counter inside the small area.

"They called him Q-Man on the streets."

"Nothing's resonating," Sandra said as she poured herself a cup of coffee. "Who was Q-Man?"

"He was going to be an informant. I stumbled on shipping him to a safe locale," Laddy said somberly as he flopped down in his chair. "I mixed Rockville Prison over in Indiana with Stateville. He was shipped to Stateville last month and was killed the day he arrived."

"Rockville is a women's prison in Indiana," Sandra snickered as she turned to face Laddy while stirring her coffee.

"I know that, okay?" Laddy stated as he leaned over and coughed repeatedly. He rose and said, "I feel bad the guy loss his life. But I can't say I feel sorry for him given the life he was living."

"You feds are all the same," Sandra stated as she shook her head from side to side. "You make promises to people, assure them of their safety and then hang them out to dry and give it no thought whatsoever."

"Q-Man came to me, okay?" Laddy justified as he righted himself. "He mentioned, he mentioned this woman Kathryn Perez having been killed by members of a group known as the Holland family," he added as he blew his nose. "God, that hurts."

Sandra perked up when she heard the name Kathryn Perez. "What else did Q-Man tell you?"

"He said whoever killed Toodie, killed this woman Desiree Abbadando over in Denver, Colorado and was also responsible for the death of his brother up in Minneapolis. Desiree and Q-Man's brother were killed by sniper shots."

"I know nothing of your ongoing investigations in Colorado or Minnesota, Agent Norcross, but I have some information that may be useful to you concerning Kathryn 'Toodie' Perez. I know her very well."

"Show me what you got," Laddy said as he eyed Sandra.

"You really should be in bed, man," Sandra said as her eyes scanned Laddy's well-toned, slender physique. "Follow me to my office, agent," she offered while blushing to herself.

Laddy and Sandra adjoined to Sandra's office where she pulled out three manila folders and set them down on her desk. "This is where it begins," she said as she pulled out a picture of Carmella Lapiente' from the top folder.

Laddy recognized Carmella right away. "This woman was mentioned as being that of a drug lord during a trial where my superior Lisa Vanguard was attempting to keep a guy named Ben Holland behind bars," he let it be known.

The name Holland didn't strike a chord with Sandra, but the name Vanguard was a name she'd never forgotten. "Vanguard?" she asked inquisitively as she raised her eyebrows. "Red-haired, petite woman? Should be in her late forties, early fifties now?"

"Yes," Laddy remarked. "You know of her?"

"Do you have a picture of Vanguard?"

"Yeah," Laddy said as he pulled out his cell phone and opened his picture application. He pulled up the latest picture he had of Lisa, which was the two of them celebrating New Year's inside Jonas', the club Lisa owned back over in Baltimore, Maryland, and showed it to Sandra as he leaned out and sneezed.

Sandra fanned the air and eyed the red-haired woman before walking off in silence. She ran her hands through her blonde hair with her back towards Laddy and said, "That woman ruined my father's career, you know?"

"Lisa?" Laddy asked baffled as he wiped his nose free of mucous. "How'd she do that?"

"June of this year will mark thirty years to the day that a woman pretending to be an Ivana Vanguard walked into robbery homicide over in Kansas City, Missouri. She was looking for a pimp named Bunny."

"Lisa wasn't a federal agent in seventy-nine. She didn't join the bureau until July of eighty-three."

"I don't know when she joined," Sandra replied as she turned and faced Laddy. "But what I do know is that my father, Hickory Cordova, gave that woman information on a Faye Bender and a Gayle McPherson. A few hours later, Gayle McPherson's parents were killed and my father never heard another word from this Ivana Vanguard ever again. He always believed and still does believe that that woman killed those two people that night back in June of seventy-nine."

"Your father didn't check credentials? Learn her superior?"

"Aww, come on, man!" Sandra scoffed in defense of her father. "Law trusted law back in those days. We were the good guys, remember?"

"I was a mere boy of nine living in Zurich, Switzerland at the time of this alleged homicide."

"And you chose to come to America and be a crime fighter?" Sandra smirked before sipping her coffee.

"Here is where the action is," Laddy remarked as he sipped his Theraflu.

"Action," Sandra said as she looked Laddy in the eyes. "For all I know it could be a coincidence. What are the chances really?"

"You've made the woman out in the picture to be that of

Lisa Vanguard, Cordova. This here situation changes everything. You're onto something. Something big."

"In what way, Agent Norcross?"

"For a while now I've been having some suspicion about Lisa Vanguard. It's like she's been keeping me out of the loop while she runs around with her new partner Tammy Moto. She's scheduled to prosecute a guy by the name of Asa Spade over in Denver come March, but I can't help but to feel as if she's purposely going to throw the trial."

"Why would she want to do that?"

"So she could do the same thing she did back in seventy-nine maybe—to kill out of spite," Laddy answered matter-of-factly. "If Lisa Vanguard has committed a double murder, she should be brought to justice—even more so than those who aren't wearing a badge and haven't taken an oath to uphold the law."

"I say it's her, but she could easily deny it." Sandra doubted.

"That she could, which is why we'll have to put all the pieces in place before we act. But I'm certain the woman that visited your father nearly thirty years ago was in fact my superior Lisa Vanguard."

"What makes you so confident that it was indeed your superior?"

"Lisa Vanguard's father's name was Ivan. She didn't deviate too far from his name because she was using his badge as her credentials is my guess for now. We'll look into it. With that aside, this thing with Q-Man and Toodie still puzzles me. I have to see it through."

"You wanna look into it while you're here, agent?"

"I sure do. You familiar with HITS?" Laddy asked.

"Damn sure am," Sandra stated proudly as she smiled while pressing her tongue to the inside of her cheek. "We just got that bad son-of-a-gun for Christmas, agent."

HITS, better known as the Homicide Information Tracking System, is a program that was started in Washington State. The database contains information on thousands of murders across the United States. What makes the program unique is that one can key in specific words relating to homicides and obtain a list of murders committed in a certain manner, i.e. asphyxiation by rope, or death by ax.

Laddy and Sandra walked over to the forensics lab where Sandra had a lab technician pull up homicides across the country that was committed via the long shot over the past ten years. They sat and waited for almost an hour, going over the events that had taken place with Sandra's father thirty years ago, before the results came back. With information in hand, the two returned to Sandra's office where Sandra pulled down a map of the United States and Laddy spread out the data sheets.

There were literally scores of assassinations committed across the country going back to 1999. The Agent and the Trooper walked around the desk eyeing the data reports. "Okay," Laddy said as he placed a check mark beside several homicides. "Call out these homicides to me and I'll mark them off on the map on the wall."

"Sure," Sandra remarked as she took the data sheet from Laddy. "April, 2002, Hayate and Isao Onishi, killed via the long shot in the towns of Kent and Bellevue, Washington respectively."

Laddy placed red dots onto the map up in the state of Washington. "A case involving JunJie Maruyama," he said. "Next?"

"September 2003, Desiree Abbadando, killed via the long shot in Denver, Colorado," Sandra remarked.

"Denver. Where Asa Spade was located," Laddy remarked as he placed a red dot on the map. "Go ahead, Cordova."

"November 2008, Daneel LuQman, killed via the long shot in Minneapolis, Minnesota."

"Minneapolis is where Q-Man and his family resided," Laddy remarked as he placed a red dot over the twin cities.

"Here's your last one," Sandra said as she set the data sheet aside. "Ricky 'RJ' Gross, killed just four days ago via the long shot in Indianapolis, Indiana."

Laddy placed a red dot over Naptown and drew a line across the map, connecting all of the dots before he placed the cap back onto the Sharpie. He stepped back and eyed the map as Sandra walked up beside him. Sandra had no clue what she was staring at exactly, but in Laddy's eyes, it seems as if the organization that JunJie Maruyama once ran had moved eastwards.

The hits started in the Seattle area, where JunJie Maruyama was once headquartered. The murders then moved down to Denver, Colorado, where Asa Spade was awaiting trial. They then traveled up to Minneapolis, where Q-Man resided. The last hit, the one in Indianapolis, he couldn't figure into the equation at the moment, but in between the last two hits, Kathryn 'Toodie' Perez had come up missing in Saint Louis. The agent's expertise told him that he was up against a highly organized criminal organization that may have ties to JunJie Maruyama. "What's their deal?" he whispered. "Who are these people that've succeeded JunJie?"

"Whoever they are, they have a well-trained assassin."

"Two assassins," Laddy countered as he stared at the map in wonderment.

"How do you know?"

"Here," Laddy said as he pointed the city of Seattle. "The Onishi brothers were killed on the same night within the same hour. There's no way one sniper could've gotten them both."

"Ben Holland. Naomi Holland," Laddy stated lowly as he looked to the floor. "Carmella Lapiente`. Kathryn Perez." he spoke lowly. The agent looked over to Casandra and asked, "Can we find out if anybody with the last name of Holland was ever killed here in Saint Louis or the surrounding areas over the past ten years?"

"You're gonna get me cussed out by the lab techs, you know?" Sandra quipped as she headed for the door.

"While you're at it we might as well get cussed out fully,"

Laddy chimed in.

"Meaning?"

"A guy by the name of Faustino 'Lucky' Cernigliaro was killed over in Saint Charles back in September of two thousand two. I killed his father just under a month ago after he'd killed a witness that mentioned the name Holland."

"You're tap dancing all around this case aren't you?" Sandra asked through an alluring smile. Laddy's insight and investigative skills was a severe turn on to the Trooper. She didn't know if he was picking up on her vibes or not, but she did nothing to hide them either. She knew he was a straight-laced man, though, but still, she could dream.

Laddy eyed the 5' 6" full-figured Hispanic woman with appreciation in return. The tight, hip-hugging beige business suit and three-inch-heeled dark brown knee-length boots she wore, coupled with her blonde hair and hazel eyes, left much to the imagination while putting just enough on display to arouse a man's curiosity.

Laddy Norcross was a married man with a young child and a wife back in Alexandria, Virginia. His wife was a homemaker; a former waitress he'd met while attending the F.B.I. Academy down in Quantico, Virginia. They'd come together over steak and eggs—numerous steak and egg breakfasts inside the diner where the woman worked.

Before long, Laddy's future bride had started having his booth and meal ready with a hot pot of hot coffee and the Washington Post waiting whenever he walked in on weekdays. The blonde-haired, petite woman from Mexico City, in fact, had asked Laddy out to dinner on a Friday morning back in June of 2003, the same month he was scheduled to graduate the academy. On the day of Laddy's graduating from the academy, the humble, husband-searching woman was the only one there to applaud for Laddy.

An early dinner and a tour of D.C., a city the woman had never toured, had set the stage for a love affair that left Laddy in awe of this lowly woman he'd been knowing for nearly a year. She became pregnant shortly into their relationship, but had loss the child after suffering a miscarriage in late 2003. To cheer his girlfriend up, Laddy had offered to take her to his homeland in Zurich to meet his parents. It was only then that the woman told Laddy she wasn't a naturalized citizen. He loved the woman so much, however, that he'd married her, thereby earning her a green card. Nearly five years later, Laddy found himself a married man, but there was no adjective to put in front of the word married as he was so involved his career that he hadn't much home time. What he was doing with Sandra Cordova was strictly job-related was what he told himself as he watched the woman sashay out of the office while swaying her hips.

A deep, involuntary swallow sent a burning sting coursing through Laddy's neck and shook him from his thoughts. He downed the remnants of his now-lukewarm Theraflu and waited patiently for Sandra's return as he leaned against her desk and eyed the map, steadily trying to put the pieces of this intriguing puzzle together.

Ten minutes, later, Sandra returned. She licked her lips as she smiled at Laddy while gently closing the door to her office. "You owe me, Laddy," she said as she looked over to the agent.

"How so?"

"I have the file on Faustino's homicide and the men that were killed right along with him in Saint Charles. They were a part of this old mafia family known as The Egan's Rats."

"How does The Egan's Rats fit into all of this?"

"They don't really. But I have a file on a Doss Dawkins and a Bena Holland. Doss Dawkins was killed outside of this club called Connections in September of two thousand six."

"Dawkins? Naomi Holland's husband," Laddy stated.

"Yes. And Bena Holland was his daughter. She was shot, but she was taken to Mercy Hospital and was treated. She survived." Sandra smiled.

"Well," Laddy said as he coughed harshly. "I think we'll pay Mercy a visit and talk to the doctor who treated Bena and see what he can tell us about this woman."

"I was thinking the same thing. You and I, sir, may have just stumbled upon the case of a lifetime. A possible dirty federal agent? A potential organized crime family operating here in Saint Louis? I want in on this!"

Laddy liked operating on his own; but Sandra had been more than helpful. To deny her would not sit right in his heart. Not to mention she could be a valuable asset as she knew the streets of Saint Louis and the surrounding areas. He knew he was walking a fine line however; he'd sensed Sandra's attraction towards him and now found himself becoming attracted to the sexy lawwoman in which he had so much in common. *"We're only working a case,"* Laddy said to himself as he eased up off the desk.

The time Laddy pushed himself forward, a sharp pain shot through his stomach. He leaned over and vomited onto Sandra's floor, regurgitating the water and Theraflu he'd consumed as he took to one knee before the desk.

Sandra didn't grow irate over Laddy's actions, which was her right to do so. Instead, she grabbed a roll of paper towels off her bookshelf and spread them out over the slime covering her tile floor. "You really should be in bed," she said as she knelt down beside Laddy. "Where're you staying?"

"The Millennium Hotel. I'm, I'm sorry about this." Laddy gasped on bended knee.

"Think nothing of it, agent."

"We have to get over to Mercy Hospital to question Bena's surgeon."

"Are you serious? In your condition? No, sir! Bed time for you, Agent Norcross. That doctor isn't going anywhere. I'll take you to your room and make sure you're tucked in. I have some antibiotics left over from a cold I had earlier this month. Are you allergic to antibiotics?"

"I'm not," Laddy grimaced.

"Good. Let's get you well before we start our journey forth and crack this career-making case wide open." Sandra ended as she helped Laddy up from the floor and readied herself to take him back over to his room inside the Millennium Hotel.

The Federal Bureau of Investigations and the Missouri State Highway Patrol was one step closer to Bena 'Bay' Holland and Tiva 'T-top' Holland courtesy of Q-Man. What becomes of the burgeoning case remains to be seen as it is still a mysterious one to Laddy Norcross and Sandra Cordova, but one fact remains certain—once the feds get involved—all bets are off, and no one's freedom, or life, for that matter, was guaranteed, not even that of Doctor Obadiah Wickenstaff, who'd treated Bay, or that of Lisa Vanguard, both of whom were on the verge of being lumped in with a bunch of violent serial killers and drug dealers running amuck in America's heartland.

****

While Laddy and Sandra were in the beginning stages of putting the pieces of a once-in-a-lifetime case together, back over in the state of Oklahoma, things were beginning to return to normal as normal could be. Spoonie was now up. She was still in a weakened state, but she was conscious and able to comprehend. She never spoke on what she now believed, that she'd heard Ne'Ne's voice, but it affected her deeply. It would be something she would hold to herself for the time being until she got back to the ranch.

Tonto Jamison's face was on every single news program. He and his unknown accomplice was being sought after for aggravated kidnapping, aggravated assault, second degree murder and second degree attempted murder. Both were considered armed and dangerous and their whereabouts were unknown.

The entire plan Tonto had thrown together was flawed from the start. First he'd used his own car, second, he'd brought along Chablis, whom he'd been bullying from day one, and had gotten him killed by Chauncey Gainey, a well-known lit fuse. As thorough as he believed himself to be, Tonto Jamison was no more than a small time punk with a reckless mindset. Everybody wants to be gangster, but not everybody's bred to live the life. Tonto would be one to learn the hard way eventually as he was now a wanted man in more ways than he could ever imagine.

Lee Sato knew the full scope. He was thinking it was best for Tonto and his associate to turn themselves in because they weren't safe on the streets by a long shot. He was waiting Ben's return from Kansas so the hunt for Tonto and his accomplice could begin as it was a job he himself wanted to handle on behalf of the family. He eased up from a sleeping Koko and walked over and sat beside Dawk, who was sitting idly staring at the wall. "You know I want this job, right, Boss?" he told Dawk.

"I already know, fam. You know we got some talkin' to do. Now just ain't the time. If Ben okay it? I want you to look after Koko and Kimi until Tonto get taken care of."

"He gone okay it, Boss. I clocked in time Samantha took flight," Lee ended as he and Dawk bumped fists.

****

Back on the ranch, meanwhile, duties still had to be performed. Siloam and several ranch hands were back on the property, as well as Irene, Francine, DeeDee and his son, and Sharona Benson. It was real awkward between Irene and Sharona inside Ponderosa. Irene was doing all she could to stay out of the woman's way and let her and DeeDee have their time with their son the few remaining days she had left in town. All she wanted to do her few days off was enjoy the peace and quiet, sip drinks and kick back. She was back and forth to the kitchen pouring herself homemade daiquiris while watching movies alone in the theater room. Going for a daiquiri refill, Irene, slightly tipsy, opened the fridge and reached for the picture of strawberry daiquiri. Unsteady hands sent the picture crashing to the floor. "Shit!" she scoffed under her breath as she jumped back, the frozen concoction coating her feet and ankles and sending a chill halfway up her legs.

"Everything okay in here?" Sharona asked, peeking into the first floor kitchen from the dining room.

"I got it!" Twiggy snapped as she moved to the pantry to retrieve a mop and broom.

"Let me help you, Irene," Sharona stated as she walked into the kitchen.

"What did I say?" Irene scoffed as she emerged from the pantry. "I can take care of my business just fine! You've helped enough!"

"Okay, this has nothing to do with the mess made," Sharona stated as she strode past the spilled liquid and stood a few feet away from Twiggy.

"I'm not afraid to say it doesn't, Sharona. DeeDee was doing just fine before you pranced back into his life."

"Pranced? Honey, I walked in like the woman I am and laid everything bare."

"I bet you did," Irene scowled as she stepped closer to Sharona.

"All I did was introduce DeeDee—"

"Back to the old pussy he had!" Irene interjected. Sharona drew back and eyed Irene in surprise. "This isn't about you and Doss' son, Sharona," she let it be known. "You walk in here and try to play for me for a fool. I can't, I can't rejoice over this as much as I want to because I know."

"Know what?" Sharona defended.

"I'm gone look you in the eyes and ask you one question— woman to woman," Irene remarked. "We're both professional women and we carry ourselves with dignity so let's be real about it."

"Let's," Sharona replied while staring Twiggy in the eyes.

"You and DeeDee still fucking?"

"I said I wasn't going to come between you and your man, Irene. DeeDee told me of you the day I told him about his son. We kissed, but that was before he spoke about you. I backed off."

"The whole time DeeDee was in Chicago the two of you never became intimate?" Irene asked in disbelief.

"We were. You want the truth, Irene? Here it is—DeeDee and I were intimate. But it was only that one time. Old feelings came back. I never wanted it to happen but it did. Now you know the truth. Now you can make your own decision about what it is you will do exactly."

"I knew it," Irene spoke lowly as her eyes watered. "The only man I ever loved, Jesus," she said as her lips trembled. "You can have him."

"I didn't tell you the truth to gain back DeeDee, Irene. I told you the truth so that when I'm gone? You won't harbor any animosity towards my son. He is part of this family and this is where I want him to grow up."

"That has nothing to do with me."

"It has everything to do with you, Irene."

"You've just told me you fucked my man. Now you try and throw your son on me? Do I look the fool I am for even considering forgiving DeeDee for what he's—"

"Irene, I'm dying of kidney failure!" Sharona blurted out.

Irene donned a confused look as she stared at Sharona. "Am I supposed to sympathize? I don't even know you."

"And you don't even have to care, Irene. All I want is for my son to grow up around a loving family. I'm all he has," Sharona said as her eyes welled up. "I don't want to have to turn him over to the state. DeeDee is up in age now and I'm afraid my son will become a statistic," Sharona said as she walked over and grabbed the broom and dust pan. "Be mad at me. Hate me if you want to, but don't hold what me and DeeDee have done against my son. As you go so does he with his kinfolk. His *kinfolk*, Irene," the woman reiterated as she began cleaning the mess on the floor.

Irene was at a loss for words. Games played by women were prevalent. Mothers wanted financially stable fathers for their children. She herself resided with a rich family and was loved by all. Had it been years ago, the woman known by all as Twiggy would've kicked Sharona's ass on the spot and then sought out DeeDee to fuck him up for playing her stupid; but this was now the woman Irene Charles. She was no longer the person she was back in Ghost Town as she'd been evolving ever since the day she'd arrived to Ponderosa eight years earlier.

The willingness to forgive under the circumstances because of the woman she now was in life had forced Irene into a rationale decision rather than devolve into the stereotypical angry black woman lashing out at her man's baby's mother. A fellow sister was dying, and she had no one to look after her son was the situation she was up against. In spite of the compunction Irene held towards Sharona for sleeping with DeeDee knowing the man had a woman, her heart was moved for the sake and the fate of an innocent little boy who hadn't transgressed against her.

"How long do you have?" Irene asked as she knelt down and assisted Sharona.

"My doctor says eighteen months max, but only because I paid him a quarter million dollars to do the best he can," Sharona chuckled.

Irene smiled to herself. "I'm still upset with you, Sharona. But for Doss the third's sake? I'll do what I can."

"We have a lot to discuss, Irene. I beg your forgiveness and I promise not to betray you again. If DeeDee tries? You'll be the first to know of it. He told me so much about you. It's some things I want to share with you right away concerning my son if it's okay?"

Irene didn't say it because it was a cruel thought—Sharona said she was dying. For someone to play around with fate, she'd never seen. She didn't wish for it, but for Sharona's sake, her ass had better been as sick as she claimed if Irene had to tell it, because if not? She was going to make her wish she'd been ill all along.

"We'll clean this up and you can join me in theater room where we can have a discussion on exactly what is going on with you and what is it that you want me to do as far as you and DeeDee's son is concerned," Irene told Sharona.

With tears in her eyes, Sharona smiled and said. "He's a good boy, Irene. He'd be the perfect son for you."

Irene didn't bother replying. She was beyond birthing

children, but the mere thought of raising a child touched her heart. "We'll see," she told Sharona as the two went on to clean up the mess. "We'll see."

****

While Irene and Sharona were making amends, Siloam Bovina, meanwhile, was out near Moses' pen. Today was they day his waste reservoir was being emptied. A large sewage truck was backed up to the pig sty and a thick hose ran from its rear and latched on to a pipe extending from the underground receptacle. The smell was so atrocious Siloam had to wear a hazmat suit and oxygen mask just to be able to withstand the rancid stench lingering in the air. Even the trucker, who'd been performing this task for years now for the family, had remarked that Moses tank was unusually foul that afternoon.

Siloam could hear the man complaining as he stood beside her; she knew Reynard's partial leftover remains that had been washed down into the tank was the reason it had such a repugnant odor on this day but she would never dare tell.

"Siloam! Senorita Bovina!" a ranch hand called out.

Siloam shut the hose she was using to wash Moses' pen and looked over to the ranch hand and raised her head slightly.

"There's a woman here that wants a word with you!" the man yelled over the truck's hydraulic pump.

Siloam looked and saw a white pickup truck at the edge of Moses' pen. She set the hose down and walked over to the edge of the fence where the smell wasn't as pungent and raised her hazmat mask. "Who is she?" she asked the ranch hand.

"She didn't say, Senorita. But she specifically asked for you."

Just then, the driver's side door on the pickup truck opened and a tall, dark-skinned woman dressed in a black denim outfit wearing knee-length black boots and a white three-quarter length leather jacket emerged. Her medium-length black hair was micro-braided to the left, resting just below her left ear and her chocolate face was round and smooth. She had a professional appeal about herself but seemed rugged in demeanor to Siloam, even though she hadn't spoken a word to her.

"Can I help you?" Siloam asked over the truck's hose that was sucking the remnants of Moses' bodily wastes up into its tank.

"You tell me, Siloam," the woman sassed as she frowned her face. "God, that's an awful smell," she complained as she fanned her face.

"How do you know my name? Who are you?"

"My name is Bianca. Detective Bianca Jacobs—Las Vegas, Nevada Police Department. How do I know you? You were the bitch fucking my father. His last move was a flight here to Oklahoma. I know he came here to see you, but he hasn't been heard from in four days and his phone is now off. Where's my father? What have you done with or to him?" Bianca asked sternly just as the sewage truck's hydraulic pump was shut down and the driver began removing the hose from Moses' underground waste bin.

To be continued.

Made in United States
Orlando, FL
10 April 2024

45642260R00310